BREAK

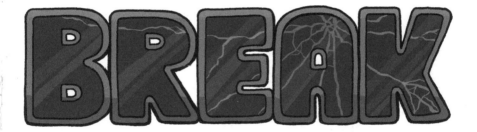

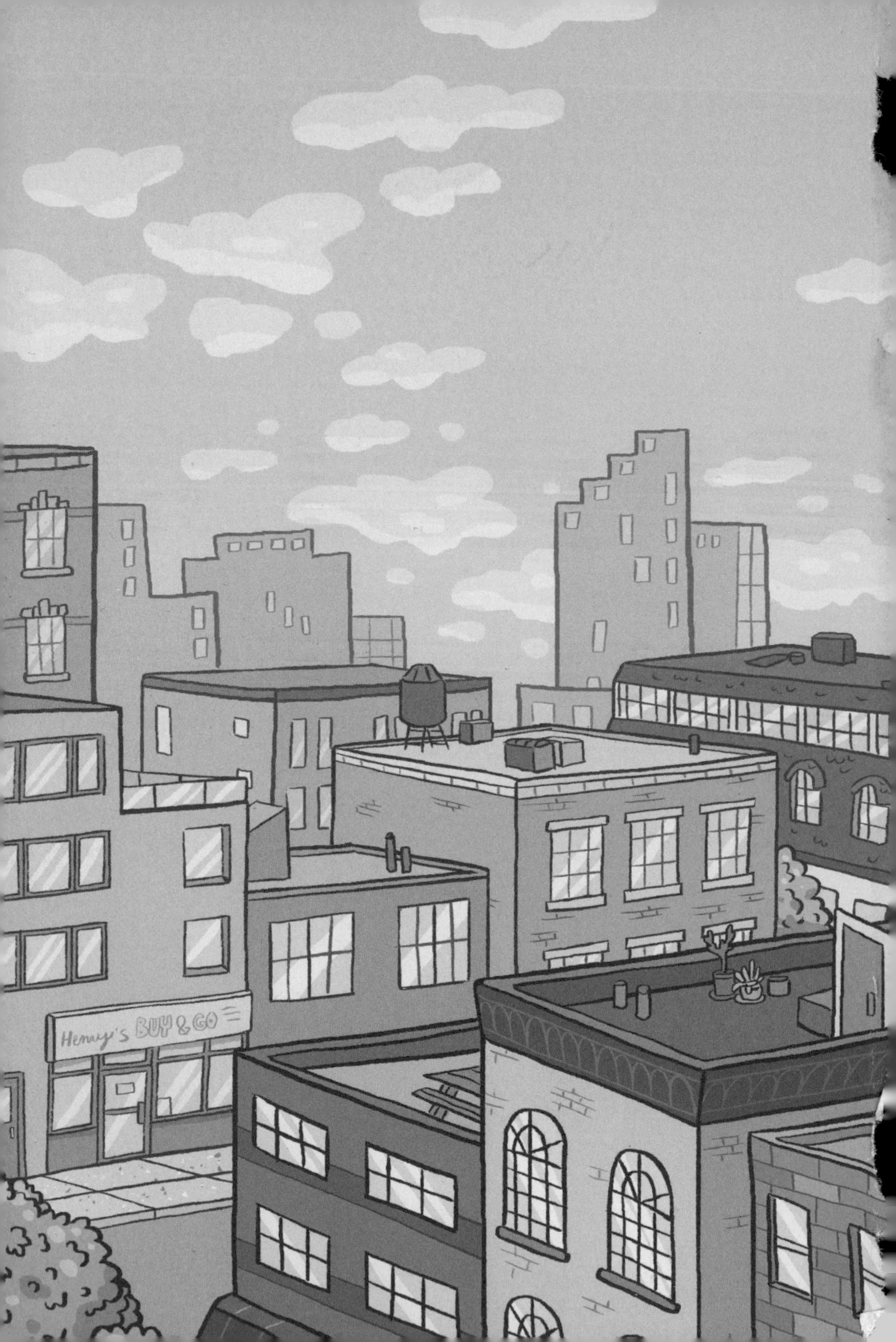
Henry's BUY & GO

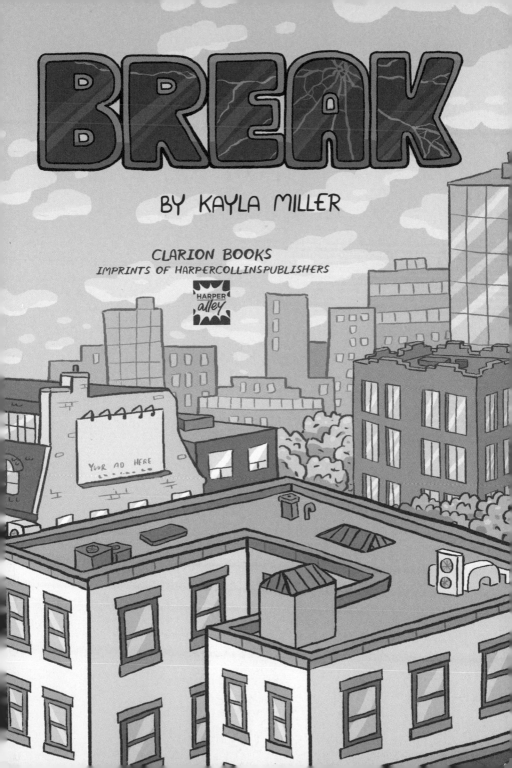

BREAK

BY KAYLA MILLER

CLARION BOOKS
IMPRINTS OF HARPERCOLLINSPUBLISHERS

HARPER alley

FOR JEFFREY. I LOVE WRITING BOOKS WITH YOU, FOR YOU, AND NEXT TO YOU. —KM

COLOR BY JESS LOME
LETTERING BY LOR PRESCOTT

Clarion Books is an imprint of HarperCollins Publishers.
HarperAlley is an imprint of HarperCollins Publishers.

Break

ISBN 978-0-35-839369-6 — ISBN 978-0-35-841422-3 (pbk)

The artist used Photoshop to create the digital illustrations for this book.
Typography by Stephanie Hays
23 24 25 26 27   GPS   10 9 8 7 6 5 4 3 2 1

First Edition

RI|||||||/||ING!

SO, WHAT IS EVERYONE DOING FOR SPRING BREAK?

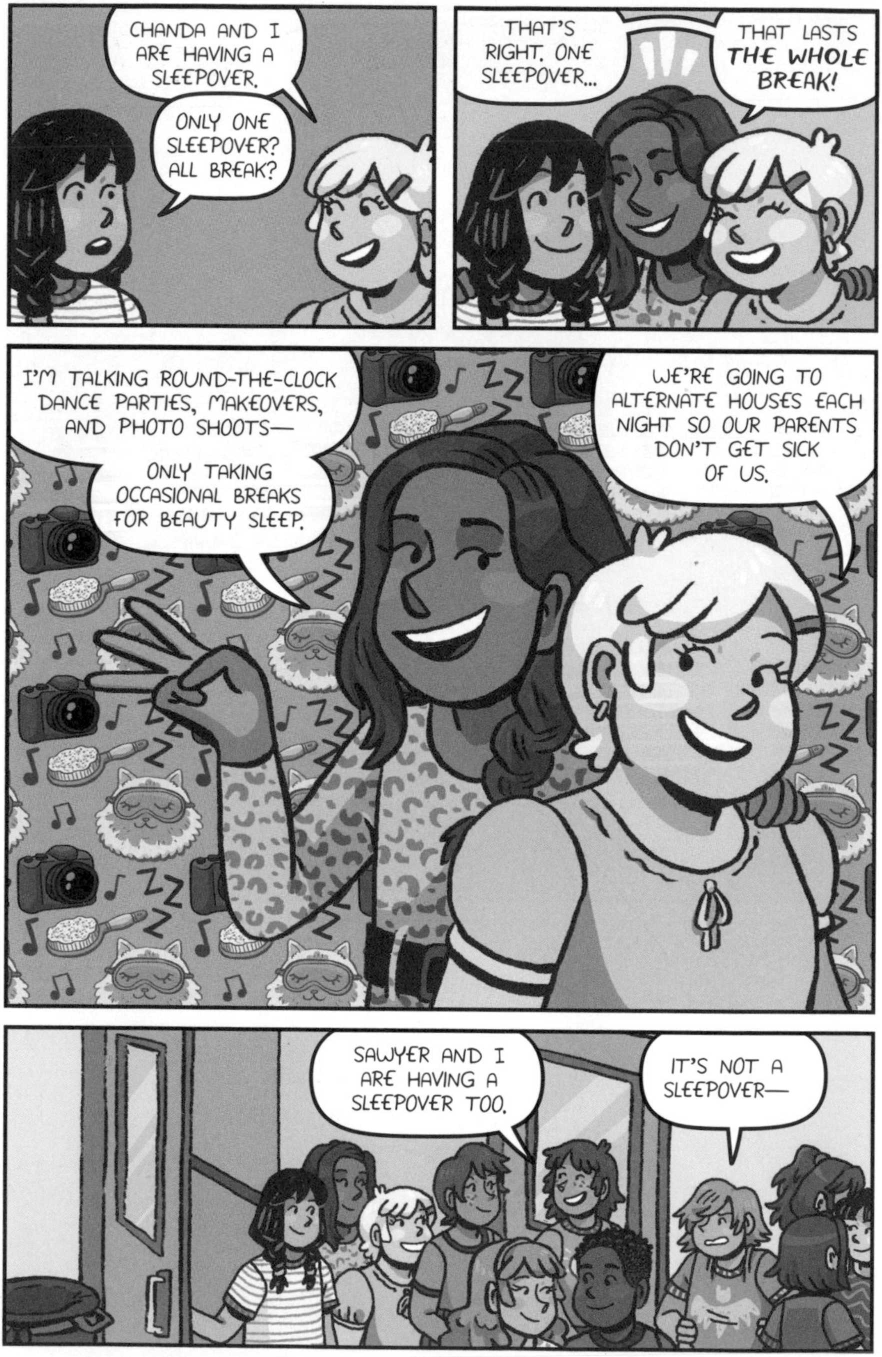
CHANDA AND I ARE HAVING A SLEEPOVER.
ONLY ONE SLEEPOVER? ALL BREAK?
THAT'S RIGHT. ONE SLEEPOVER...
THAT LASTS **THE WHOLE BREAK!**
I'M TALKING ROUND-THE-CLOCK DANCE PARTIES, MAKEOVERS, AND PHOTO SHOOTS—
ONLY TAKING OCCASIONAL BREAKS FOR BEAUTY SLEEP.
WE'RE GOING TO ALTERNATE HOUSES EACH NIGHT SO OUR PARENTS DON'T GET SICK OF US.
SAWYER AND I ARE HAVING A SLEEPOVER TOO.
IT'S NOT A SLEEPOVER—

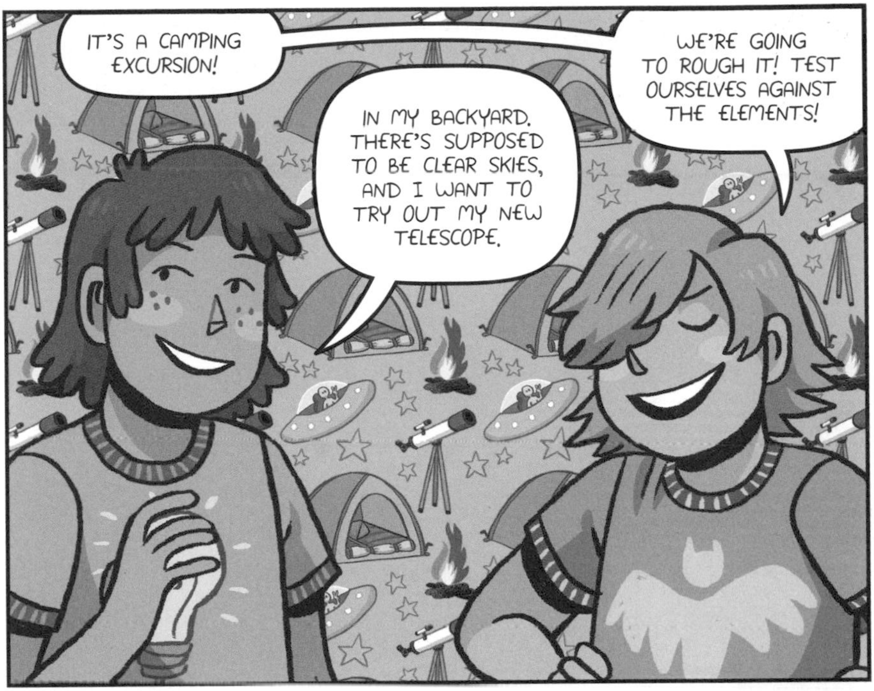
IT'S A CAMPING EXCURSION!
IN MY BACKYARD. THERE'S SUPPOSED TO BE CLEAR SKIES, AND I WANT TO TRY OUT MY NEW TELESCOPE.
WE'RE GOING TO ROUGH IT! TEST OURSELVES AGAINST THE ELEMENTS!

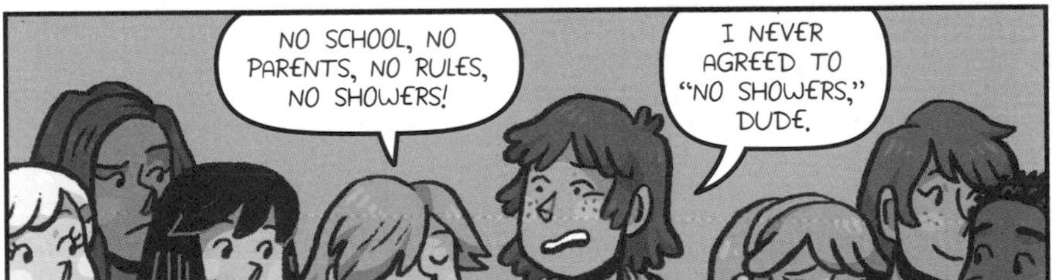
NO SCHOOL, NO PARENTS, NO RULES, NO SHOWERS!
I NEVER AGREED TO "NO SHOWERS," DUDE.

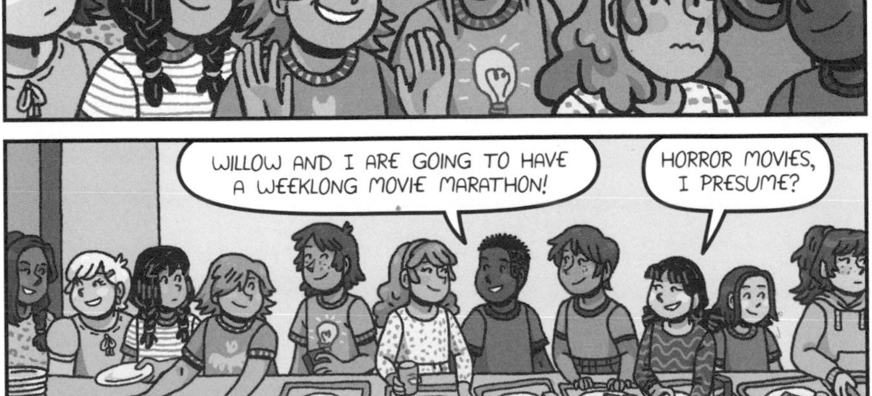
WILLOW AND I ARE GOING TO HAVE A WEEKLONG MOVIE MARATHON!
HORROR MOVIES, I PRESUME?

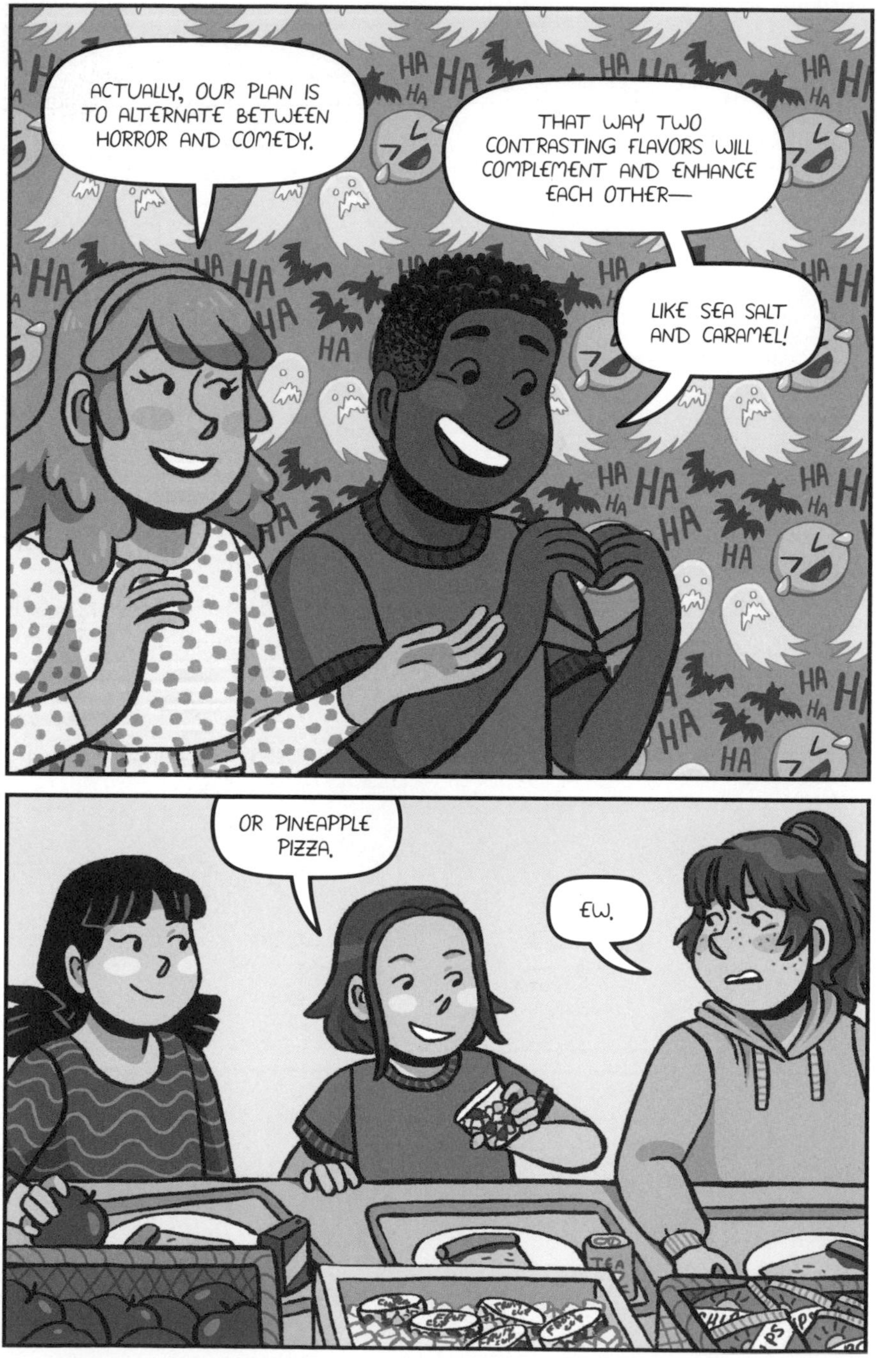
ACTUALLY, OUR PLAN IS TO ALTERNATE BETWEEN HORROR AND COMEDY.
THAT WAY TWO CONTRASTING FLAVORS WILL COMPLEMENT AND ENHANCE EACH OTHER—
LIKE SEA SALT AND CARAMEL!
OR PINEAPPLE PIZZA.
EW.

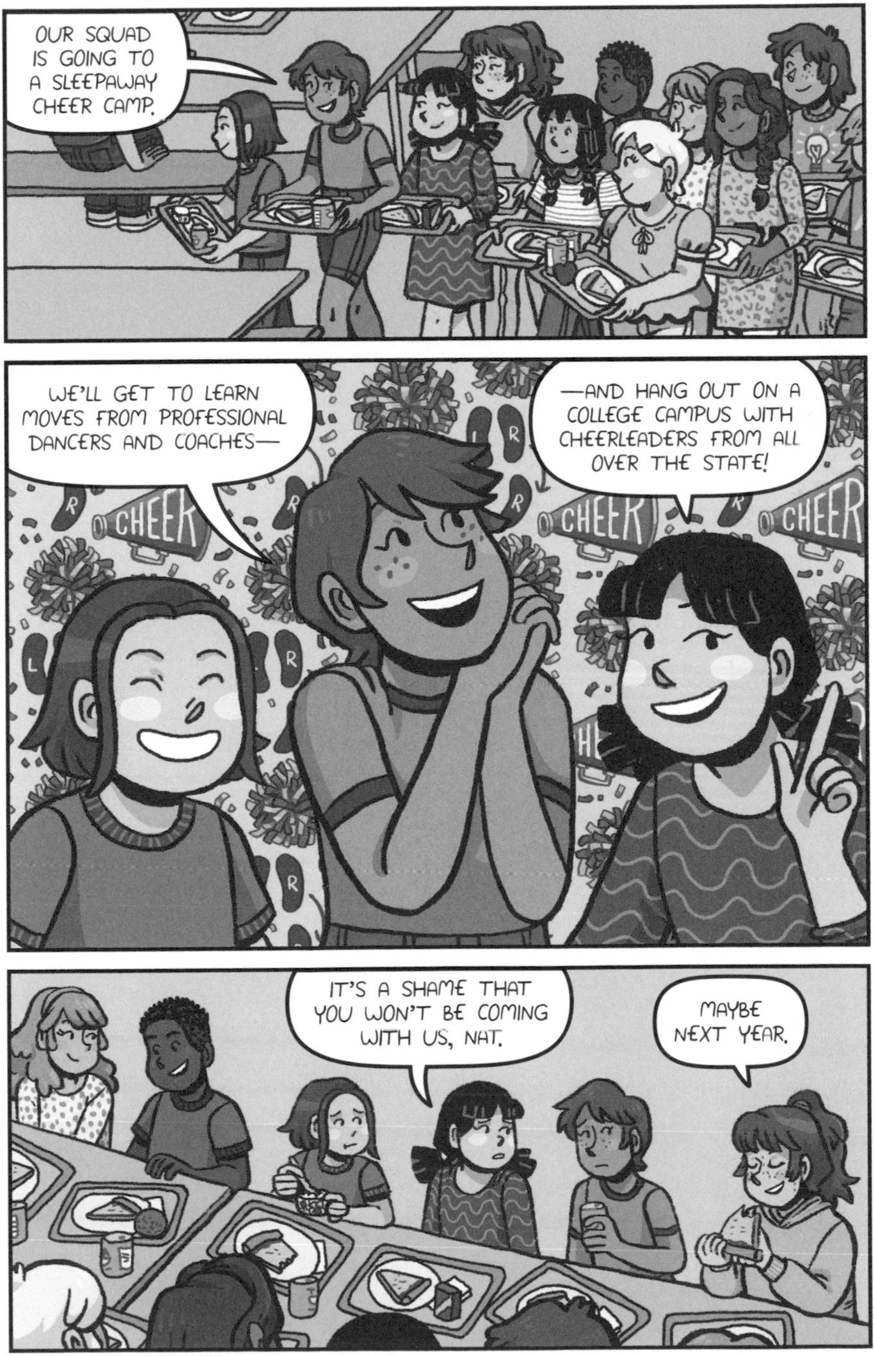
OUR SQUAD IS GOING TO A SLEEPAWAY CHEER CAMP.
WE'LL GET TO LEARN MOVES FROM PROFESSIONAL DANCERS AND COACHES—
—AND HANG OUT ON A COLLEGE CAMPUS WITH CHEERLEADERS FROM ALL OVER THE STATE!
CHEER
CHEER
CHEER
IT'S A SHAME THAT YOU WON'T BE COMING WITH US, NAT.
MAYBE NEXT YEAR.

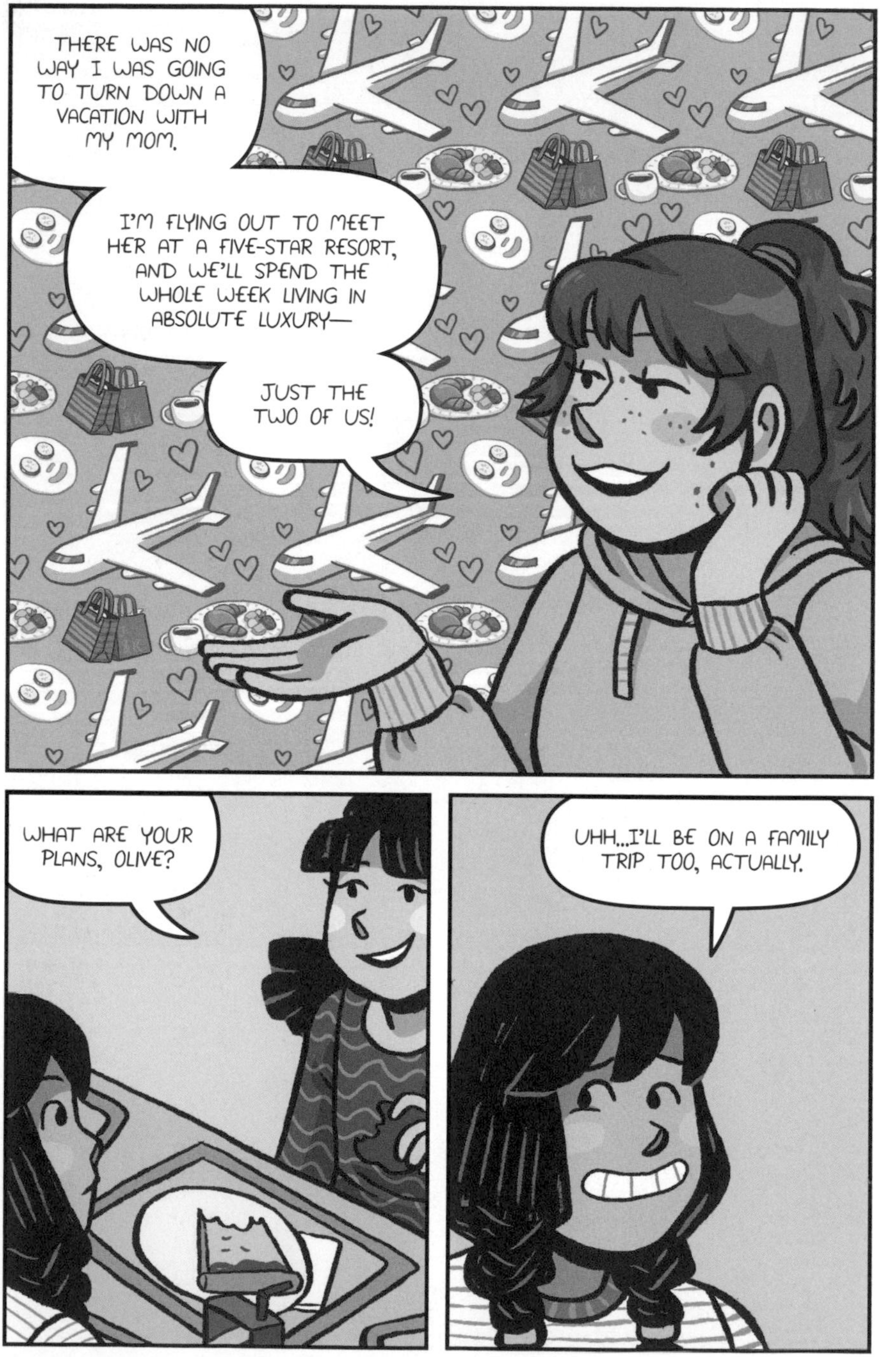
THERE WAS NO WAY I WAS GOING TO TURN DOWN A VACATION WITH MY MOM.
I'M FLYING OUT TO MEET HER AT A FIVE-STAR RESORT, AND WE'LL SPEND THE WHOLE WEEK LIVING IN ABSOLUTE LUXURY—
JUST THE TWO OF US!
WHAT ARE YOUR PLANS, OLIVE?
UHH...I'LL BE ON A FAMILY TRIP TOO, ACTUALLY.

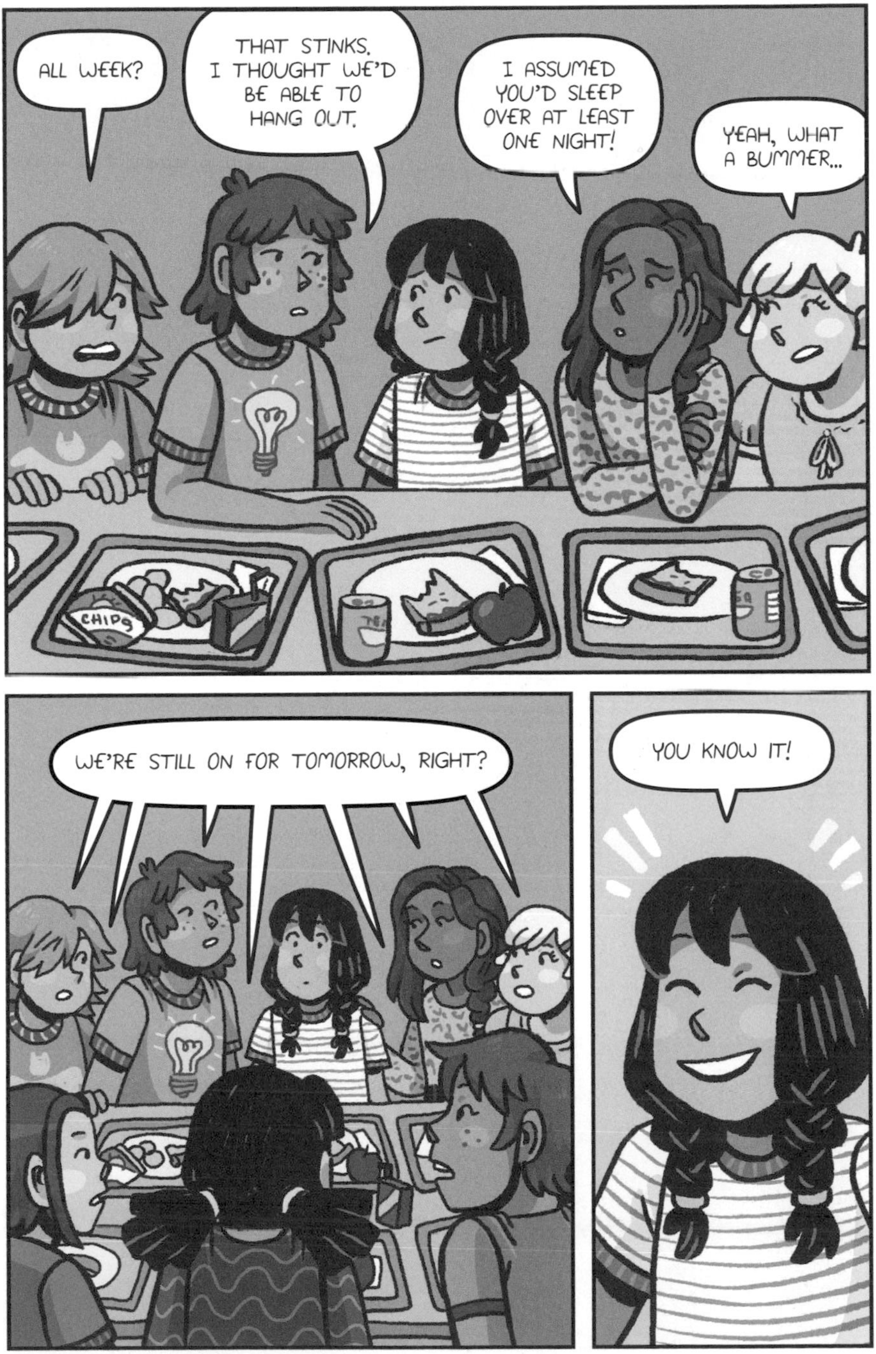
ALL WEEK?
THAT STINKS. I THOUGHT WE'D BE ABLE TO HANG OUT.
I ASSUMED YOU'D SLEEP OVER AT LEAST ONE NIGHT!
YEAH, WHAT A BUMMER...
CHIPS
WE'RE STILL ON FOR TOMORROW, RIGHT?
YOU KNOW IT!

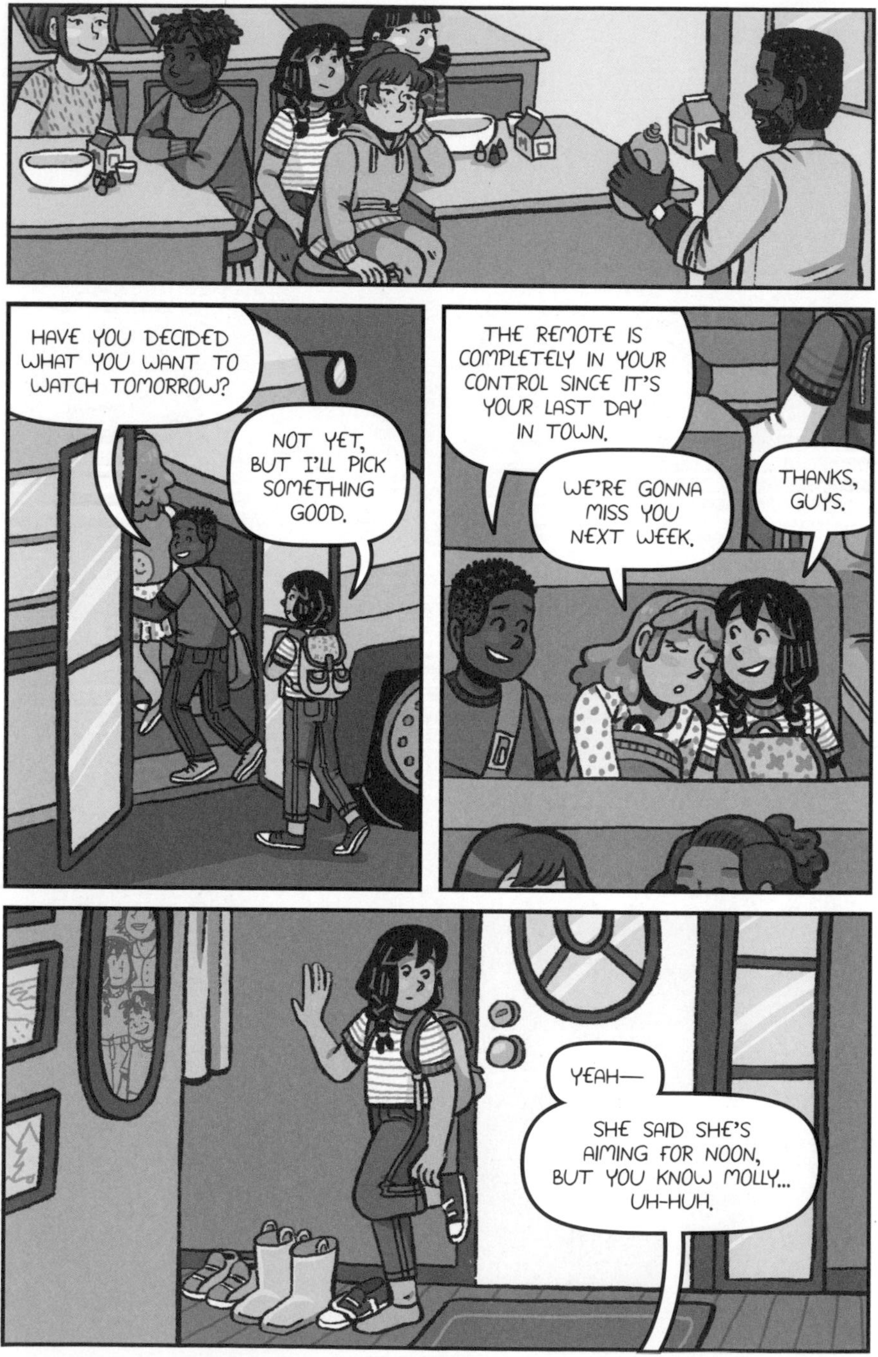
HAVE YOU DECIDED WHAT YOU WANT TO WATCH TOMORROW?
NOT YET, BUT I'LL PICK SOMETHING GOOD.
THE REMOTE IS COMPLETELY IN YOUR CONTROL SINCE IT'S YOUR LAST DAY IN TOWN.
WE'RE GONNA MISS YOU NEXT WEEK.
THANKS, GUYS.
YEAH—
SHE SAID SHE'S AIMING FOR NOON, BUT YOU KNOW MOLLY... UH-HUH.

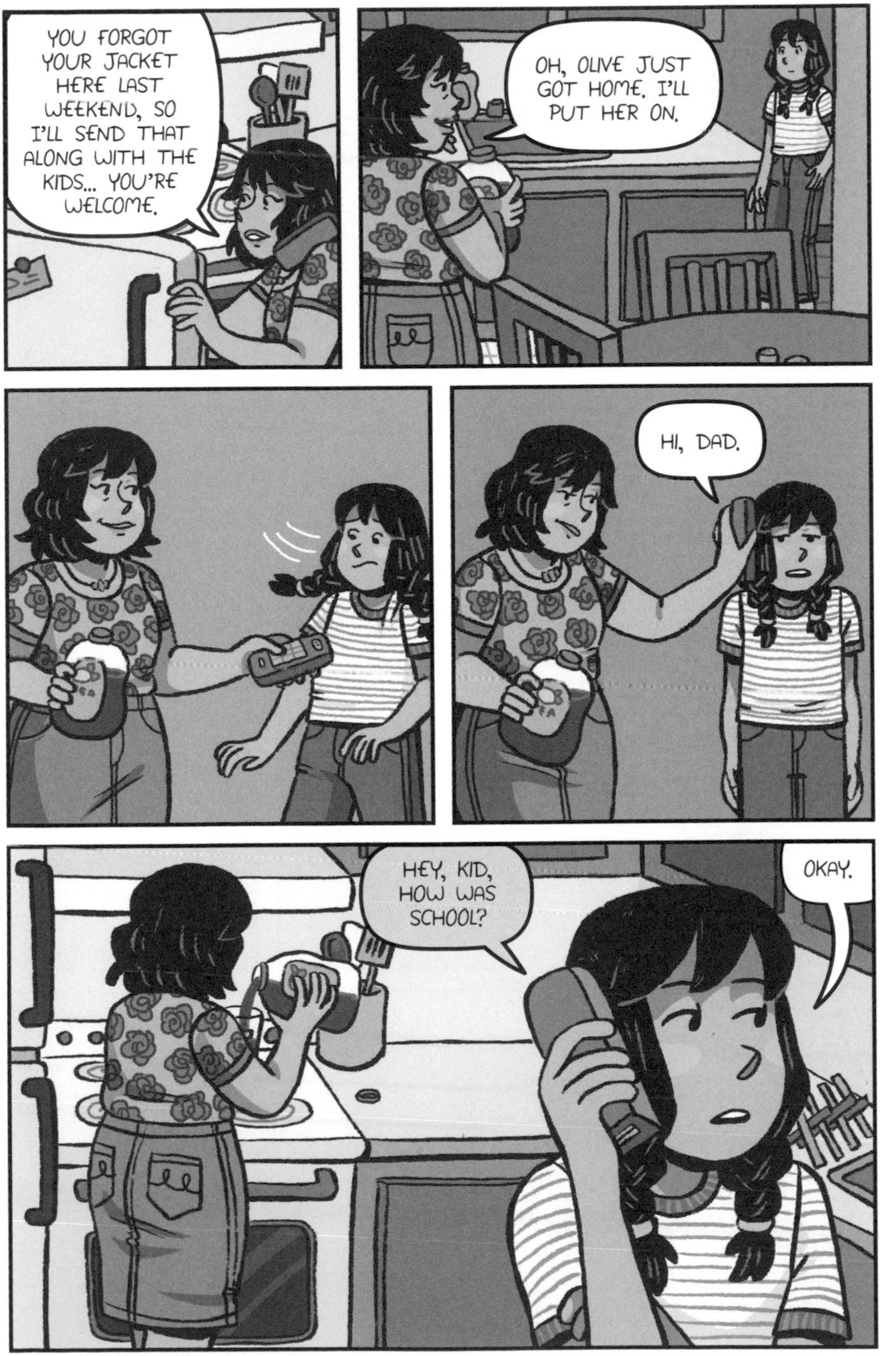

YOU FORGOT YOUR JACKET HERE LAST WEEKEND, SO I'LL SEND THAT ALONG WITH THE KIDS... YOU'RE WELCOME.
OH, OLIVE JUST GOT HOME. I'LL PUT HER ON.
HI, DAD.
HEY, KID, HOW WAS SCHOOL?
OKAY.

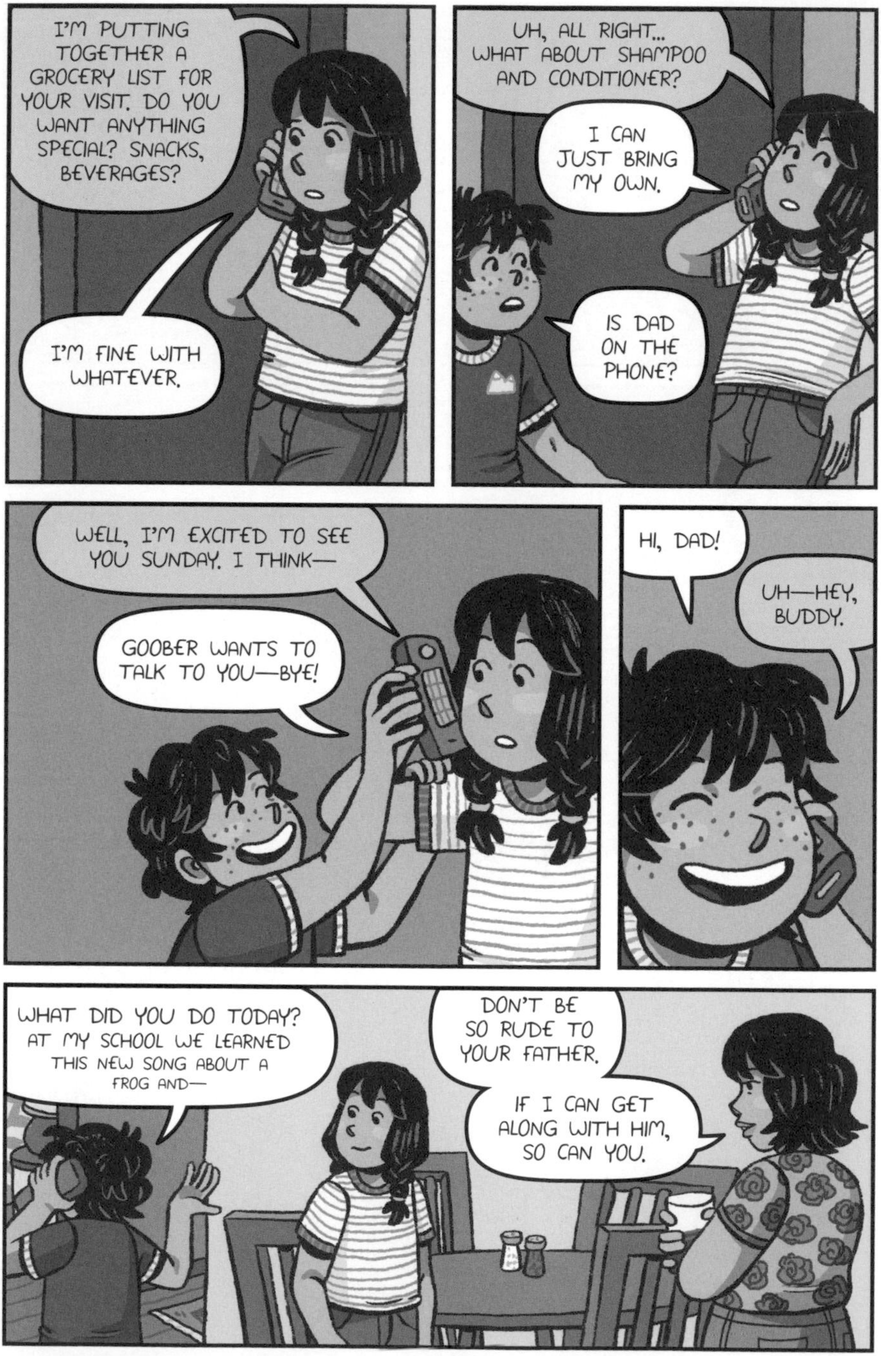
I'M PUTTING TOGETHER A GROCERY LIST FOR YOUR VISIT. DO YOU WANT ANYTHING SPECIAL? SNACKS, BEVERAGES?
I'M FINE WITH WHATEVER.
UH, ALL RIGHT... WHAT ABOUT SHAMPOO AND CONDITIONER?
I CAN JUST BRING MY OWN.
IS DAD ON THE PHONE?
WELL, I'M EXCITED TO SEE YOU SUNDAY. I THINK—
GOOBER WANTS TO TALK TO YOU—BYE!
HI, DAD!
UH—HEY, BUDDY.
WHAT DID YOU DO TODAY? AT MY SCHOOL WE LEARNED THIS NEW SONG ABOUT A FROG AND—
DON'T BE SO RUDE TO YOUR FATHER.
IF I CAN GET ALONG WITH HIM, SO CAN YOU.

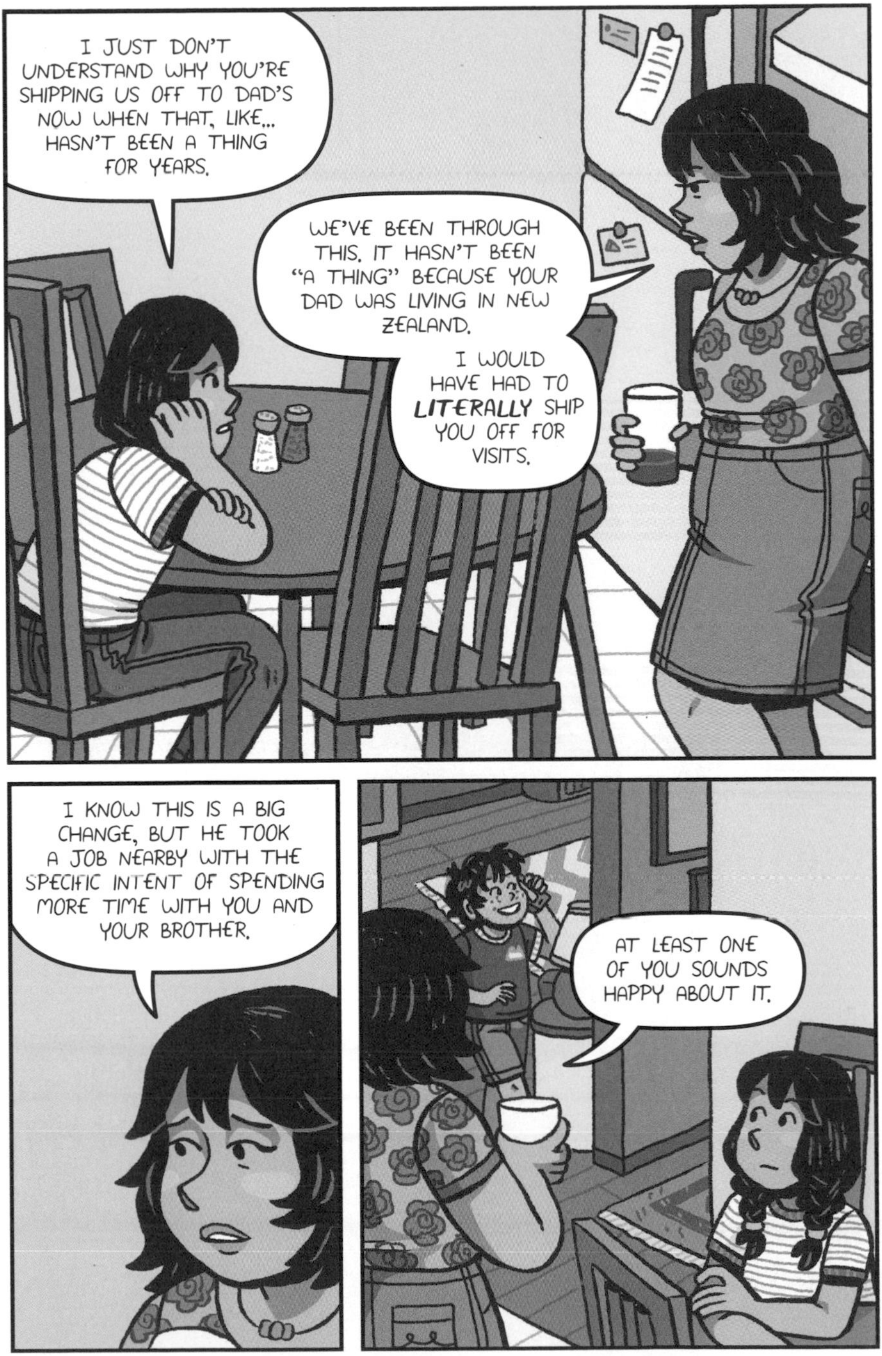
I JUST DON'T UNDERSTAND WHY YOU'RE SHIPPING US OFF TO DAD'S NOW WHEN THAT, LIKE... HASN'T BEEN A THING FOR YEARS.
WE'VE BEEN THROUGH THIS. IT HASN'T BEEN "A THING" BECAUSE YOUR DAD WAS LIVING IN NEW ZEALAND.
I WOULD HAVE HAD TO **LITERALLY** SHIP YOU OFF FOR VISITS.
I KNOW THIS IS A BIG CHANGE, BUT HE TOOK A JOB NEARBY WITH THE SPECIFIC INTENT OF SPENDING MORE TIME WITH YOU AND YOUR BROTHER.
AT LEAST ONE OF YOU SOUNDS HAPPY ABOUT IT.

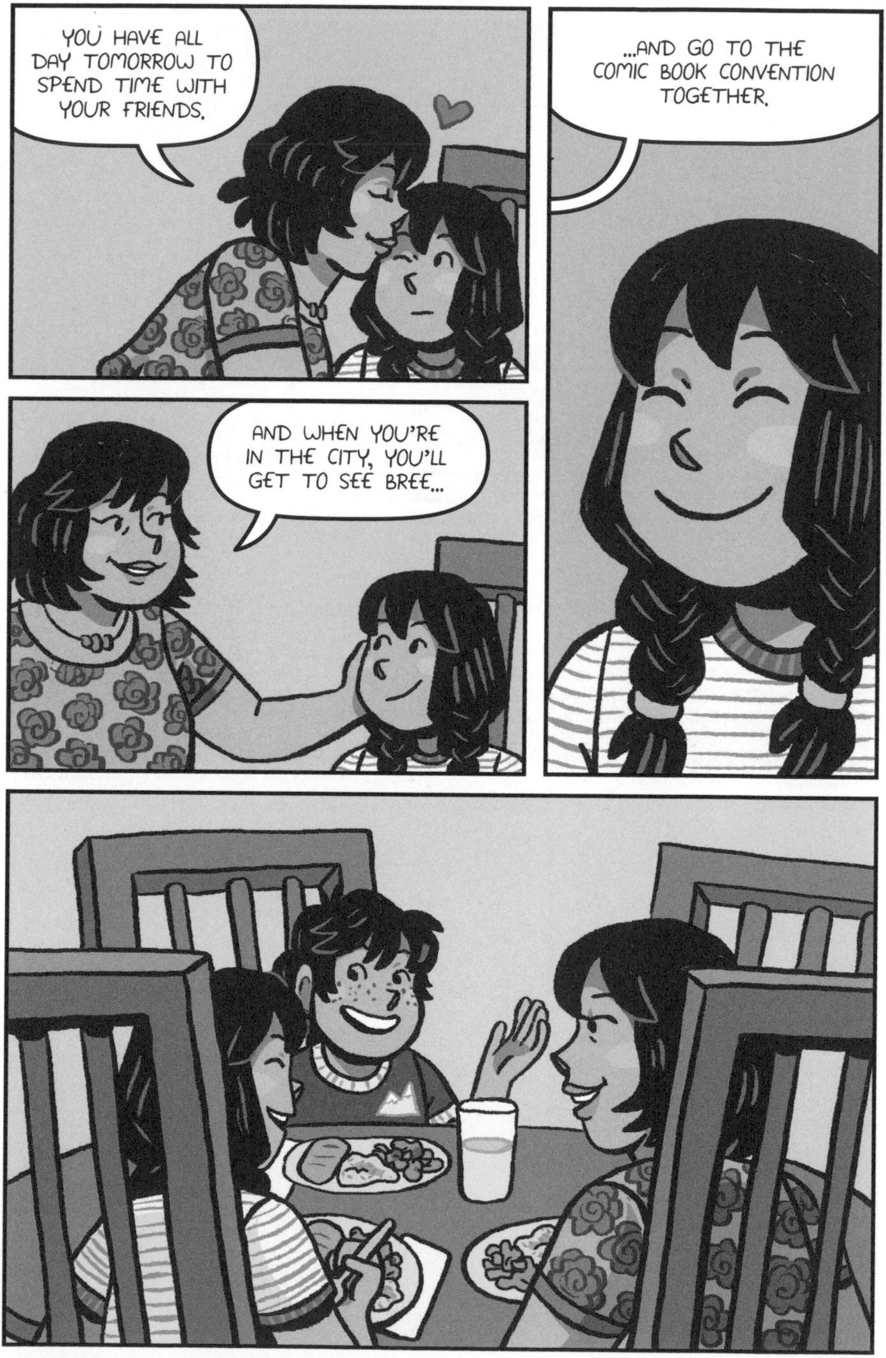
YOU HAVE ALL DAY TOMORROW TO SPEND TIME WITH YOUR FRIENDS.
AND WHEN YOU'RE IN THE CITY, YOU'LL GET TO SEE BREE...
...AND GO TO THE COMIC BOOK CONVENTION TOGETHER.

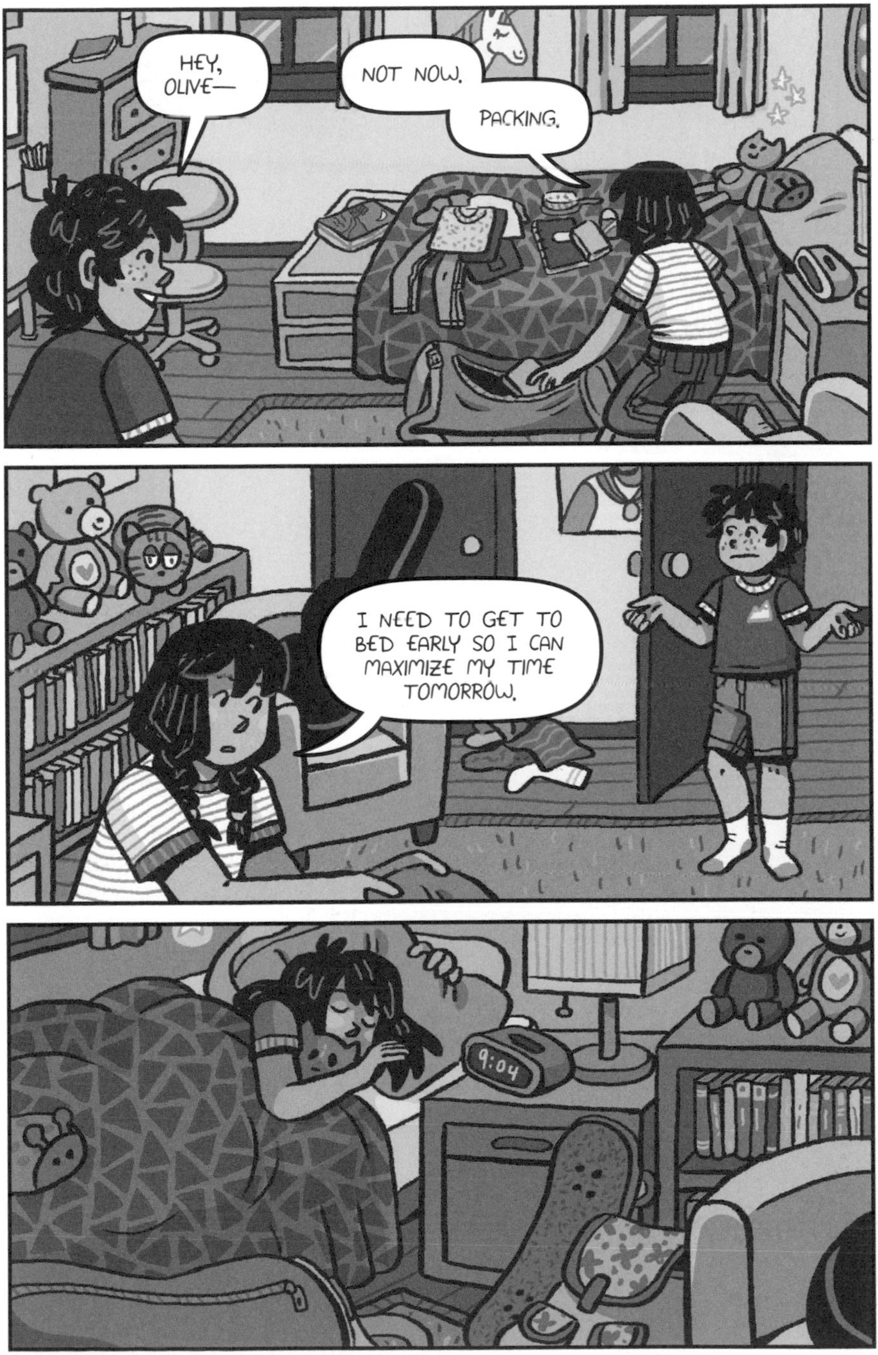
HEY, OLIVE—
NOT NOW.
PACKING.
I NEED TO GET TO BED EARLY SO I CAN MAXIMIZE MY TIME TOMORROW.
9:04

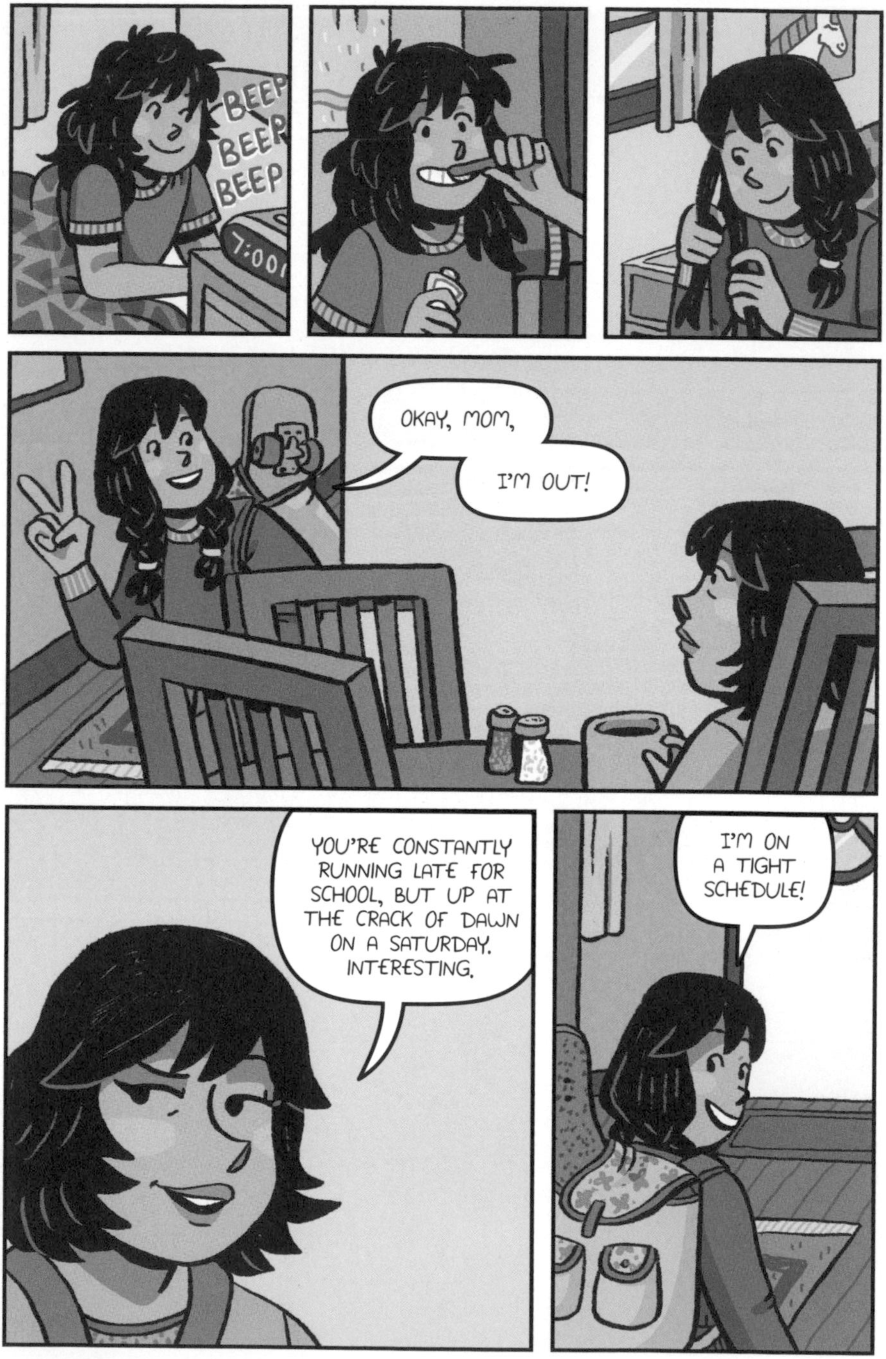
BEEP
BEEP
BEEP
7:00
OKAY, MOM,
I'M OUT!
YOU'RE CONSTANTLY RUNNING LATE FOR SCHOOL, BUT UP AT THE CRACK OF DAWN ON A SATURDAY. INTERESTING.
I'M ON A TIGHT SCHEDULE!

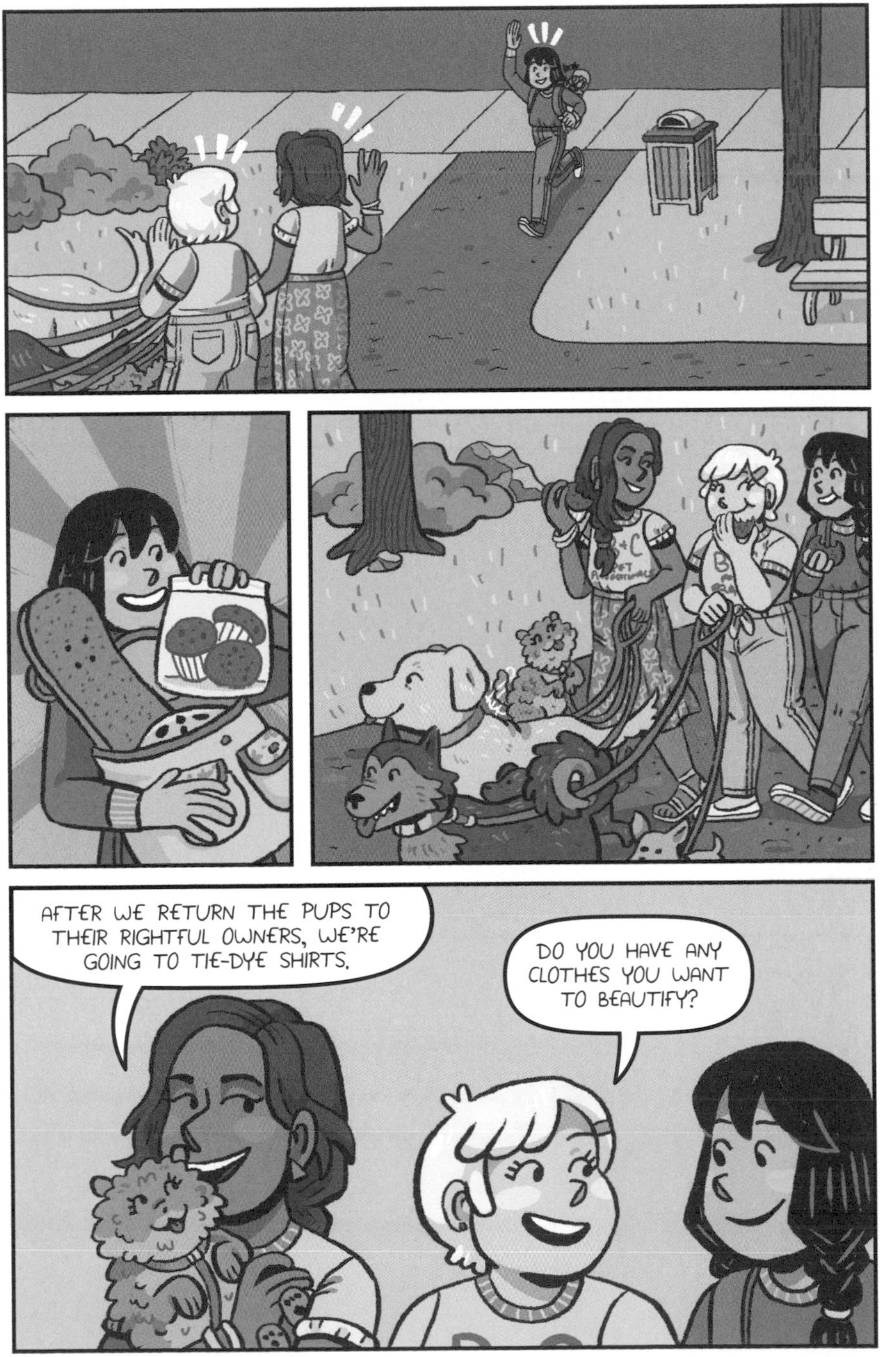
AFTER WE RETURN THE PUPS TO THEIR RIGHTFUL OWNERS, WE'RE GOING TO TIE-DYE SHIRTS.
DO YOU HAVE ANY CLOTHES YOU WANT TO BEAUTIFY?

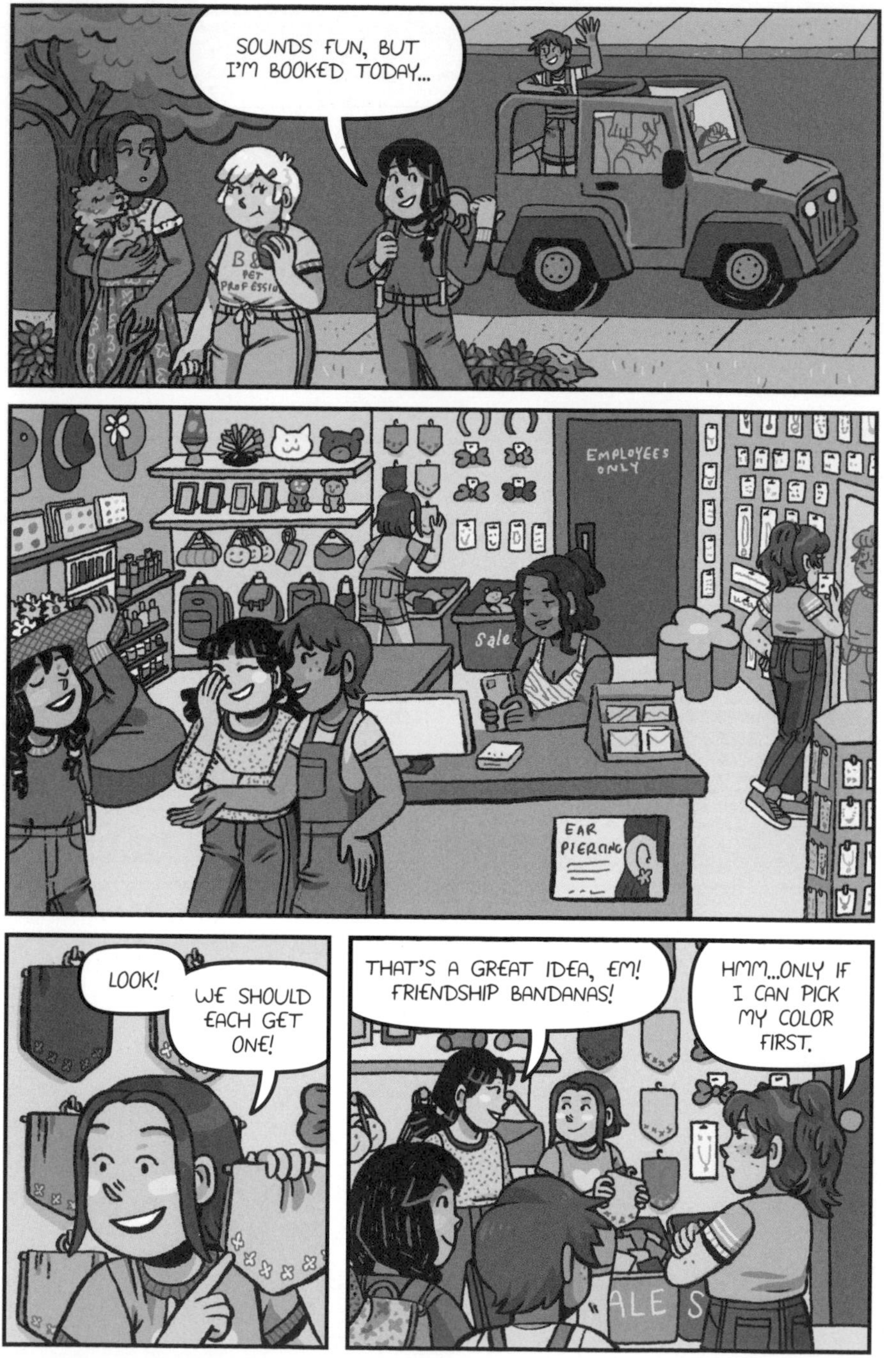
SOUNDS FUN, BUT I'M BOOKED TODAY...
B&
PET PROFESSIO
EMPLOYEES ONLY
SALE
EAR PIERCING
LOOK!
WE SHOULD EACH GET ONE!
THAT'S A GREAT IDEA, EM! FRIENDSHIP BANDANAS!
HMM...ONLY IF I CAN PICK MY COLOR FIRST.
ALE S

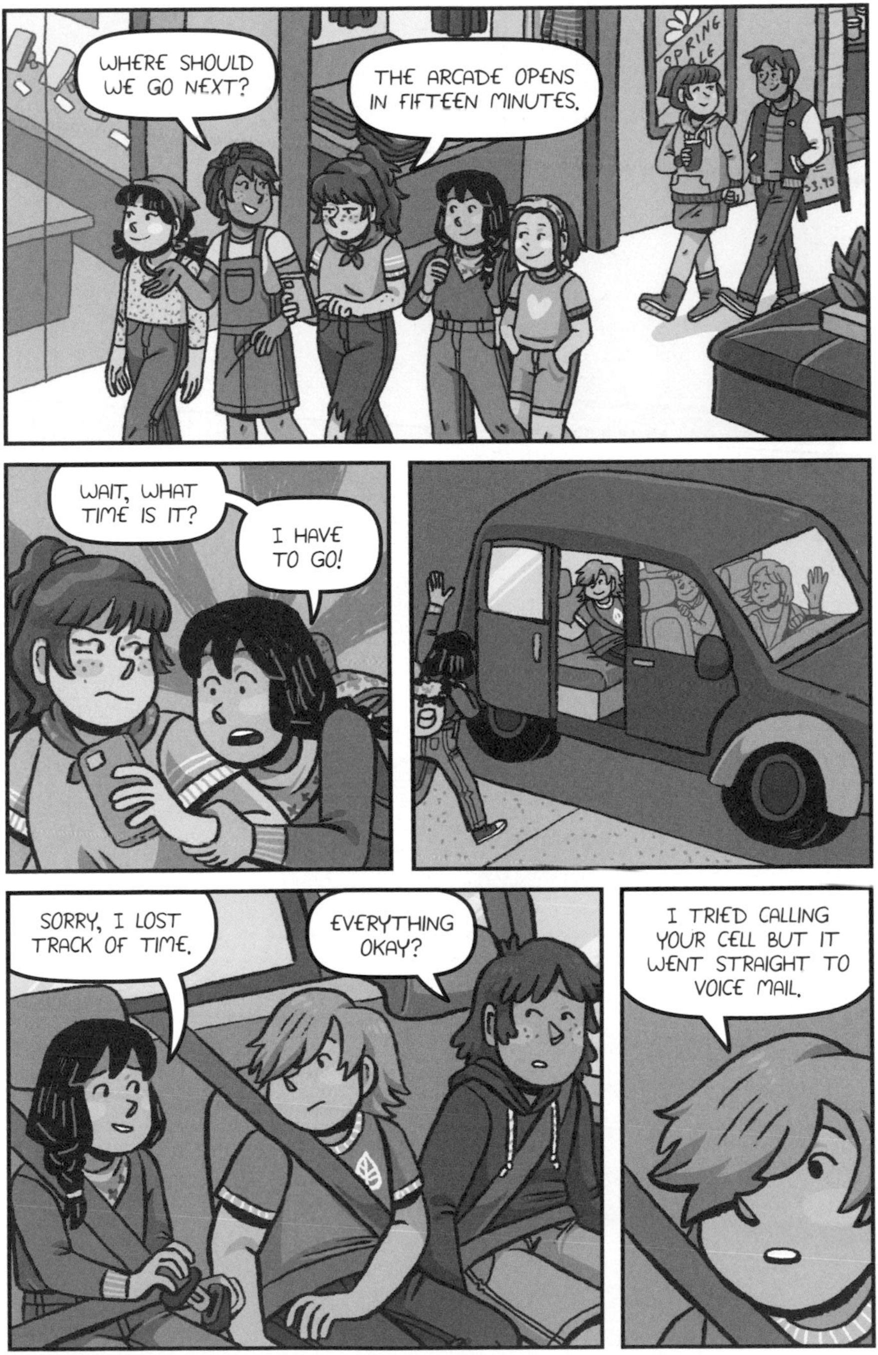
WHERE SHOULD WE GO NEXT?
THE ARCADE OPENS IN FIFTEEN MINUTES.
SPRING SALE
WAIT, WHAT TIME IS IT?
I HAVE TO GO!
SORRY, I LOST TRACK OF TIME.
EVERYTHING OKAY?
I TRIED CALLING YOUR CELL BUT IT WENT STRAIGHT TO VOICE MAIL.

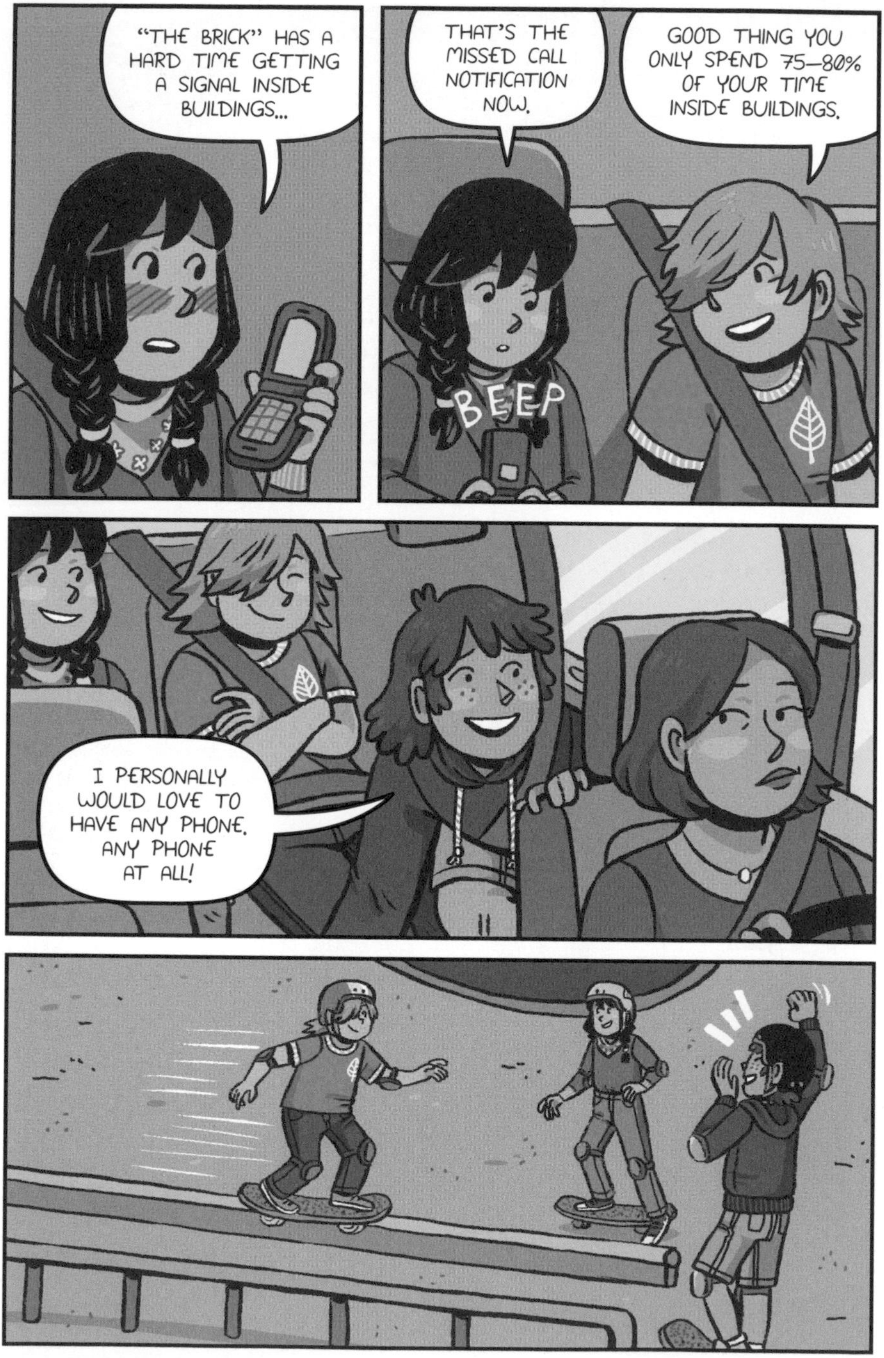
"THE BRICK" HAS A HARD TIME GETTING A SIGNAL INSIDE BUILDINGS...
THAT'S THE MISSED CALL NOTIFICATION NOW.
GOOD THING YOU ONLY SPEND 75–80% OF YOUR TIME INSIDE BUILDINGS.
BEEP
I PERSONALLY WOULD LOVE TO HAVE ANY PHONE. ANY PHONE AT ALL!

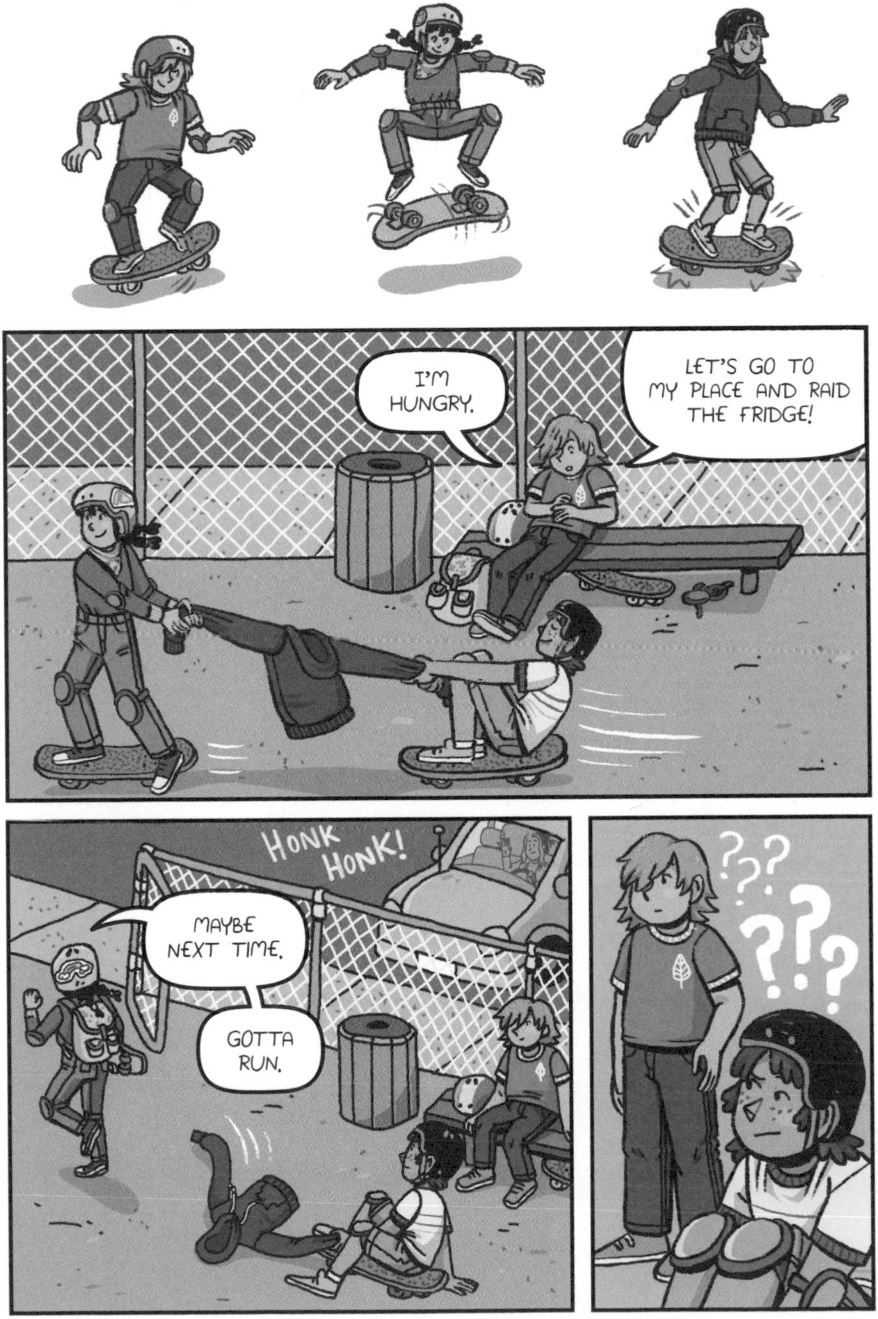
I'M HUNGRY.
LET'S GO TO MY PLACE AND RAID THE FRIDGE!
HONK HONK!
MAYBE NEXT TIME.
GOTTA RUN.
???
???

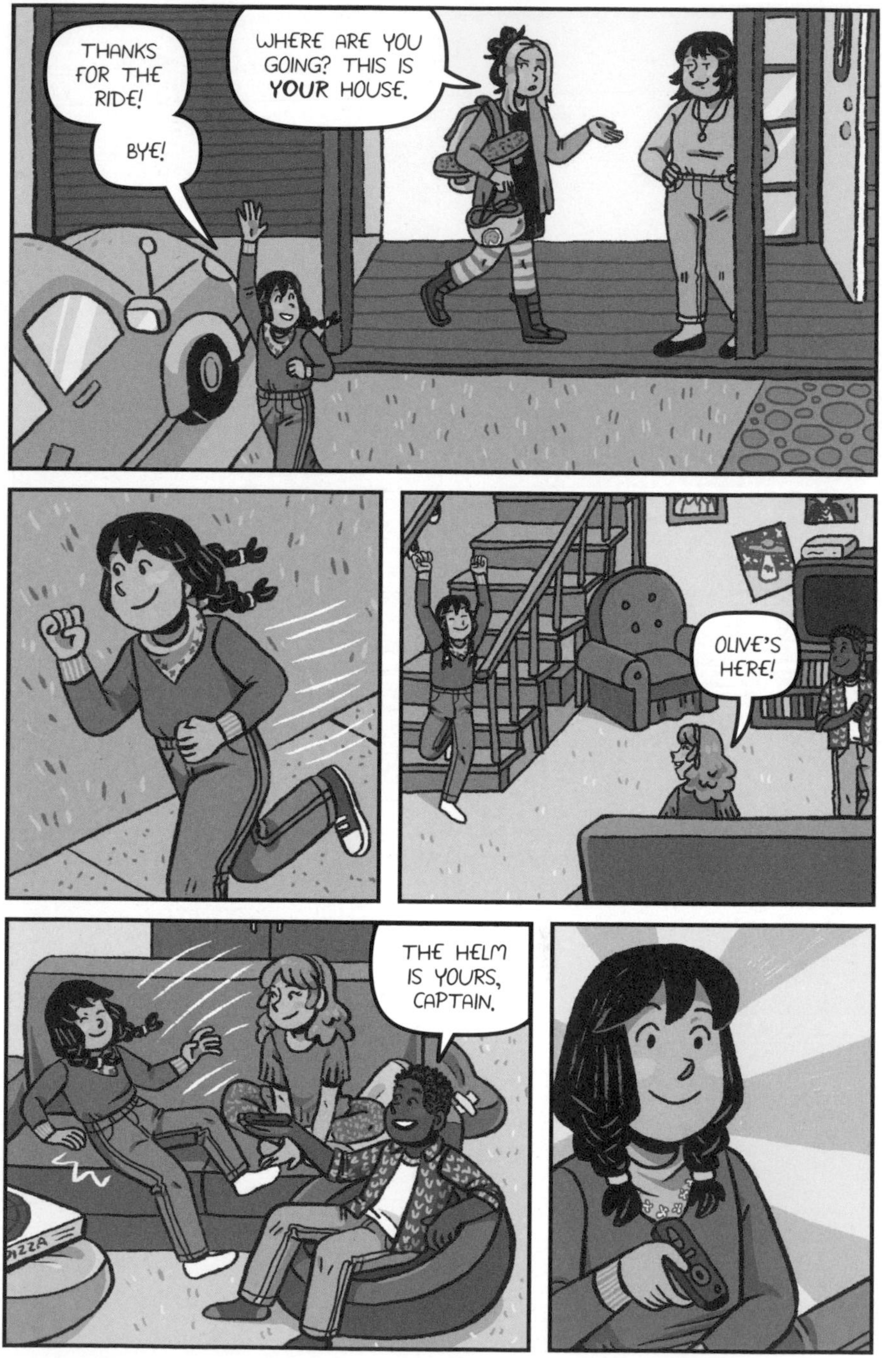
THANKS FOR THE RIDE!
BYE!
WHERE ARE YOU GOING? THIS IS **YOUR** HOUSE.
OLIVE'S HERE!
THE HELM IS YOURS, CAPTAIN.
PIZZA

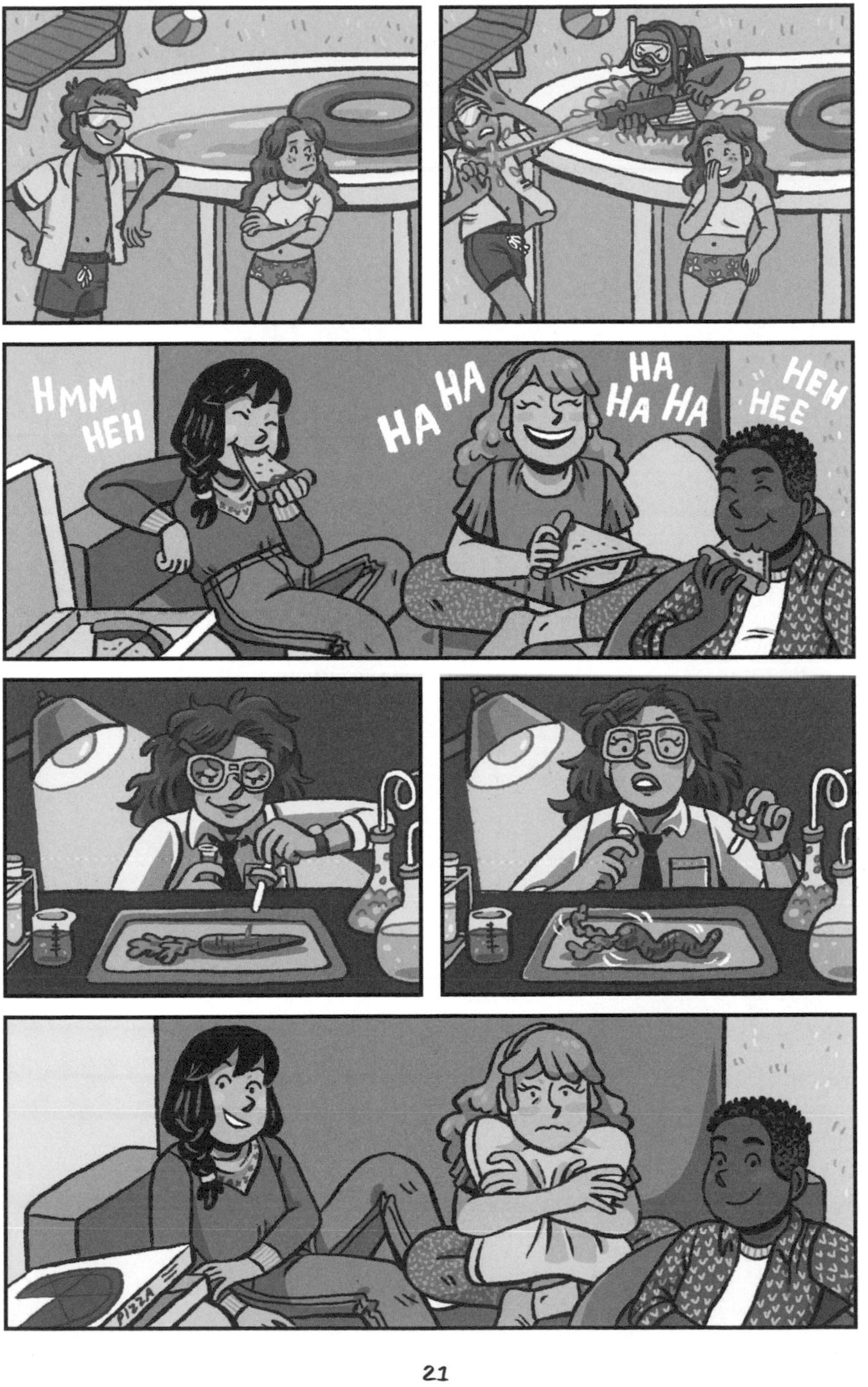
HMM
HEH
HA HA
HA
HA HA
HEH
HEE
PIZZA

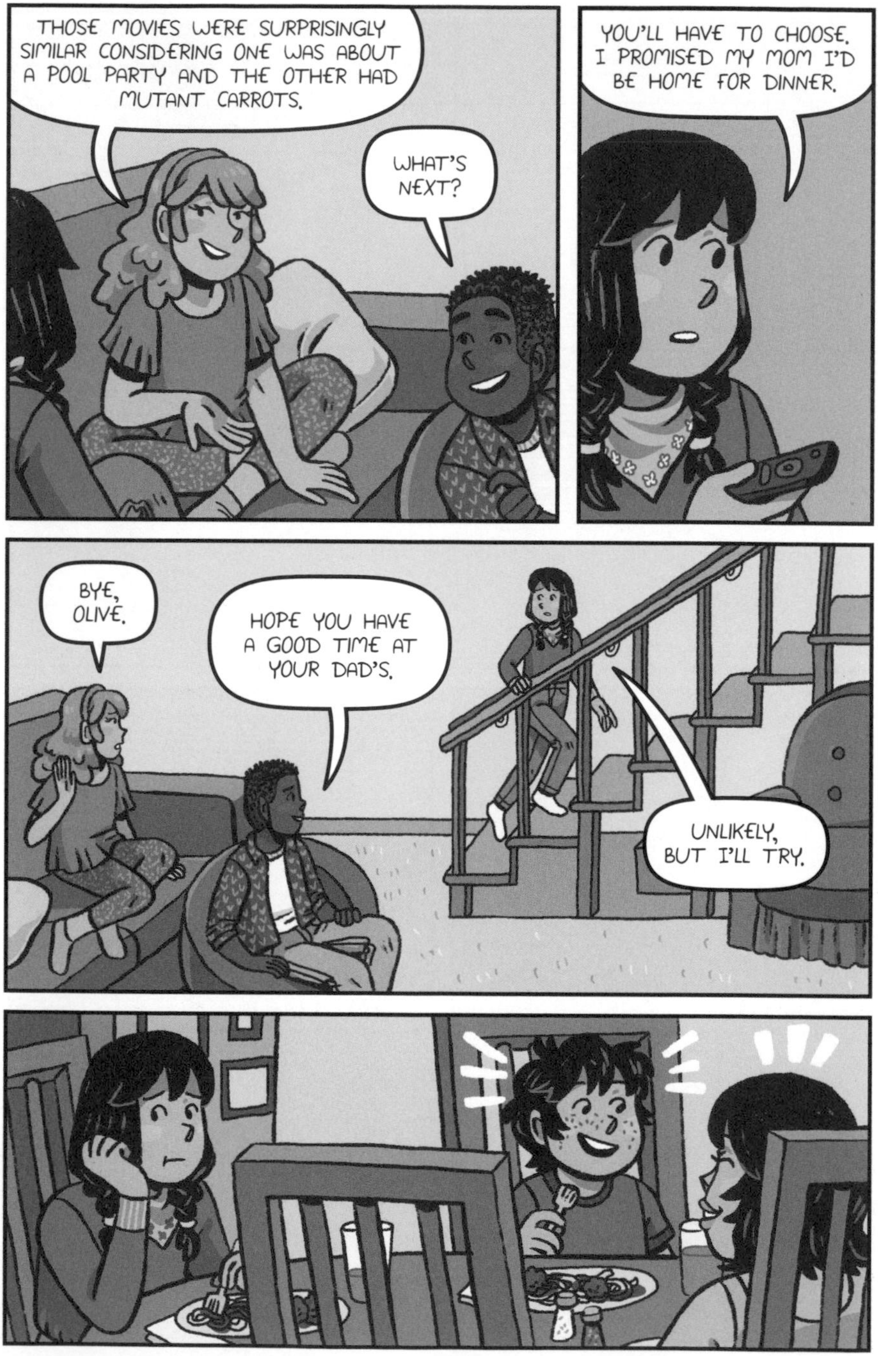
THOSE MOVIES WERE SURPRISINGLY SIMILAR CONSIDERING ONE WAS ABOUT A POOL PARTY AND THE OTHER HAD MUTANT CARROTS.
WHAT'S NEXT?
YOU'LL HAVE TO CHOOSE. I PROMISED MY MOM I'D BE HOME FOR DINNER.
BYE, OLIVE.
HOPE YOU HAVE A GOOD TIME AT YOUR DAD'S.
UNLIKELY, BUT I'LL TRY.

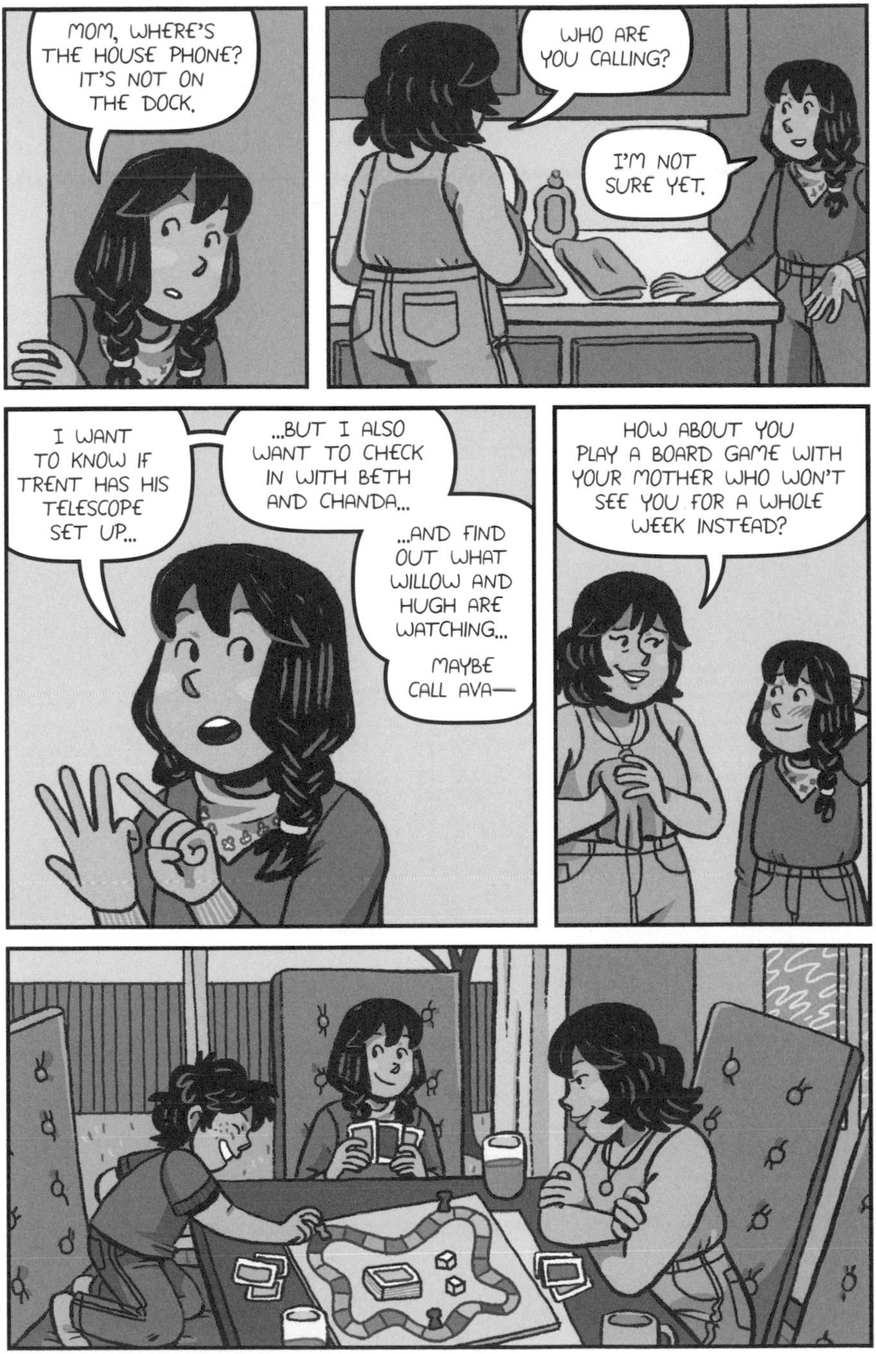

MOM, WHERE'S THE HOUSE PHONE? IT'S NOT ON THE DOCK.
WHO ARE YOU CALLING?
I'M NOT SURE YET.
I WANT TO KNOW IF TRENT HAS HIS TELESCOPE SET UP...
...BUT I ALSO WANT TO CHECK IN WITH BETH AND CHANDA...
...AND FIND OUT WHAT WILLOW AND HUGH ARE WATCHING...
MAYBE CALL AVA—
HOW ABOUT YOU PLAY A BOARD GAME WITH YOUR MOTHER WHO WON'T SEE YOU FOR A WHOLE WEEK INSTEAD?

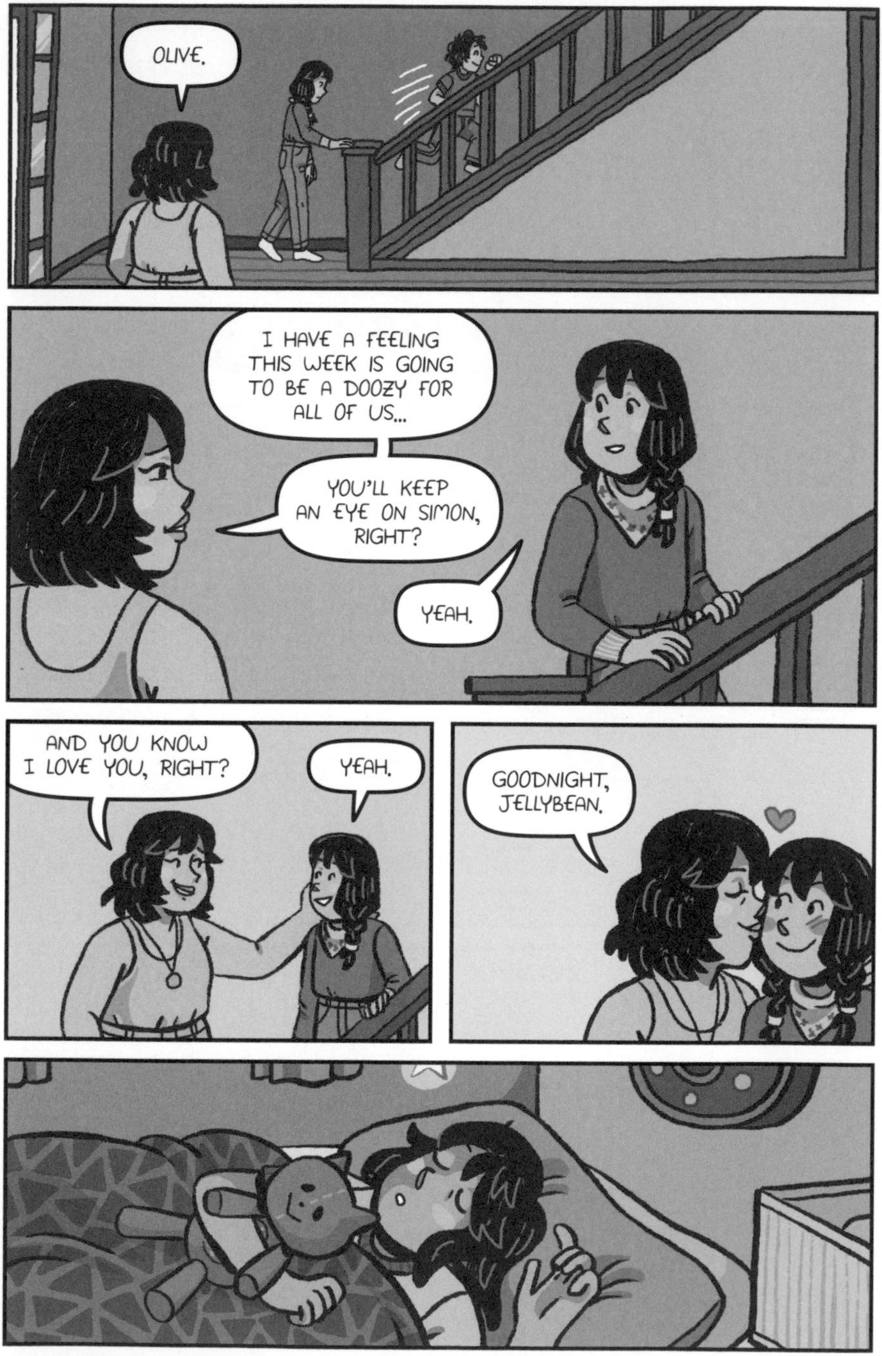
OLIVE.
I HAVE A FEELING THIS WEEK IS GOING TO BE A DOOZY FOR ALL OF US...
YOU'LL KEEP AN EYE ON SIMON, RIGHT?
YEAH.
AND YOU KNOW I LOVE YOU, RIGHT?
YEAH.
GOODNIGHT, JELLYBEAN.

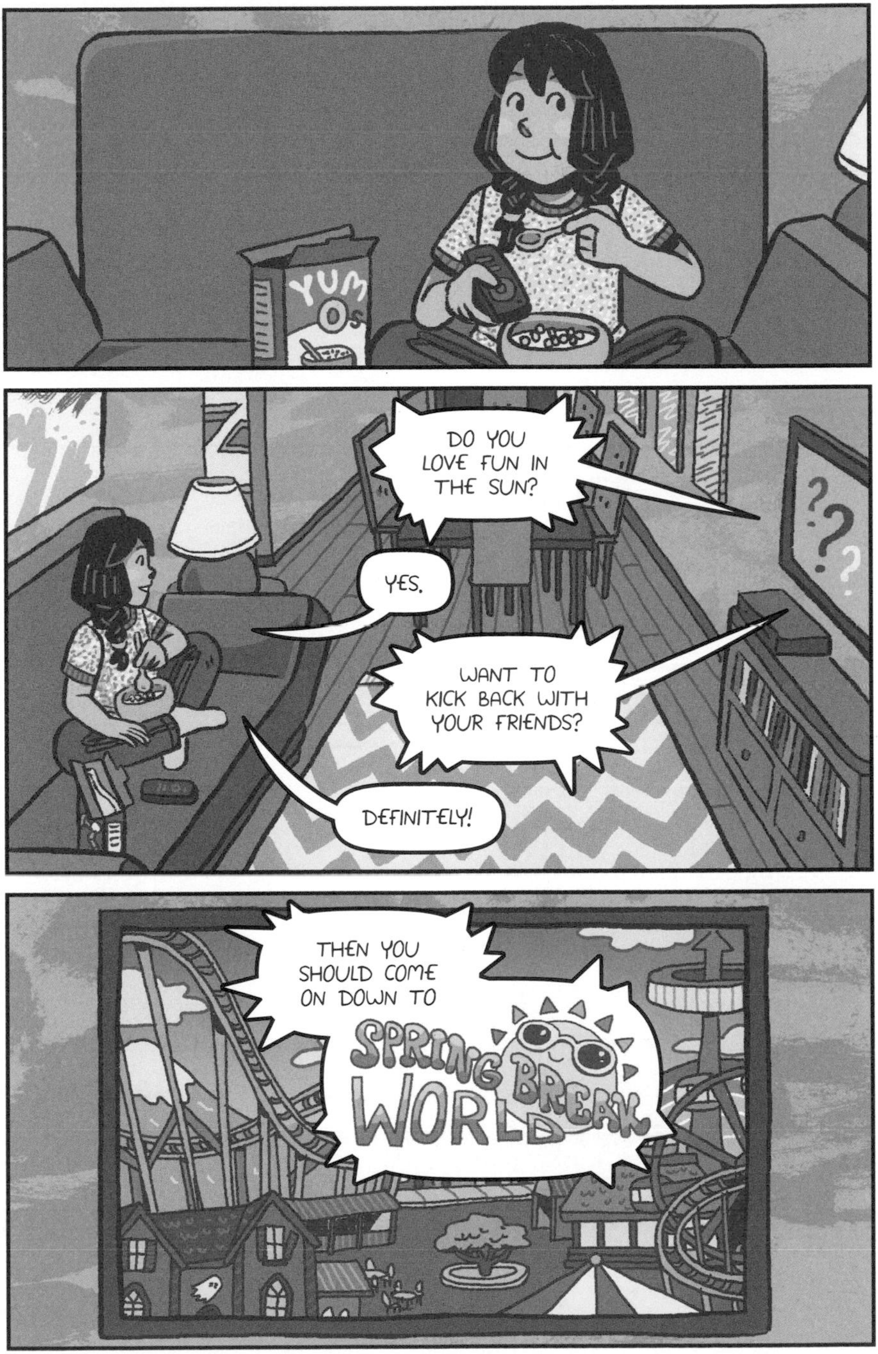
YUM Os
DO YOU LOVE FUN IN THE SUN?
YES.
WANT TO KICK BACK WITH YOUR FRIENDS?
DEFINITELY!
THEN YOU SHOULD COME ON DOWN TO
SPRING BREAK WORLD

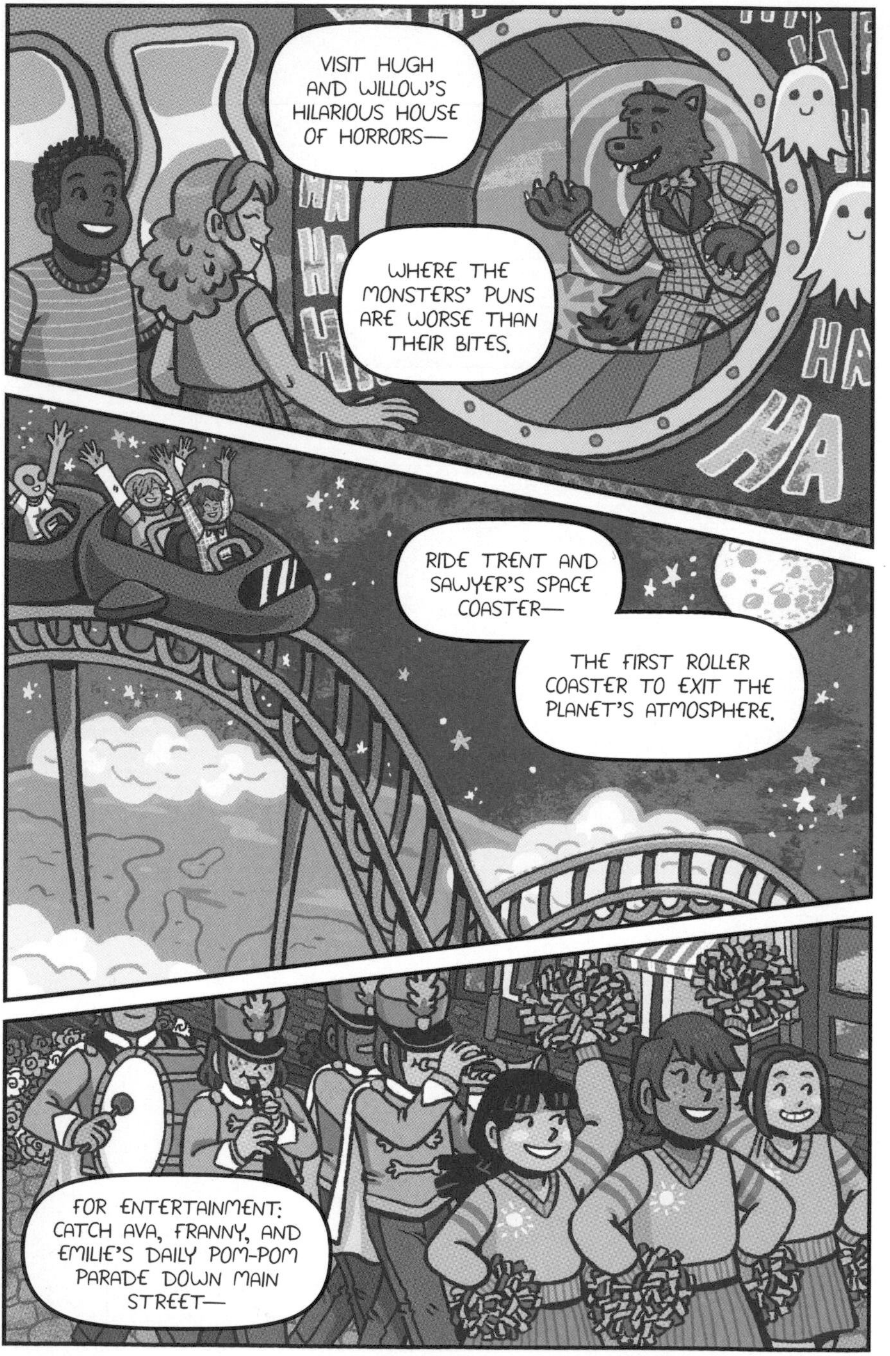
VISIT HUGH AND WILLOW'S HILARIOUS HOUSE OF HORRORS—
WHERE THE MONSTERS' PUNS ARE WORSE THAN THEIR BITES.
HA HA HA HA
HA HA
RIDE TRENT AND SAWYER'S SPACE COASTER—
THE FIRST ROLLER COASTER TO EXIT THE PLANET'S ATMOSPHERE.
FOR ENTERTAINMENT: CATCH AVA, FRANNY, AND EMILIE'S DAILY POM-POM PARADE DOWN MAIN STREET—

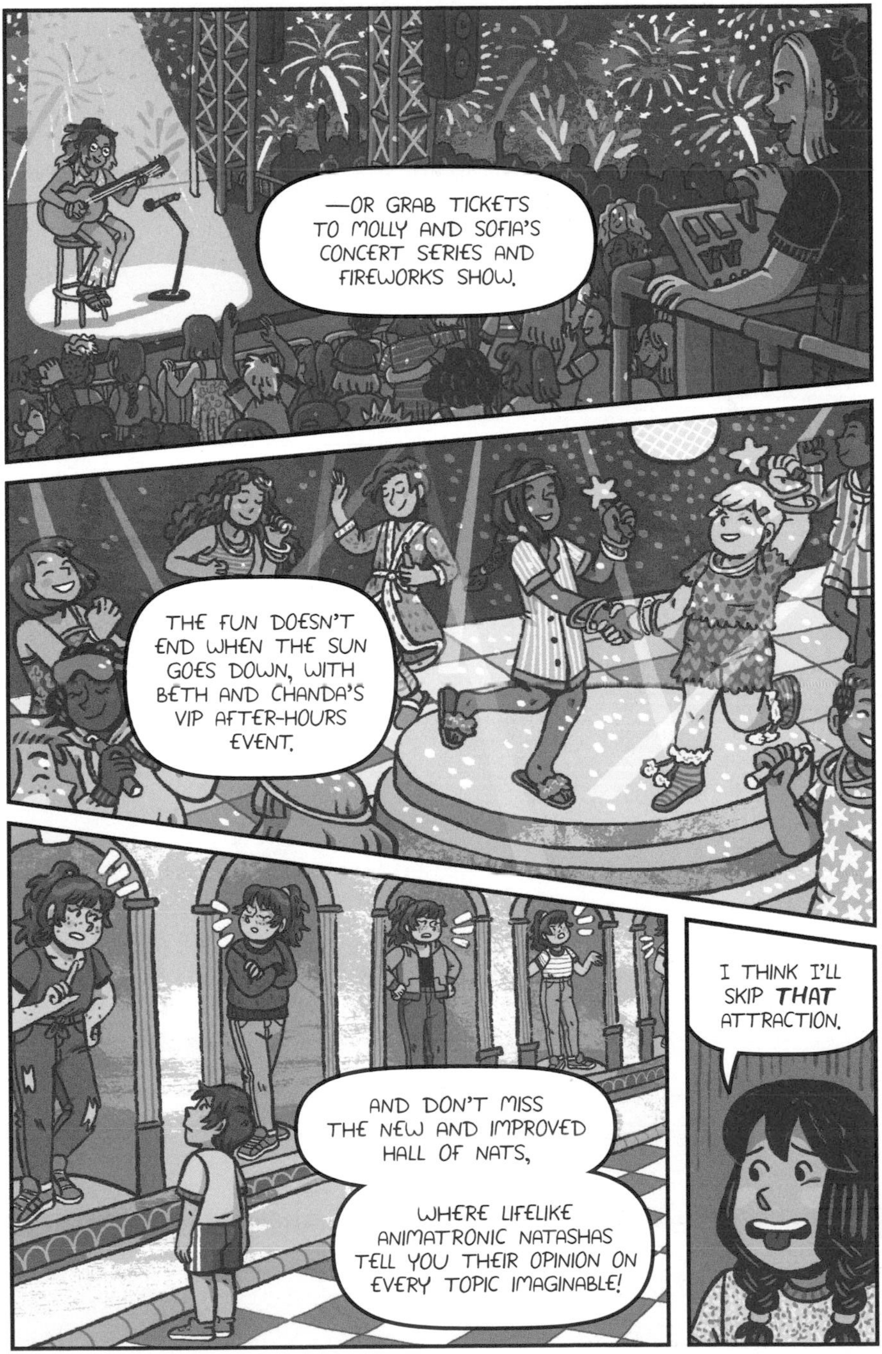
—OR GRAB TICKETS TO MOLLY AND SOFIA'S CONCERT SERIES AND FIREWORKS SHOW.
THE FUN DOESN'T END WHEN THE SUN GOES DOWN, WITH BETH AND CHANDA'S VIP AFTER-HOURS EVENT.
AND DON'T MISS THE NEW AND IMPROVED HALL OF NATS,
WHERE LIFELIKE ANIMATRONIC NATASHAS TELL YOU THEIR OPINION ON EVERY TOPIC IMAGINABLE!
I THINK I'LL SKIP **THAT** ATTRACTION.

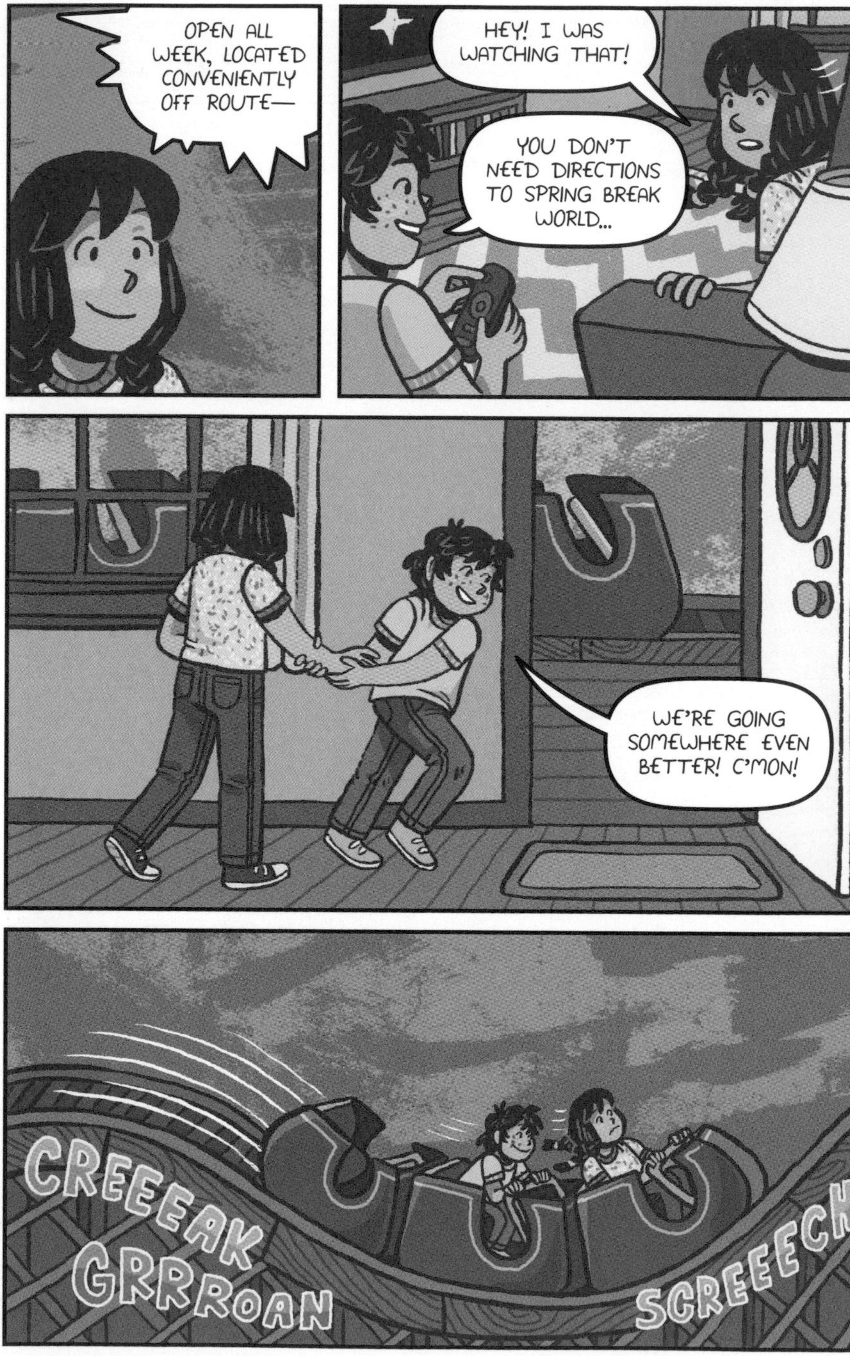
OPEN ALL WEEK, LOCATED CONVENIENTLY OFF ROUTE—
HEY! I WAS WATCHING THAT!
YOU DON'T NEED DIRECTIONS TO SPRING BREAK WORLD...
WE'RE GOING SOMEWHERE EVEN BETTER! C'MON!
CREEEAK
GRRROAN
SCREEECH

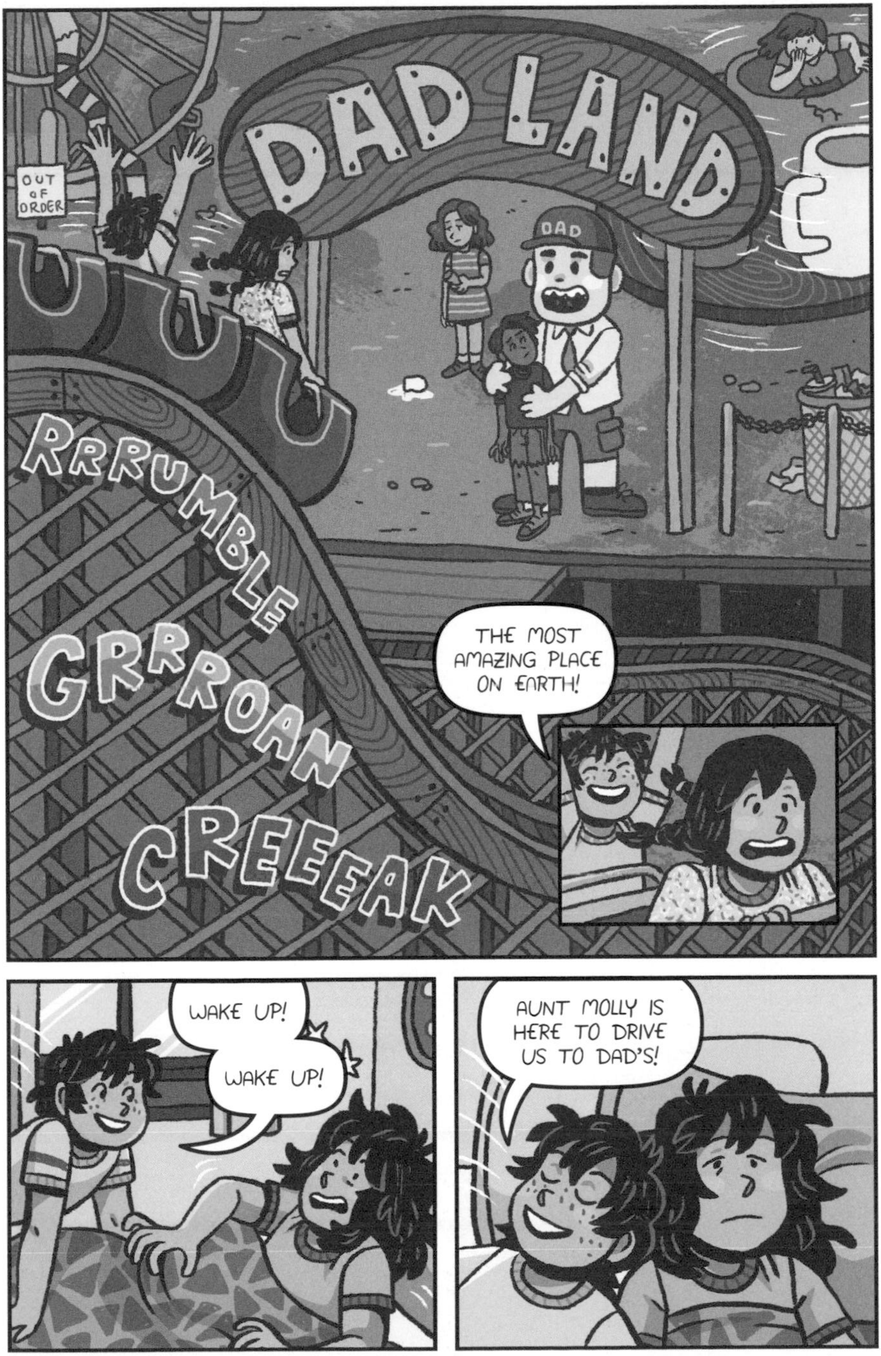
DAD LAND
OUT OF ORDER
DAD
RRRUMBLE
GRRROAN
CREEEAK
THE MOST AMAZING PLACE ON EARTH!
WAKE UP!
WAKE UP!
AUNT MOLLY IS HERE TO DRIVE US TO DAD'S!

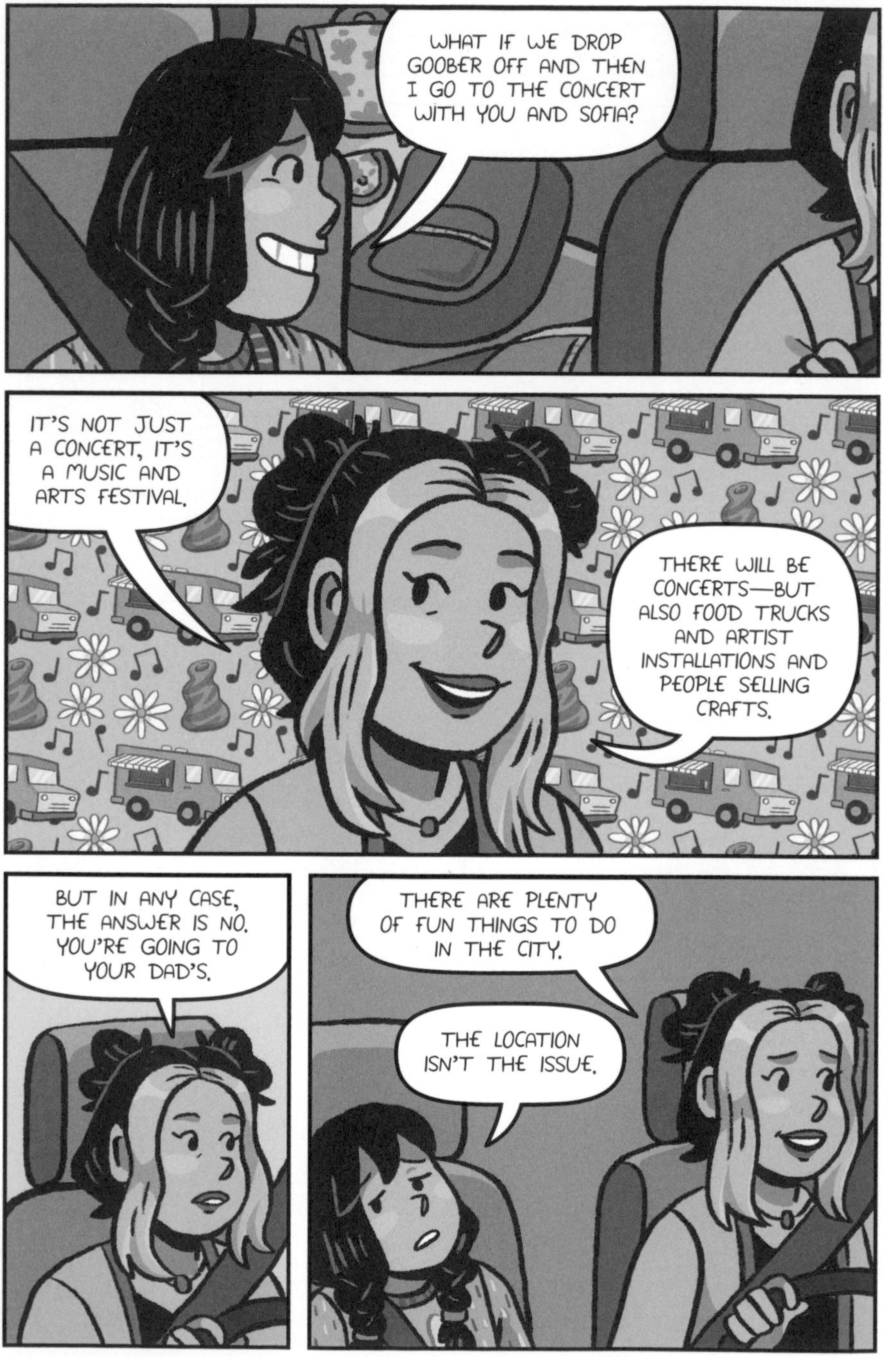
WHAT IF WE DROP GOOBER OFF AND THEN I GO TO THE CONCERT WITH YOU AND SOFIA?
IT'S NOT JUST A CONCERT, IT'S A MUSIC AND ARTS FESTIVAL.
THERE WILL BE CONCERTS—BUT ALSO FOOD TRUCKS AND ARTIST INSTALLATIONS AND PEOPLE SELLING CRAFTS.
BUT IN ANY CASE, THE ANSWER IS NO. YOU'RE GOING TO YOUR DAD'S.
THERE ARE PLENTY OF FUN THINGS TO DO IN THE CITY.
THE LOCATION ISN'T THE ISSUE.

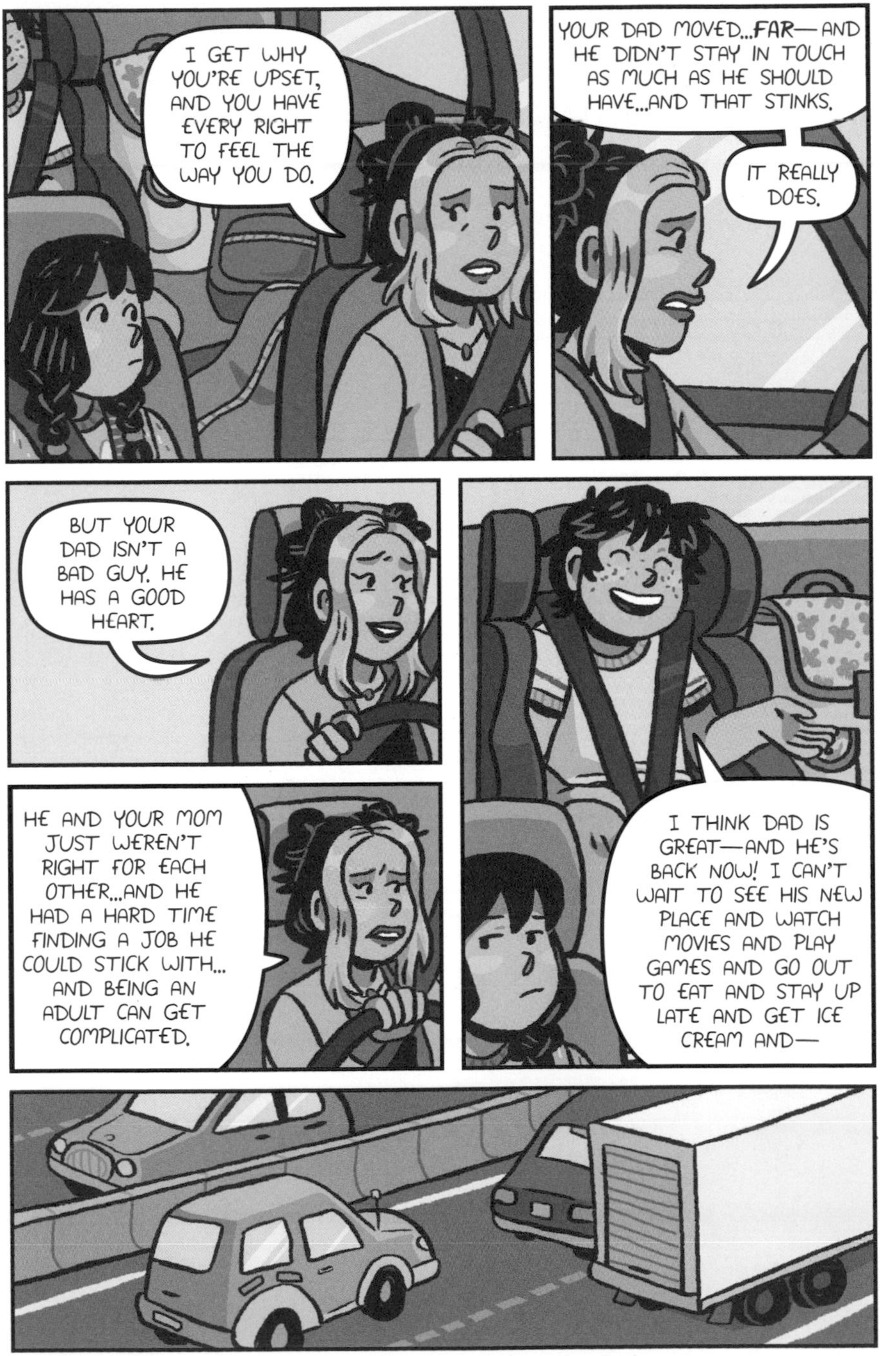
I GET WHY YOU'RE UPSET, AND YOU HAVE EVERY RIGHT TO FEEL THE WAY YOU DO.
YOUR DAD MOVED...**FAR**— AND HE DIDN'T STAY IN TOUCH AS MUCH AS HE SHOULD HAVE...AND THAT STINKS.
IT REALLY DOES.
BUT YOUR DAD ISN'T A BAD GUY. HE HAS A GOOD HEART.
HE AND YOUR MOM JUST WEREN'T RIGHT FOR EACH OTHER...AND HE HAD A HARD TIME FINDING A JOB HE COULD STICK WITH... AND BEING AN ADULT CAN GET COMPLICATED.
I THINK DAD IS GREAT—AND HE'S BACK NOW! I CAN'T WAIT TO SEE HIS NEW PLACE AND WATCH MOVIES AND PLAY GAMES AND GO OUT TO EAT AND STAY UP LATE AND GET ICE CREAM AND—

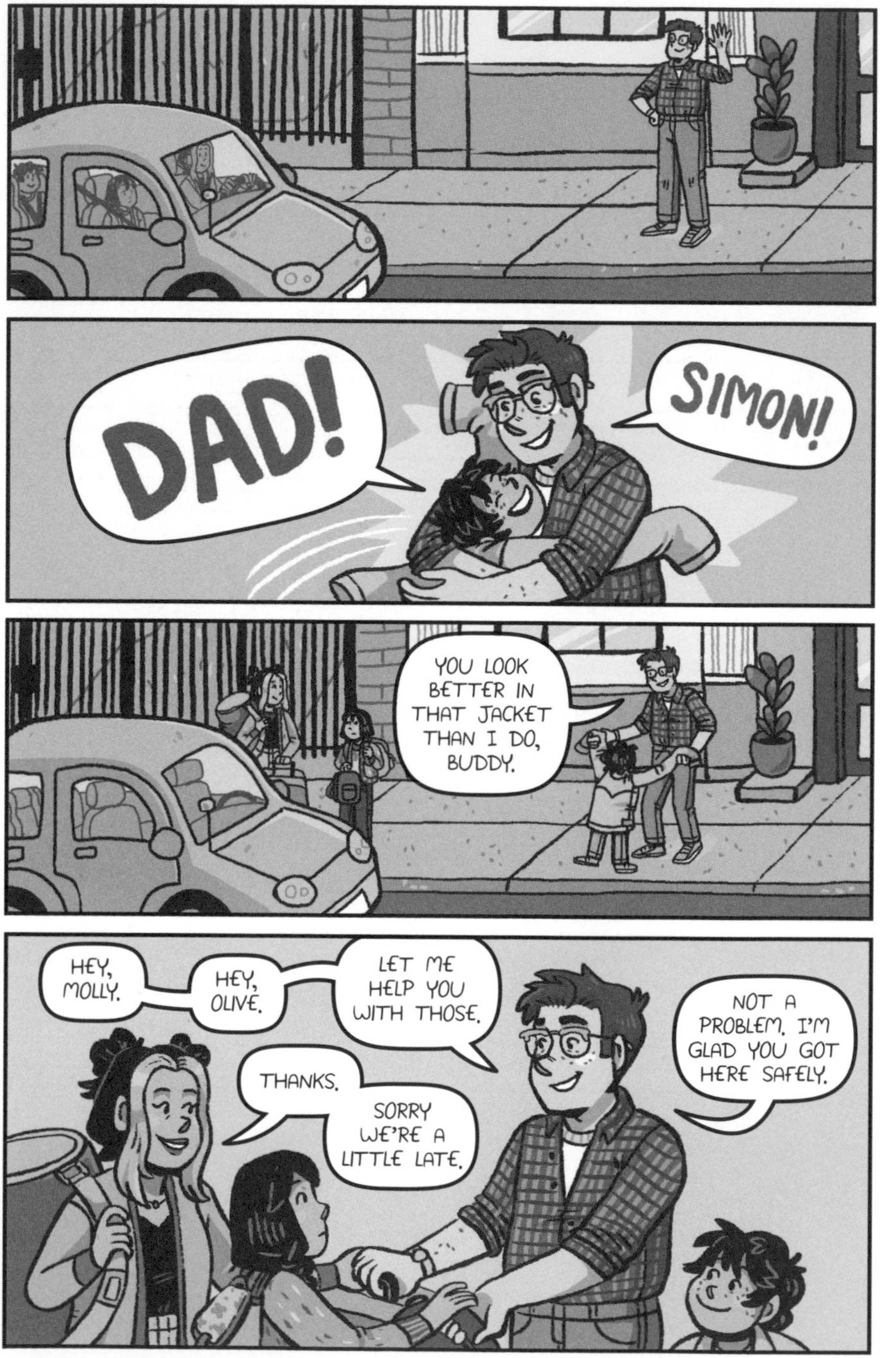
DAD!
SIMON!
YOU LOOK BETTER IN THAT JACKET THAN I DO, BUDDY.
HEY, MOLLY.
HEY, OLIVE.
LET ME HELP YOU WITH THOSE.
THANKS.
SORRY WE'RE A LITTLE LATE.
NOT A PROBLEM. I'M GLAD YOU GOT HERE SAFELY.

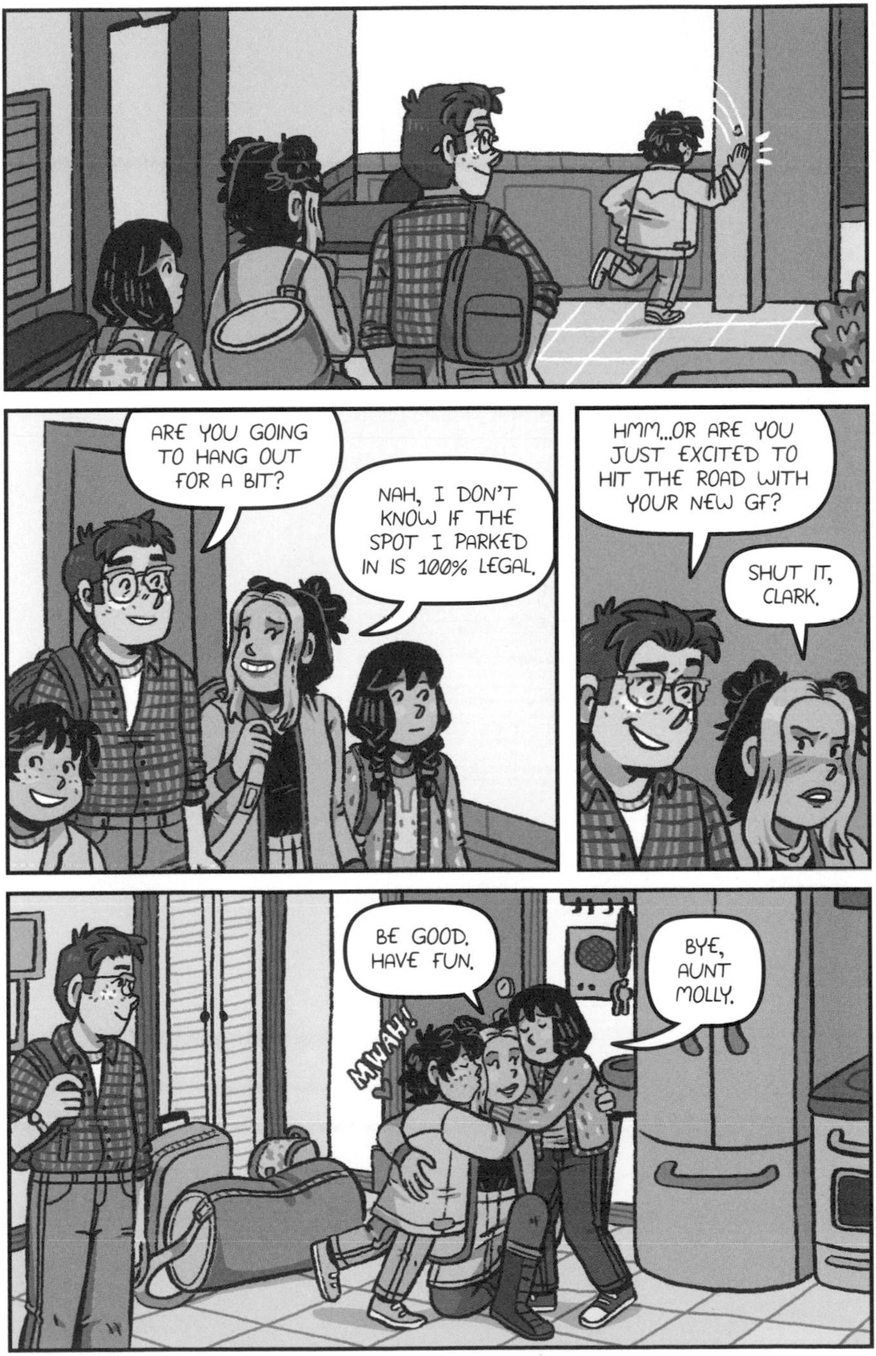
ARE YOU GOING TO HANG OUT FOR A BIT?
NAH, I DON'T KNOW IF THE SPOT I PARKED IN IS 100% LEGAL.
HMM...OR ARE YOU JUST EXCITED TO HIT THE ROAD WITH YOUR NEW GF?
SHUT IT, CLARK.
BE GOOD. HAVE FUN.
BYE, AUNT MOLLY.
MWAH!

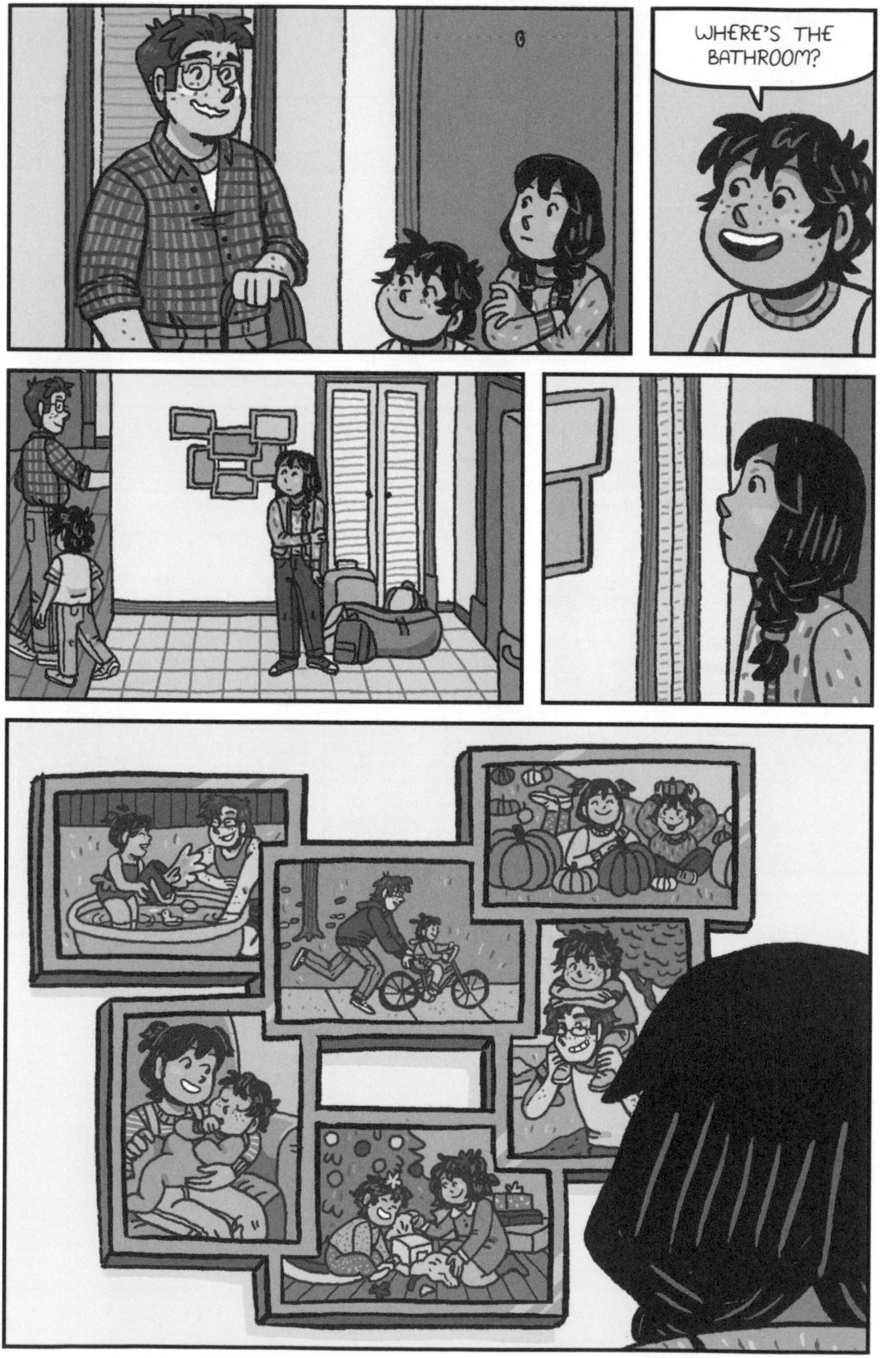
WHERE'S THE BATHROOM?

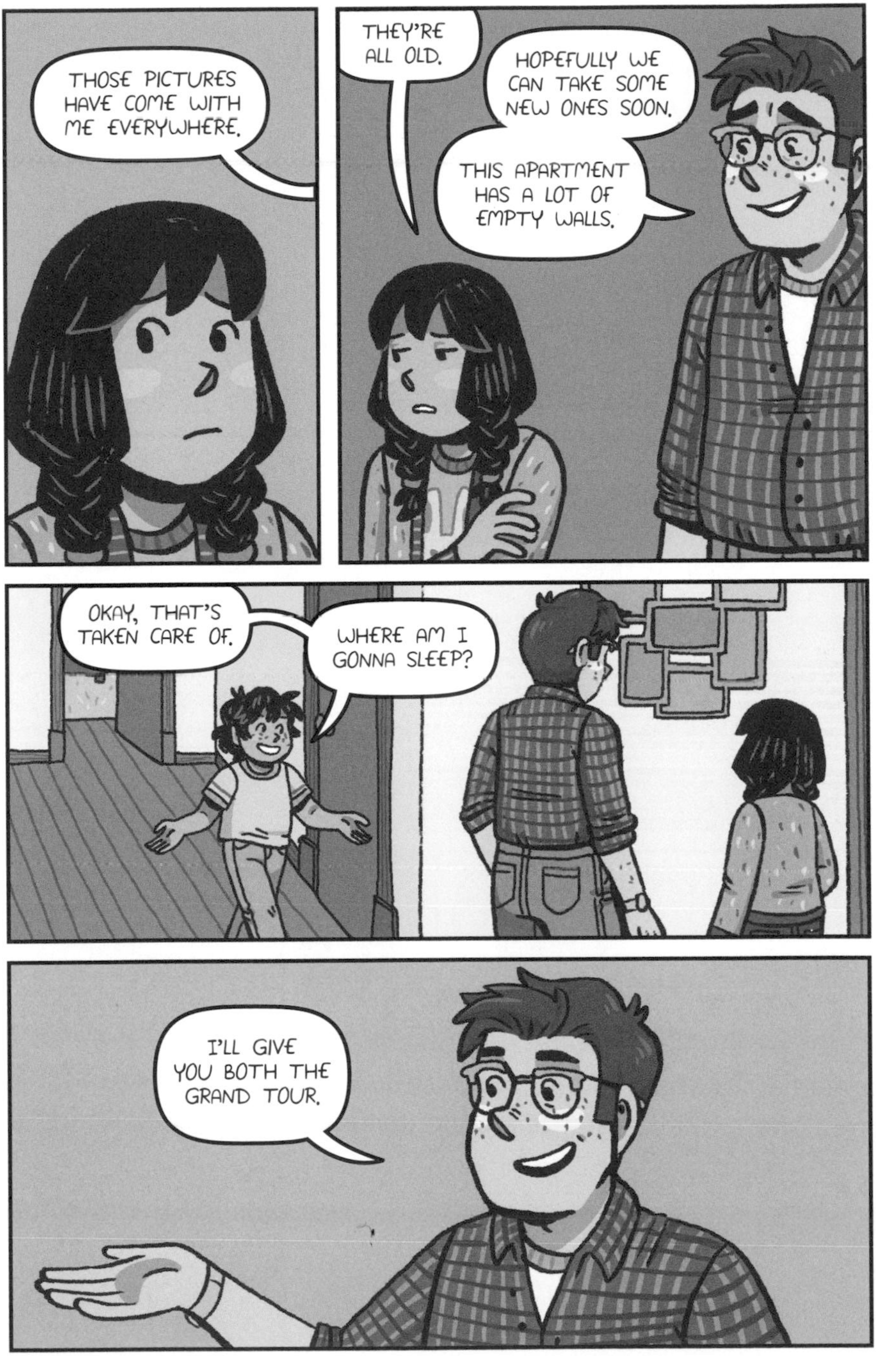
THOSE PICTURES HAVE COME WITH ME EVERYWHERE.
THEY'RE ALL OLD.
HOPEFULLY WE CAN TAKE SOME NEW ONES SOON.
THIS APARTMENT HAS A LOT OF EMPTY WALLS.
OKAY, THAT'S TAKEN CARE OF.
WHERE AM I GONNA SLEEP?
I'LL GIVE YOU BOTH THE GRAND TOUR.

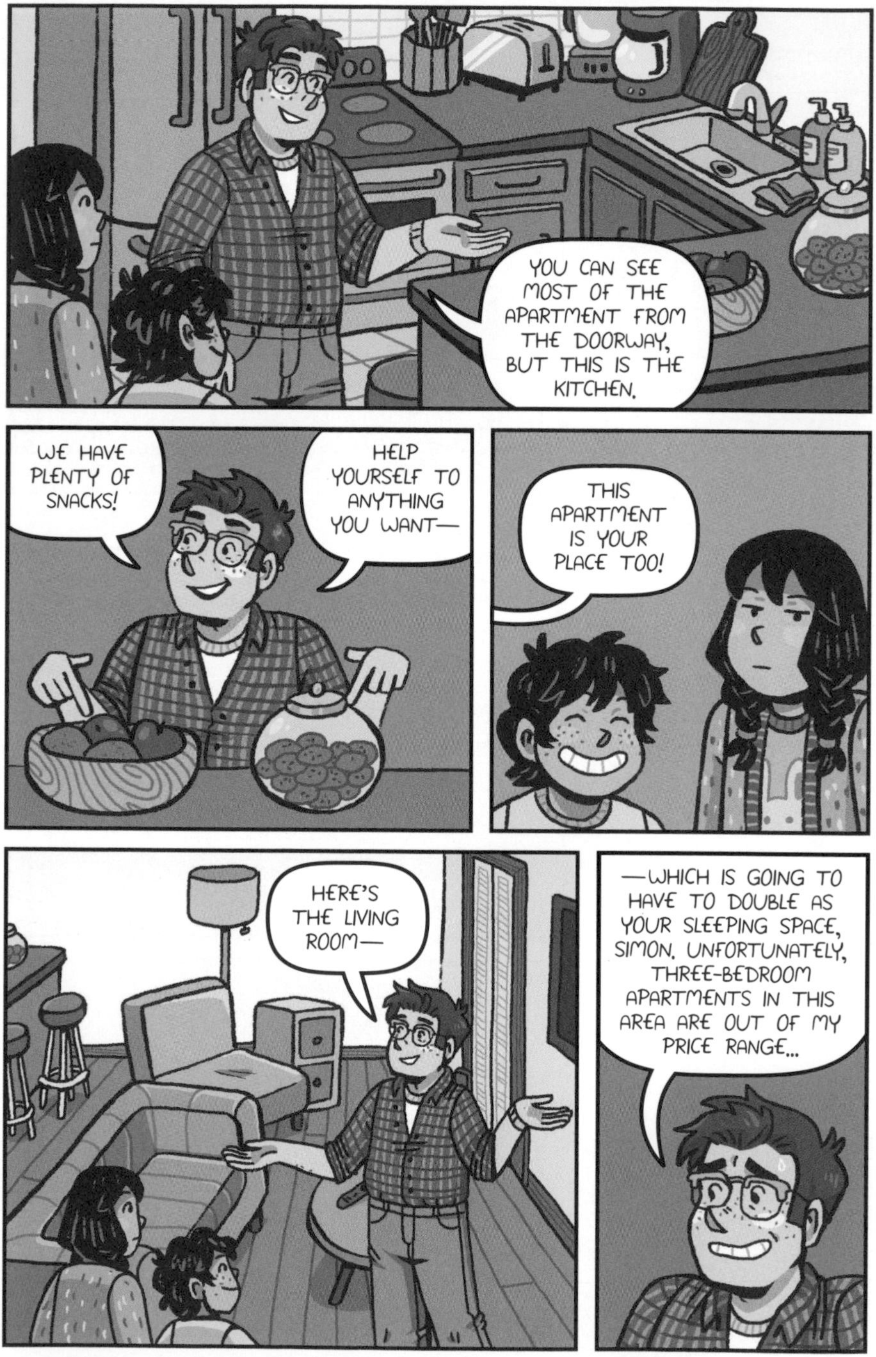
YOU CAN SEE MOST OF THE APARTMENT FROM THE DOORWAY, BUT THIS IS THE KITCHEN.
WE HAVE PLENTY OF SNACKS!
HELP YOURSELF TO ANYTHING YOU WANT—
THIS APARTMENT IS YOUR PLACE TOO!
HERE'S THE LIVING ROOM—
—WHICH IS GOING TO HAVE TO DOUBLE AS YOUR SLEEPING SPACE, SIMON. UNFORTUNATELY, THREE-BEDROOM APARTMENTS IN THIS AREA ARE OUT OF MY PRICE RANGE...

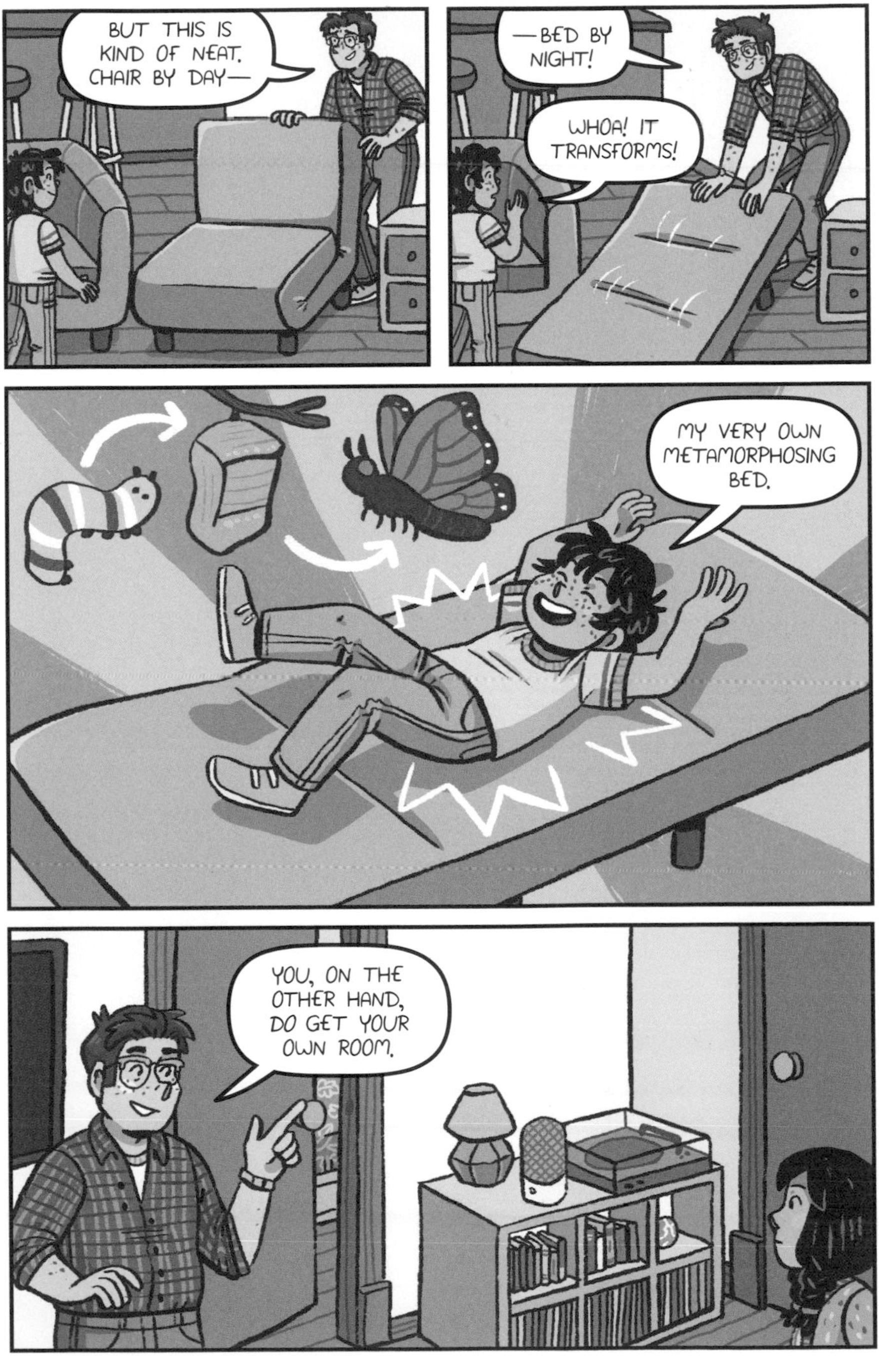
BUT THIS IS KIND OF NEAT. CHAIR BY DAY—
—BED BY NIGHT!
WHOA! IT TRANSFORMS!
MY VERY OWN METAMORPHOSING BED.
YOU, ON THE OTHER HAND, DO GET YOUR OWN ROOM.

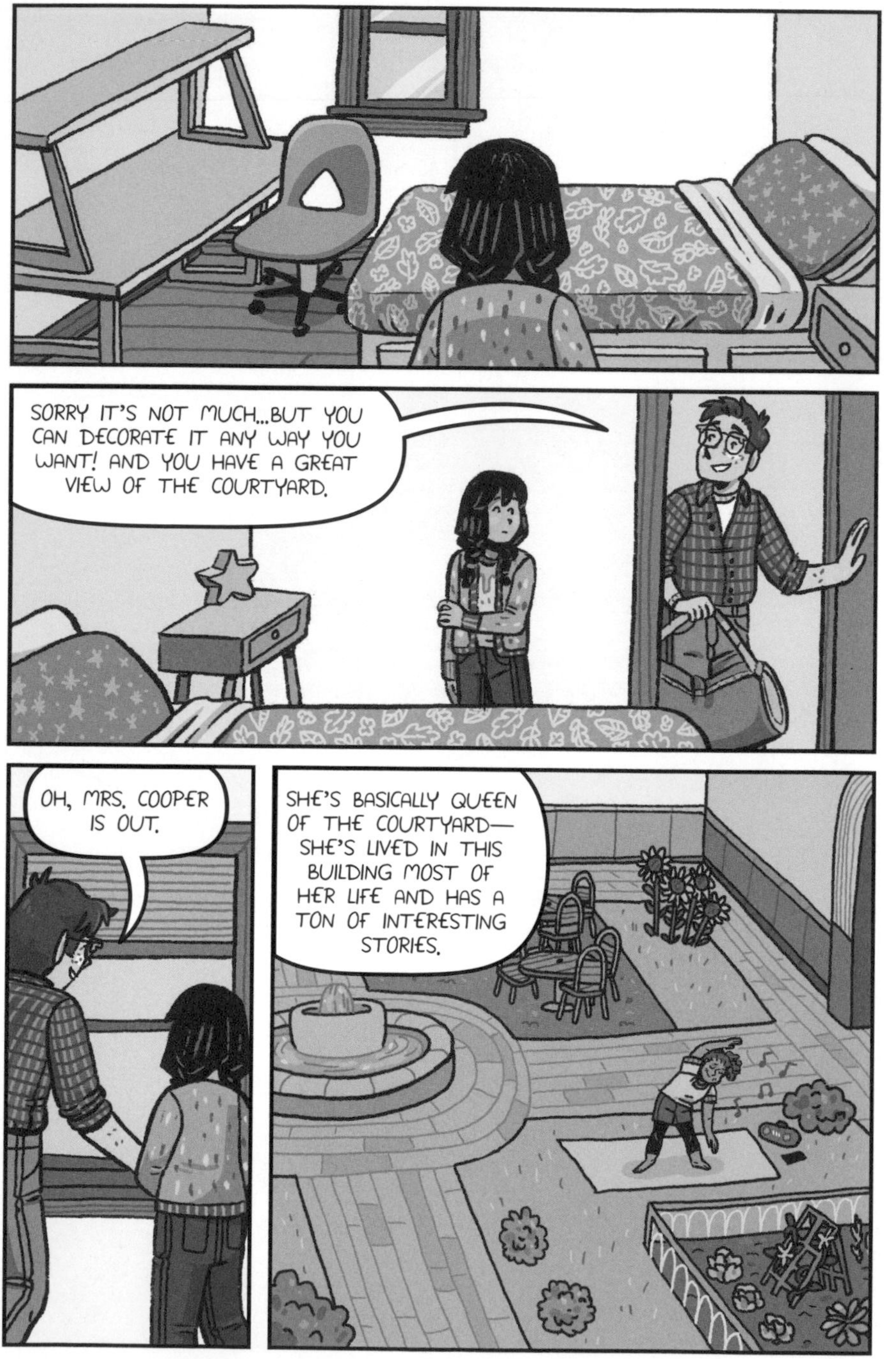
SORRY IT'S NOT MUCH...BUT YOU CAN DECORATE IT ANY WAY YOU WANT! AND YOU HAVE A GREAT VIEW OF THE COURTYARD.
OH, MRS. COOPER IS OUT.
SHE'S BASICALLY QUEEN OF THE COURTYARD— SHE'S LIVED IN THIS BUILDING MOST OF HER LIFE AND HAS A TON OF INTERESTING STORIES.

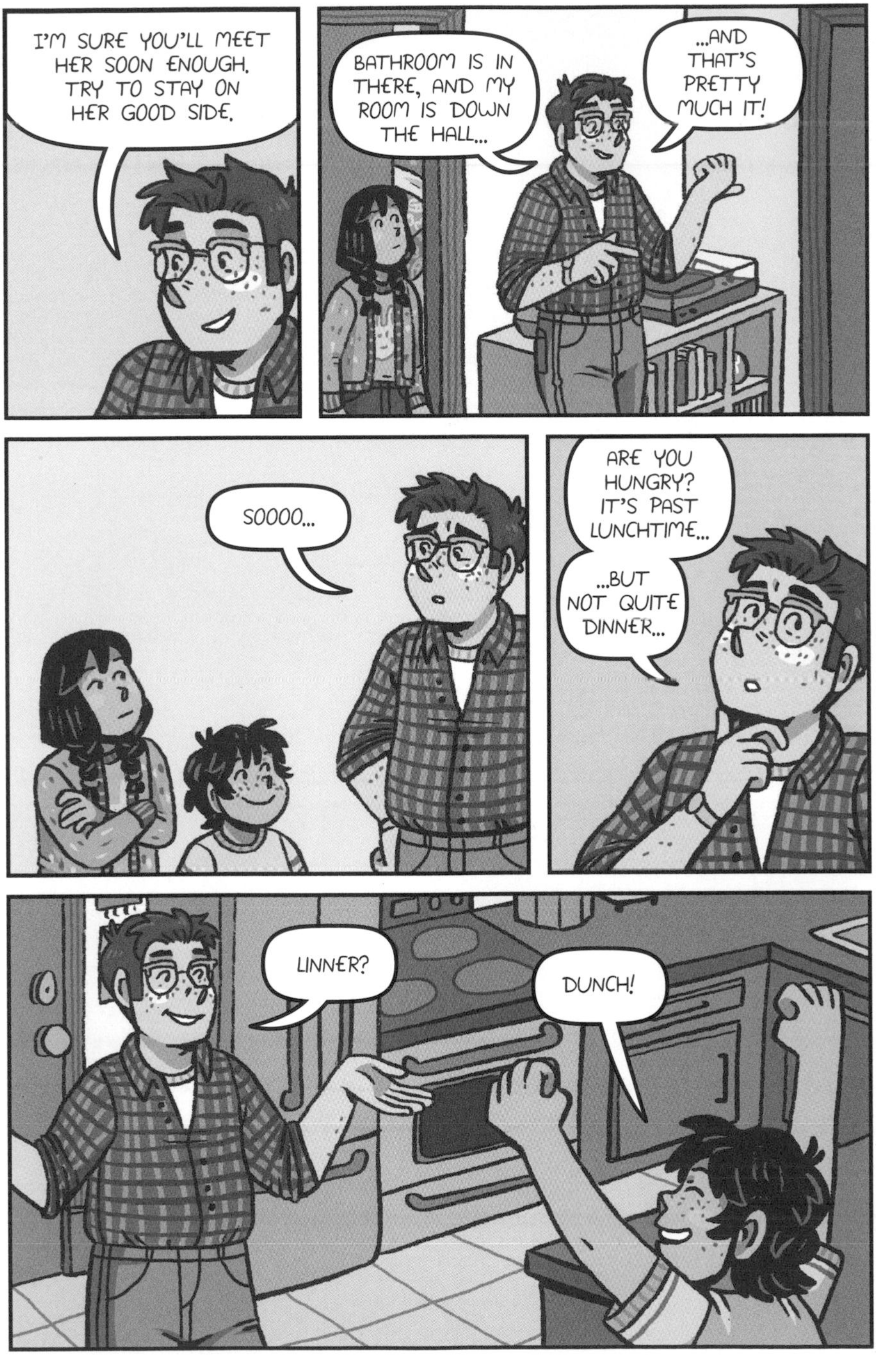
I'M SURE YOU'LL MEET HER SOON ENOUGH. TRY TO STAY ON HER GOOD SIDE.
BATHROOM IS IN THERE, AND MY ROOM IS DOWN THE HALL...
...AND THAT'S PRETTY MUCH IT!
SOOOO...
ARE YOU HUNGRY? IT'S PAST LUNCHTIME...
...BUT NOT QUITE DINNER...
LINNER?
DUNCH!

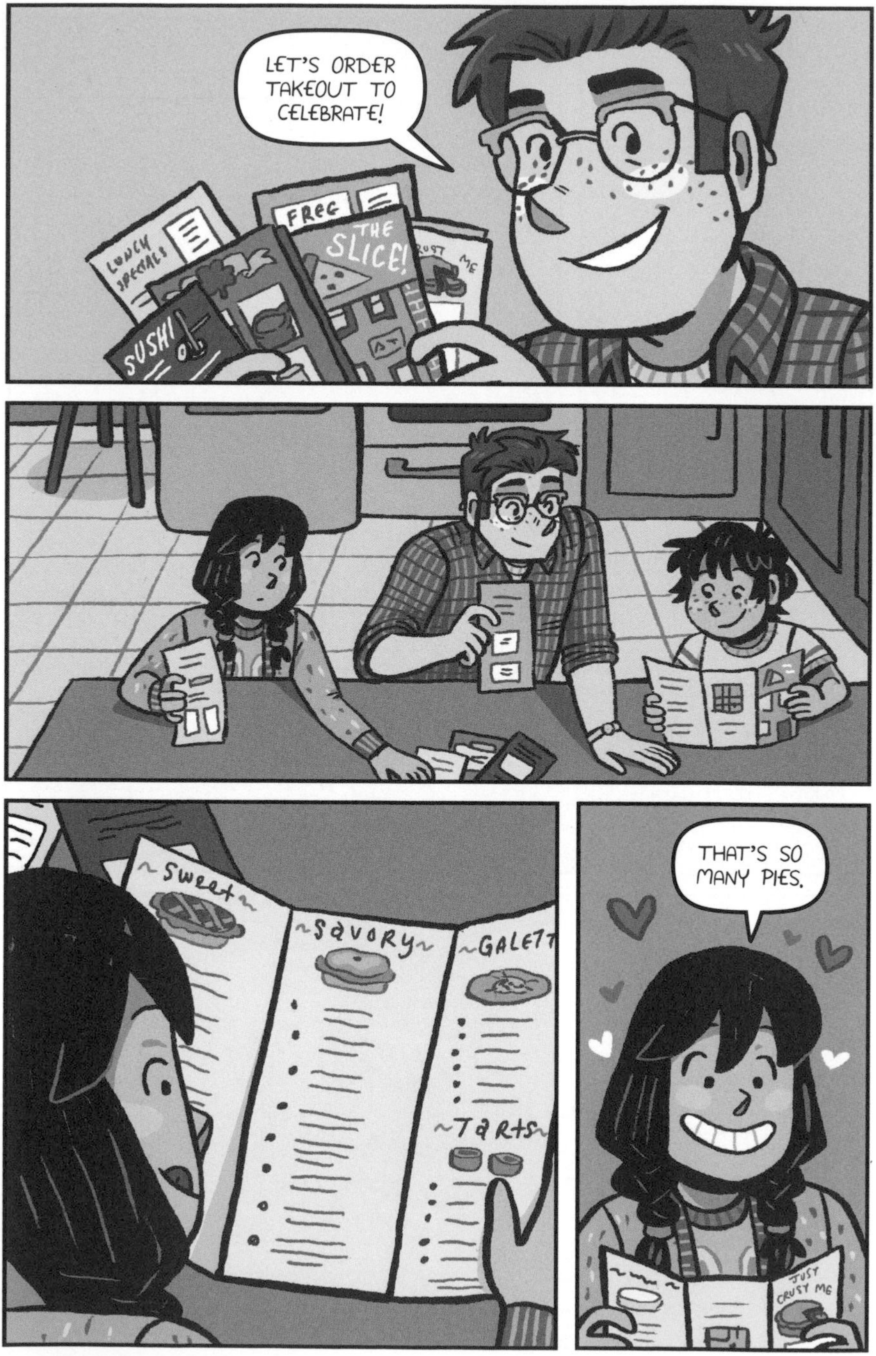
LET'S ORDER TAKEOUT TO CELEBRATE!
LUNCH SPECIALS
THE SLICE!
SUSHI
Sweet
savory
Tarts
THAT'S SO MANY PIES.
JUST CRUSTY ME

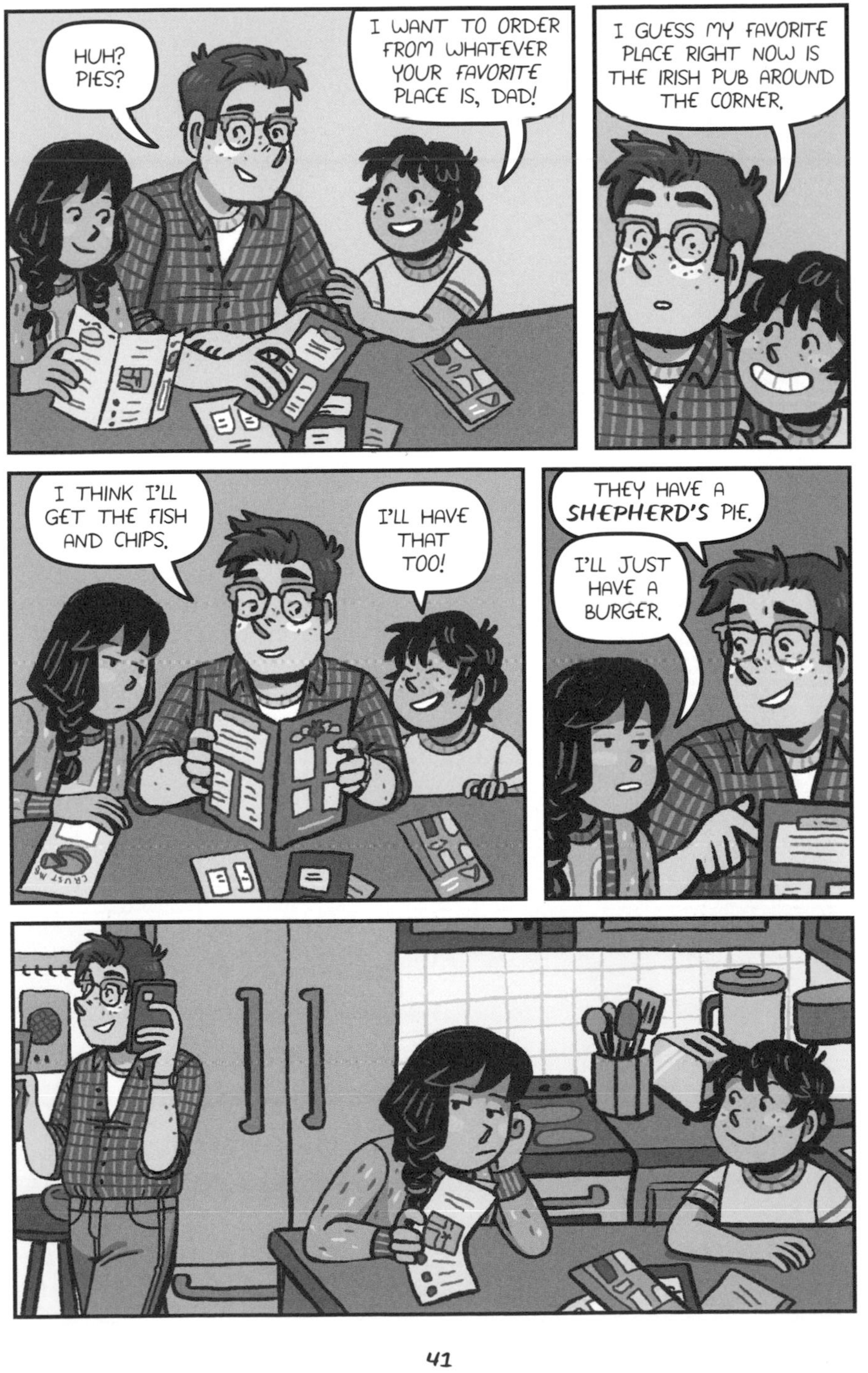

HUH? PIES?
I WANT TO ORDER FROM WHATEVER YOUR *FAVORITE* PLACE IS, DAD!
I GUESS MY FAVORITE PLACE RIGHT NOW IS THE IRISH PUB AROUND THE CORNER.
I THINK I'LL GET THE FISH AND CHIPS.
I'LL HAVE THAT TOO!
CRUST ME
THEY HAVE A **SHEPHERD'S** PIE.
I'LL JUST HAVE A BURGER.

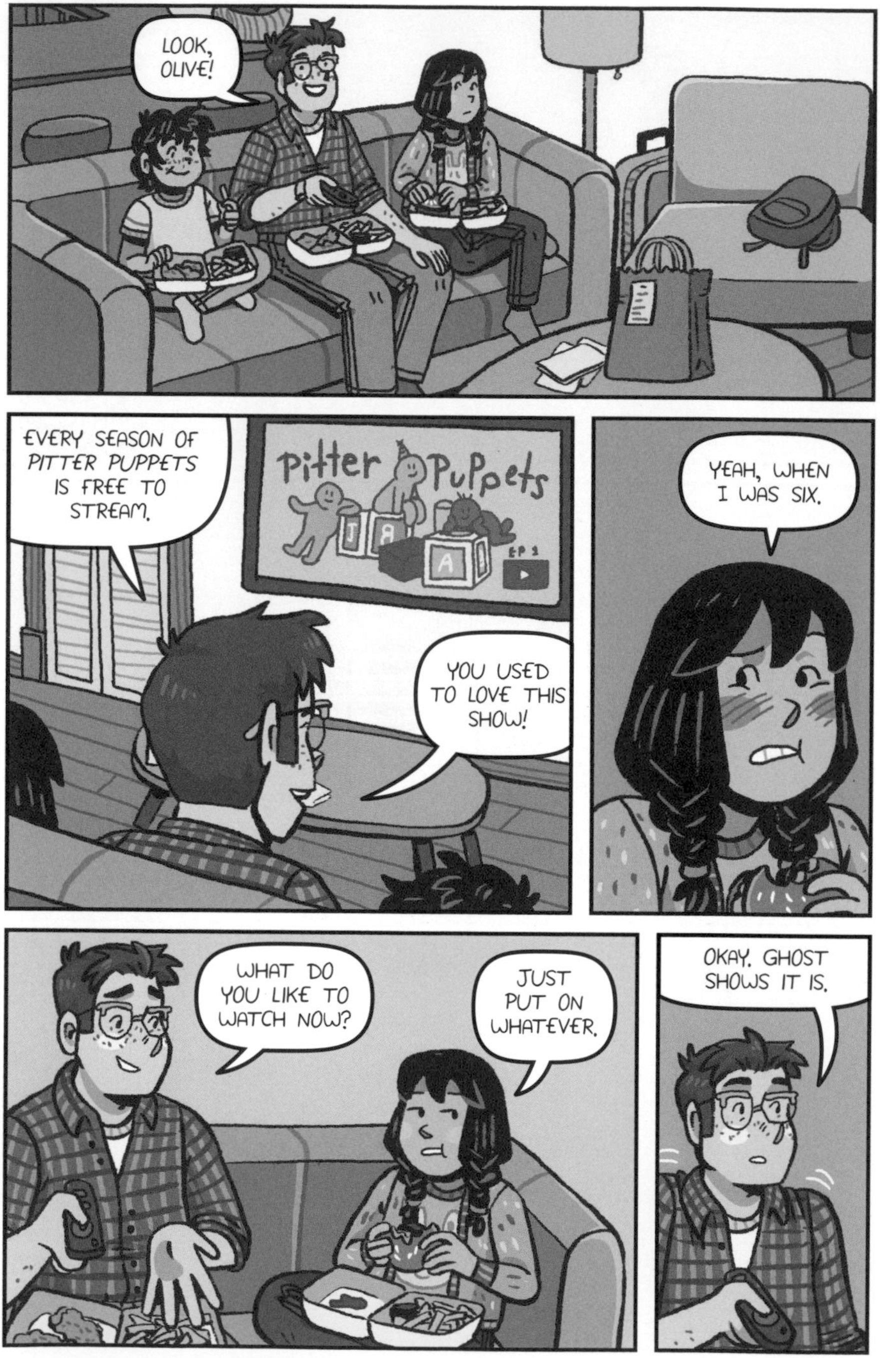
LOOK, OLIVE!
EVERY SEASON OF PITTER PUPPETS IS FREE TO STREAM.
pitter Puppets
EP 1
YOU USED TO LOVE THIS SHOW!
YEAH, WHEN I WAS SIX.
WHAT DO YOU LIKE TO WATCH NOW?
JUST PUT ON WHATEVER.
OKAY. GHOST SHOWS IT IS.

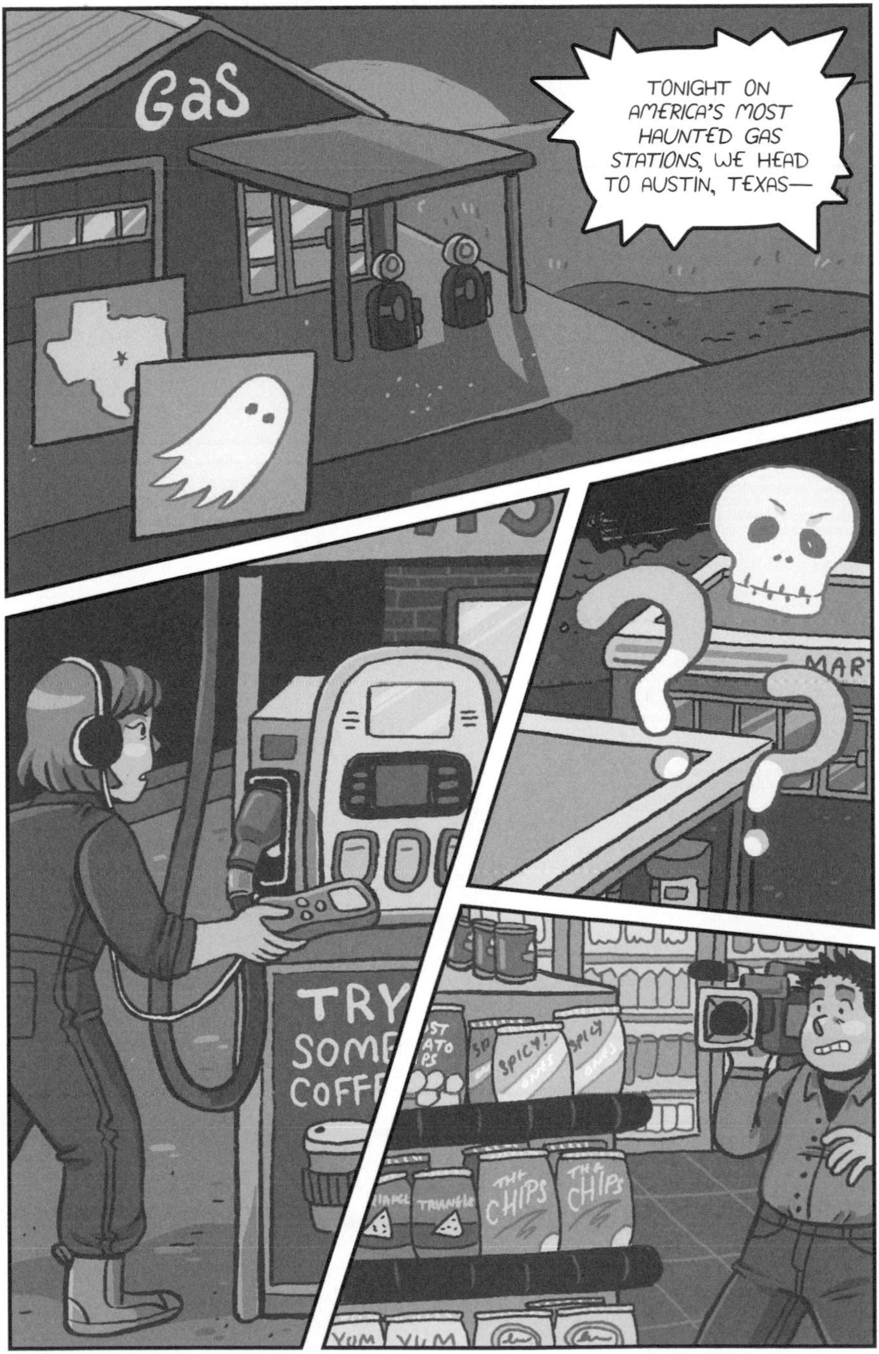
Gas
TONIGHT ON AMERICA'S MOST HAUNTED GAS STATIONS, WE HEAD TO AUSTIN, TEXAS—
MART
TRY
SPICY!
THE CHIPS
THE CHIPS
TRIANGLE
YUM

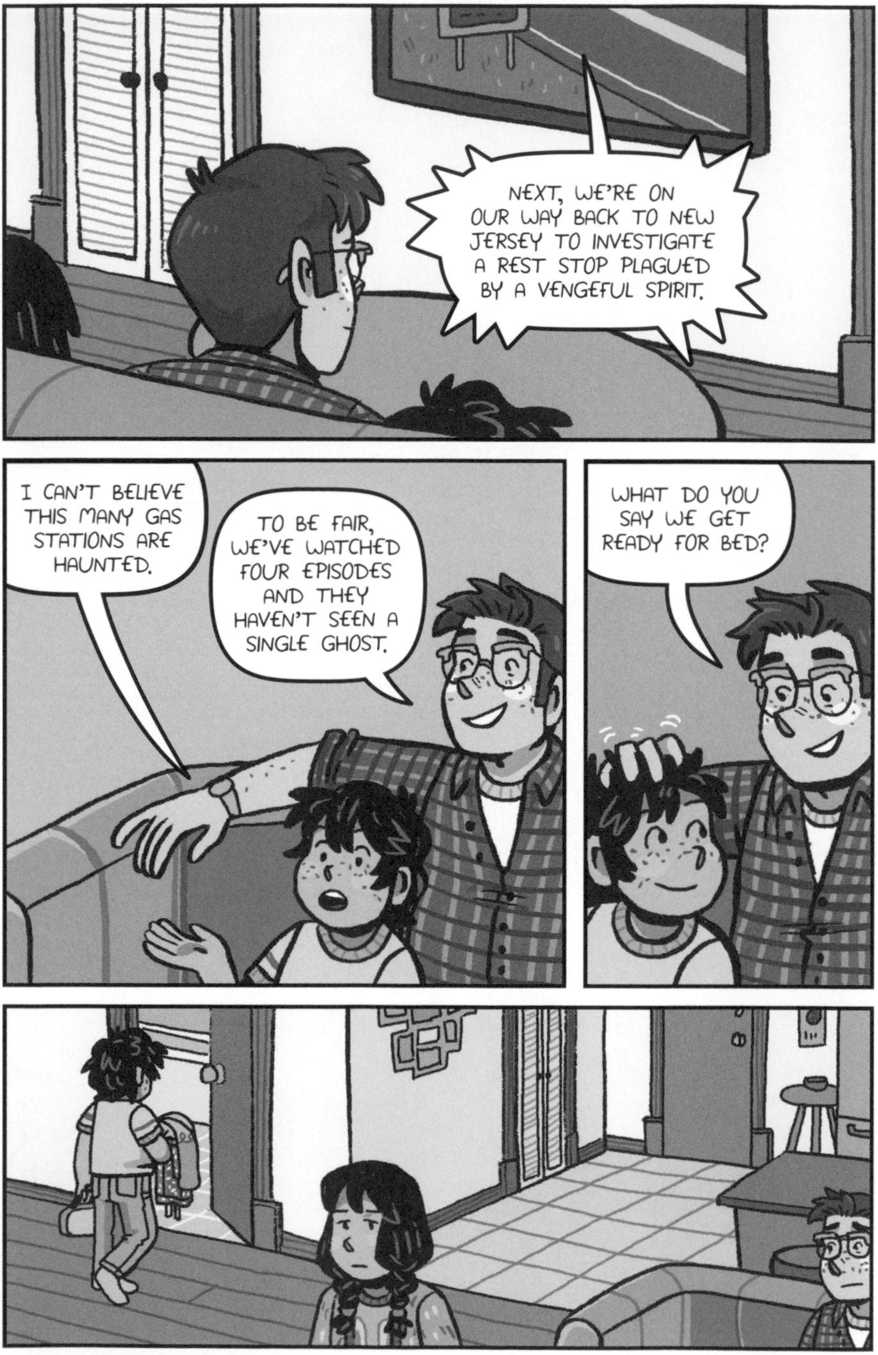
NEXT, WE'RE ON OUR WAY BACK TO NEW JERSEY TO INVESTIGATE A REST STOP PLAGUED BY A VENGEFUL SPIRIT.
I CAN'T BELIEVE THIS MANY GAS STATIONS ARE HAUNTED.
TO BE FAIR, WE'VE WATCHED FOUR EPISODES AND THEY HAVEN'T SEEN A SINGLE GHOST.
WHAT DO YOU SAY WE GET READY FOR BED?

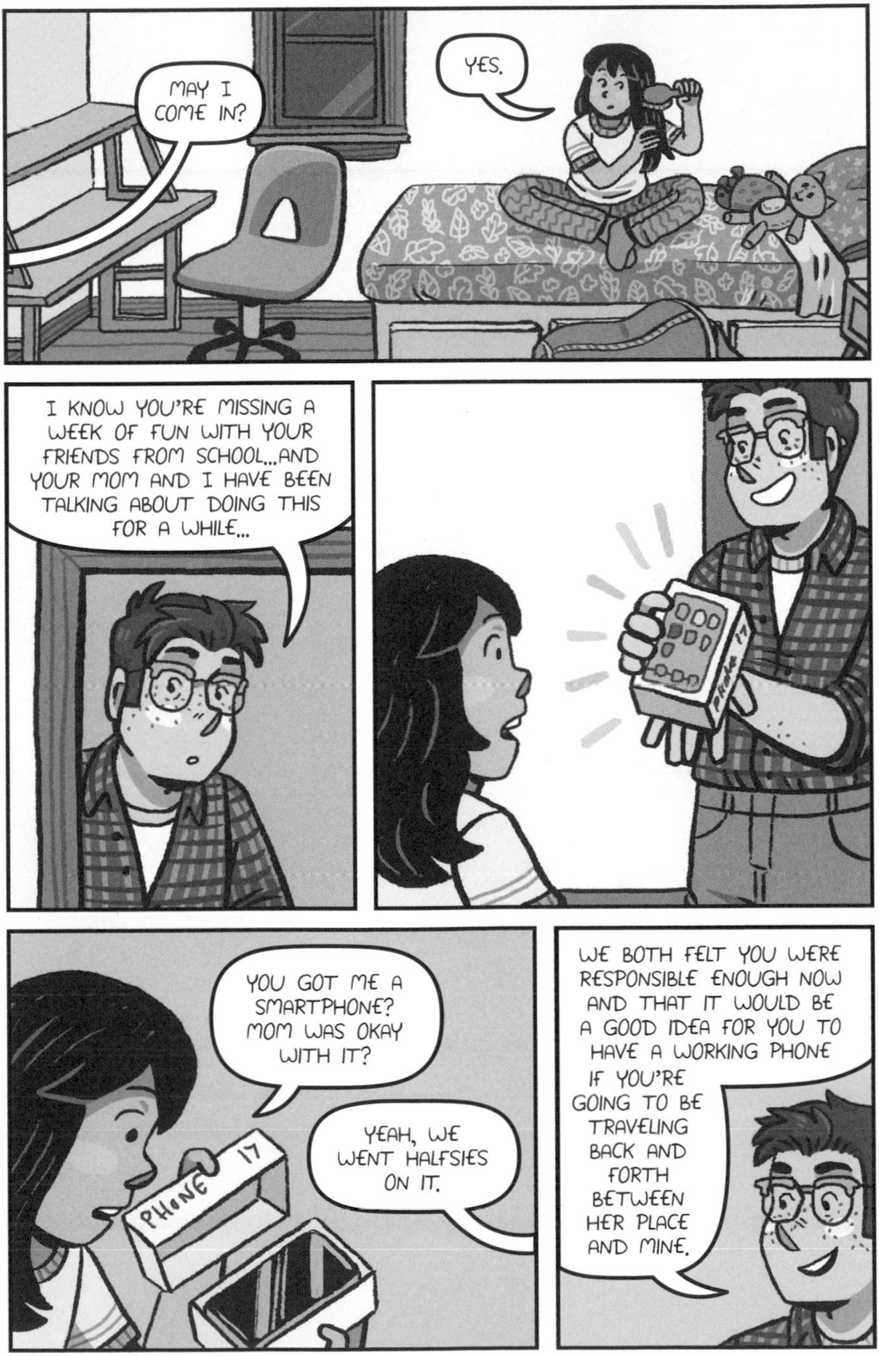
MAY I COME IN?
YES.
I KNOW YOU'RE MISSING A WEEK OF FUN WITH YOUR FRIENDS FROM SCHOOL...AND YOUR MOM AND I HAVE BEEN TALKING ABOUT DOING THIS FOR A WHILE...
PHONE 17
YOU GOT ME A SMARTPHONE? MOM WAS OKAY WITH IT?
YEAH, WE WENT HALFSIES ON IT.
PHONE 17
WE BOTH FELT YOU WERE RESPONSIBLE ENOUGH NOW AND THAT IT WOULD BE A GOOD IDEA FOR YOU TO HAVE A WORKING PHONE
IF YOU'RE GOING TO BE TRAVELING BACK AND FORTH BETWEEN HER PLACE AND MINE.

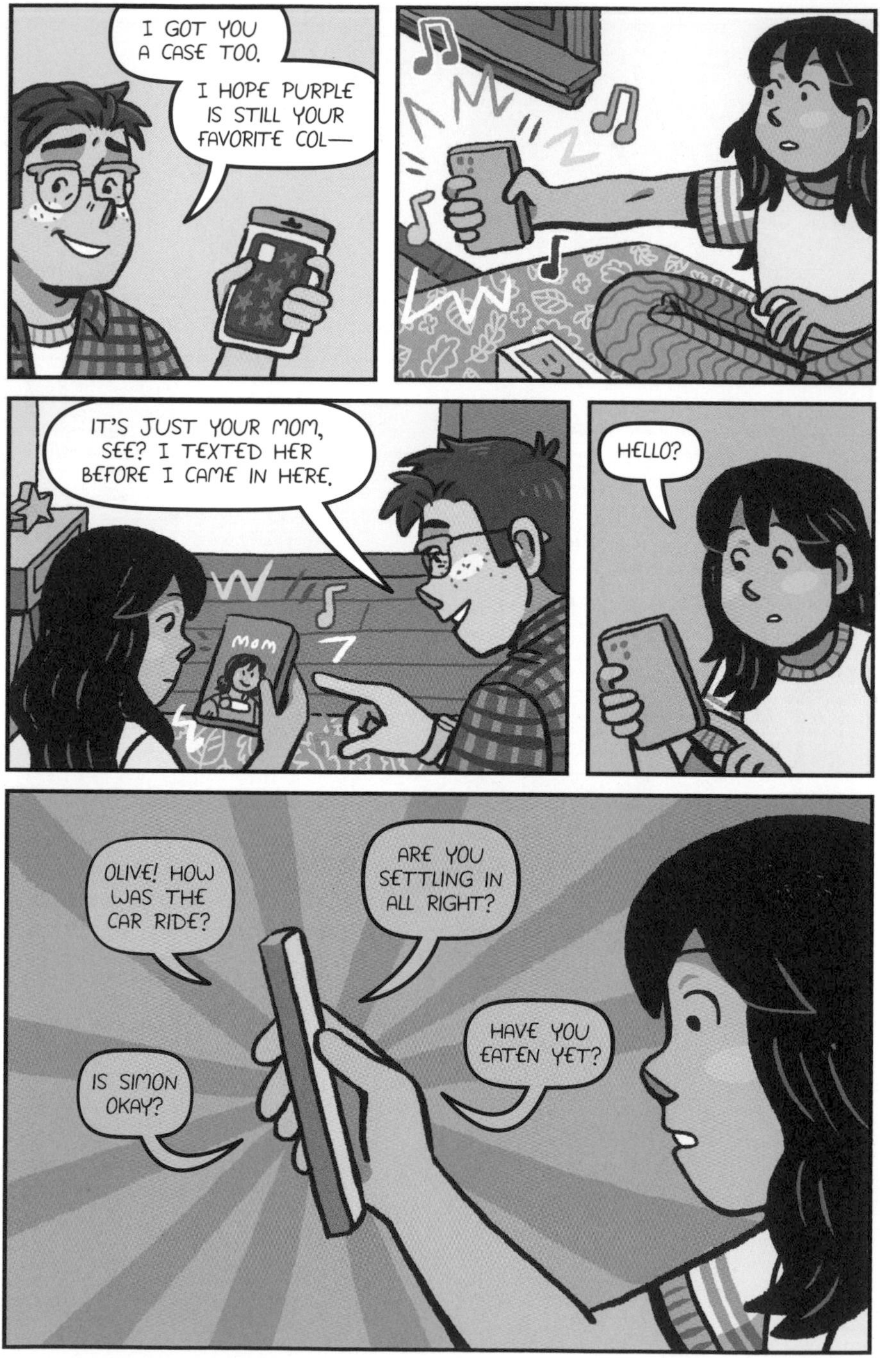
I GOT YOU A CASE TOO.
I HOPE PURPLE IS STILL YOUR FAVORITE COL—
IT'S JUST YOUR MOM, SEE? I TEXTED HER BEFORE I CAME IN HERE.
MOM
HELLO?
OLIVE! HOW WAS THE CAR RIDE?
ARE YOU SETTLING IN ALL RIGHT?
IS SIMON OKAY?
HAVE YOU EATEN YET?

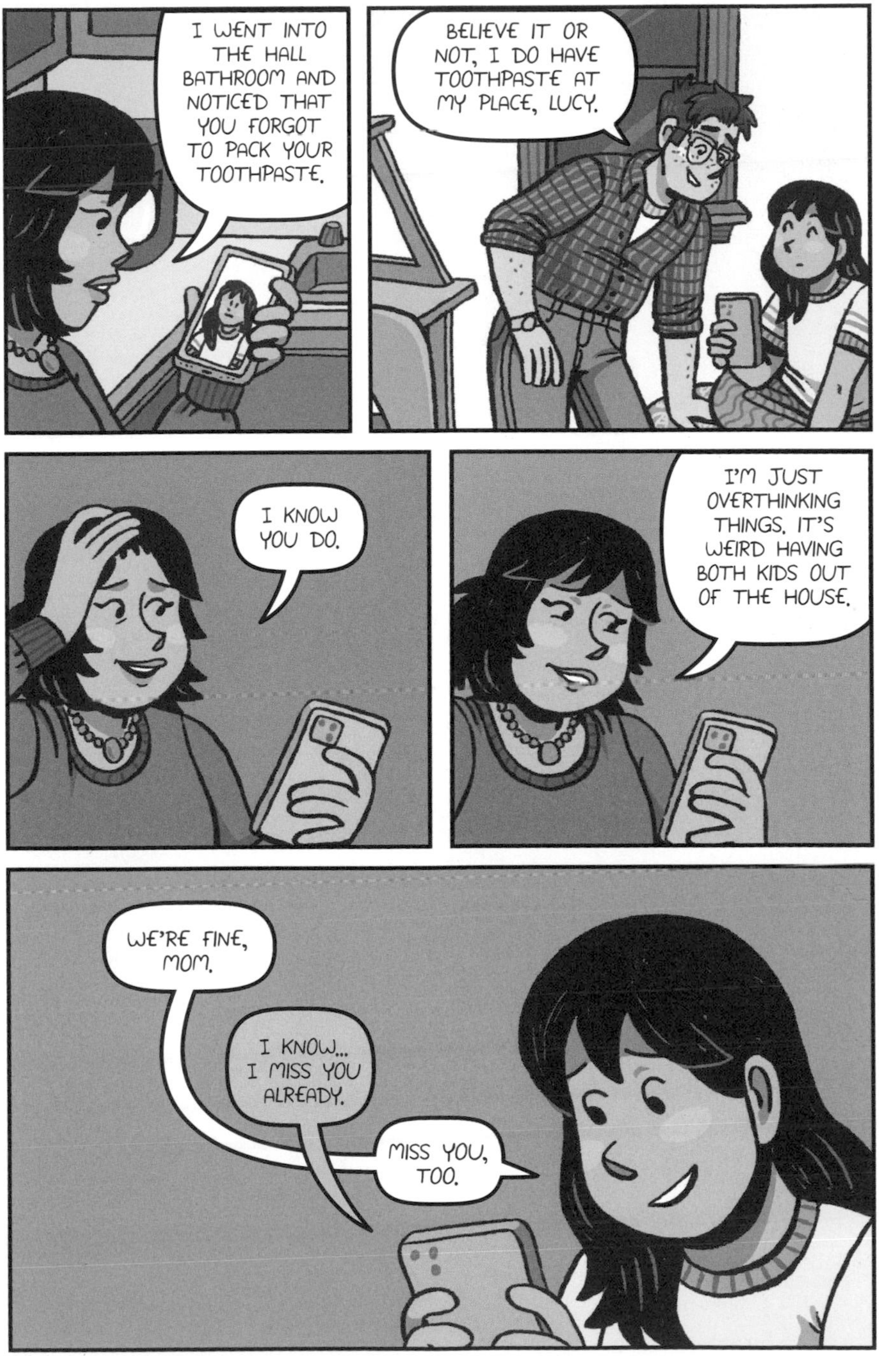
I WENT INTO THE HALL BATHROOM AND NOTICED THAT YOU FORGOT TO PACK YOUR TOOTHPASTE.
BELIEVE IT OR NOT, I DO HAVE TOOTHPASTE AT MY PLACE, LUCY.
I KNOW YOU DO.
I'M JUST OVERTHINKING THINGS. IT'S WEIRD HAVING BOTH KIDS OUT OF THE HOUSE.
WE'RE FINE, MOM.
I KNOW... I MISS YOU ALREADY.
MISS YOU, TOO.

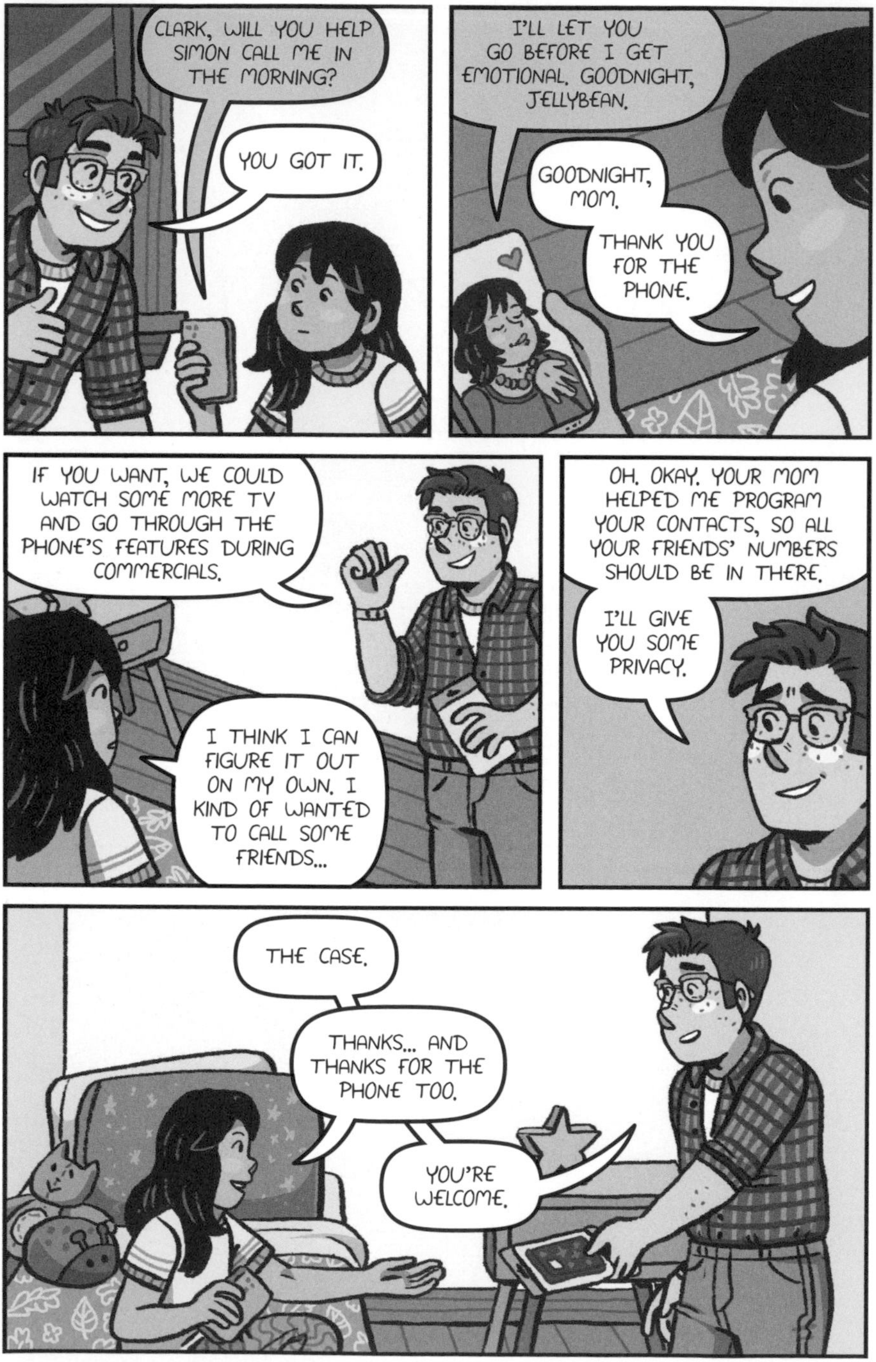
CLARK, WILL YOU HELP SIMON CALL ME IN THE MORNING?
YOU GOT IT.
I'LL LET YOU GO BEFORE I GET EMOTIONAL. GOODNIGHT, JELLYBEAN.
GOODNIGHT, MOM.
THANK YOU FOR THE PHONE.
IF YOU WANT, WE COULD WATCH SOME MORE TV AND GO THROUGH THE PHONE'S FEATURES DURING COMMERCIALS.
I THINK I CAN FIGURE IT OUT ON MY OWN. I KIND OF WANTED TO CALL SOME FRIENDS...
OH. OKAY. YOUR MOM HELPED ME PROGRAM YOUR CONTACTS, SO ALL YOUR FRIENDS' NUMBERS SHOULD BE IN THERE.
I'LL GIVE YOU SOME PRIVACY.
THE CASE.
THANKS... AND THANKS FOR THE PHONE TOO.
YOU'RE WELCOME.

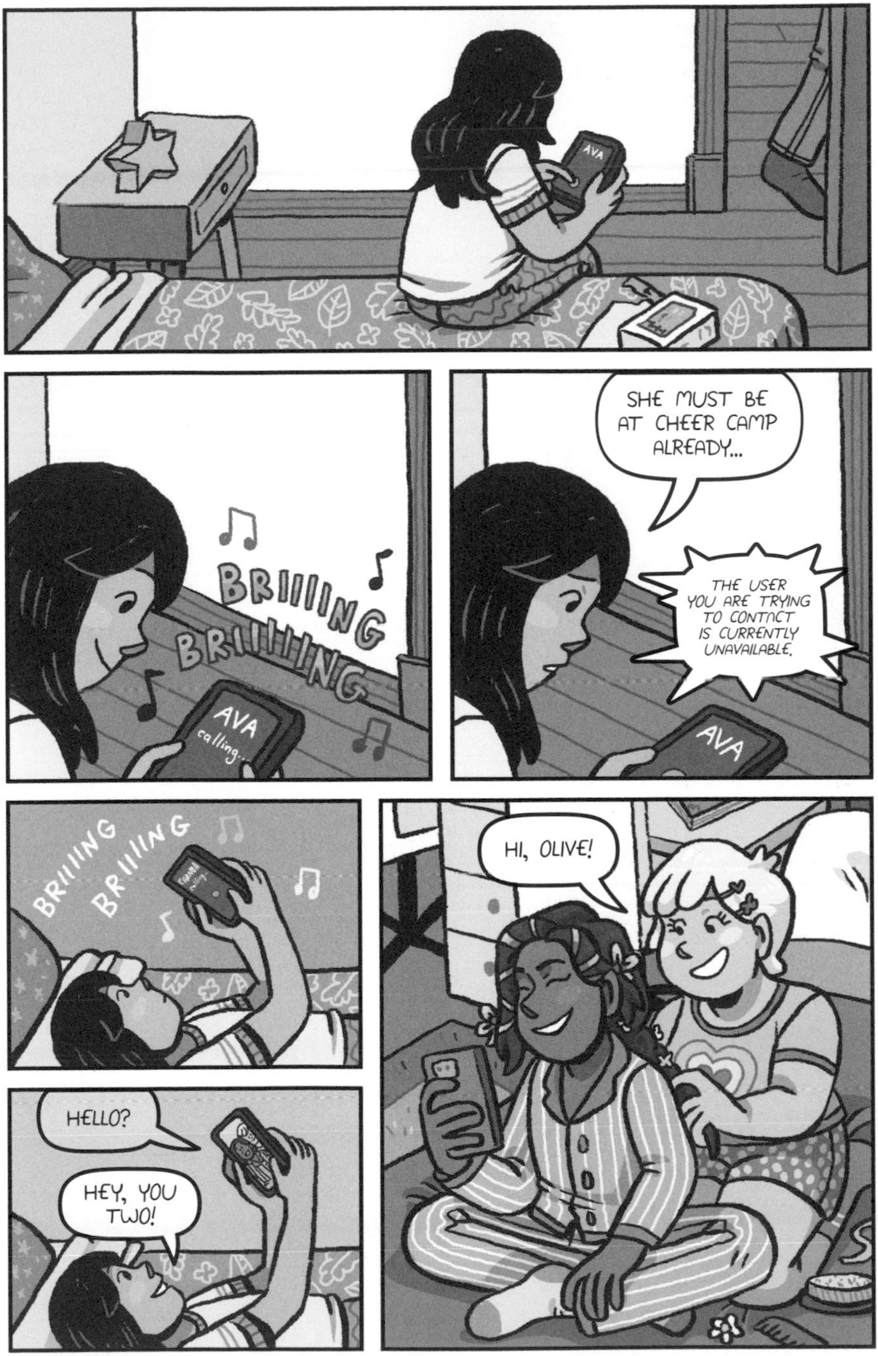
AVA
BRIIIING
BRIIIING
AVA
calling...
SHE MUST BE AT CHEER CAMP ALREADY...
THE USER YOU ARE TRYING TO CONTACT IS CURRENTLY UNAVAILABLE.
AVA
BRIIIING
BRIIIING
HELLO?
HEY, YOU TWO!
HI, OLIVE!

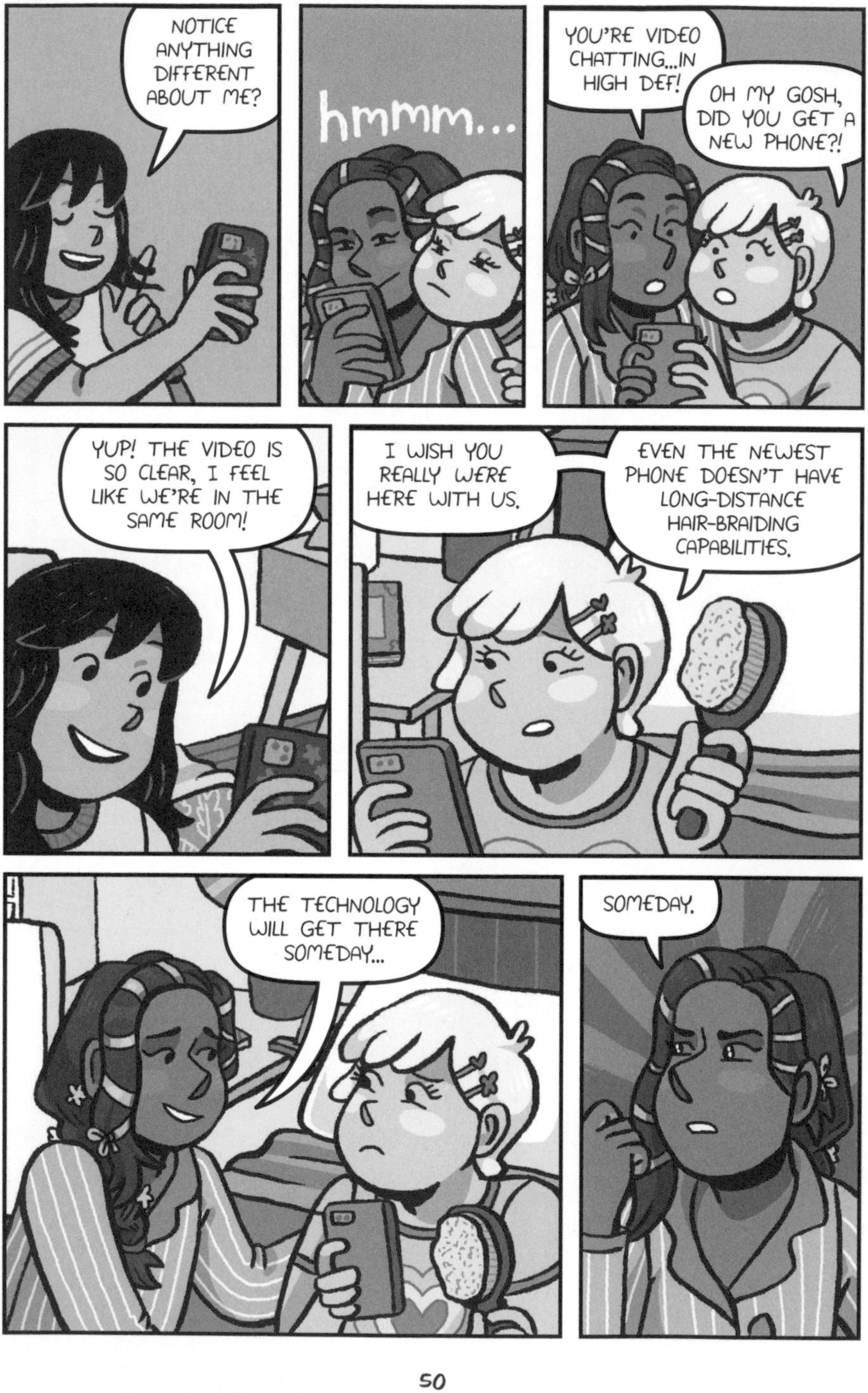
NOTICE ANYTHING DIFFERENT ABOUT ME?
hmmm...
YOU'RE VIDEO CHATTING...IN HIGH DEF!
OH MY GOSH, DID YOU GET A NEW PHONE?!
YUP! THE VIDEO IS SO CLEAR, I FEEL LIKE WE'RE IN THE SAME ROOM!
I WISH YOU REALLY WERE HERE WITH US.
EVEN THE NEWEST PHONE DOESN'T HAVE LONG-DISTANCE HAIR-BRAIDING CAPABILITIES.
THE TECHNOLOGY WILL GET THERE SOMEDAY...
SOMEDAY.

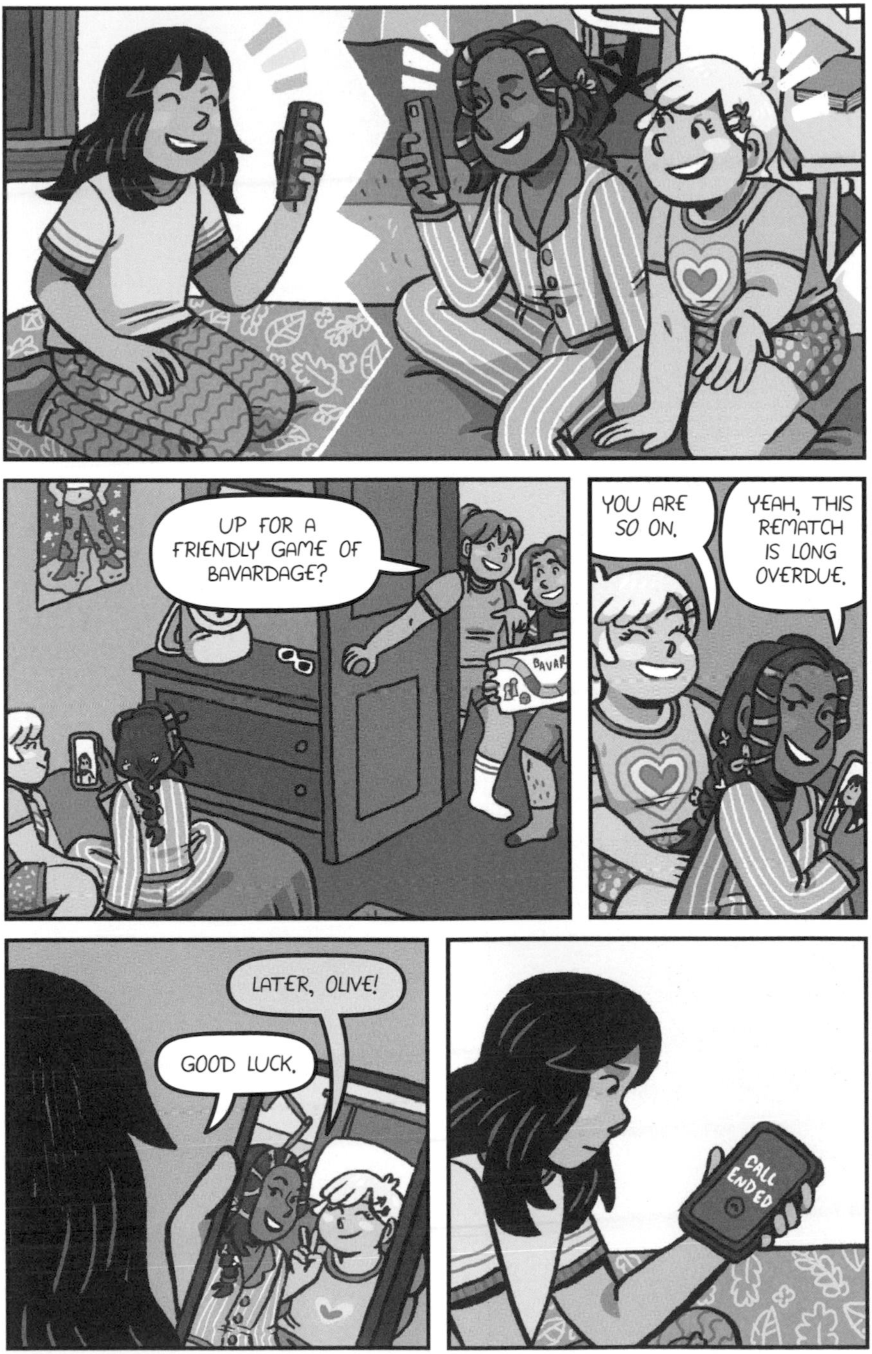
UP FOR A FRIENDLY GAME OF BAVARDAGE?
BAVAR
YOU ARE SO ON.
YEAH, THIS REMATCH IS LONG OVERDUE.
LATER, OLIVE!
GOOD LUCK.
CALL ENDED

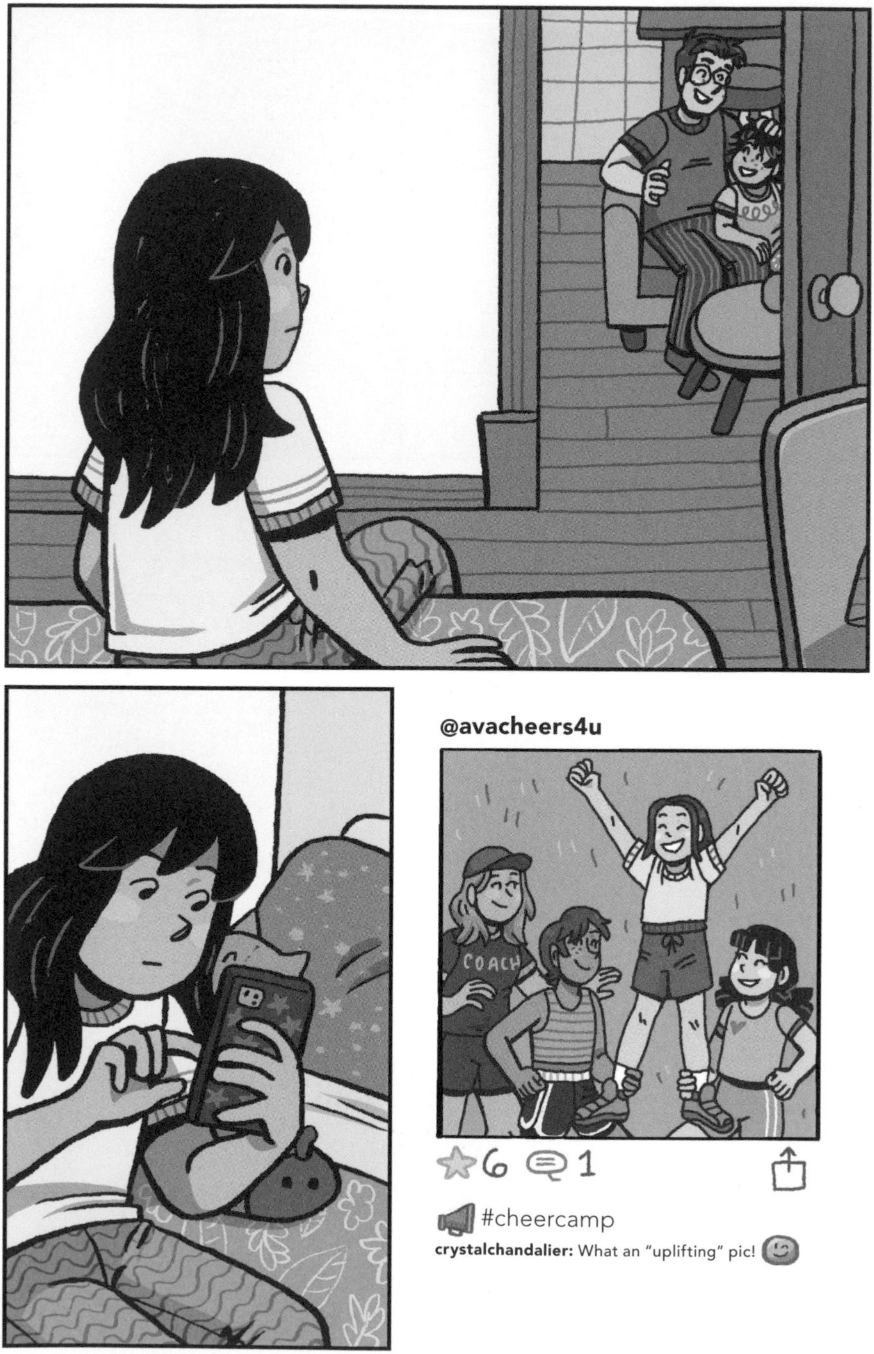
@avacheers4u
COACH
6
1
#cheercamp
crystalchandalier: What an "uplifting" pic!

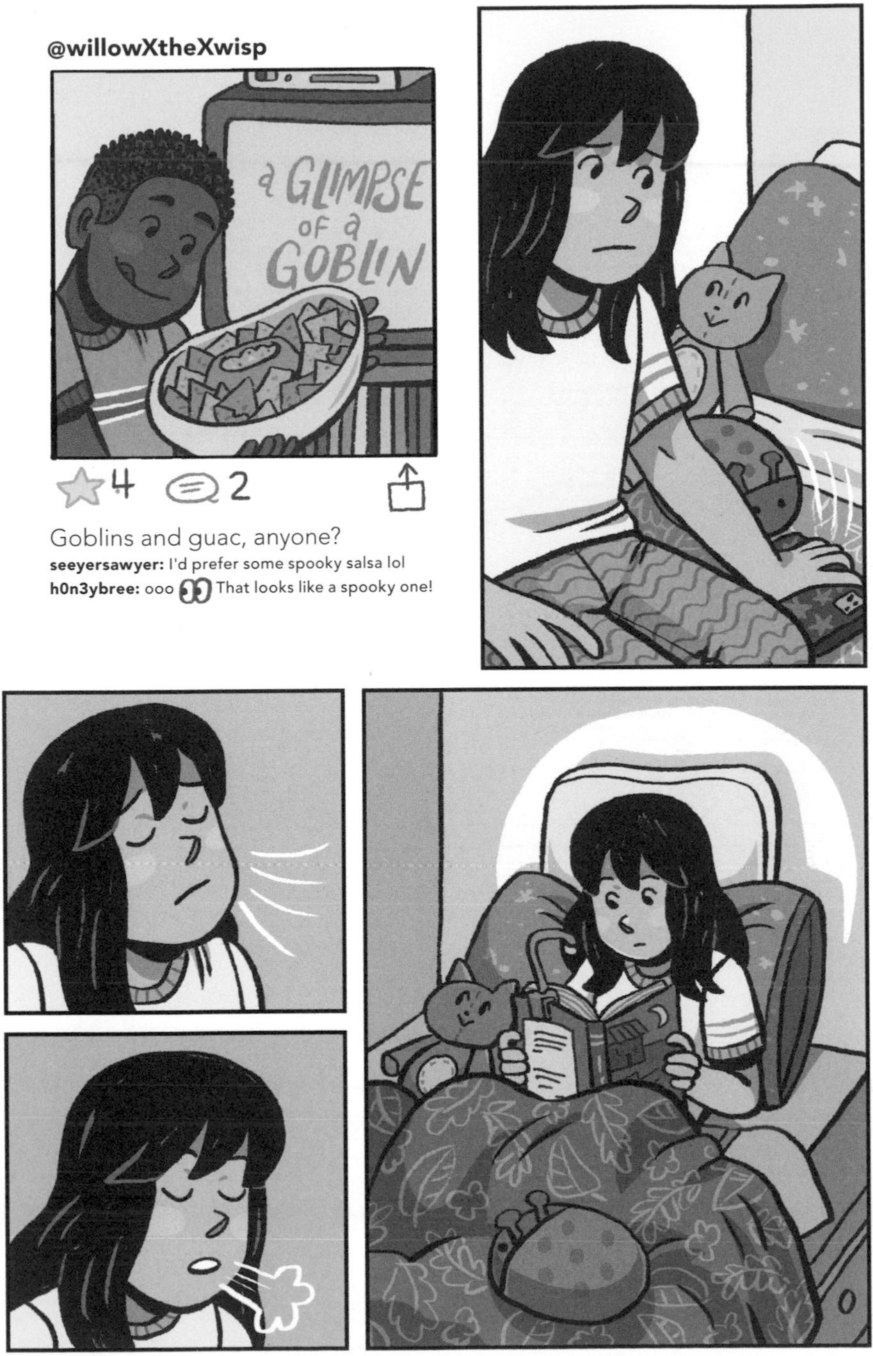
@willowXtheXwisp
a GLIMPSE of a GOBLIN
4
2
Goblins and guac, anyone?
seeyersawyer: I'd prefer some spooky salsa lol
h0n3ybree: ooo That looks like a spooky one!

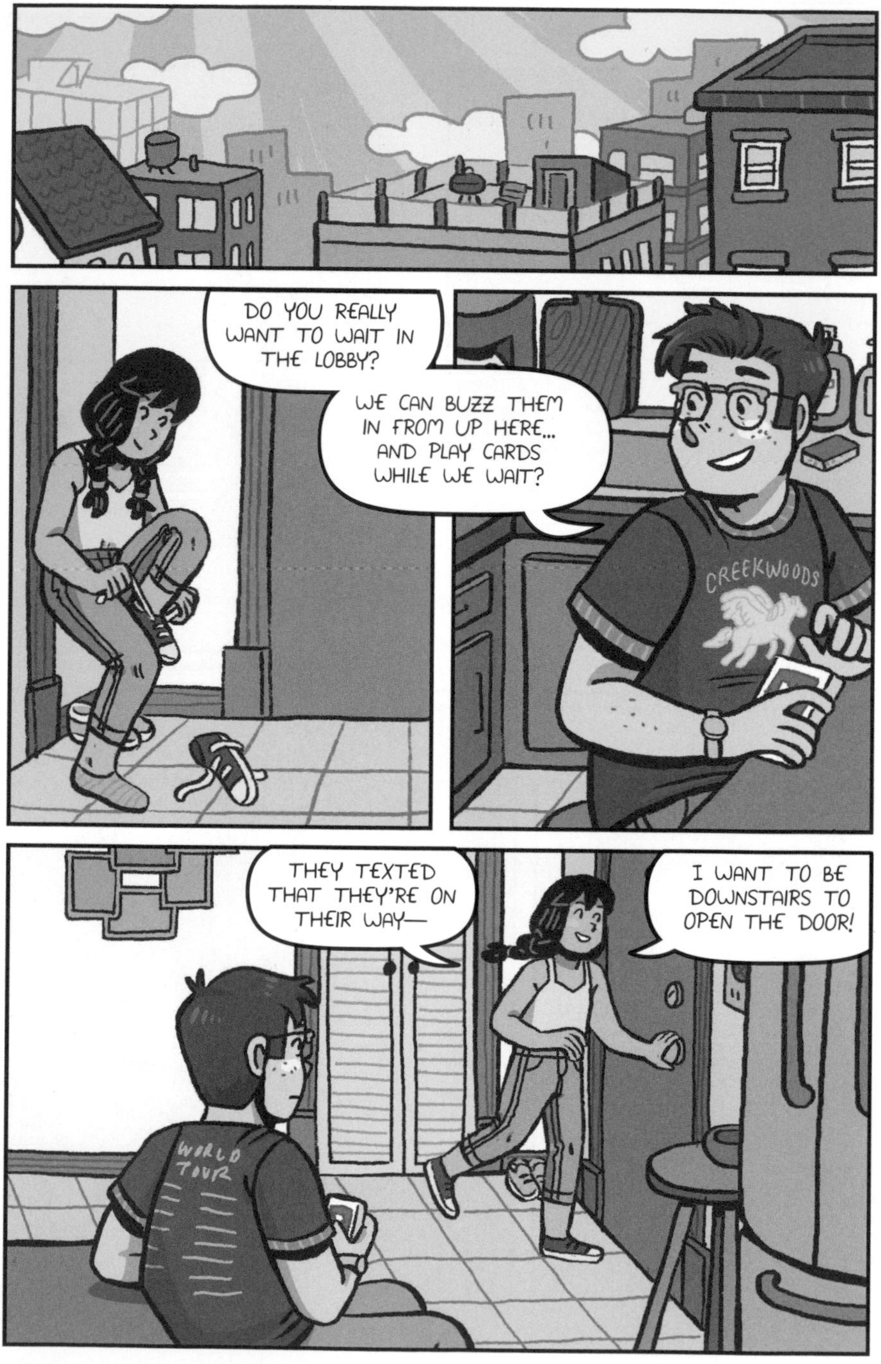
DO YOU REALLY WANT TO WAIT IN THE LOBBY?
WE CAN BUZZ THEM IN FROM UP HERE... AND PLAY CARDS WHILE WE WAIT?
CREEKWOODS
THEY TEXTED THAT THEY'RE ON THEIR WAY—
I WANT TO BE DOWNSTAIRS TO OPEN THE DOOR!
WORLD TOUR

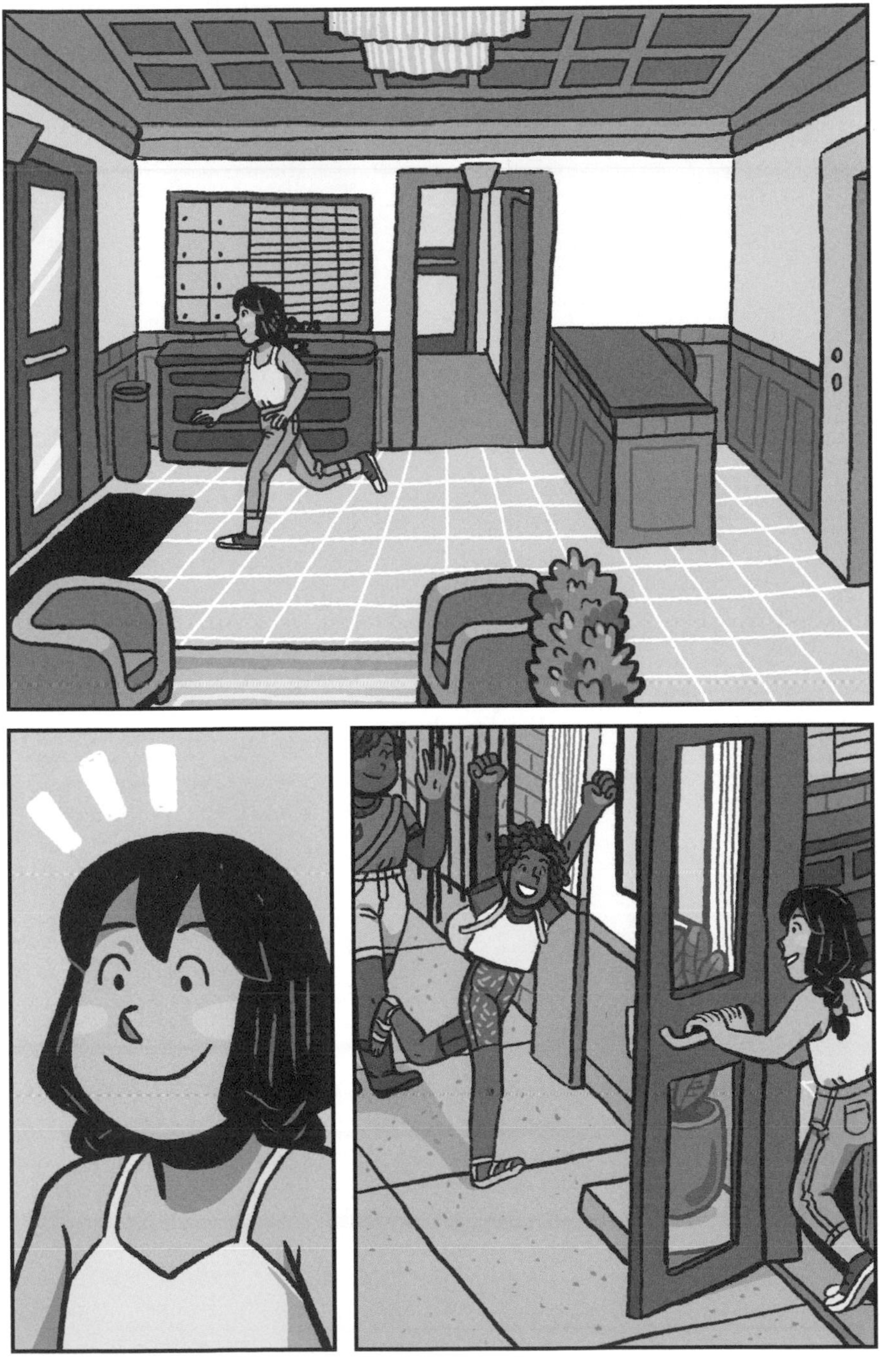

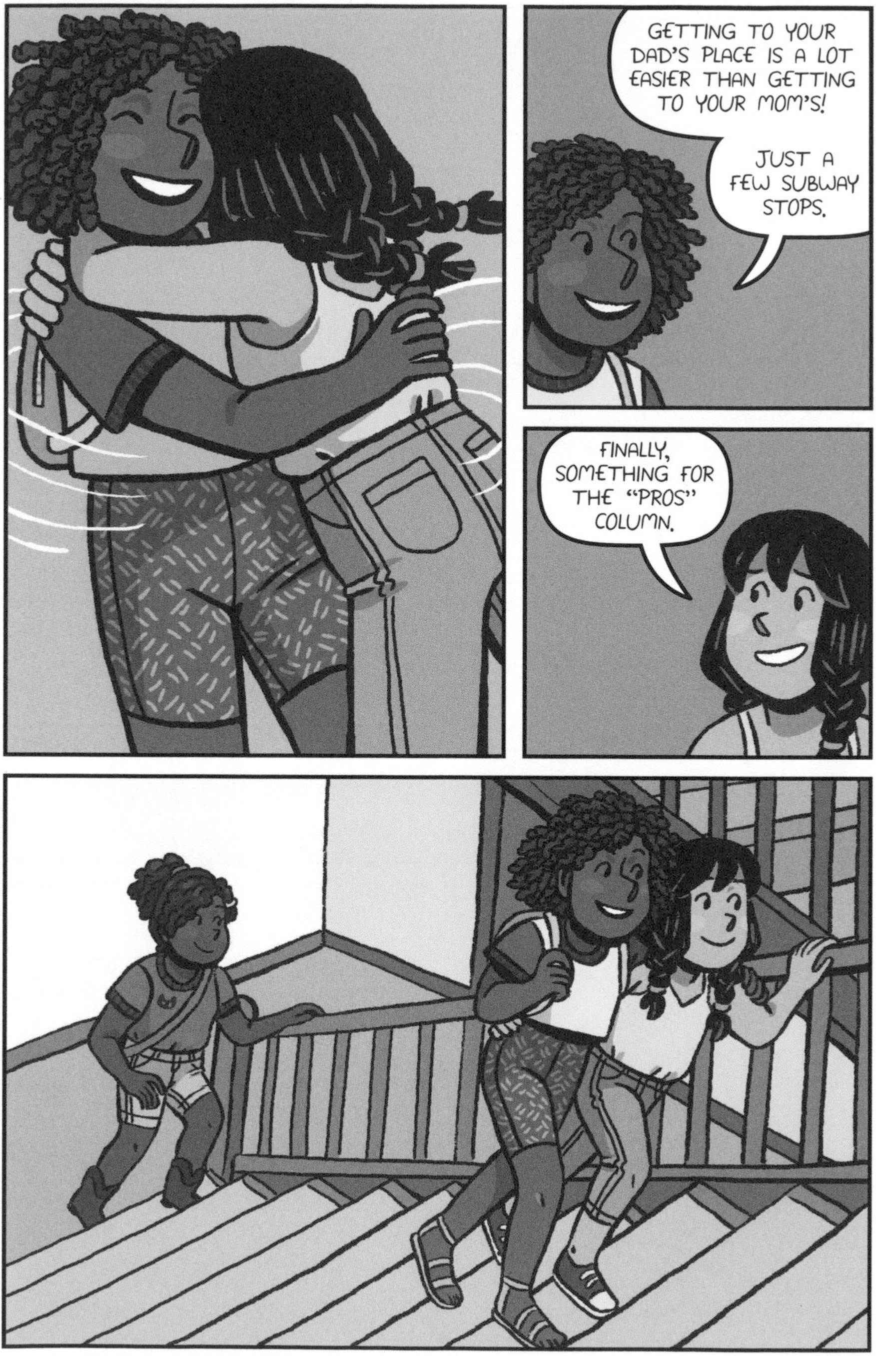
GETTING TO YOUR DAD'S PLACE IS A LOT EASIER THAN GETTING TO YOUR MOM'S!
JUST A FEW SUBWAY STOPS.
FINALLY, SOMETHING FOR THE "PROS" COLUMN.

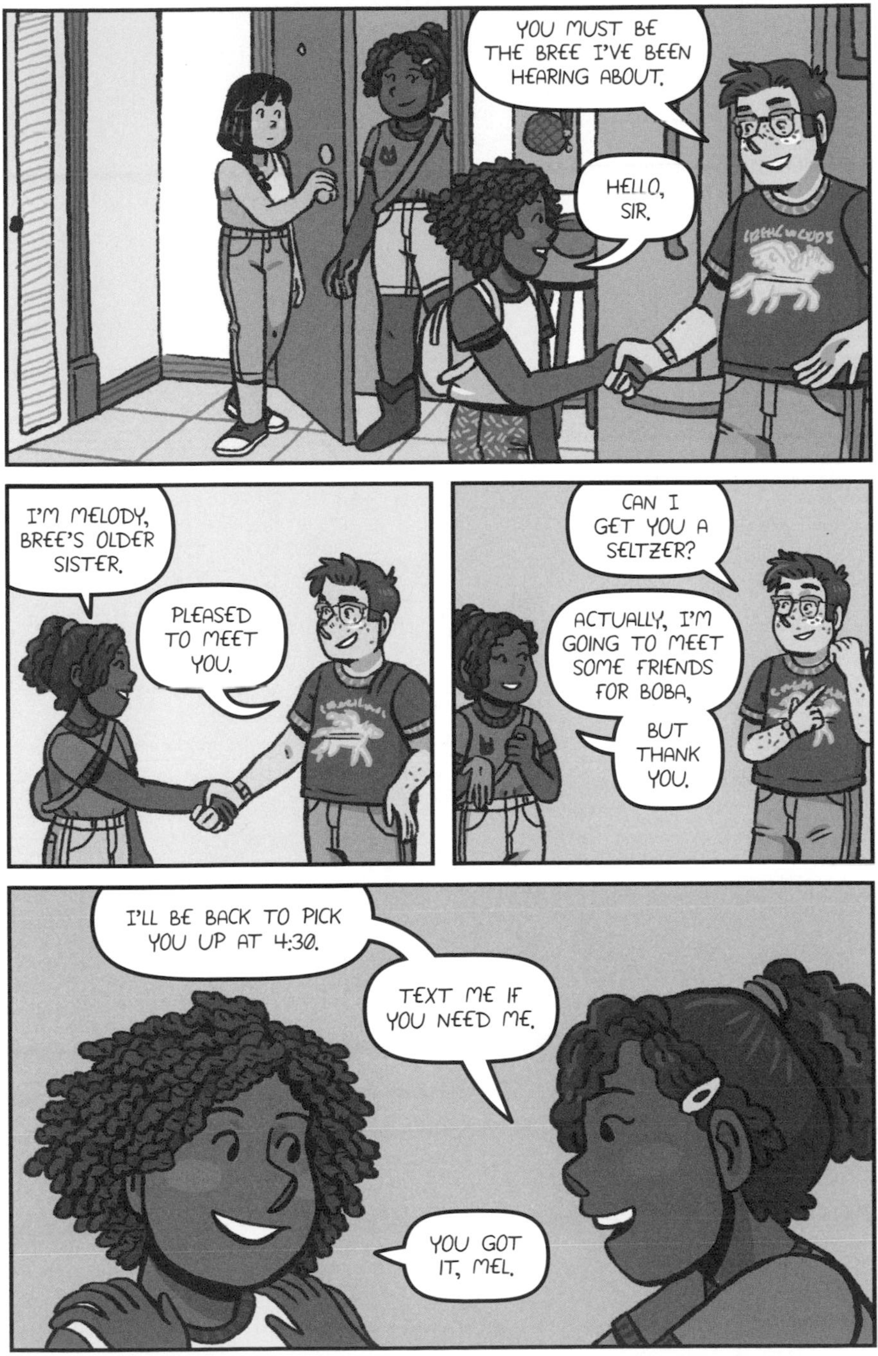
YOU MUST BE THE BREE I'VE BEEN HEARING ABOUT.
HELLO, SIR.
I'M MELODY, BREE'S OLDER SISTER.
PLEASED TO MEET YOU.
CAN I GET YOU A SELTZER?
ACTUALLY, I'M GOING TO MEET SOME FRIENDS FOR BOBA,
BUT THANK YOU.
I'LL BE BACK TO PICK YOU UP AT 4:30.
TEXT ME IF YOU NEED ME.
YOU GOT IT, MEL.

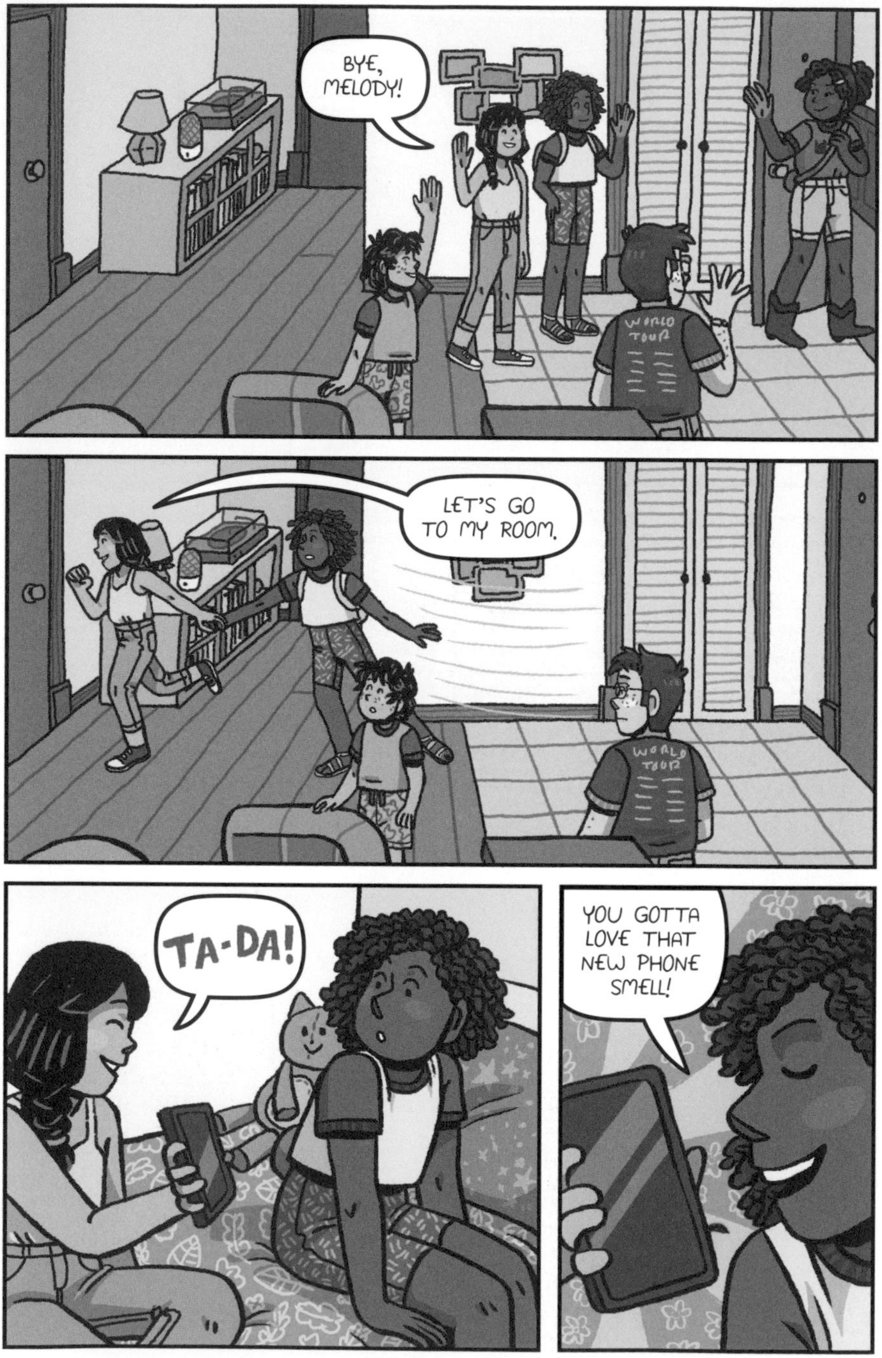
BYE, MELODY!
LET'S GO TO MY ROOM.
TA-DA!
YOU GOTTA LOVE THAT NEW PHONE SMELL!

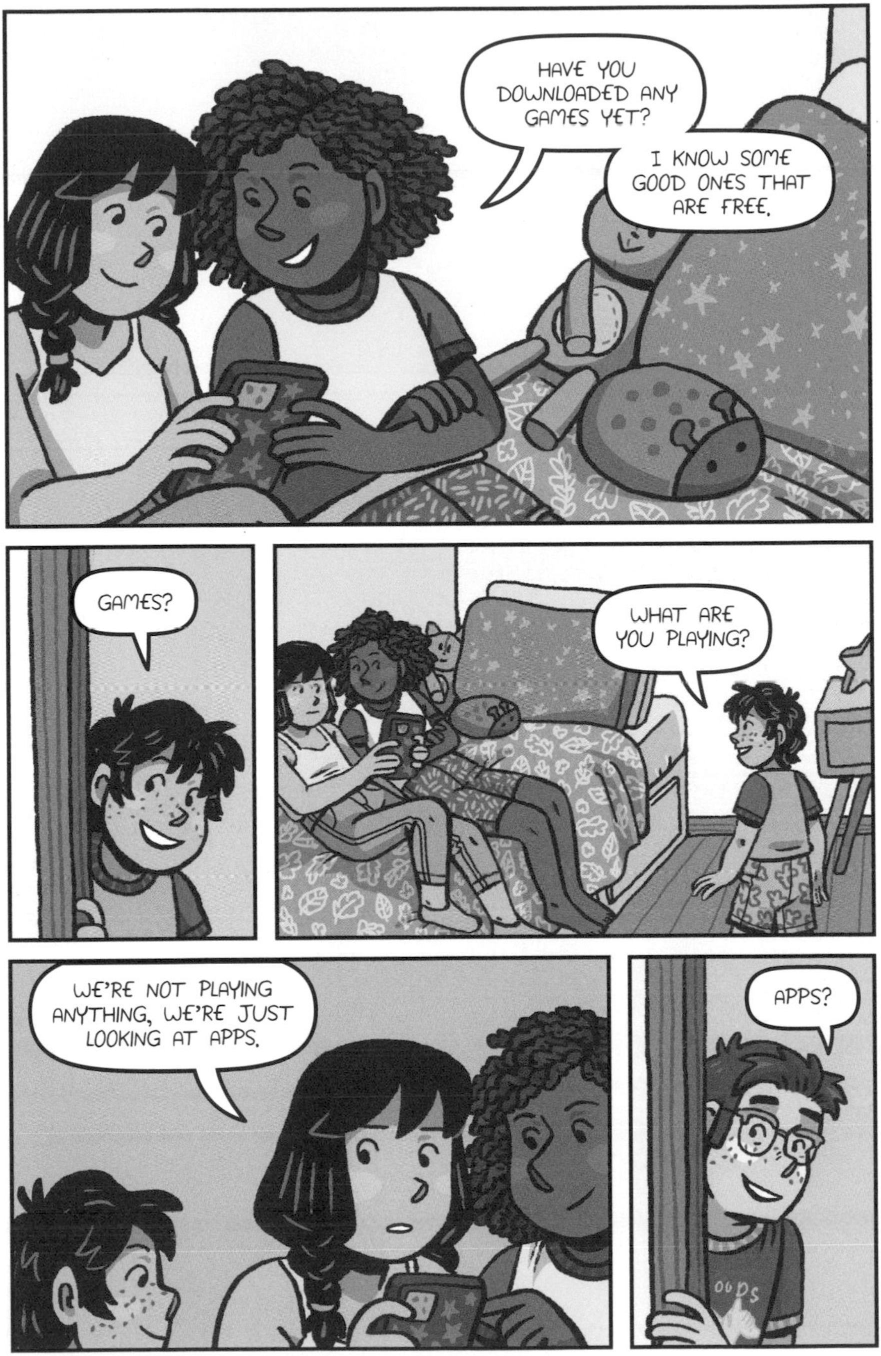
HAVE YOU DOWNLOADED ANY GAMES YET?
I KNOW SOME GOOD ONES THAT ARE FREE.
GAMES?
WHAT ARE YOU PLAYING?
WE'RE NOT PLAYING ANYTHING, WE'RE JUST LOOKING AT APPS.
APPS?

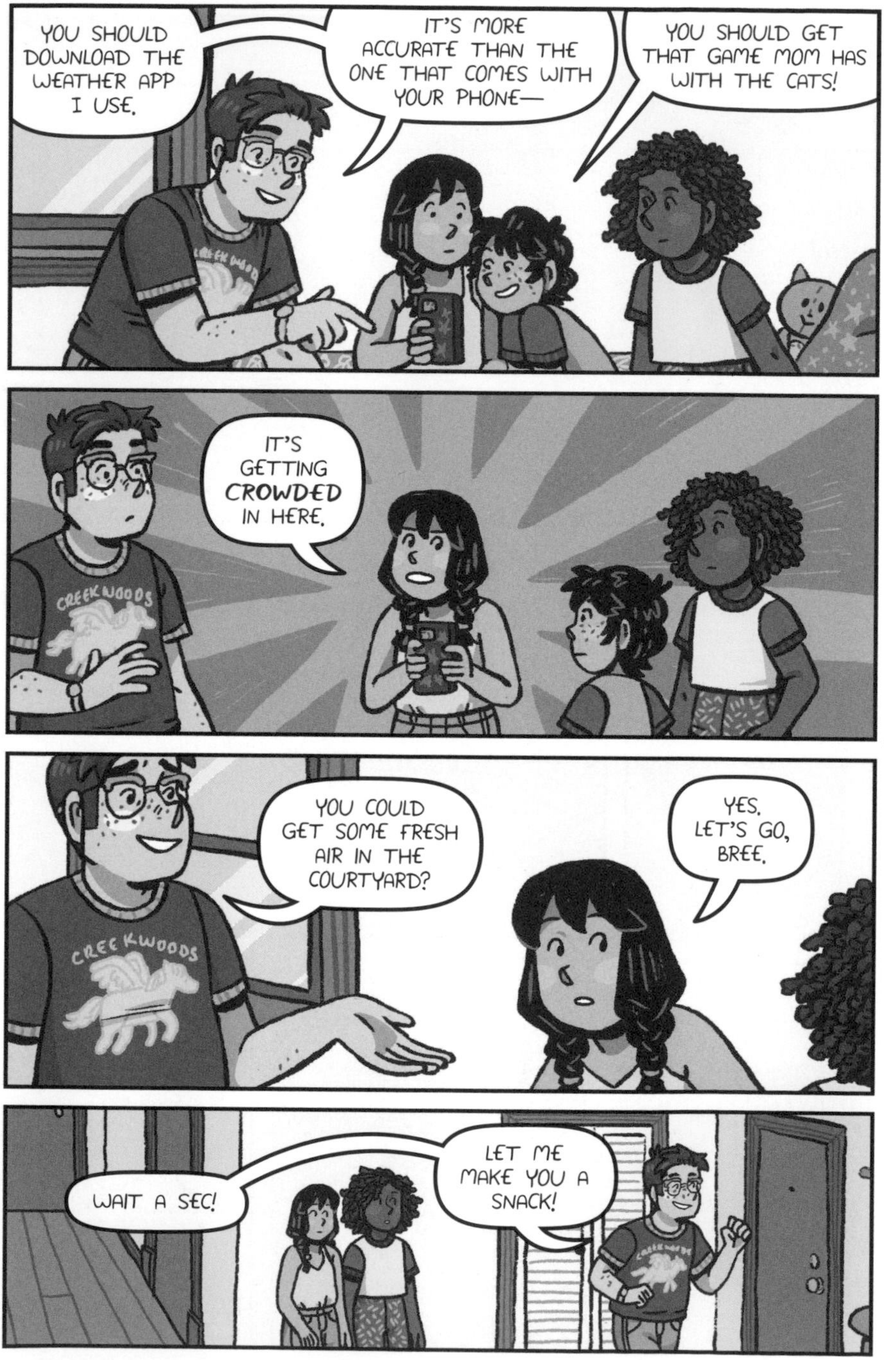
YOU SHOULD DOWNLOAD THE WEATHER APP I USE.
IT'S MORE ACCURATE THAN THE ONE THAT COMES WITH YOUR PHONE—
YOU SHOULD GET THAT GAME MOM HAS WITH THE CATS!
IT'S GETTING CROWDED IN HERE.
YOU COULD GET SOME FRESH AIR IN THE COURTYARD?
YES. LET'S GO, BREE.
WAIT A SEC!
LET ME MAKE YOU A SNACK!

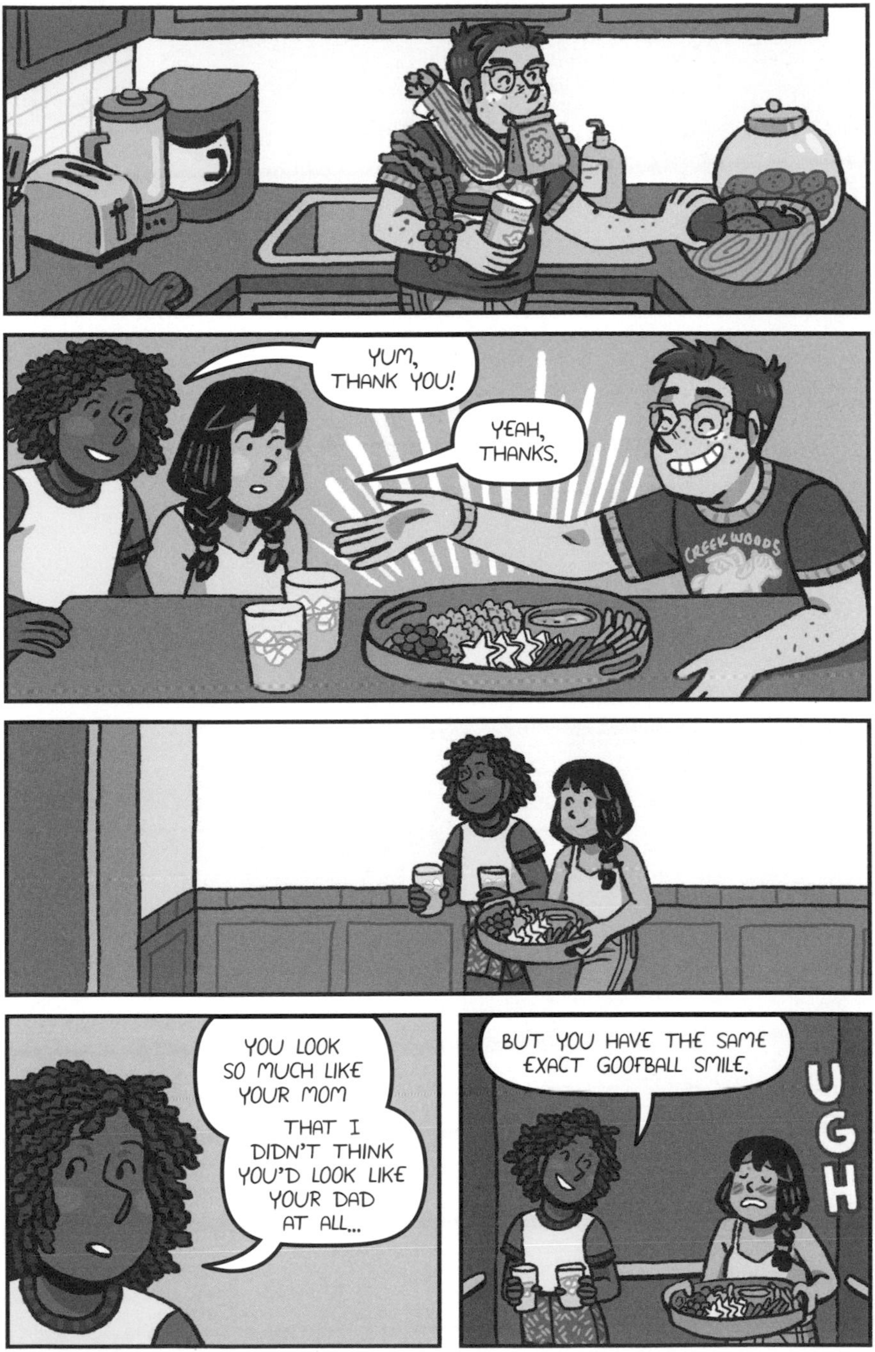
YUM, THANK YOU!
YEAH, THANKS.
CREEKWOODS
YOU LOOK SO MUCH LIKE YOUR MOM
THAT I DIDN'T THINK YOU'D LOOK LIKE YOUR DAD AT ALL...
BUT YOU HAVE THE SAME EXACT GOOFBALL SMILE.
UGH

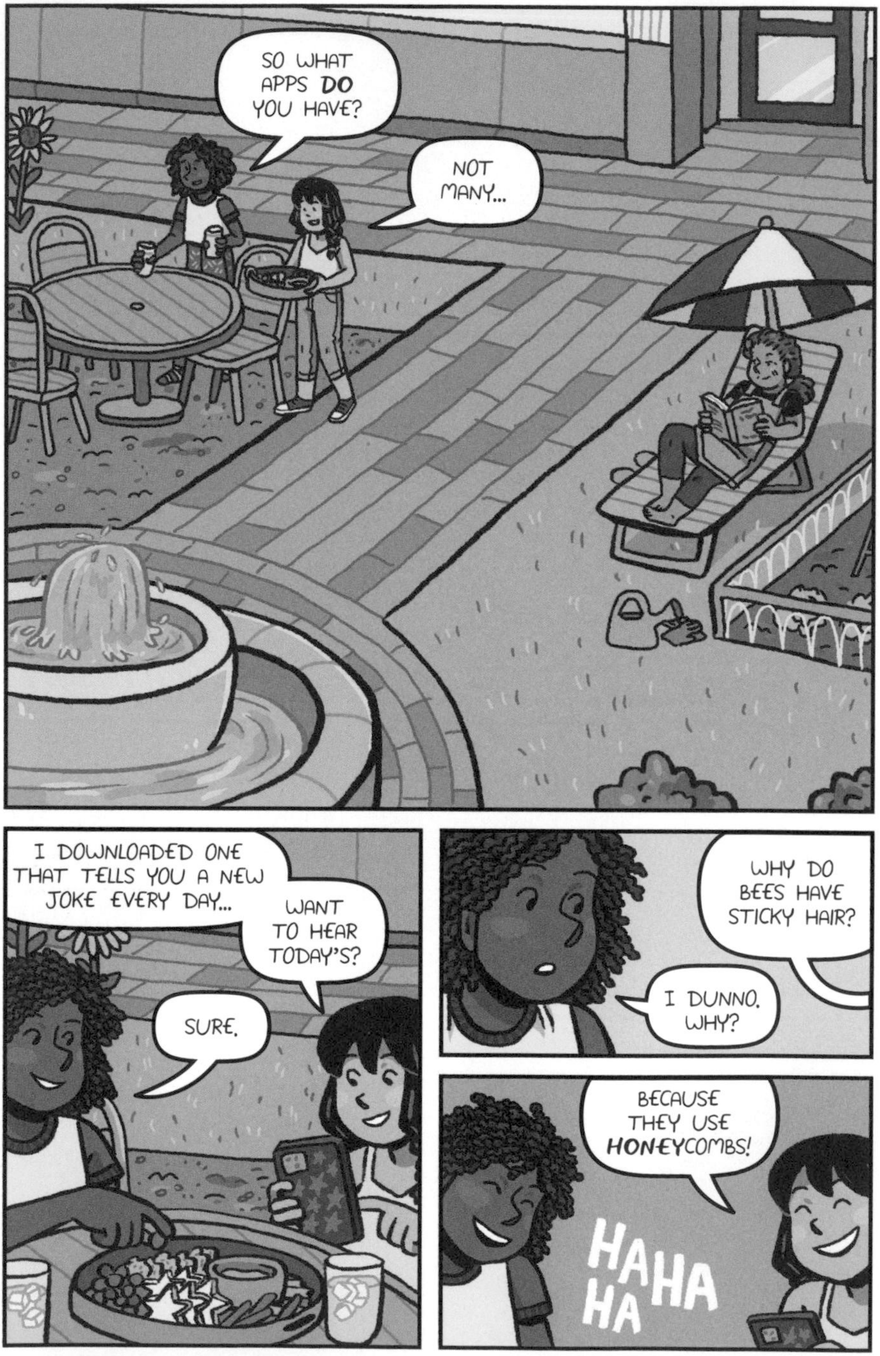
SO WHAT APPS **DO** YOU HAVE?
NOT MANY...
I DOWNLOADED ONE THAT TELLS YOU A NEW JOKE EVERY DAY...
WANT TO HEAR TODAY'S?
SURE.
WHY DO BEES HAVE STICKY HAIR?
I DUNNO. WHY?
BECAUSE THEY USE **HONEY**COMBS!
HAHA HA HA

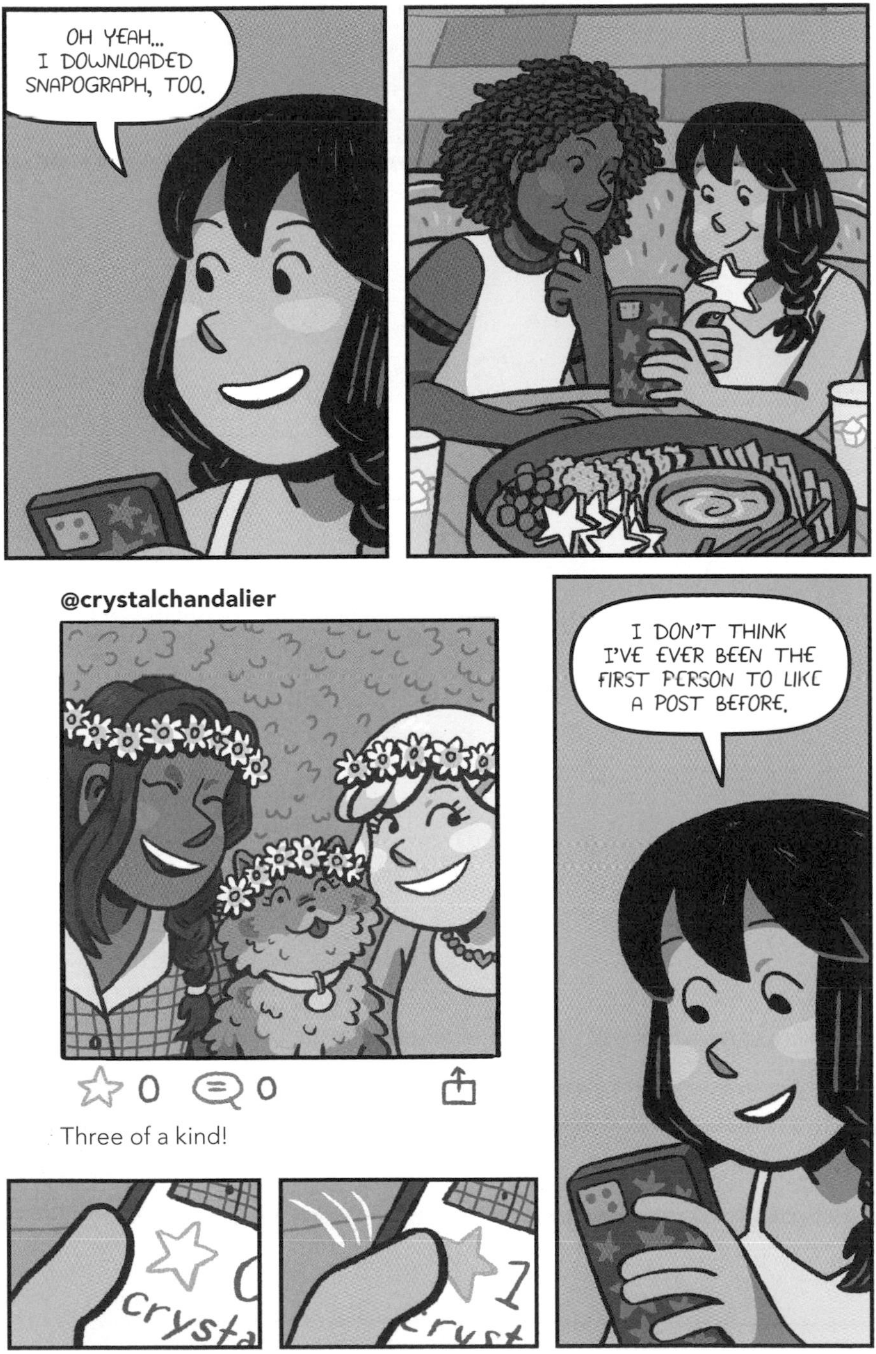

OH YEAH... I DOWNLOADED SNAPOGRAPH, TOO.
@crystalchandalier
0
0
Three of a kind!
I DON'T THINK I'VE EVER BEEN THE FIRST PERSON TO LIKE A POST BEFORE.
1

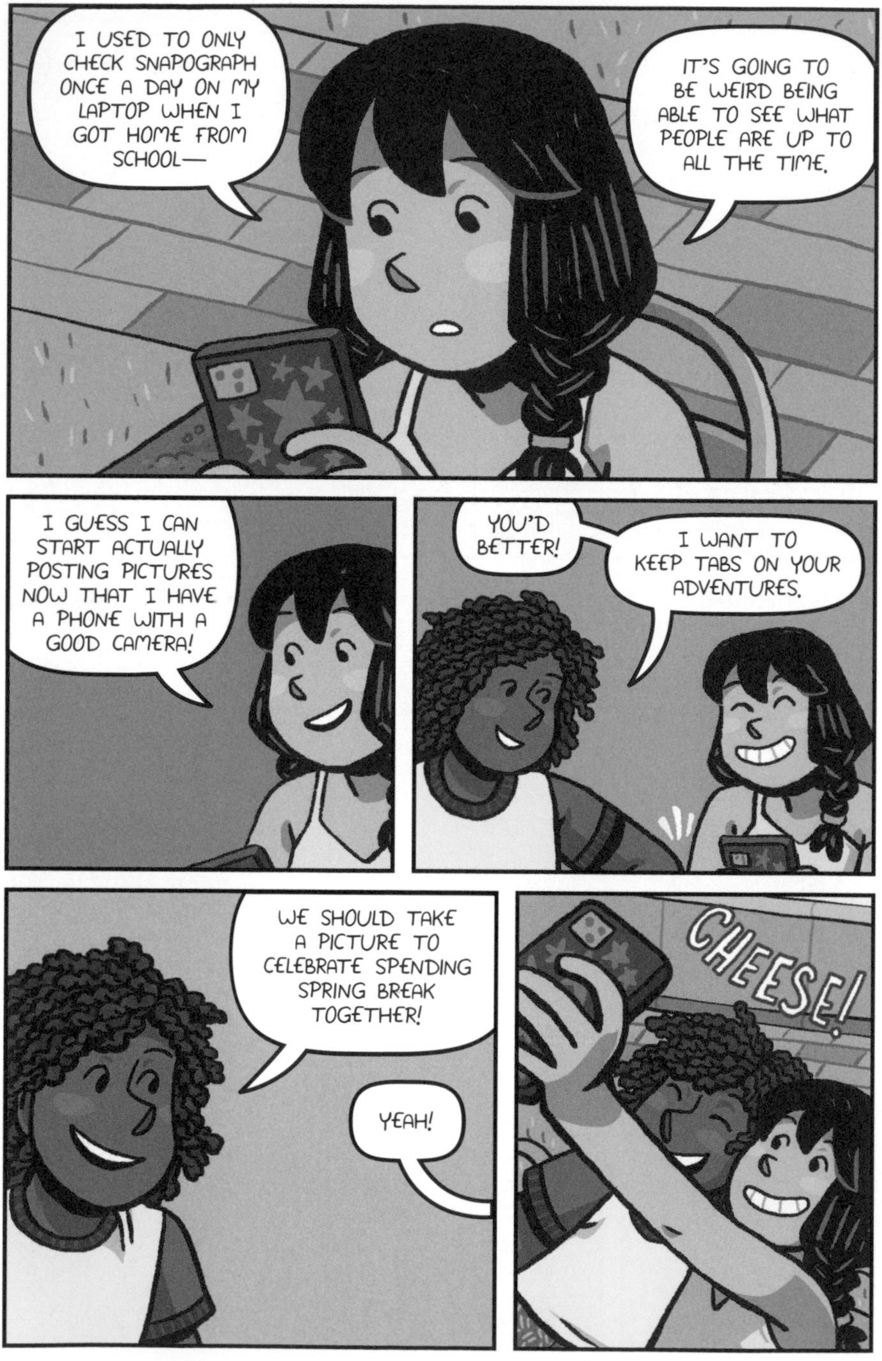
I USED TO ONLY CHECK SNAPOGRAPH ONCE A DAY ON MY LAPTOP WHEN I GOT HOME FROM SCHOOL—
IT'S GOING TO BE WEIRD BEING ABLE TO SEE WHAT PEOPLE ARE UP TO ALL THE TIME.
I GUESS I CAN START ACTUALLY POSTING PICTURES NOW THAT I HAVE A PHONE WITH A GOOD CAMERA!
YOU'D BETTER!
I WANT TO KEEP TABS ON YOUR ADVENTURES.
WE SHOULD TAKE A PICTURE TO CELEBRATE SPENDING SPRING BREAK TOGETHER!
YEAH!
CHEESE!

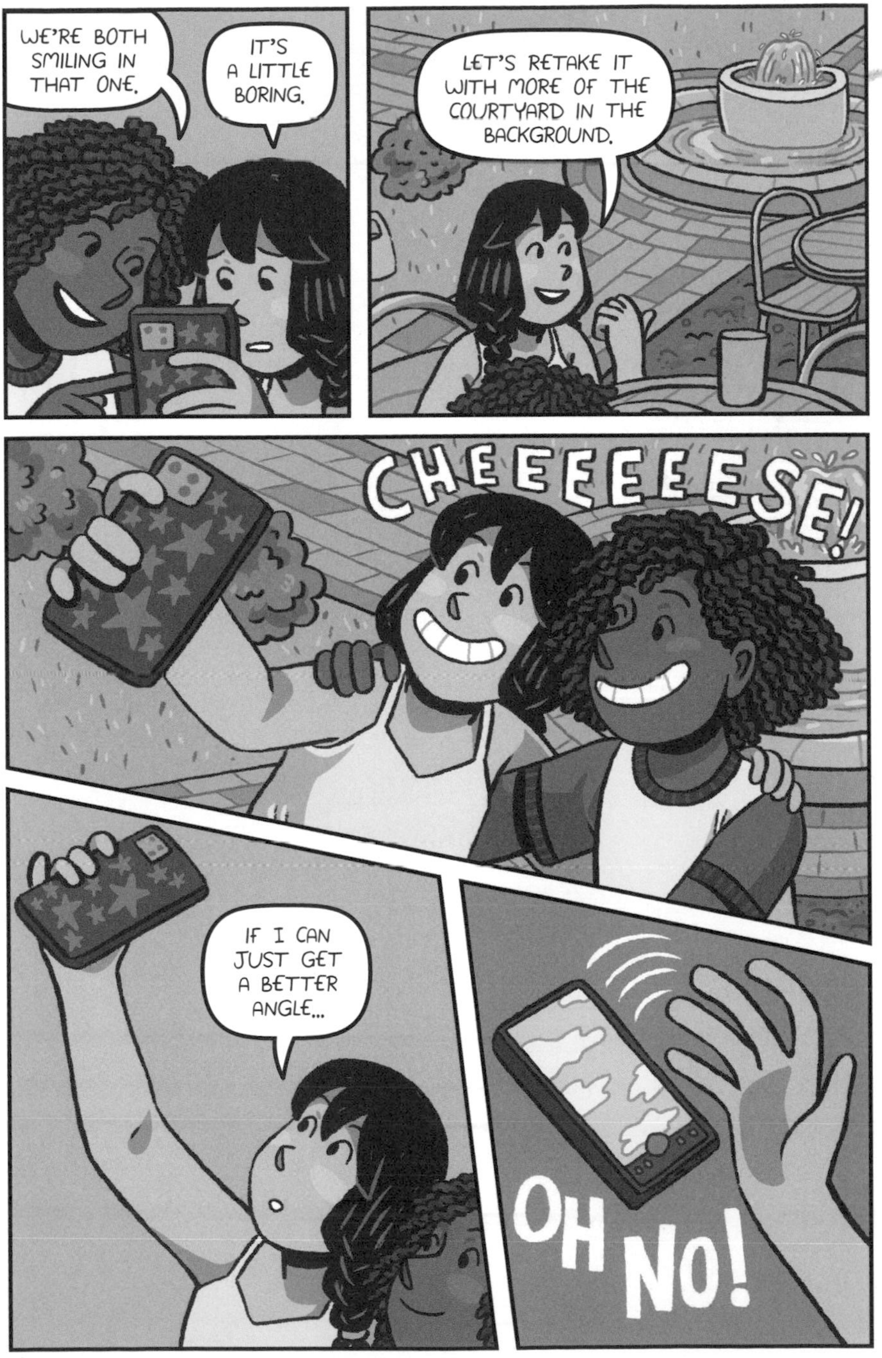
WE'RE BOTH SMILING IN THAT ONE.
IT'S A LITTLE BORING.
LET'S RETAKE IT WITH MORE OF THE COURTYARD IN THE BACKGROUND.
CHEEEEEESE!
IF I CAN JUST GET A BETTER ANGLE...
OH NO!

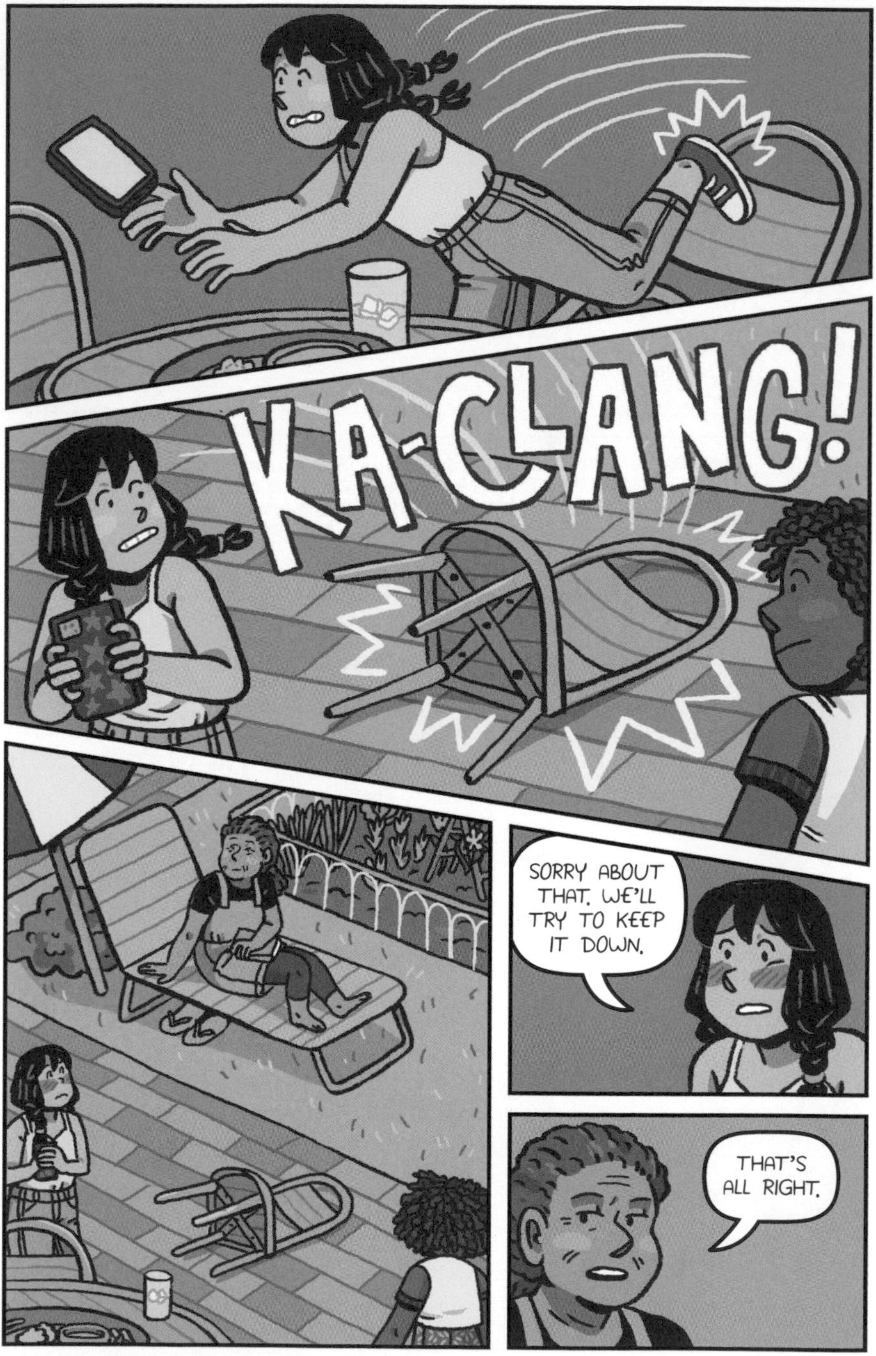
KA-CLANG!
SORRY ABOUT THAT. WE'LL TRY TO KEEP IT DOWN.
THAT'S ALL RIGHT.

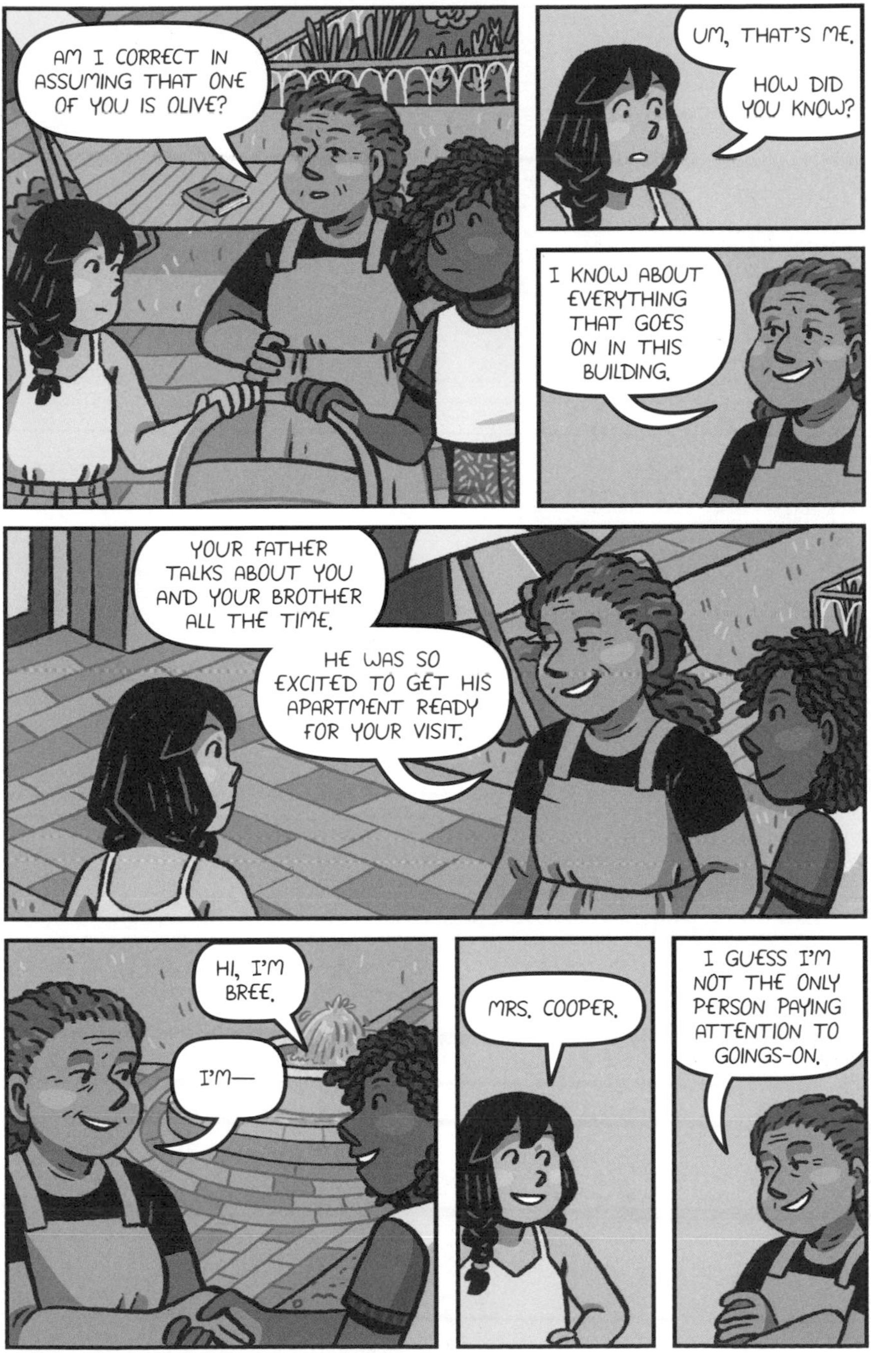
AM I CORRECT IN ASSUMING THAT ONE OF YOU IS OLIVE?
UM, THAT'S ME.
HOW DID YOU KNOW?
I KNOW ABOUT EVERYTHING THAT GOES ON IN THIS BUILDING.
YOUR FATHER TALKS ABOUT YOU AND YOUR BROTHER ALL THE TIME.
HE WAS SO EXCITED TO GET HIS APARTMENT READY FOR YOUR VISIT.
HI, I'M BREE.
I'M—
MRS. COOPER.
I GUESS I'M NOT THE ONLY PERSON PAYING ATTENTION TO GOINGS-ON.

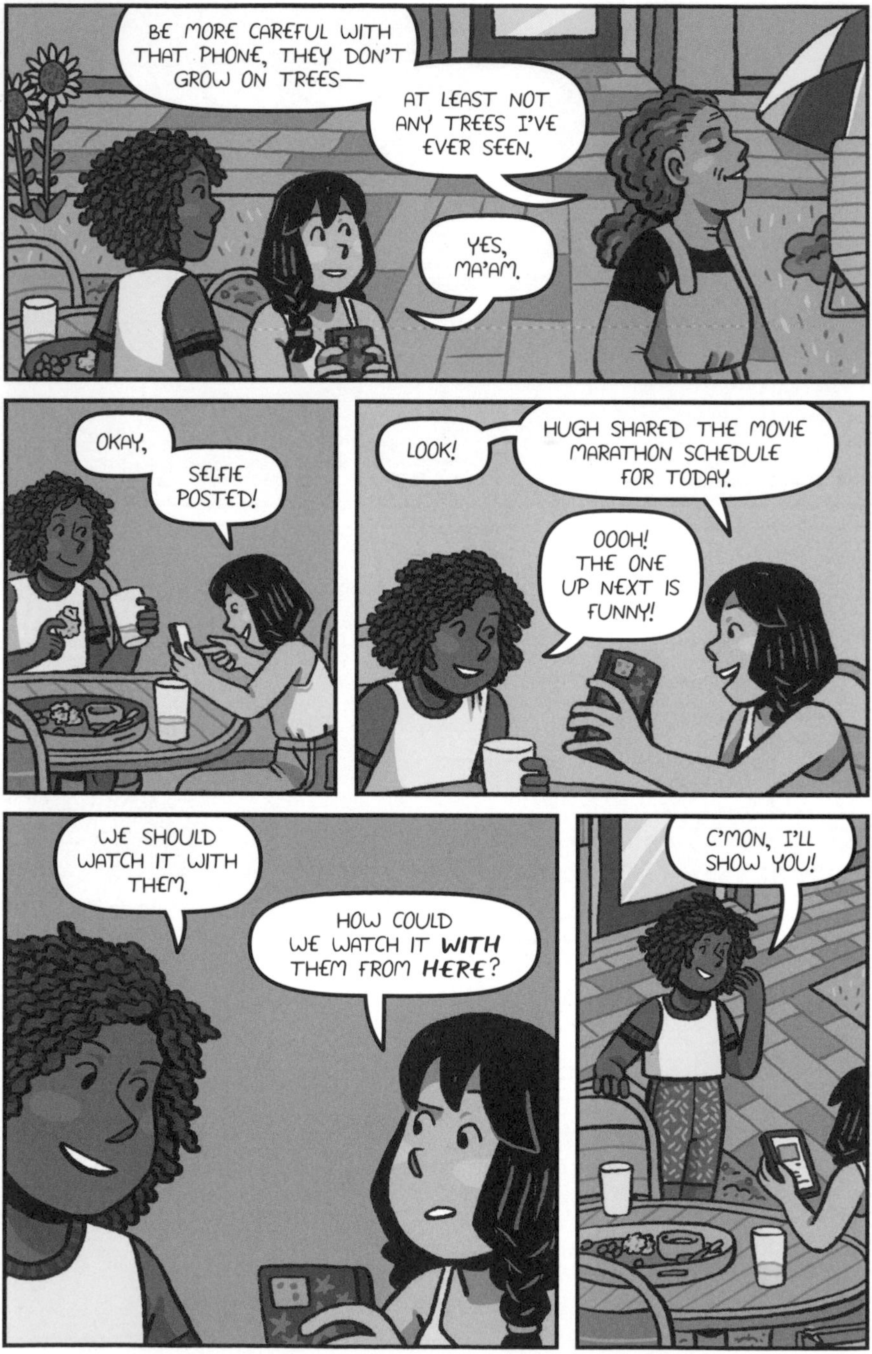
BE MORE CAREFUL WITH THAT PHONE, THEY DON'T GROW ON TREES—
AT LEAST NOT ANY TREES I'VE EVER SEEN.
YES, MA'AM.
OKAY,
SELFIE POSTED!
LOOK!
HUGH SHARED THE MOVIE MARATHON SCHEDULE FOR TODAY.
OOOH! THE ONE UP NEXT IS FUNNY!
WE SHOULD WATCH IT WITH THEM.
HOW COULD WE WATCH IT **WITH** THEM FROM **HERE**?
C'MON, I'LL SHOW YOU!

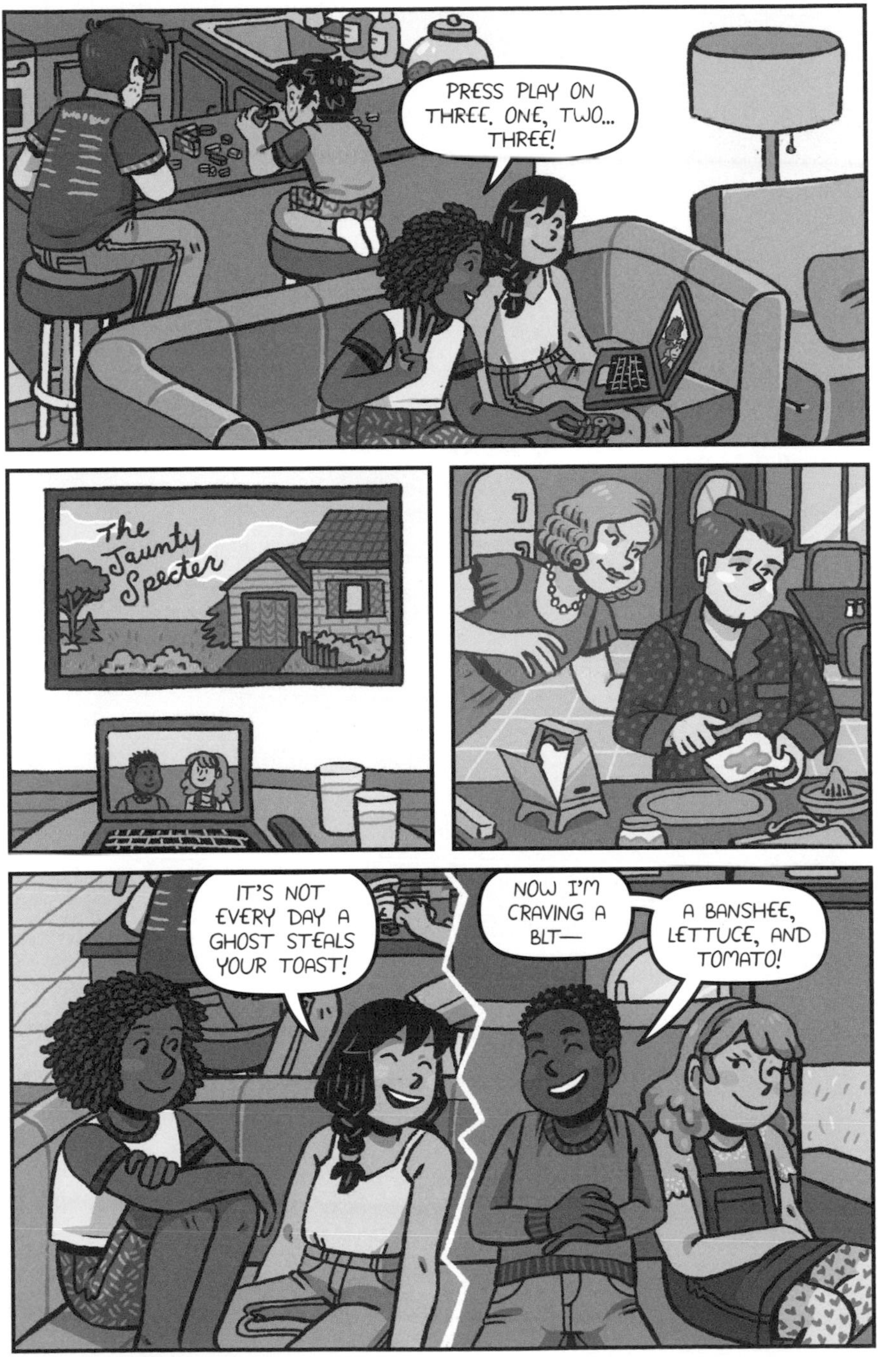
PRESS PLAY ON THREE. ONE, TWO... THREE!
The Jaunty Specter
IT'S NOT EVERY DAY A GHOST STEALS YOUR TOAST!
NOW I'M CRAVING A BLT—
A BANSHEE, LETTUCE, AND TOMATO!

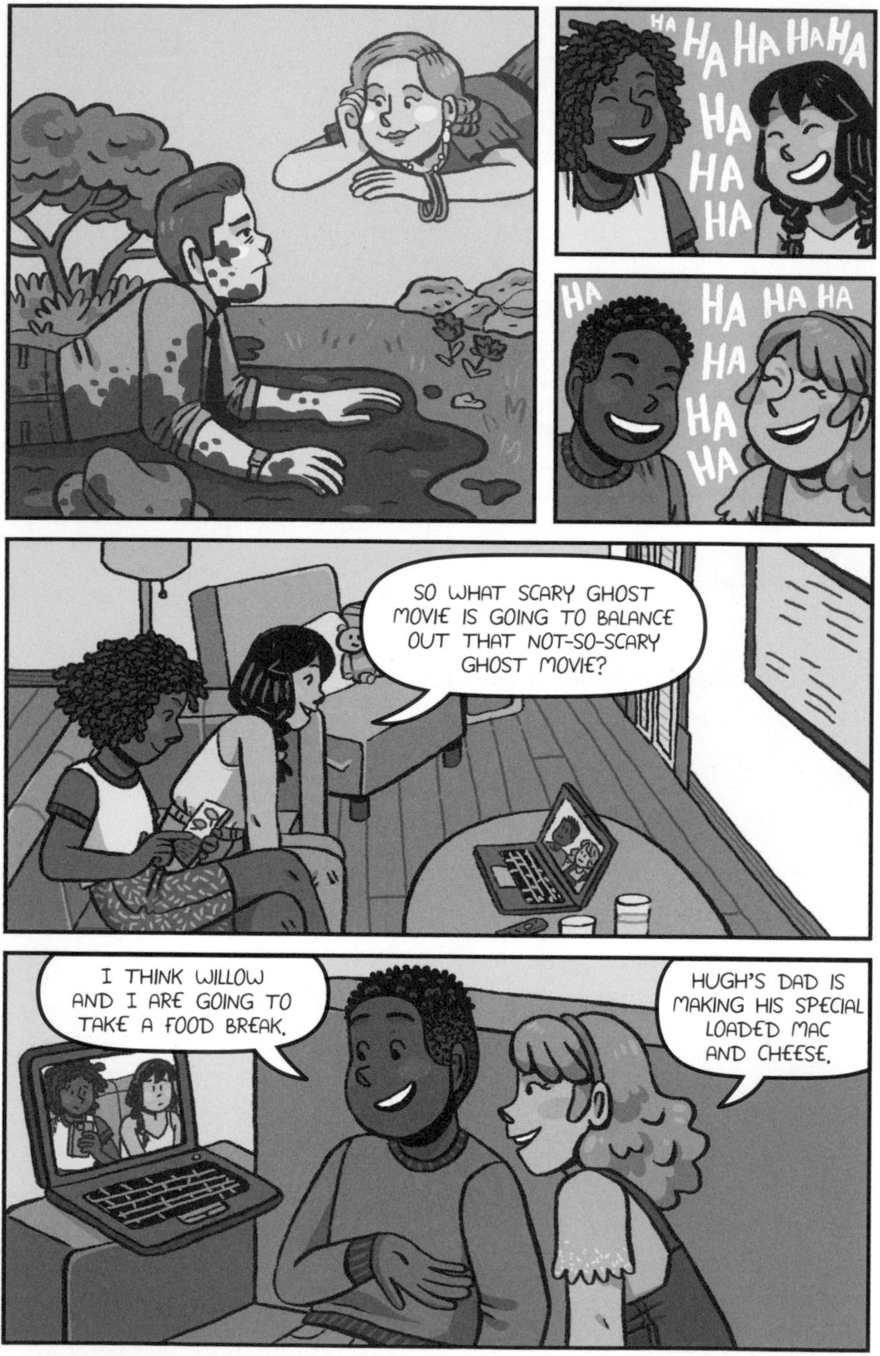
HA HA HA HA HA HA HA HA HA
HA HA HA HA HA HA HA
SO WHAT SCARY GHOST MOVIE IS GOING TO BALANCE OUT THAT NOT-SO-SCARY GHOST MOVIE?
I THINK WILLOW AND I ARE GOING TO TAKE A FOOD BREAK.
HUGH'S DAD IS MAKING HIS SPECIAL LOADED MAC AND CHEESE.

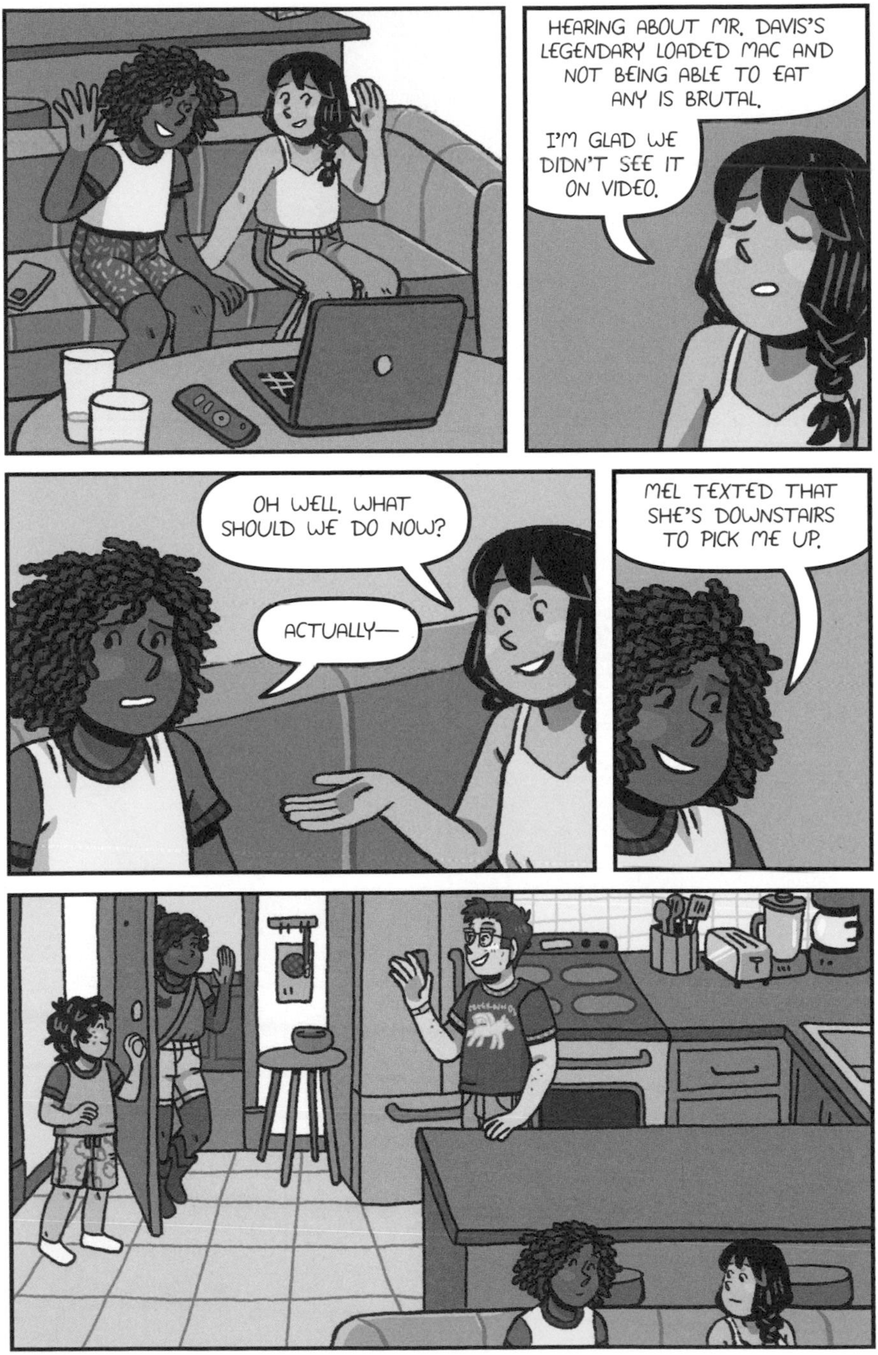
HEARING ABOUT MR. DAVIS'S LEGENDARY LOADED MAC AND NOT BEING ABLE TO EAT ANY IS BRUTAL.
I'M GLAD WE DIDN'T SEE IT ON VIDEO.
OH WELL. WHAT SHOULD WE DO NOW?
ACTUALLY—
MEL TEXTED THAT SHE'S DOWNSTAIRS TO PICK ME UP.

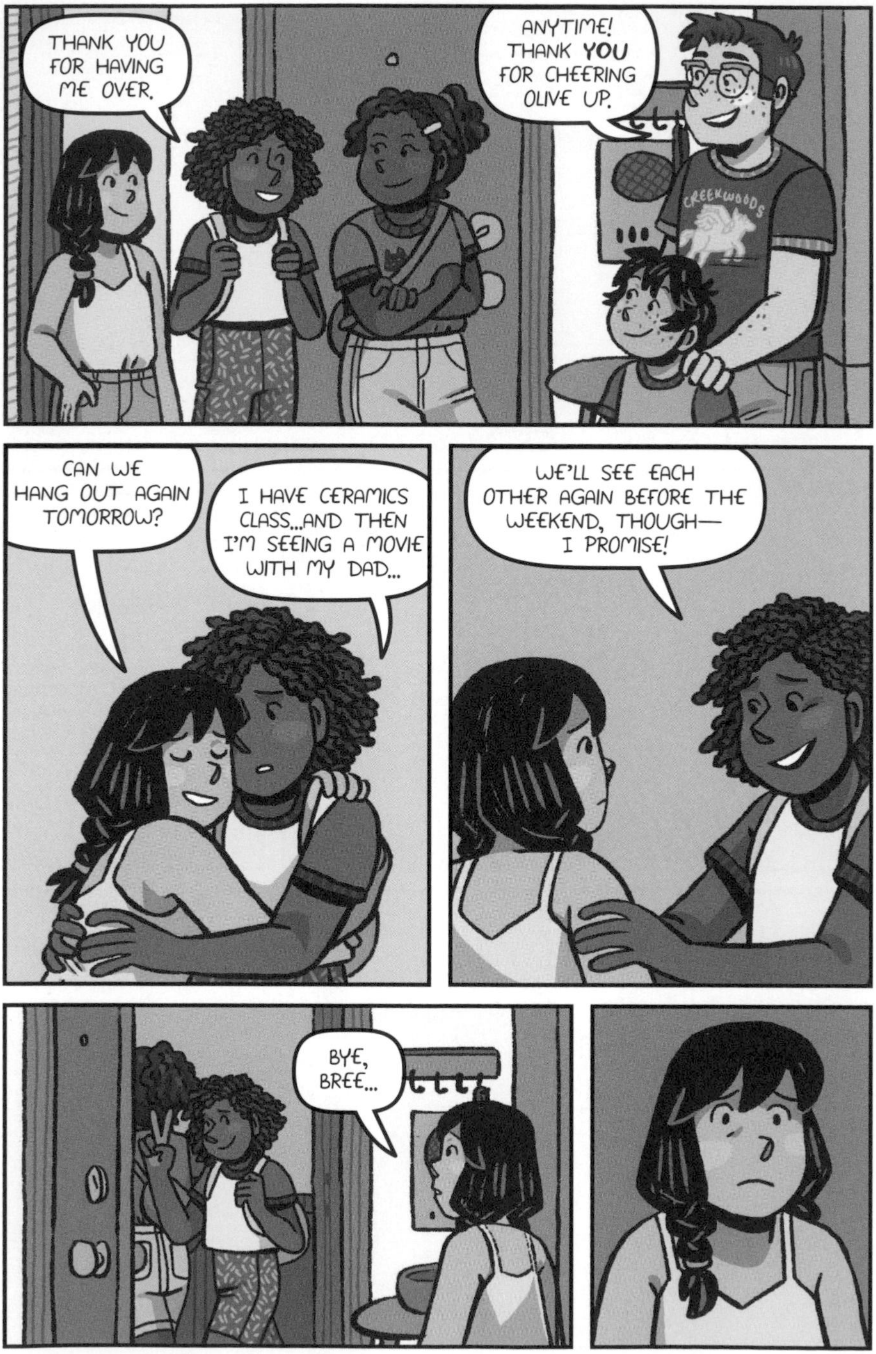

THANK YOU FOR HAVING ME OVER.
ANYTIME! THANK **YOU** FOR CHEERING OLIVE UP.
CREEKWOODS
CAN WE HANG OUT AGAIN TOMORROW?
I HAVE CERAMICS CLASS...AND THEN I'M SEEING A MOVIE WITH MY DAD...
WE'LL SEE EACH OTHER AGAIN BEFORE THE WEEKEND, THOUGH— I PROMISE!
BYE, BREE...

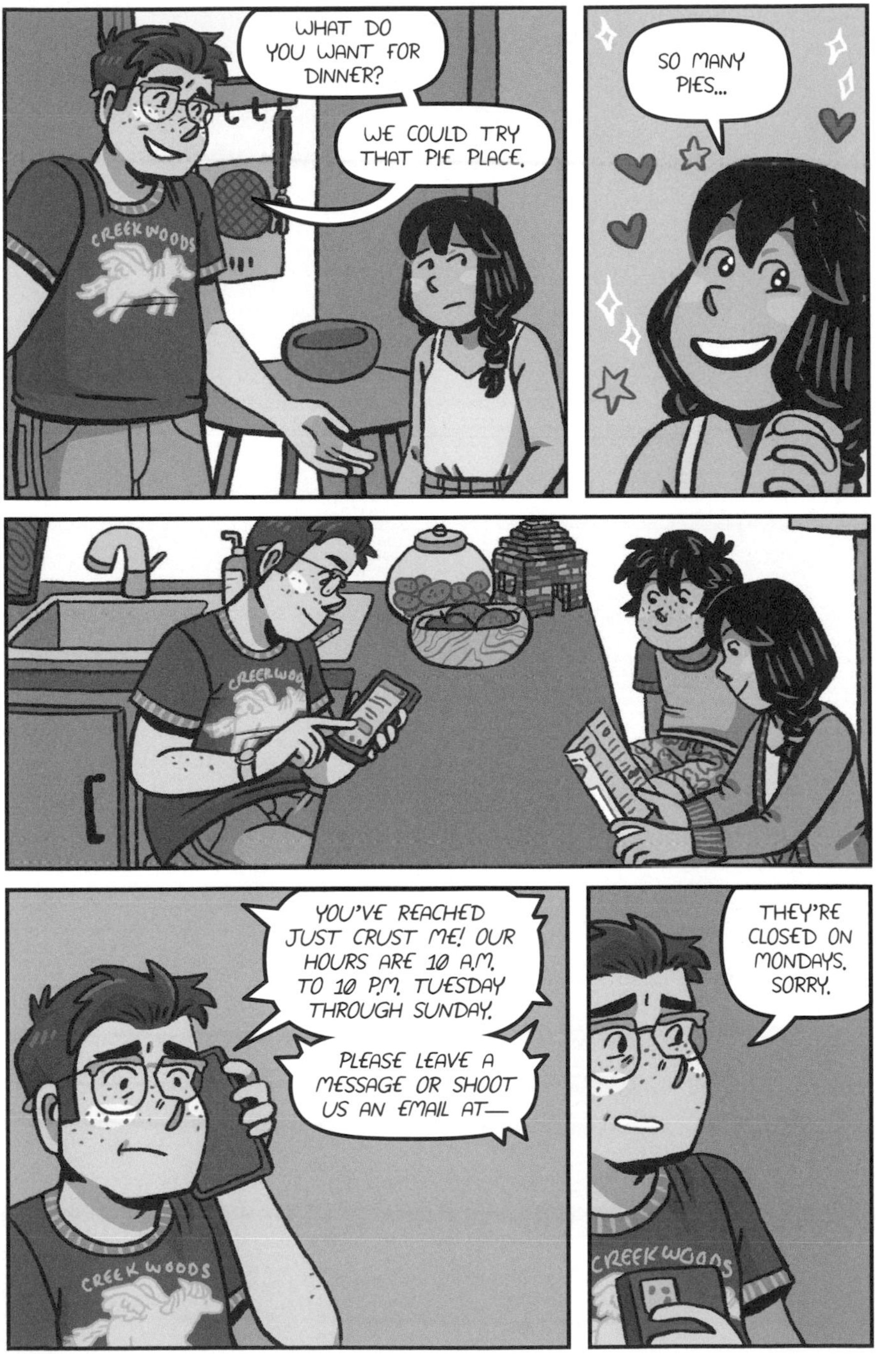
WHAT DO YOU WANT FOR DINNER?
WE COULD TRY THAT PIE PLACE.
SO MANY PIES...
CREEKWOODS
YOU'VE REACHED JUST CRUST ME! OUR HOURS ARE 10 A.M. TO 10 P.M. TUESDAY THROUGH SUNDAY.
PLEASE LEAVE A MESSAGE OR SHOOT US AN EMAIL AT—
THEY'RE CLOSED ON MONDAYS. SORRY.

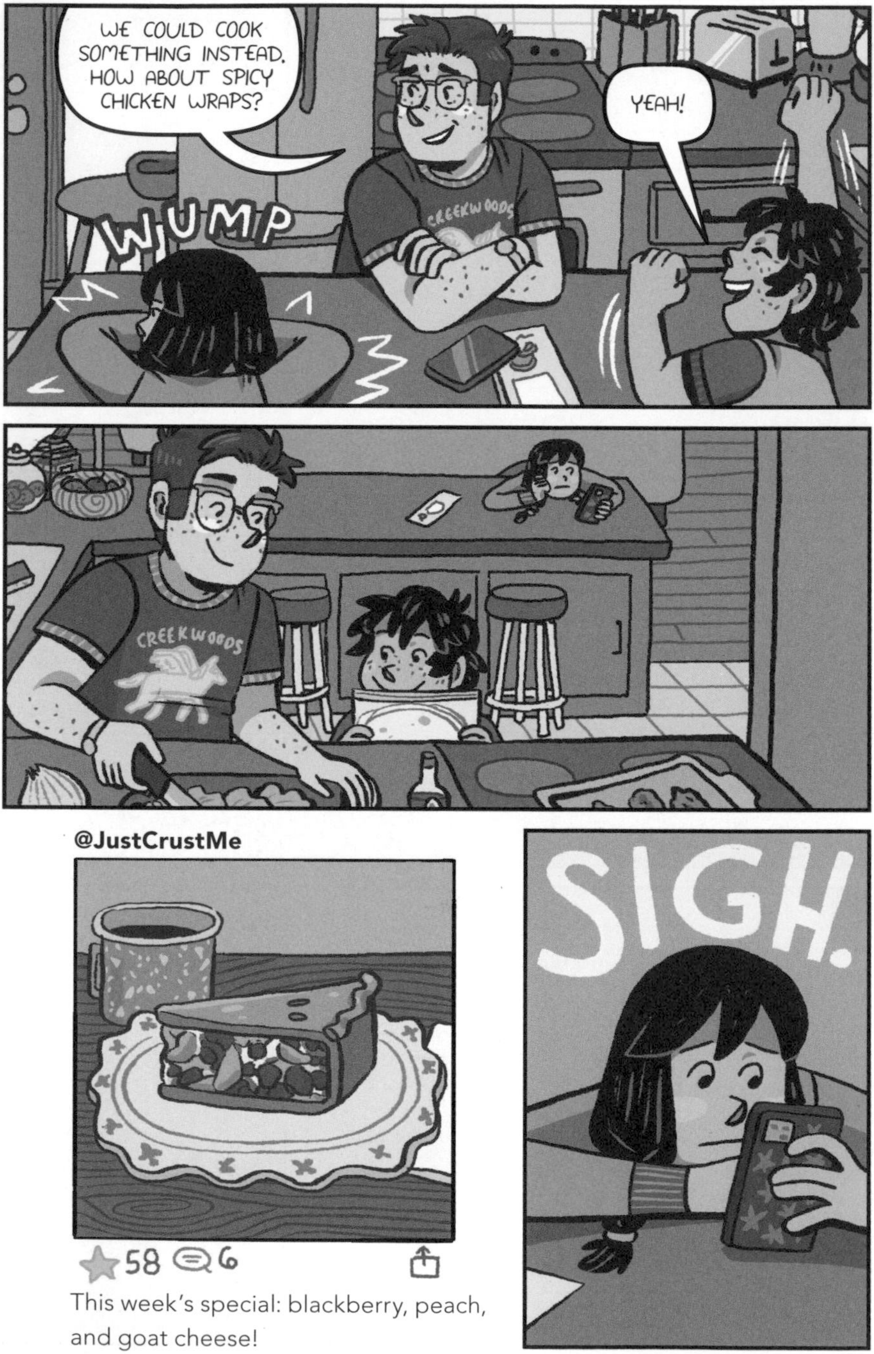
WE COULD COOK SOMETHING INSTEAD. HOW ABOUT SPICY CHICKEN WRAPS?
WUMP
CREEKWOODS
YEAH!
CREEKWOODS
@JustCrustMe
58
6
This week's special: blackberry, peach, and goat cheese!
READ MORE...
SIGH.

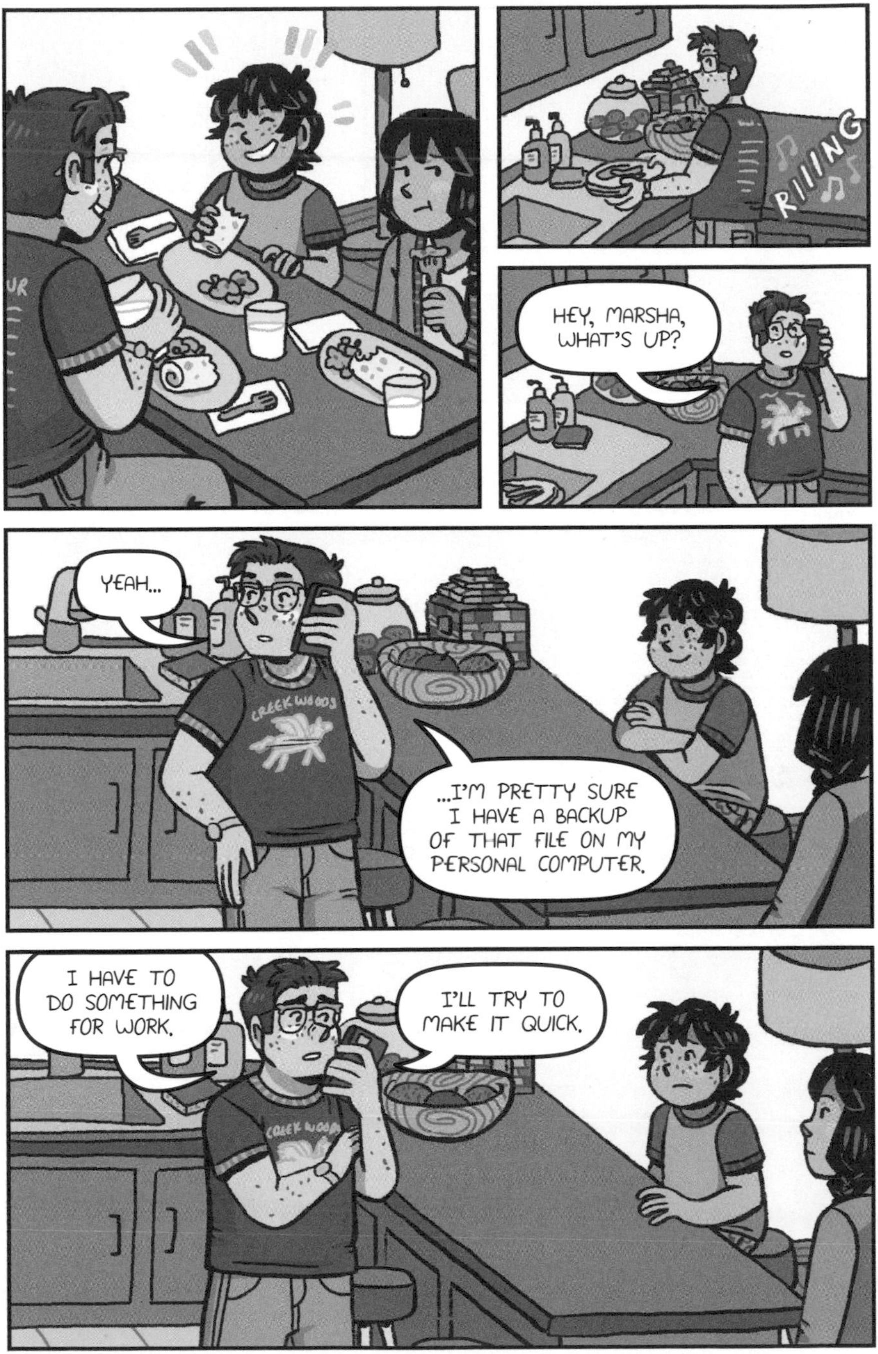
RIIING
HEY, MARSHA, WHAT'S UP?
YEAH...
...I'M PRETTY SURE I HAVE A BACKUP OF THAT FILE ON MY PERSONAL COMPUTER.
CREEK WOODS
I HAVE TO DO SOMETHING FOR WORK.
I'LL TRY TO MAKE IT QUICK.

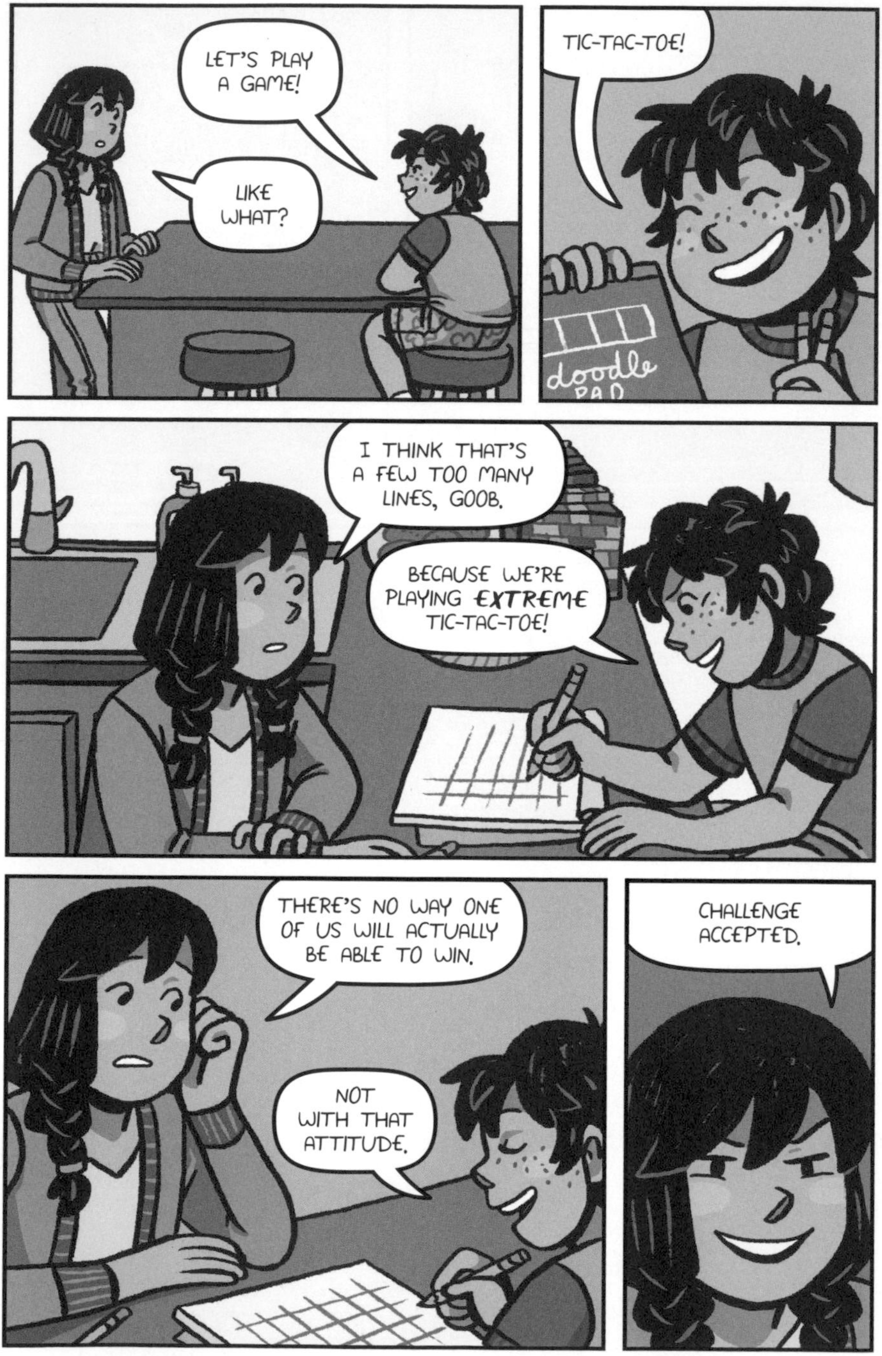
LET'S PLAY A GAME!
LIKE WHAT?
TIC-TAC-TOE!
doodle PAD
I THINK THAT'S A FEW TOO MANY LINES, GOOB.
BECAUSE WE'RE PLAYING EXTREME TIC-TAC-TOE!
THERE'S NO WAY ONE OF US WILL ACTUALLY BE ABLE TO WIN.
NOT WITH THAT ATTITUDE.
CHALLENGE ACCEPTED.

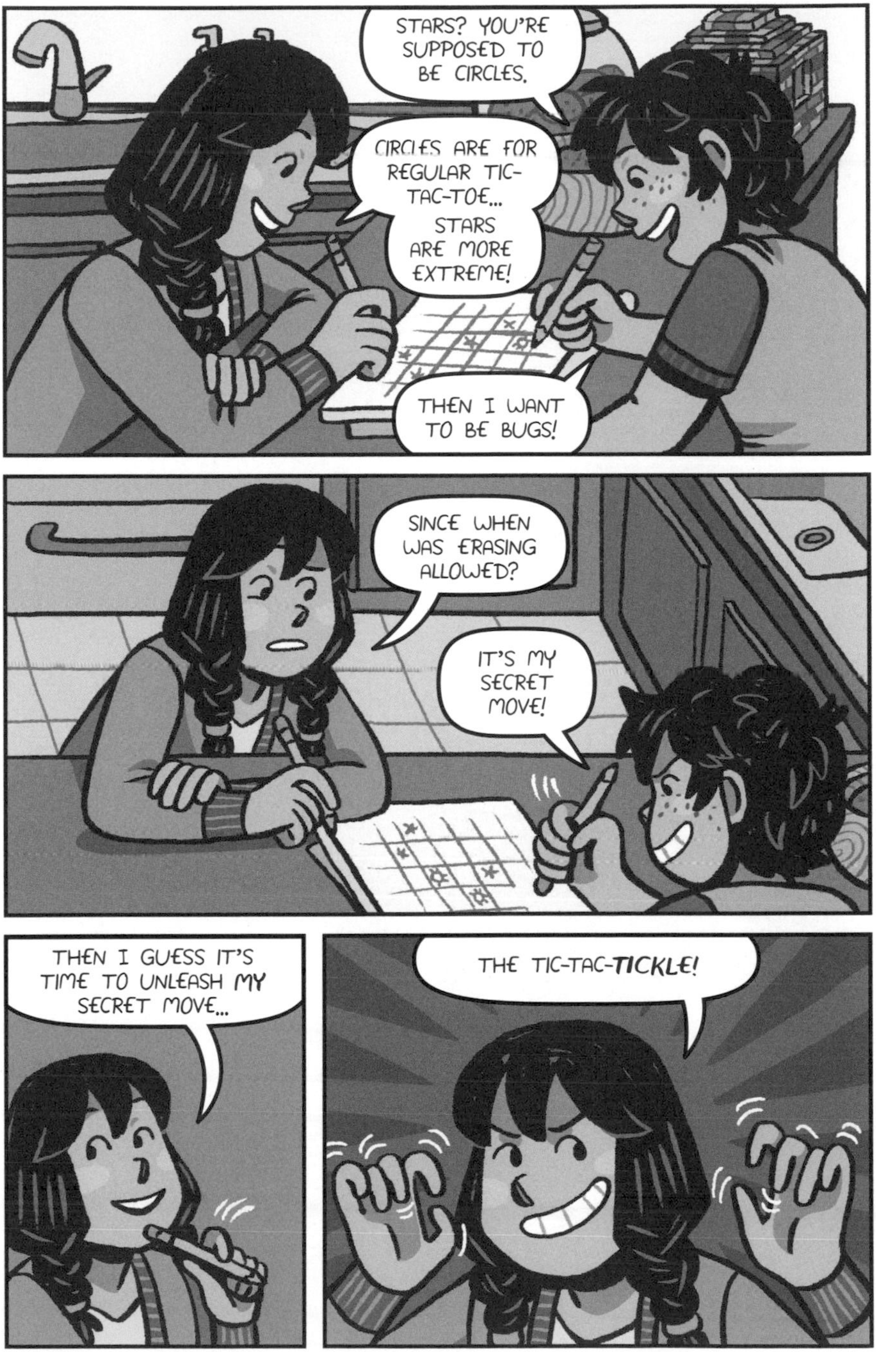
STARS? YOU'RE SUPPOSED TO BE CIRCLES.
CIRCLES ARE FOR REGULAR TIC-TAC-TOE...
STARS ARE MORE EXTREME!
THEN I WANT TO BE BUGS!
SINCE WHEN WAS ERASING ALLOWED?
IT'S MY SECRET MOVE!
THEN I GUESS IT'S TIME TO UNLEASH **MY** SECRET MOVE...
THE TIC-TAC-**TICKLE**!

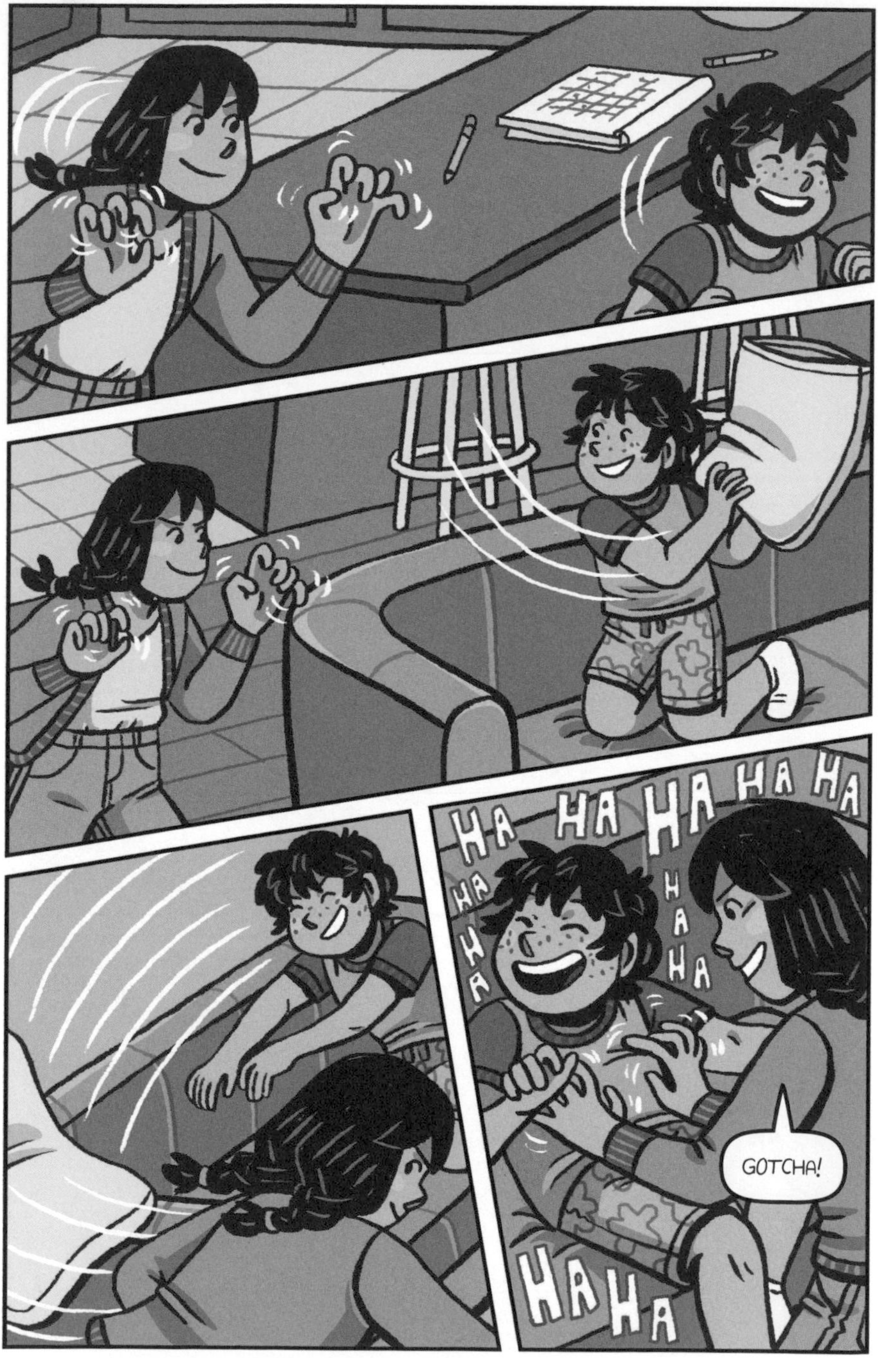
HA HA HA HA HA
HA HA HA
HA HA HA
GOTCHA!
HA HA HA

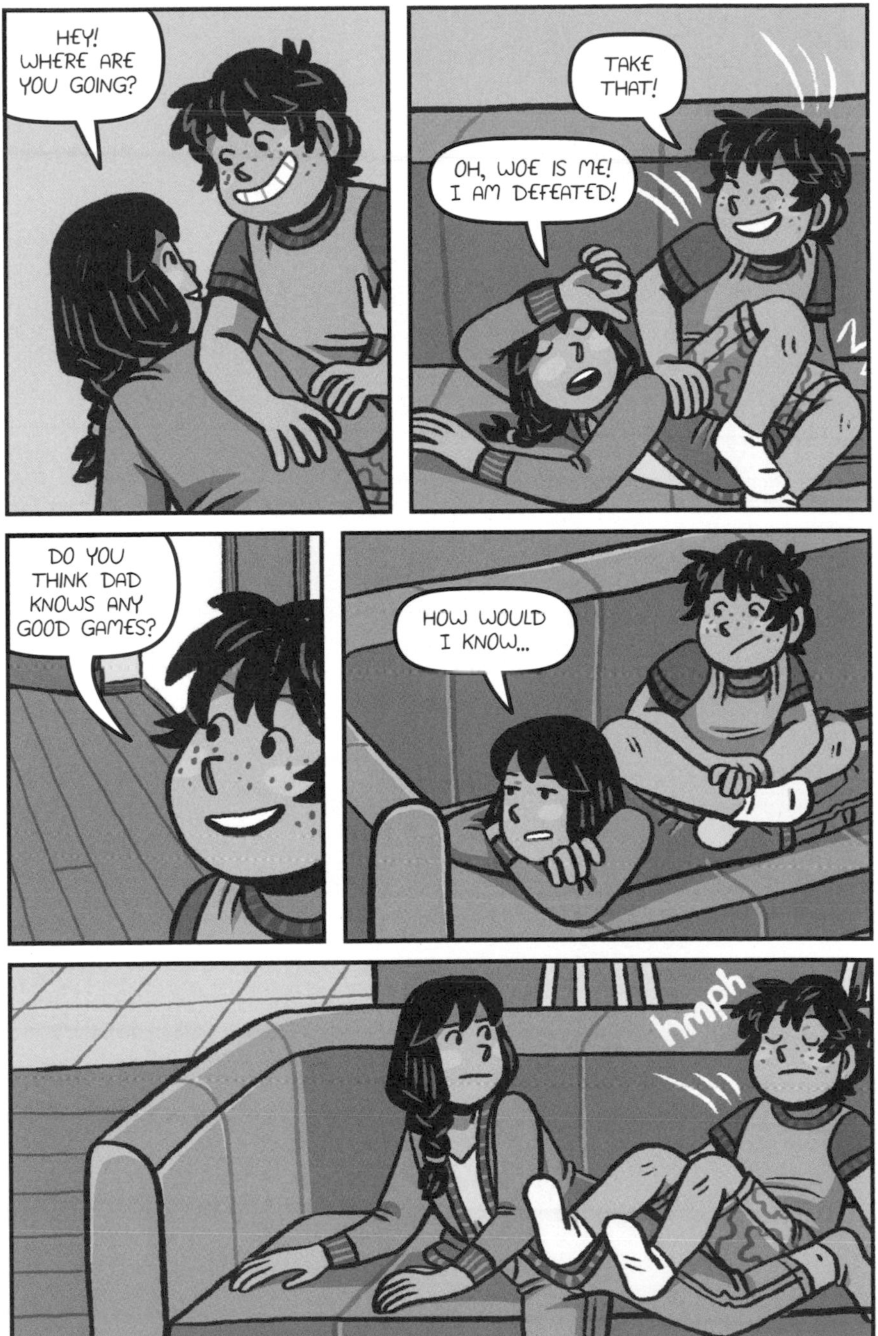
HEY! WHERE ARE YOU GOING?
TAKE THAT!
OH, WOE IS ME! I AM DEFEATED!
DO YOU THINK DAD KNOWS ANY GOOD GAMES?
HOW WOULD I KNOW...
hmph

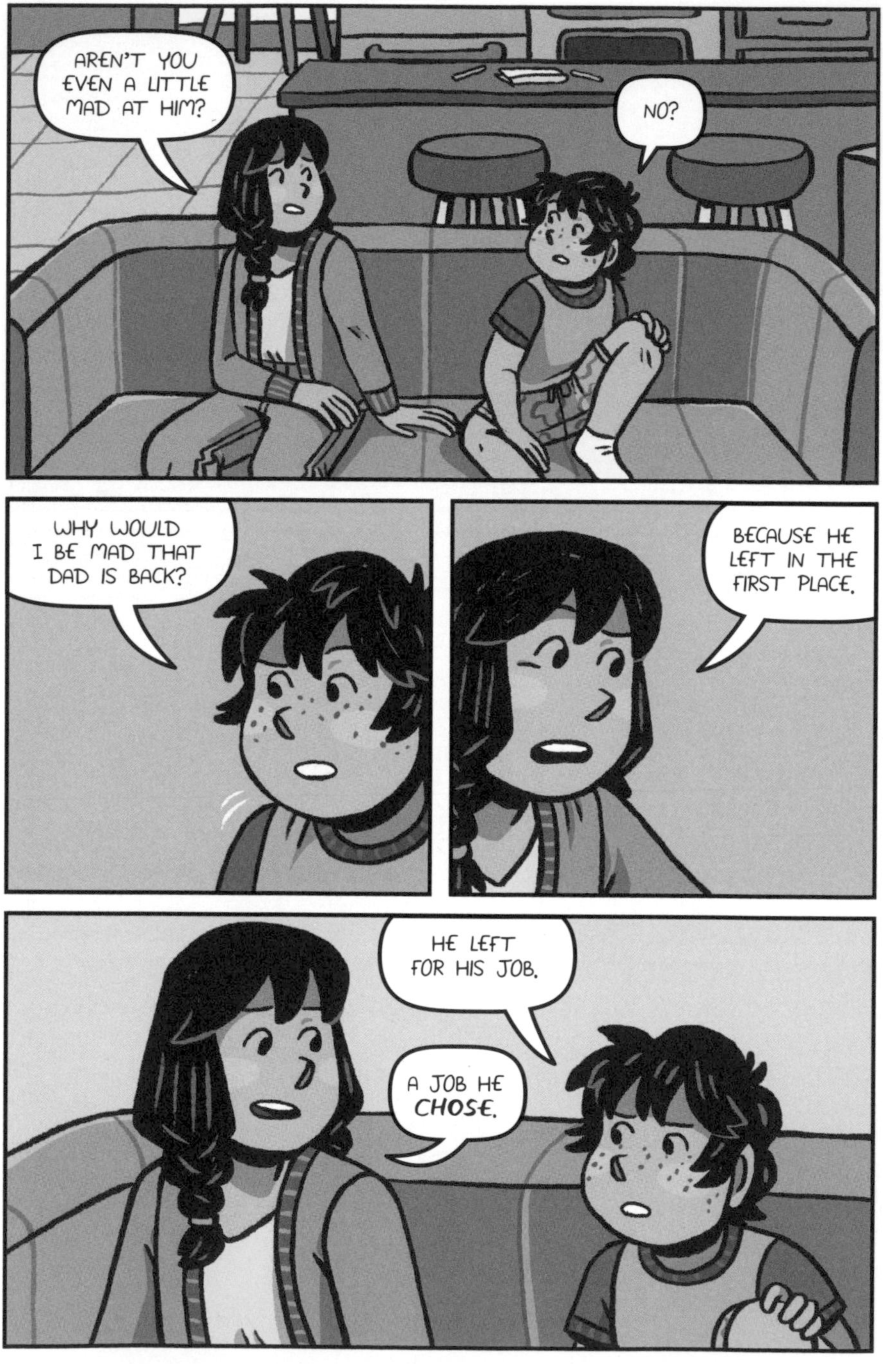
AREN'T YOU EVEN A LITTLE MAD AT HIM?
NO?
WHY WOULD I BE MAD THAT DAD IS BACK?
BECAUSE HE LEFT IN THE FIRST PLACE.
HE LEFT FOR HIS JOB.
A JOB HE **CHOSE**.

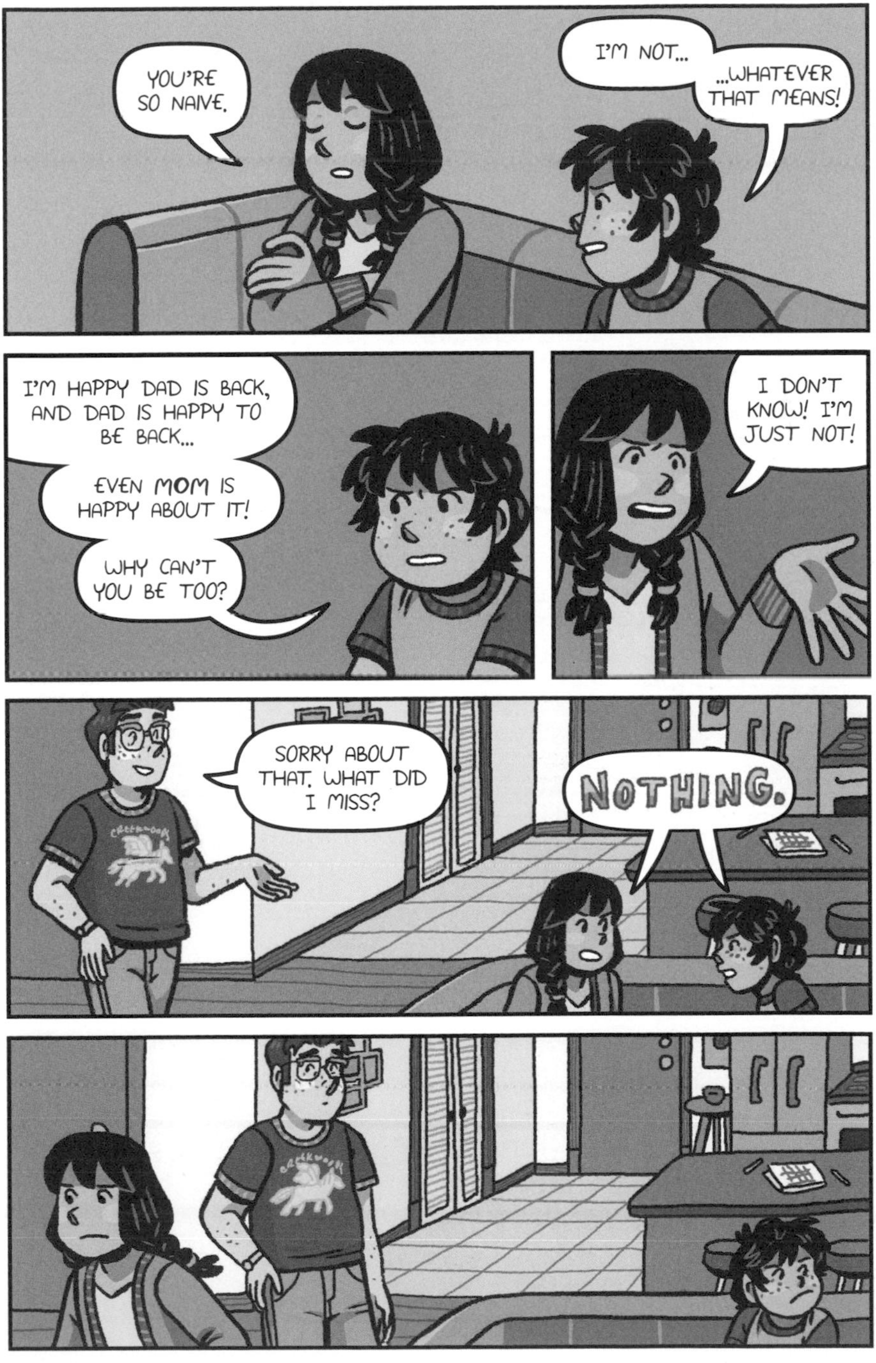
YOU'RE SO NAIVE.
I'M NOT...
...WHATEVER THAT MEANS!
I'M HAPPY DAD IS BACK, AND DAD IS HAPPY TO BE BACK...
EVEN MOM IS HAPPY ABOUT IT!
WHY CAN'T YOU BE TOO?
I DON'T KNOW! I'M JUST NOT!
SORRY ABOUT THAT. WHAT DID I MISS?
NOTHING.

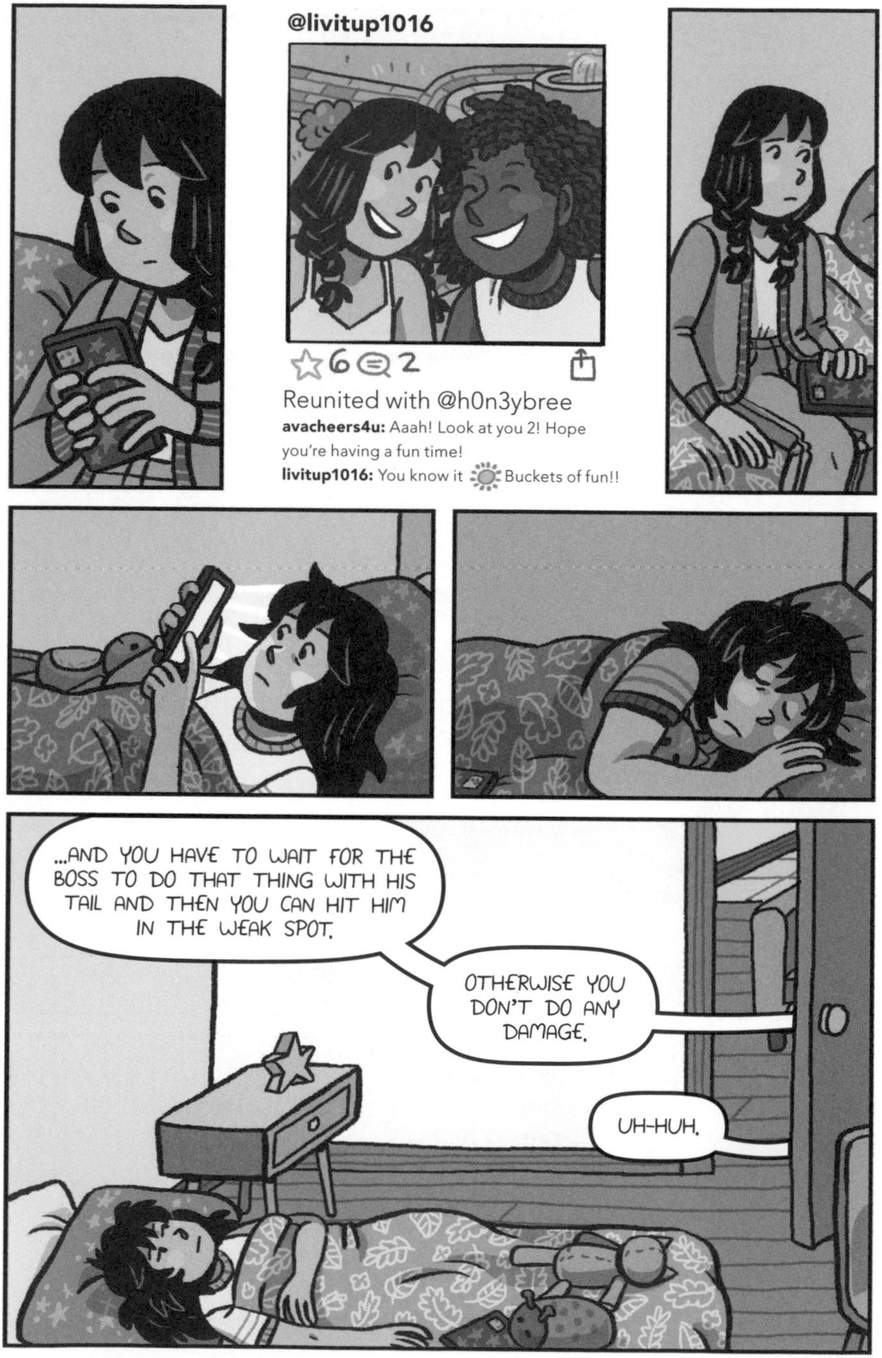
@livitup1016
6 2
Reunited with @h0n3ybree
avacheers4u: Aaah! Look at you 2! Hope you're having a fun time!
livitup1016: You know it Buckets of fun!!
...AND YOU HAVE TO WAIT FOR THE BOSS TO DO THAT THING WITH HIS TAIL AND THEN YOU CAN HIT HIM IN THE WEAK SPOT.
OTHERWISE YOU DON'T DO ANY DAMAGE.
UH-HUH.

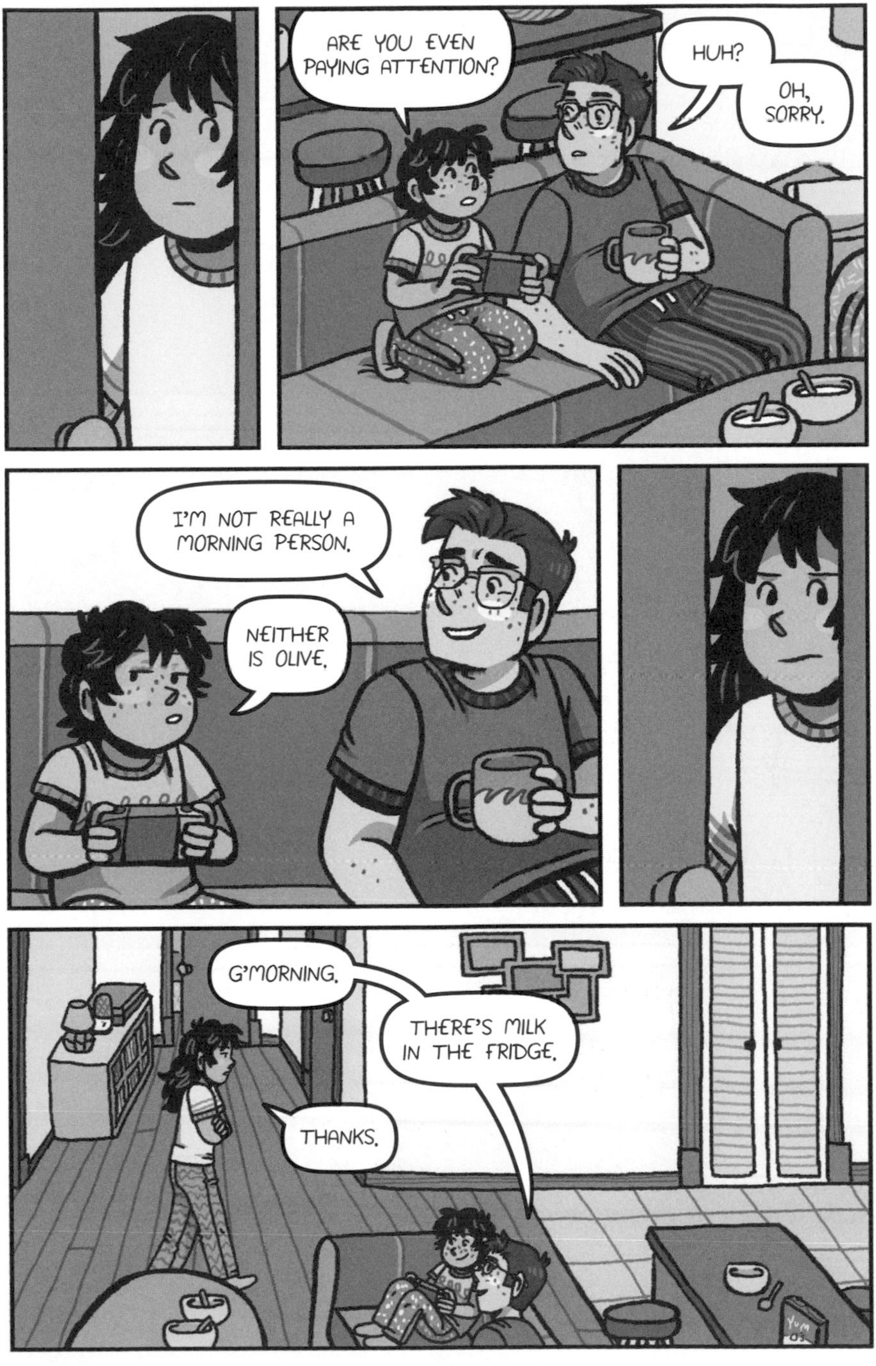
ARE YOU EVEN PAYING ATTENTION?
HUH?
OH, SORRY.
I'M NOT REALLY A MORNING PERSON.
NEITHER IS OLIVE.
G'MORNING.
THERE'S MILK IN THE FRIDGE.
THANKS.

SO, WHAT SHOULD WE DO TODAY?

I TOOK THE WHOLE WEEK OFF FROM WORK, SO WE HAVE A LOT OF TIME TO FILL.

I WANT TO EAT... DOG FROM A HOTDOG CART! AND RIDE IN A RICKSHAW! AND VISIT YOUR... ALL YOUR WORK FRIENDS! AND FEED A PIGEON! AND ...NT MOLLY... ...ST OF ALL THE DIFFERENT KINDS OF BUGS THAT LIV... ...N THE PARK... ...GO TO THE PARK AND TRY TO FIND AS MANY AS W... CAN! AND I... ...TOGETHER A PUZZLE! AND I WANT... ...CH MORE... GHOST... ...ANT TO SHOW YOU MY FAVOR... THE... ...A CAT ARE SIBLINGS AND THE... ...OG... ...SOCCER TEAM! OR WE COULD... ...FA... ...H SONGS BUT I ALSO LIKE SOME... ...AVE... SONG... ...SOMETHING TOGETHER! I LIKE... ...MOM DOES... ...KITCHEN BECAUSE WHEN I COOK TH... ...E CAN MAKE DINN...

WHOA THERE, BUD! SLOW DOWN.

I'M SURE WE CAN MAKE AT LEAST **SOME** OF THAT HAPPEN THIS WEEK.

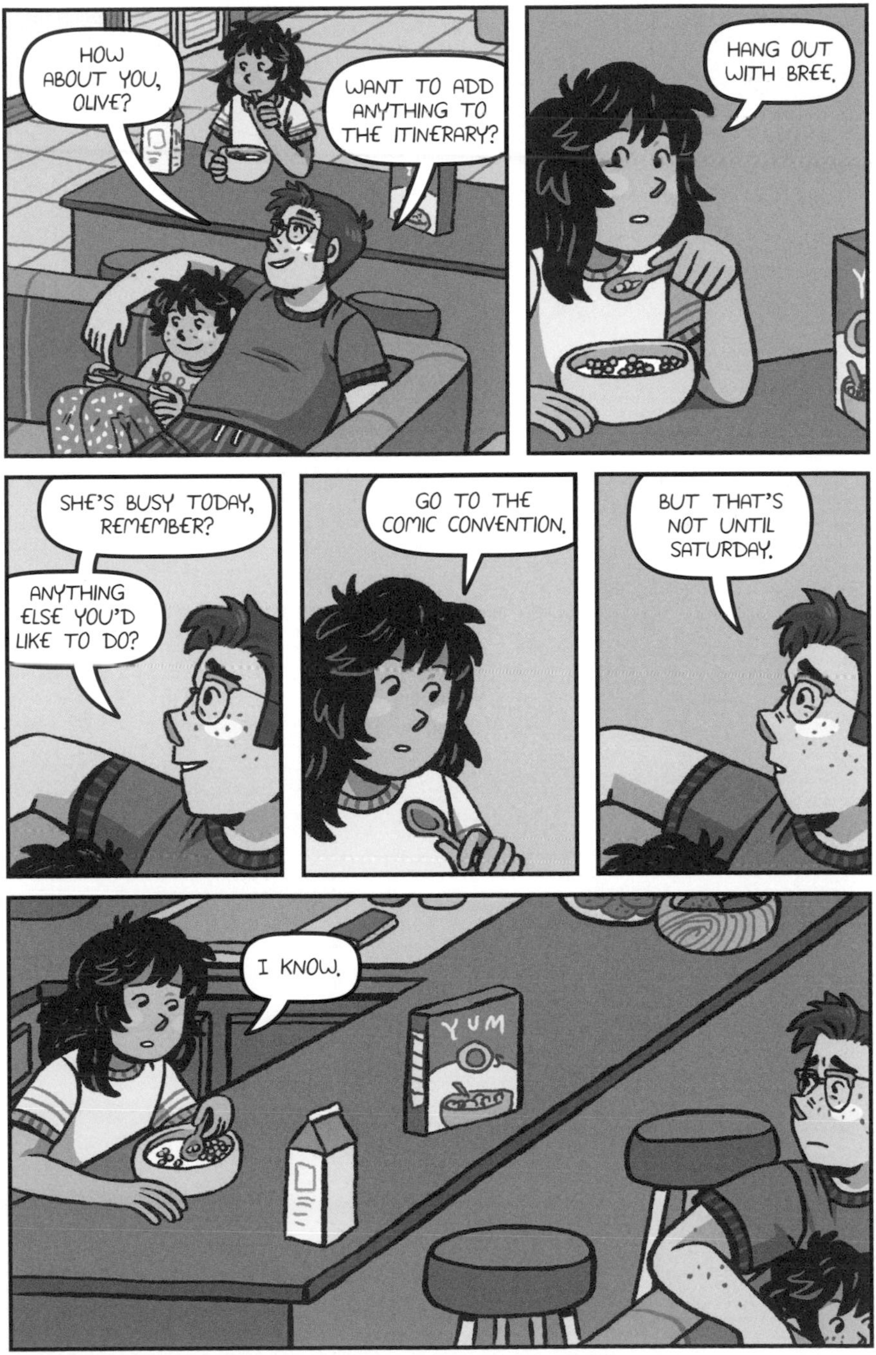
HOW ABOUT YOU, OLIVE?
WANT TO ADD ANYTHING TO THE ITINERARY?
HANG OUT WITH BREE.
SHE'S BUSY TODAY, REMEMBER?
ANYTHING ELSE YOU'D LIKE TO DO?
GO TO THE COMIC CONVENTION.
BUT THAT'S NOT UNTIL SATURDAY.
I KNOW.
YUM

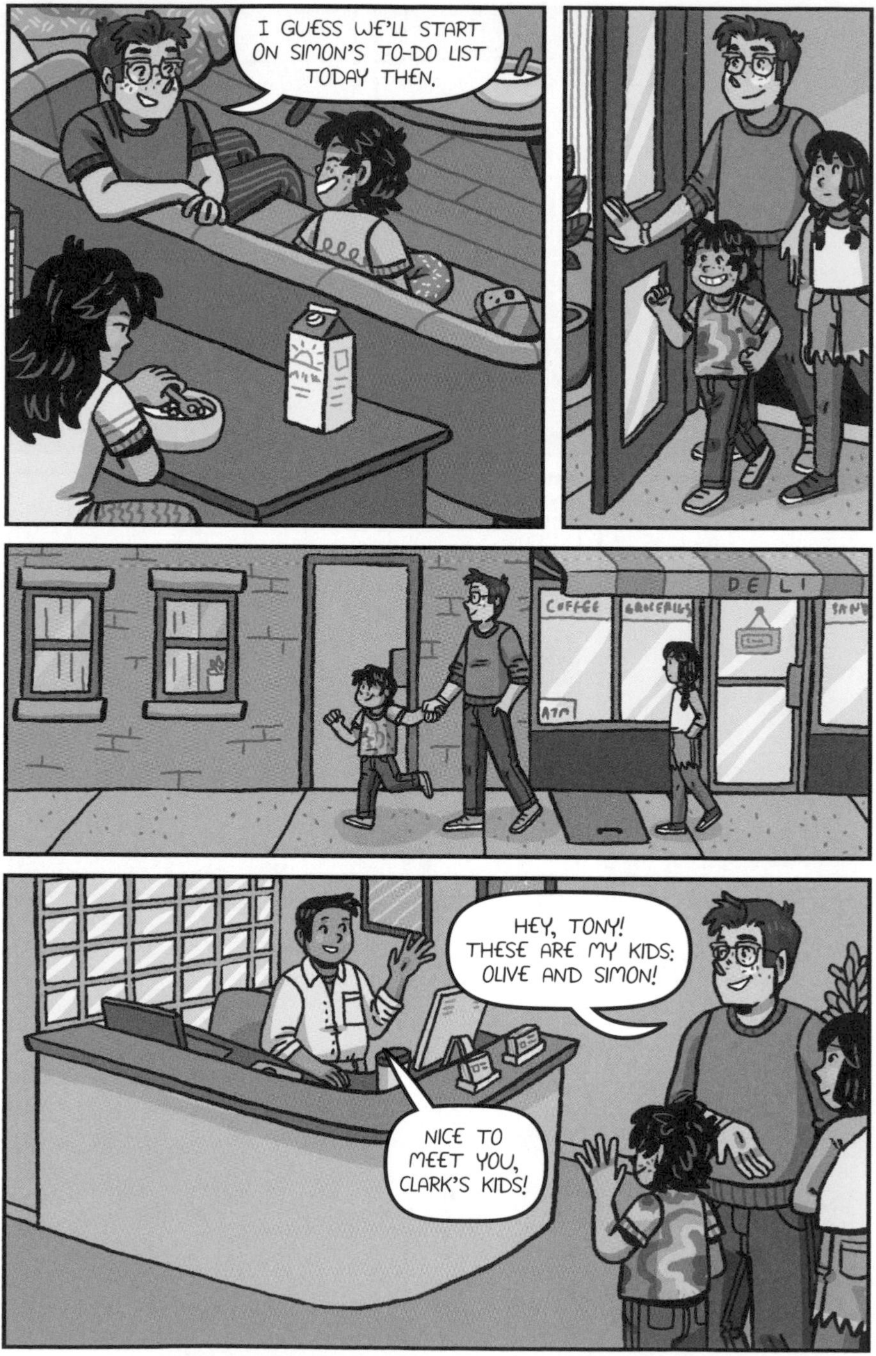
I GUESS WE'LL START ON SIMON'S TO-DO LIST TODAY THEN.
DELI
COFFEE
ATM
HEY, TONY! THESE ARE MY KIDS: OLIVE AND SIMON!
NICE TO MEET YOU, CLARK'S KIDS!

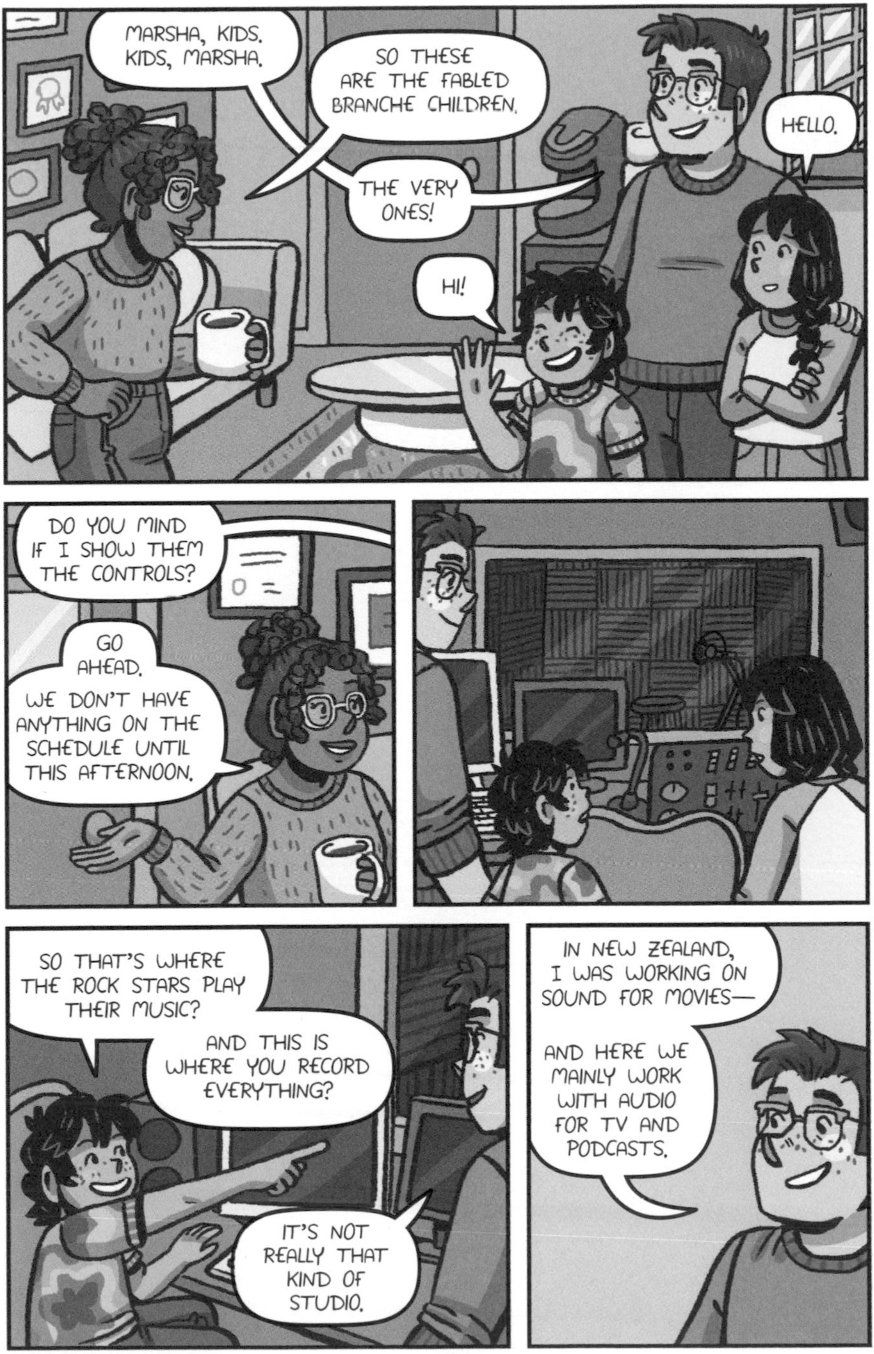
MARSHA, KIDS. KIDS, MARSHA.
SO THESE ARE THE FABLED BRANCHE CHILDREN.
THE VERY ONES!
HELLO.
HI!
DO YOU MIND IF I SHOW THEM THE CONTROLS?
GO AHEAD.
WE DON'T HAVE ANYTHING ON THE SCHEDULE UNTIL THIS AFTERNOON.
SO THAT'S WHERE THE ROCK STARS PLAY THEIR MUSIC?
AND THIS IS WHERE YOU RECORD EVERYTHING?
IT'S NOT REALLY THAT KIND OF STUDIO.
IN NEW ZEALAND, I WAS WORKING ON SOUND FOR MOVIES—
AND HERE WE MAINLY WORK WITH AUDIO FOR TV AND PODCASTS.

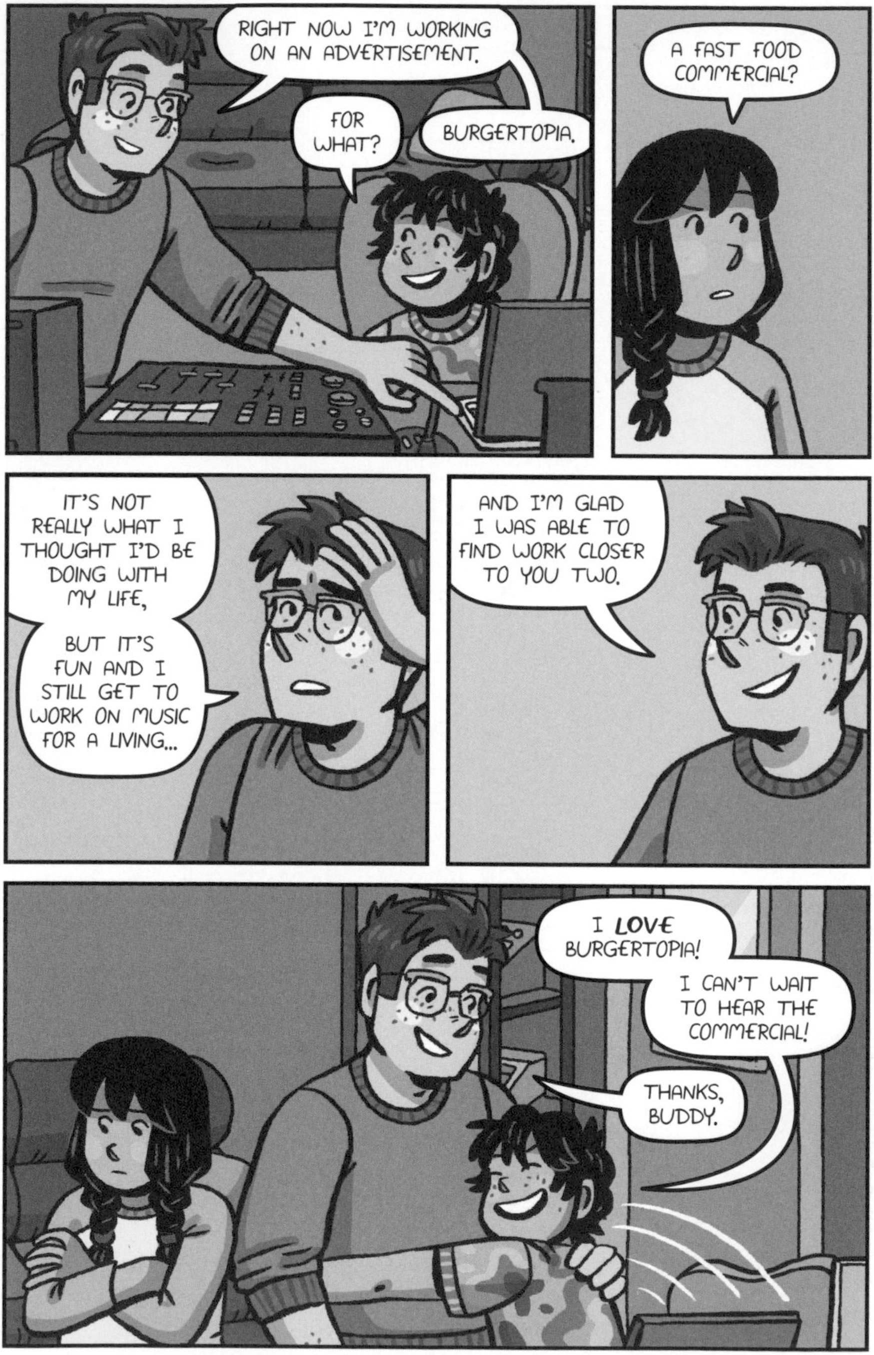
RIGHT NOW I'M WORKING ON AN ADVERTISEMENT.
FOR WHAT?
BURGERTOPIA.
A FAST FOOD COMMERCIAL?
IT'S NOT REALLY WHAT I THOUGHT I'D BE DOING WITH MY LIFE,
BUT IT'S FUN AND I STILL GET TO WORK ON MUSIC FOR A LIVING...
AND I'M GLAD I WAS ABLE TO FIND WORK CLOSER TO YOU TWO.
I **LOVE** BURGERTOPIA!
I CAN'T WAIT TO HEAR THE COMMERCIAL!
THANKS, BUDDY.

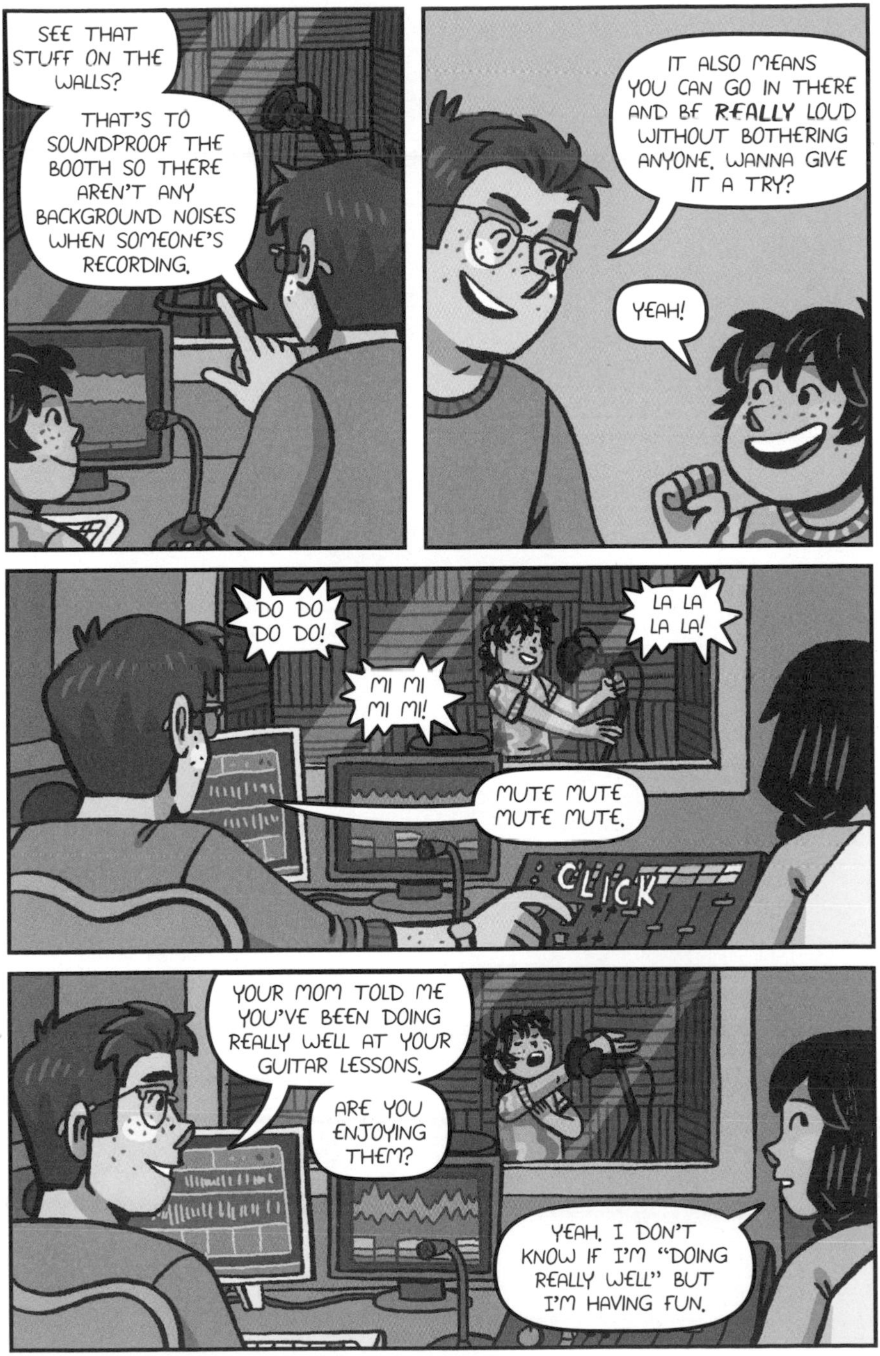
SEE THAT STUFF ON THE WALLS?
THAT'S TO SOUNDPROOF THE BOOTH SO THERE AREN'T ANY BACKGROUND NOISES WHEN SOMEONE'S RECORDING.
IT ALSO MEANS YOU CAN GO IN THERE AND BE REALLY LOUD WITHOUT BOTHERING ANYONE. WANNA GIVE IT A TRY?
YEAH!
DO DO DO DO!
MI MI MI MI!
LA LA LA LA!
MUTE MUTE MUTE MUTE.
CLICK
YOUR MOM TOLD ME YOU'VE BEEN DOING REALLY WELL AT YOUR GUITAR LESSONS.
ARE YOU ENJOYING THEM?
YEAH. I DON'T KNOW IF I'M "DOING REALLY WELL" BUT I'M HAVING FUN.

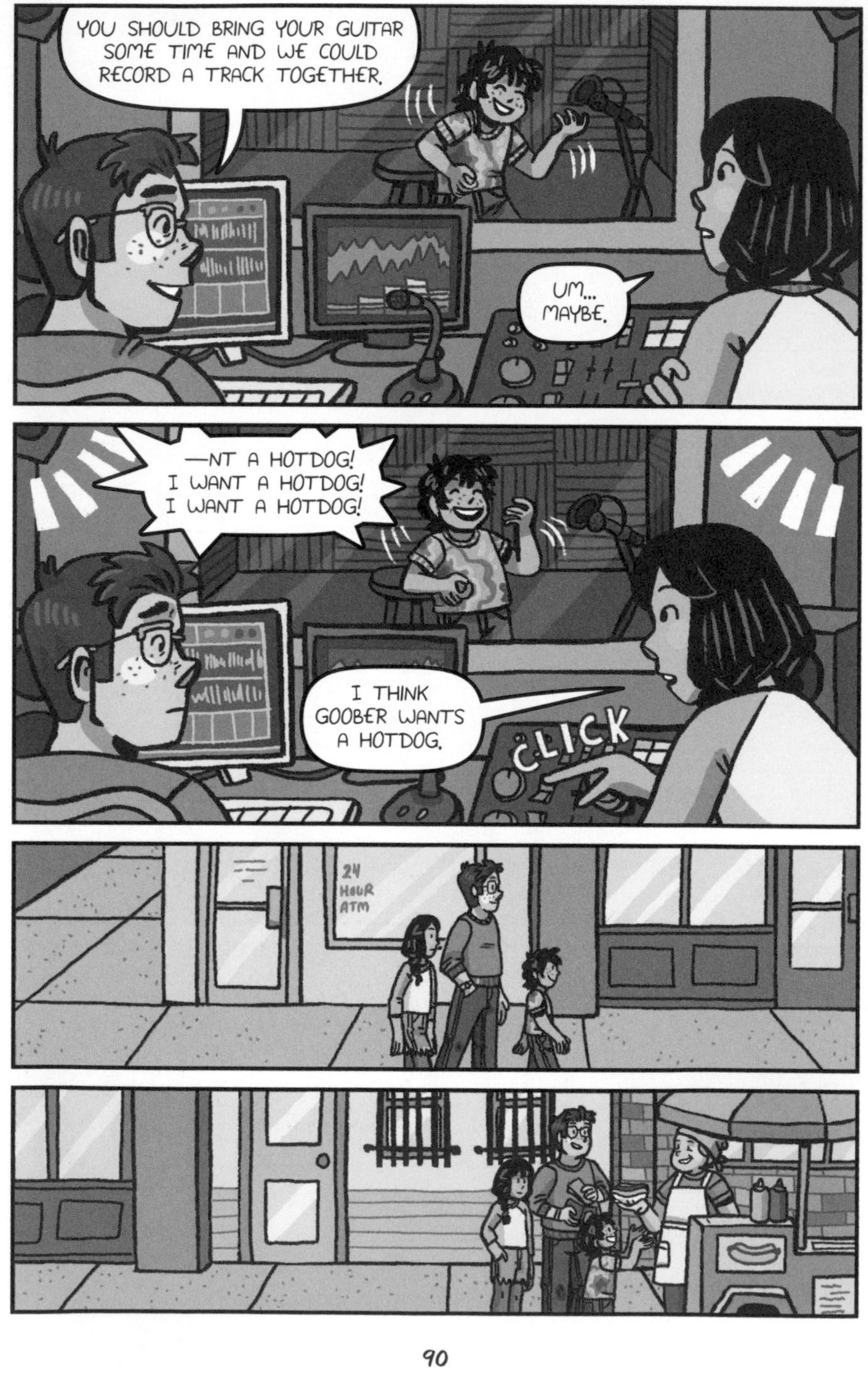
YOU SHOULD BRING YOUR GUITAR SOME TIME AND WE COULD RECORD A TRACK TOGETHER.
UM... MAYBE.
—NT A HOTDOG! I WANT A HOTDOG! I WANT A HOTDOG!
I THINK GOOBER WANTS A HOTDOG.
CLICK
24 HOUR ATM

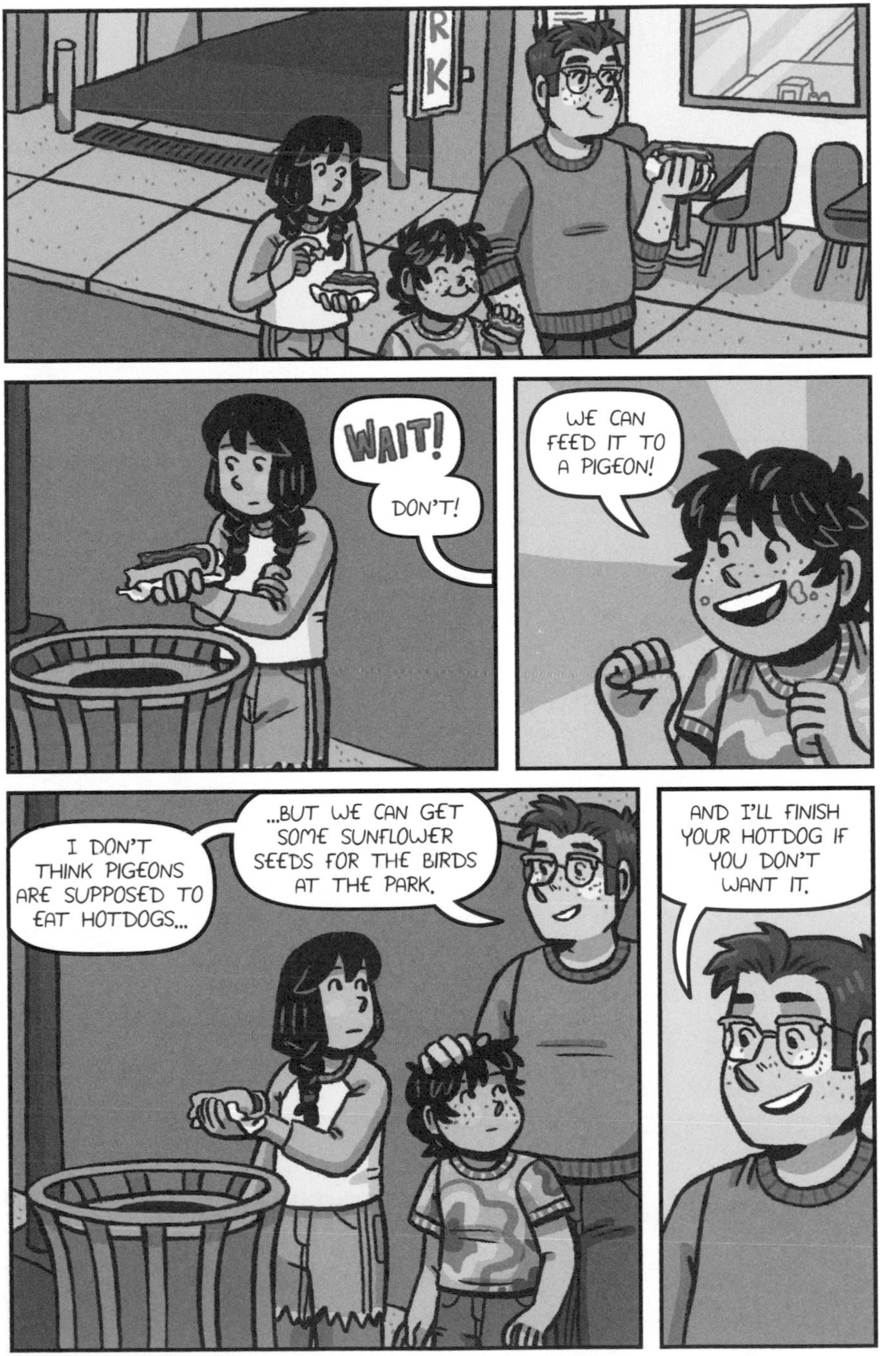
WAIT!
DON'T!
WE CAN FEED IT TO A PIGEON!
I DON'T THINK PIGEONS ARE SUPPOSED TO EAT HOTDOGS...
...BUT WE CAN GET SOME SUNFLOWER SEEDS FOR THE BIRDS AT THE PARK.
AND I'LL FINISH YOUR HOTDOG IF YOU DON'T WANT IT.

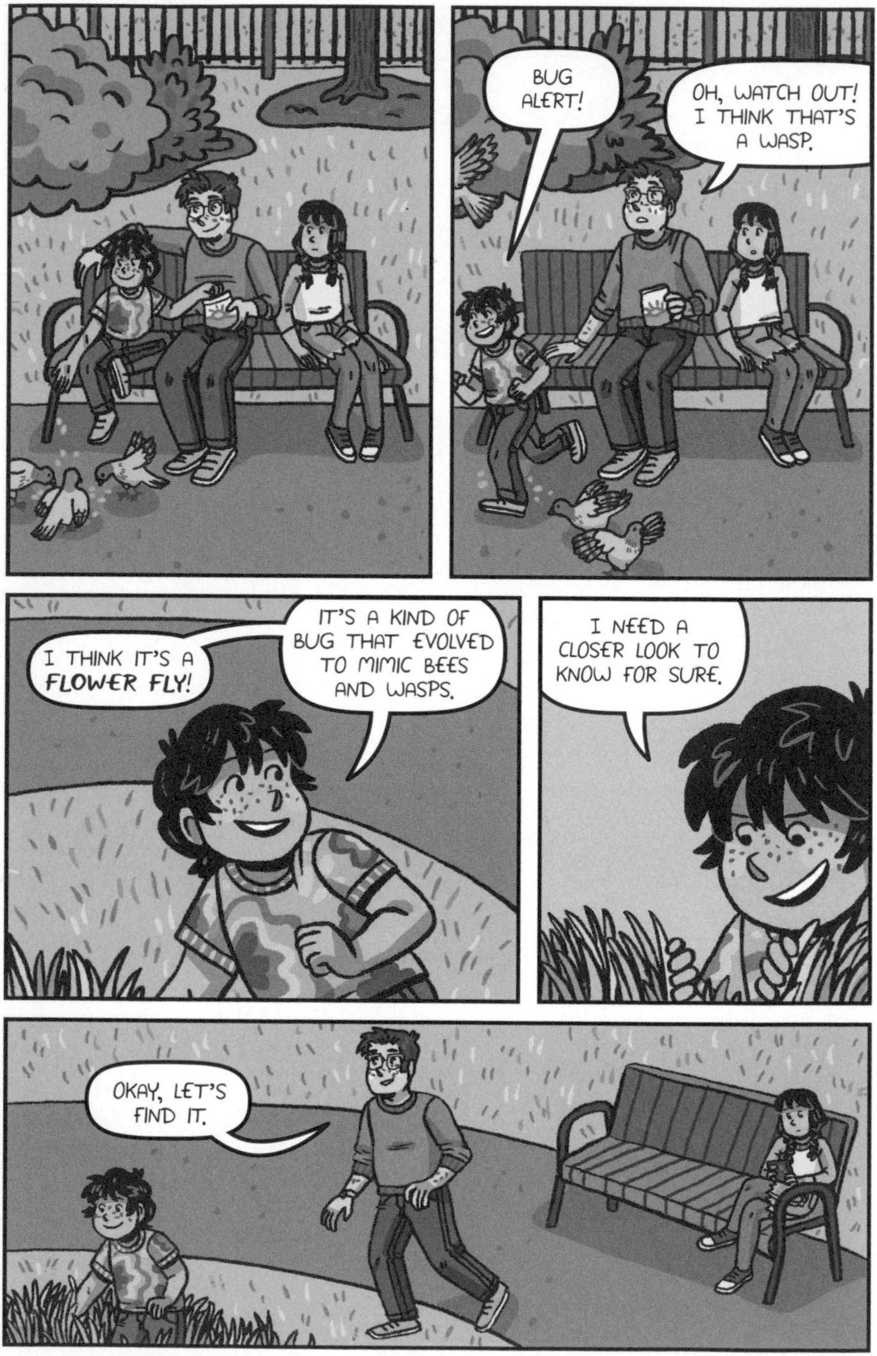
BUG ALERT!
OH, WATCH OUT! I THINK THAT'S A WASP.
I THINK IT'S A FLOWER FLY!
IT'S A KIND OF BUG THAT EVOLVED TO MIMIC BEES AND WASPS.
I NEED A CLOSER LOOK TO KNOW FOR SURE.
OKAY, LET'S FIND IT.

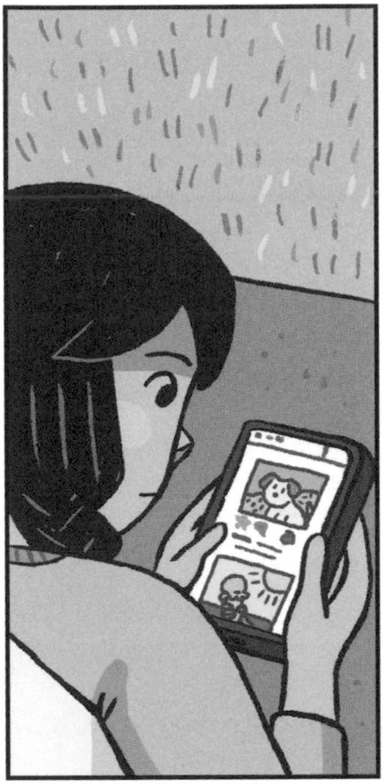

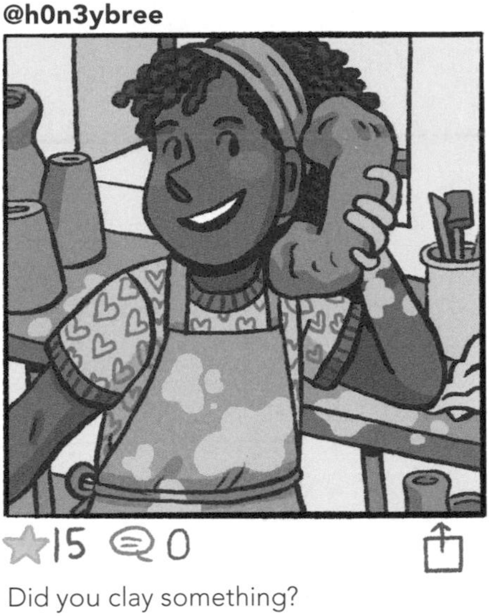
@h0n3ybree
15 0
Did you clay something?

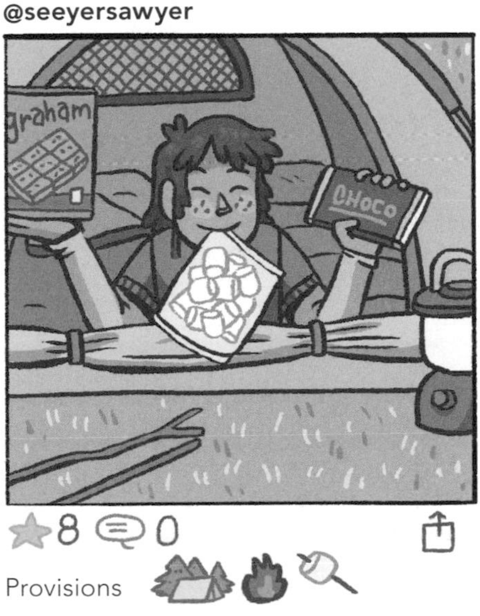
@seeyersawyer
graham
CHOCO
8 0
Provisions

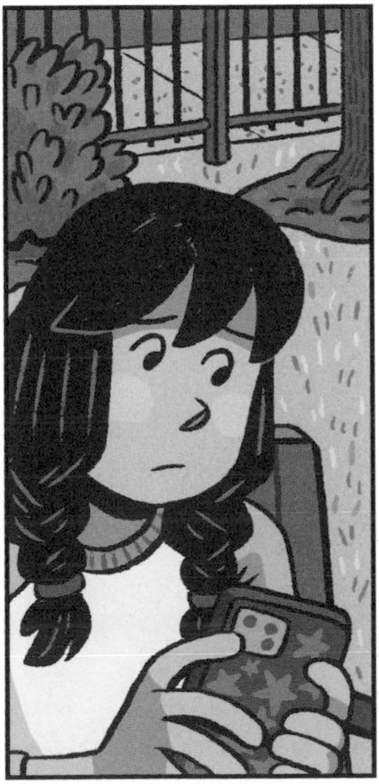

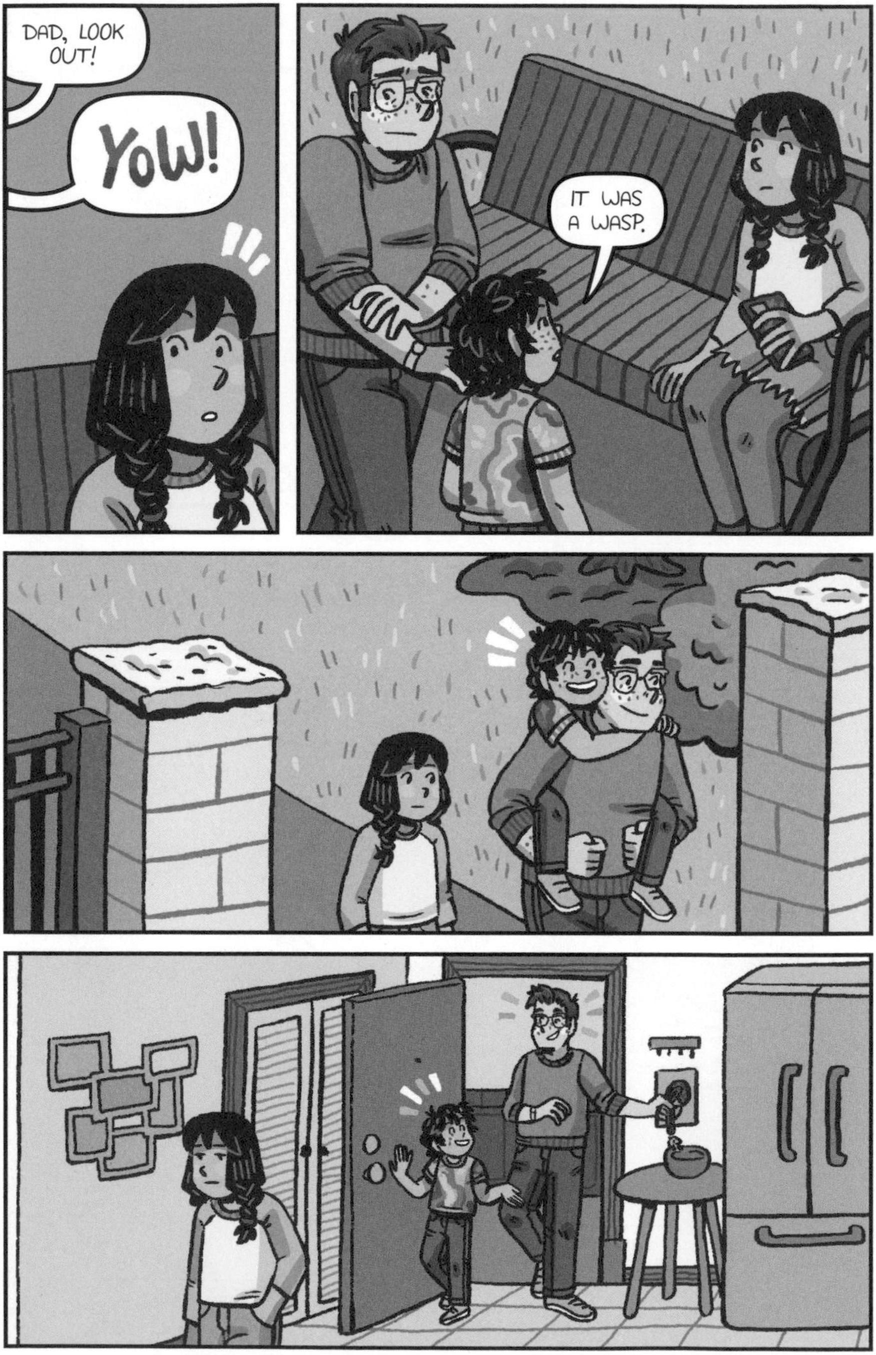
DAD, LOOK OUT!
YOW!
IT WAS A WASP.

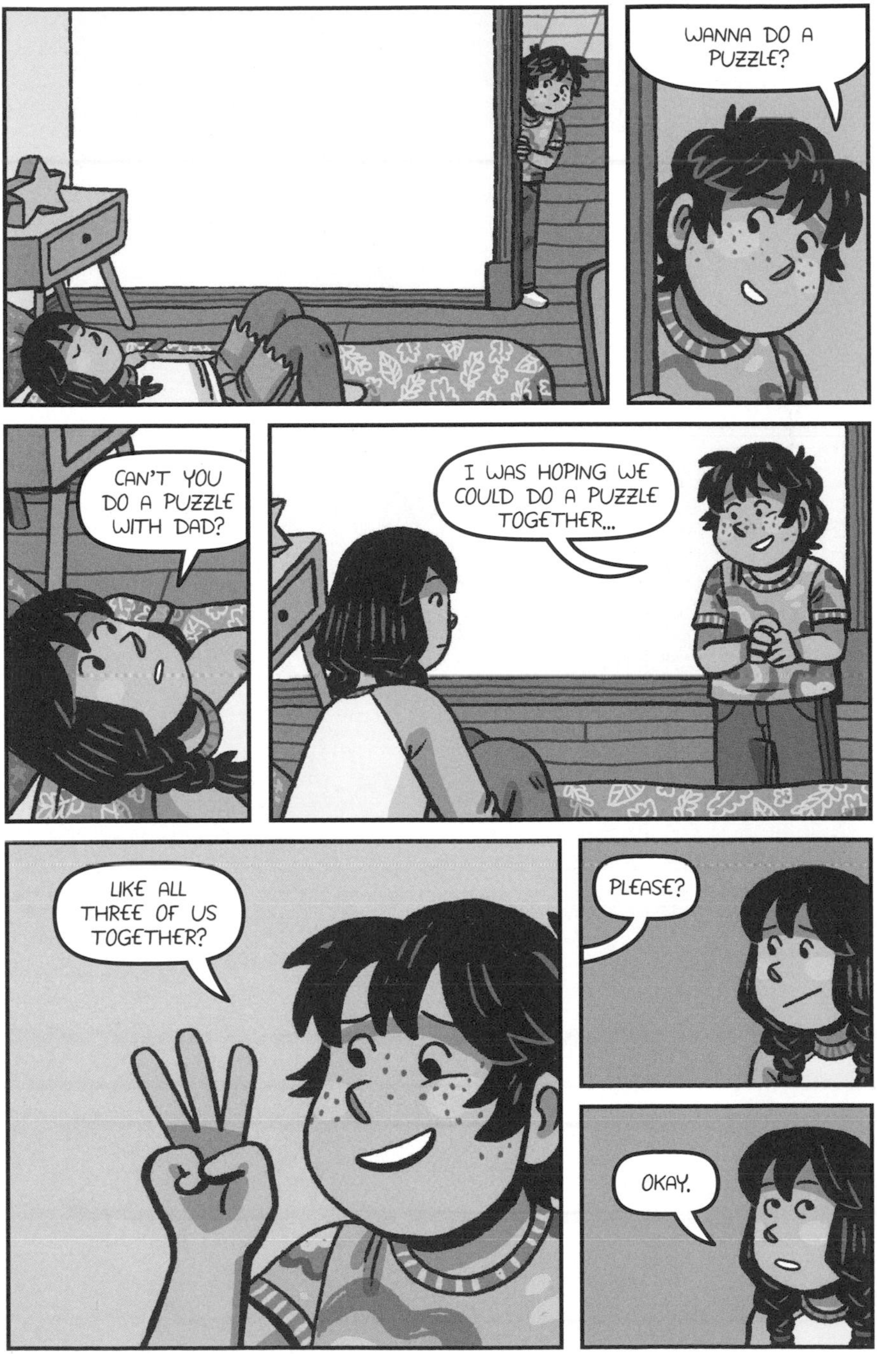
WANNA DO A PUZZLE?
CAN'T YOU DO A PUZZLE WITH DAD?
I WAS HOPING WE COULD DO A PUZZLE TOGETHER...
LIKE ALL THREE OF US TOGETHER?
PLEASE?
OKAY.

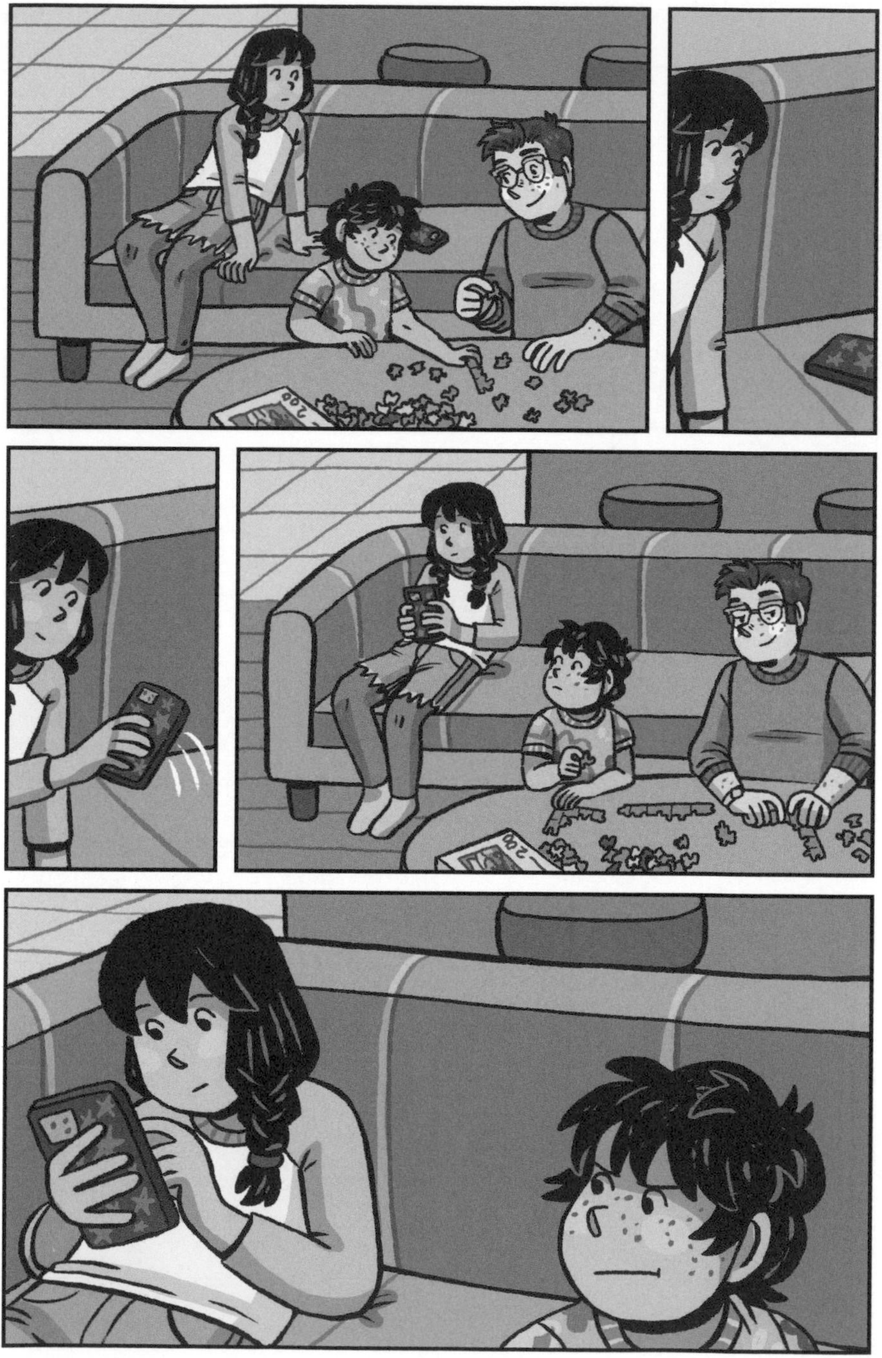

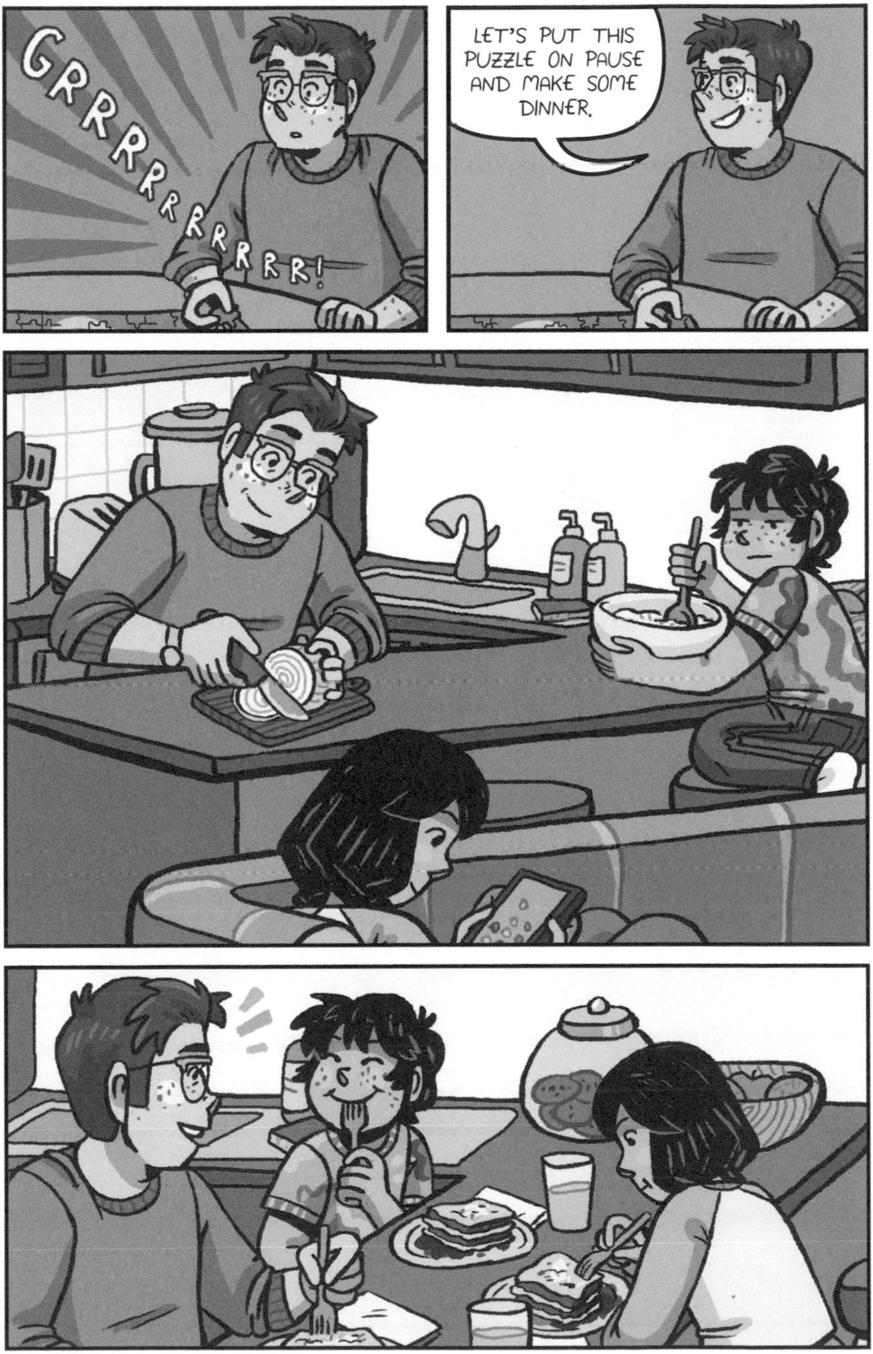
GRRRRRRRRRRRR!
LET'S PUT THIS PUZZLE ON PAUSE AND MAKE SOME DINNER.

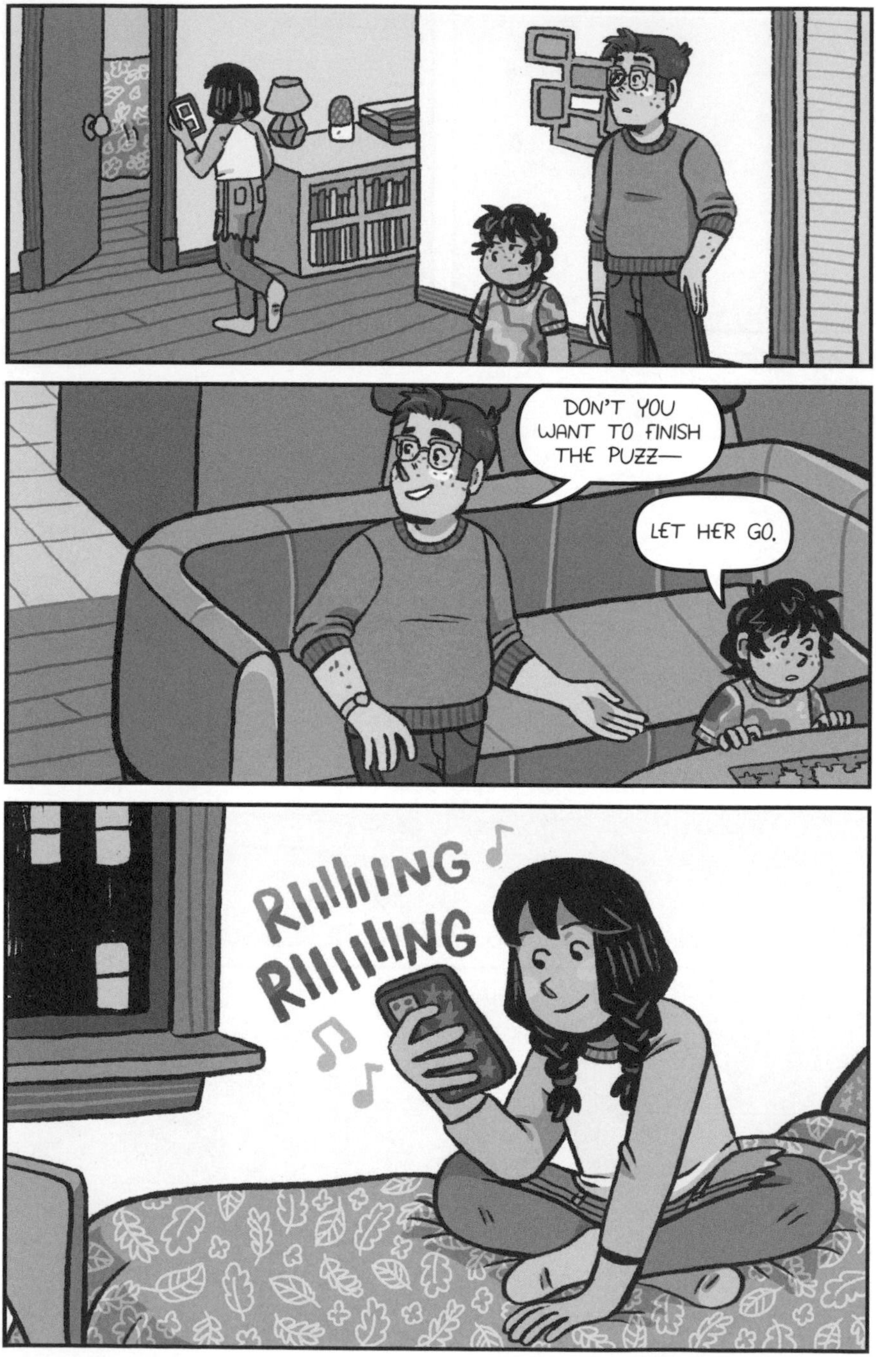
DON'T YOU WANT TO FINISH THE PUZZ—
LET HER GO.
RIIIIING
RIIIIIING

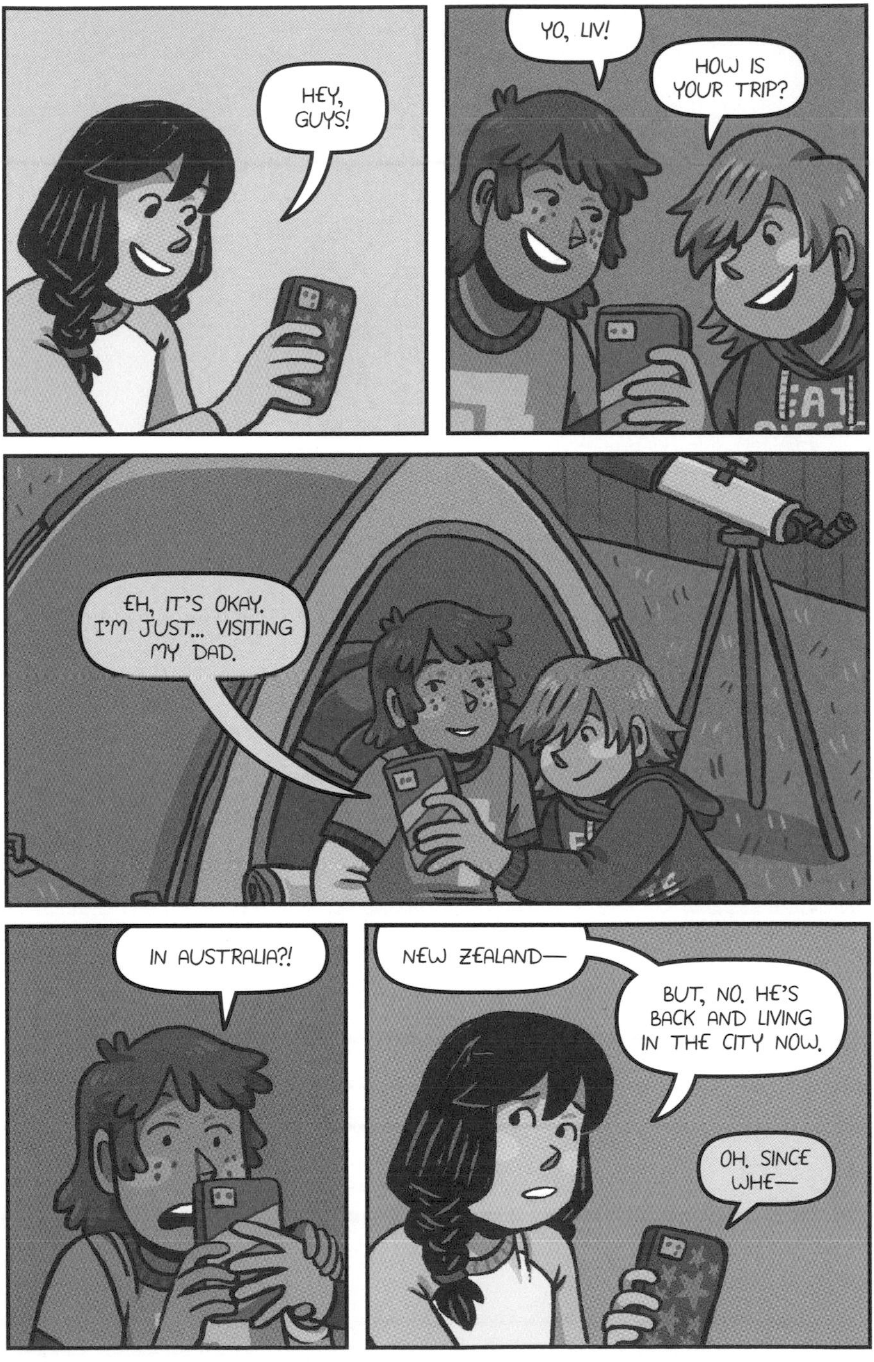
HEY, GUYS!
YO, LIV!
HOW IS YOUR TRIP?
EH, IT'S OKAY. I'M JUST... VISITING MY DAD.
IN AUSTRALIA?!
NEW ZEALAND—
BUT, NO. HE'S BACK AND LIVING IN THE CITY NOW.
OH. SINCE WHE—

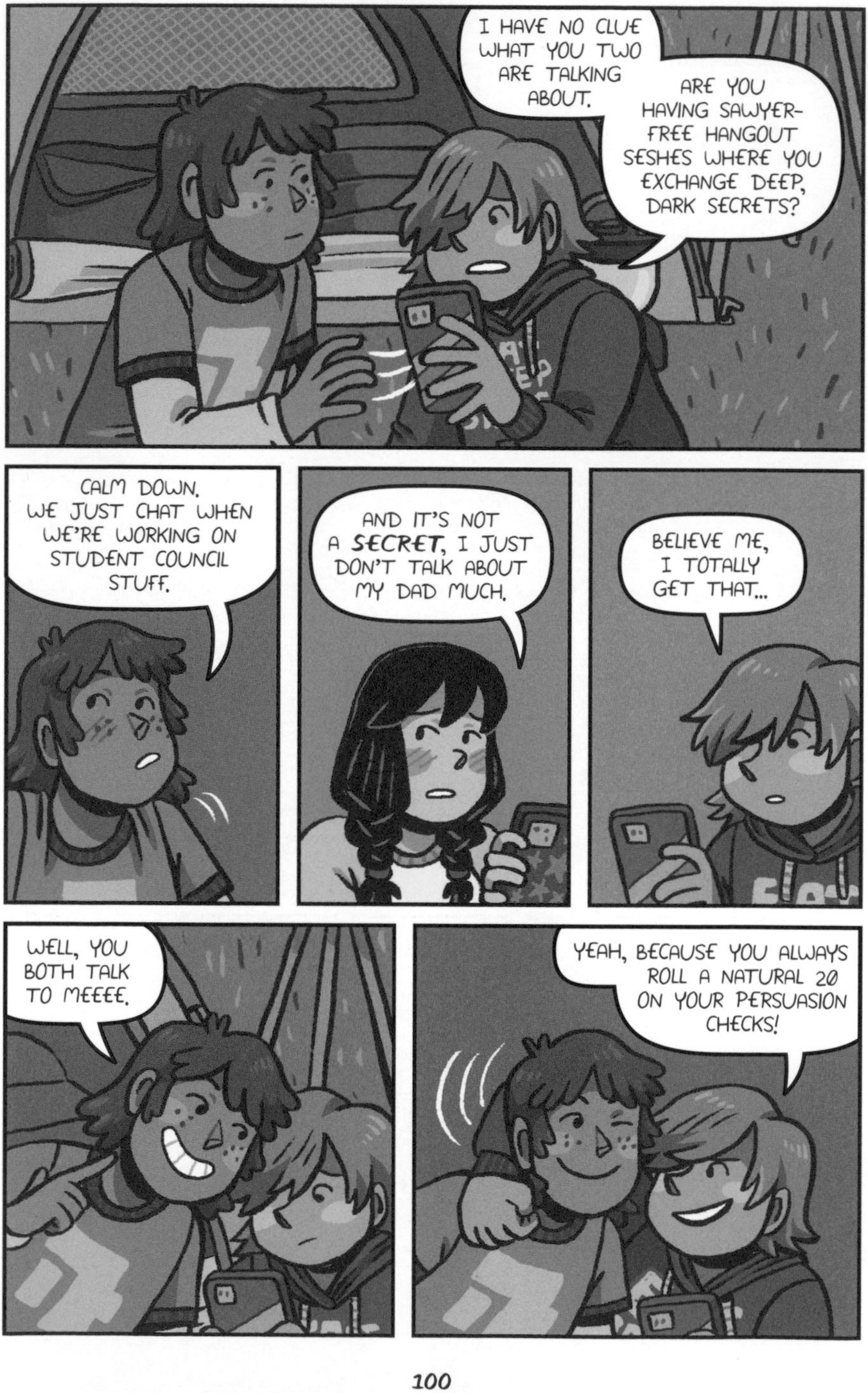
I HAVE NO CLUE WHAT YOU TWO ARE TALKING ABOUT.
ARE YOU HAVING SAWYER-FREE HANGOUT SESHES WHERE YOU EXCHANGE DEEP, DARK SECRETS?
CALM DOWN. WE JUST CHAT WHEN WE'RE WORKING ON STUDENT COUNCIL STUFF.
AND IT'S NOT A **SECRET**, I JUST DON'T TALK ABOUT MY DAD MUCH.
BELIEVE ME, I TOTALLY GET THAT...
WELL, YOU BOTH TALK TO MEEEE.
YEAH, BECAUSE YOU ALWAYS ROLL A NATURAL 20 ON YOUR PERSUASION CHECKS!

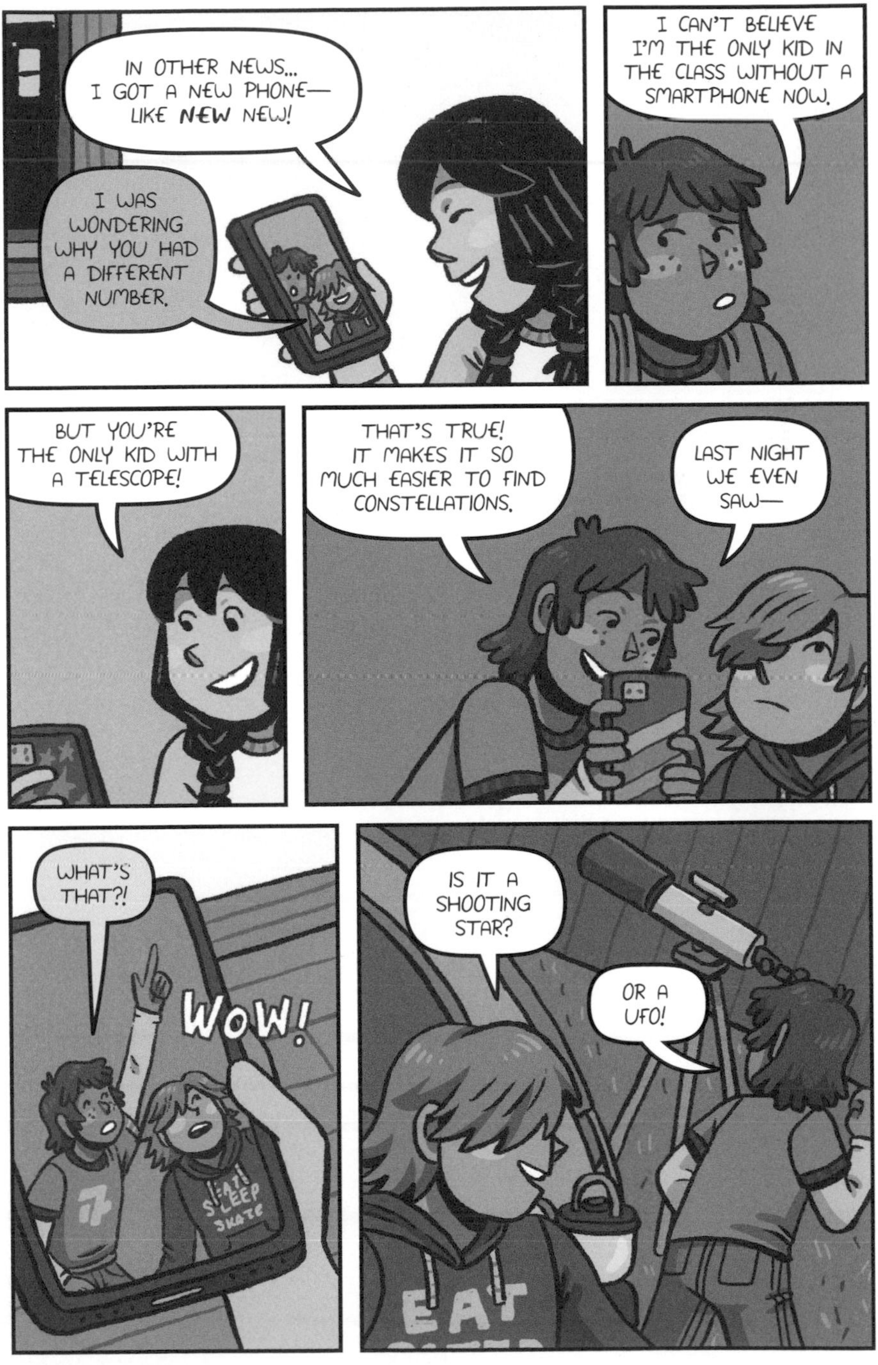
IN OTHER NEWS... I GOT A NEW PHONE— LIKE **NEW** NEW!
I WAS WONDERING WHY YOU HAD A DIFFERENT NUMBER.
I CAN'T BELIEVE I'M THE ONLY KID IN THE CLASS WITHOUT A SMARTPHONE NOW.
BUT YOU'RE THE ONLY KID WITH A TELESCOPE!
THAT'S TRUE! IT MAKES IT SO MUCH EASIER TO FIND CONSTELLATIONS.
LAST NIGHT WE EVEN SAW—
WHAT'S THAT?!
WOW!
EAT SLEEP SKATE
IS IT A SHOOTING STAR?
OR A UFO!
EAT

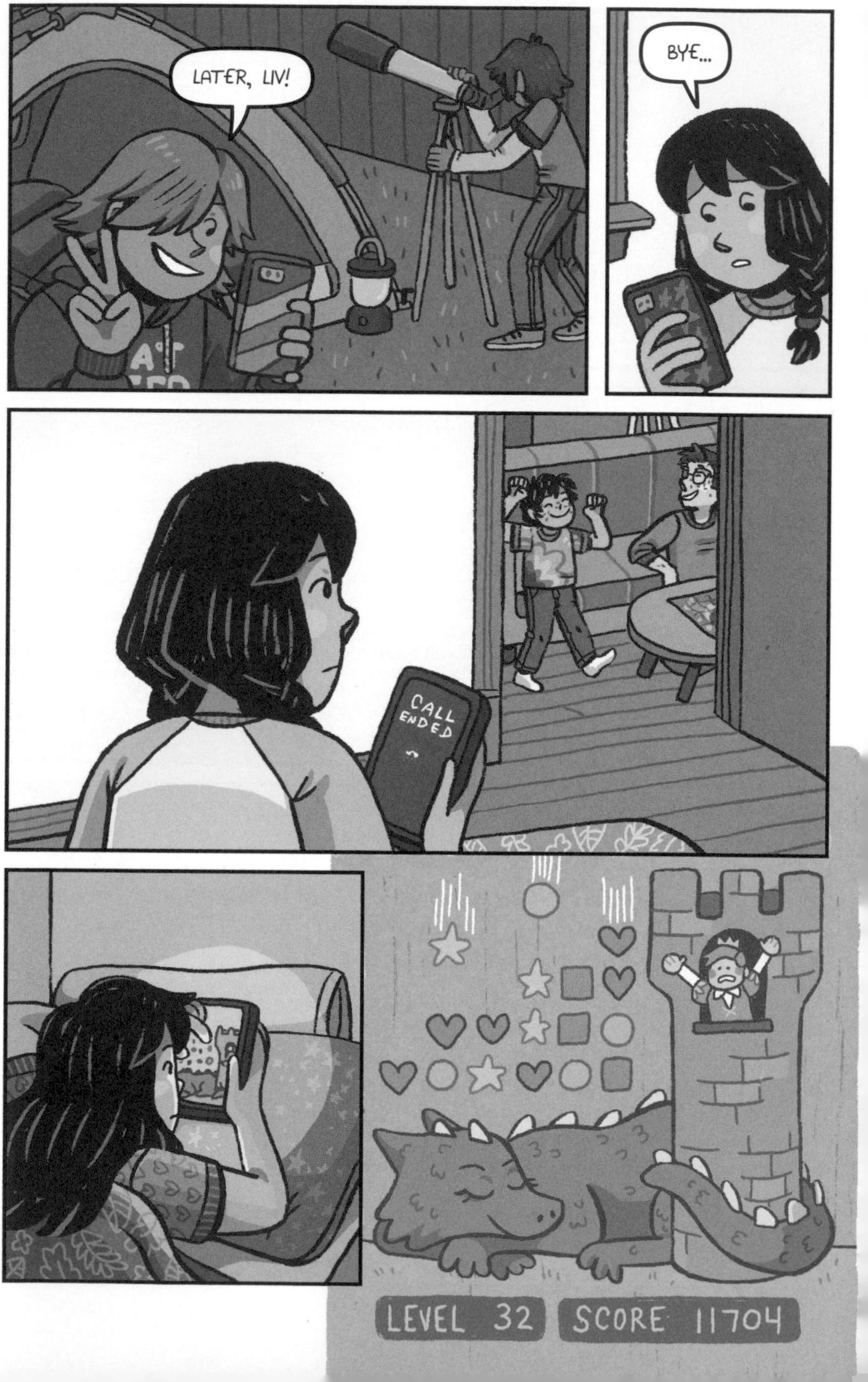
LATER, LIV!
BYE...
CALL ENDED
LEVEL 32
SCORE 11704

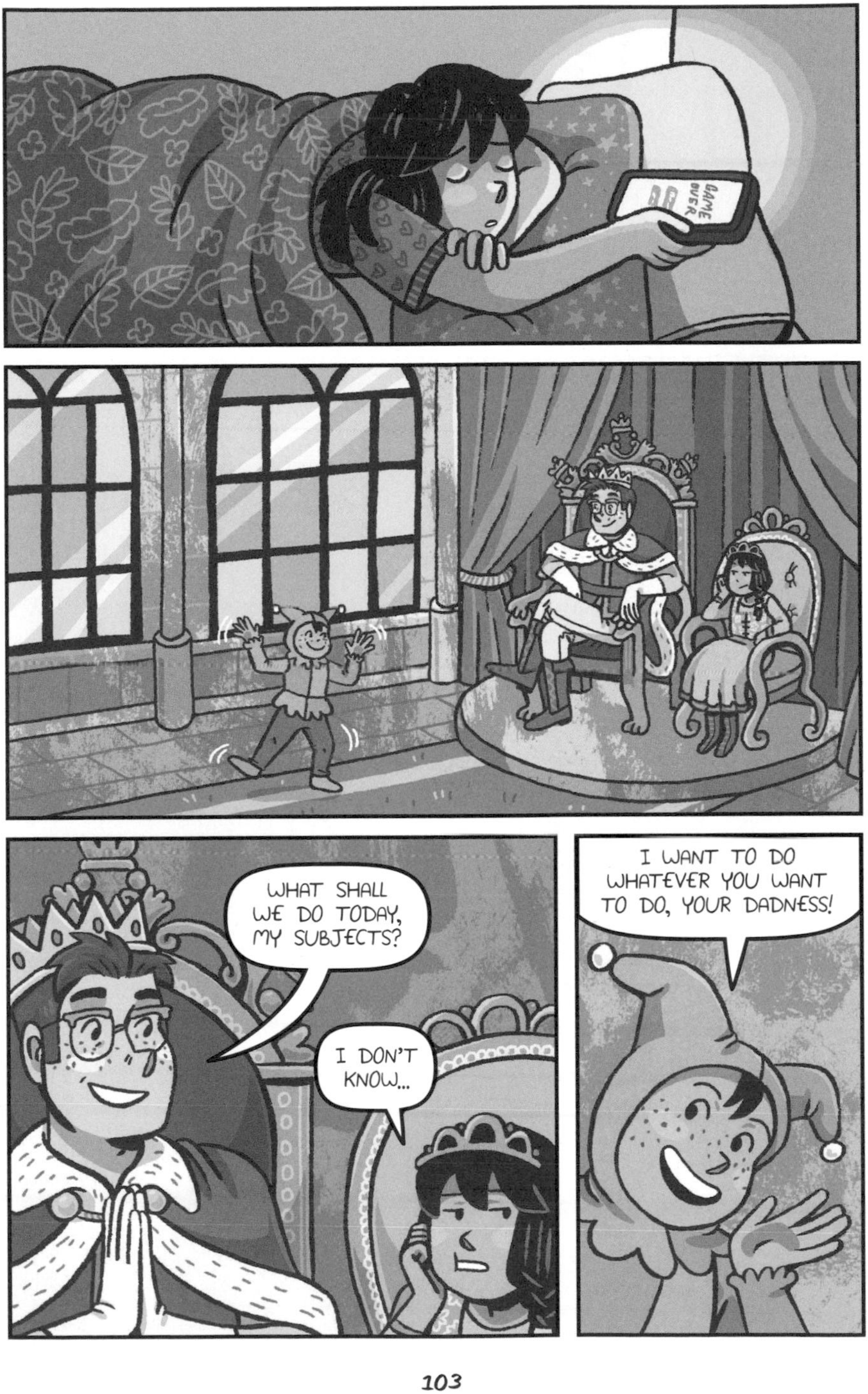
GAME OVER
WHAT SHALL WE DO TODAY, MY SUBJECTS?
I DON'T KNOW...
I WANT TO DO WHATEVER YOU WANT TO DO, YOUR DADNESS!

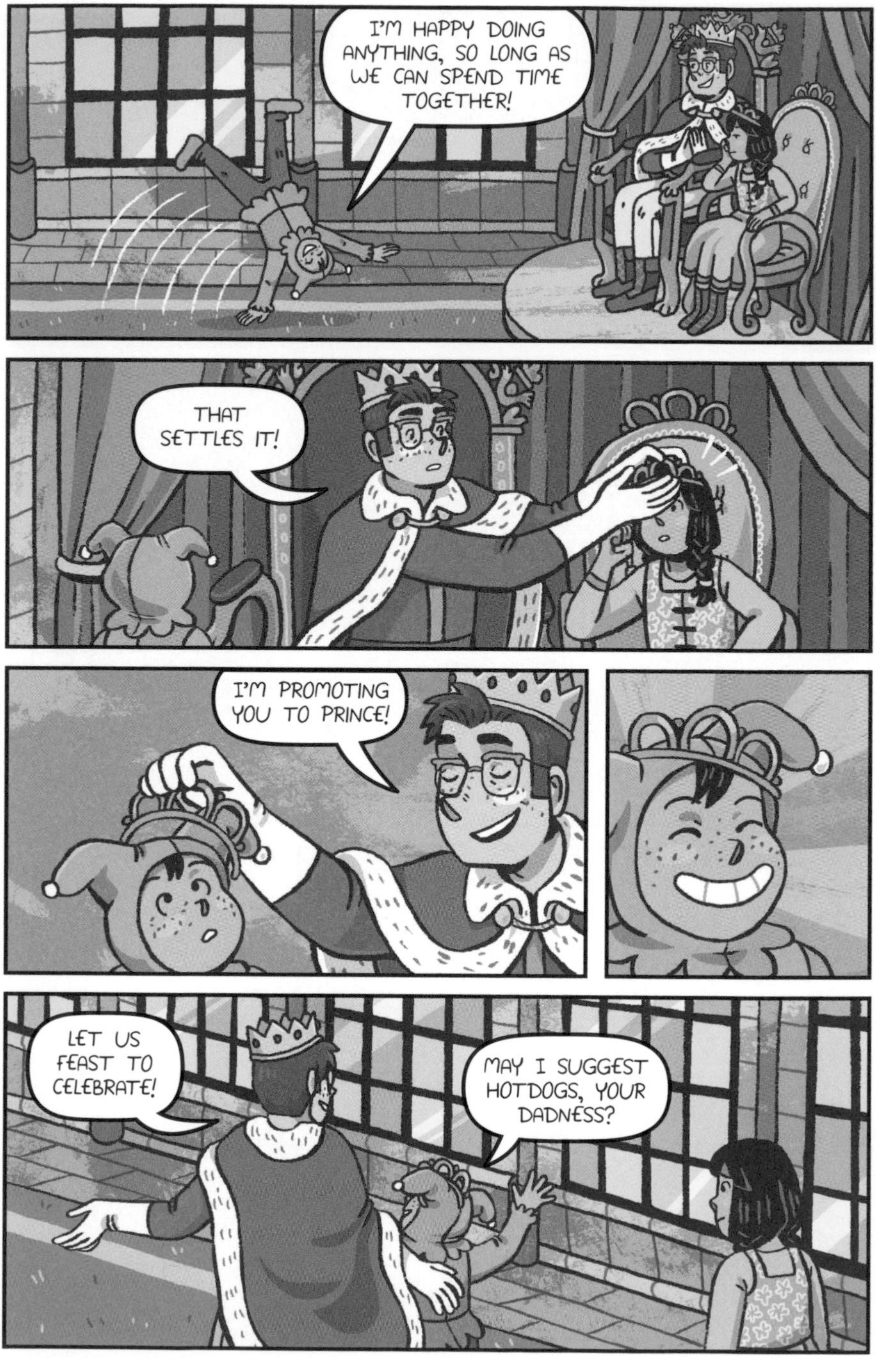
I'M HAPPY DOING ANYTHING, SO LONG AS WE CAN SPEND TIME TOGETHER!
THAT SETTLES IT!
I'M PROMOTING YOU TO PRINCE!
LET US FEAST TO CELEBRATE!
MAY I SUGGEST HOTDOGS, YOUR DADNESS?

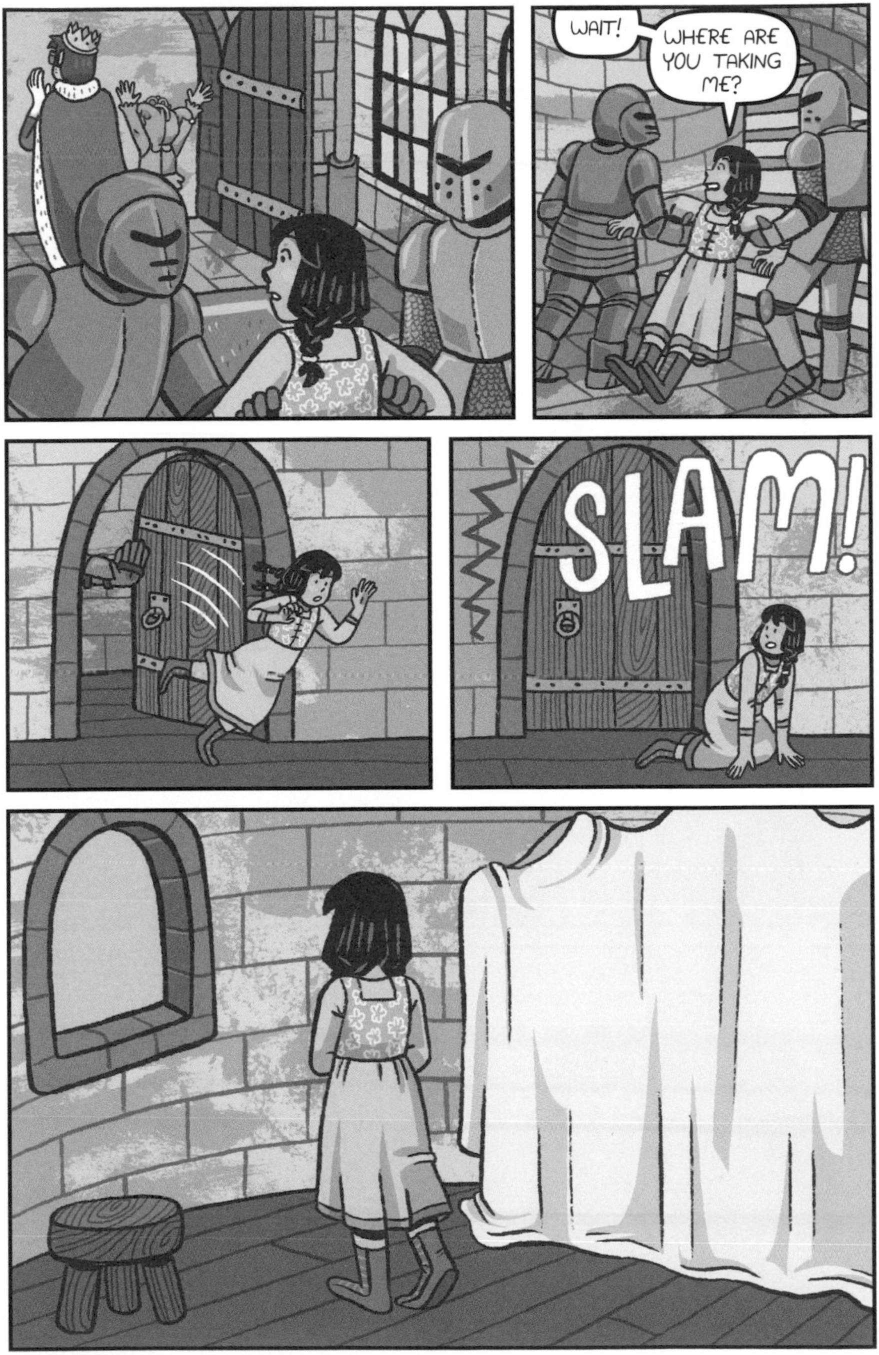
WAIT!
WHERE ARE YOU TAKING ME?
SLAM!

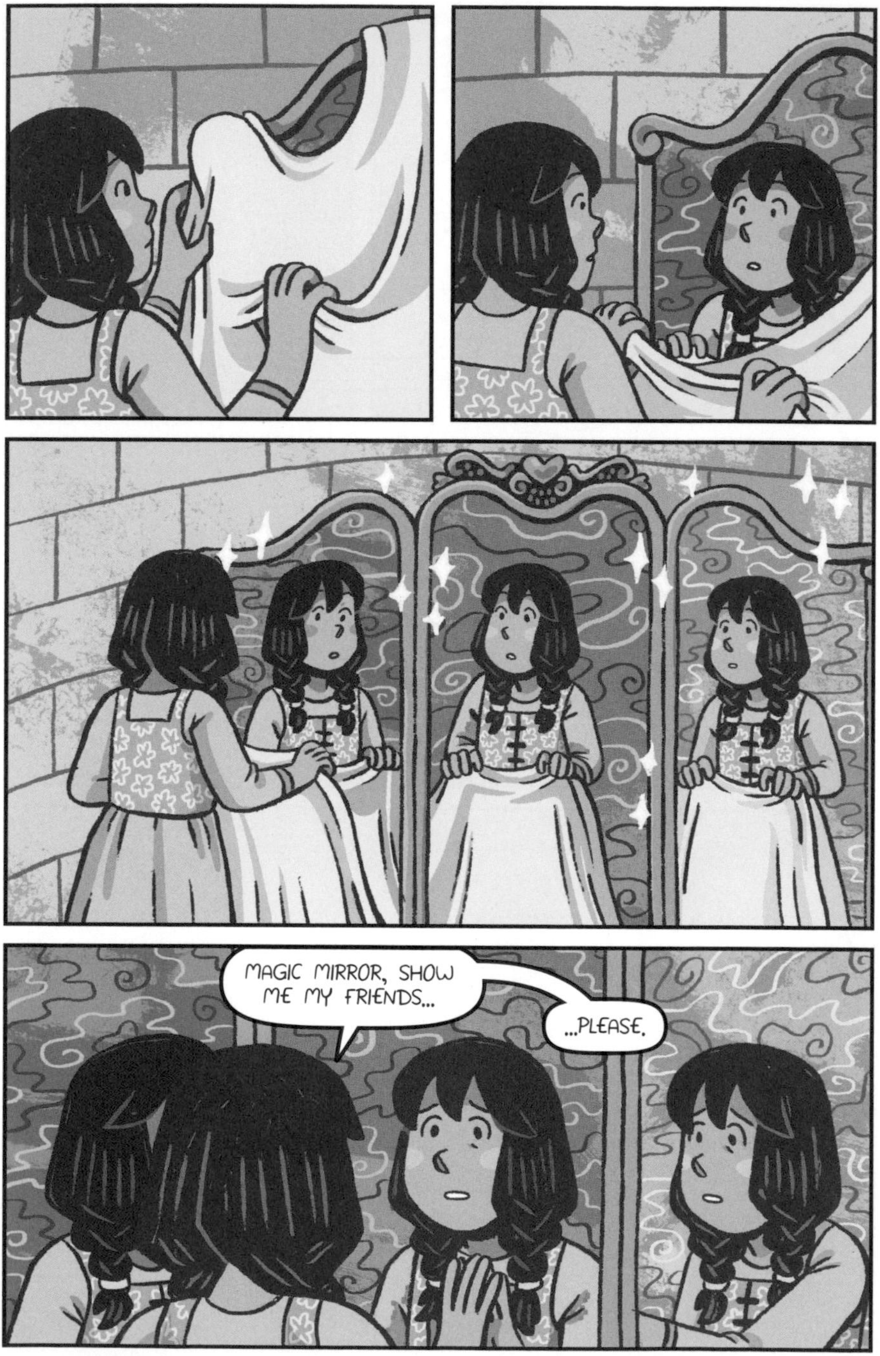
MAGIC MIRROR, SHOW ME MY FRIENDS...
...PLEASE.

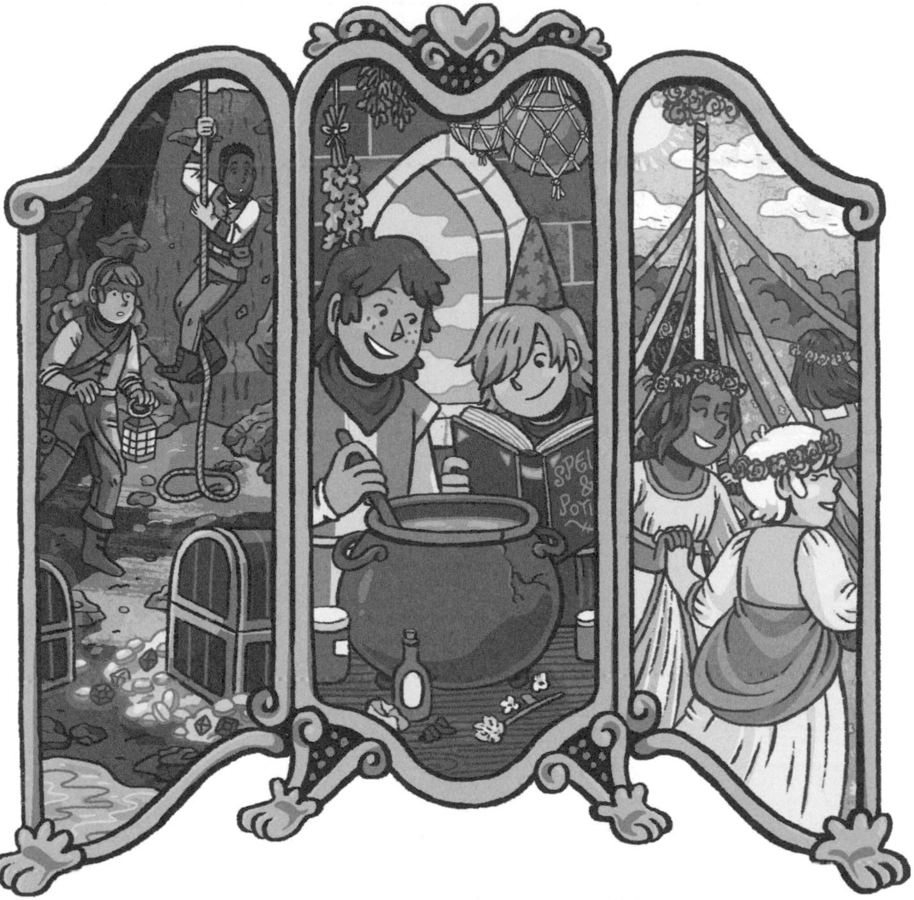

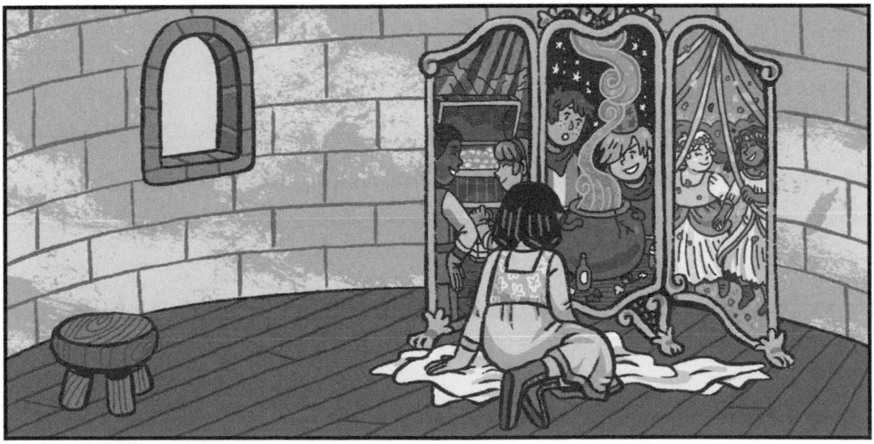

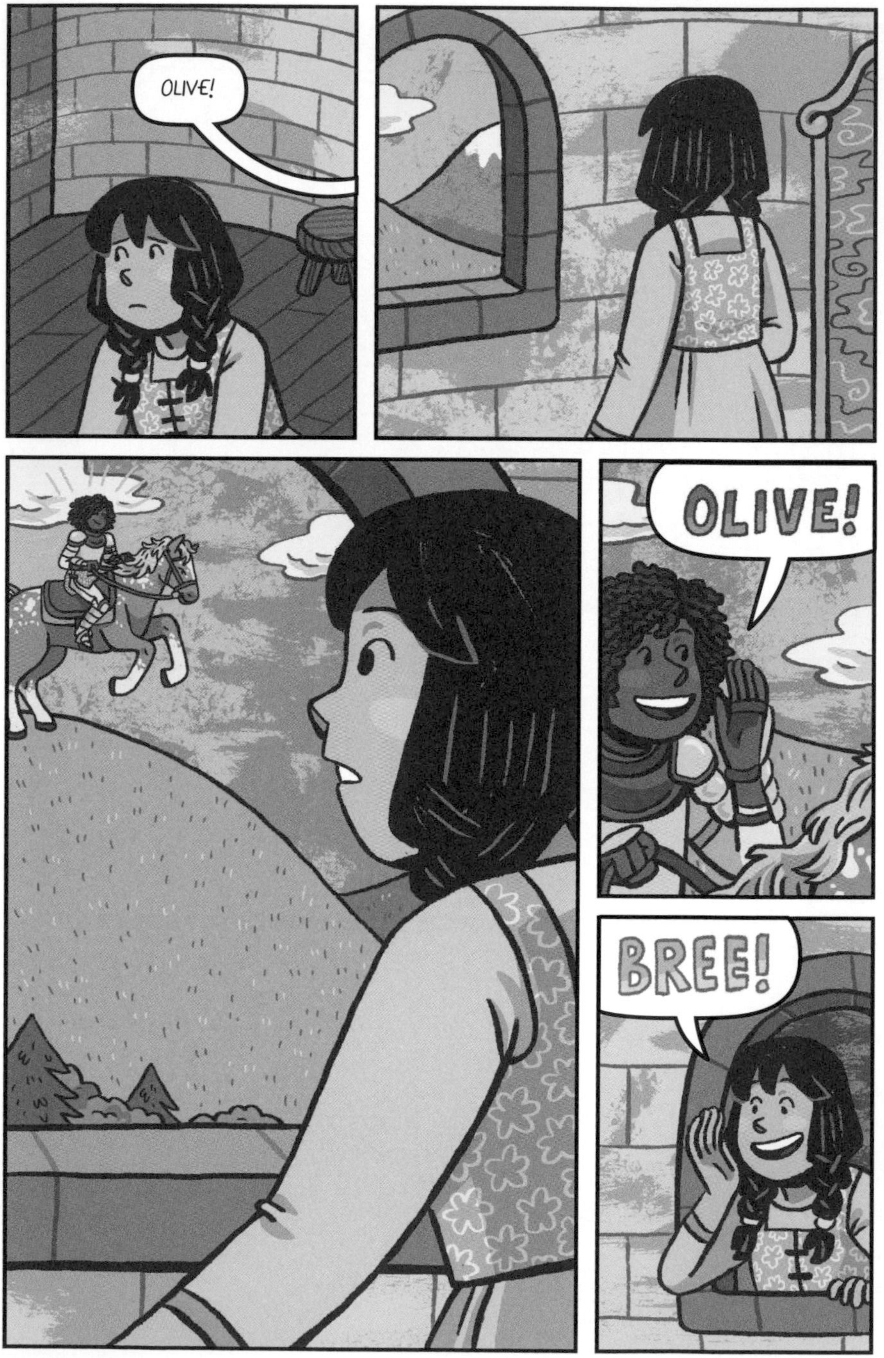
OLIVE!
OLIVE!
BREE!

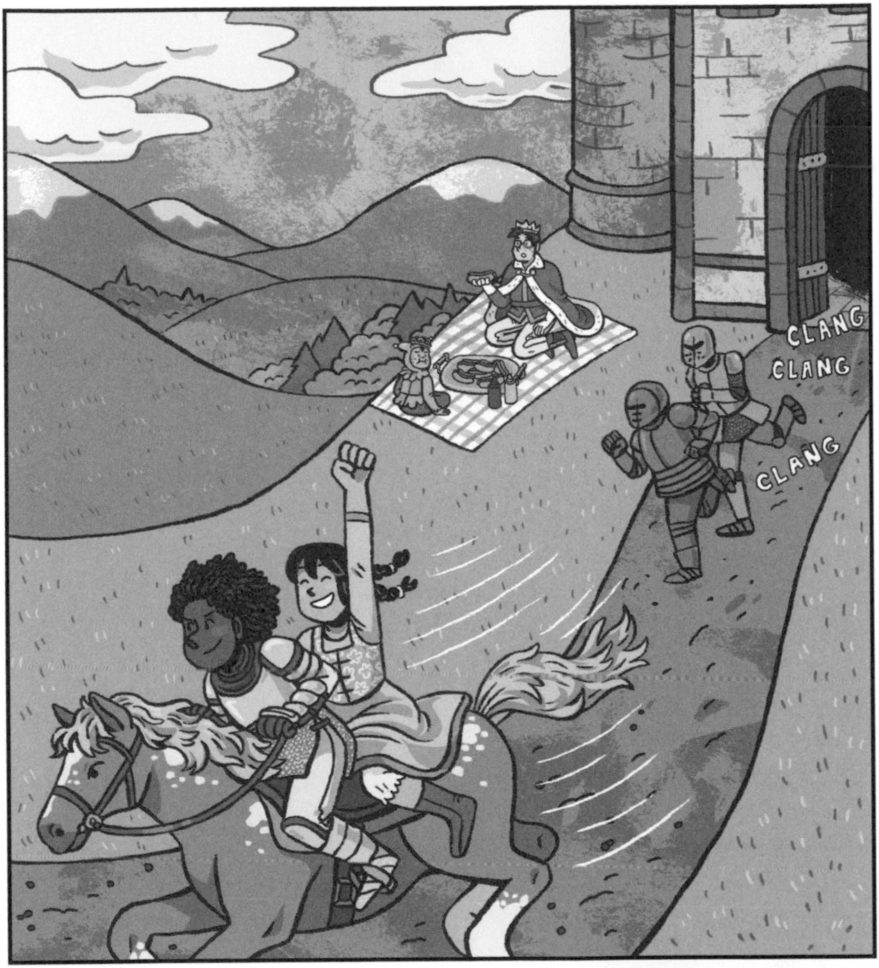
CLANG
CLANG
CLANG

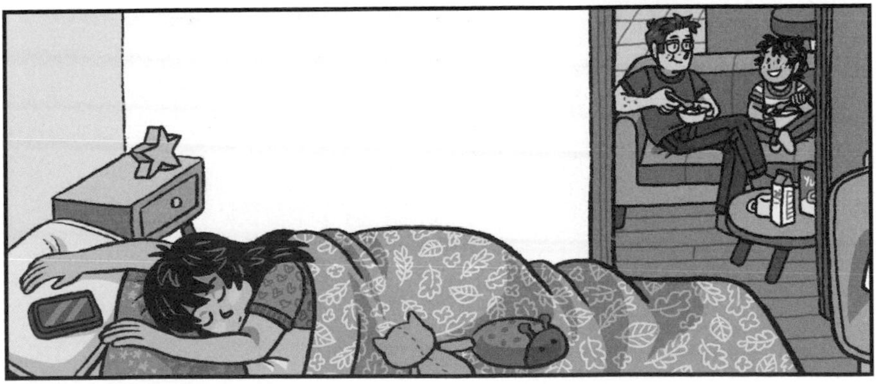

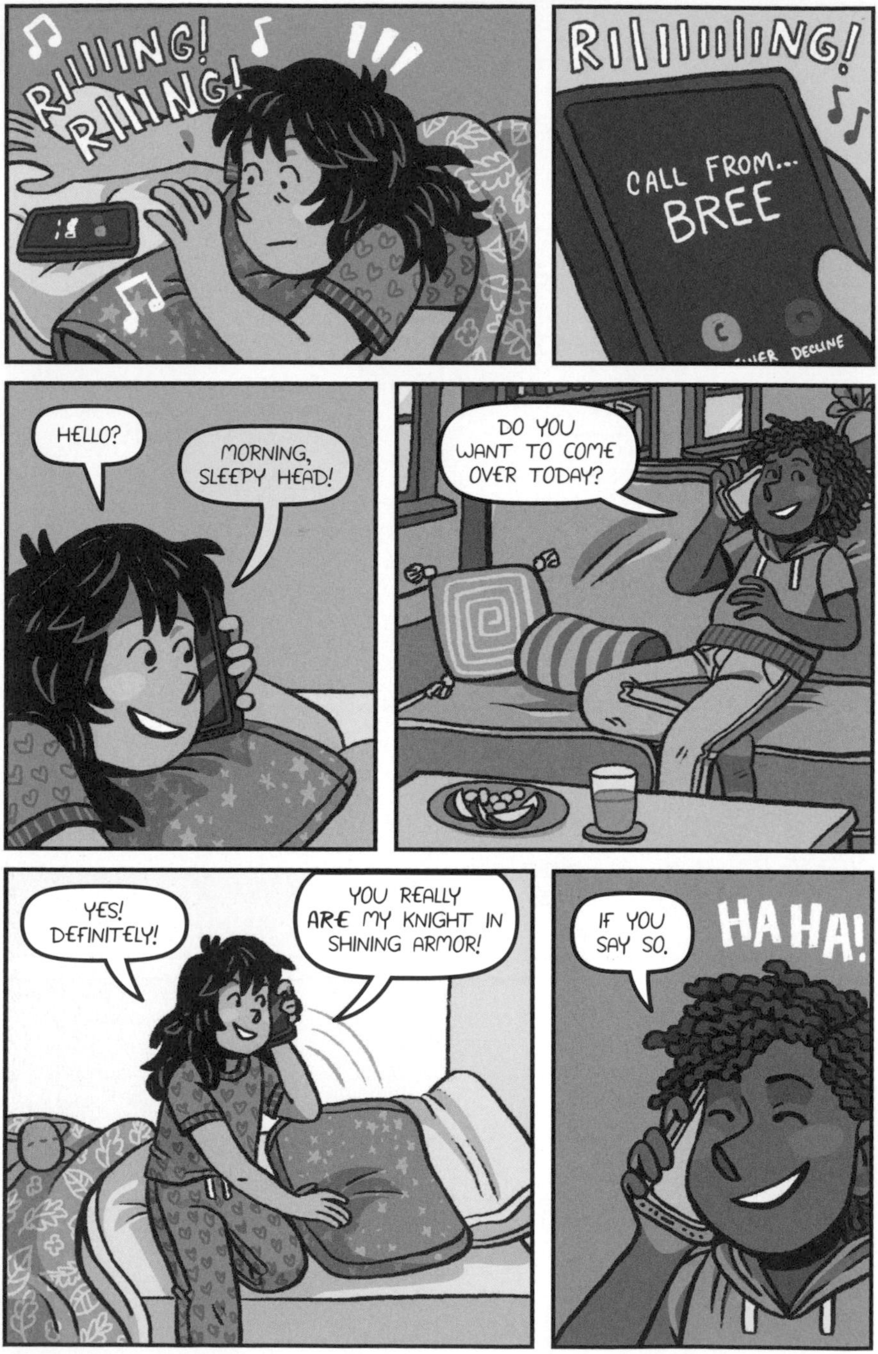
RIIIING!
RIIING!
RIIIIIIIIING!
CALL FROM... BREE
DECLINE
HELLO?
MORNING, SLEEPY HEAD!
DO YOU WANT TO COME OVER TODAY?
YES! DEFINITELY!
YOU REALLY ARE MY KNIGHT IN SHINING ARMOR!
IF YOU SAY SO.
HAHA!

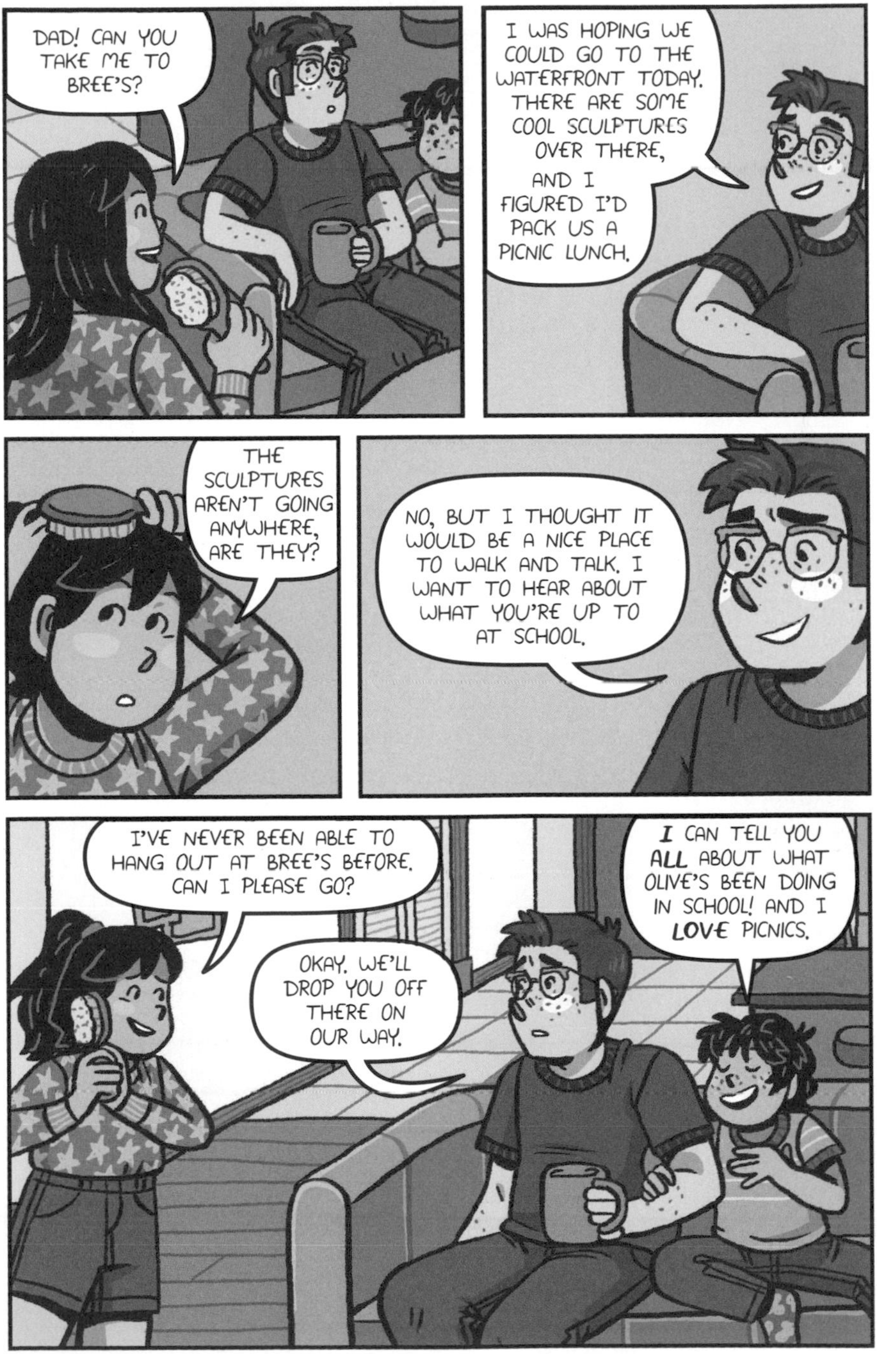
DAD! CAN YOU TAKE ME TO BREE'S?
I WAS HOPING WE COULD GO TO THE WATERFRONT TODAY. THERE ARE SOME COOL SCULPTURES OVER THERE,
AND I FIGURED I'D PACK US A PICNIC LUNCH.
THE SCULPTURES AREN'T GOING ANYWHERE, ARE THEY?
NO, BUT I THOUGHT IT WOULD BE A NICE PLACE TO WALK AND TALK. I WANT TO HEAR ABOUT WHAT YOU'RE UP TO AT SCHOOL.
I'VE NEVER BEEN ABLE TO HANG OUT AT BREE'S BEFORE. CAN I PLEASE GO?
OKAY. WE'LL DROP YOU OFF THERE ON OUR WAY.
I CAN TELL YOU ALL ABOUT WHAT OLIVE'S BEEN DOING IN SCHOOL! AND I LOVE PICNICS.

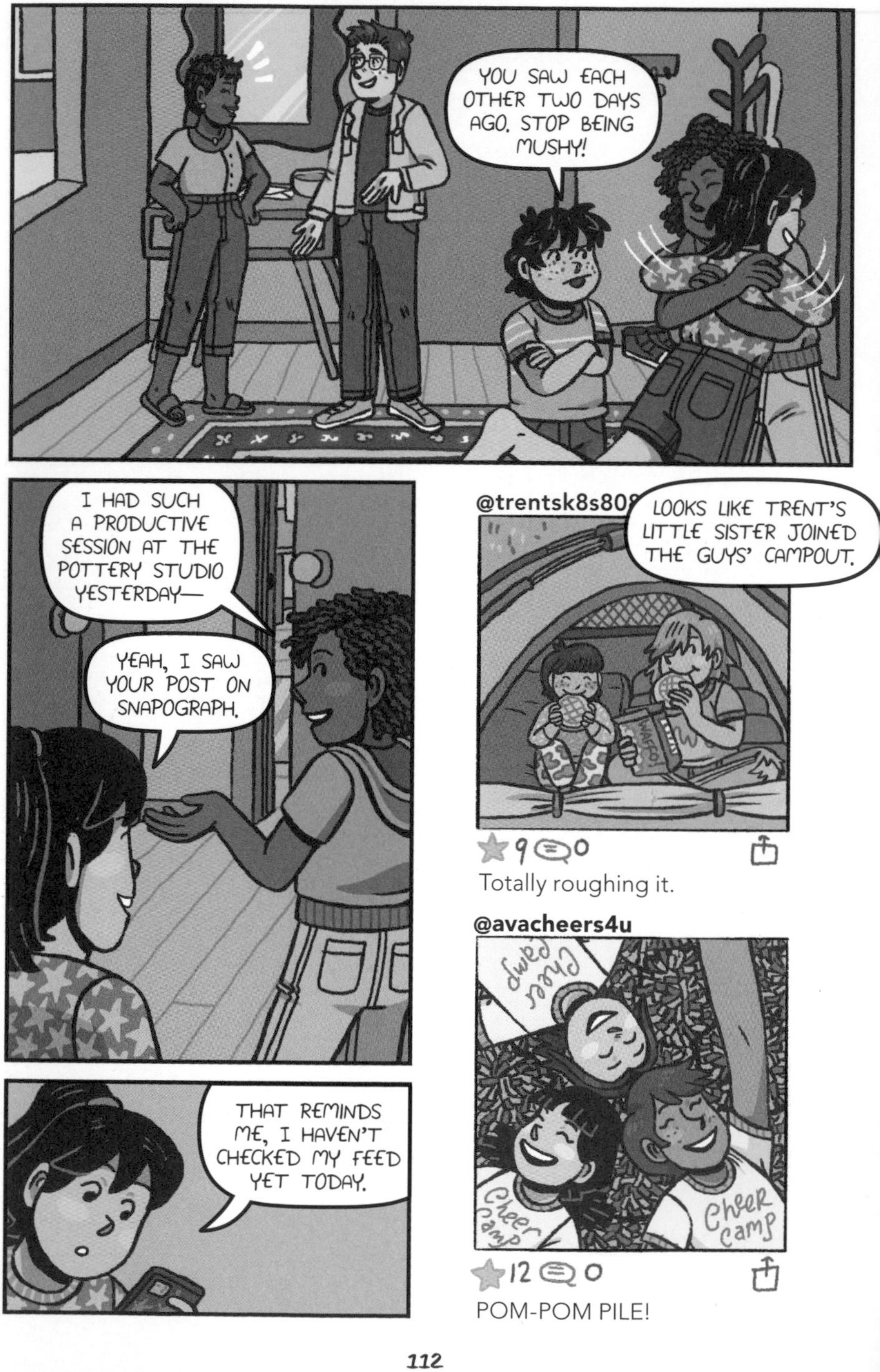
YOU SAW EACH OTHER TWO DAYS AGO. STOP BEING MUSHY!
I HAD SUCH A PRODUCTIVE SESSION AT THE POTTERY STUDIO YESTERDAY—
YEAH, I SAW YOUR POST ON SNAPOGRAPH.
THAT REMINDS ME, I HAVEN'T CHECKED MY FEED YET TODAY.
@trentsk8s80
LOOKS LIKE TRENT'S LITTLE SISTER JOINED THE GUYS' CAMPOUT.
WAFFO
9 0
Totally roughing it.
@avacheers4u
Cheer camp
Cheer camp
Cheer camp
12 0
POM-POM PILE!

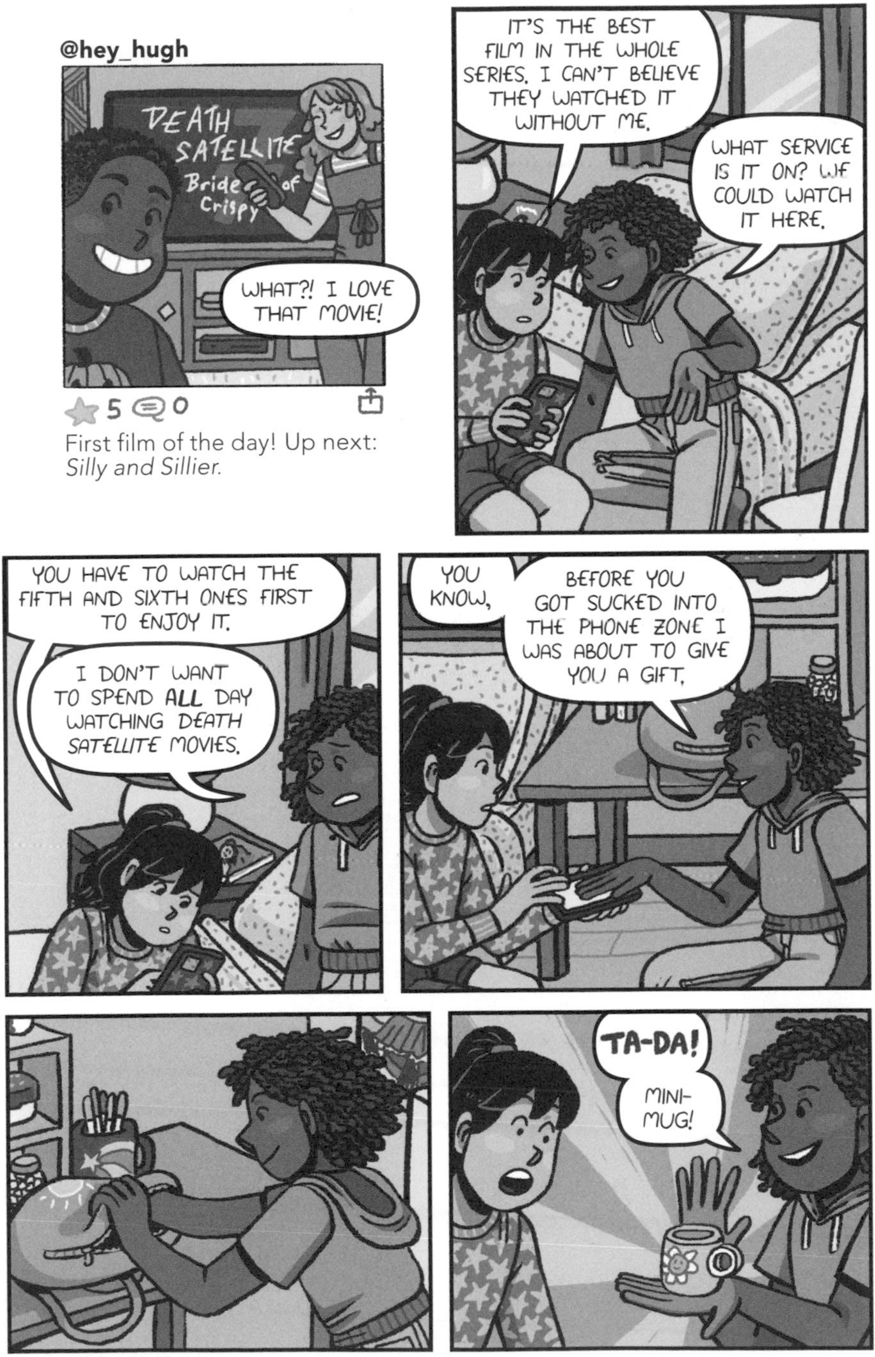
@hey_hugh
DEATH SATELLITE Bride of Crispy
WHAT?! I LOVE THAT MOVIE!
5 0
First film of the day! Up next: *Silly and Sillier.*
IT'S THE BEST FILM IN THE WHOLE SERIES. I CAN'T BELIEVE THEY WATCHED IT WITHOUT ME.
WHAT SERVICE IS IT ON? WE COULD WATCH IT HERE.
YOU HAVE TO WATCH THE FIFTH AND SIXTH ONES FIRST TO ENJOY IT.
I DON'T WANT TO SPEND **ALL** DAY WATCHING *DEATH SATELLITE* MOVIES.
YOU KNOW,
BEFORE YOU GOT SUCKED INTO THE PHONE ZONE I WAS ABOUT TO GIVE YOU A GIFT.
TA-DA!
MINI-MUG!

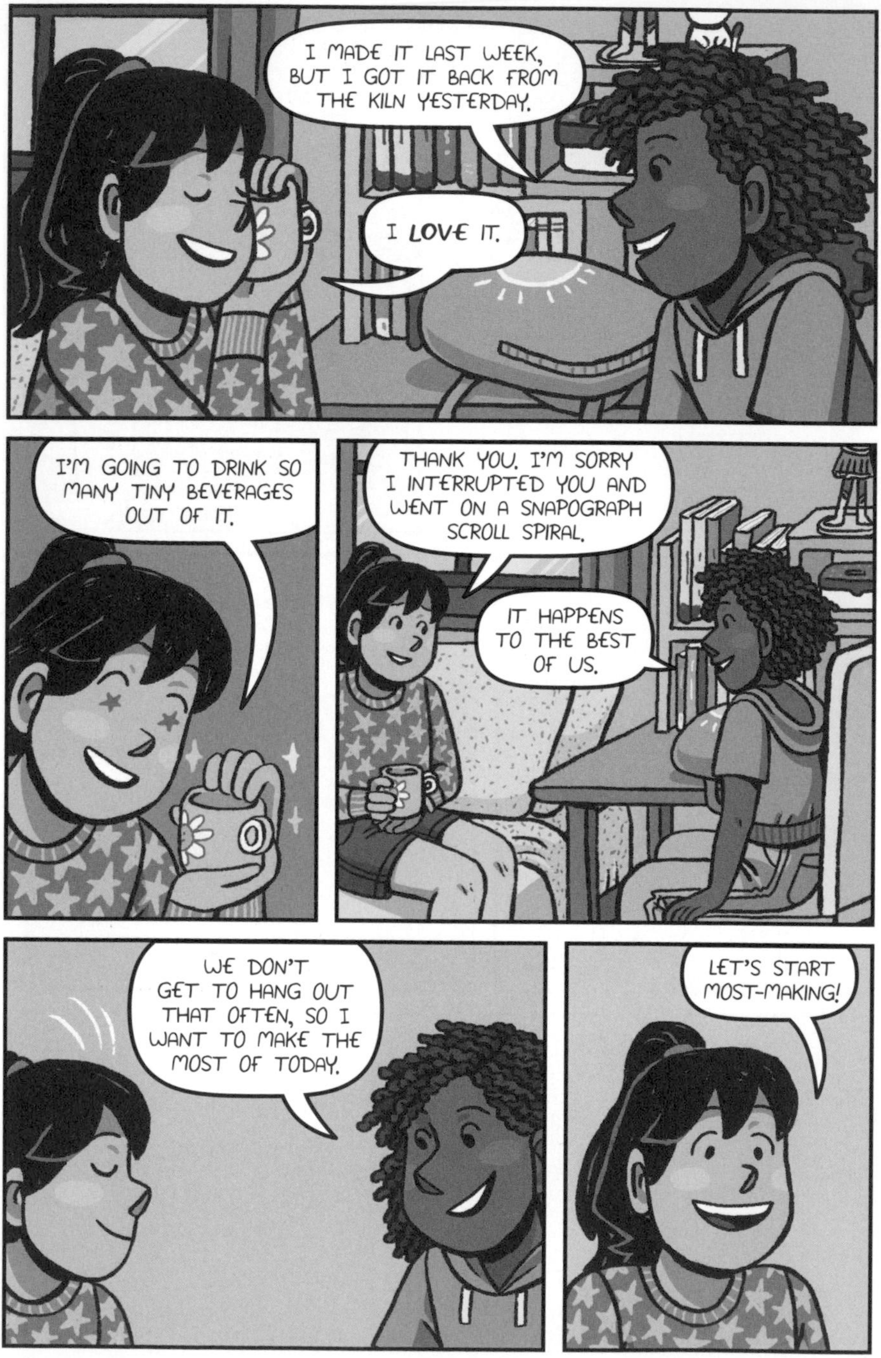
I MADE IT LAST WEEK, BUT I GOT IT BACK FROM THE KILN YESTERDAY.
I **LOVE** IT.
I'M GOING TO DRINK SO MANY TINY BEVERAGES OUT OF IT.
THANK YOU. I'M SORRY I INTERRUPTED YOU AND WENT ON A SNAPOGRAPH SCROLL SPIRAL.
IT HAPPENS TO THE BEST OF US.
WE DON'T GET TO HANG OUT THAT OFTEN, SO I WANT TO MAKE THE MOST OF TODAY.
LET'S START MOST-MAKING!

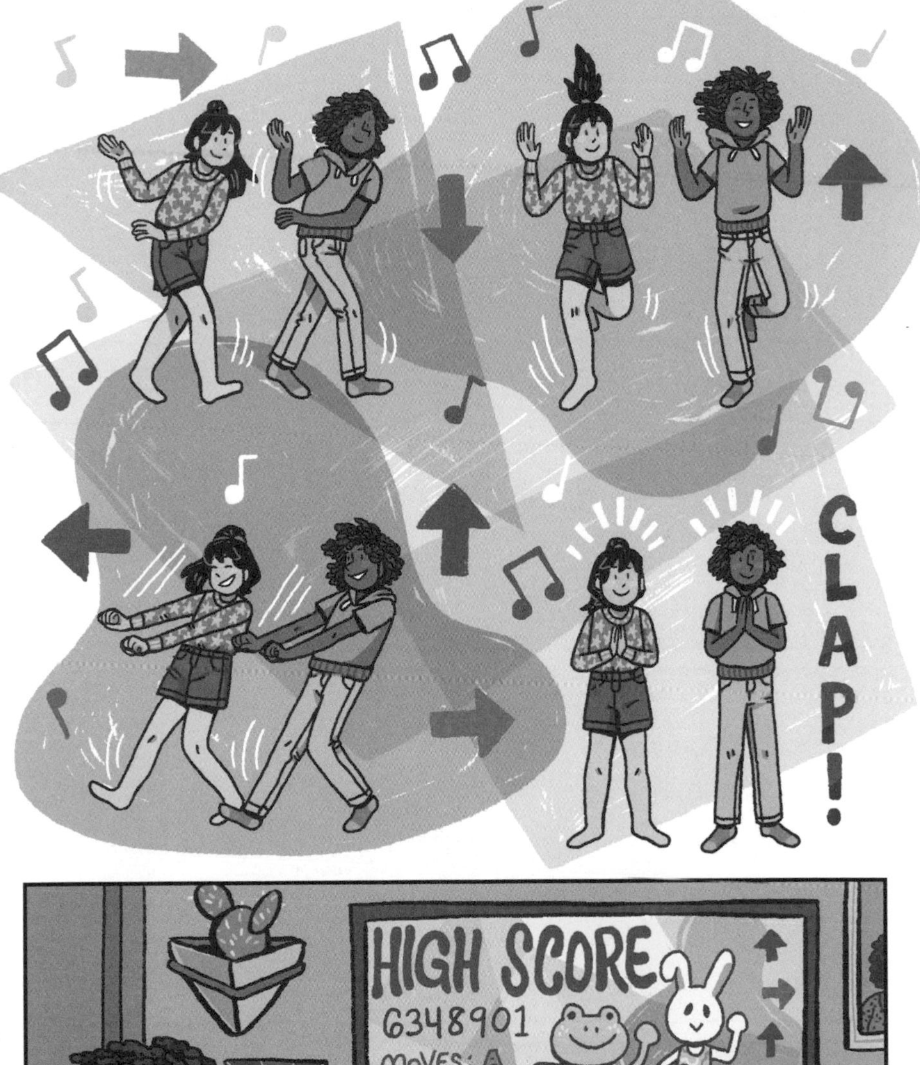
CLAP!

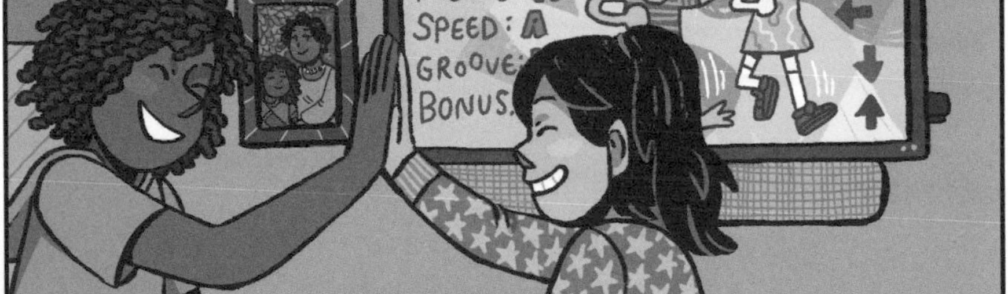
HIGH SCORE
6348901
MOVES: A
SPEED: A
GROOVE:
BONUS:

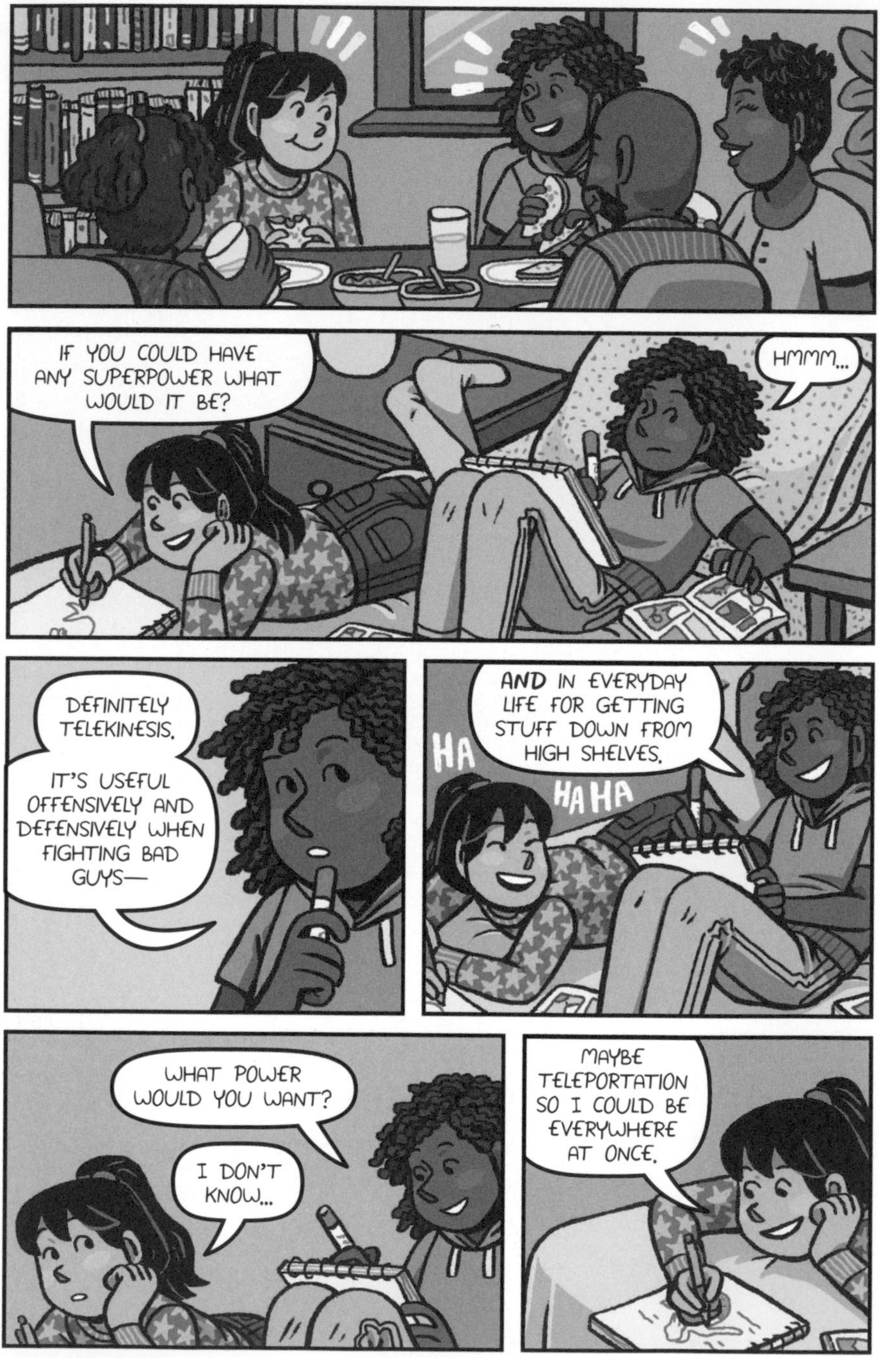
IF YOU COULD HAVE ANY SUPERPOWER WHAT WOULD IT BE?
HMMM...
DEFINITELY TELEKINESIS.
IT'S USEFUL OFFENSIVELY AND DEFENSIVELY WHEN FIGHTING BAD GUYS—
AND IN EVERYDAY LIFE FOR GETTING STUFF DOWN FROM HIGH SHELVES.
HA
HA HA
WHAT POWER WOULD YOU WANT?
I DON'T KNOW...
MAYBE TELEPORTATION SO I COULD BE EVERYWHERE AT ONCE.

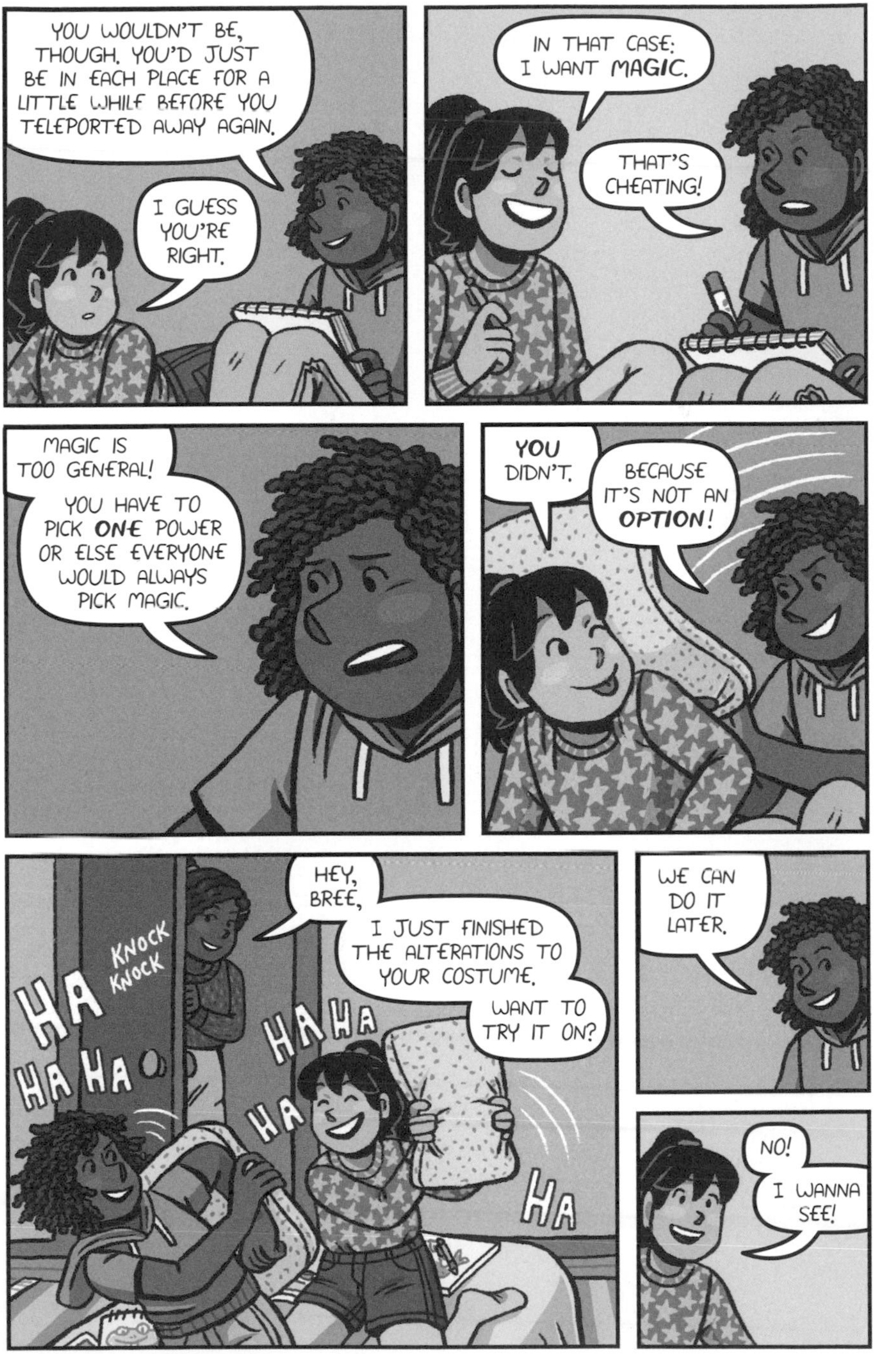
YOU WOULDN'T BE, THOUGH. YOU'D JUST BE IN EACH PLACE FOR A LITTLE WHILE BEFORE YOU TELEPORTED AWAY AGAIN.
I GUESS YOU'RE RIGHT.
IN THAT CASE: I WANT **MAGIC**.
THAT'S CHEATING!
MAGIC IS TOO GENERAL!
YOU HAVE TO PICK **ONE** POWER OR ELSE EVERYONE WOULD ALWAYS PICK MAGIC.
YOU DIDN'T.
BECAUSE IT'S NOT AN **OPTION**!
KNOCK KNOCK
HA HA HA
HAHAHA
HA
HA
HEY, BREE,
I JUST FINISHED THE ALTERATIONS TO YOUR COSTUME.
WANT TO TRY IT ON?
WE CAN DO IT LATER.
NO!
I WANNA SEE!

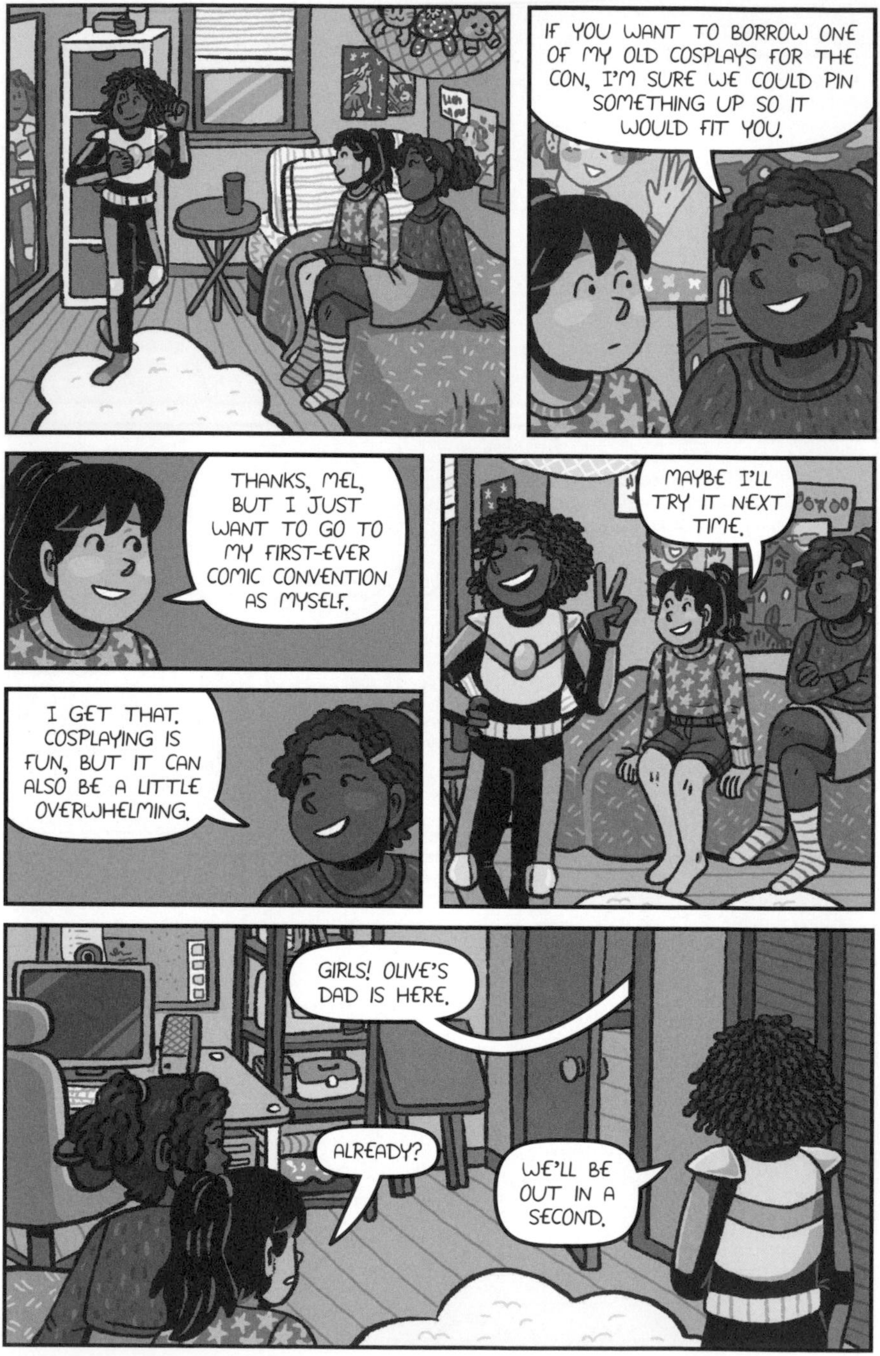
IF YOU WANT TO BORROW ONE OF MY OLD COSPLAYS FOR THE CON, I'M SURE WE COULD PIN SOMETHING UP SO IT WOULD FIT YOU.
THANKS, MEL, BUT I JUST WANT TO GO TO MY FIRST-EVER COMIC CONVENTION AS MYSELF.
I GET THAT. COSPLAYING IS FUN, BUT IT CAN ALSO BE A LITTLE OVERWHELMING.
MAYBE I'LL TRY IT NEXT TIME.
GIRLS! OLIVE'S DAD IS HERE.
ALREADY?
WE'LL BE OUT IN A SECOND.

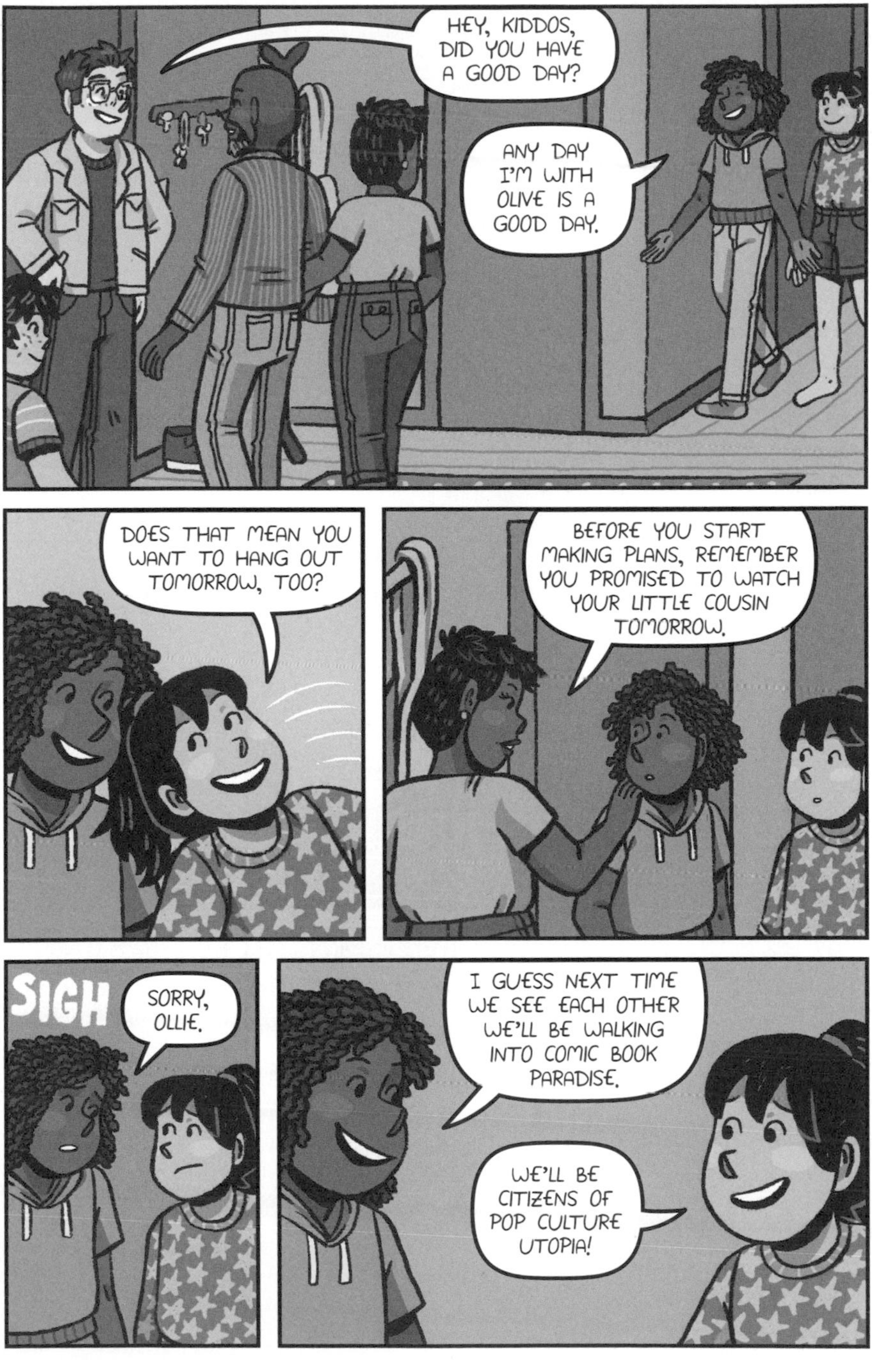
HEY, KIDDOS, DID YOU HAVE A GOOD DAY?
ANY DAY I'M WITH OLIVE IS A GOOD DAY.
DOES THAT MEAN YOU WANT TO HANG OUT TOMORROW, TOO?
BEFORE YOU START MAKING PLANS, REMEMBER YOU PROMISED TO WATCH YOUR LITTLE COUSIN TOMORROW.
SIGH
SORRY, OLLIE.
I GUESS NEXT TIME WE SEE EACH OTHER WE'LL BE WALKING INTO COMIC BOOK PARADISE.
WE'LL BE CITIZENS OF POP CULTURE UTOPIA!

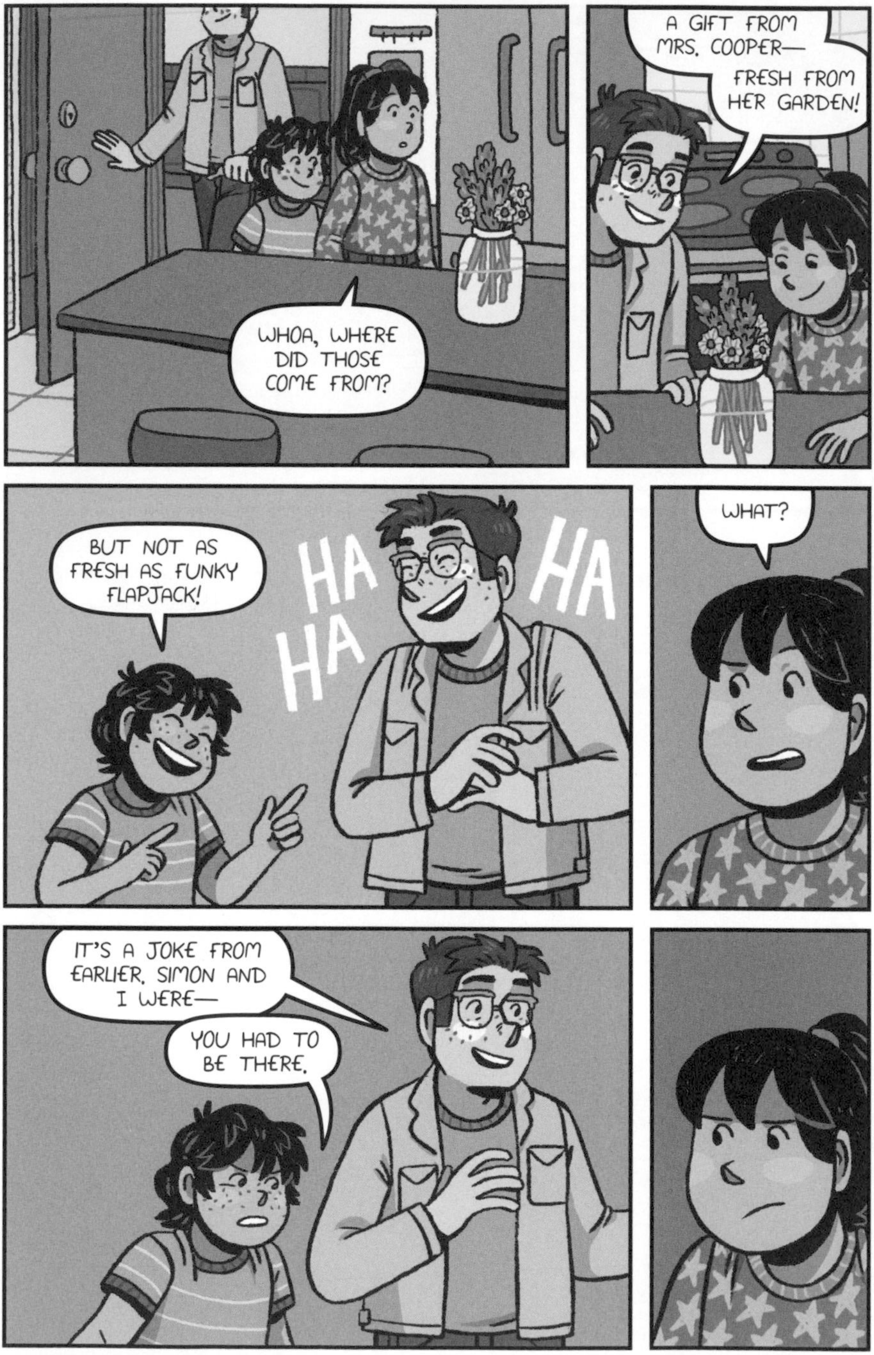
WHOA, WHERE DID THOSE COME FROM?
A GIFT FROM MRS. COOPER—
FRESH FROM HER GARDEN!
BUT NOT AS FRESH AS FUNKY FLAPJACK!
HA HA HA
WHAT?
IT'S A JOKE FROM EARLIER. SIMON AND I WERE—
YOU HAD TO BE THERE.

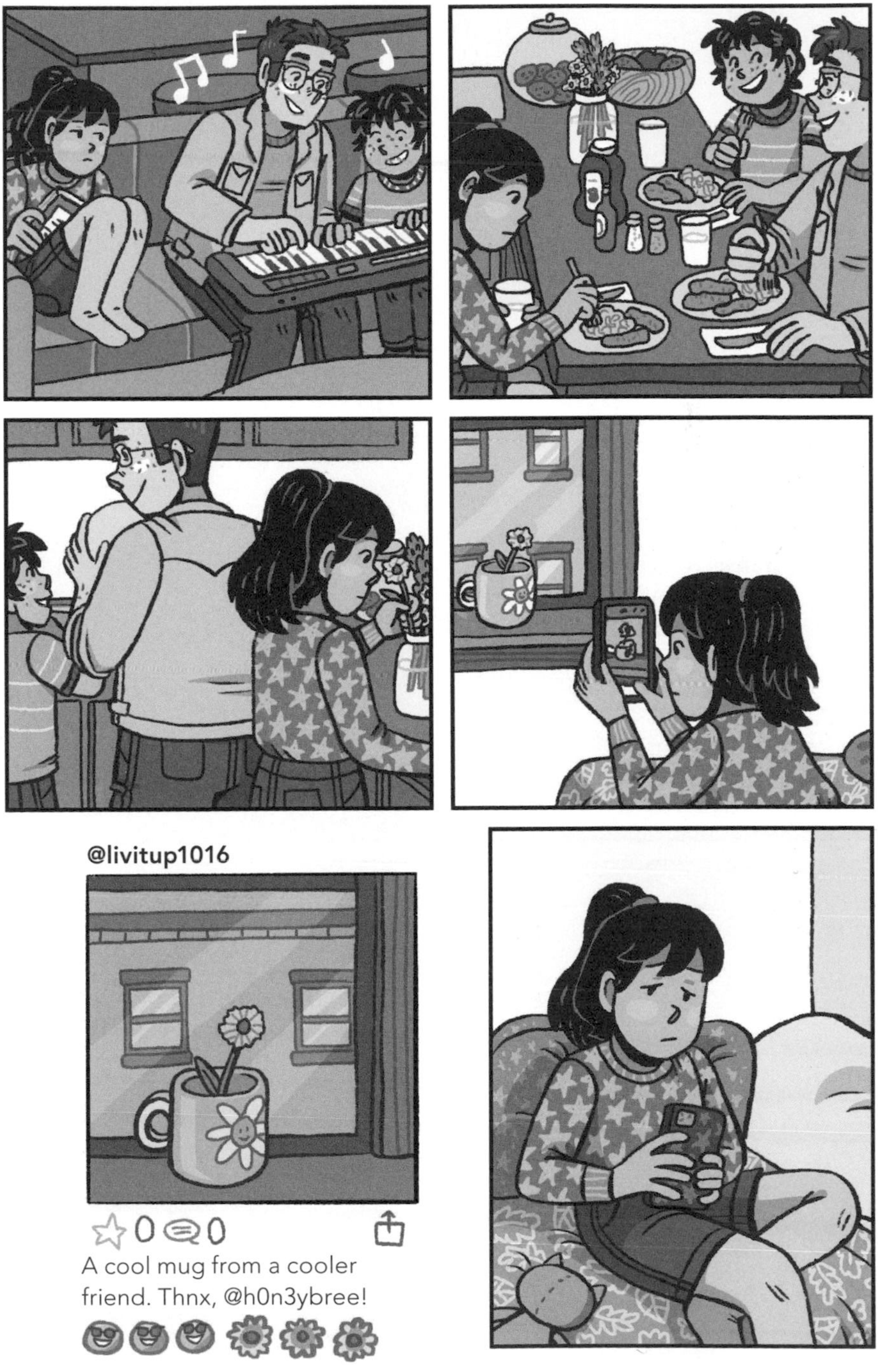
@livitup1016
0 0
A cool mug from a cooler friend. Thnx, @h0n3ybree!

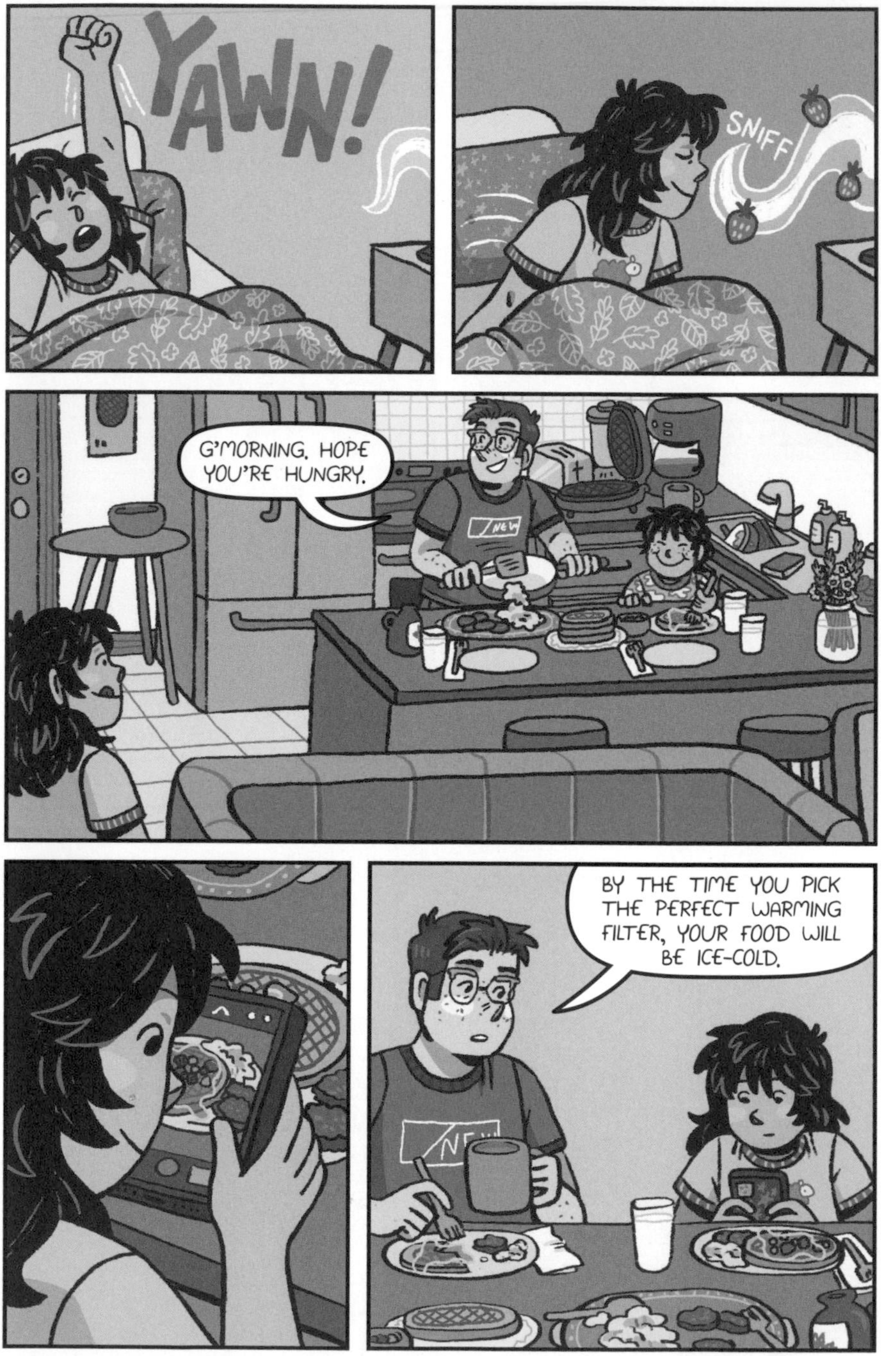
YAWN!
SNIFF
G'MORNING. HOPE YOU'RE HUNGRY.
NEW
BY THE TIME YOU PICK THE PERFECT WARMING FILTER, YOUR FOOD WILL BE ICE-COLD.

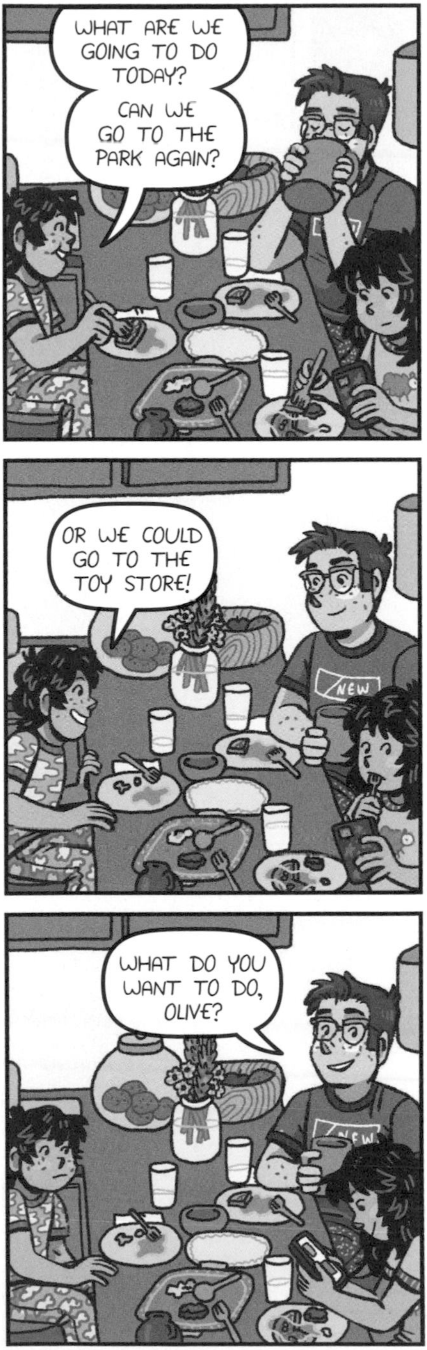
WHAT ARE WE GOING TO DO TODAY?
CAN WE GO TO THE PARK AGAIN?
OR WE COULD GO TO THE TOY STORE!
NEW
WHAT DO YOU WANT TO DO, OLIVE?
NEW

@livitup1016

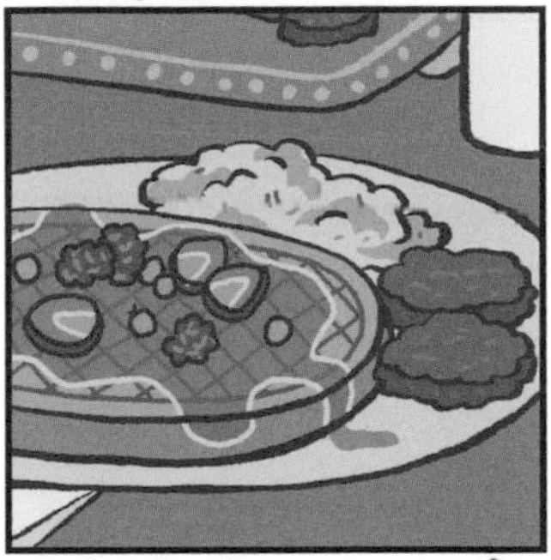

☆3 0

@crystalchandalier

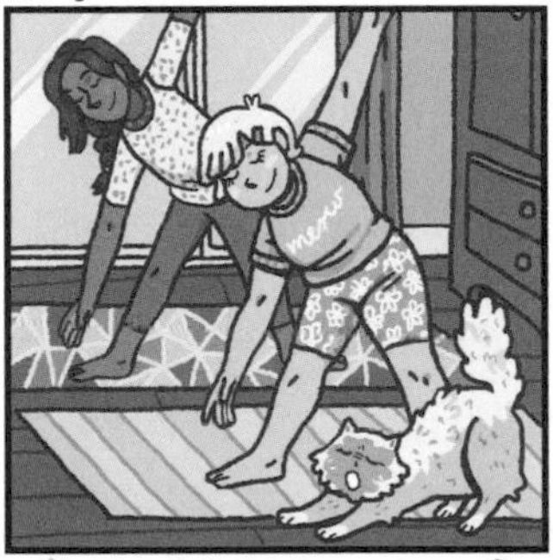
meow

★5 0

Getting centered with my girls.

@naturalbornchiller

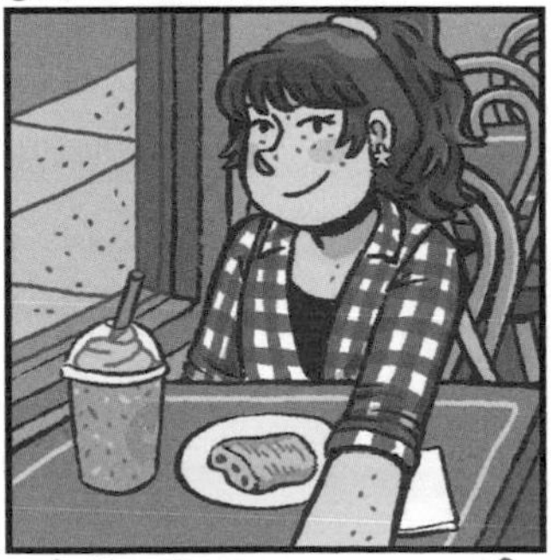

☆4 0

In the 🏙 today. Fueling up for some serious art appreciation.

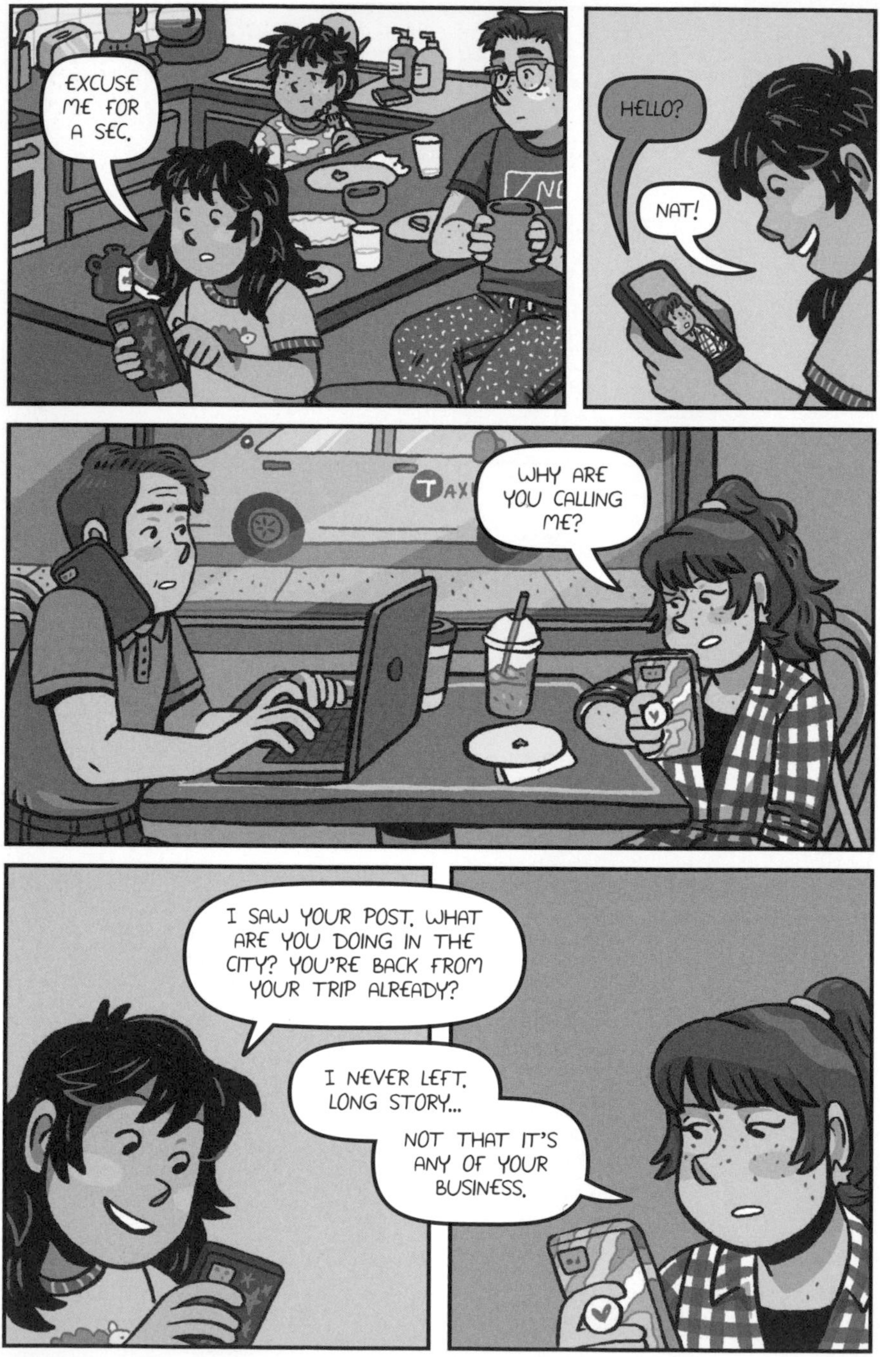
EXCUSE ME FOR A SEC.
HELLO?
NAT!
WHY ARE YOU CALLING ME?
I SAW YOUR POST. WHAT ARE YOU DOING IN THE CITY? YOU'RE BACK FROM YOUR TRIP ALREADY?
I NEVER LEFT. LONG STORY...
NOT THAT IT'S ANY OF YOUR BUSINESS.

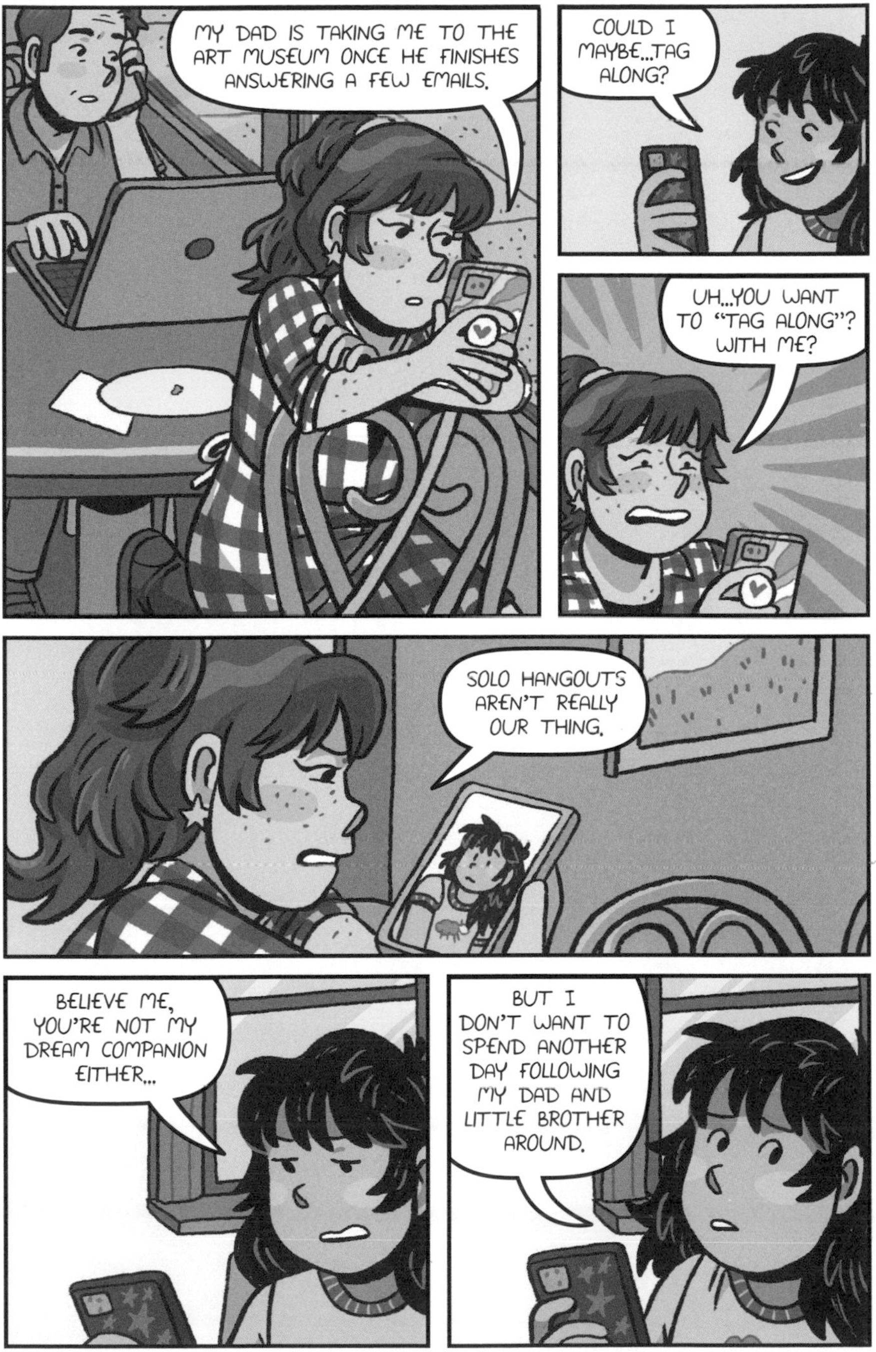
MY DAD IS TAKING ME TO THE ART MUSEUM ONCE HE FINISHES ANSWERING A FEW EMAILS.
COULD I MAYBE...TAG ALONG?
UH...YOU WANT TO "TAG ALONG"? WITH ME?
SOLO HANGOUTS AREN'T REALLY OUR THING.
BELIEVE ME, YOU'RE NOT MY DREAM COMPANION EITHER...
BUT I DON'T WANT TO SPEND ANOTHER DAY FOLLOWING MY DAD AND LITTLE BROTHER AROUND.

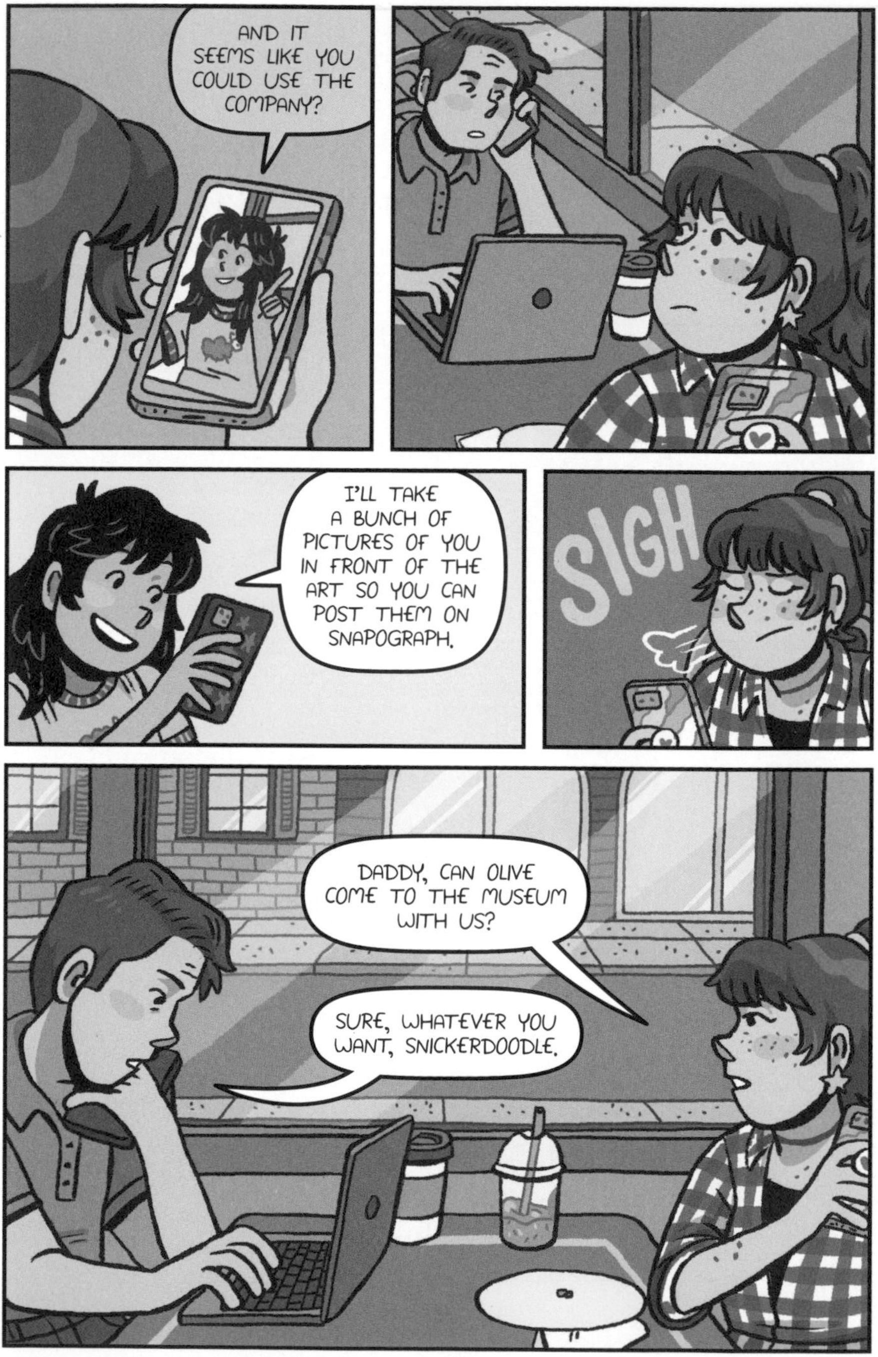
AND IT SEEMS LIKE YOU COULD USE THE COMPANY?
I'LL TAKE A BUNCH OF PICTURES OF YOU IN FRONT OF THE ART SO YOU CAN POST THEM ON SNAPOGRAPH.
SIGH
DADDY, CAN OLIVE COME TO THE MUSEUM WITH US?
SURE, WHATEVER YOU WANT, SNICKERDOODLE.

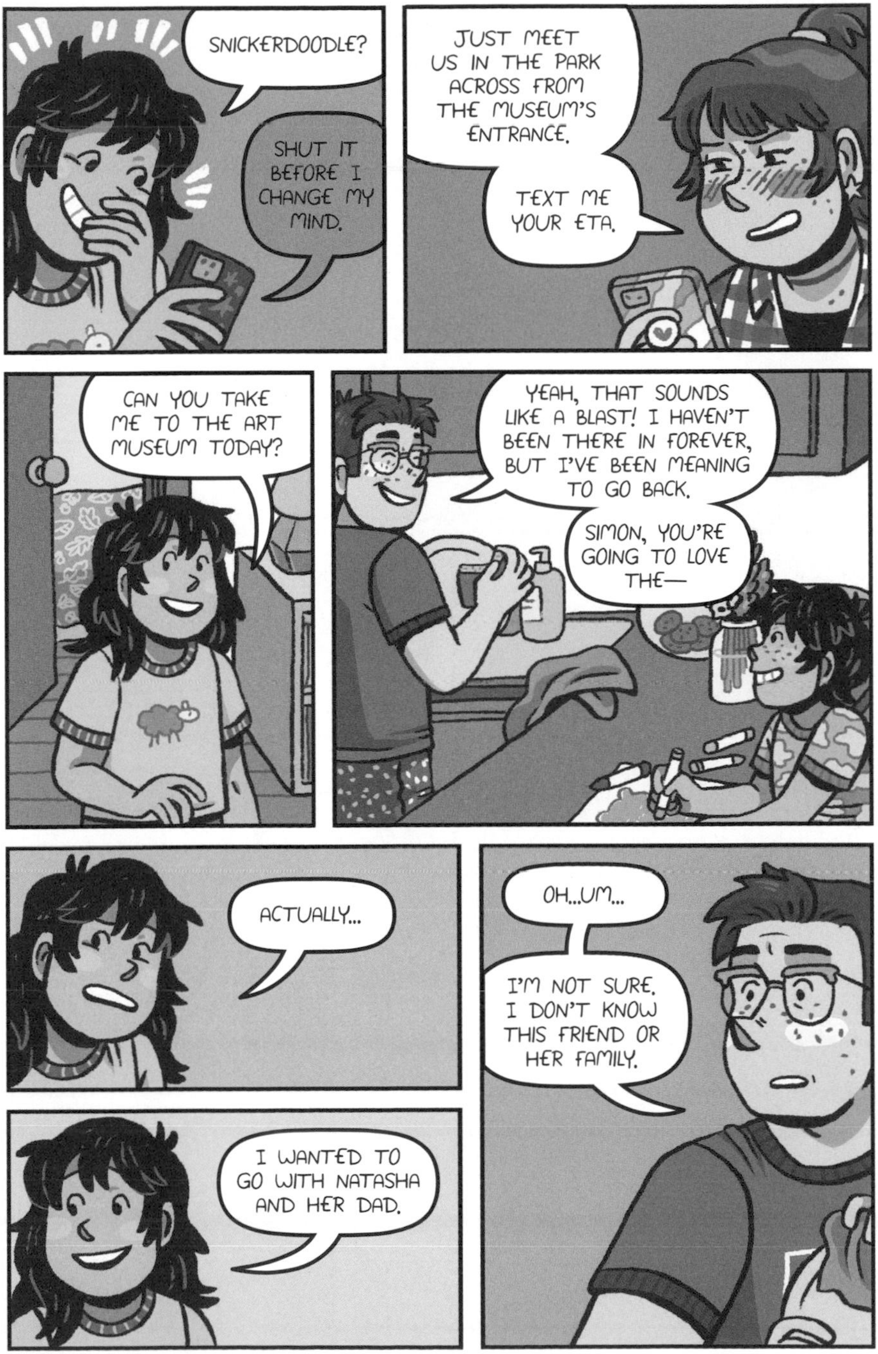
SNICKERDOODLE?
SHUT IT BEFORE I CHANGE MY MIND.
JUST MEET US IN THE PARK ACROSS FROM THE MUSEUM'S ENTRANCE.
TEXT ME YOUR ETA.
CAN YOU TAKE ME TO THE ART MUSEUM TODAY?
YEAH, THAT SOUNDS LIKE A BLAST! I HAVEN'T BEEN THERE IN FOREVER, BUT I'VE BEEN MEANING TO GO BACK.
SIMON, YOU'RE GOING TO LOVE THE—
ACTUALLY...
I WANTED TO GO WITH NATASHA AND HER DAD.
OH...UM...
I'M NOT SURE. I DON'T KNOW THIS FRIEND OR HER FAMILY.

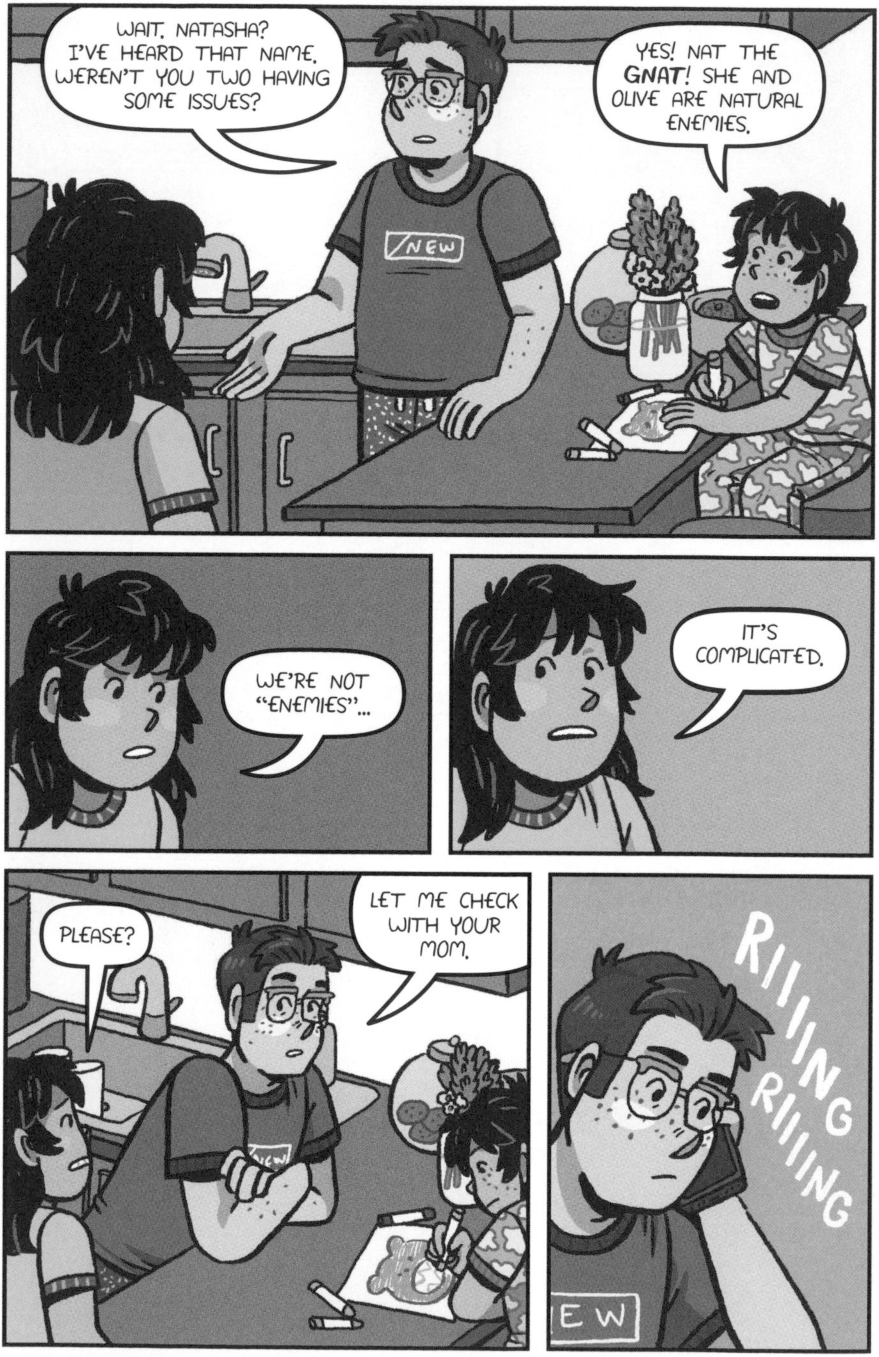
WAIT. NATASHA? I'VE HEARD THAT NAME. WEREN'T YOU TWO HAVING SOME ISSUES?
YES! NAT THE **GNAT**! SHE AND OLIVE ARE NATURAL ENEMIES.
NEW
WE'RE NOT "ENEMIES"...
IT'S COMPLICATED.
PLEASE?
LET ME CHECK WITH YOUR MOM.
RIIIING RIIIING

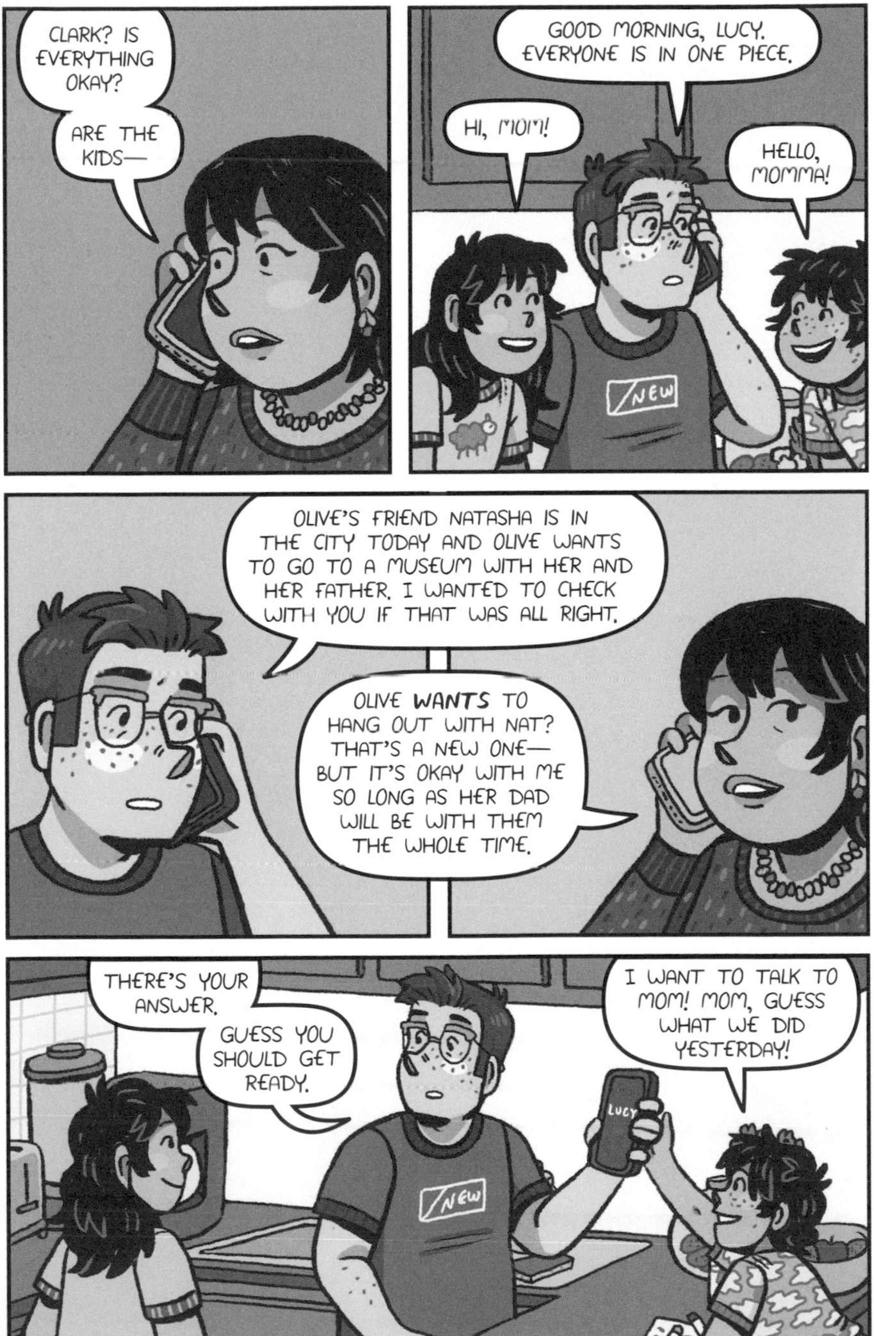
CLARK? IS EVERYTHING OKAY?
ARE THE KIDS—
GOOD MORNING, LUCY. EVERYONE IS IN ONE PIECE.
HI, MOM!
HELLO, MOMMA!
NEW
OLIVE'S FRIEND NATASHA IS IN THE CITY TODAY AND OLIVE WANTS TO GO TO A MUSEUM WITH HER AND HER FATHER. I WANTED TO CHECK WITH YOU IF THAT WAS ALL RIGHT.
OLIVE **WANTS** TO HANG OUT WITH NAT? THAT'S A NEW ONE—BUT IT'S OKAY WITH ME SO LONG AS HER DAD WILL BE WITH THEM THE WHOLE TIME.
THERE'S YOUR ANSWER.
GUESS YOU SHOULD GET READY.
I WANT TO TALK TO MOM! MOM, GUESS WHAT WE DID YESTERDAY!
LUCY
NEW

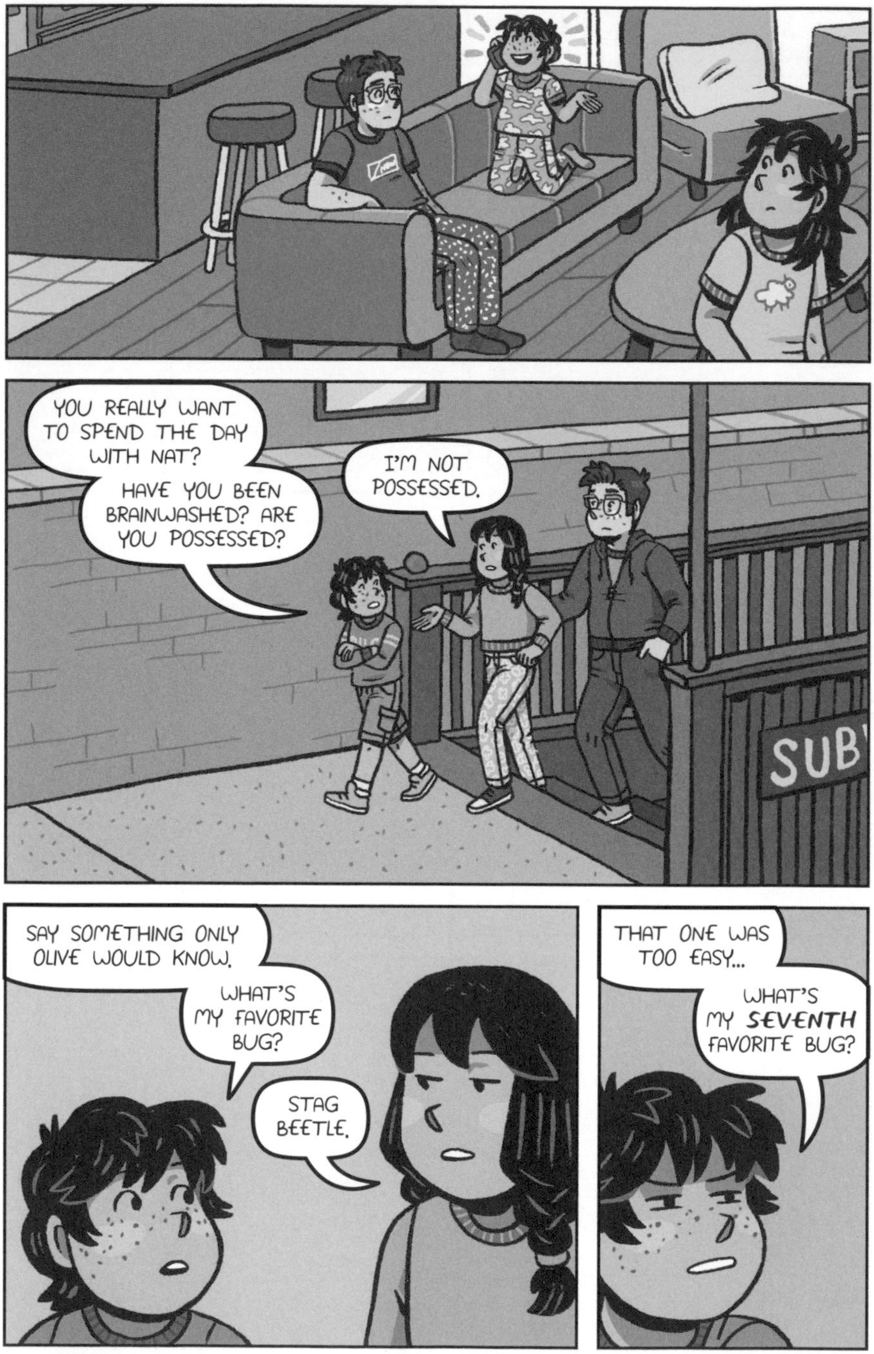
YOU REALLY WANT TO SPEND THE DAY WITH NAT?
HAVE YOU BEEN BRAINWASHED? ARE YOU POSSESSED?
I'M NOT POSSESSED.
SUB
SAY SOMETHING ONLY OLIVE WOULD KNOW.
WHAT'S MY FAVORITE BUG?
STAG BEETLE.
THAT ONE WAS TOO EASY...
WHAT'S MY **SEVENTH** FAVORITE BUG?

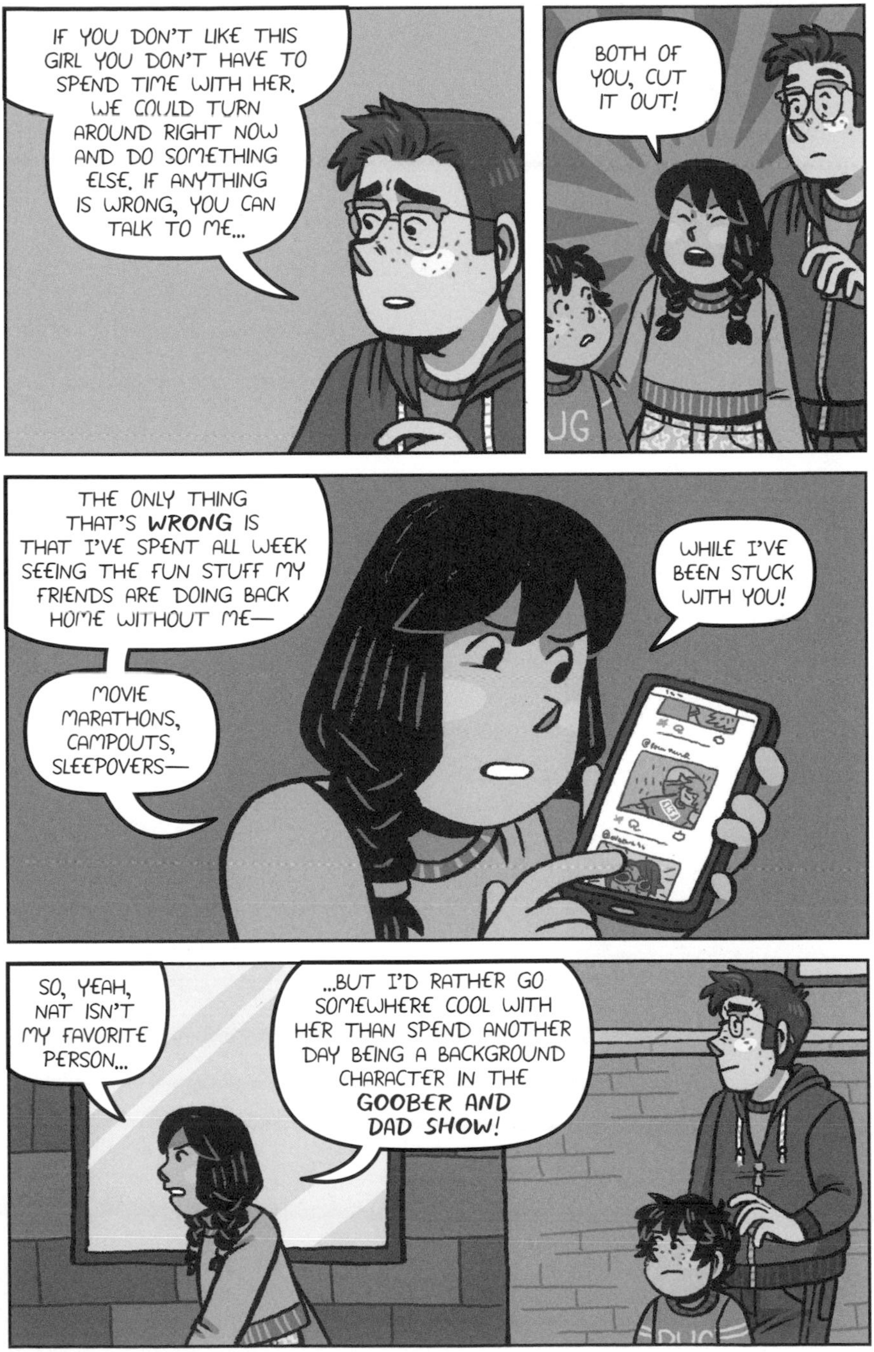
IF YOU DON'T LIKE THIS GIRL YOU DON'T HAVE TO SPEND TIME WITH HER. WE COULD TURN AROUND RIGHT NOW AND DO SOMETHING ELSE. IF ANYTHING IS WRONG, YOU CAN TALK TO ME...
BOTH OF YOU, CUT IT OUT!
THE ONLY THING THAT'S **WRONG** IS THAT I'VE SPENT ALL WEEK SEEING THE FUN STUFF MY FRIENDS ARE DOING BACK HOME WITHOUT ME—
MOVIE MARATHONS, CAMPOUTS, SLEEPOVERS—
WHILE I'VE BEEN STUCK WITH YOU!
SO, YEAH, NAT ISN'T MY FAVORITE PERSON...
...BUT I'D RATHER GO SOMEWHERE COOL WITH HER THAN SPEND ANOTHER DAY BEING A BACKGROUND CHARACTER IN THE **GOOBER AND DAD SHOW!**

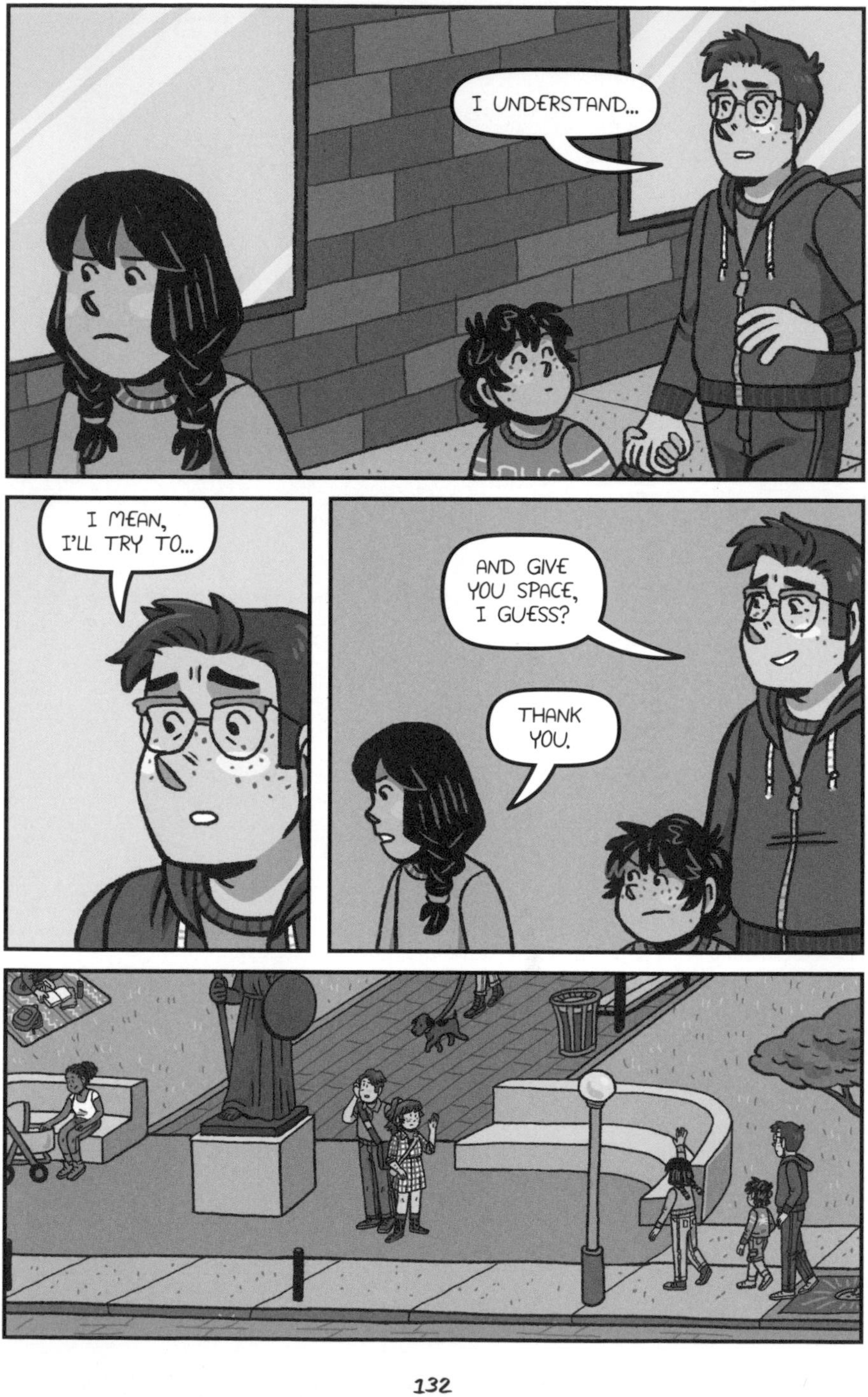
I UNDERSTAND...
I MEAN, I'LL TRY TO...
AND GIVE YOU SPACE, I GUESS?
THANK YOU.

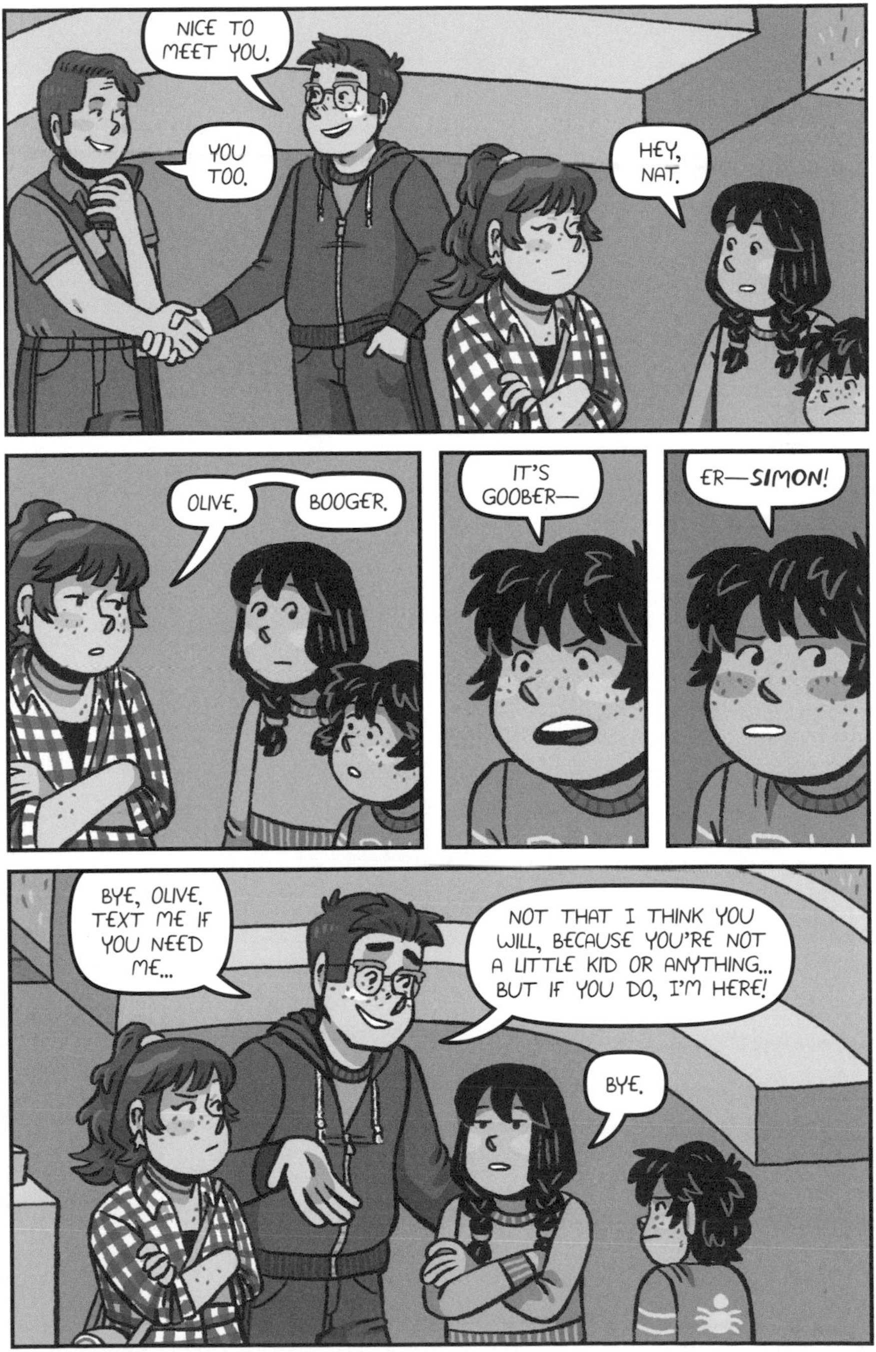
NICE TO MEET YOU.
YOU TOO.
HEY, NAT.
OLIVE.
BOOGER.
IT'S GOOBER—
ER—**SIMON!**
BYE, OLIVE. TEXT ME IF YOU NEED ME...
NOT THAT I THINK YOU WILL, BECAUSE YOU'RE NOT A LITTLE KID OR ANYTHING... BUT IF YOU DO, I'M HERE!
BYE.

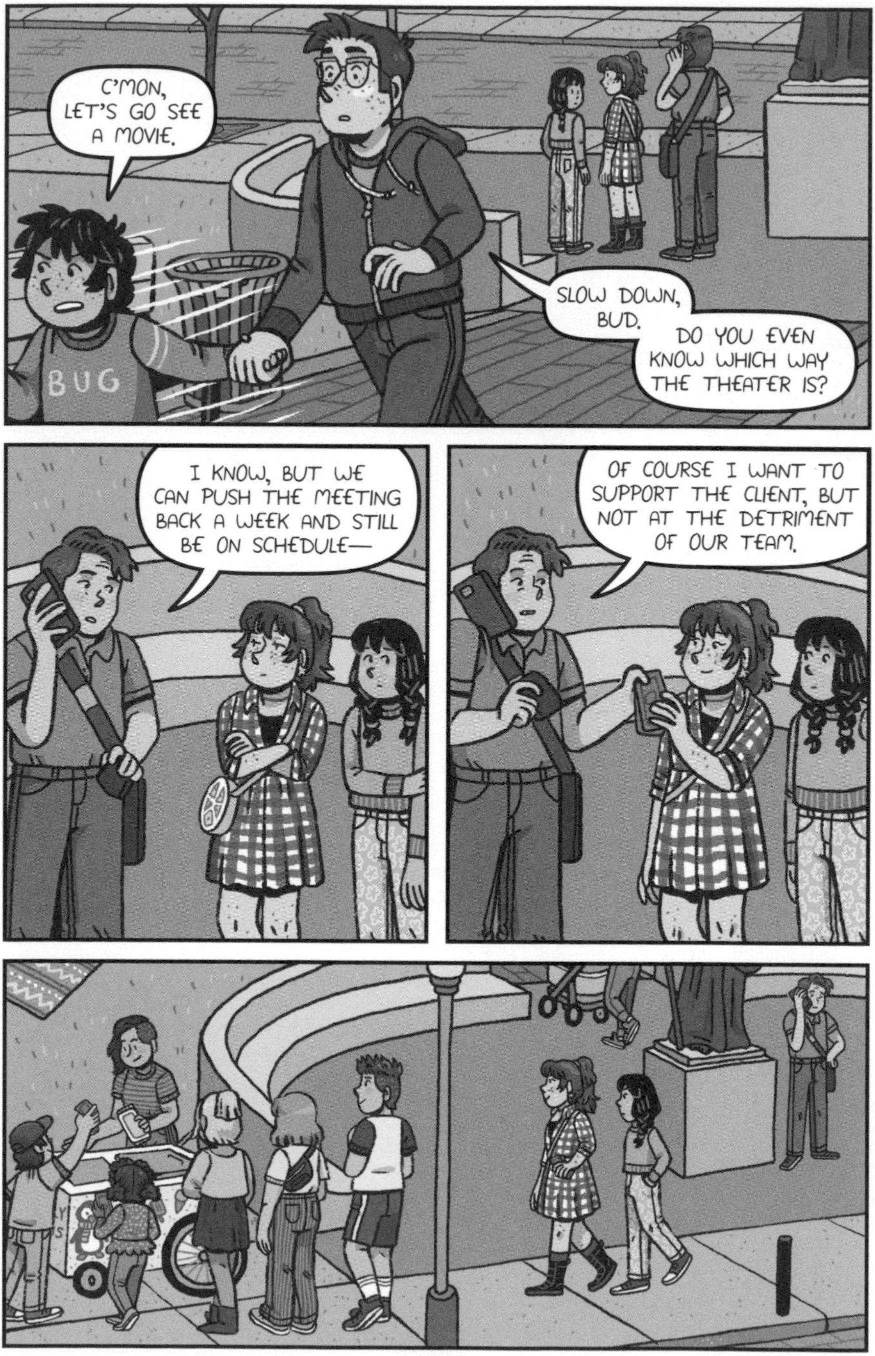
C'MON, LET'S GO SEE A MOVIE.
SLOW DOWN, BUD.
DO YOU EVEN KNOW WHICH WAY THE THEATER IS?
BUG
I KNOW, BUT WE CAN PUSH THE MEETING BACK A WEEK AND STILL BE ON SCHEDULE—
OF COURSE I WANT TO SUPPORT THE CLIENT, BUT NOT AT THE DETRIMENT OF OUR TEAM.

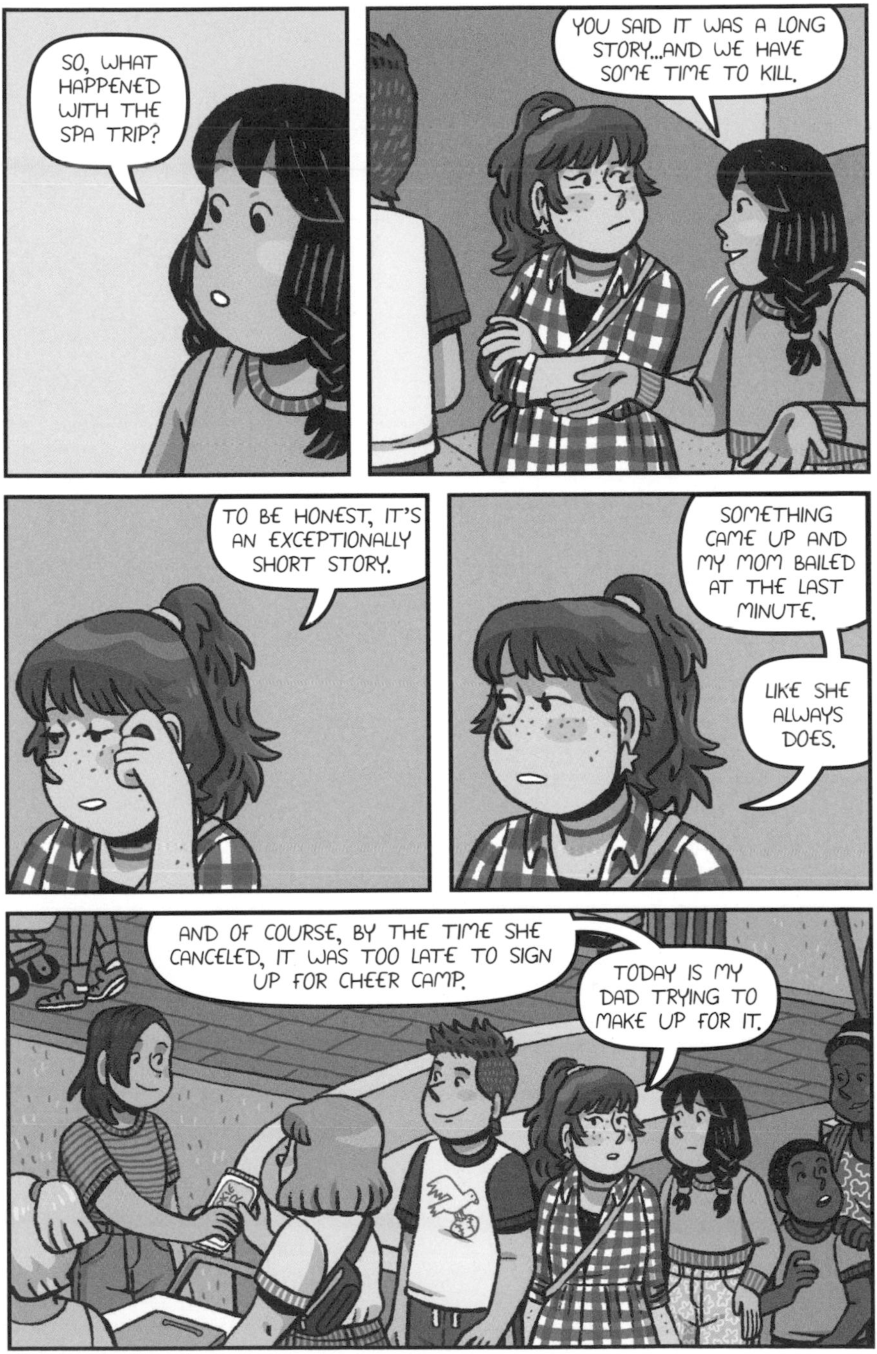
SO, WHAT HAPPENED WITH THE SPA TRIP?
YOU SAID IT WAS A LONG STORY...AND WE HAVE SOME TIME TO KILL.
TO BE HONEST, IT'S AN EXCEPTIONALLY SHORT STORY.
SOMETHING CAME UP AND MY MOM BAILED AT THE LAST MINUTE.
LIKE SHE ALWAYS DOES.
AND OF COURSE, BY THE TIME SHE CANCELED, IT WAS TOO LATE TO SIGN UP FOR CHEER CAMP.
TODAY IS MY DAD TRYING TO MAKE UP FOR IT.

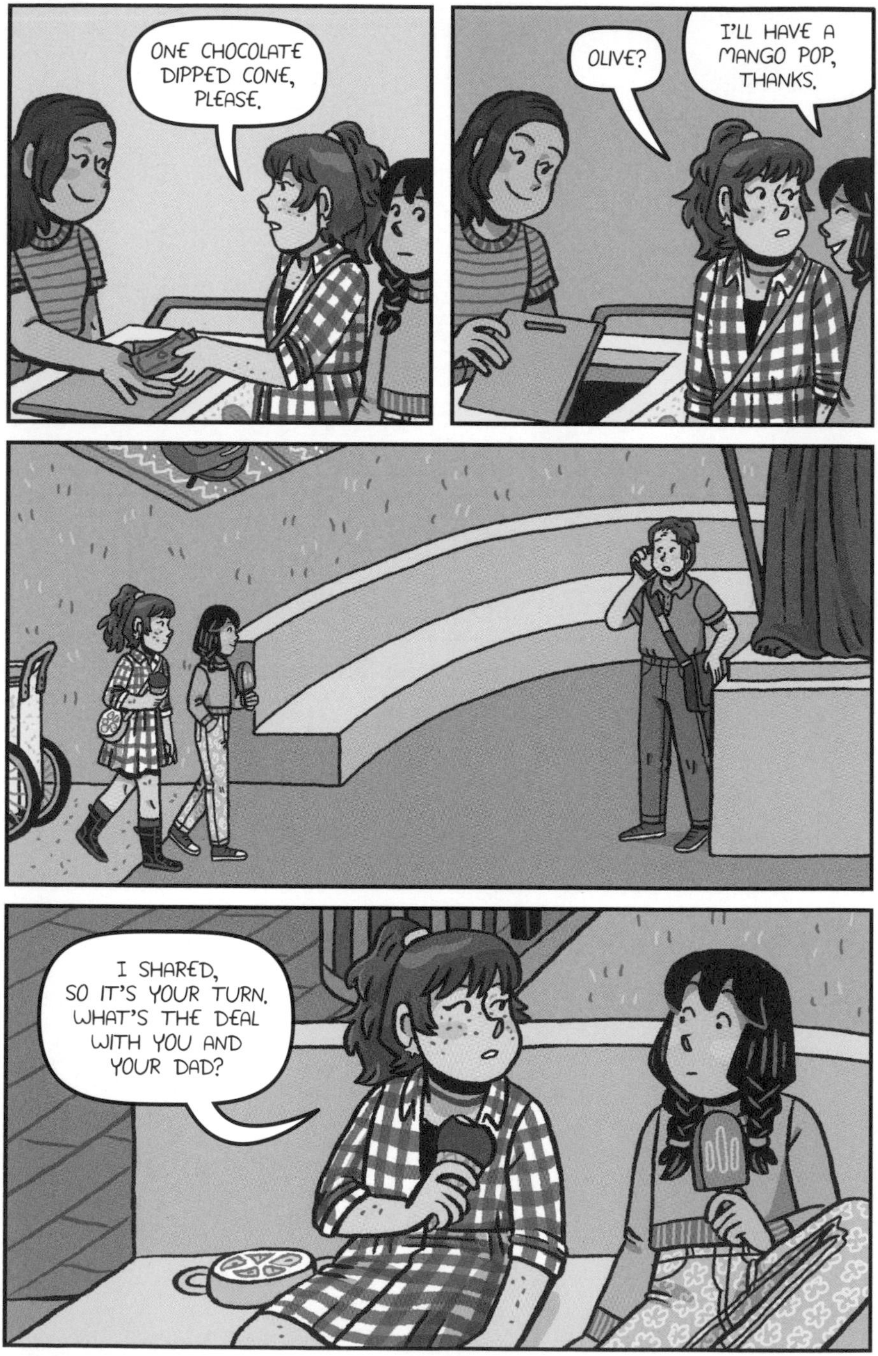
ONE CHOCOLATE DIPPED CONE, PLEASE.
OLIVE?
I'LL HAVE A MANGO POP, THANKS.
I SHARED, SO IT'S YOUR TURN. WHAT'S THE DEAL WITH YOU AND YOUR DAD?

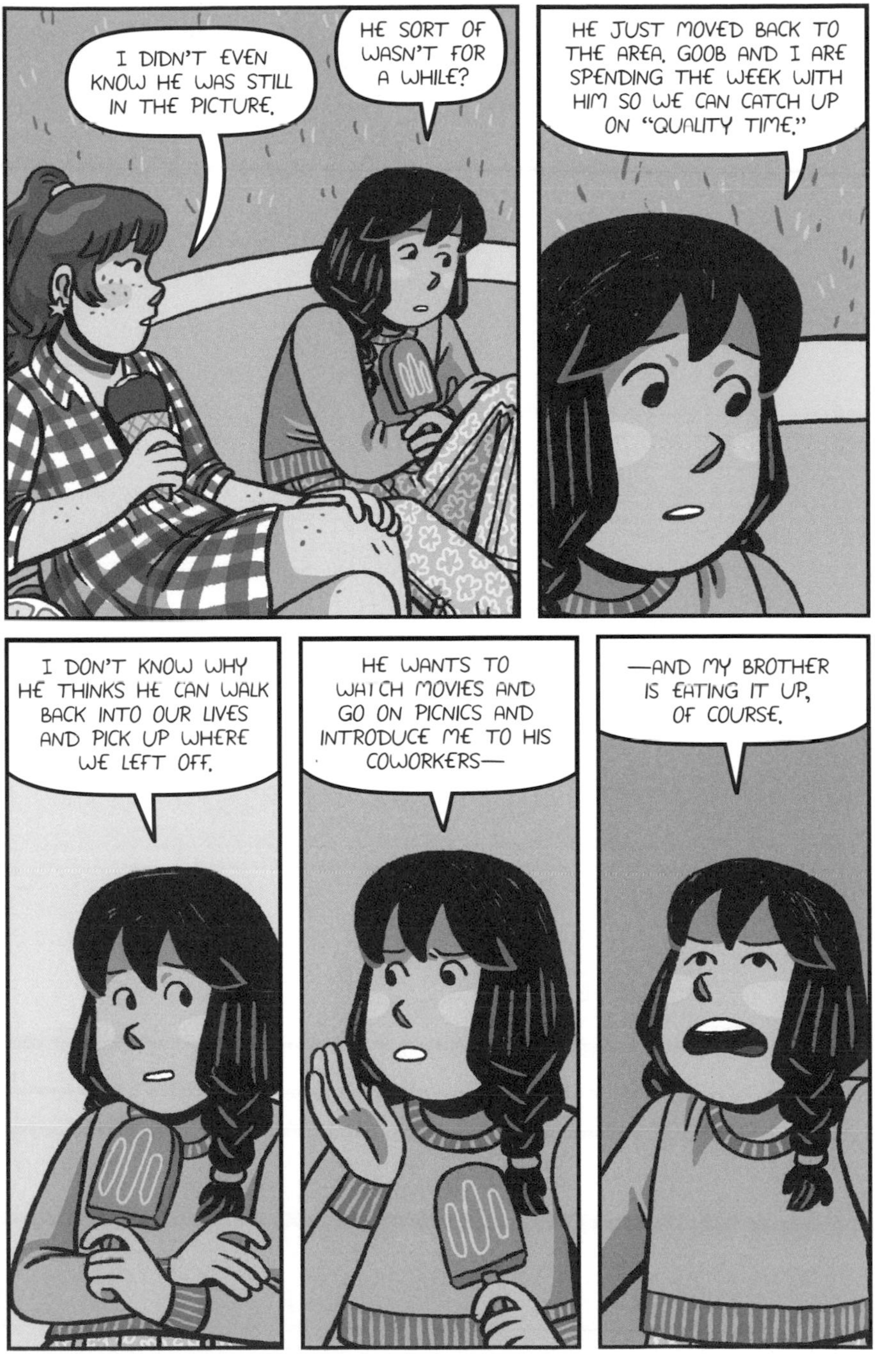
I DIDN'T EVEN KNOW HE WAS STILL IN THE PICTURE.
HE SORT OF WASN'T FOR A WHILE?
HE JUST MOVED BACK TO THE AREA. GOOB AND I ARE SPENDING THE WEEK WITH HIM SO WE CAN CATCH UP ON "QUALITY TIME."
I DON'T KNOW WHY HE THINKS HE CAN WALK BACK INTO OUR LIVES AND PICK UP WHERE WE LEFT OFF.
HE WANTS TO WATCH MOVIES AND GO ON PICNICS AND INTRODUCE ME TO HIS COWORKERS—
—AND MY BROTHER IS EATING IT UP, OF COURSE.

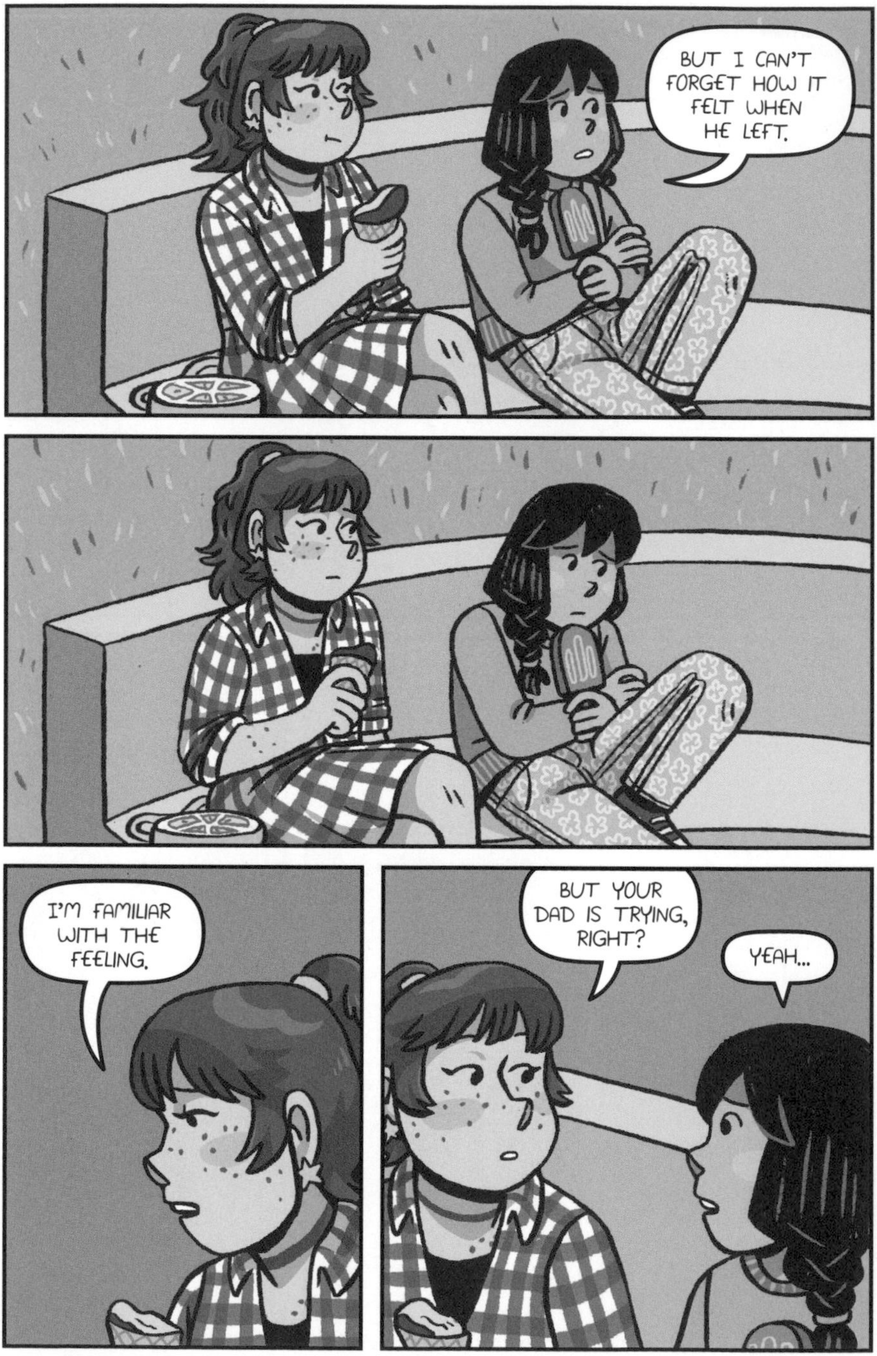
BUT I CAN'T FORGET HOW IT FELT WHEN HE LEFT.
I'M FAMILIAR WITH THE FEELING.
BUT YOUR DAD IS TRYING, RIGHT?
YEAH...

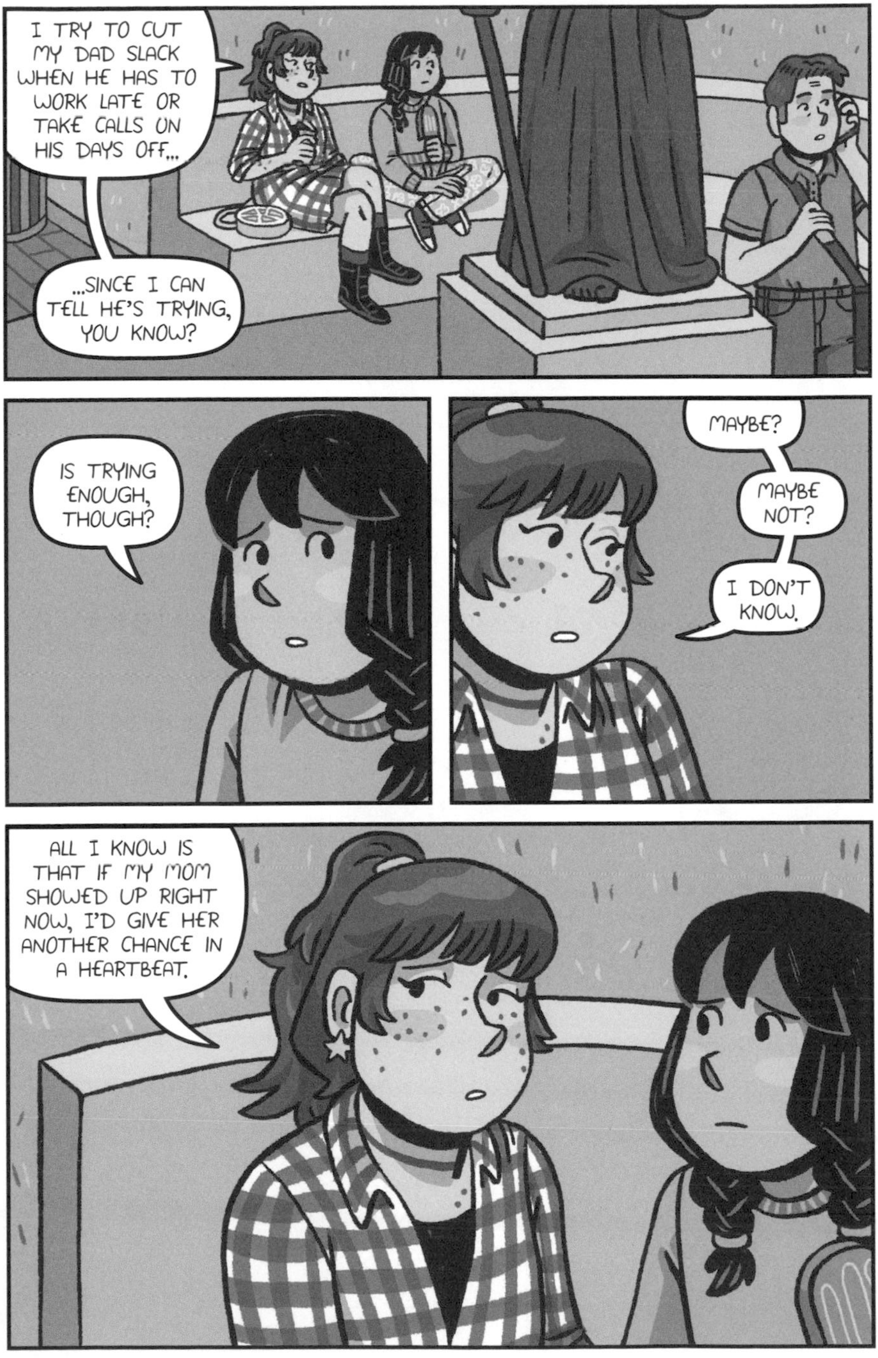
I TRY TO CUT MY DAD SLACK WHEN HE HAS TO WORK LATE OR TAKE CALLS ON HIS DAYS OFF...
...SINCE I CAN TELL HE'S TRYING, YOU KNOW?
IS TRYING ENOUGH, THOUGH?
MAYBE?
MAYBE NOT?
I DON'T KNOW.
ALL I KNOW IS THAT IF MY MOM SHOWED UP RIGHT NOW, I'D GIVE HER ANOTHER CHANCE IN A HEARTBEAT.

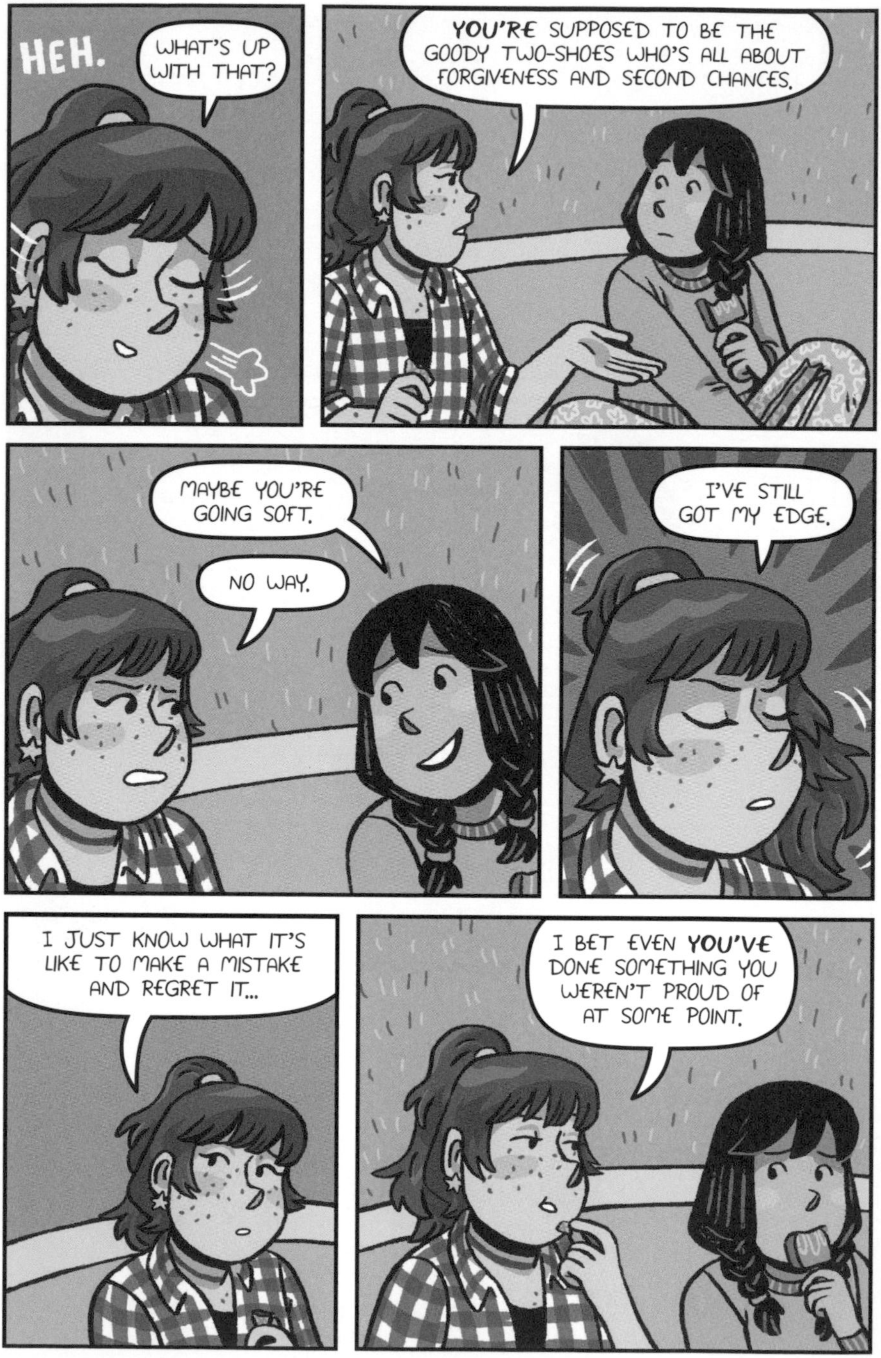

HEH.
WHAT'S UP WITH THAT?
YOU'RE SUPPOSED TO BE THE GOODY TWO-SHOES WHO'S ALL ABOUT FORGIVENESS AND SECOND CHANCES.
MAYBE YOU'RE GOING SOFT.
NO WAY.
I'VE STILL GOT MY EDGE.
I JUST KNOW WHAT IT'S LIKE TO MAKE A MISTAKE AND REGRET IT...
I BET EVEN **YOU'VE** DONE SOMETHING YOU WEREN'T PROUD OF AT SOME POINT.

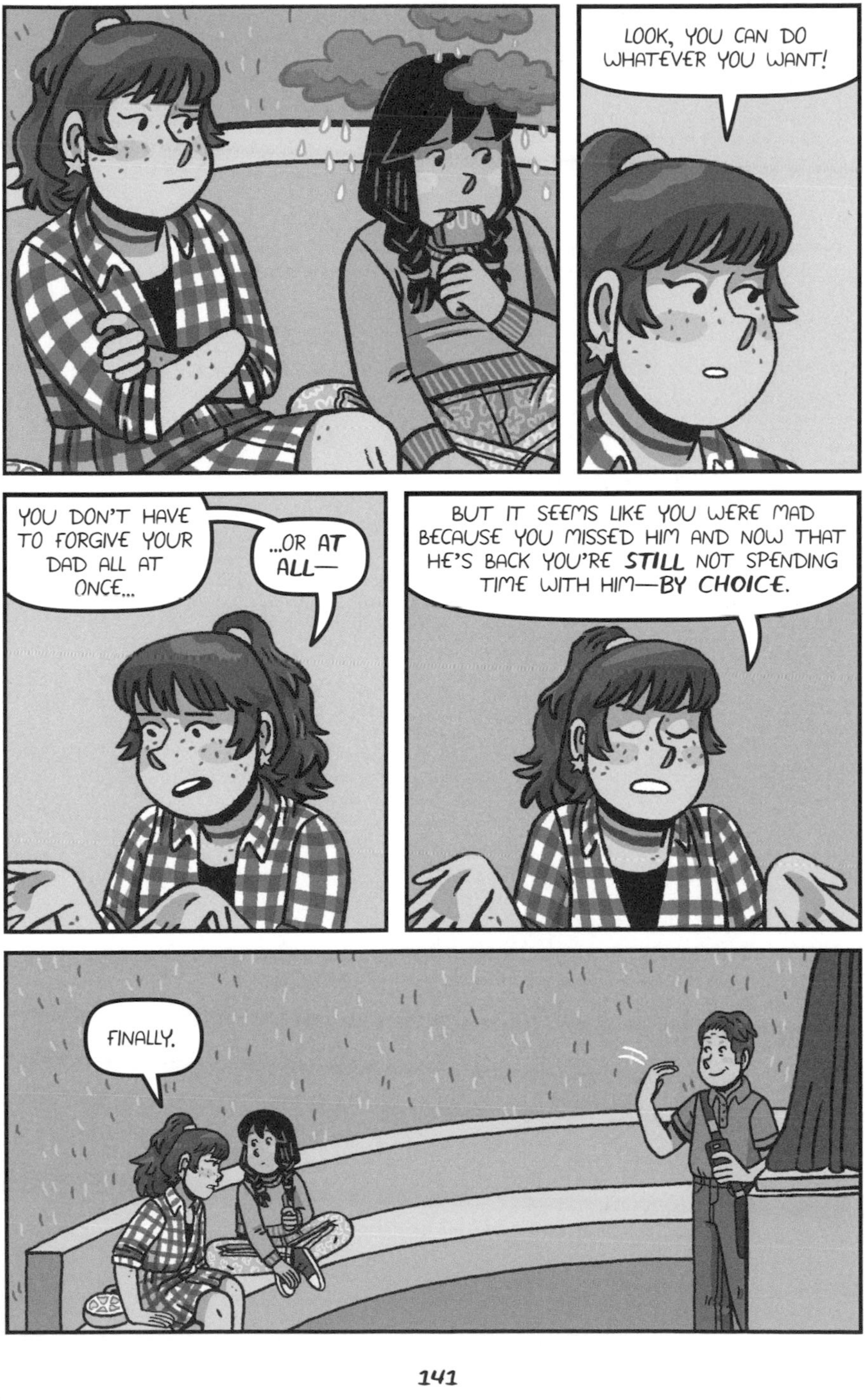
LOOK, YOU CAN DO WHATEVER YOU WANT!
YOU DON'T HAVE TO FORGIVE YOUR DAD ALL AT ONCE...
...OR **AT ALL**—
BUT IT SEEMS LIKE YOU WERE MAD BECAUSE YOU MISSED HIM AND NOW THAT HE'S BACK YOU'RE **STILL** NOT SPENDING TIME WITH HIM—**BY CHOICE**.
FINALLY.

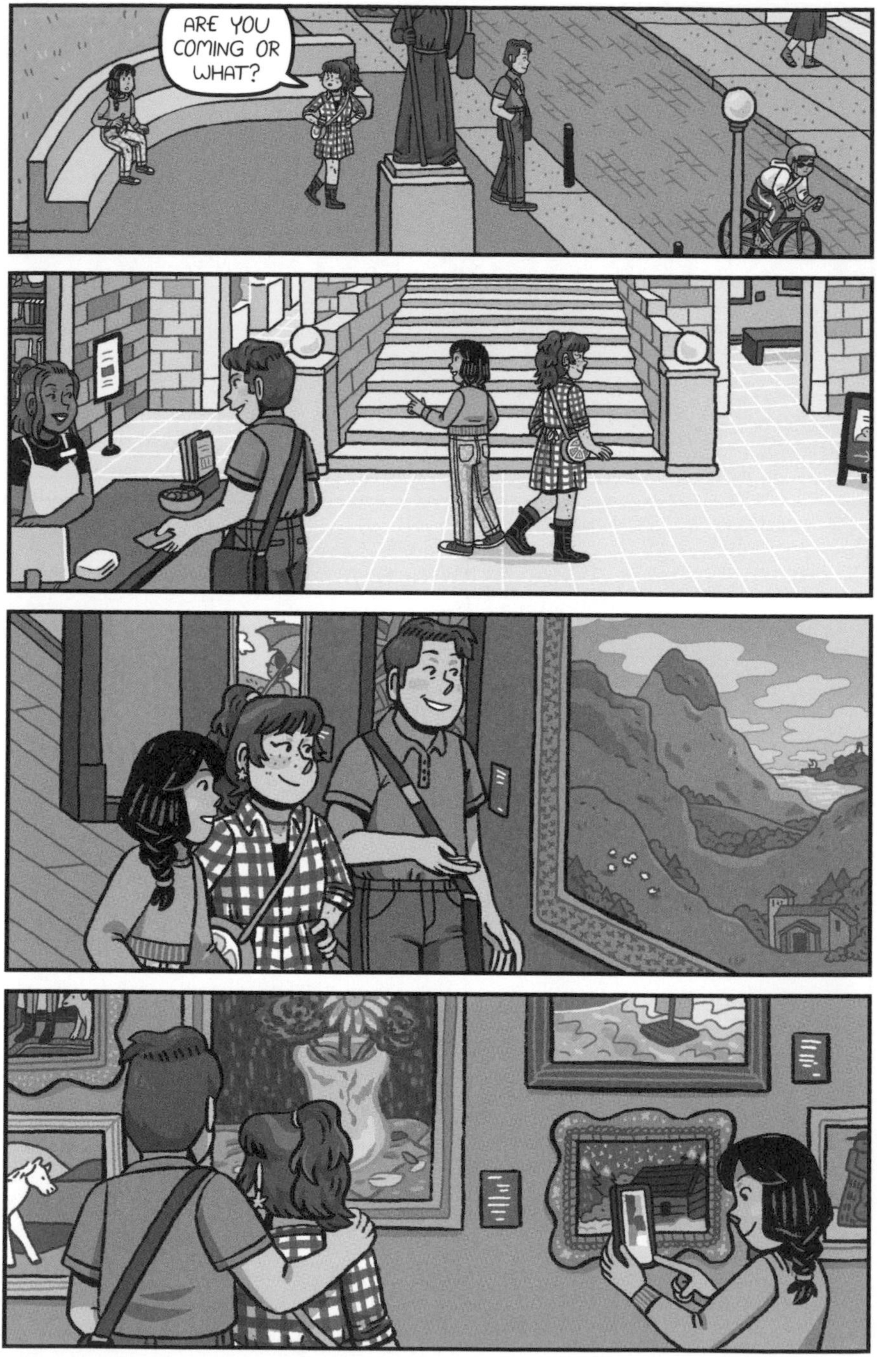
ARE YOU COMING OR WHAT?

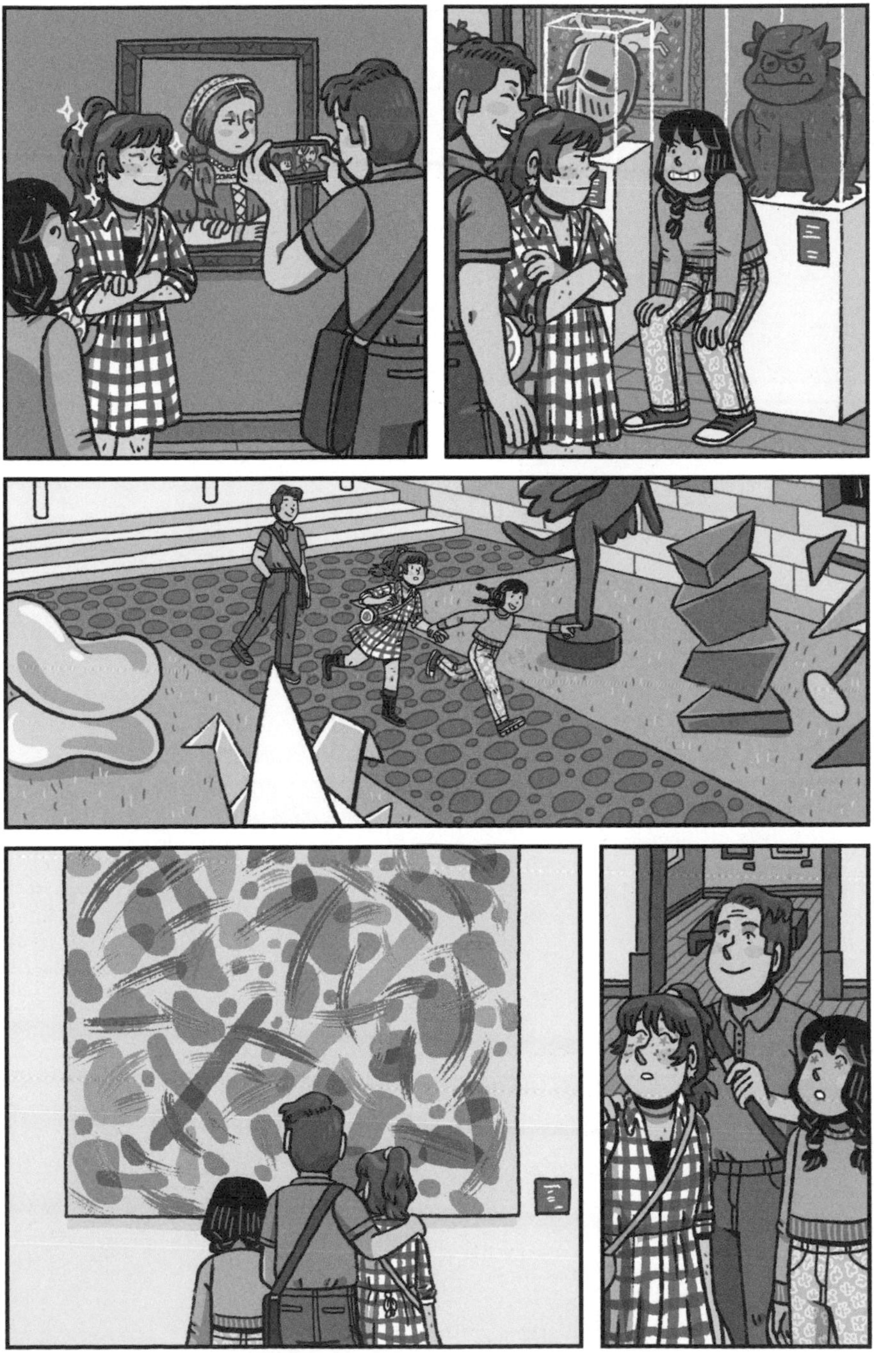

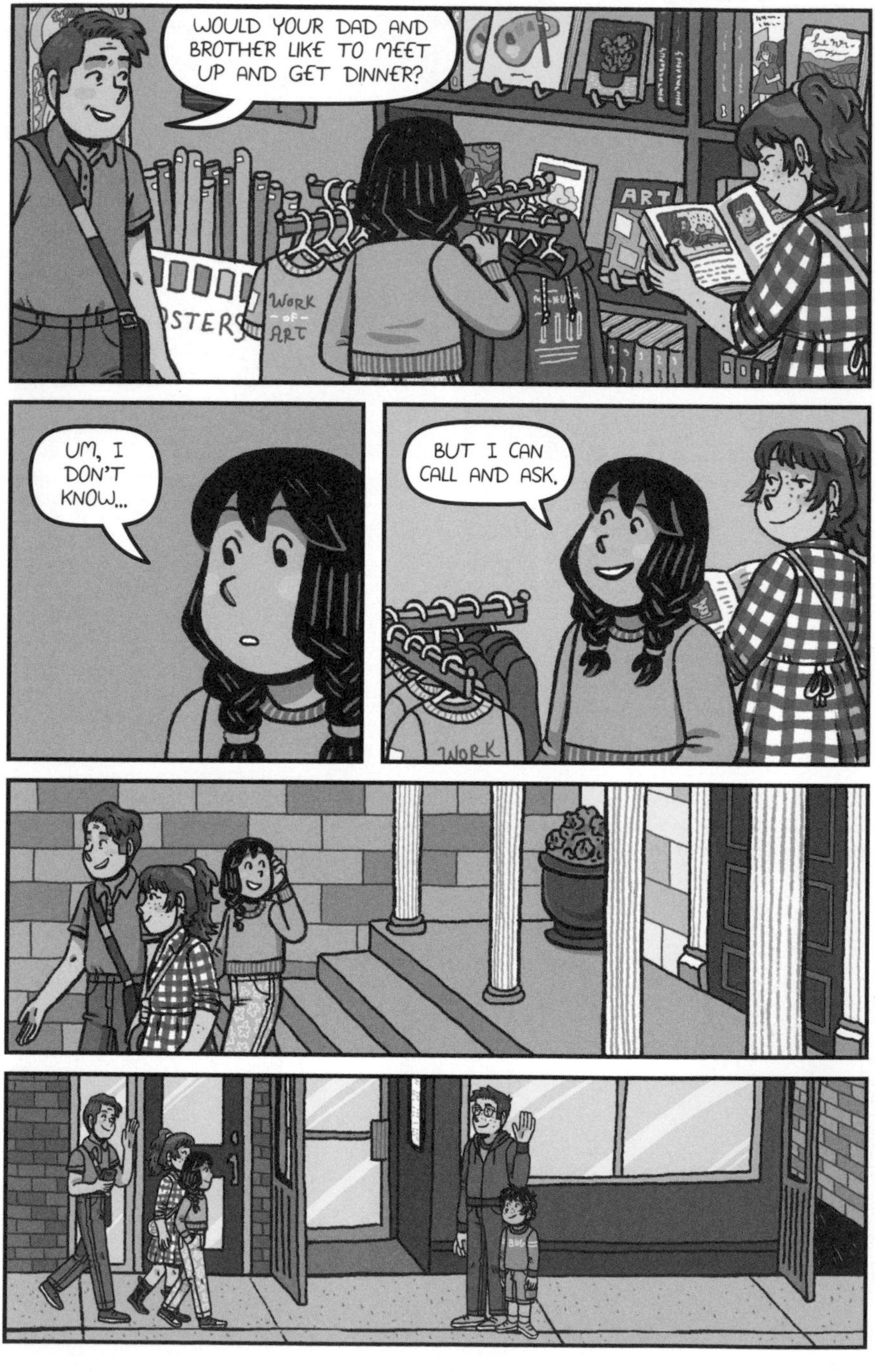
WOULD YOUR DAD AND BROTHER LIKE TO MEET UP AND GET DINNER?
UM, I DON'T KNOW...
BUT I CAN CALL AND ASK.

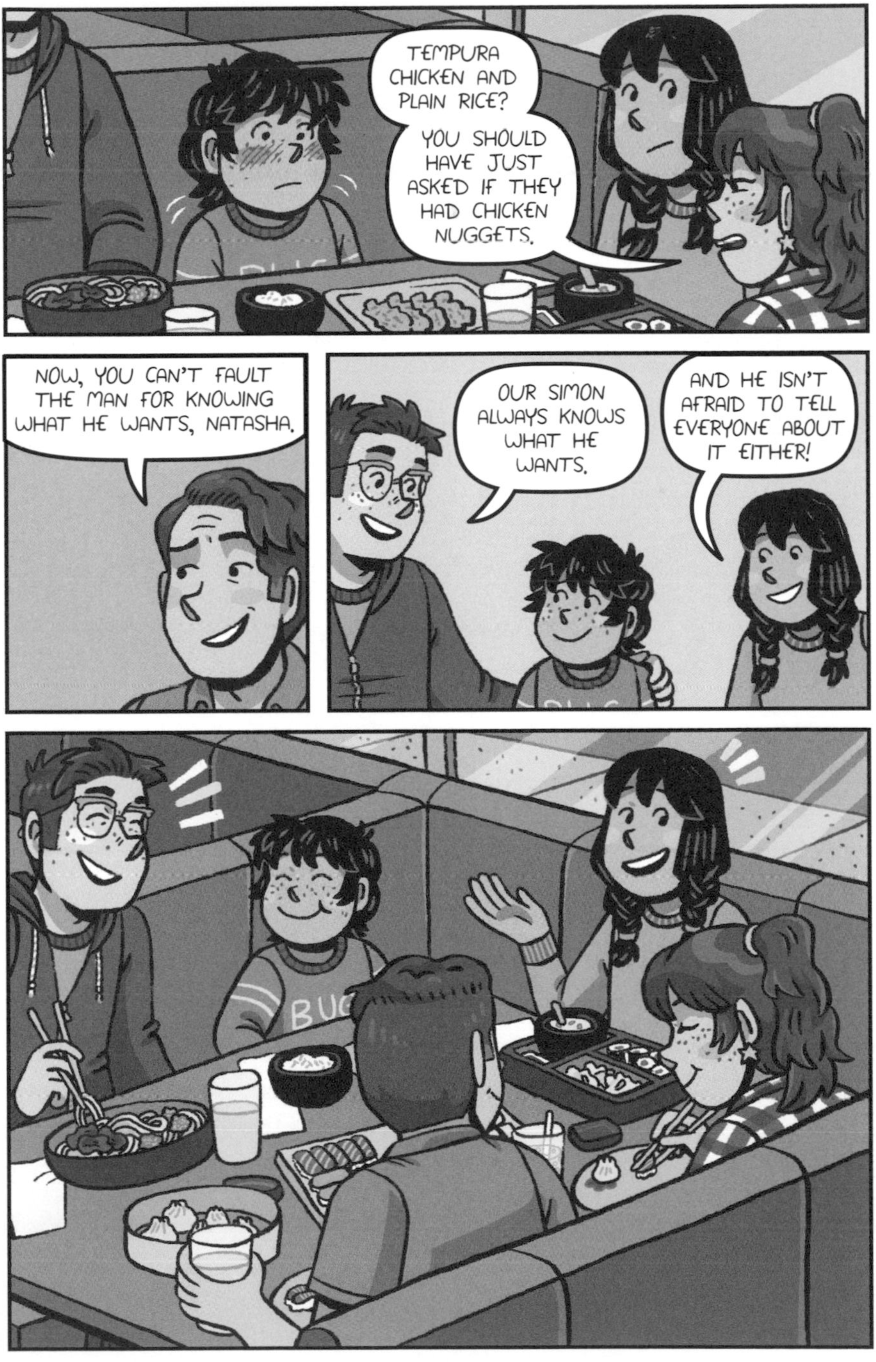
TEMPURA CHICKEN AND PLAIN RICE?
YOU SHOULD HAVE JUST ASKED IF THEY HAD CHICKEN NUGGETS.
NOW, YOU CAN'T FAULT THE MAN FOR KNOWING WHAT HE WANTS, NATASHA.
OUR SIMON ALWAYS KNOWS WHAT HE WANTS.
AND HE ISN'T AFRAID TO TELL EVERYONE ABOUT IT EITHER!
BUG

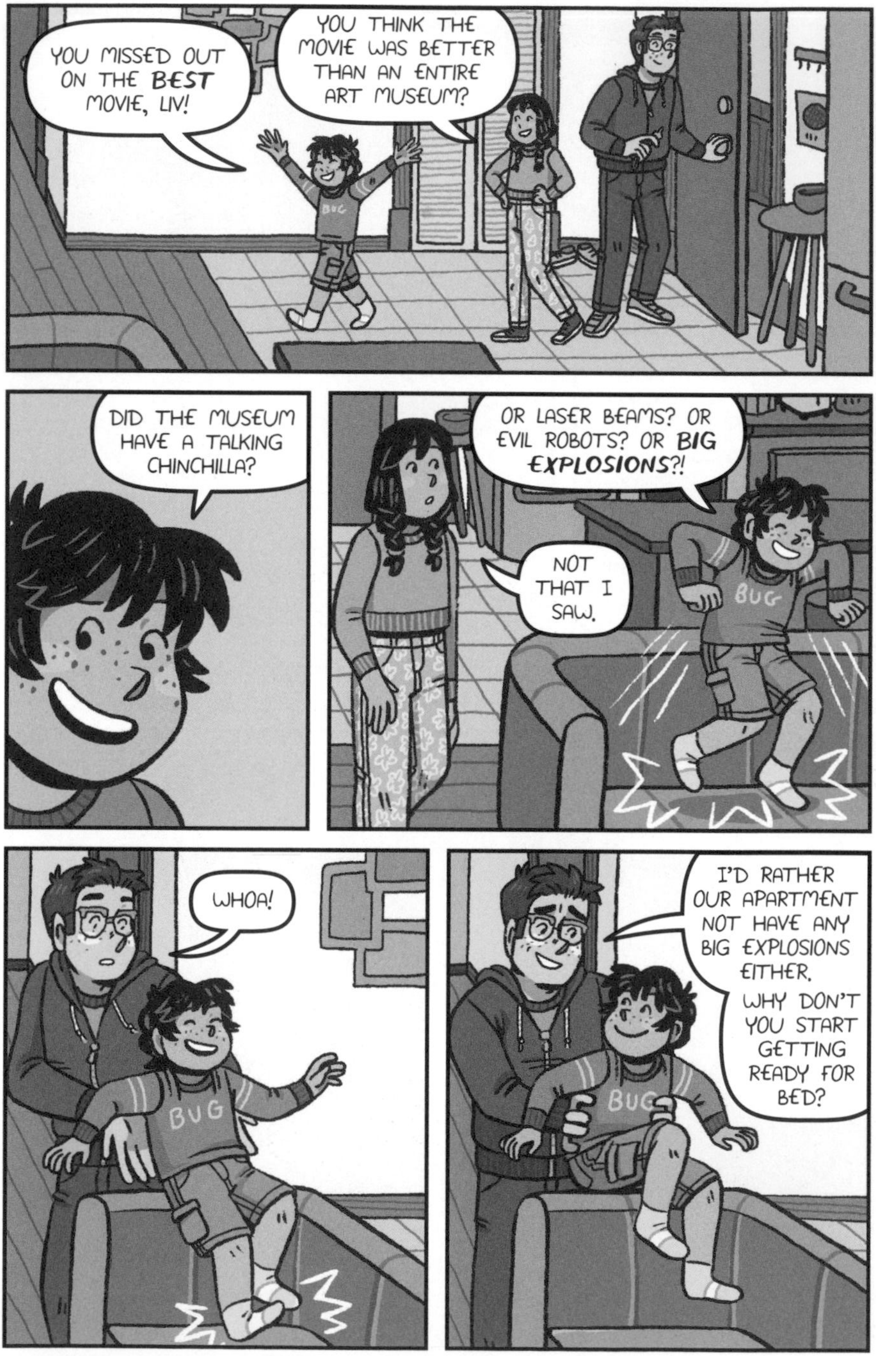
YOU MISSED OUT ON THE **BEST** MOVIE, LIV!
YOU THINK THE MOVIE WAS BETTER THAN AN ENTIRE ART MUSEUM?
BUG
DID THE MUSEUM HAVE A TALKING CHINCHILLA?
OR LASER BEAMS? OR EVIL ROBOTS? OR **BIG EXPLOSIONS**?!
NOT THAT I SAW.
BUG
WHOA!
BUG
I'D RATHER OUR APARTMENT NOT HAVE ANY BIG EXPLOSIONS EITHER.
WHY DON'T YOU START GETTING READY FOR BED?
BUG

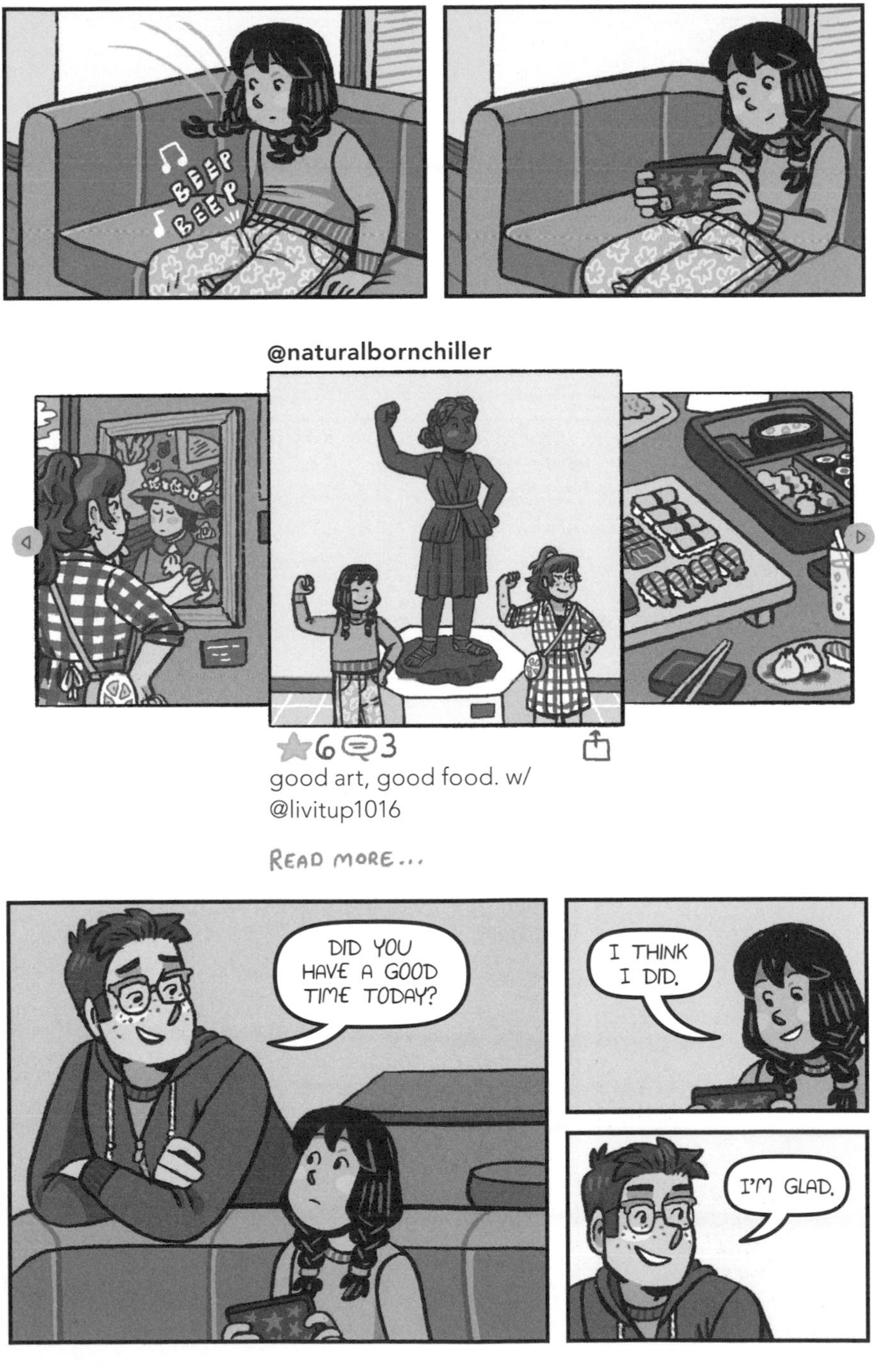
BEEP BEEP
@naturalbornchiller
6 3
good art, good food. w/
@livitup1016
READ MORE...
DID YOU HAVE A GOOD TIME TODAY?
I THINK I DID.
I'M GLAD.

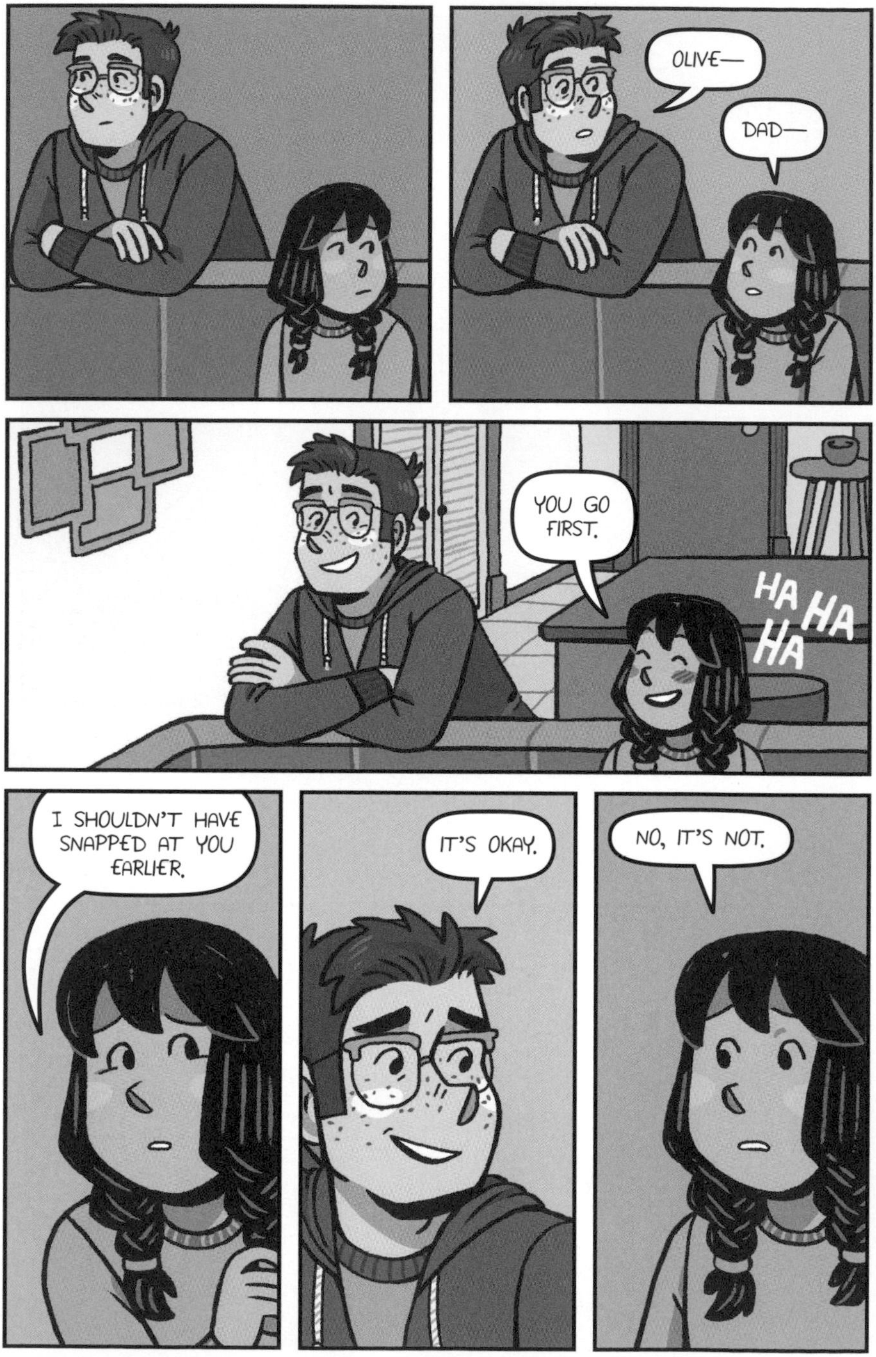
OLIVE—
DAD—
YOU GO FIRST.
HA HA HA
I SHOULDN'T HAVE SNAPPED AT YOU EARLIER.
IT'S OKAY.
NO, IT'S NOT.

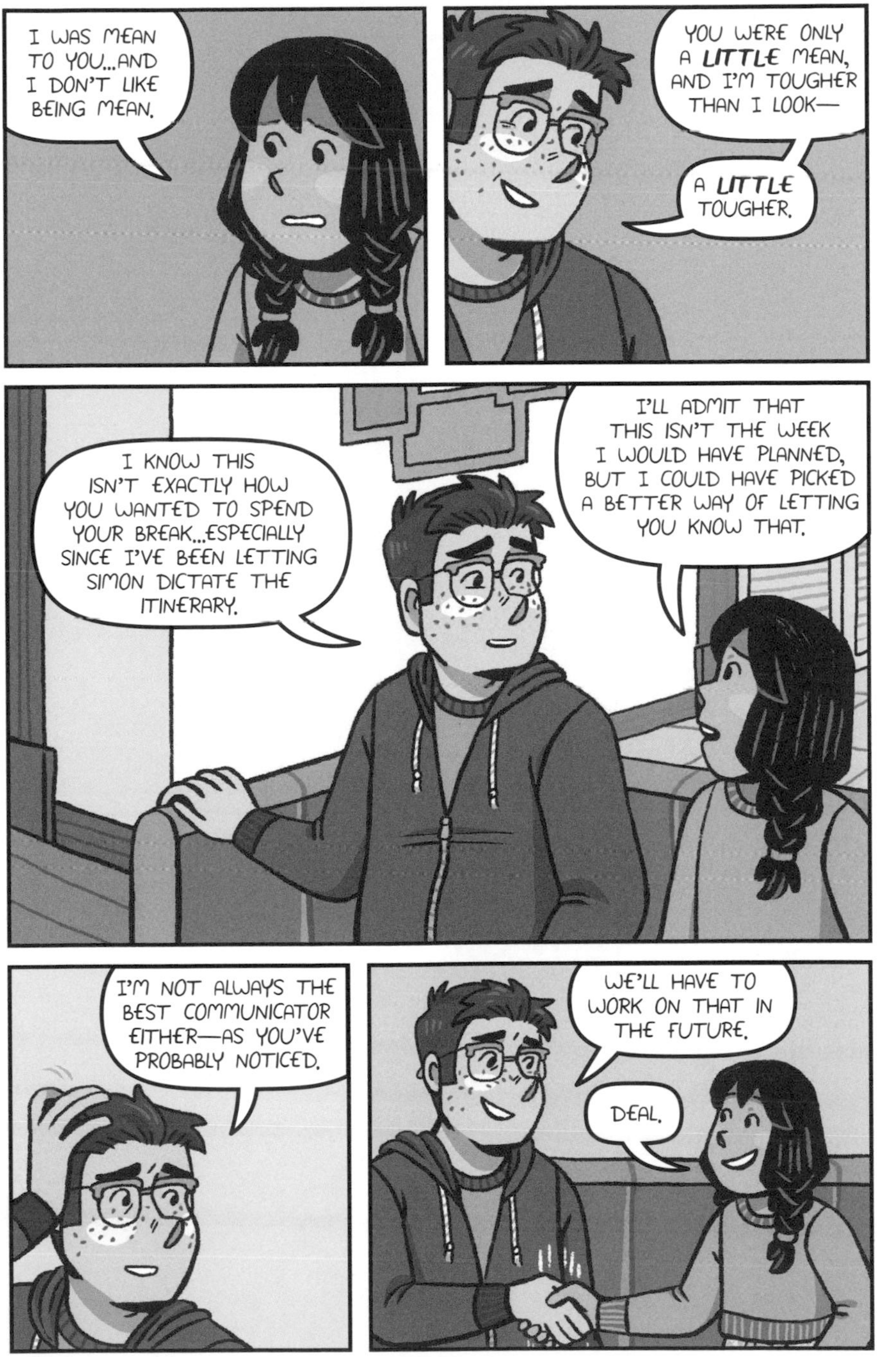
I WAS MEAN TO YOU...AND I DON'T LIKE BEING MEAN.
YOU WERE ONLY A **LITTLE** MEAN, AND I'M TOUGHER THAN I LOOK—
A **LITTLE** TOUGHER.
I KNOW THIS ISN'T EXACTLY HOW YOU WANTED TO SPEND YOUR BREAK...ESPECIALLY SINCE I'VE BEEN LETTING SIMON DICTATE THE ITINERARY.
I'LL ADMIT THAT THIS ISN'T THE WEEK I WOULD HAVE PLANNED, BUT I COULD HAVE PICKED A BETTER WAY OF LETTING YOU KNOW THAT.
I'M NOT ALWAYS THE BEST COMMUNICATOR EITHER—AS YOU'VE PROBABLY NOTICED.
WE'LL HAVE TO WORK ON THAT IN THE FUTURE.
DEAL.

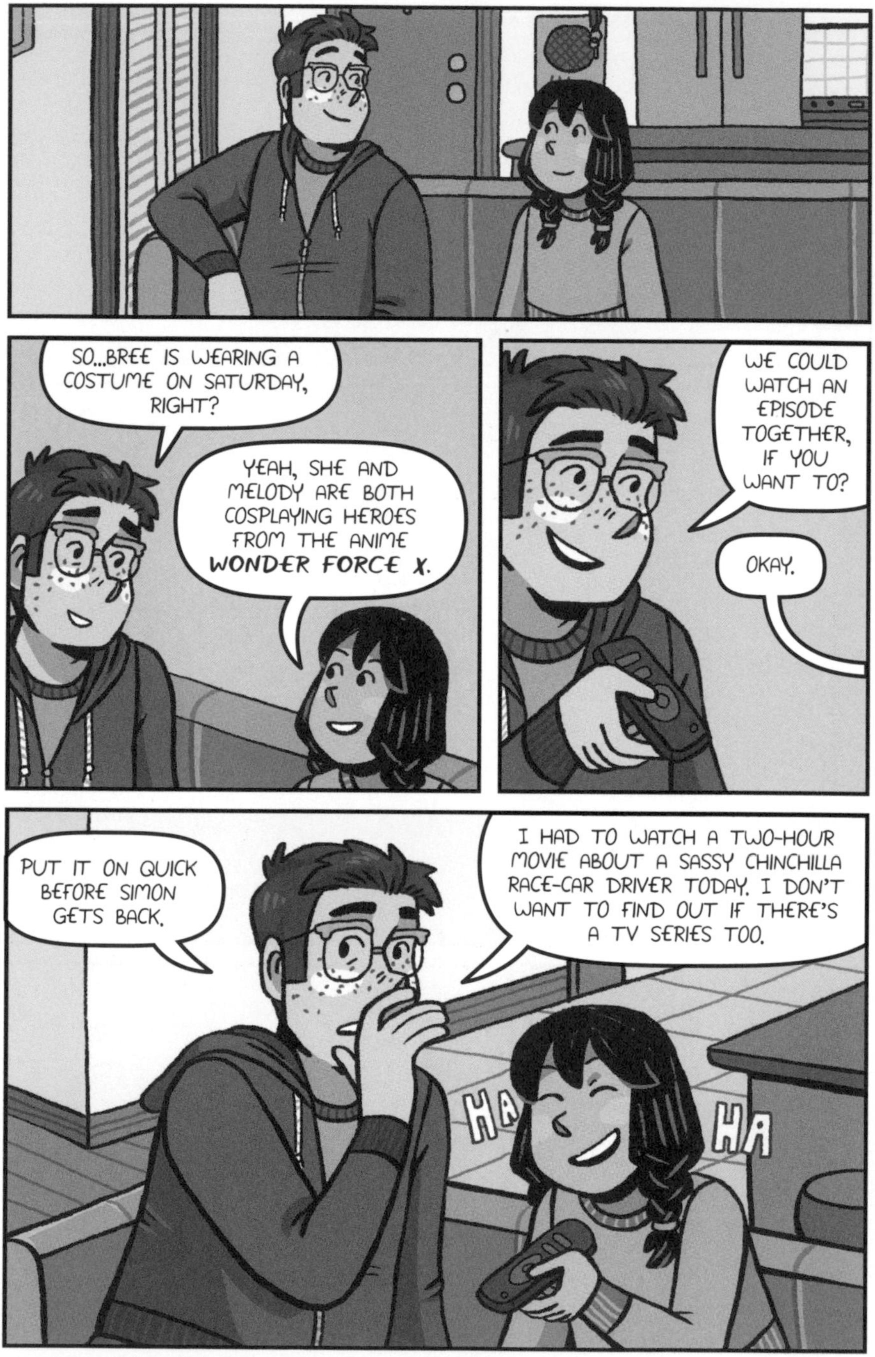
SO...BREE IS WEARING A COSTUME ON SATURDAY, RIGHT?
YEAH, SHE AND MELODY ARE BOTH COSPLAYING HEROES FROM THE ANIME **WONDER FORCE X**.
WE COULD WATCH AN EPISODE TOGETHER, IF YOU WANT TO?
OKAY.
PUT IT ON QUICK BEFORE SIMON GETS BACK.
I HAD TO WATCH A TWO-HOUR MOVIE ABOUT A SASSY CHINCHILLA RACE-CAR DRIVER TODAY. I DON'T WANT TO FIND OUT IF THERE'S A TV SERIES TOO.
HA
HA

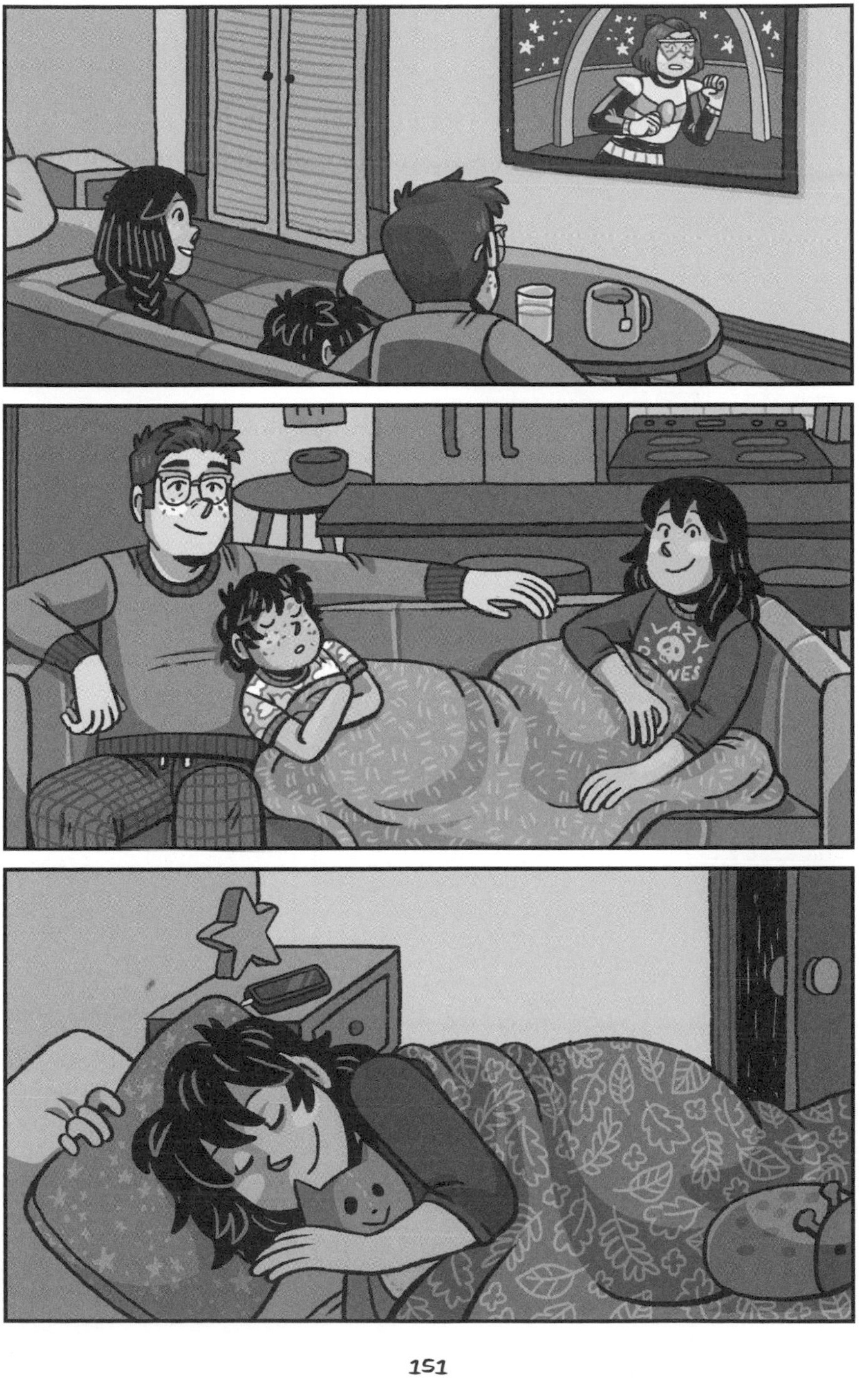
LAZY

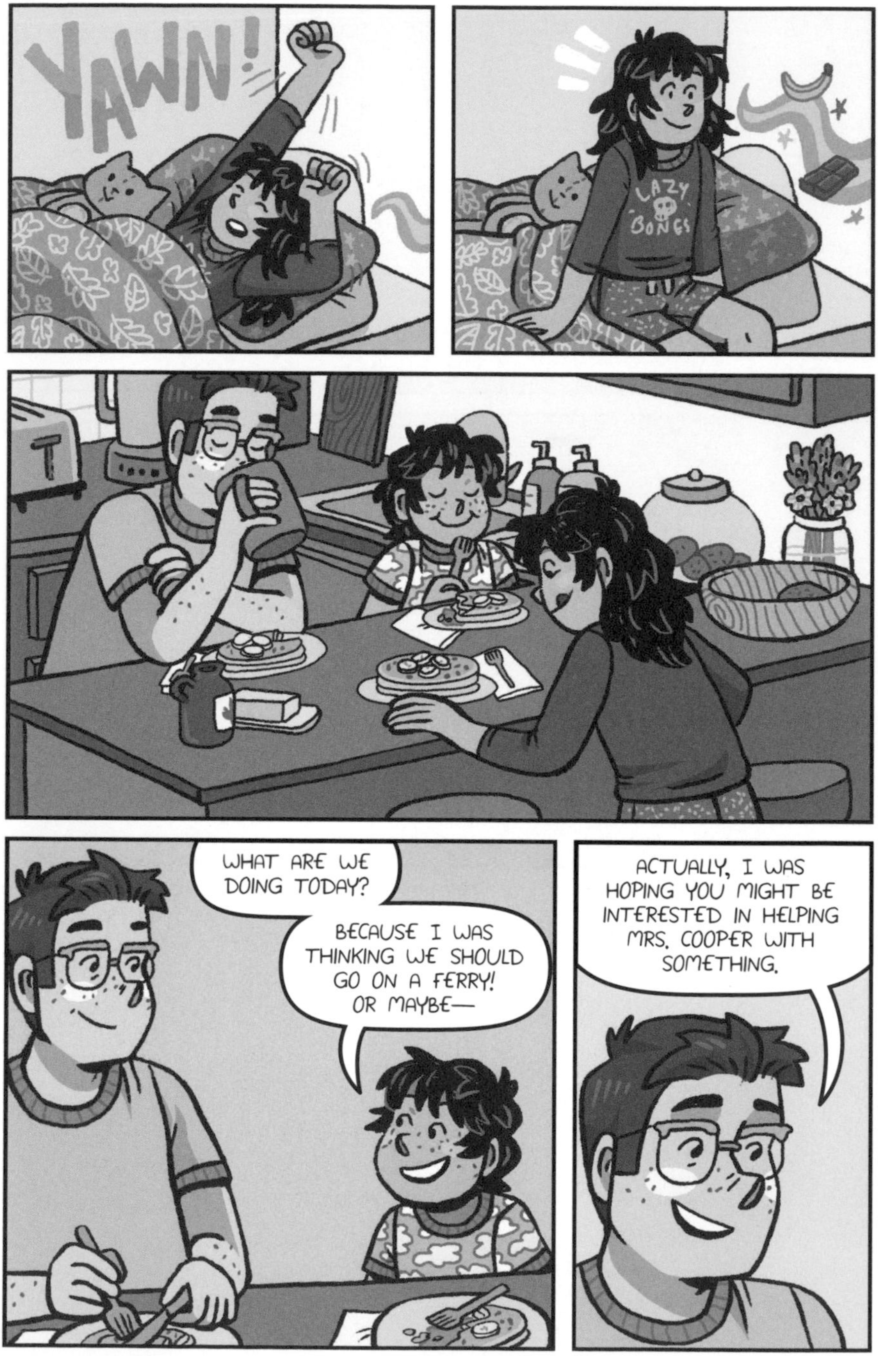
YAWN!
LAZY BONES
WHAT ARE WE DOING TODAY?
BECAUSE I WAS THINKING WE SHOULD GO ON A FERRY! OR MAYBE—
ACTUALLY, I WAS HOPING YOU MIGHT BE INTERESTED IN HELPING MRS. COOPER WITH SOMETHING.

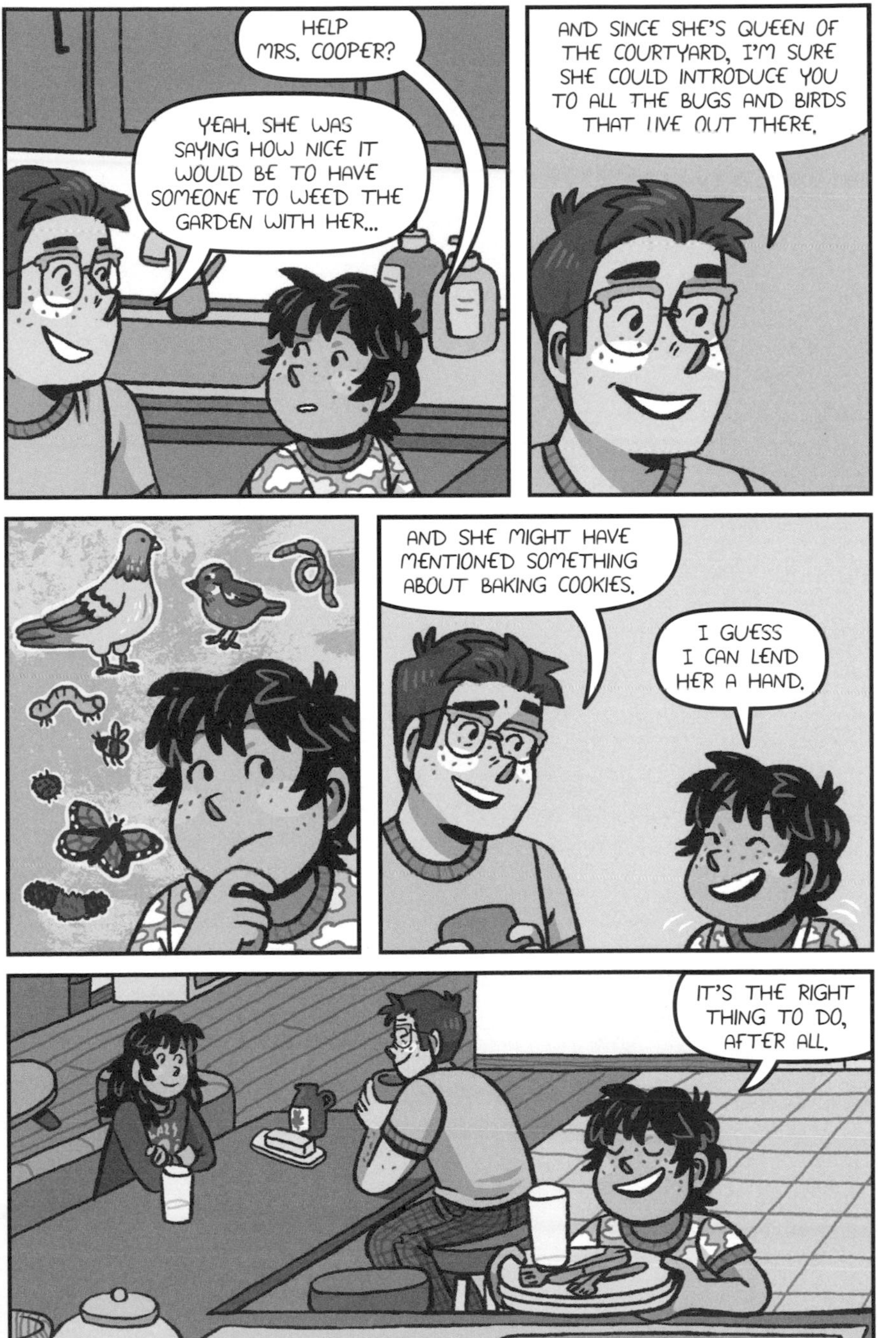
HELP MRS. COOPER?
YEAH. SHE WAS SAYING HOW NICE IT WOULD BE TO HAVE SOMEONE TO WEED THE GARDEN WITH HER...
AND SINCE SHE'S QUEEN OF THE COURTYARD, I'M SURE SHE COULD INTRODUCE YOU TO ALL THE BUGS AND BIRDS THAT LIVE OUT THERE.
AND SHE MIGHT HAVE MENTIONED SOMETHING ABOUT BAKING COOKIES.
I GUESS I CAN LEND HER A HAND.
IT'S THE RIGHT THING TO DO, AFTER ALL.

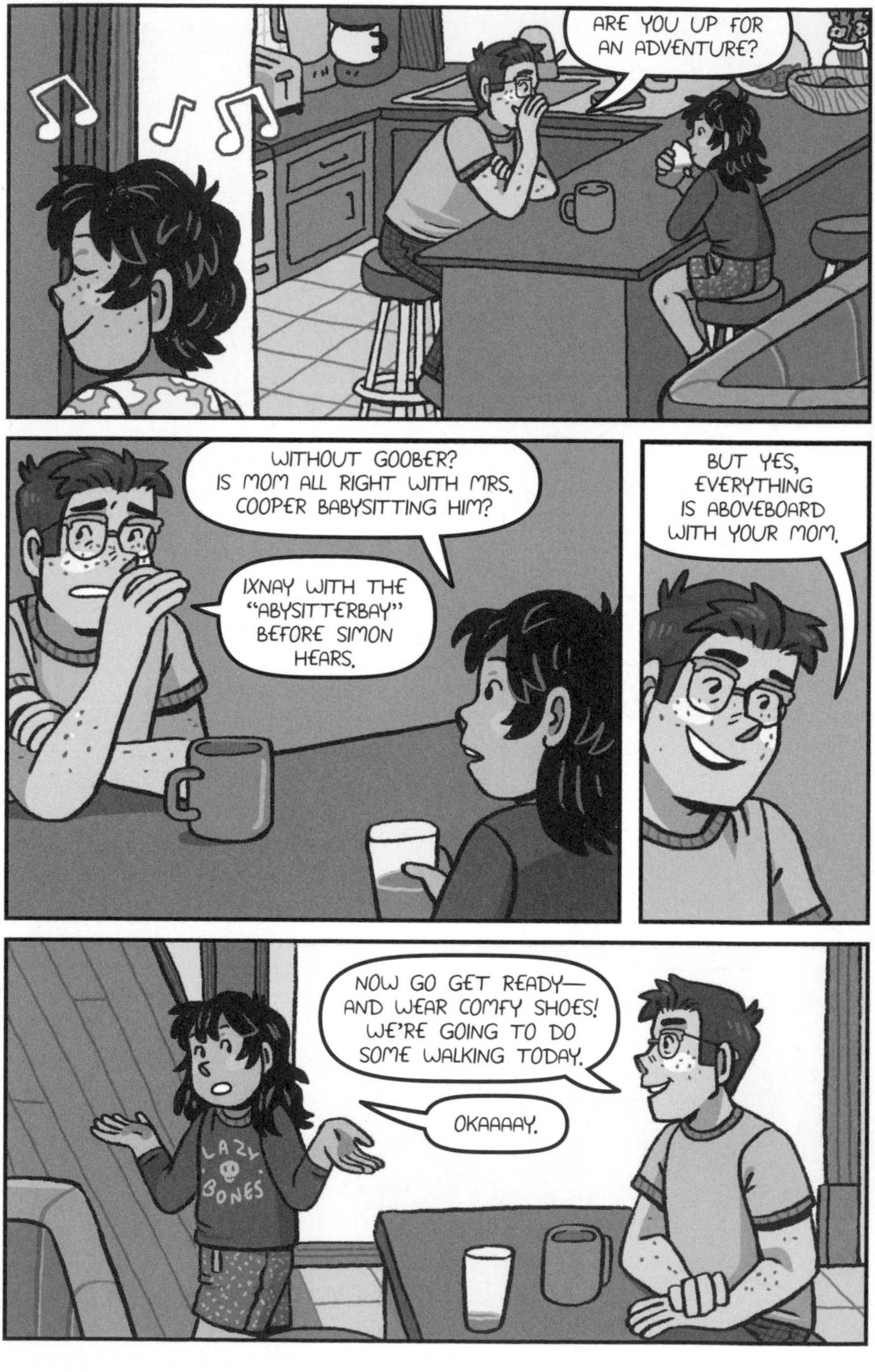
ARE YOU UP FOR AN ADVENTURE?
WITHOUT GOOBER? IS MOM ALL RIGHT WITH MRS. COOPER BABYSITTING HIM?
IXNAY WITH THE "ABYSITTERBAY" BEFORE SIMON HEARS.
BUT YES, EVERYTHING IS ABOVEBOARD WITH YOUR MOM.
NOW GO GET READY— AND WEAR COMFY SHOES! WE'RE GOING TO DO SOME WALKING TODAY.
OKAAAAY.
LAZY BONES

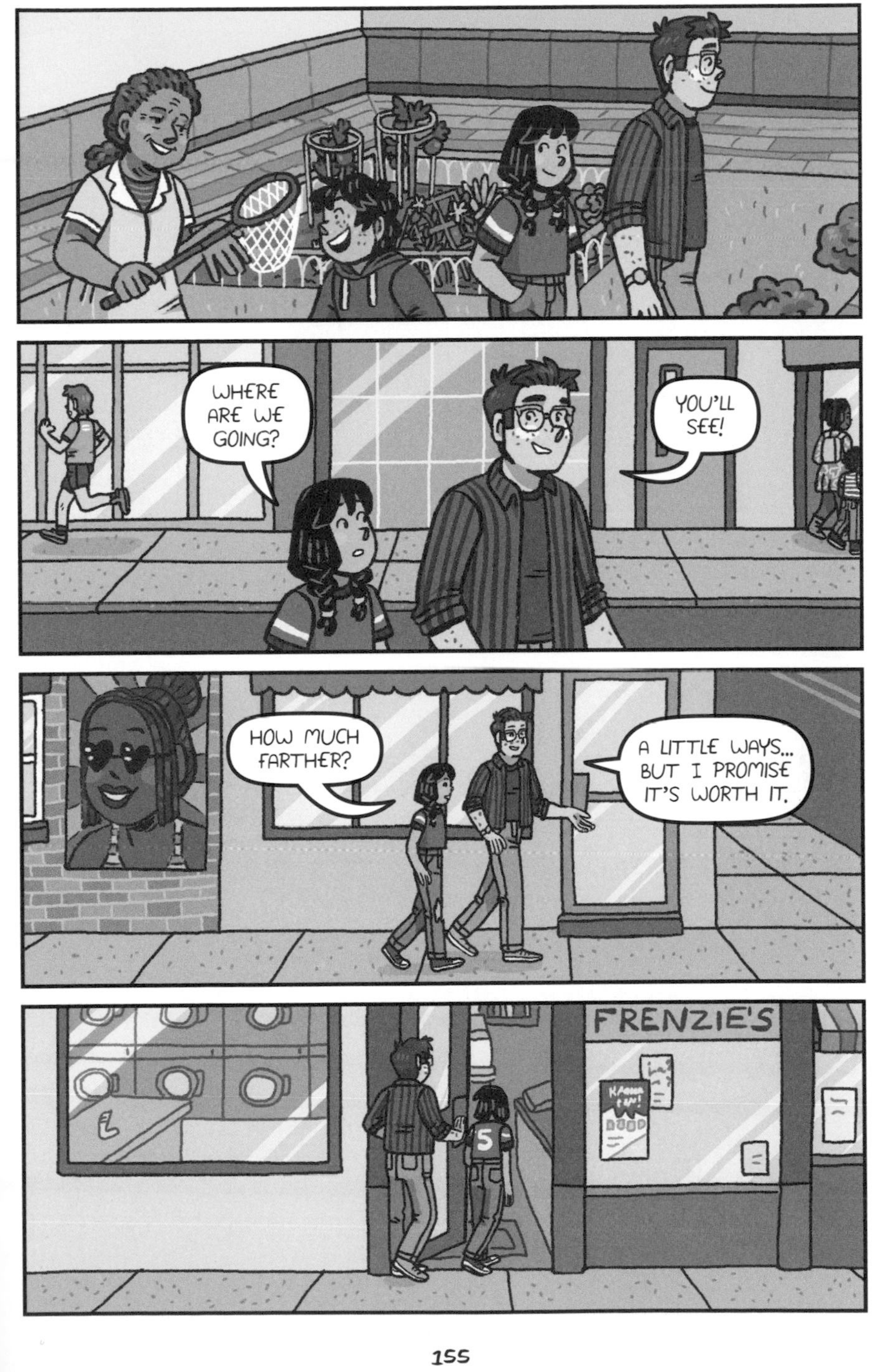
WHERE ARE WE GOING?
YOU'LL SEE!
HOW MUCH FARTHER?
A LITTLE WAYS... BUT I PROMISE IT'S WORTH IT.
FRENZIE'S

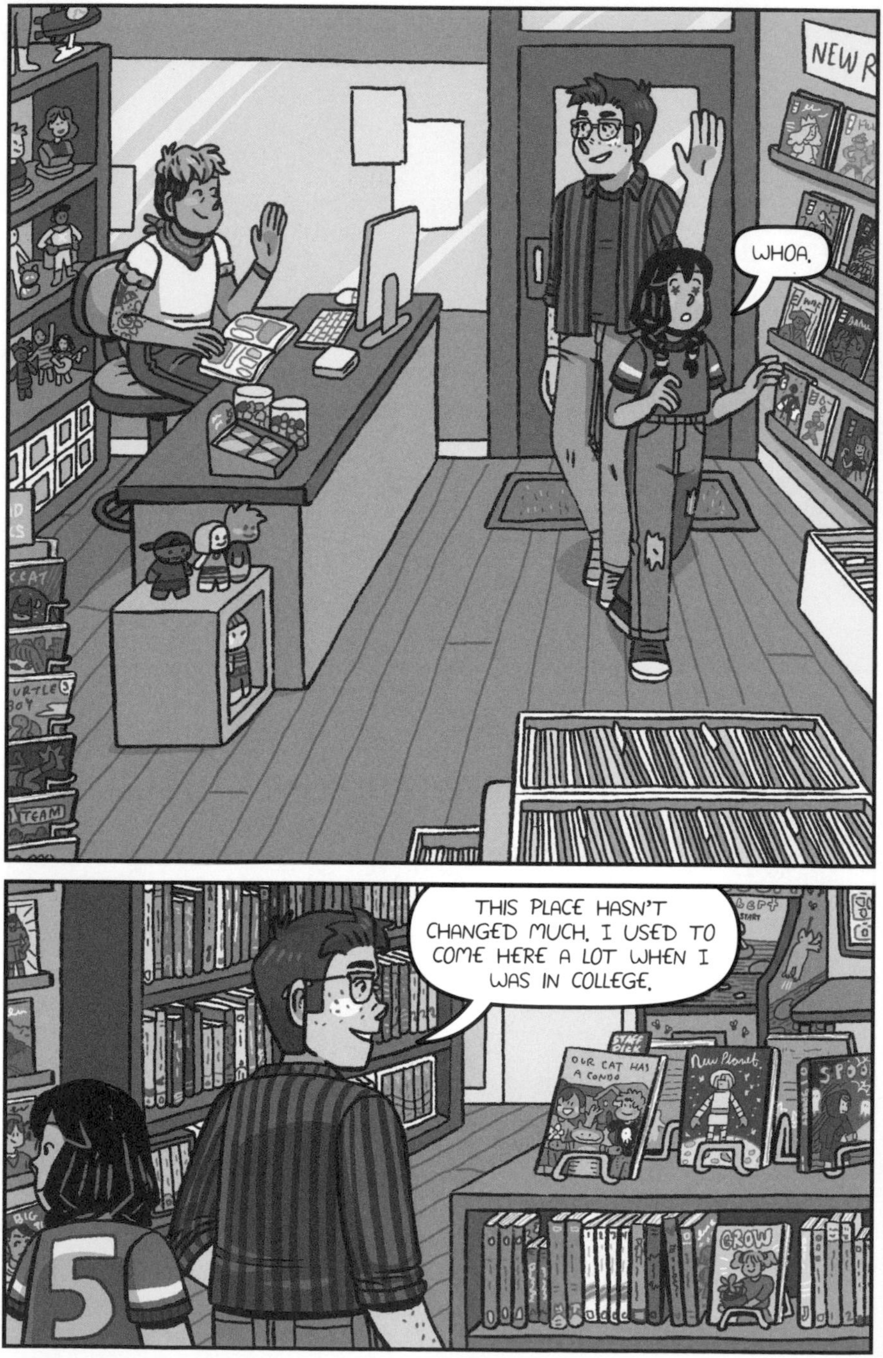
WHOA.
THIS PLACE HASN'T CHANGED MUCH. I USED TO COME HERE A LOT WHEN I WAS IN COLLEGE.
OUR CAT HAS A CONDO
New Planet
GROW

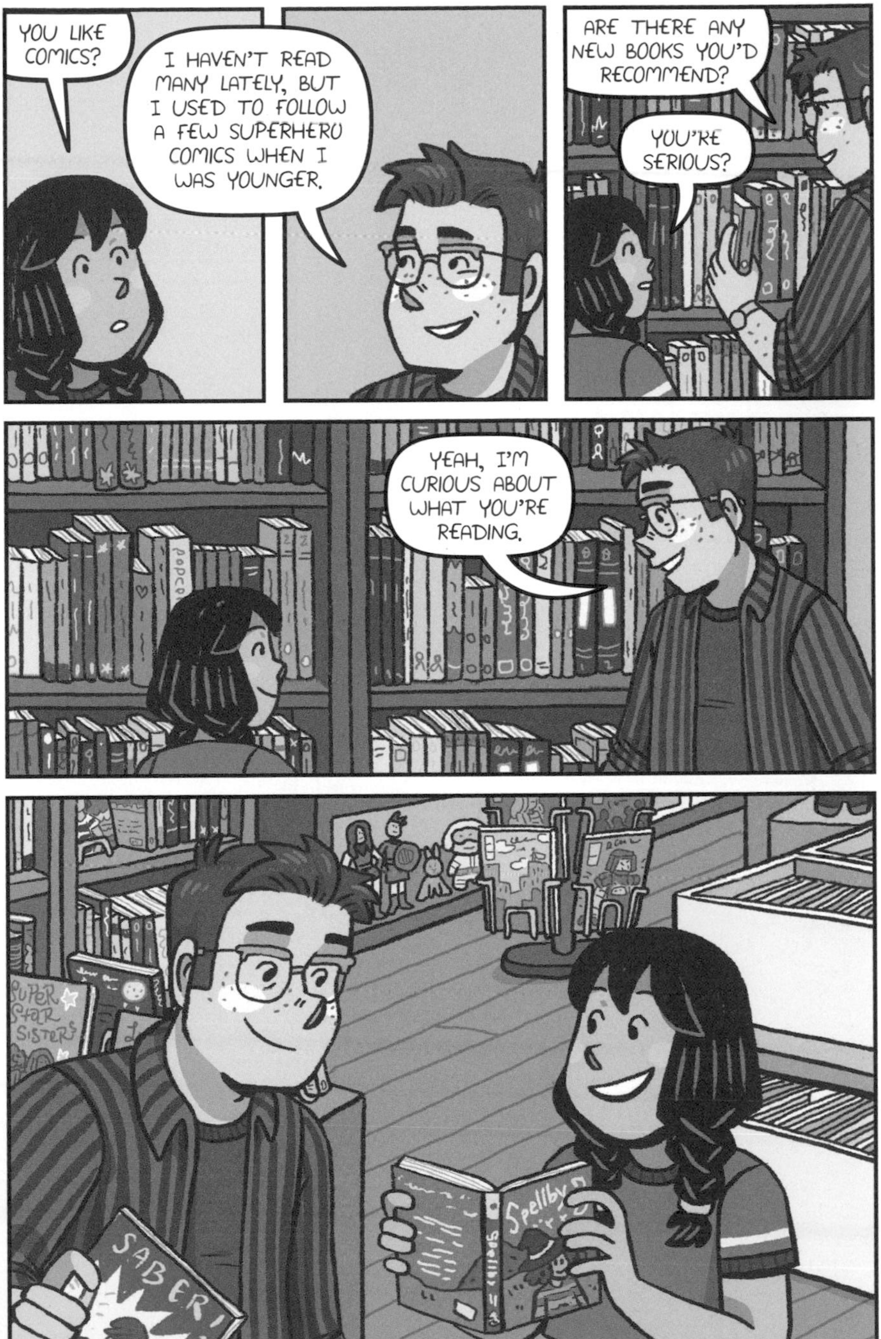
YOU LIKE COMICS?
I HAVEN'T READ MANY LATELY, BUT I USED TO FOLLOW A FEW SUPERHERO COMICS WHEN I WAS YOUNGER.
ARE THERE ANY NEW BOOKS YOU'D RECOMMEND?
YOU'RE SERIOUS?
YEAH, I'M CURIOUS ABOUT WHAT YOU'RE READING.
SUPER STAR SISTERS
SABER!

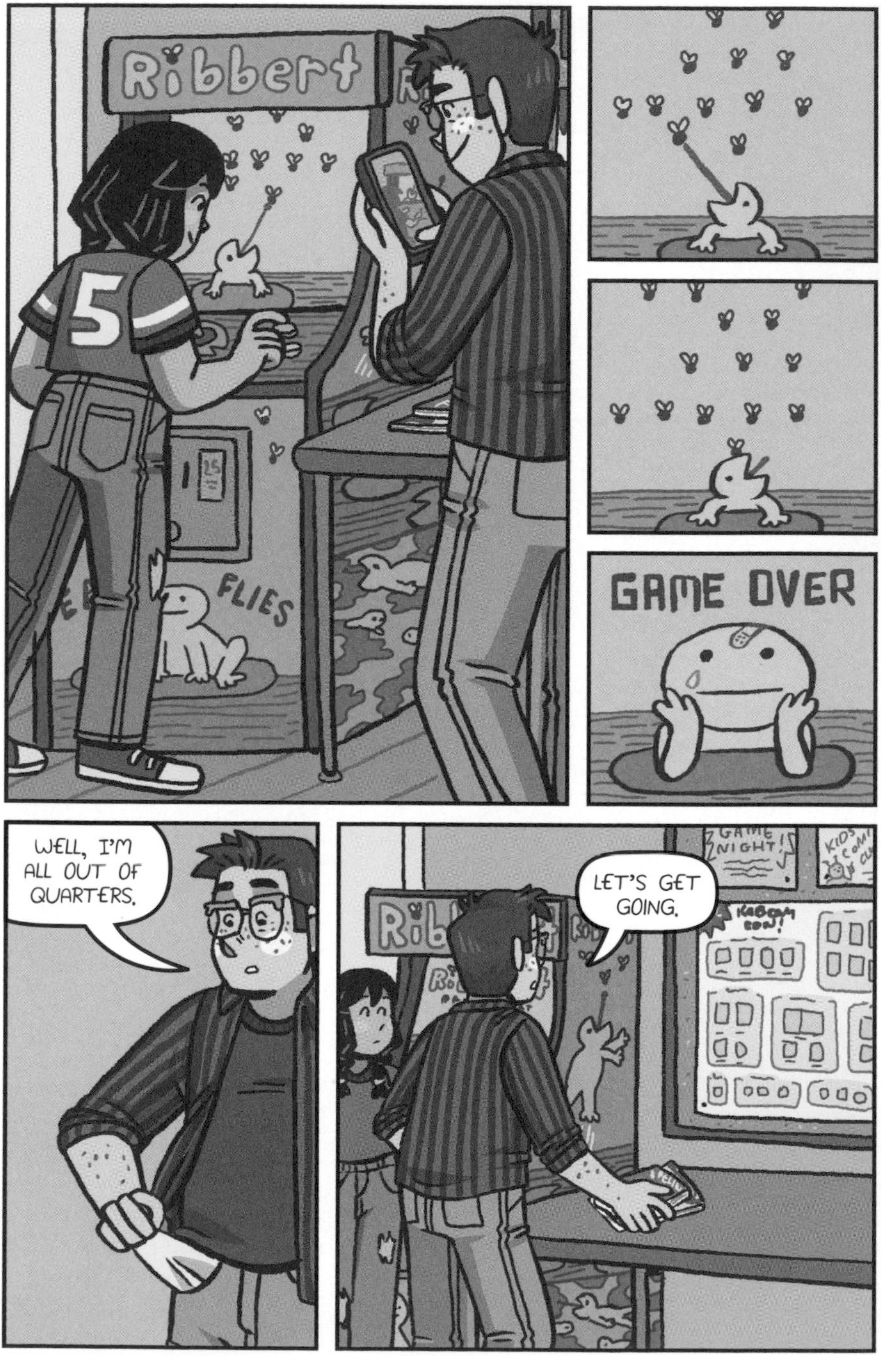
Ribbert
FLIES
GAME OVER
WELL, I'M ALL OUT OF QUARTERS.
LET'S GET GOING.
GAME NIGHT!

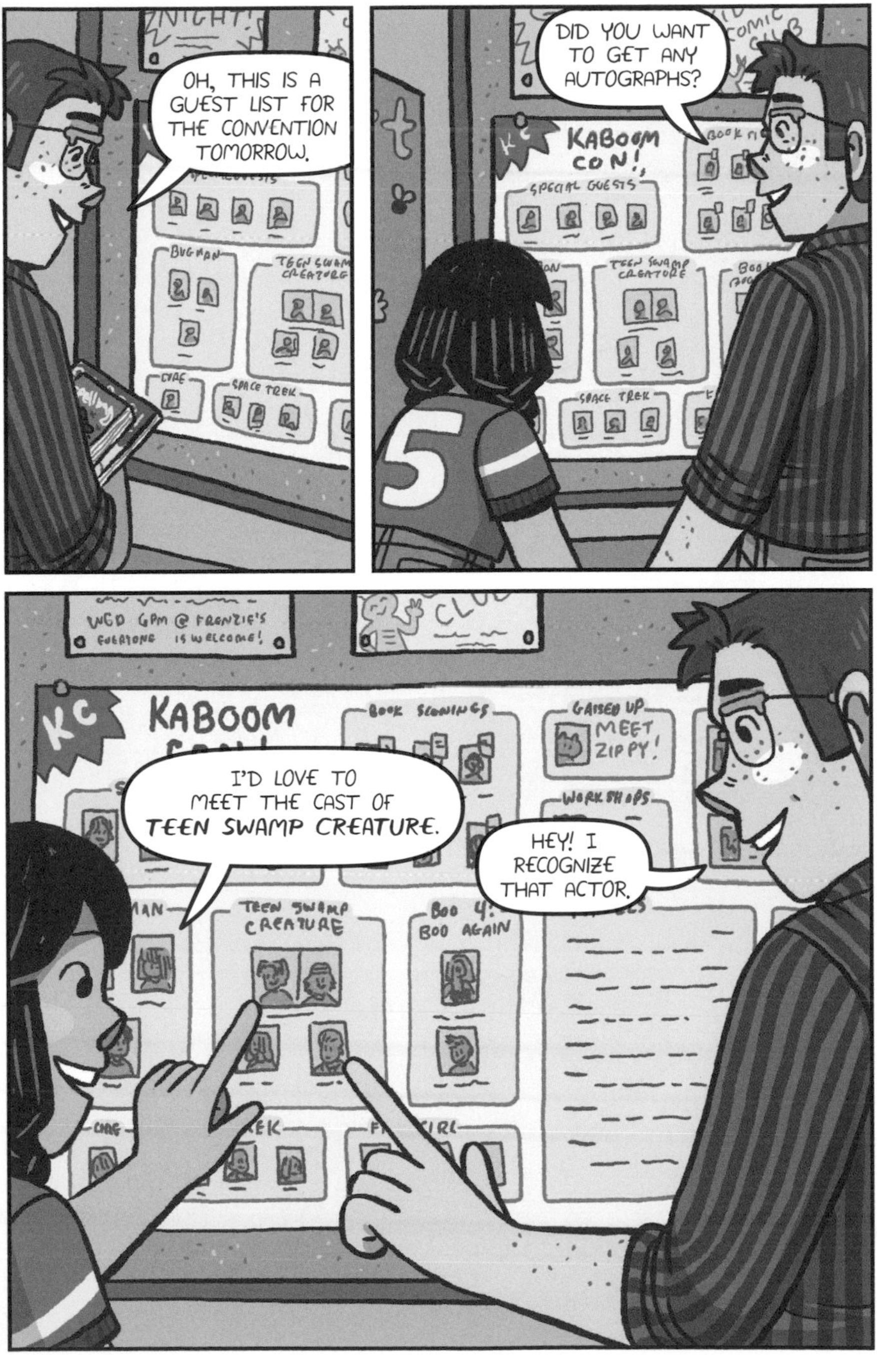
OH, THIS IS A GUEST LIST FOR THE CONVENTION TOMORROW.
DID YOU WANT TO GET ANY AUTOGRAPHS?
KABOOM CON!
SPECIAL GUESTS
TEEN SWAMP CREATURE
SPACE TREK
I'D LOVE TO MEET THE CAST OF TEEN SWAMP CREATURE.
HEY! I RECOGNIZE THAT ACTOR.
BOOK SIGNINGS
GAISED UP
MEET ZIPPY!
WORKSHOPS
BOO 4: BOO AGAIN

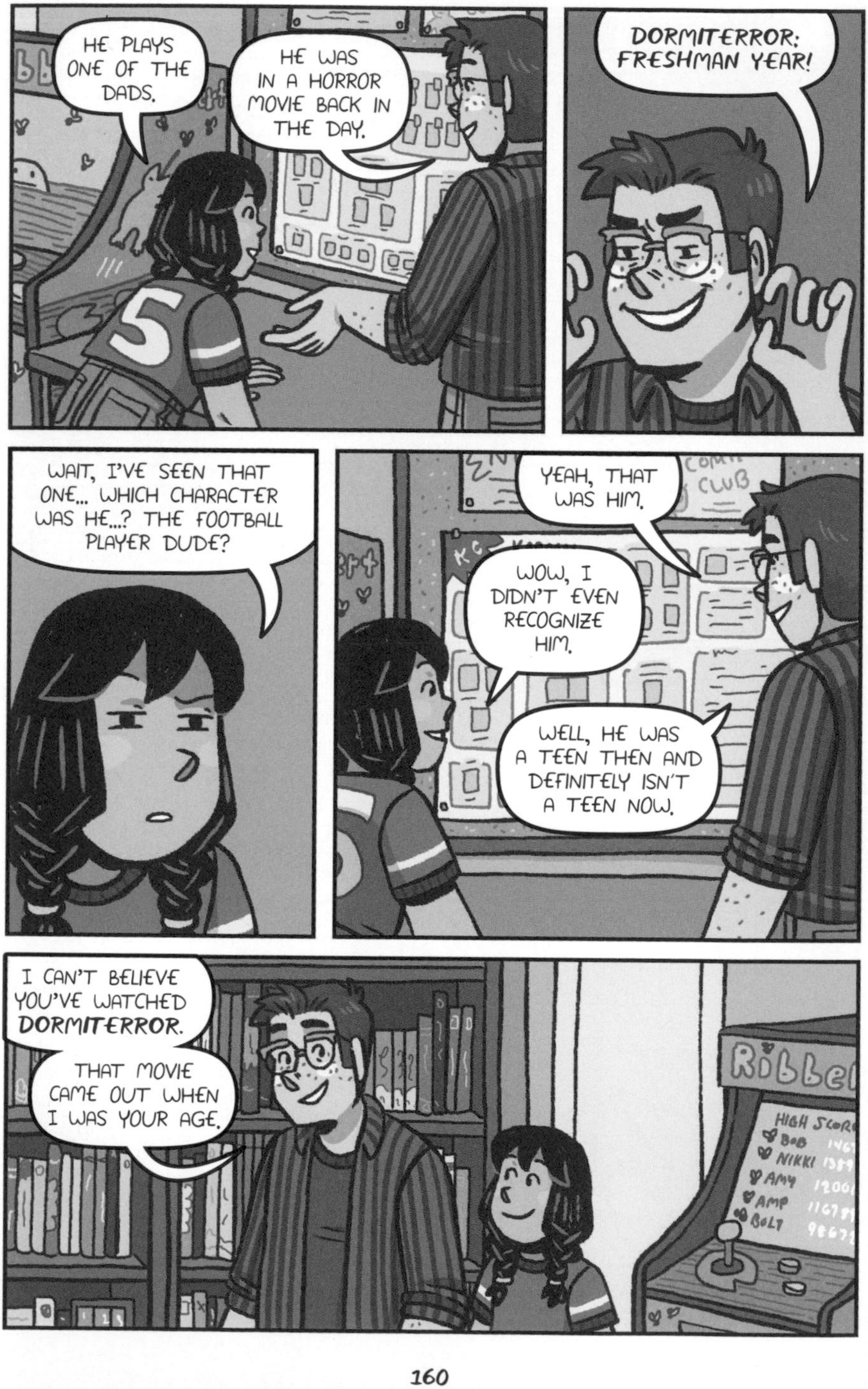
HE PLAYS ONE OF THE DADS.
HE WAS IN A HORROR MOVIE BACK IN THE DAY.
DORMITERROR: FRESHMAN YEAR!
WAIT, I'VE SEEN THAT ONE... WHICH CHARACTER WAS HE...? THE FOOTBALL PLAYER DUDE?
YEAH, THAT WAS HIM.
WOW, I DIDN'T EVEN RECOGNIZE HIM.
WELL, HE WAS A TEEN THEN AND DEFINITELY ISN'T A TEEN NOW.
I CAN'T BELIEVE YOU'VE WATCHED **DORMITERROR**.
THAT MOVIE CAME OUT WHEN I WAS YOUR AGE.
HIGH SCORE
BOB
NIKKI
AMY
AMP
BOLT

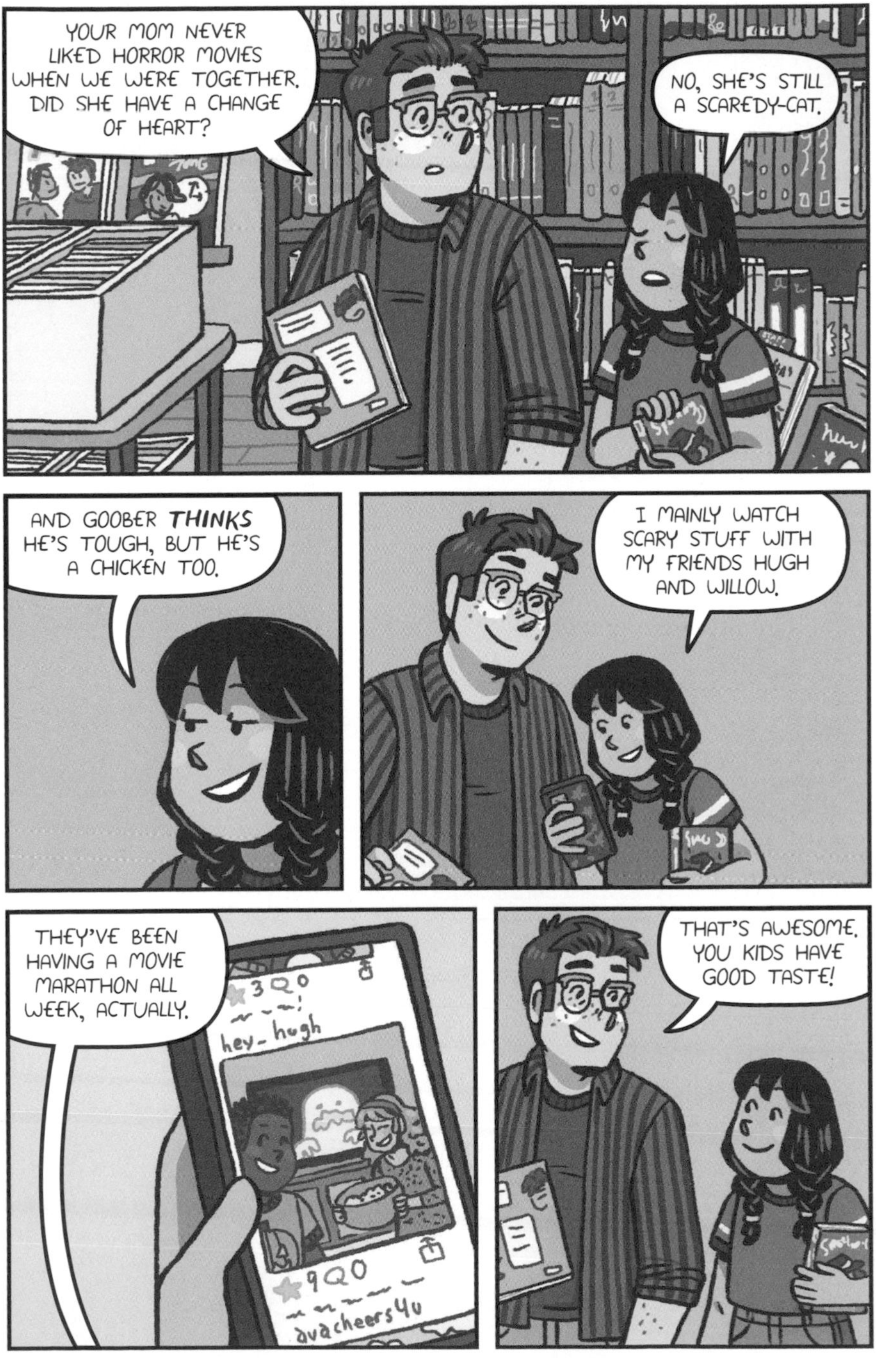
YOUR MOM NEVER LIKED HORROR MOVIES WHEN WE WERE TOGETHER. DID SHE HAVE A CHANGE OF HEART?
NO, SHE'S STILL A SCAREDY-CAT.
AND GOOBER **THINKS** HE'S TOUGH, BUT HE'S A CHICKEN TOO.
I MAINLY WATCH SCARY STUFF WITH MY FRIENDS HUGH AND WILLOW.
THEY'VE BEEN HAVING A MOVIE MARATHON ALL WEEK, ACTUALLY.
hey_hugh
avacheers4u
THAT'S AWESOME. YOU KIDS HAVE GOOD TASTE!

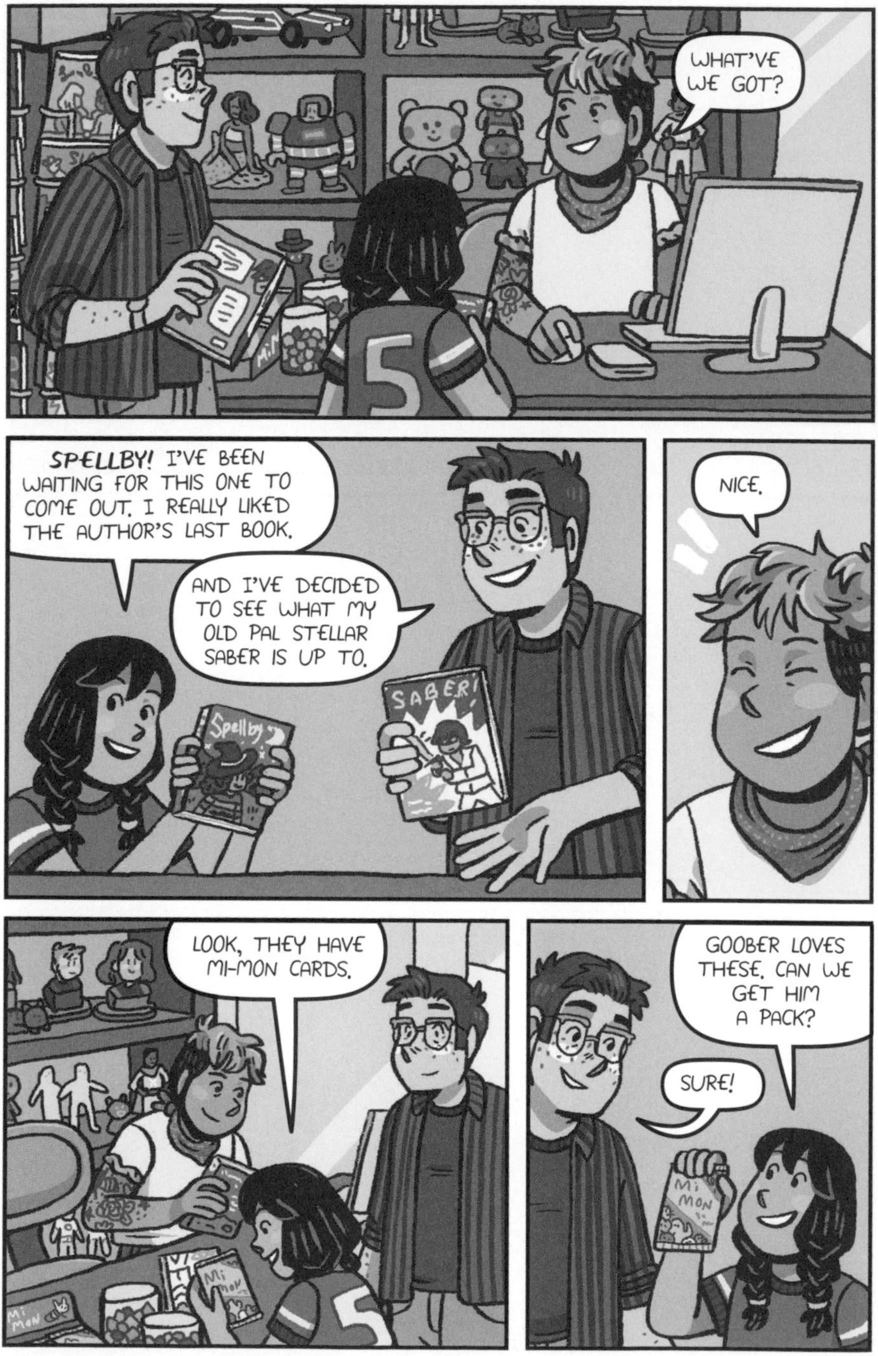
WHAT'VE WE GOT?
SPELLBY! I'VE BEEN WAITING FOR THIS ONE TO COME OUT. I REALLY LIKED THE AUTHOR'S LAST BOOK.
AND I'VE DECIDED TO SEE WHAT MY OLD PAL STELLAR SABER IS UP TO.
Spellby
SABER!
NICE.
LOOK, THEY HAVE MI-MON CARDS.
GOOBER LOVES THESE. CAN WE GET HIM A PACK?
SURE!
Mi MON

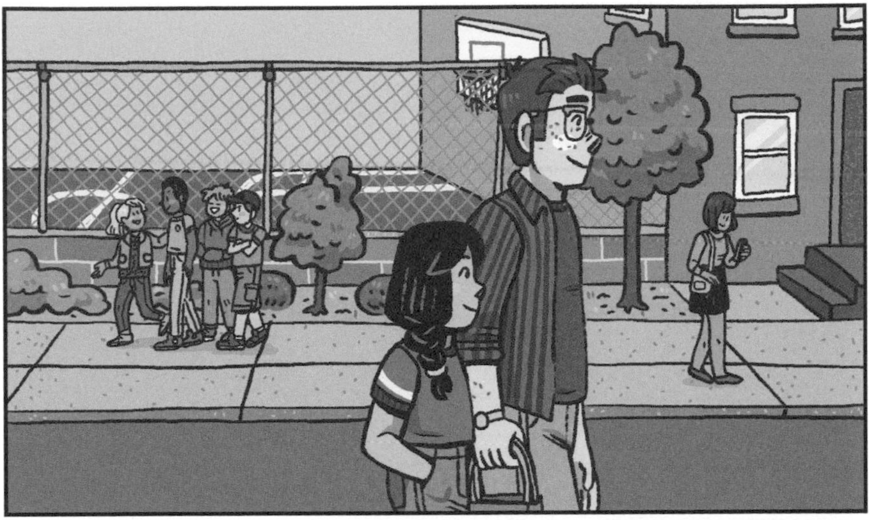

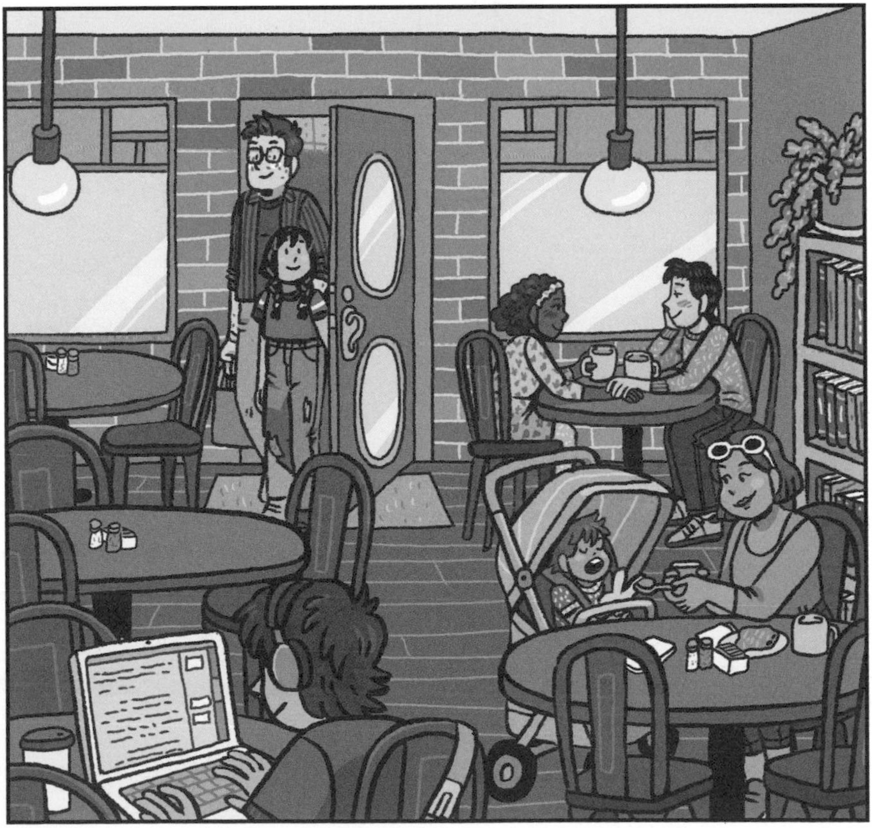

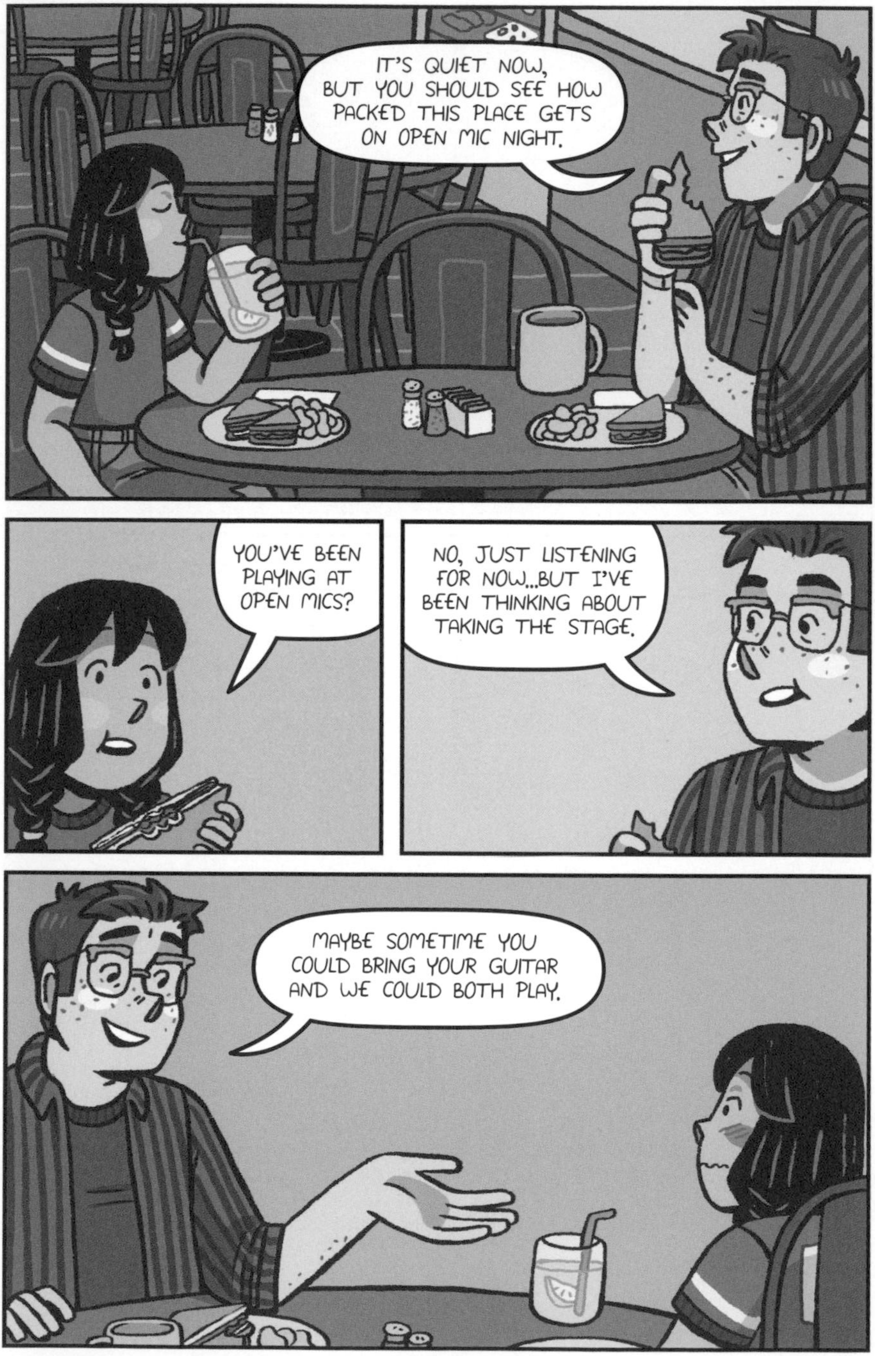
IT'S QUIET NOW, BUT YOU SHOULD SEE HOW PACKED THIS PLACE GETS ON OPEN MIC NIGHT.
YOU'VE BEEN PLAYING AT OPEN MICS?
NO, JUST LISTENING FOR NOW...BUT I'VE BEEN THINKING ABOUT TAKING THE STAGE.
MAYBE SOMETIME YOU COULD BRING YOUR GUITAR AND WE COULD BOTH PLAY.

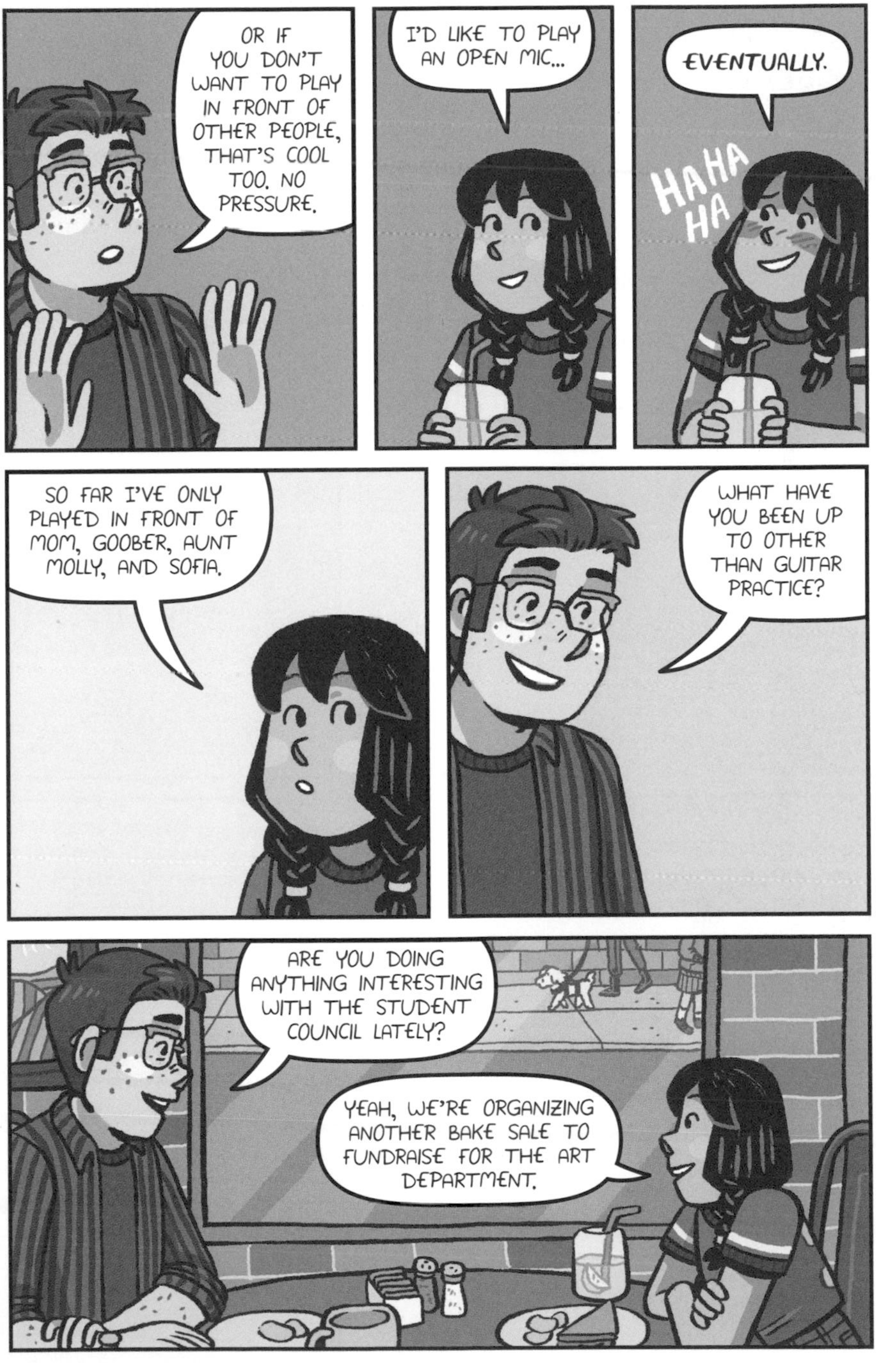
OR IF YOU DON'T WANT TO PLAY IN FRONT OF OTHER PEOPLE, THAT'S COOL TOO. NO PRESSURE.
I'D LIKE TO PLAY AN OPEN MIC...
EVENTUALLY.
HAHA HA
SO FAR I'VE ONLY PLAYED IN FRONT OF MOM, GOOBER, AUNT MOLLY, AND SOFIA.
WHAT HAVE YOU BEEN UP TO OTHER THAN GUITAR PRACTICE?
ARE YOU DOING ANYTHING INTERESTING WITH THE STUDENT COUNCIL LATELY?
YEAH, WE'RE ORGANIZING ANOTHER BAKE SALE TO FUNDRAISE FOR THE ART DEPARTMENT.

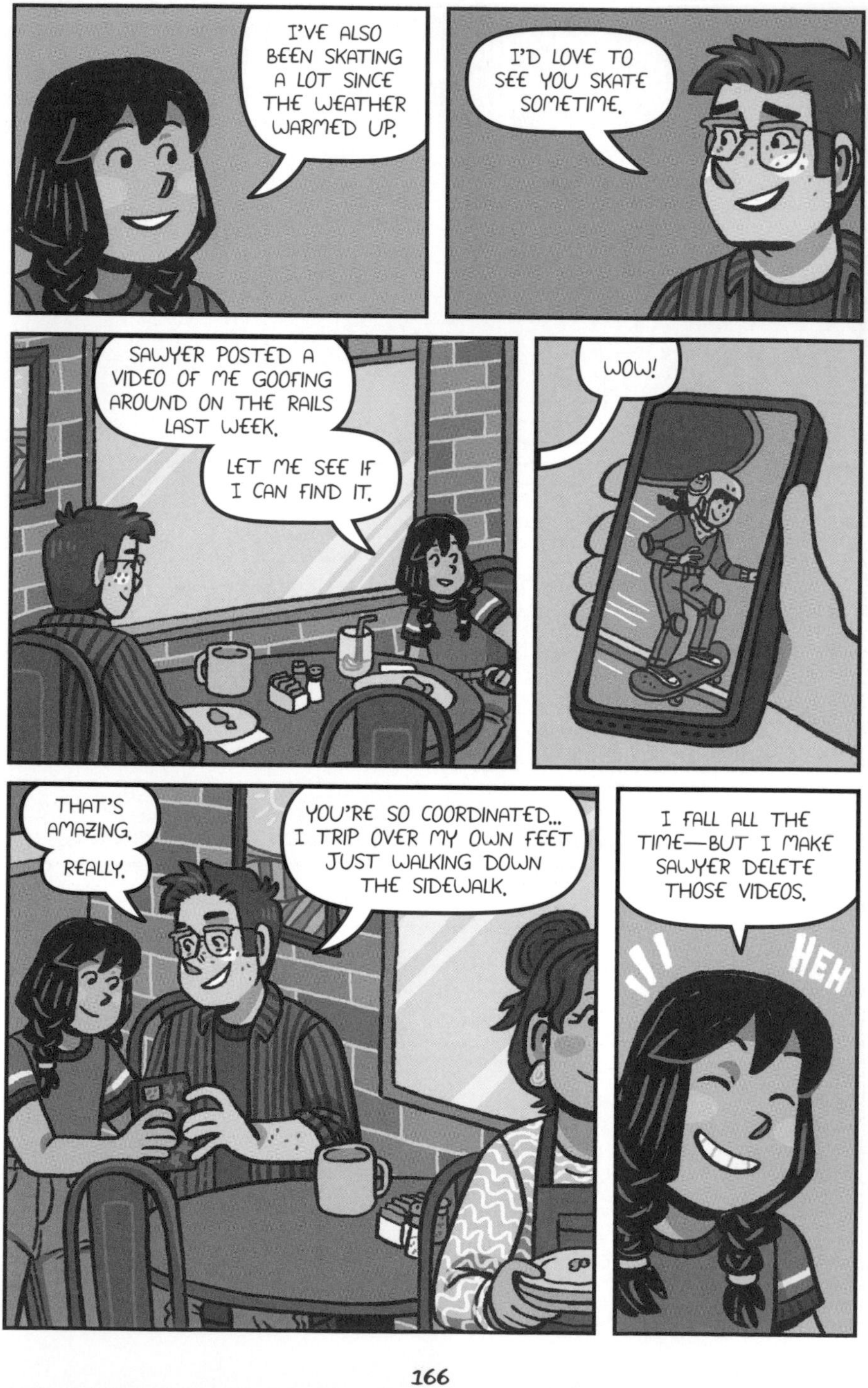
I'VE ALSO BEEN SKATING A LOT SINCE THE WEATHER WARMED UP.
I'D LOVE TO SEE YOU SKATE SOMETIME.
SAWYER POSTED A VIDEO OF ME GOOFING AROUND ON THE RAILS LAST WEEK.
LET ME SEE IF I CAN FIND IT.
WOW!
THAT'S AMAZING.
REALLY.
YOU'RE SO COORDINATED... I TRIP OVER MY OWN FEET JUST WALKING DOWN THE SIDEWALK.
I FALL ALL THE TIME—BUT I MAKE SAWYER DELETE THOSE VIDEOS.
HEH

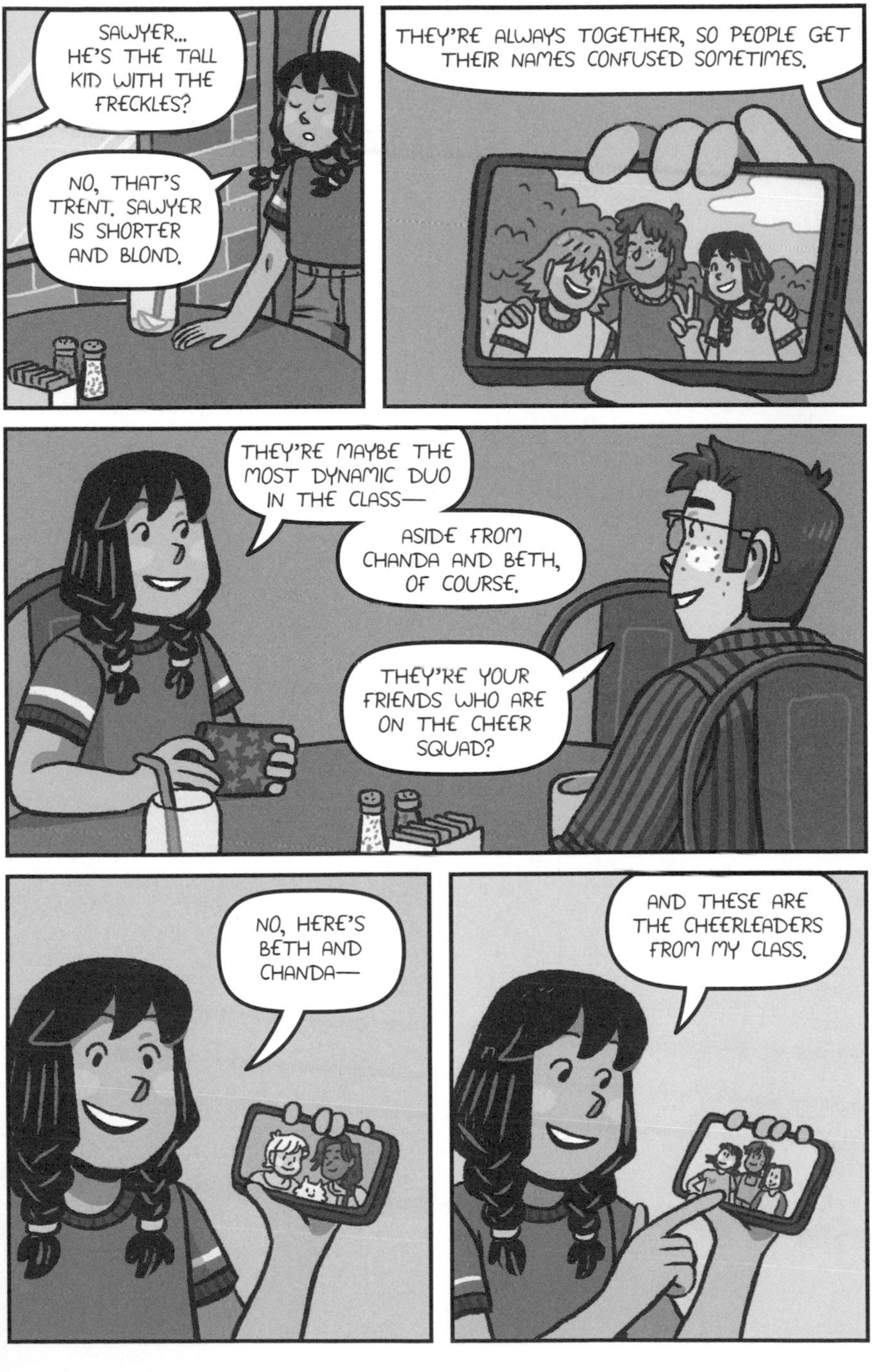
SAWYER... HE'S THE TALL KID WITH THE FRECKLES?
NO, THAT'S TRENT. SAWYER IS SHORTER AND BLOND.
THEY'RE ALWAYS TOGETHER, SO PEOPLE GET THEIR NAMES CONFUSED SOMETIMES.
THEY'RE MAYBE THE MOST DYNAMIC DUO IN THE CLASS—
ASIDE FROM CHANDA AND BETH, OF COURSE.
THEY'RE YOUR FRIENDS WHO ARE ON THE CHEER SQUAD?
NO, HERE'S BETH AND CHANDA—
AND THESE ARE THE CHEERLEADERS FROM MY CLASS.

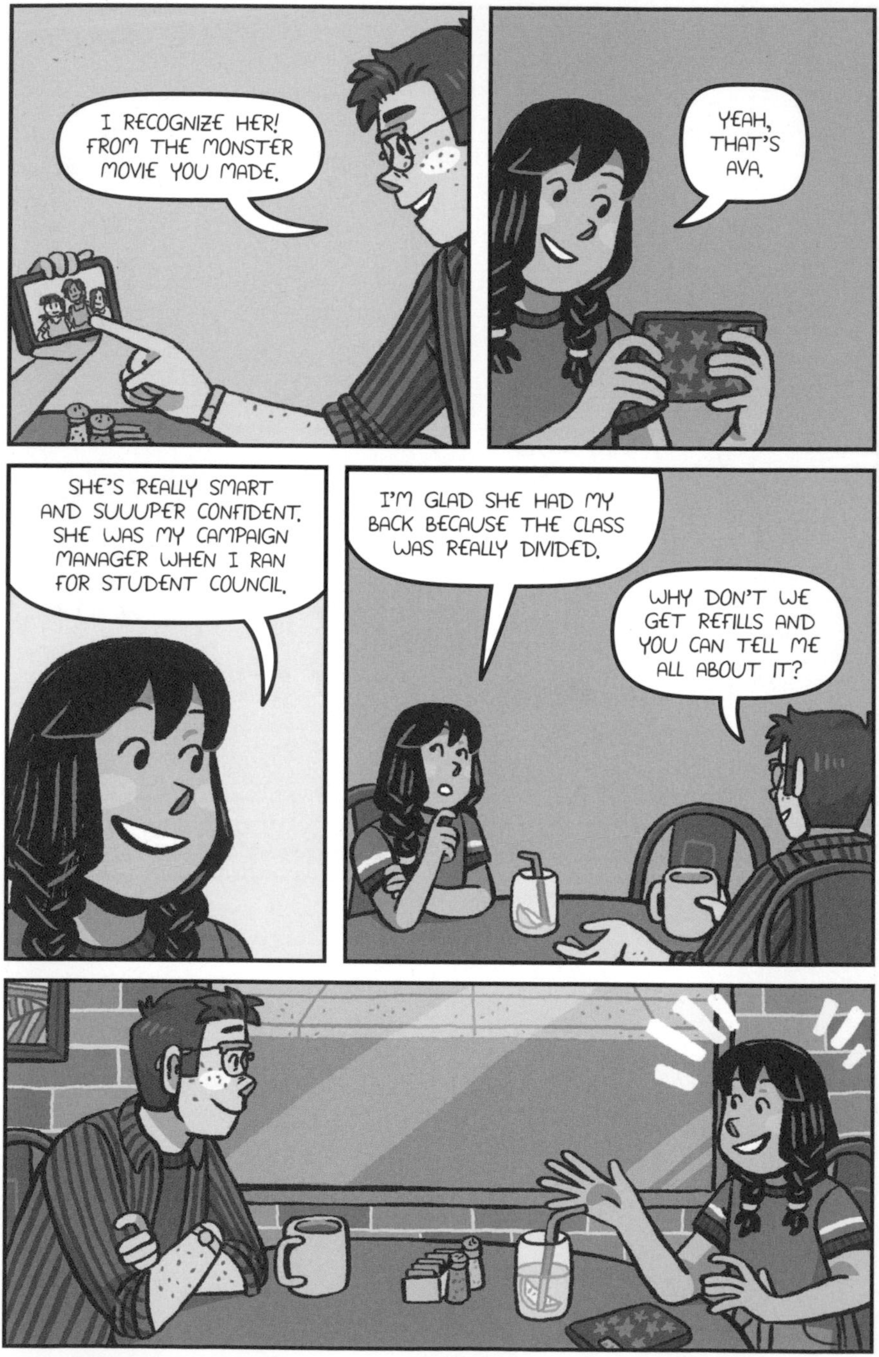
I RECOGNIZE HER! FROM THE MONSTER MOVIE YOU MADE.
YEAH, THAT'S AVA.
SHE'S REALLY SMART AND SUUUPER CONFIDENT. SHE WAS MY CAMPAIGN MANAGER WHEN I RAN FOR STUDENT COUNCIL.
I'M GLAD SHE HAD MY BACK BECAUSE THE CLASS WAS REALLY DIVIDED.
WHY DON'T WE GET REFILLS AND YOU CAN TELL ME ALL ABOUT IT?

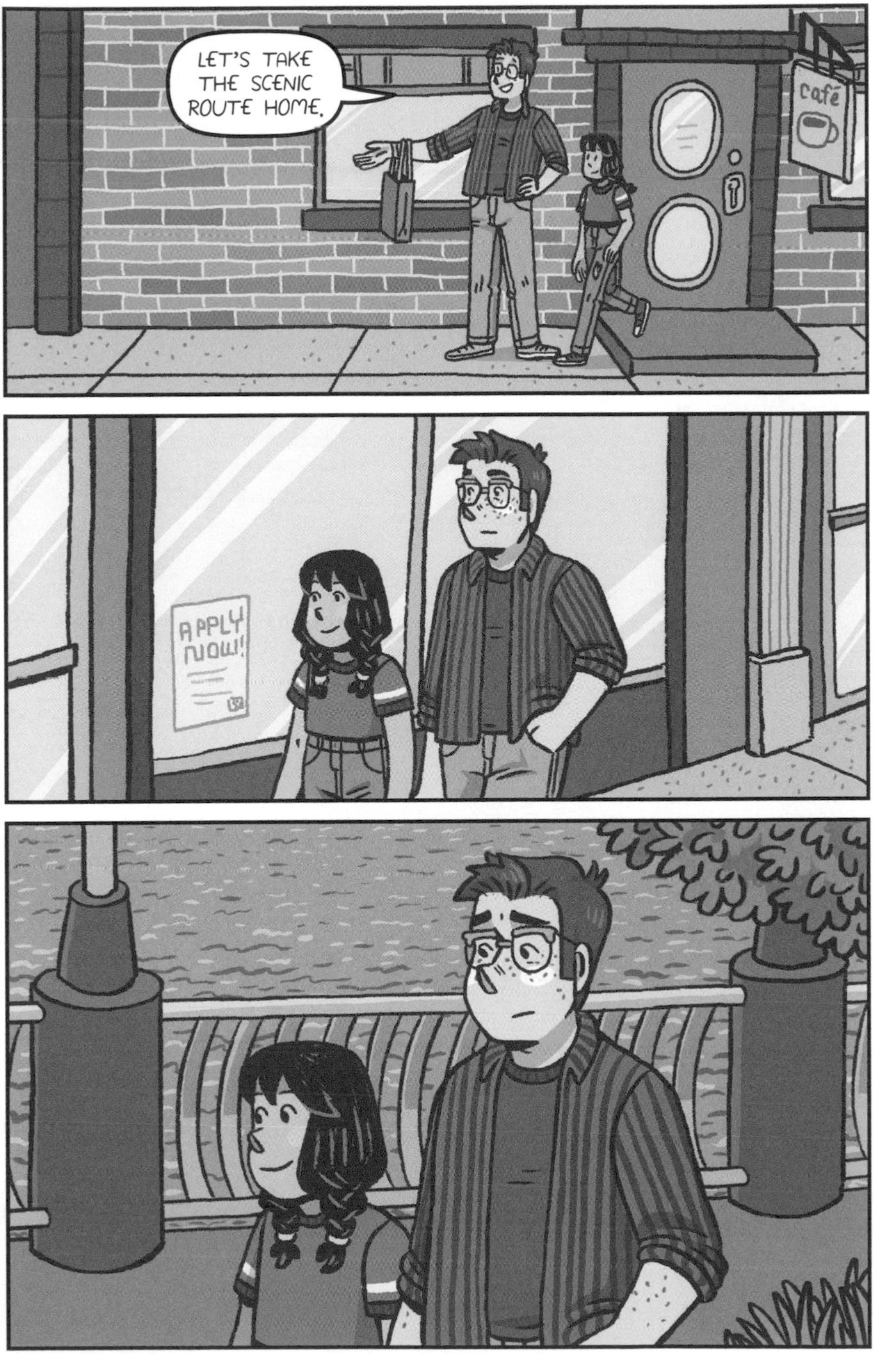
LET'S TAKE THE SCENIC ROUTE HOME.
café
APPLY NOW!

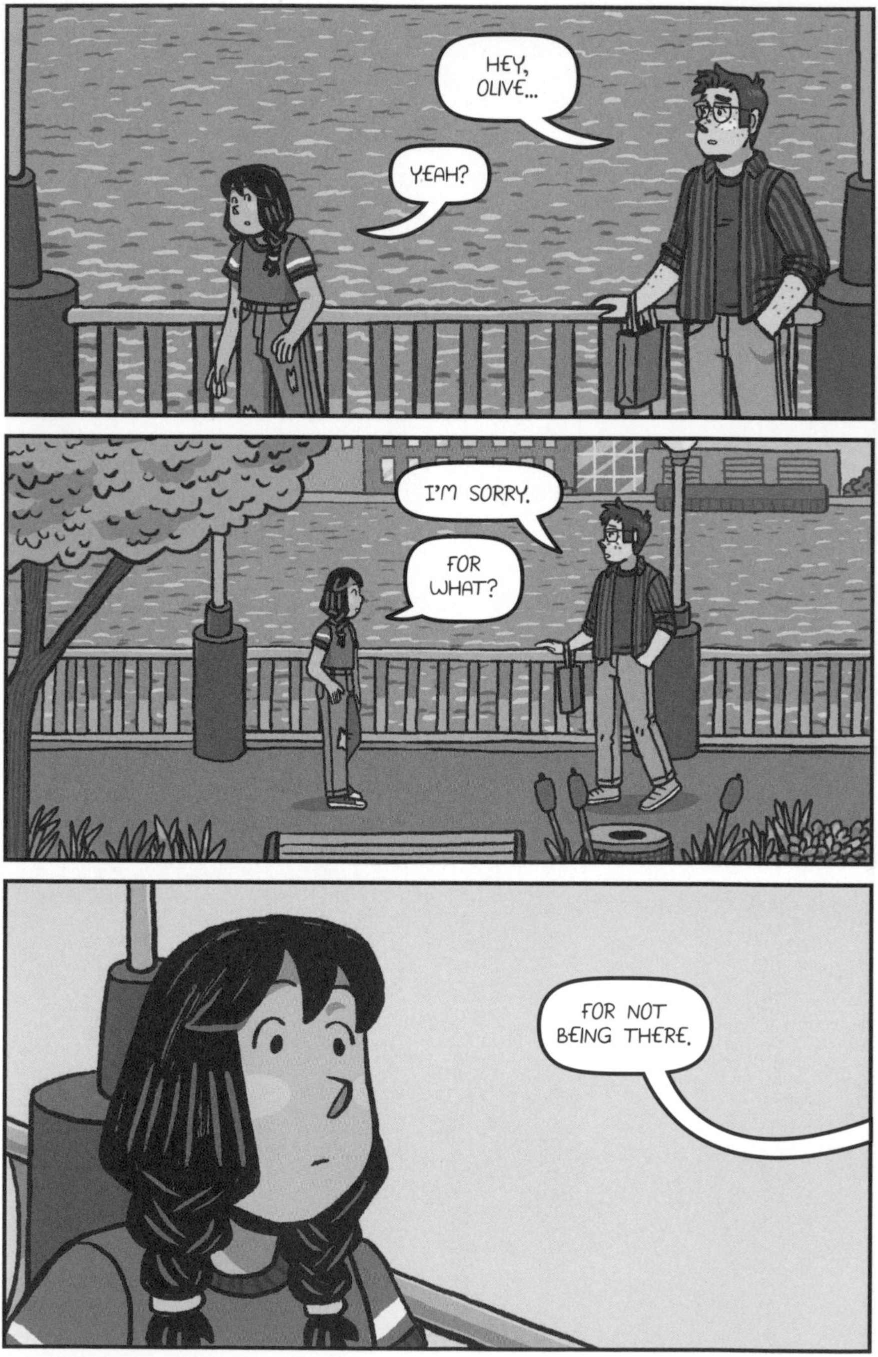
HEY, OLIVE...
YEAH?
I'M SORRY.
FOR WHAT?
FOR NOT BEING THERE.

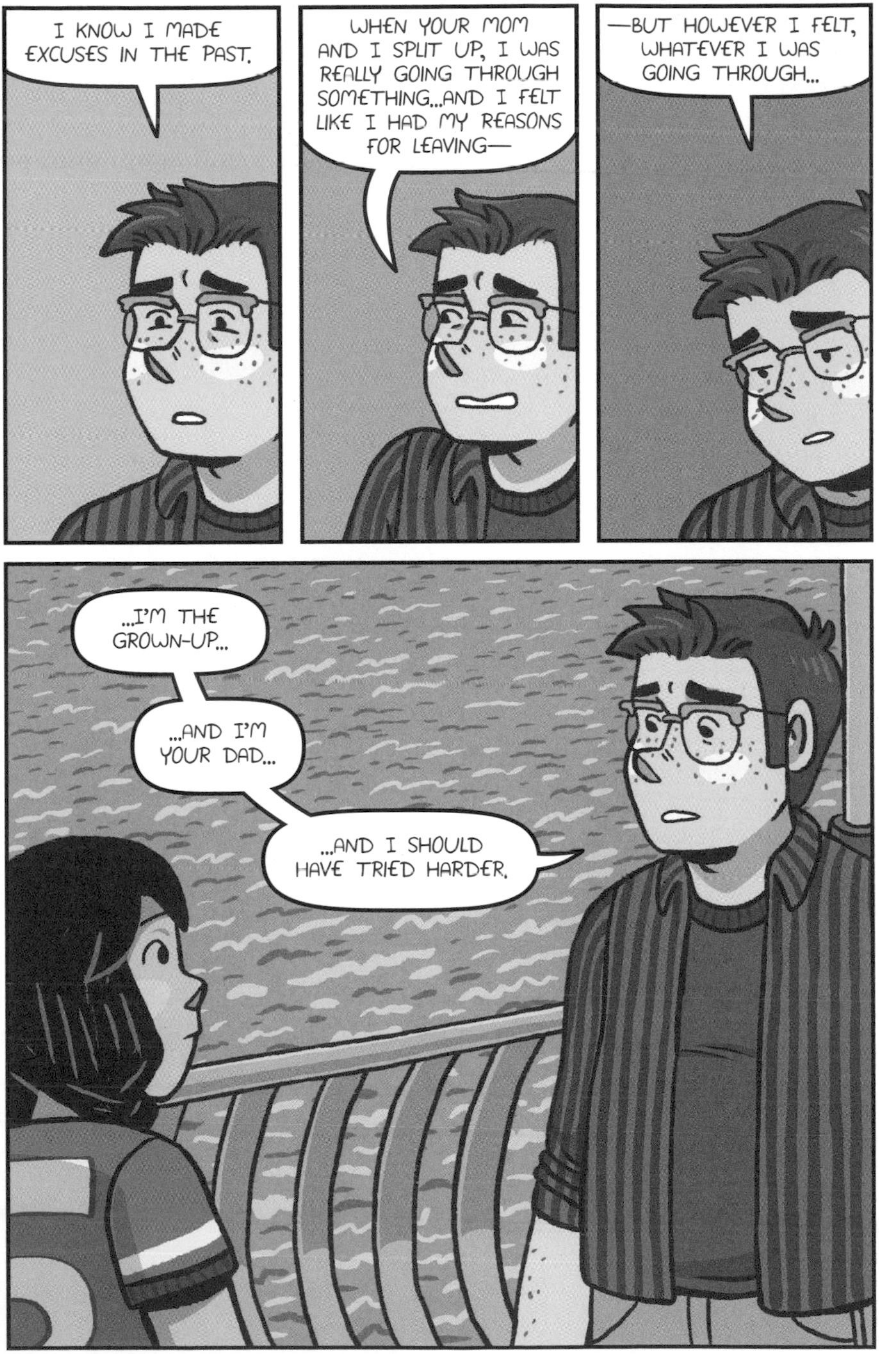
I KNOW I MADE EXCUSES IN THE PAST.
WHEN YOUR MOM AND I SPLIT UP, I WAS REALLY GOING THROUGH SOMETHING...AND I FELT LIKE I HAD MY REASONS FOR LEAVING—
—BUT HOWEVER I FELT, WHATEVER I WAS GOING THROUGH...
...I'M THE GROWN-UP...
...AND I'M YOUR DAD...
...AND I SHOULD HAVE TRIED HARDER.

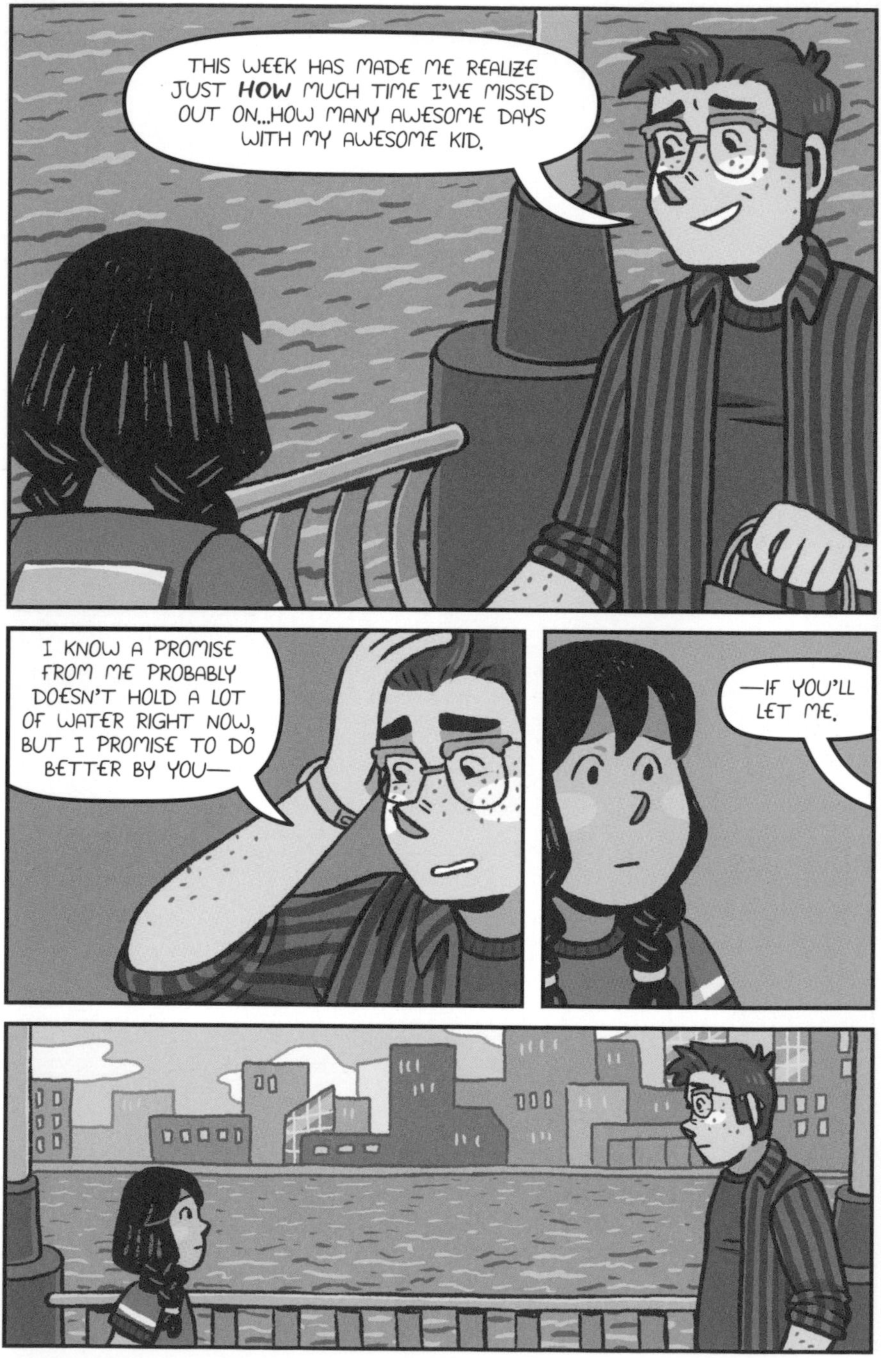
THIS WEEK HAS MADE ME REALIZE JUST **HOW** MUCH TIME I'VE MISSED OUT ON...HOW MANY AWESOME DAYS WITH MY AWESOME KID.
I KNOW A PROMISE FROM ME PROBABLY DOESN'T HOLD A LOT OF WATER RIGHT NOW, BUT I PROMISE TO DO BETTER BY YOU—
—IF YOU'LL LET ME.

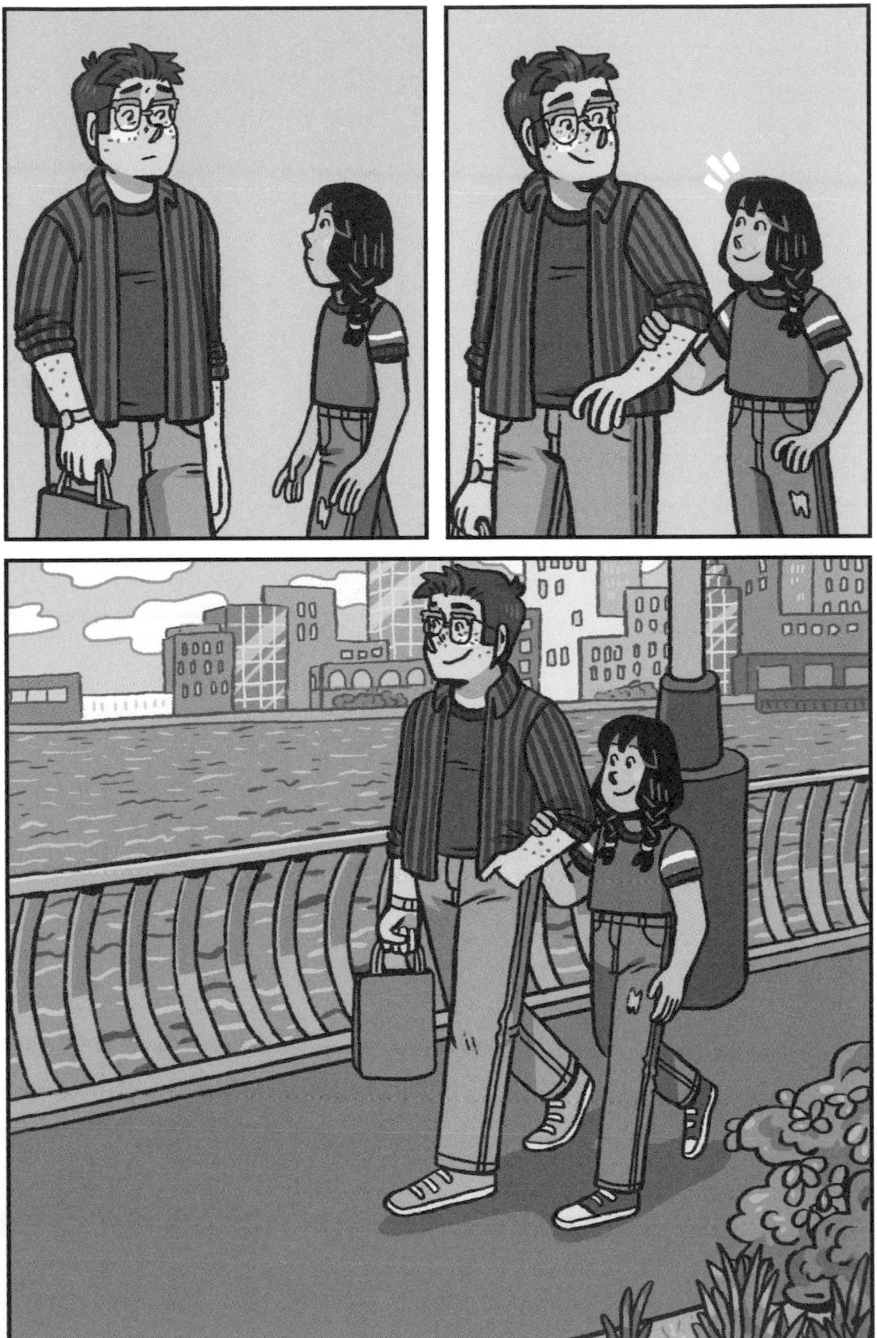

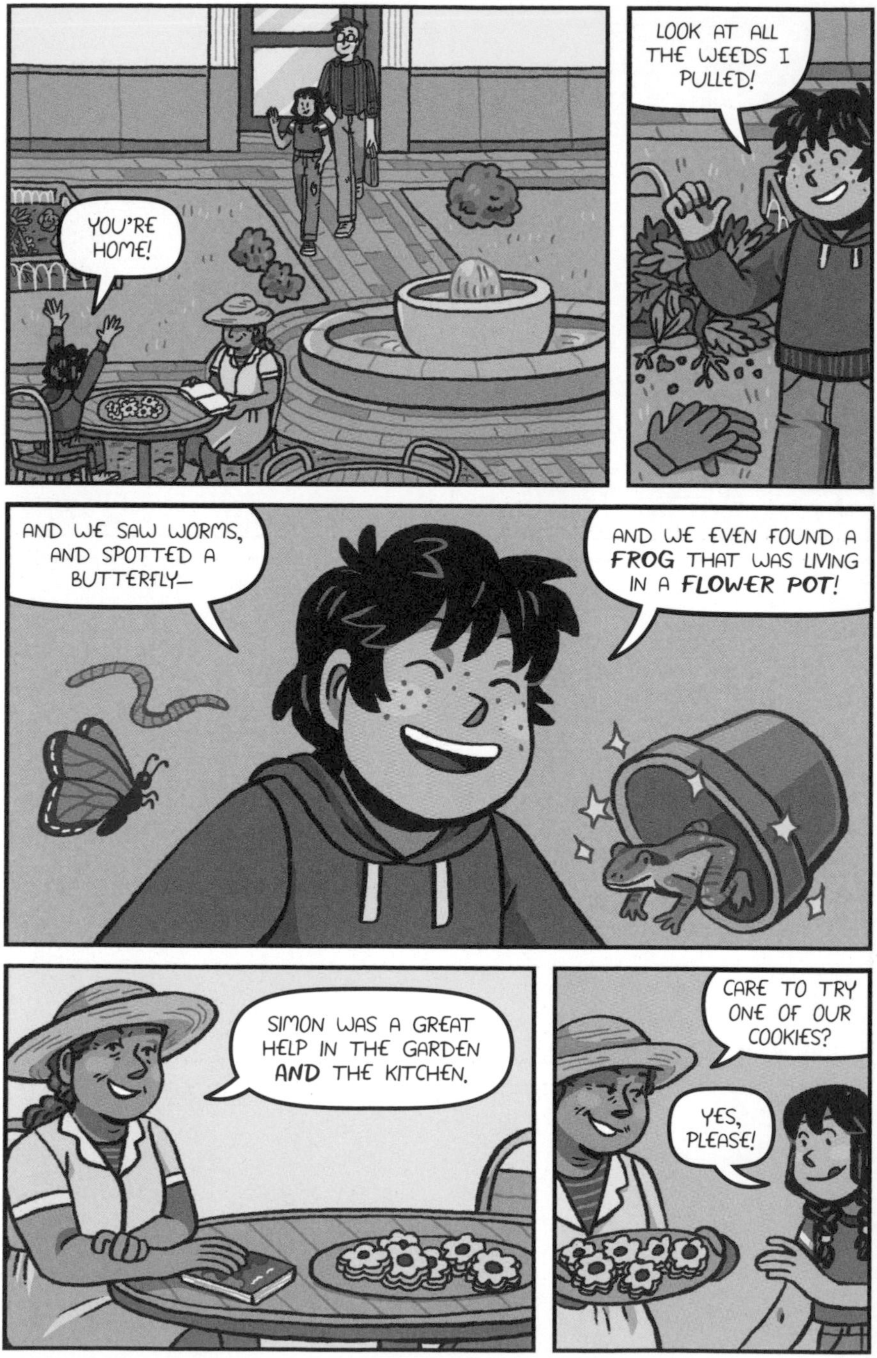

YOU'RE HOME!
LOOK AT ALL THE WEEDS I PULLED!
AND WE SAW WORMS, AND SPOTTED A BUTTERFLY—
AND WE EVEN FOUND A **FROG** THAT WAS LIVING IN A **FLOWER POT**!
SIMON WAS A GREAT HELP IN THE GARDEN **AND** THE KITCHEN.
CARE TO TRY ONE OF OUR COOKIES?
YES, PLEASE!

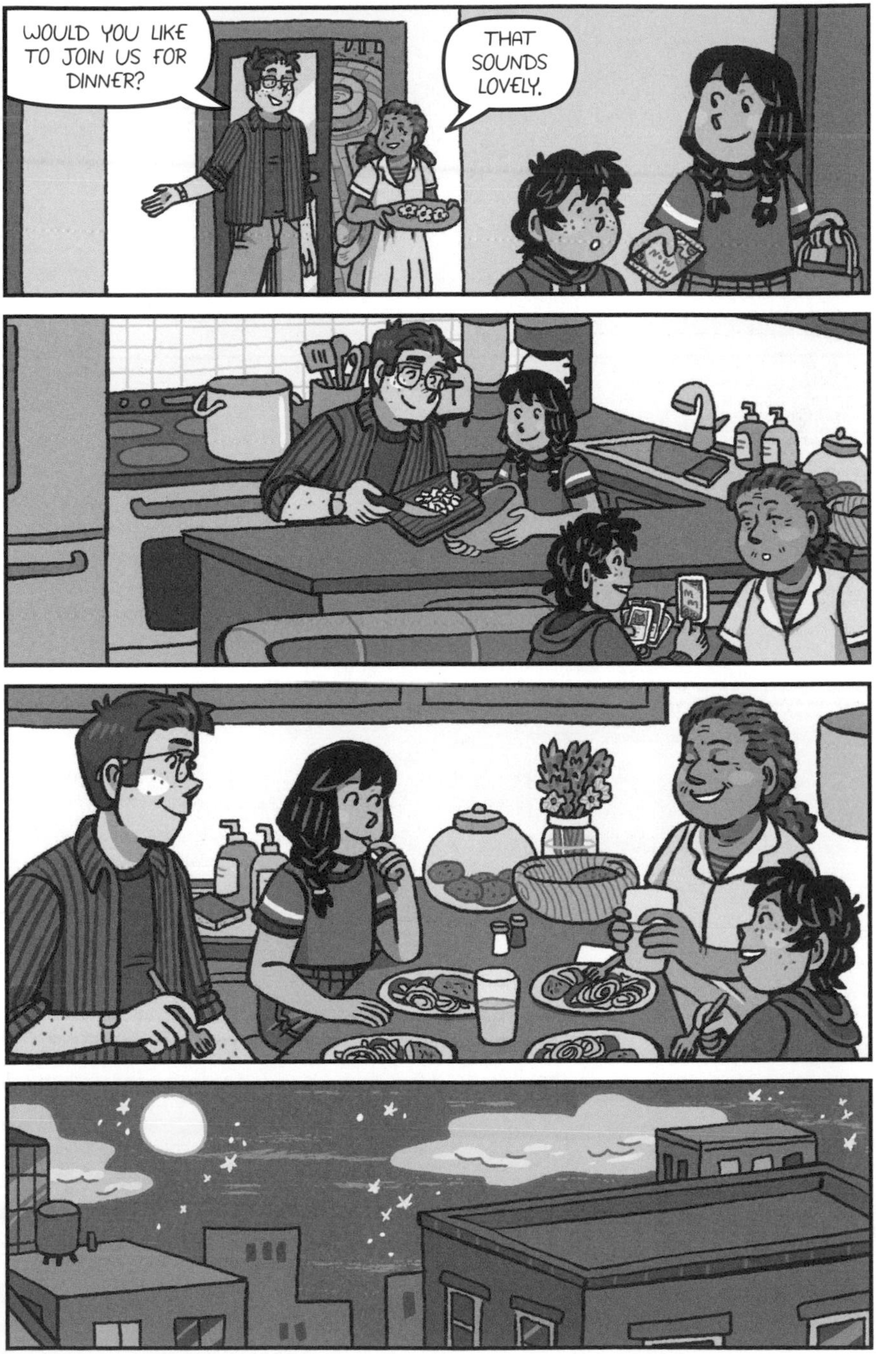
WOULD YOU LIKE TO JOIN US FOR DINNER?
THAT SOUNDS LOVELY.

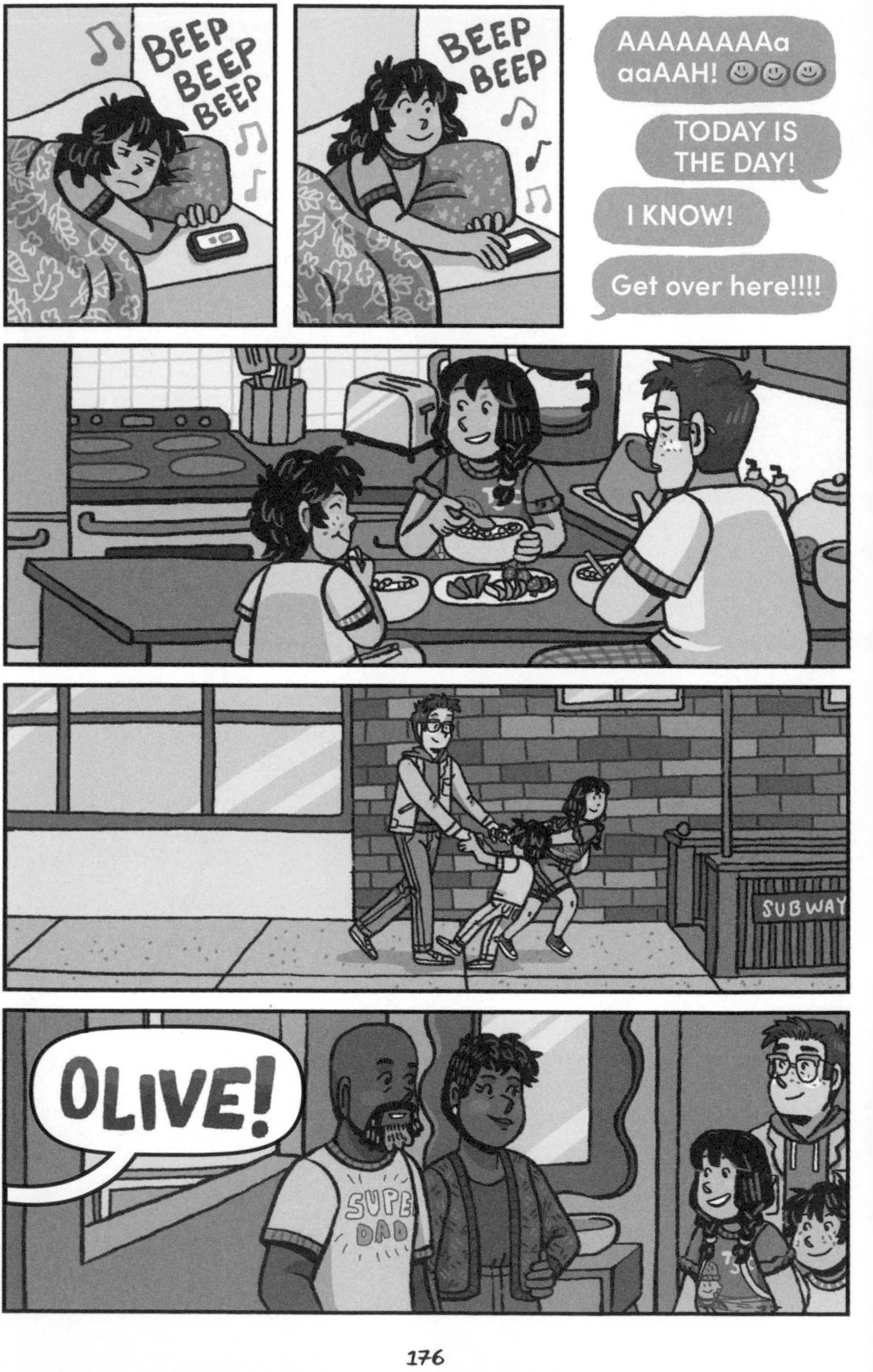
BEEP BEEP BEEP
BEEP BEEP
AAAAAAAAa aaAAH!
TODAY IS THE DAY!
I KNOW!
Get over here!!!!
SUBWAY
OLIVE!

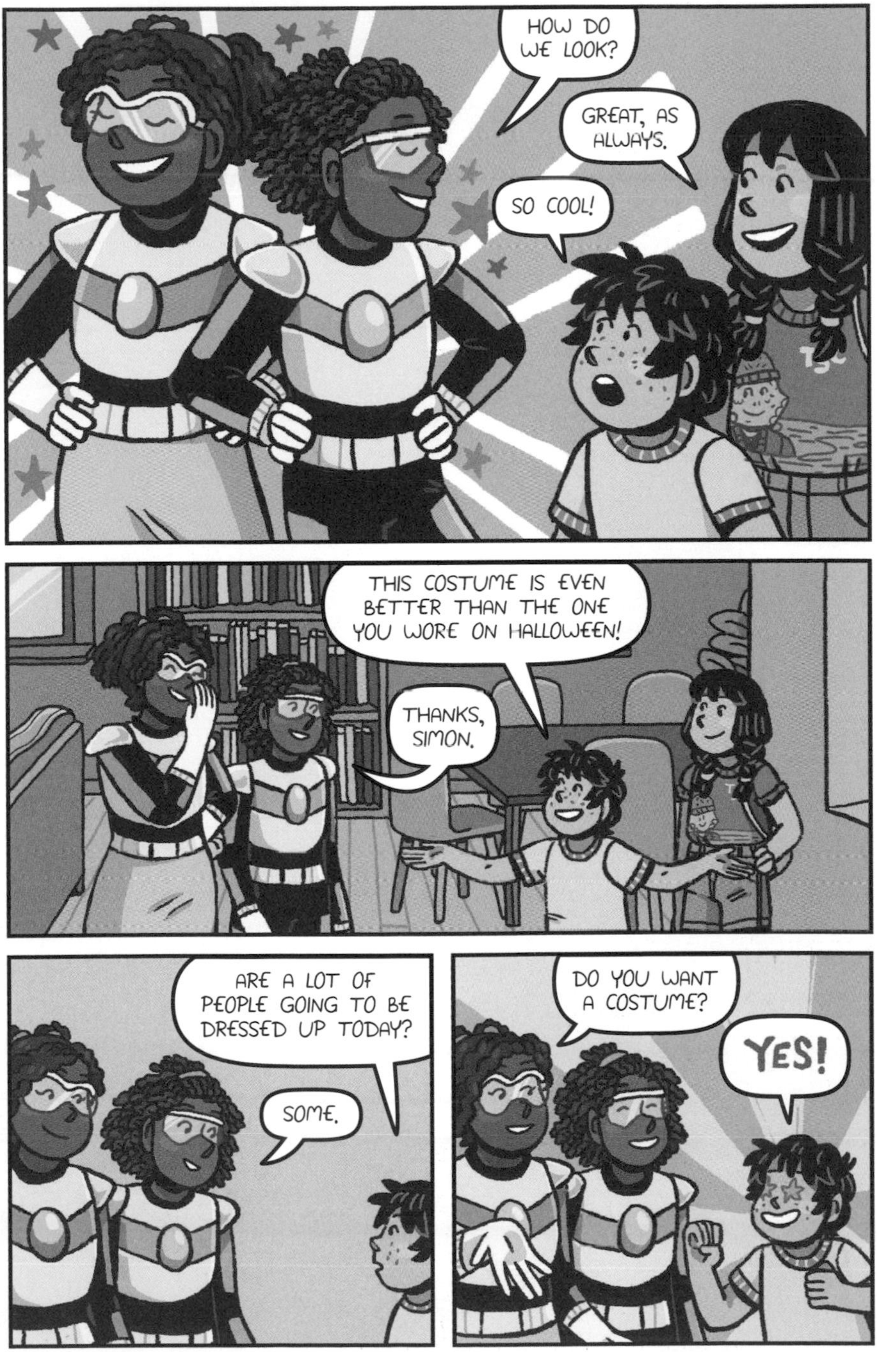
HOW DO WE LOOK?
GREAT, AS ALWAYS.
SO COOL!
THIS COSTUME IS EVEN BETTER THAN THE ONE YOU WORE ON HALLOWEEN!
THANKS, SIMON.
ARE A LOT OF PEOPLE GOING TO BE DRESSED UP TODAY?
SOME.
DO YOU WANT A COSTUME?
YES!

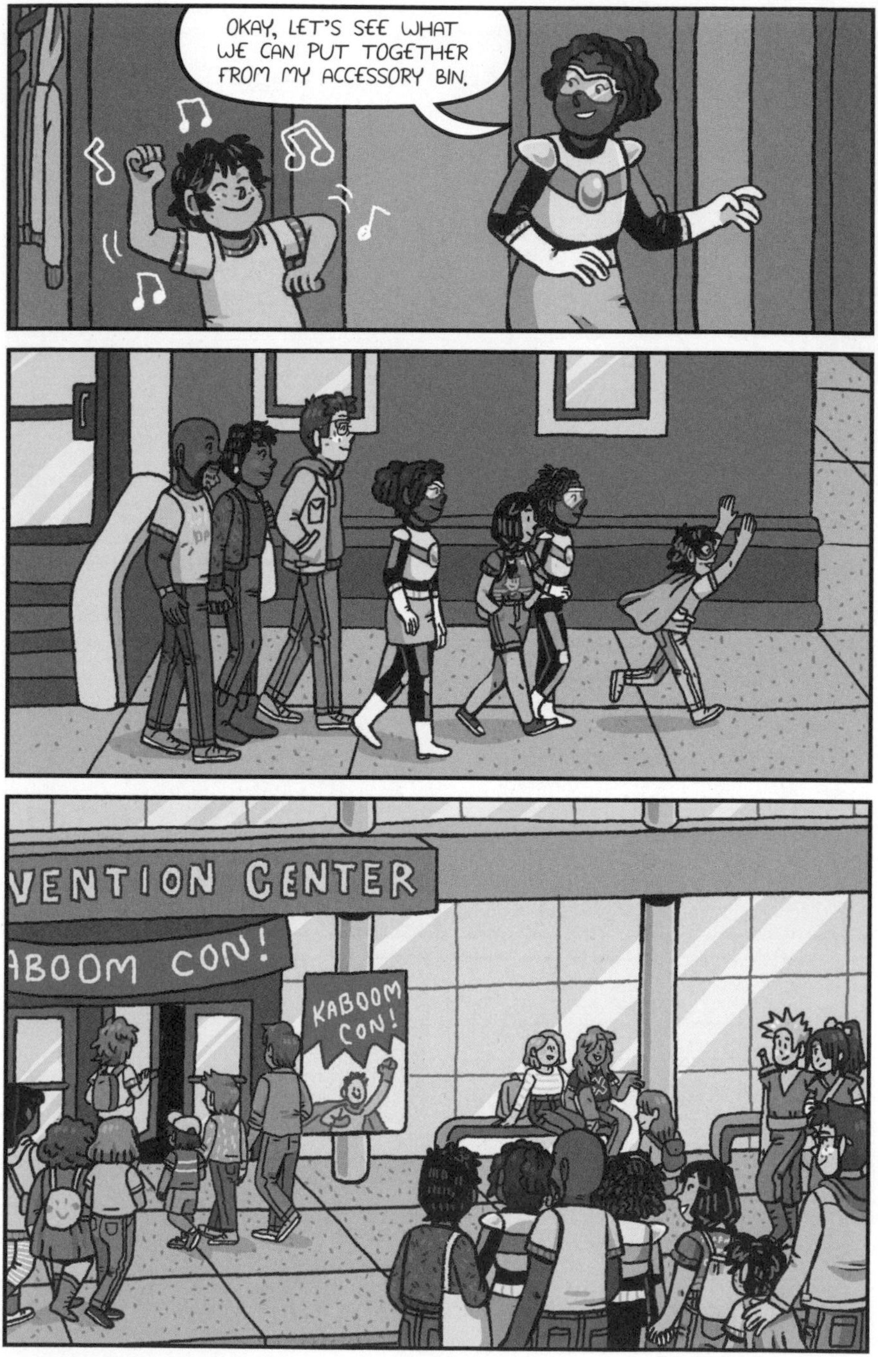
OKAY, LET'S SEE WHAT WE CAN PUT TOGETHER FROM MY ACCESSORY BIN.
VENTION CENTER
ABOOM CON!
KABOOM CON!

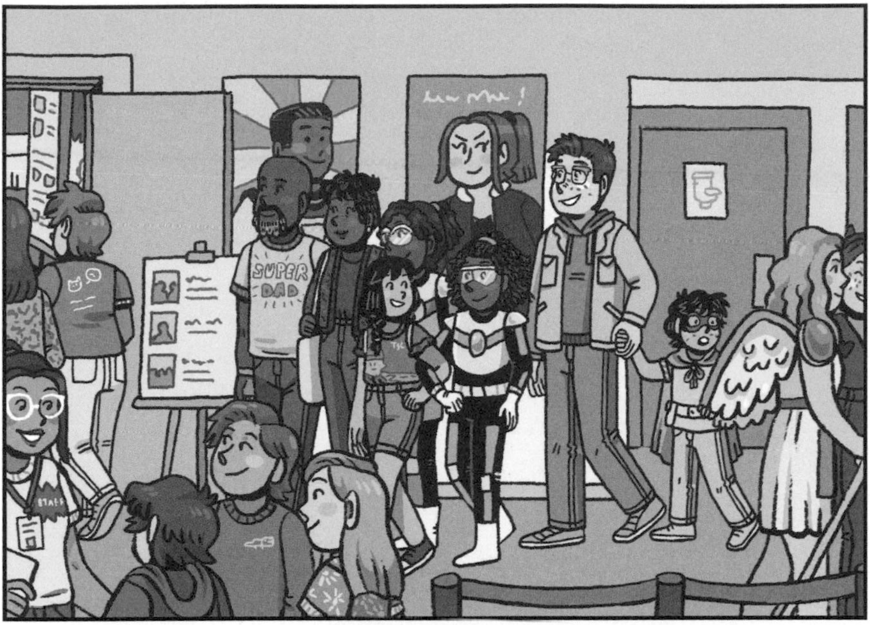
SUPER DAD

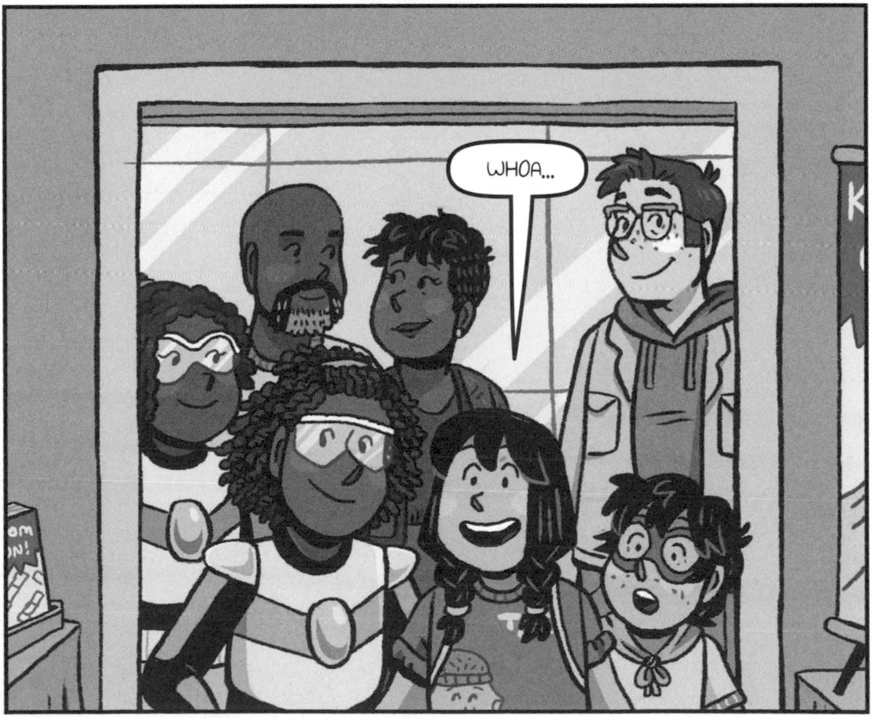
WHOA...

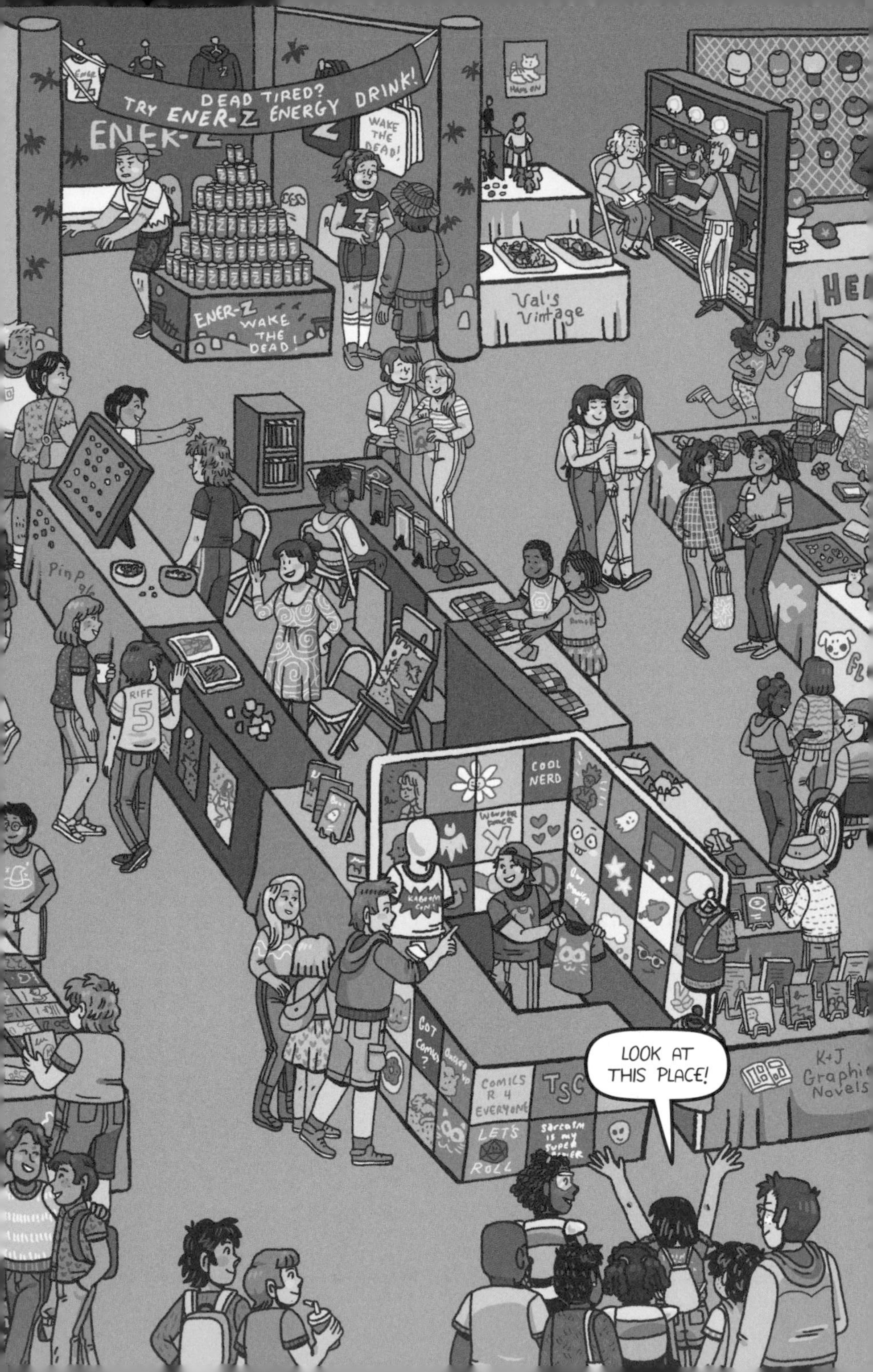
DEAD TIRED? TRY ENER-Z ENERGY DRINK!
ENER-Z
WAKE THE DEAD!
ENER-Z WAKE THE DEAD!
Val's Vintage
COOL NERD
GOT COMICS?
COMICS R 4 EVERYONE
TSC
LET'S ROLL
Sarcasm is my super power
K+J Graphic Novels
LOOK AT THIS PLACE!

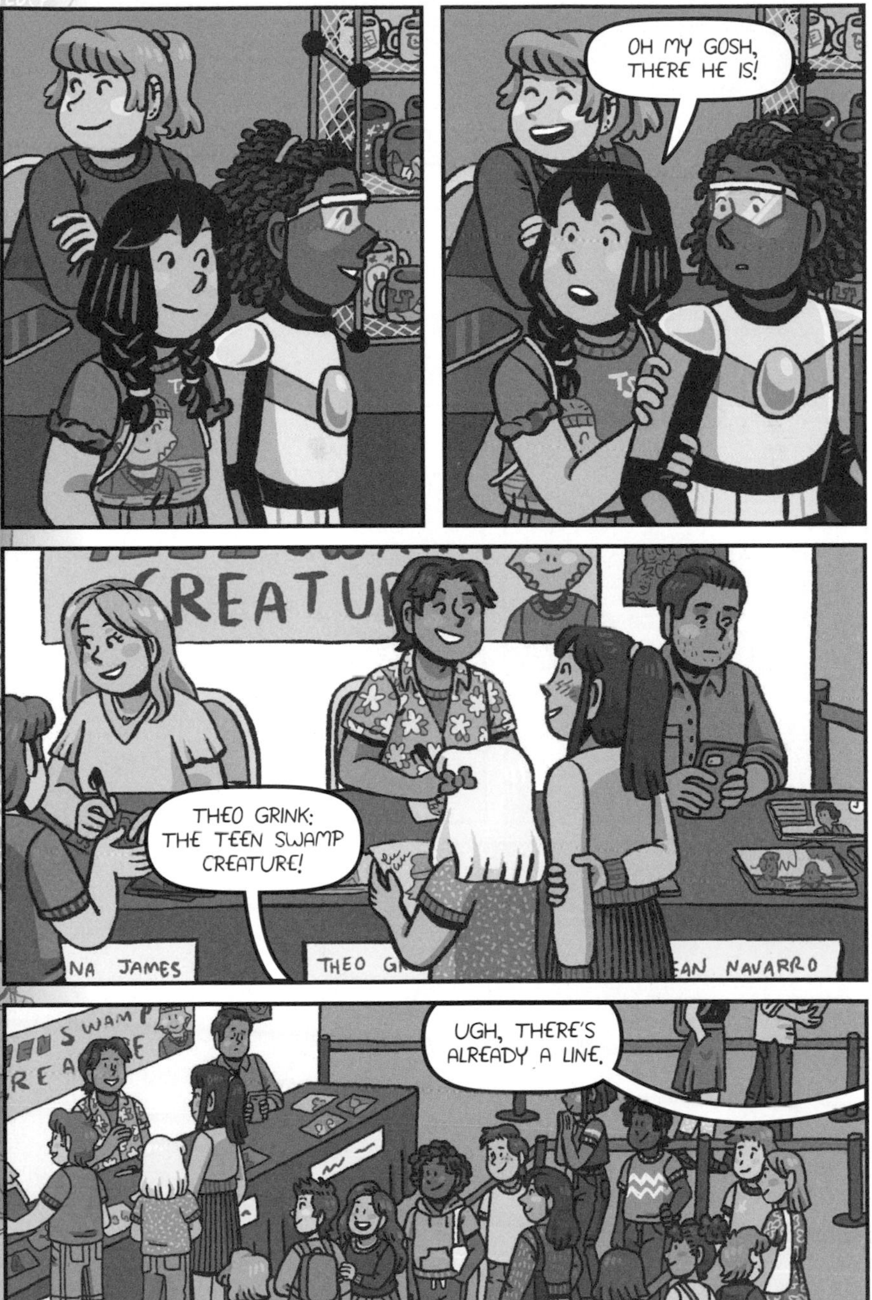
OH MY GOSH, THERE HE IS!
CREATU
THEO GRINK: THE TEEN SWAMP CREATURE!
NA JAMES
THEO G
EAN NAVARRO
UGH, THERE'S ALREADY A LINE.

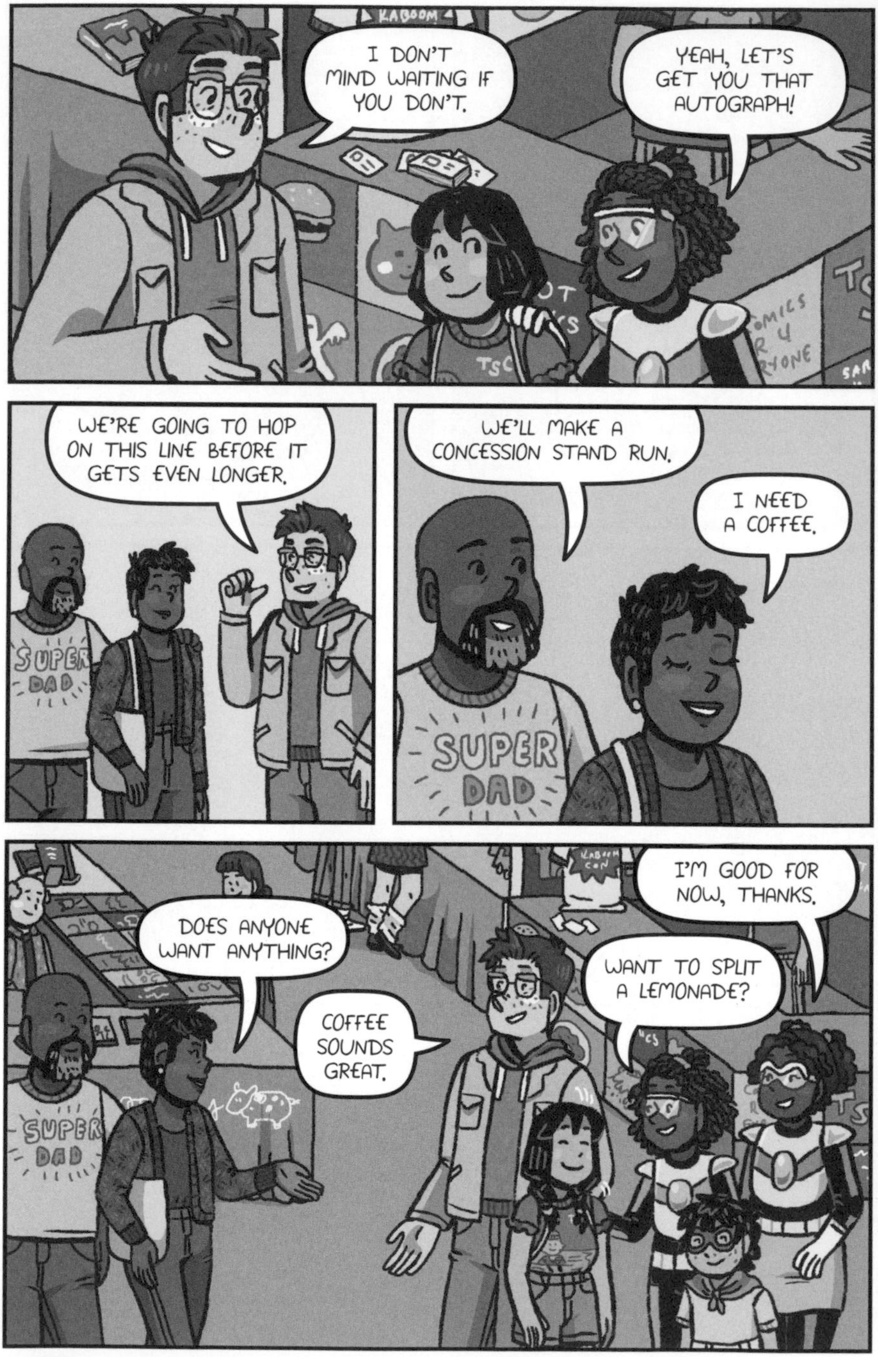
I DON'T MIND WAITING IF YOU DON'T.
YEAH, LET'S GET YOU THAT AUTOGRAPH!
KABOOM
WE'RE GOING TO HOP ON THIS LINE BEFORE IT GETS EVEN LONGER.
SUPER DAD
WE'LL MAKE A CONCESSION STAND RUN.
I NEED A COFFEE.
SUPER DAD
DOES ANYONE WANT ANYTHING?
COFFEE SOUNDS GREAT.
I'M GOOD FOR NOW, THANKS.
WANT TO SPLIT A LEMONADE?
SUPER DAD

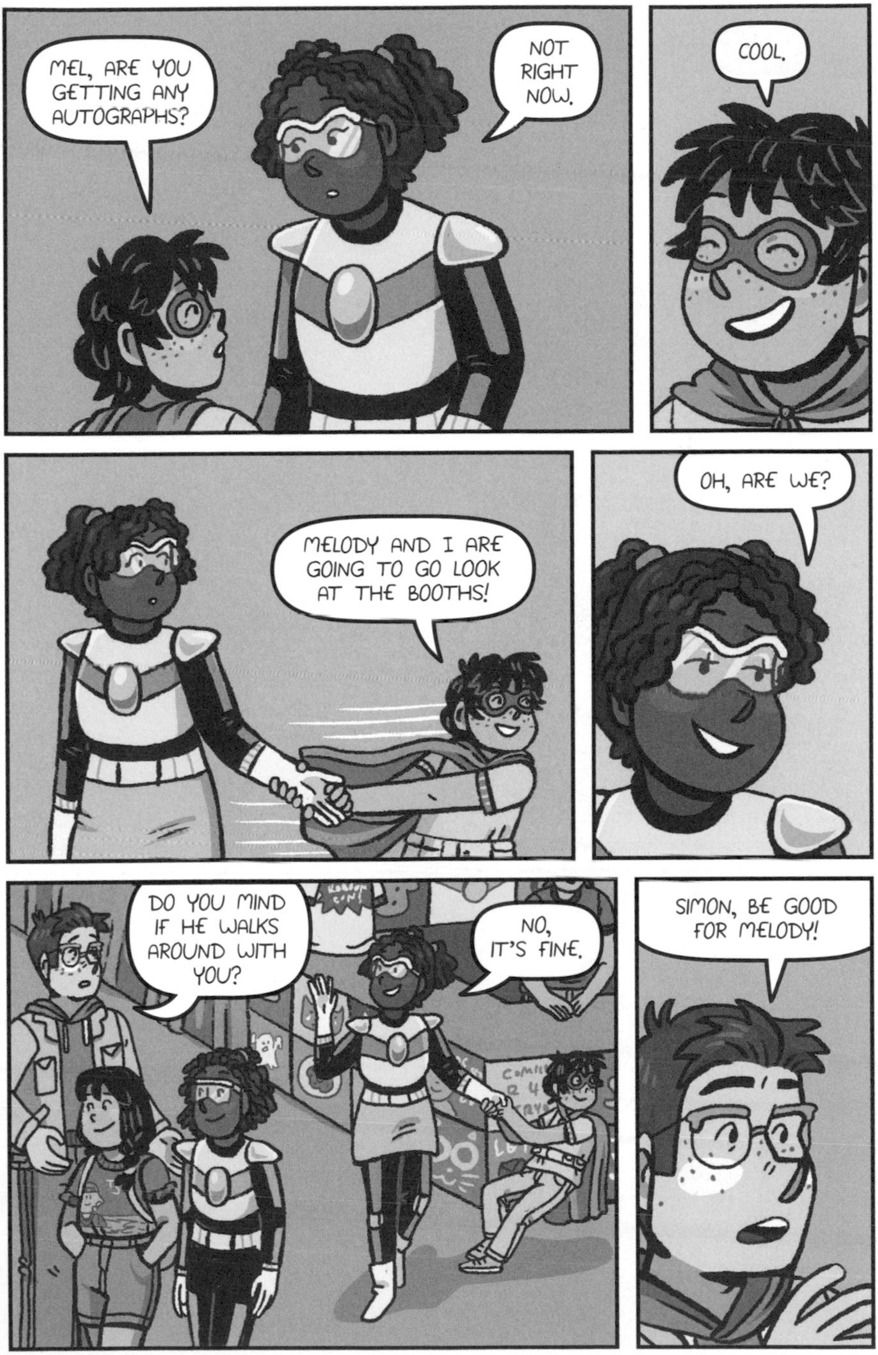
MEL, ARE YOU GETTING ANY AUTOGRAPHS?
NOT RIGHT NOW.
COOL.
MELODY AND I ARE GOING TO GO LOOK AT THE BOOTHS!
OH, ARE WE?
DO YOU MIND IF HE WALKS AROUND WITH YOU?
NO, IT'S FINE.
SIMON, BE GOOD FOR MELODY!

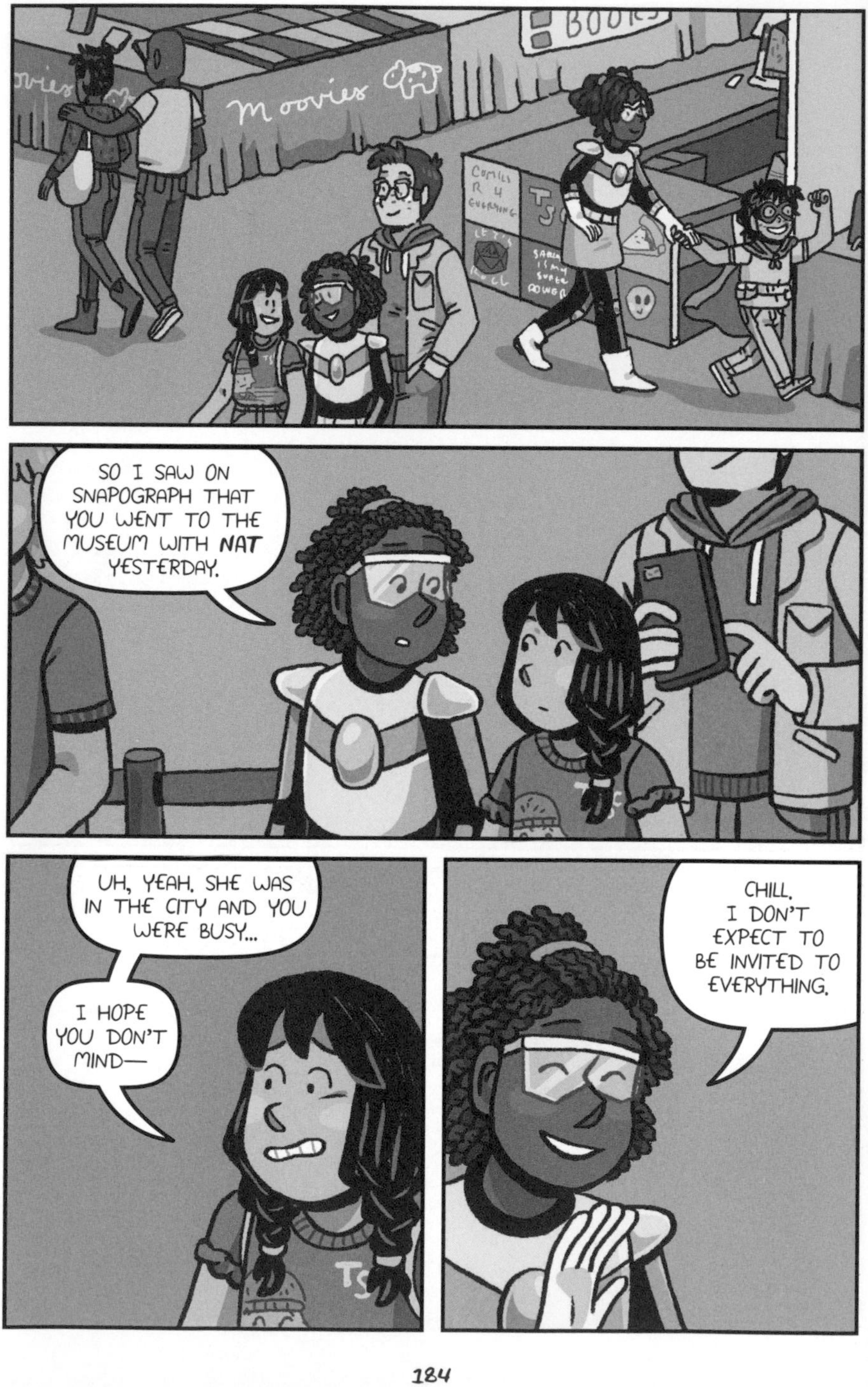
BOOKS
Moovies
COMICS R 4 EVERYTHING
LET'S ROLL
SARCASM IS MY SUPER POWER
SO I SAW ON SNAPOGRAPH THAT YOU WENT TO THE MUSEUM WITH **NAT** YESTERDAY.
UH, YEAH. SHE WAS IN THE CITY AND YOU WERE BUSY...
I HOPE YOU DON'T MIND—
CHILL. I DON'T EXPECT TO BE INVITED TO EVERYTHING.

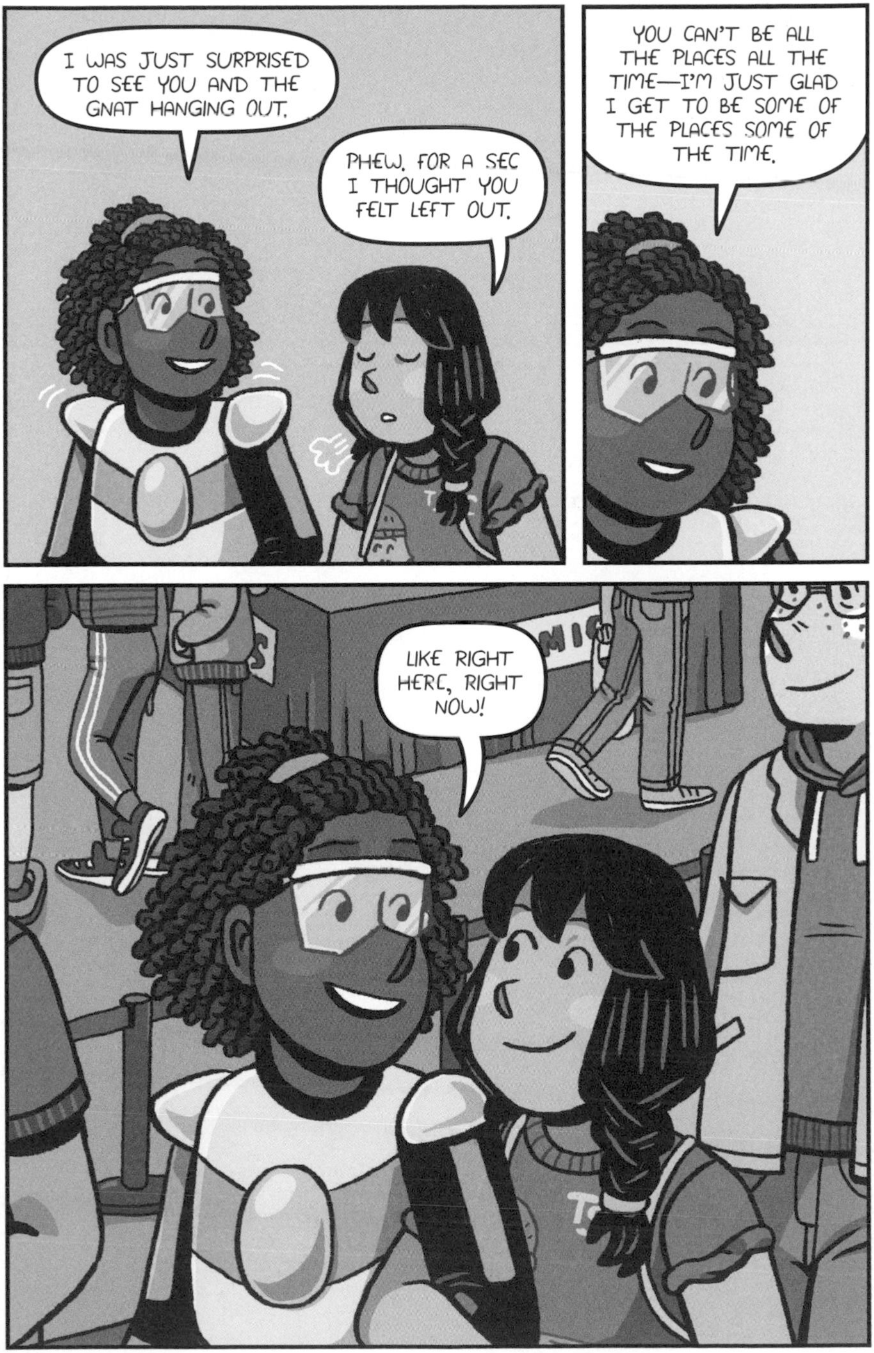
I WAS JUST SURPRISED TO SEE YOU AND THE GNAT HANGING OUT.
PHEW. FOR A SEC I THOUGHT YOU FELT LEFT OUT.
YOU CAN'T BE ALL THE PLACES ALL THE TIME—I'M JUST GLAD I GET TO BE SOME OF THE PLACES SOME OF THE TIME.
LIKE RIGHT HERE, RIGHT NOW!

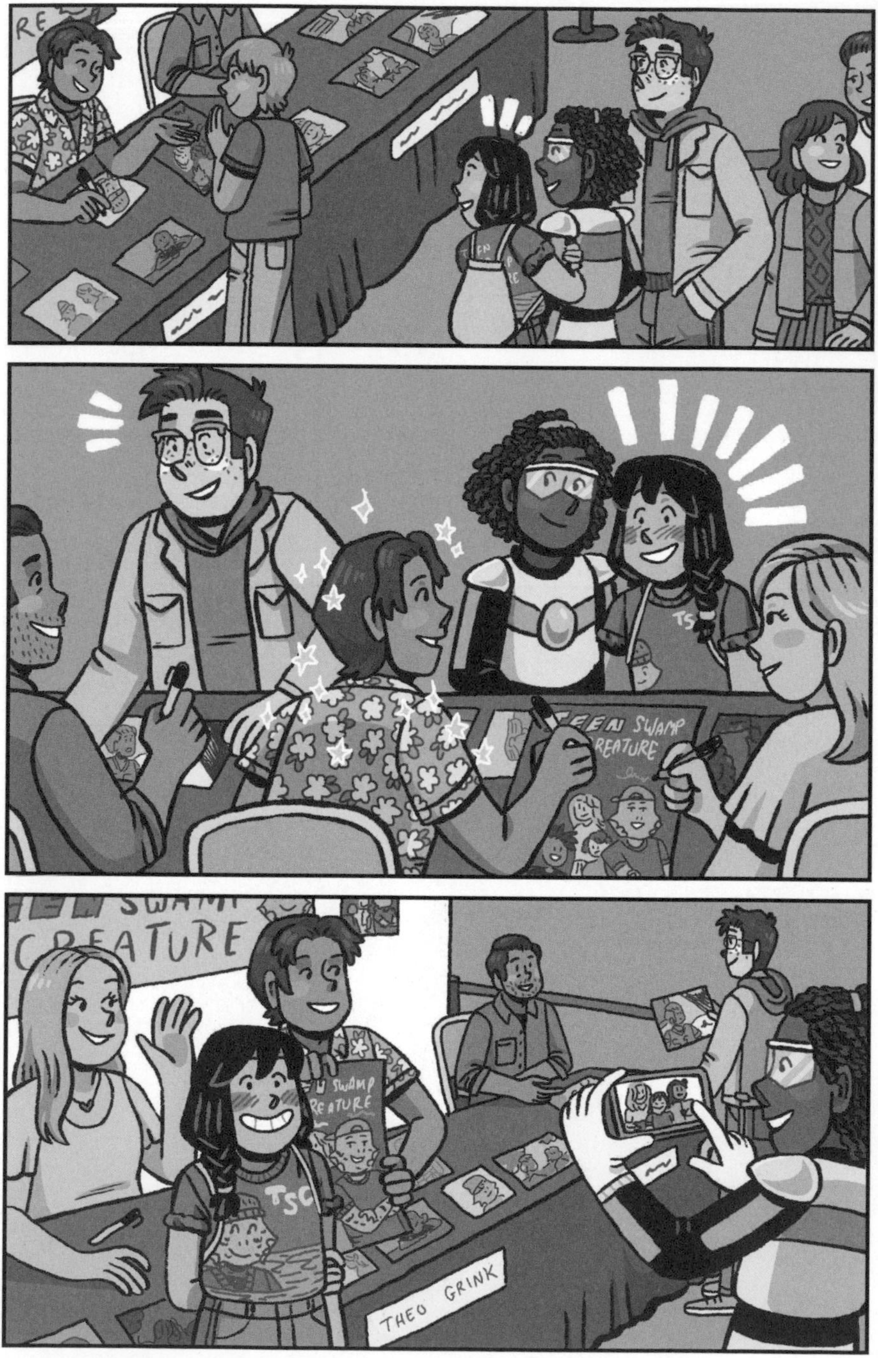
TEEN SWAMP CREATURE
TSC
CREATURE
SWAMP REATURE
TSC
THEO GRINK

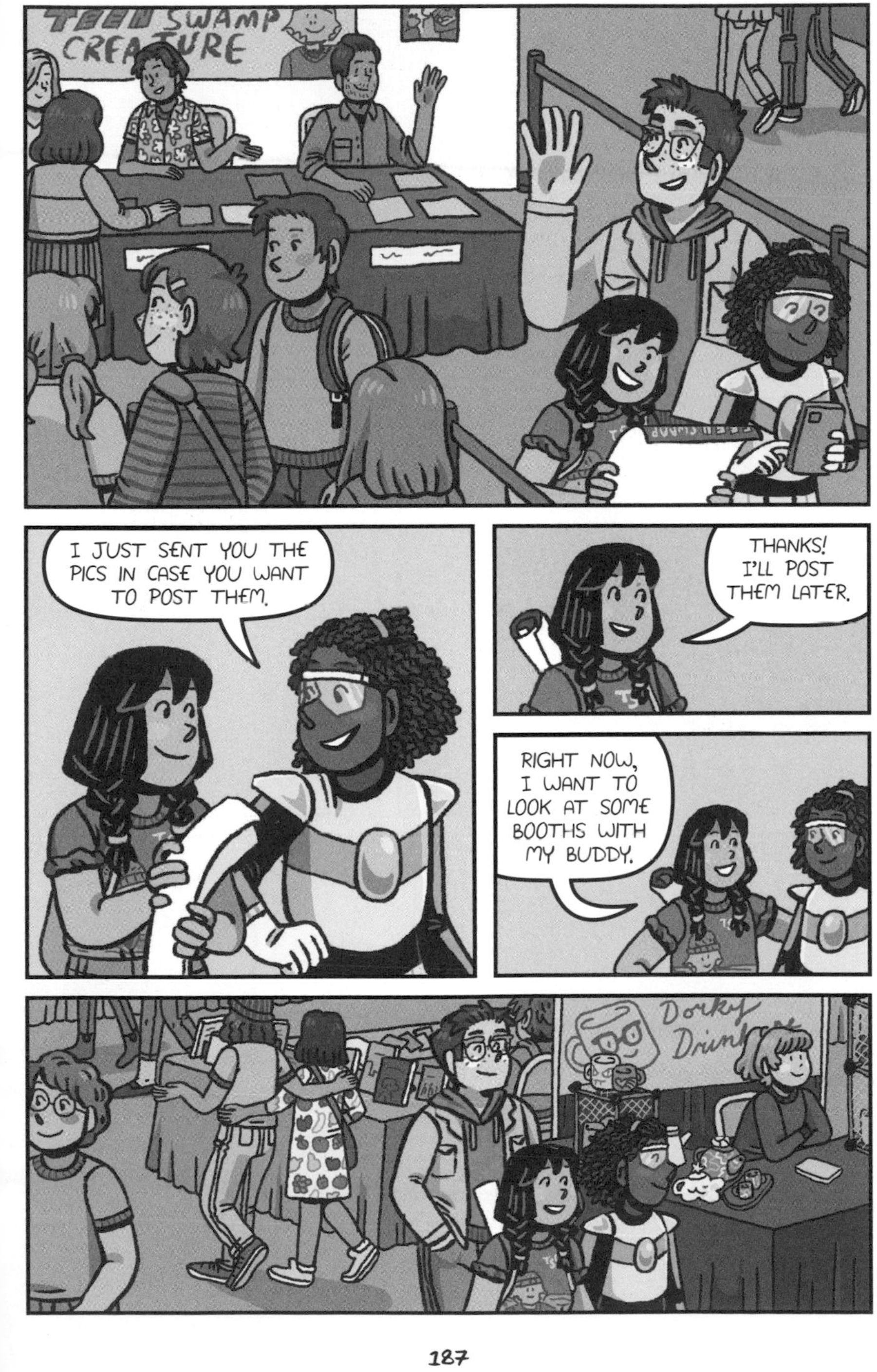
TEEN SWAMP CREATURE
I JUST SENT YOU THE PICS IN CASE YOU WANT TO POST THEM.
THANKS! I'LL POST THEM LATER.
RIGHT NOW, I WANT TO LOOK AT SOME BOOTHS WITH MY BUDDY.
Dorky Drink

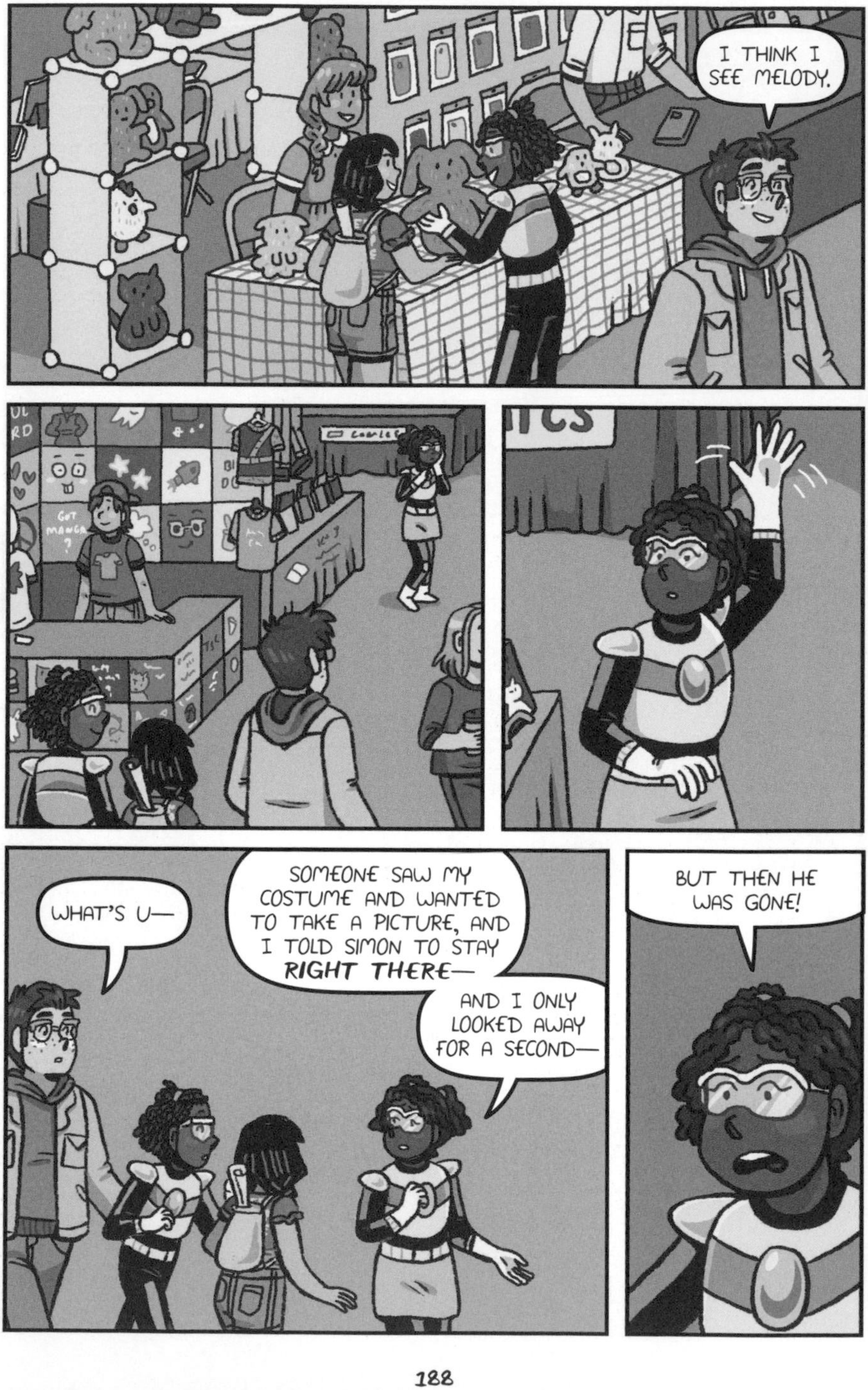
I THINK I SEE MELODY.
WHAT'S U—
SOMEONE SAW MY COSTUME AND WANTED TO TAKE A PICTURE, AND I TOLD SIMON TO STAY **RIGHT THERE**—
AND I ONLY LOOKED AWAY FOR A SECOND—
BUT THEN HE WAS GONE!

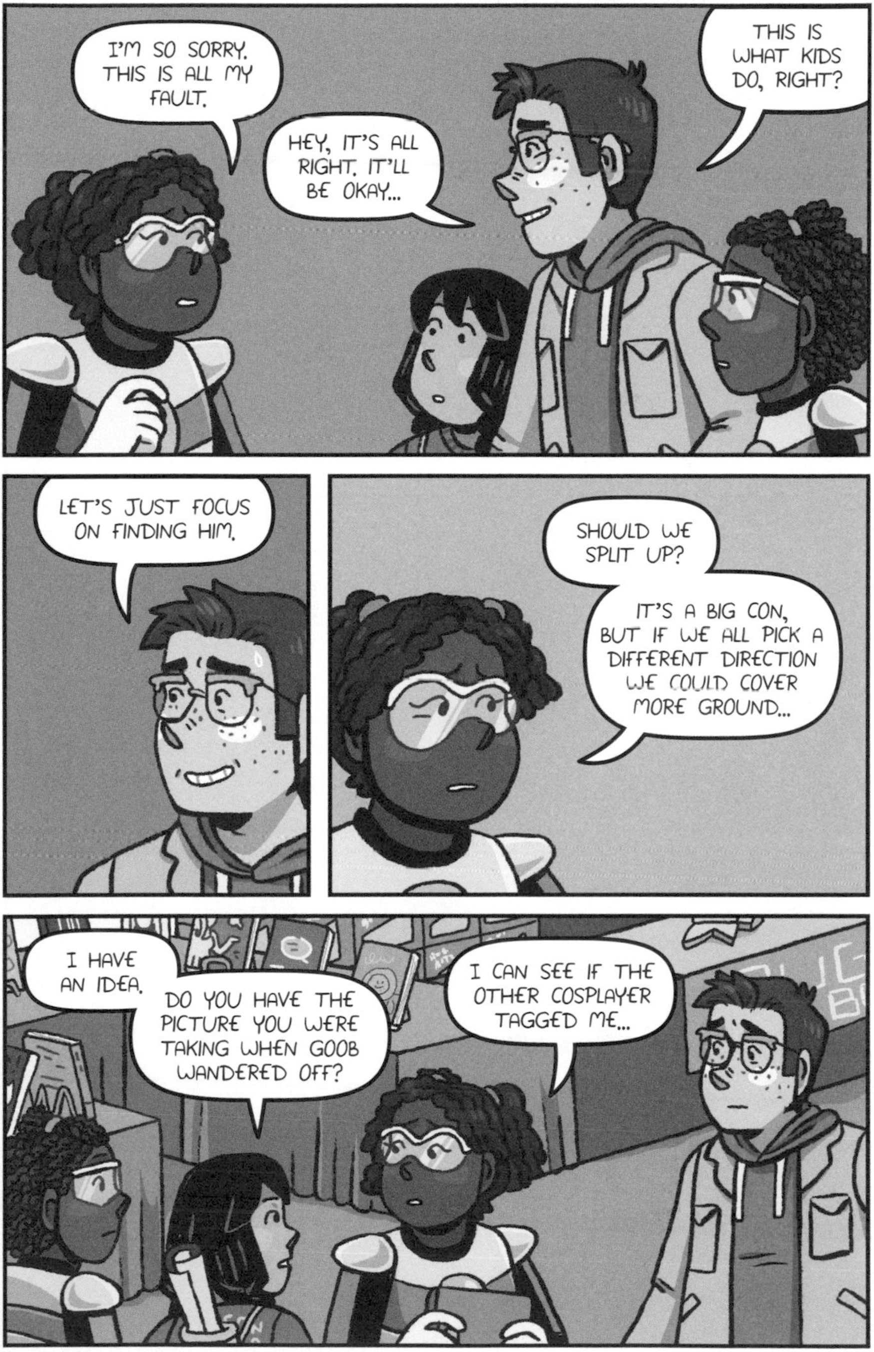
I'M SO SORRY. THIS IS ALL MY FAULT.
HEY, IT'S ALL RIGHT. IT'LL BE OKAY...
THIS IS WHAT KIDS DO, RIGHT?
LET'S JUST FOCUS ON FINDING HIM.
SHOULD WE SPLIT UP?
IT'S A BIG CON, BUT IF WE ALL PICK A DIFFERENT DIRECTION WE COULD COVER MORE GROUND...
I HAVE AN IDEA.
DO YOU HAVE THE PICTURE YOU WERE TAKING WHEN GOOB WANDERED OFF?
I CAN SEE IF THE OTHER COSPLAYER TAGGED ME...

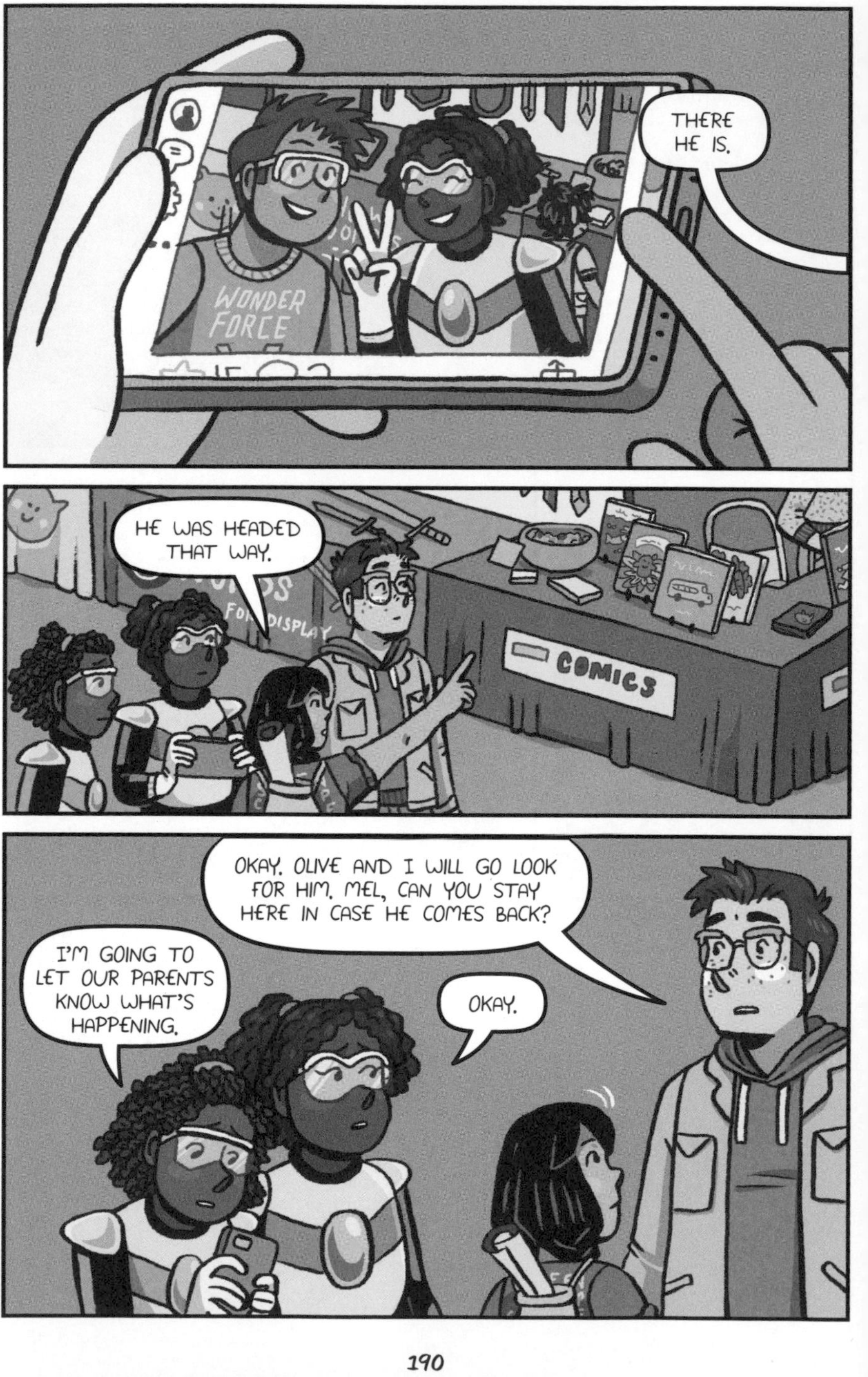
WONDER FORCE
THERE HE IS.
HE WAS HEADED THAT WAY.
COMICS
OKAY. OLIVE AND I WILL GO LOOK FOR HIM. MEL, CAN YOU STAY HERE IN CASE HE COMES BACK?
I'M GOING TO LET OUR PARENTS KNOW WHAT'S HAPPENING.
OKAY.

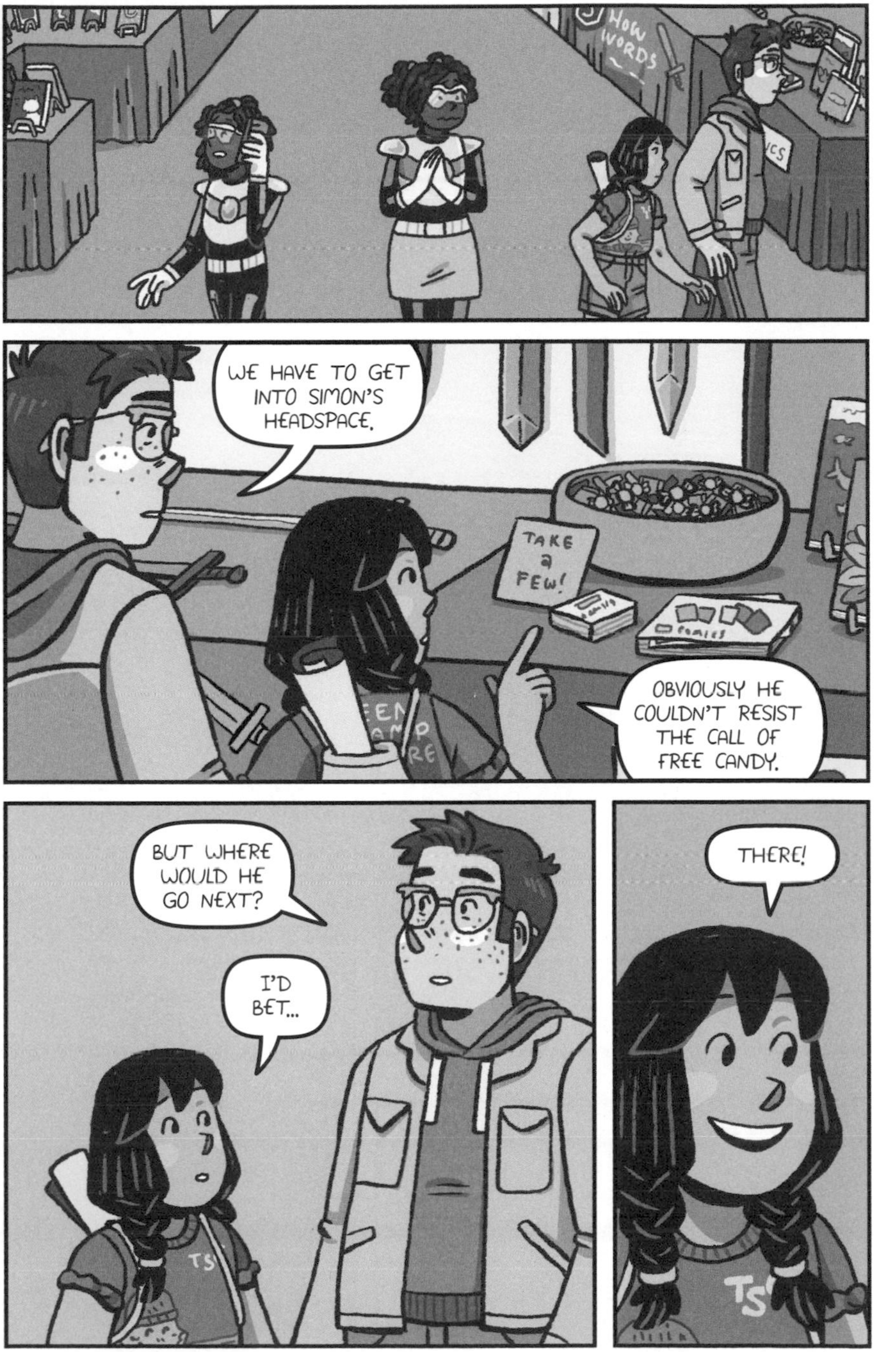
HOW WORDS
WE HAVE TO GET INTO SIMON'S HEADSPACE.
TAKE a FEW!
OBVIOUSLY HE COULDN'T RESIST THE CALL OF FREE CANDY.
BUT WHERE WOULD HE GO NEXT?
I'D BET...
THERE!

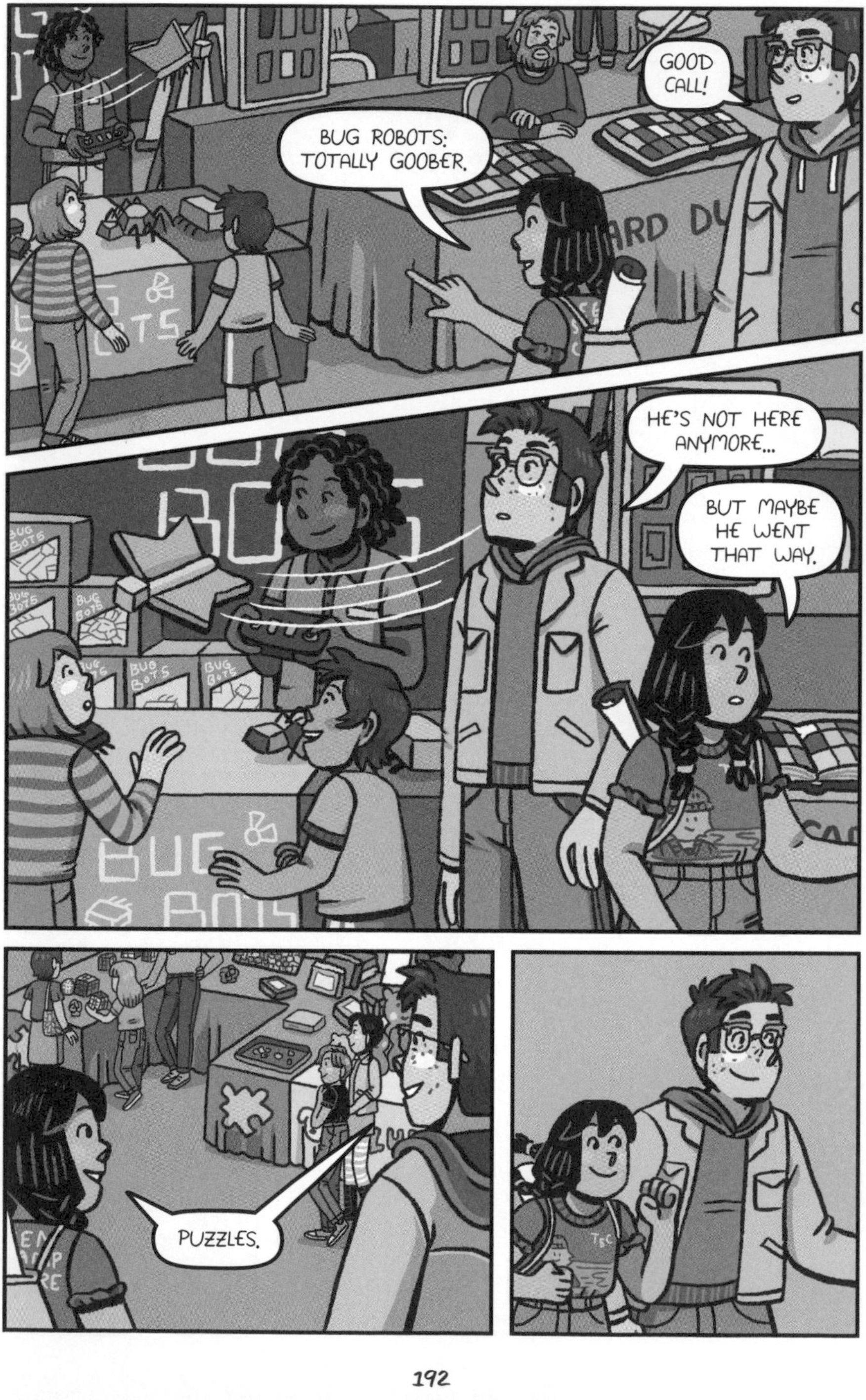
BUG ROBOTS: TOTALLY GOOBER.
GOOD CALL!
HE'S NOT HERE ANYMORE...
BUT MAYBE HE WENT THAT WAY.
PUZZLES.

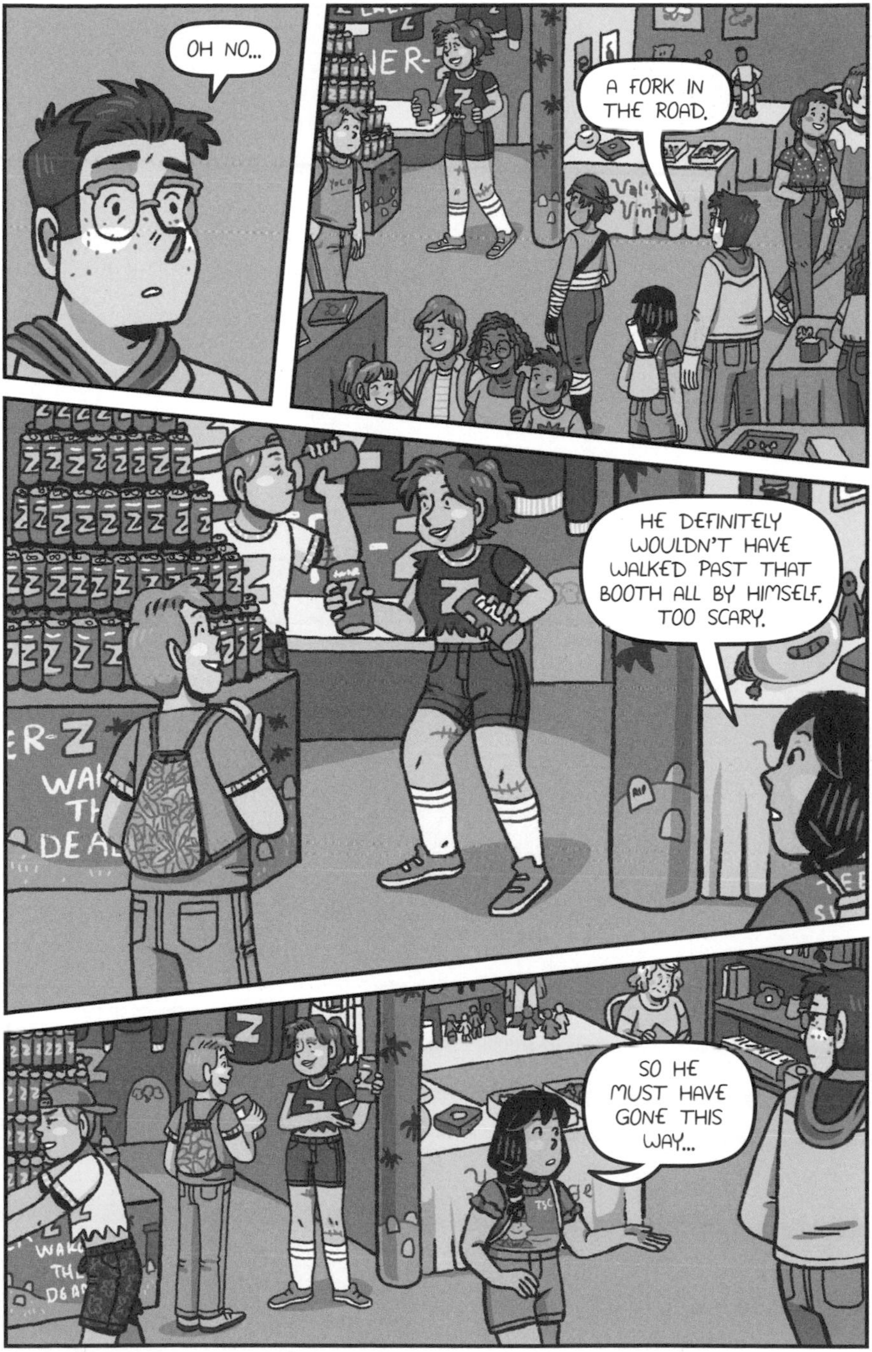
OH NO...
A FORK IN THE ROAD.
HE DEFINITELY WOULDN'T HAVE WALKED PAST THAT BOOTH ALL BY HIMSELF. TOO SCARY.
SO HE MUST HAVE GONE THIS WAY...

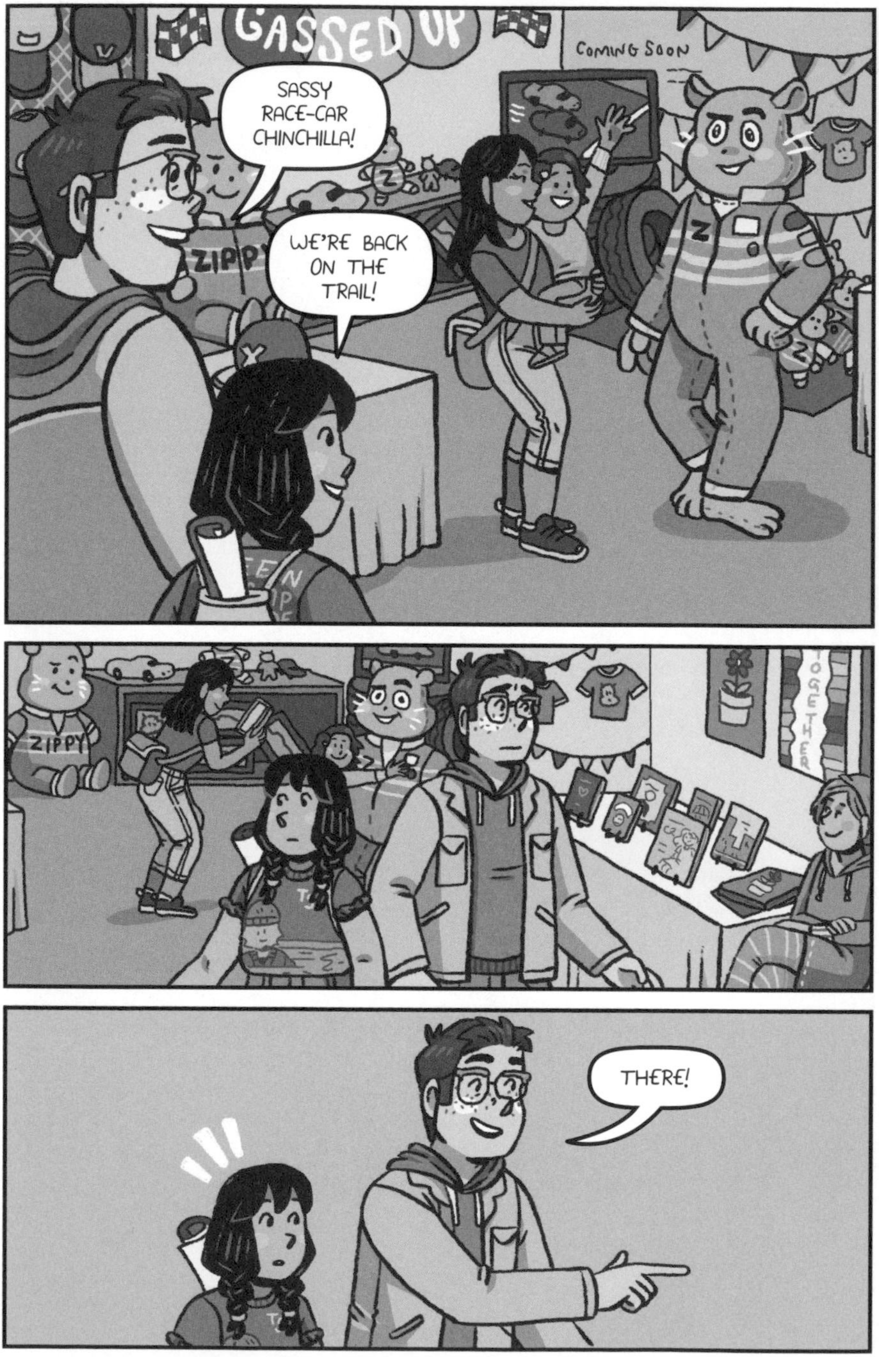
GASSED UP
COMING SOON
SASSY RACE-CAR CHINCHILLA!
WE'RE BACK ON THE TRAIL!
ZIPPY
ZIPPY
TOGETHER
THERE!

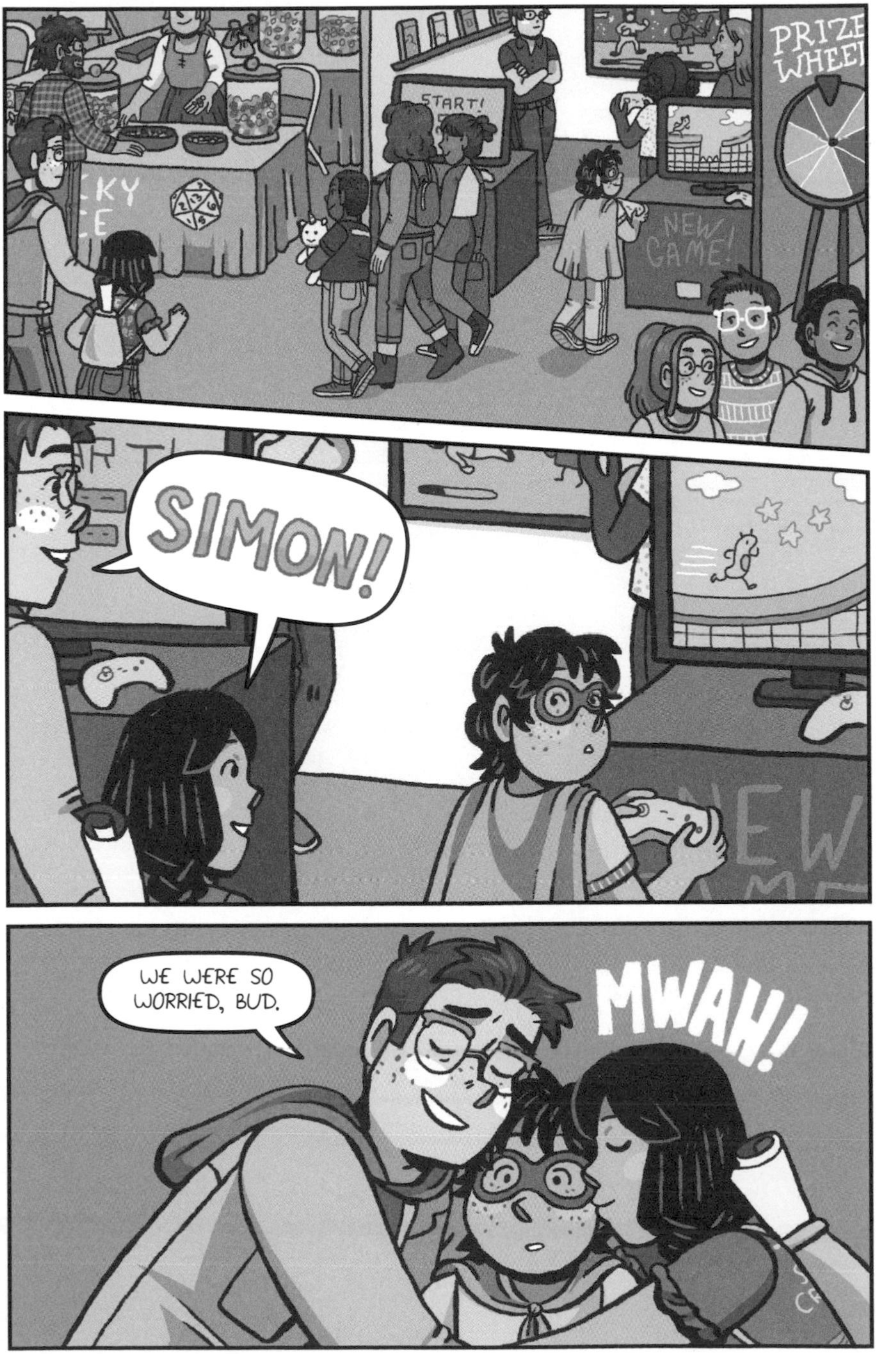
PRIZE WHEEL
START!
NEW GAME!
SIMON!
NEW
WE WERE SO WORRIED, BUD.
MWAH!

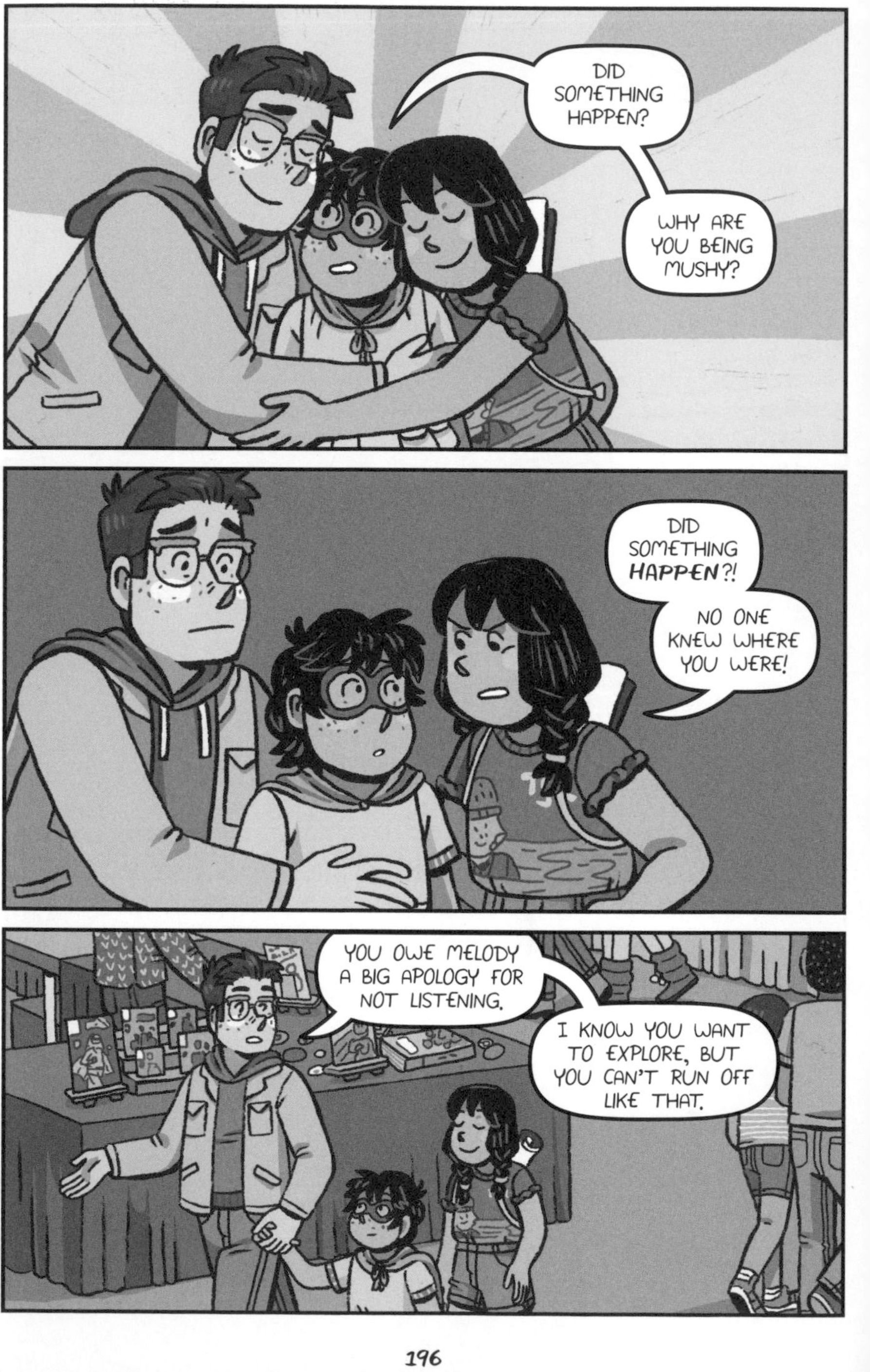
DID SOMETHING HAPPEN?
WHY ARE YOU BEING MUSHY?
DID SOMETHING **HAPPEN**?!
NO ONE KNEW WHERE YOU WERE!
YOU OWE MELODY A BIG APOLOGY FOR NOT LISTENING.
I KNOW YOU WANT TO EXPLORE, BUT YOU CAN'T RUN OFF LIKE THAT.

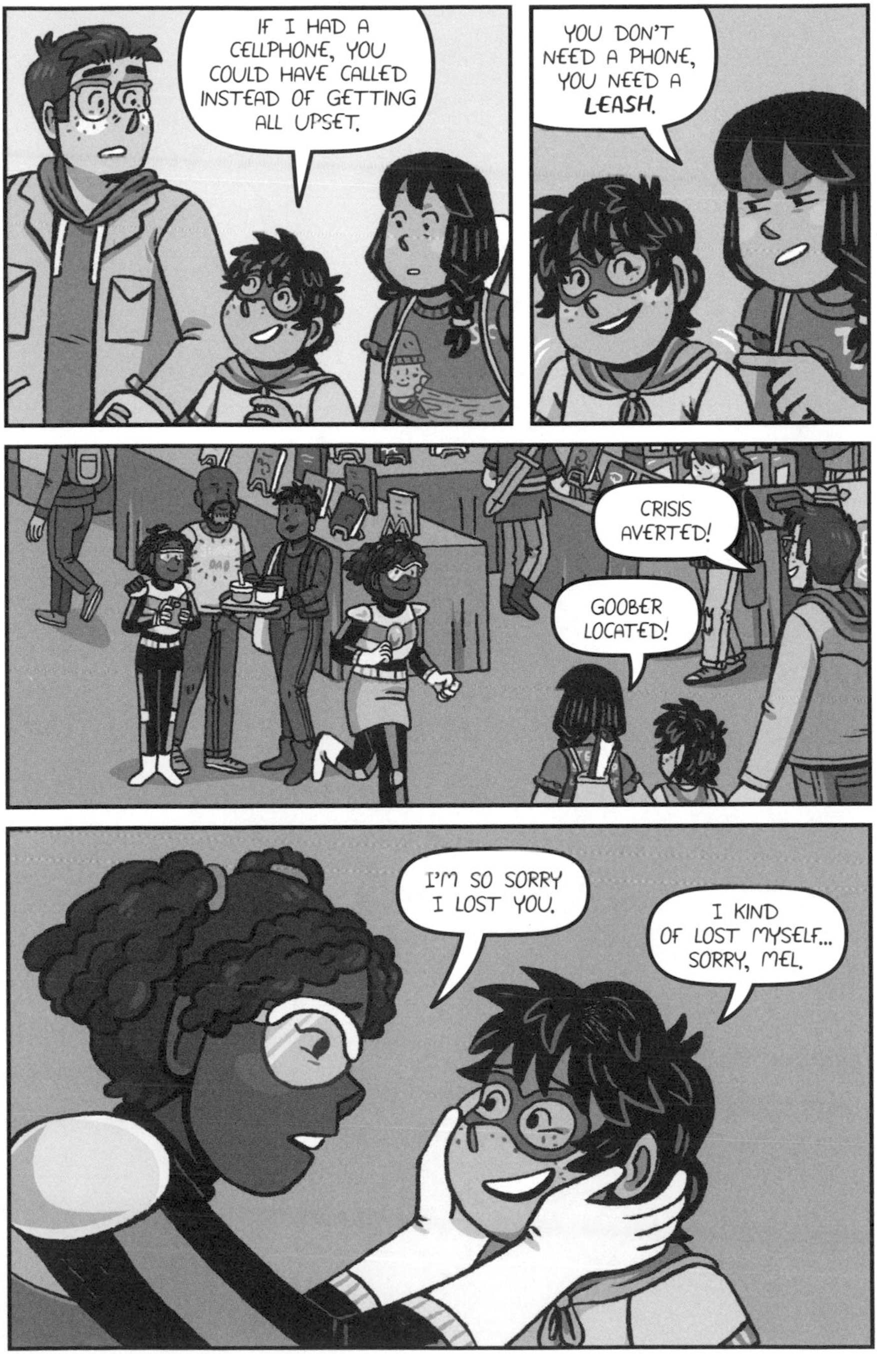
IF I HAD A CELLPHONE, YOU COULD HAVE CALLED INSTEAD OF GETTING ALL UPSET.
YOU DON'T NEED A PHONE, YOU NEED A **LEASH.**
CRISIS AVERTED!
GOOBER LOCATED!
I'M SO SORRY I LOST YOU.
I KIND OF LOST MYSELF... SORRY, MEL.

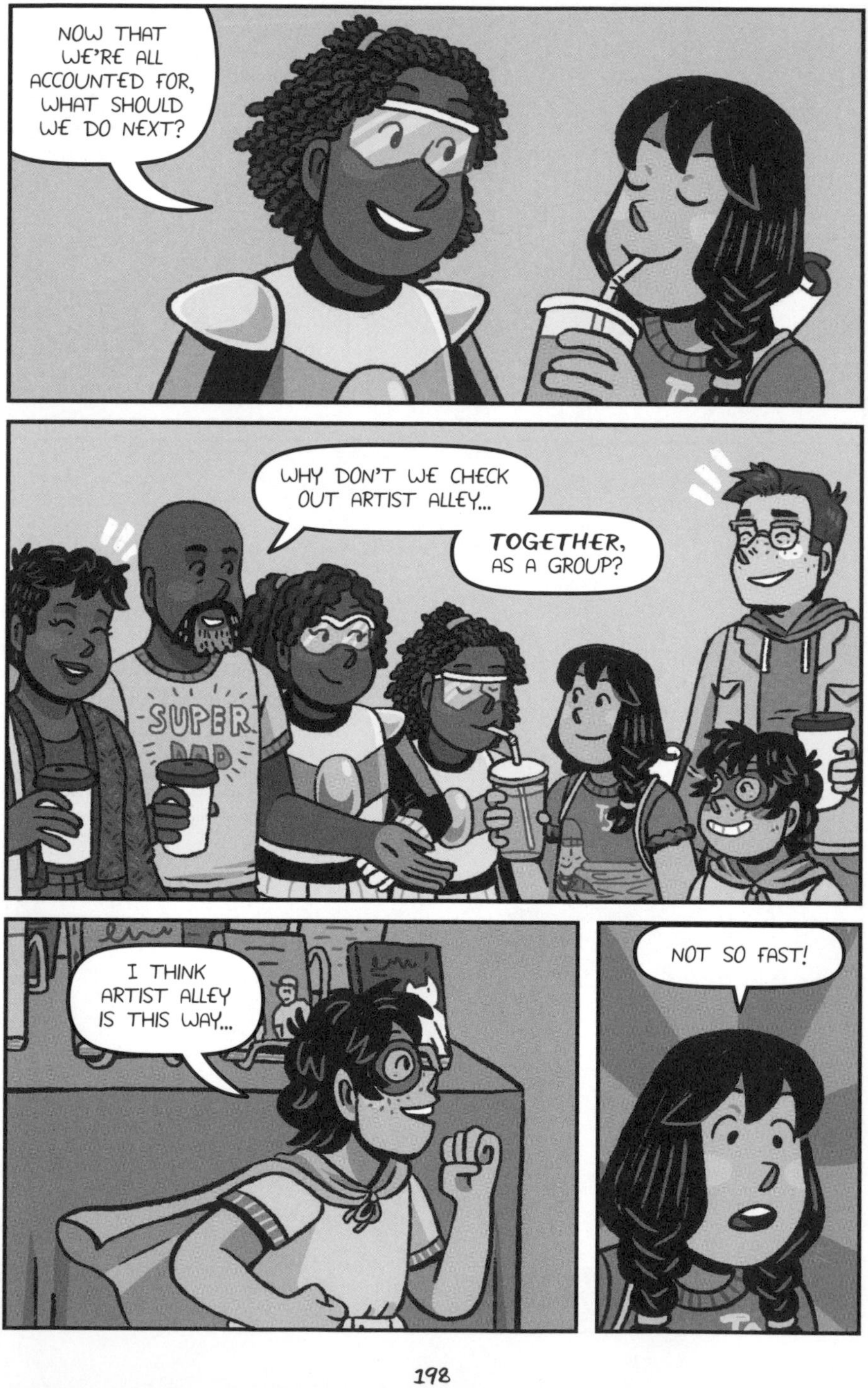
NOW THAT WE'RE ALL ACCOUNTED FOR, WHAT SHOULD WE DO NEXT?
WHY DON'T WE CHECK OUT ARTIST ALLEY...
TOGETHER, AS A GROUP?
SUPER DAD
I THINK ARTIST ALLEY IS THIS WAY...
NOT SO FAST!

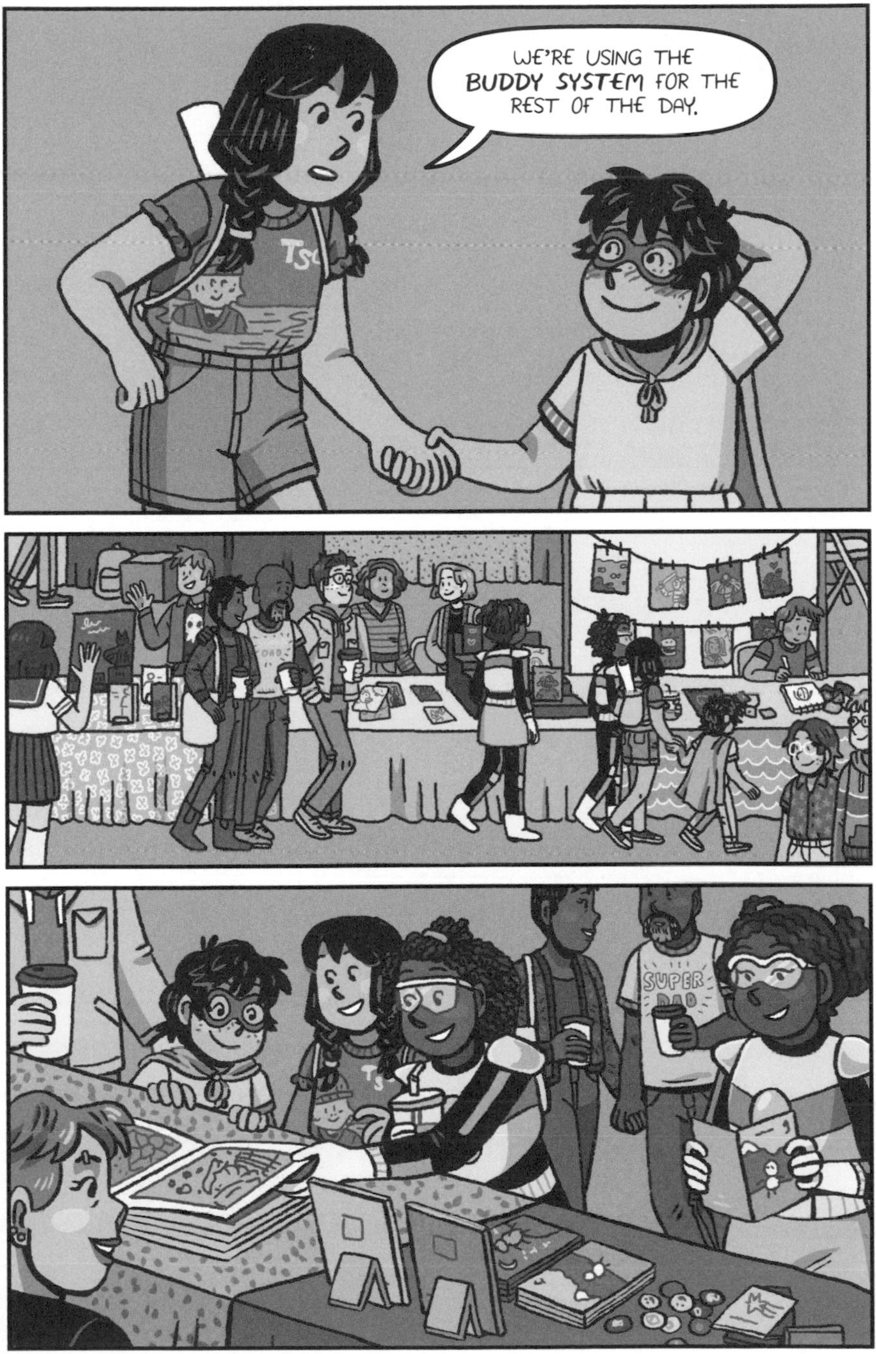
WE'RE USING THE **BUDDY SYSTEM** FOR THE REST OF THE DAY.
SUPER DAD

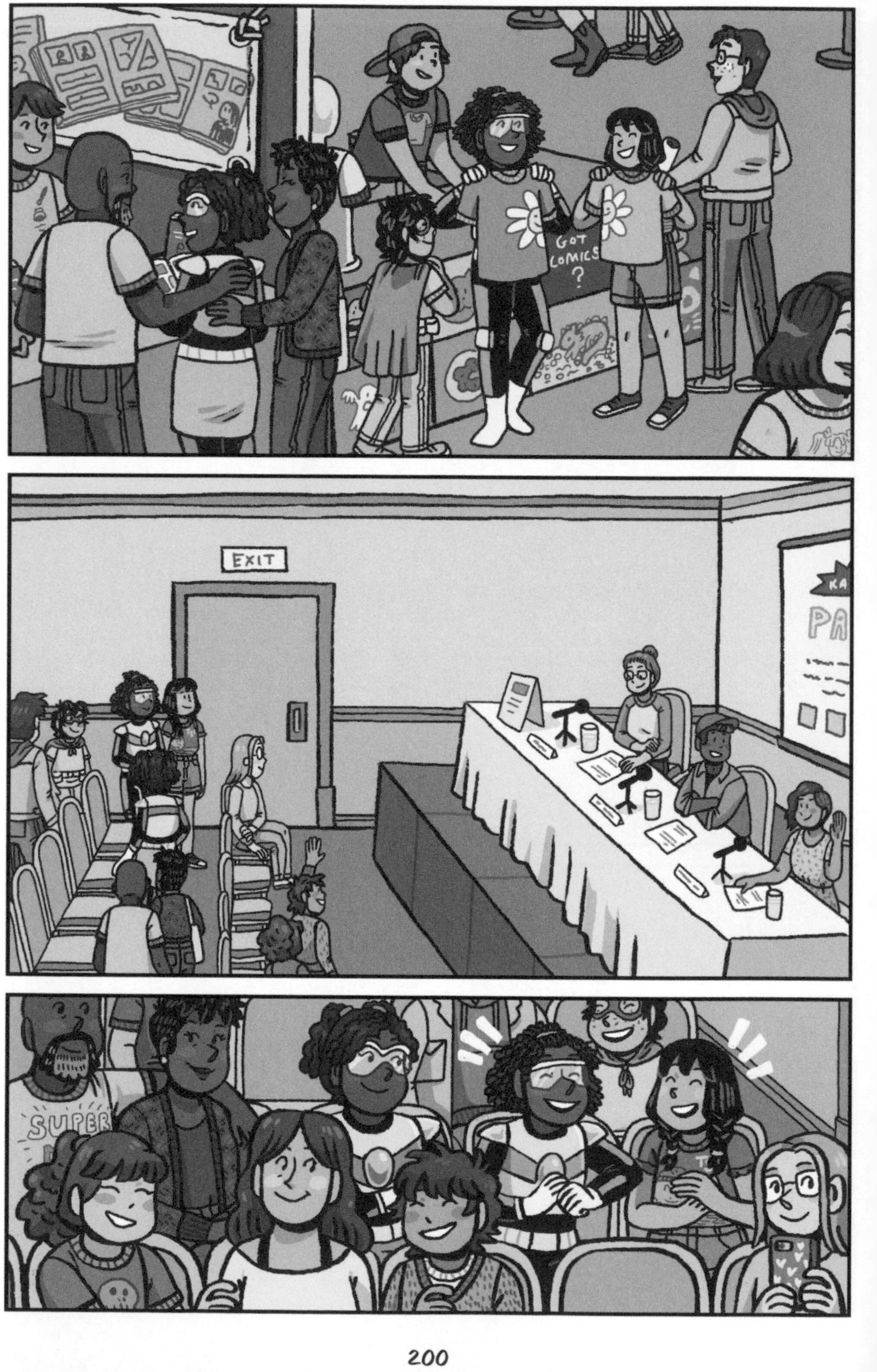
GOT COMICS ?
EXIT
SUPER

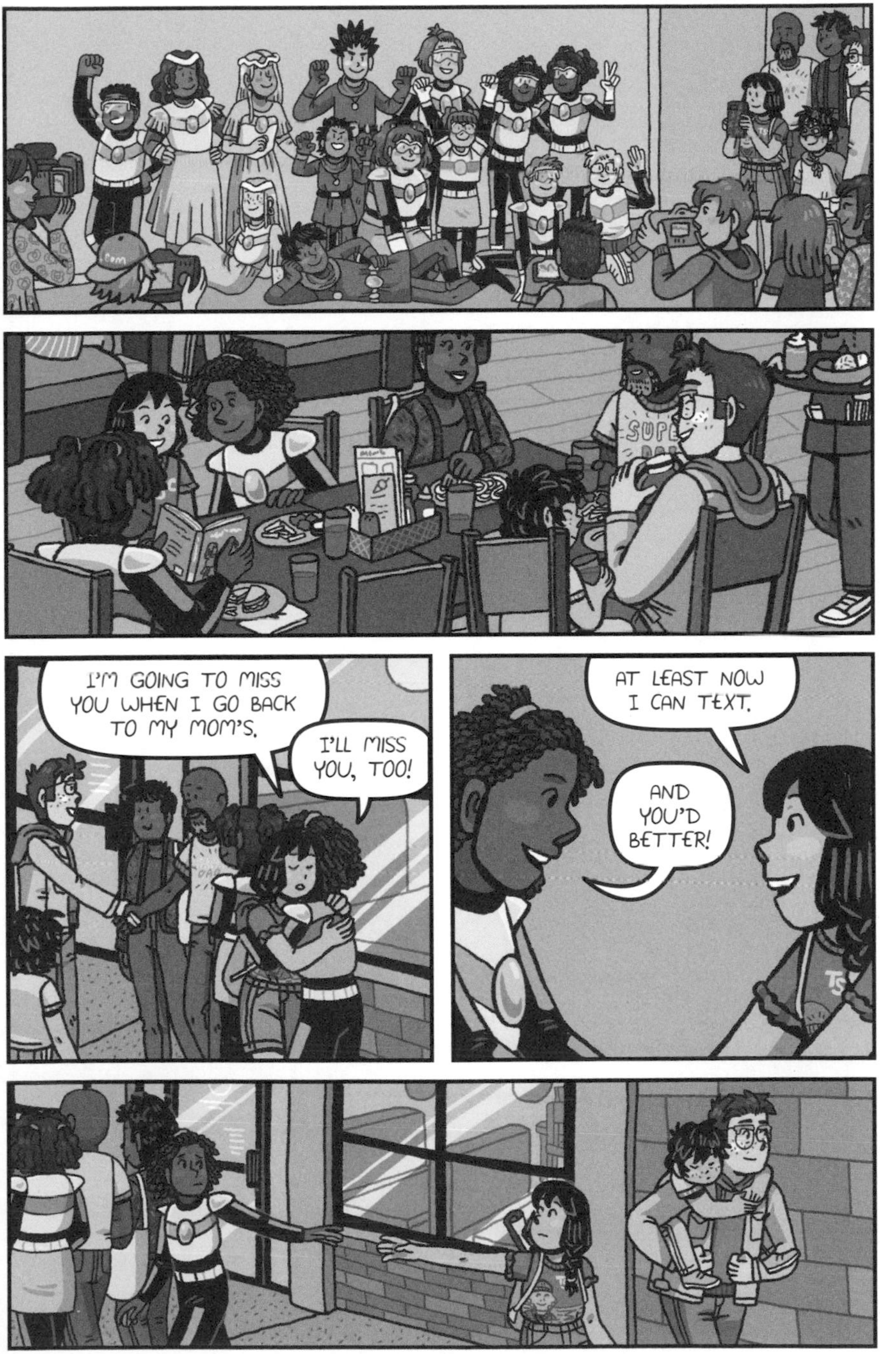
I'M GOING TO MISS YOU WHEN I GO BACK TO MY MOM'S.
I'LL MISS YOU, TOO!
AT LEAST NOW I CAN TEXT.
AND YOU'D BETTER!

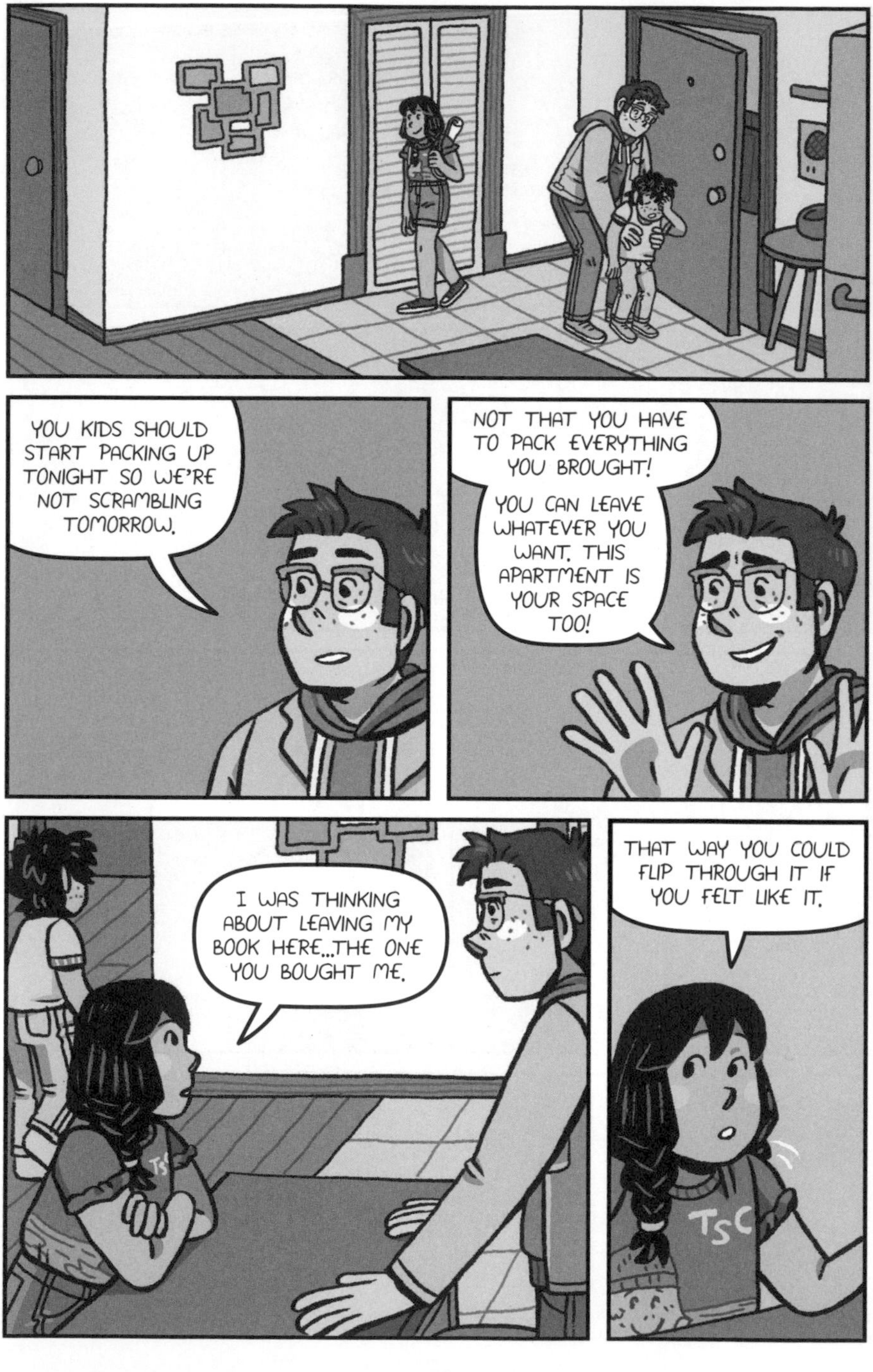
YOU KIDS SHOULD START PACKING UP TONIGHT SO WE'RE NOT SCRAMBLING TOMORROW.
NOT THAT YOU HAVE TO PACK EVERYTHING YOU BROUGHT!
YOU CAN LEAVE WHATEVER YOU WANT. THIS APARTMENT IS YOUR SPACE TOO!
I WAS THINKING ABOUT LEAVING MY BOOK HERE...THE ONE YOU BOUGHT ME.
THAT WAY YOU COULD FLIP THROUGH IT IF YOU FELT LIKE IT.
TSC
TSC

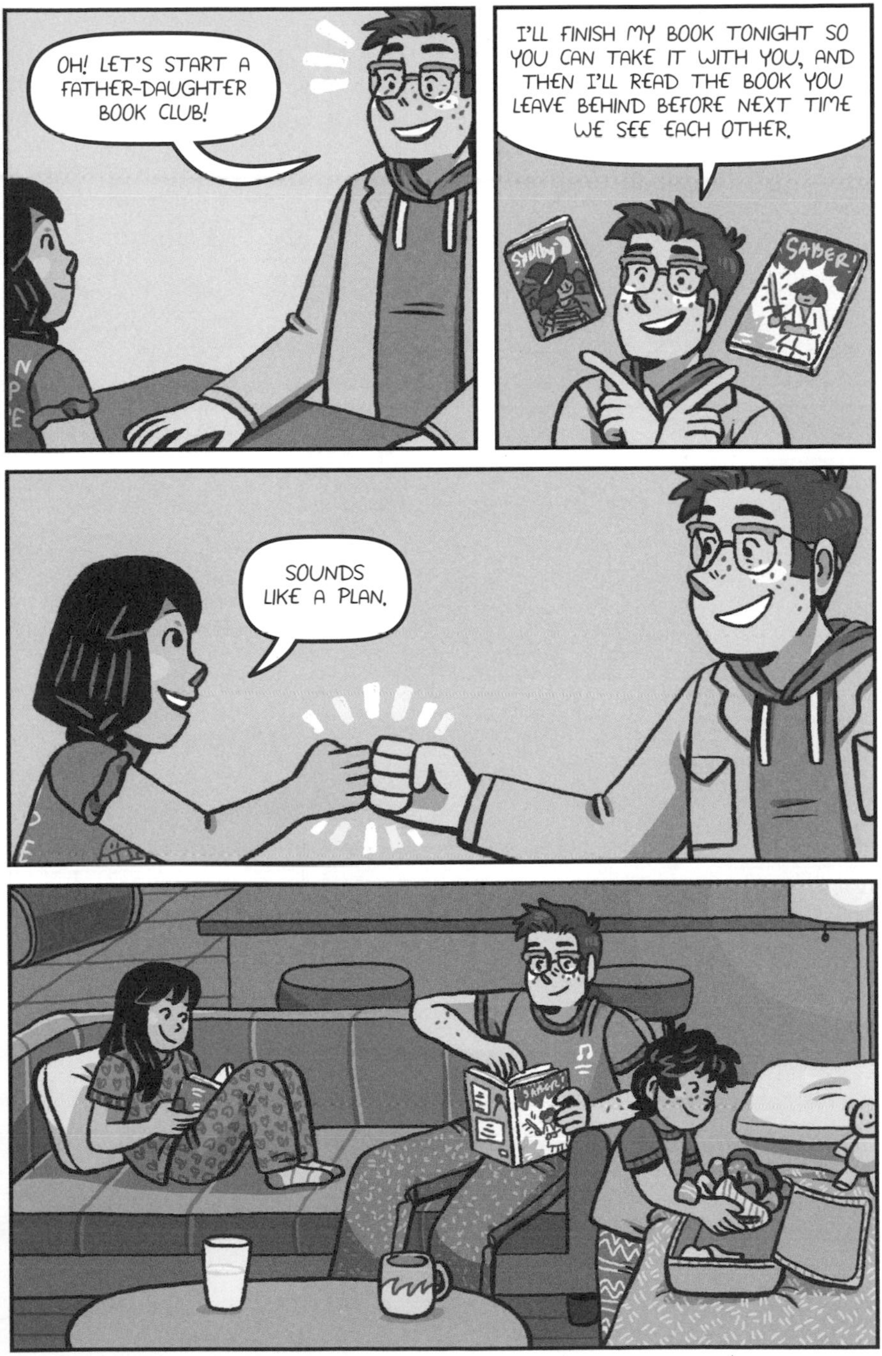
OH! LET'S START A FATHER-DAUGHTER BOOK CLUB!
I'LL FINISH MY BOOK TONIGHT SO YOU CAN TAKE IT WITH YOU, AND THEN I'LL READ THE BOOK YOU LEAVE BEHIND BEFORE NEXT TIME WE SEE EACH OTHER.
SABER!
SOUNDS LIKE A PLAN.

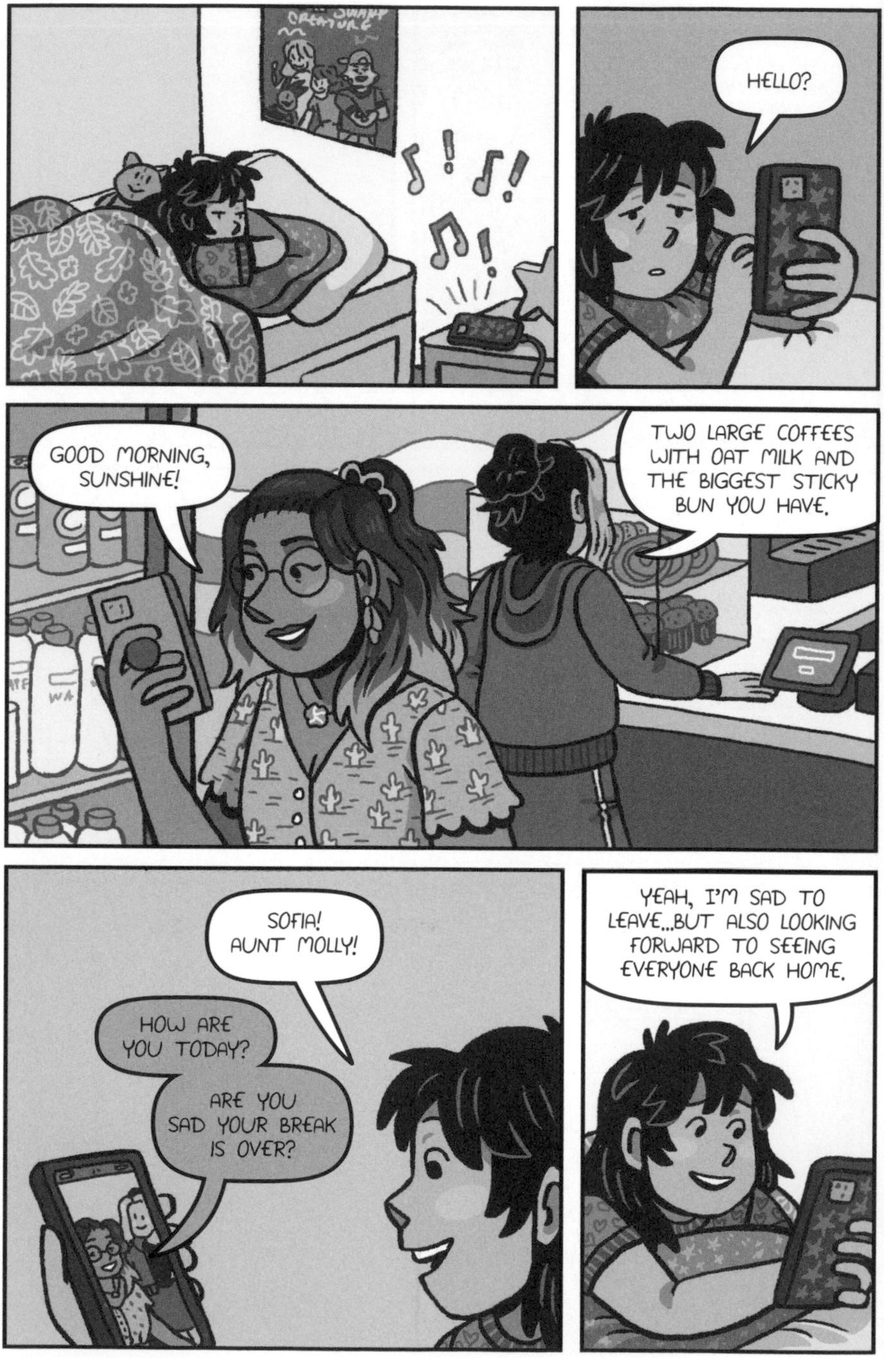
HELLO?
GOOD MORNING, SUNSHINE!
TWO LARGE COFFEES WITH OAT MILK AND THE BIGGEST STICKY BUN YOU HAVE.
SOFIA! AUNT MOLLY!
HOW ARE YOU TODAY?
ARE YOU SAD YOUR BREAK IS OVER?
YEAH, I'M SAD TO LEAVE...BUT ALSO LOOKING FORWARD TO SEEING EVERYONE BACK HOME.

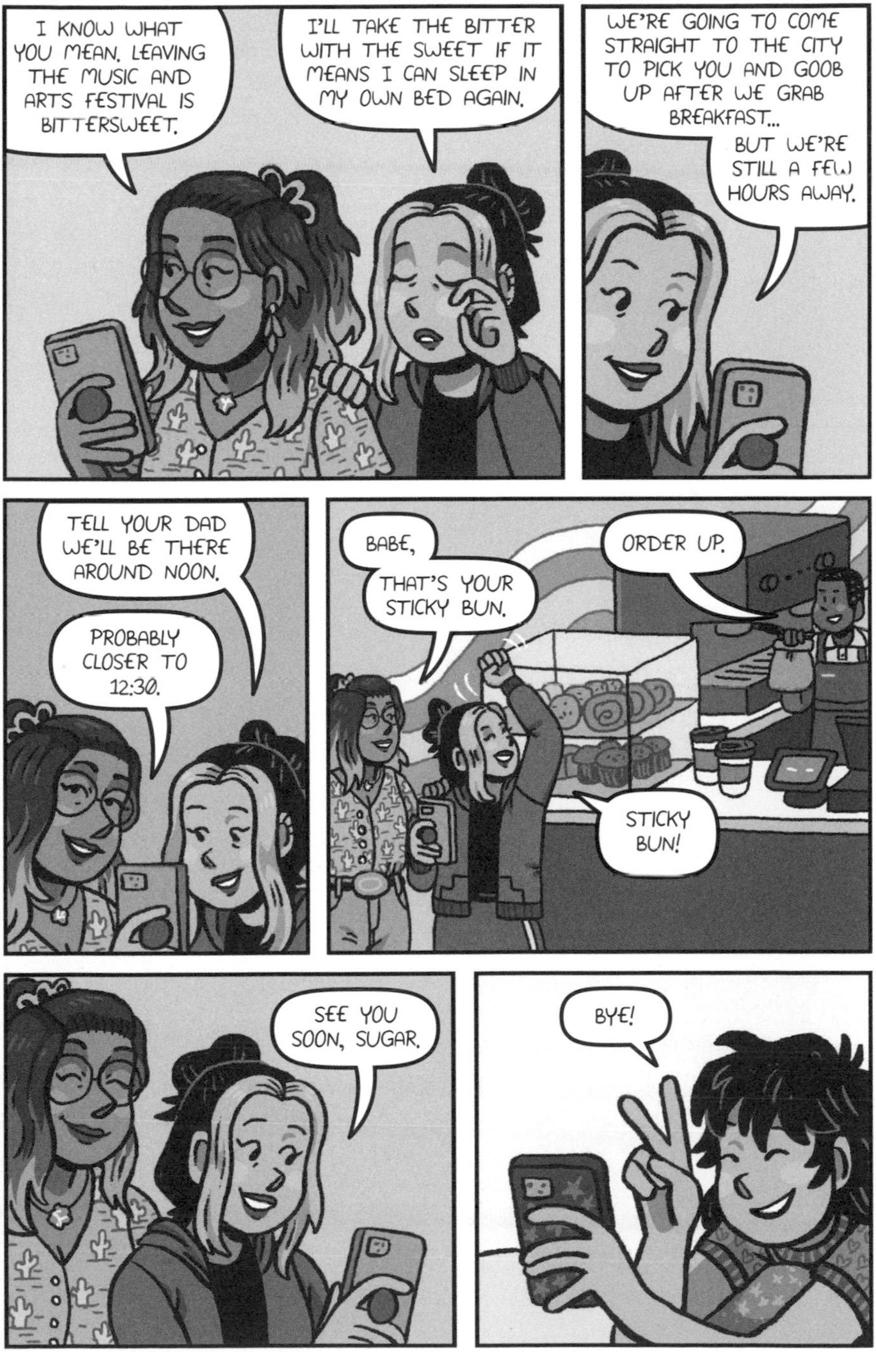
I KNOW WHAT YOU MEAN. LEAVING THE MUSIC AND ARTS FESTIVAL IS BITTERSWEET.
I'LL TAKE THE BITTER WITH THE SWEET IF IT MEANS I CAN SLEEP IN MY OWN BED AGAIN.
WE'RE GOING TO COME STRAIGHT TO THE CITY TO PICK YOU AND GOOB UP AFTER WE GRAB BREAKFAST...
BUT WE'RE STILL A FEW HOURS AWAY.
TELL YOUR DAD WE'LL BE THERE AROUND NOON.
PROBABLY CLOSER TO 12:30.
BABE,
THAT'S YOUR STICKY BUN.
ORDER UP.
STICKY BUN!
SEE YOU SOON, SUGAR.
BYE!

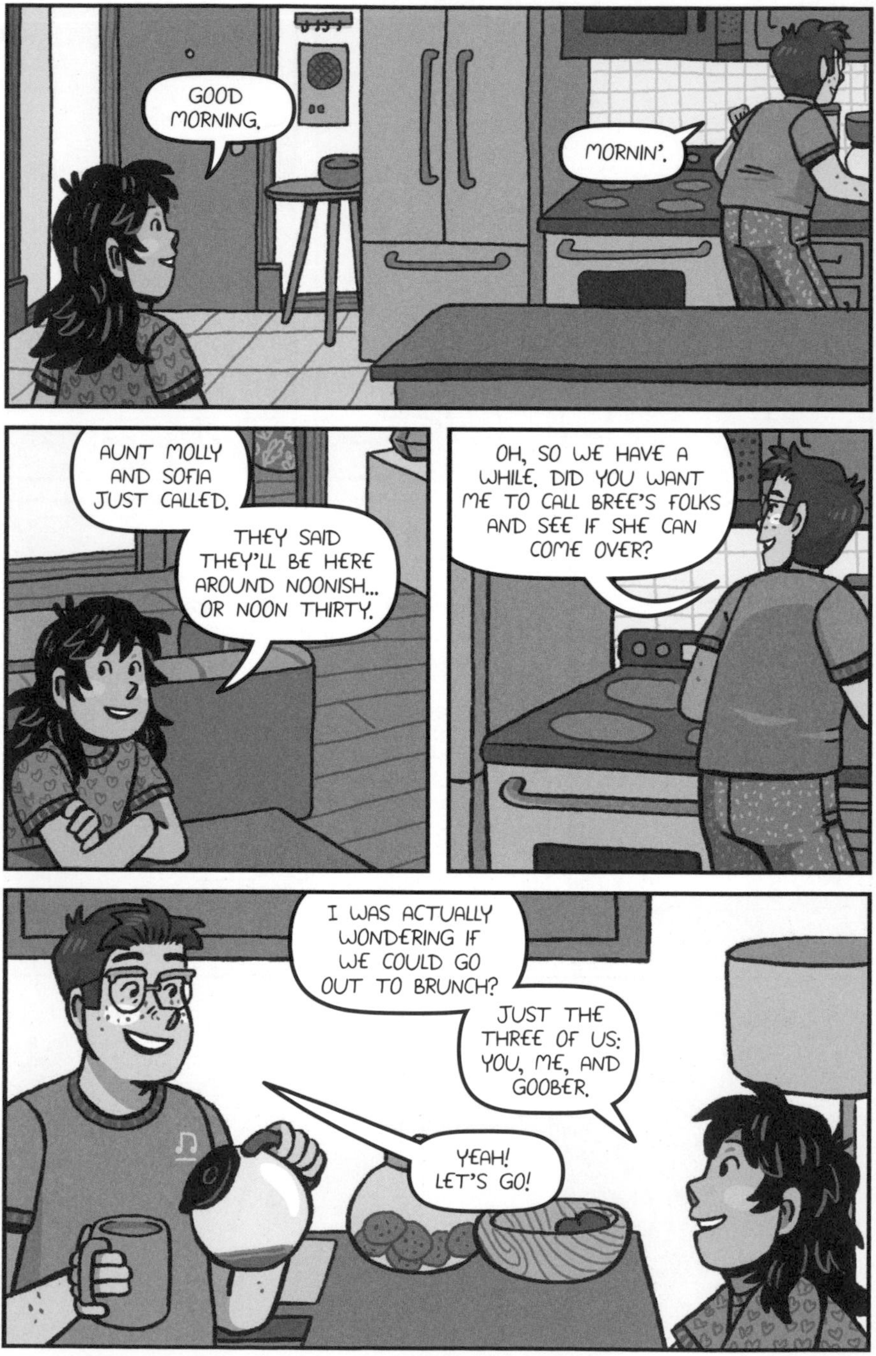
GOOD MORNING.
MORNIN'.
AUNT MOLLY AND SOFIA JUST CALLED.
THEY SAID THEY'LL BE HERE AROUND NOONISH... OR NOON THIRTY.
OH, SO WE HAVE A WHILE. DID YOU WANT ME TO CALL BREE'S FOLKS AND SEE IF SHE CAN COME OVER?
I WAS ACTUALLY WONDERING IF WE COULD GO OUT TO BRUNCH?
JUST THE THREE OF US: YOU, ME, AND GOOBER.
YEAH! LET'S GO!

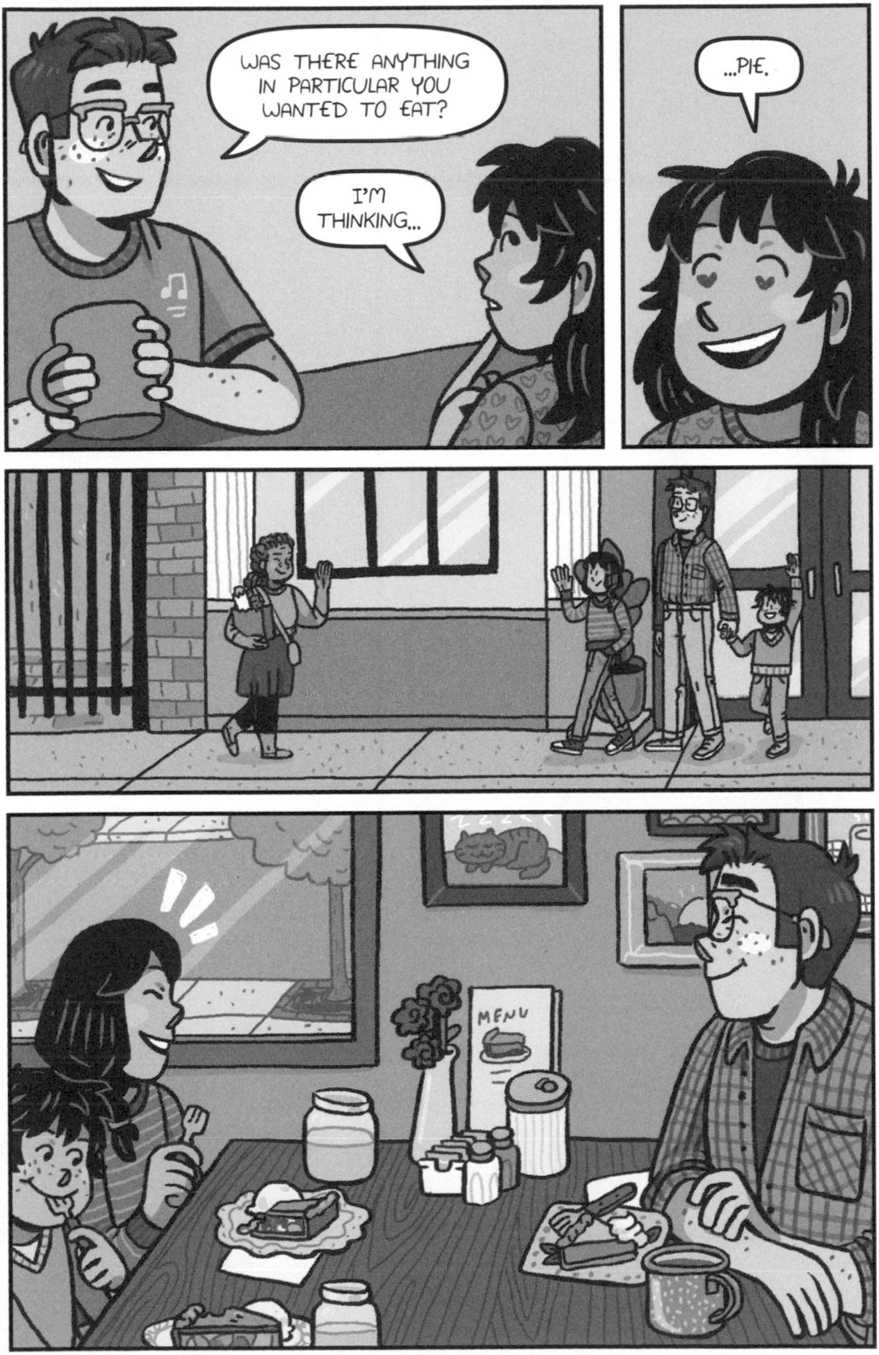
WAS THERE ANYTHING IN PARTICULAR YOU WANTED TO EAT?
I'M THINKING...
...PIE.
MENU

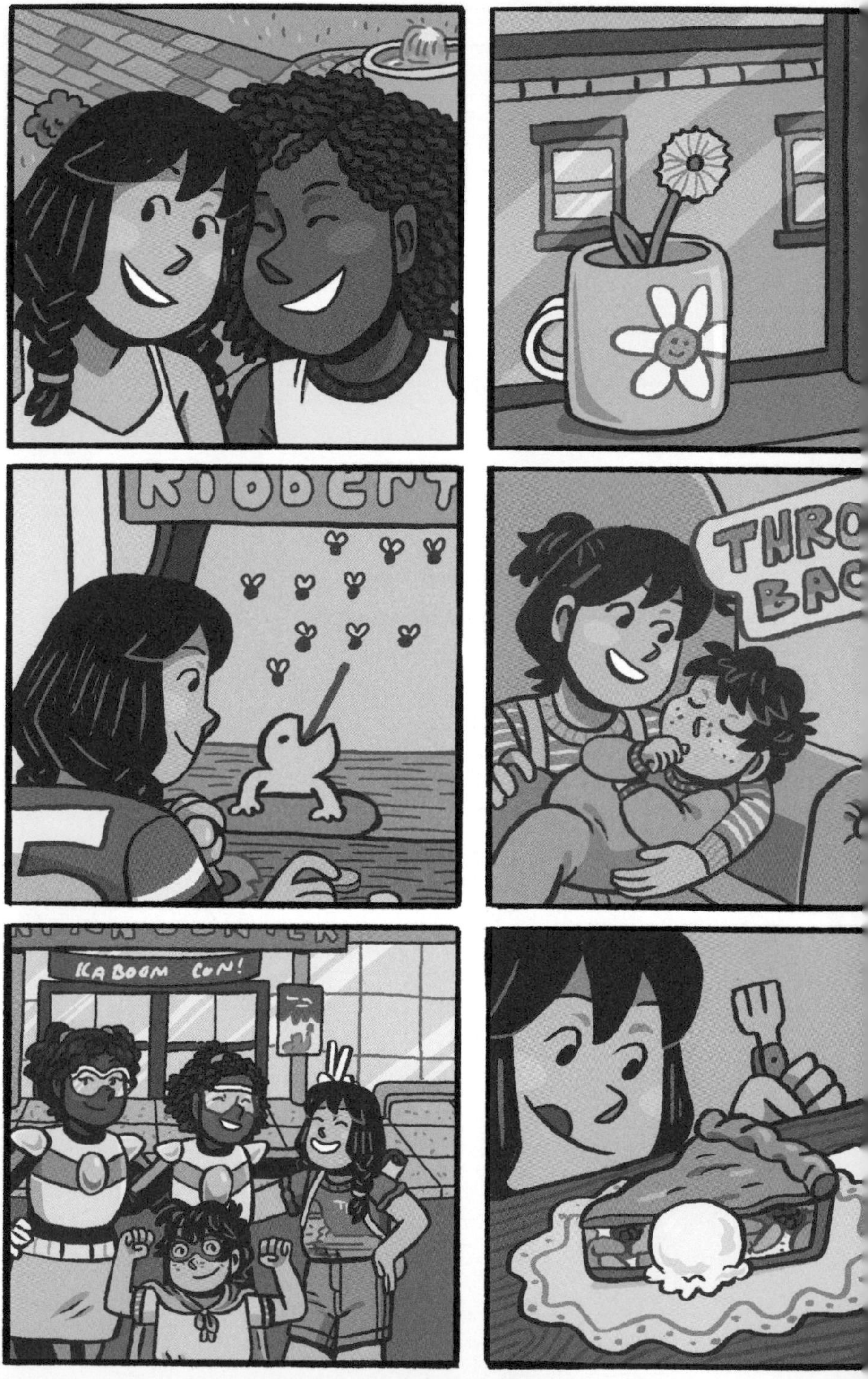
KA BOOM CON!

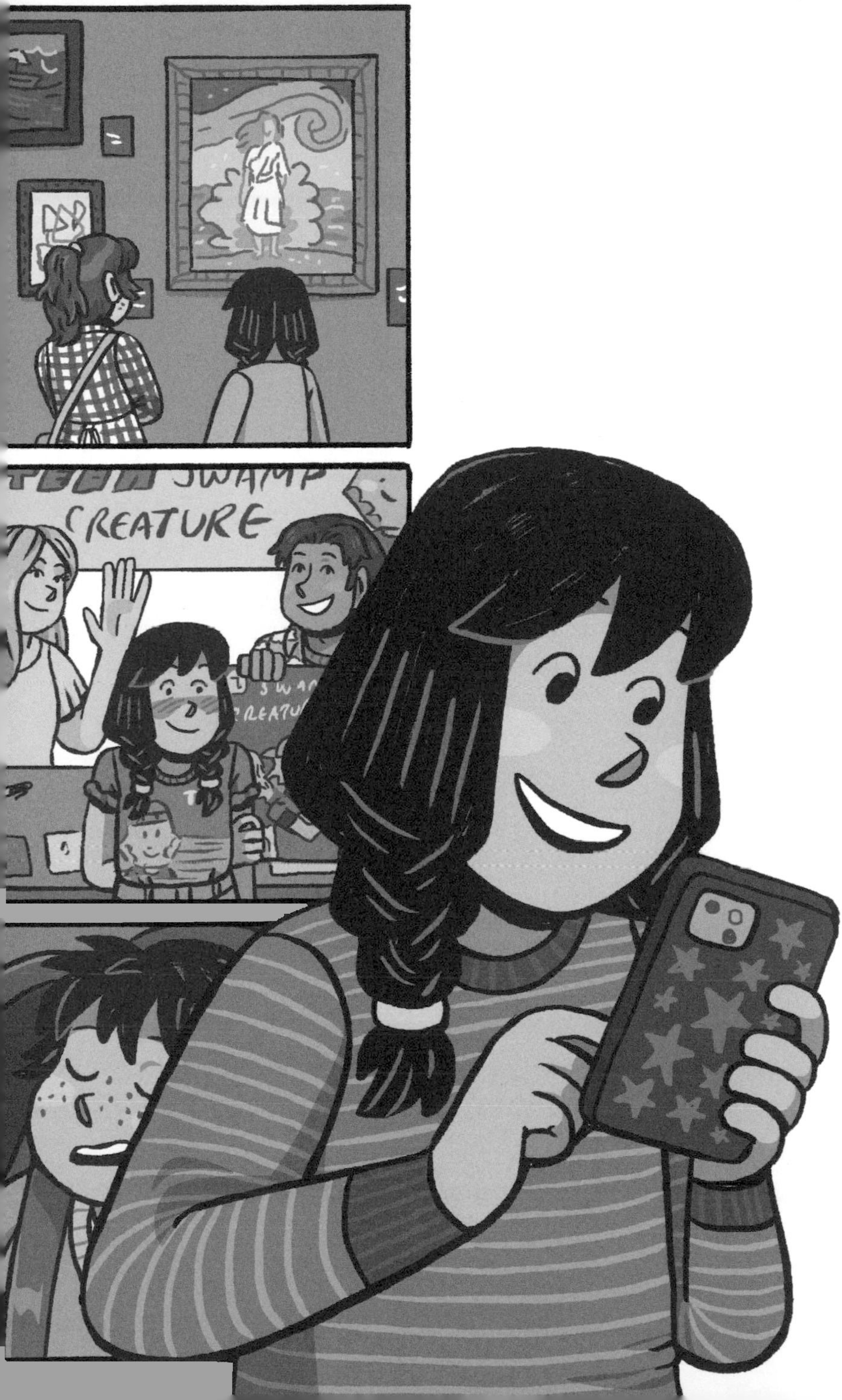
SWAMP
CREATURE

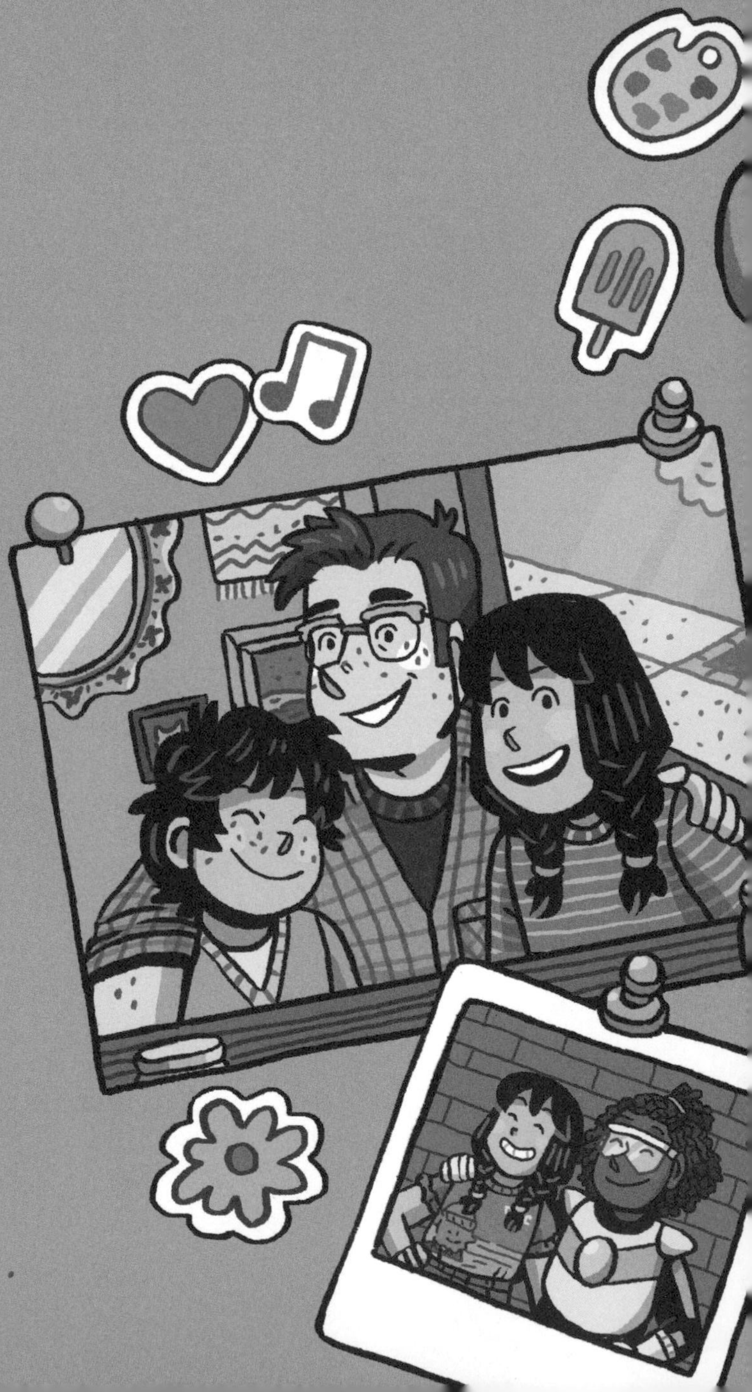

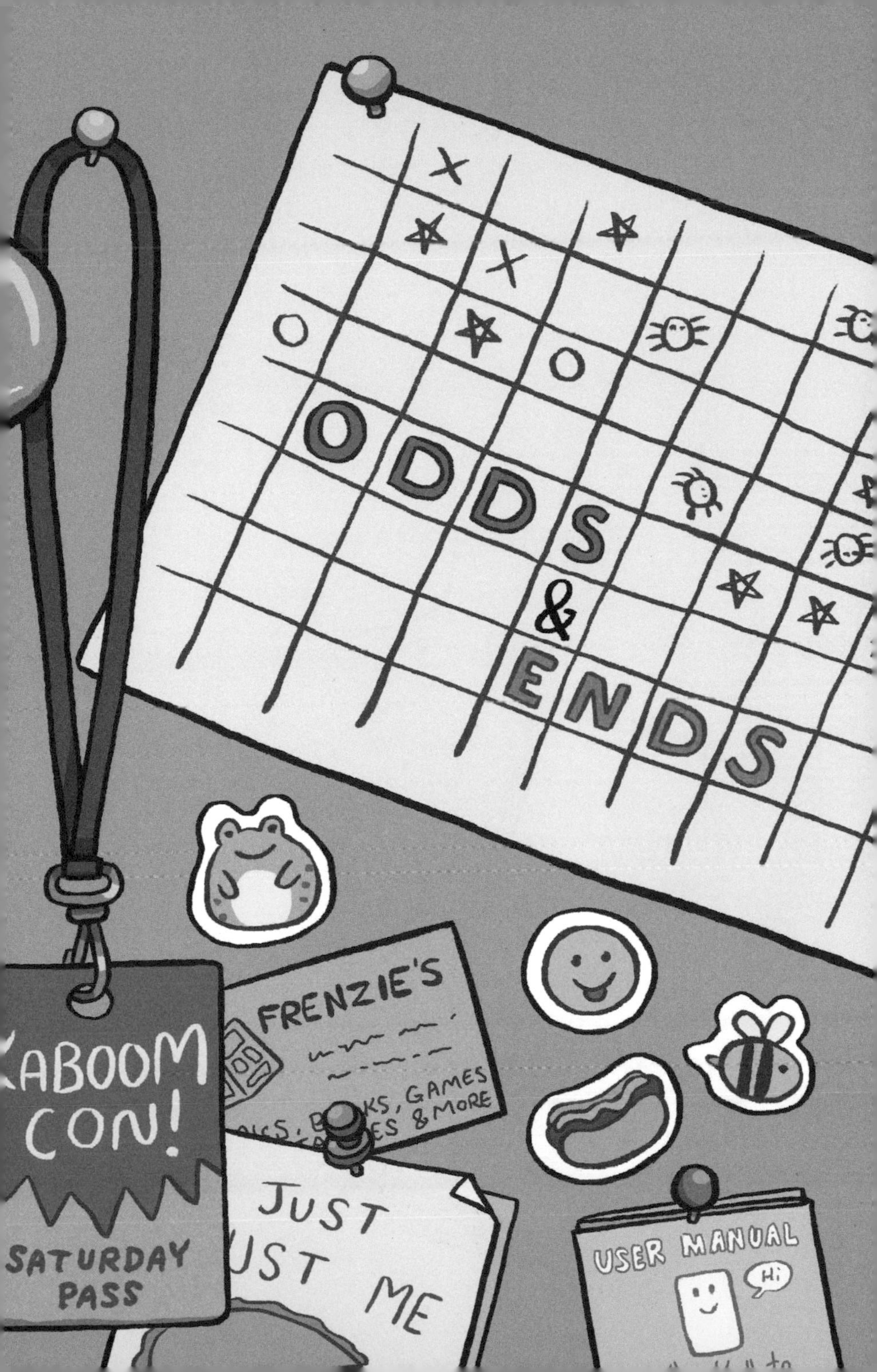
ODDS & ENDS
FRENZIE'S
KS, GAMES
ES & MORE
ABOOM CON!
SATURDAY PASS
JUST
UST ME
USER MANUAL
Hi

SOCIAL MEDIA DOs and DON'Ts

DON'T: BE IN A RUSH TO SIGN UP

IT MIGHT SEEM LIKE EVERYONE YOU KNOW HAS SOCIAL MEDIA, BUT HUMANS SURVIVED FOR CENTURIES WITHOUT ONLINE PROFILES—AND YOU CAN SURVIVE TOO! THE AGE REQUIREMENTS FOR WEBSITES ARE THERE FOR A REASON. IF YOU ARE OLD ENOUGH TO SIGN UP, CONSIDER WHETHER BEING ON A CERTAIN PLATFORM WILL BE BENEFICIAL TO YOU.

DO: CONSIDER USING A CREATIVE SCREEN NAME

PICKING OUT A SCREEN NAME THAT ISN'T YOUR REAL NAME CAN BE A GOOD WAY TO PROTECT YOUR IDENTITY...BUT ALSO A FUN WAY TO EXPRESS YOURSELF.

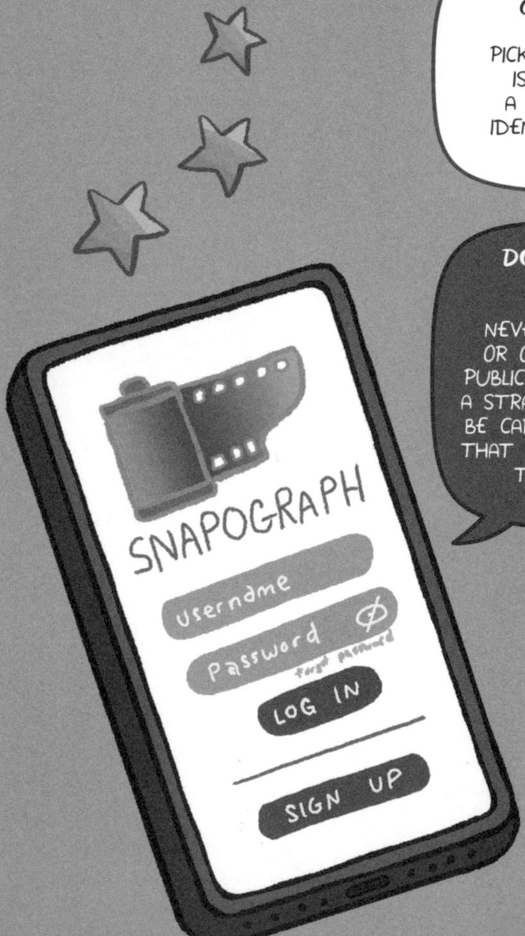
SNAPOGRAPH
username
password
LOG IN
SIGN UP

DON'T: SHARE PERSONAL INFORMATION

NEVER GIVE OUT YOUR ADDRESS OR OTHER IDENTIFYING INFO IN A PUBLIC POST. IF YOU WOULDN'T TELL A STRANGER, DON'T POST IT ONLINE! BE CAREFUL ABOUT SHARING PHOTOS THAT MIGHT HAVE YOUR ADDRESS IN THE BACKGROUND—LIKE ON A PIECE OF MAIL!

DO: SPREAD POSITIVITY

IT DOESN'T COST ANYTHING TO BE NICE! IF SOMEONE YOU KNOW POSTS A SELFIE OR A WORK OF ART OR A CUTE PIC OF THEIR PET, YOU COULD MAKE THEIR DAY BY SAYING SOMETHING NICE IN THE COMMENTS OR SIMPLY GIVING IT A "LIKE."

DON'T: RESPOND TO DMS FROM PEOPLE YOU DON'T KNOW

YOU DON'T HAVE TO RESPOND TO EVERY MESSAGE THAT POPS UP IN YOUR INBOX, AND IF THEY'RE FROM A STRANGER, YOU DON'T EVEN HAVE TO OPEN THEM. IT'S NOT RUDE TO FILTER YOUR MESSAGES.

@seeyersawyer

☆5 💬0   📤

DO: KNOW WHO CAN SEE YOUR POSTS

MOST PLATFORMS HAVE PRIVATE MODES WHERE YOU CAN CONTROL WHO IS SEEING WHAT YOU POST OR WAYS TO SHARE CONTENT WITH ONLY CERTAIN GROUPS OF PEOPLE. IF YOU'RE POSTING PUBLICLY THERE'S THE POTENTIAL FOR ANYONE TO SEE YOUR POSTS, SO DON'T SHARE ANYTHING YOU WOULDN'T WANT YOUR GRANDPARENTS, YOUR CRUSH, OR THE PRESIDENT TO SEE.

@crystalchandalier

☆7 💬0   📤

DON'T: COMPARE YOURSELF TO OTHERS

IT MIGHT SEEM LIKE EVERYONE ONLINE IS LOOKING CUTE, DOING EXCITING ACTIVITIES, AND LIVING THEIR BEST LIVES...BUT REMEMBER, IT ONLY SEEMS THAT WAY BECAUSE PEOPLE ARE MORE INCLINED TO SHARE THE GOOD STUFF!! NOT MANY PEOPLE POST ABOUT GETTING SPINACH IN THEIR TEETH, BUT IT HAPPENS TO THE BEST OF US.

DO: BE YOURSELF

YOUR ONLINE PRESENCE SHOULD BE A REFLECTION OF YOU, SO DON'T STRESS OUT TRYING TO BE SOMEONE YOU'RE NOT. POST ABOUT WHAT YOU CARE ABOUT AND WHAT MAKES YOU HAPPY AND YOU'LL FIND OUT WHO SHARES THOSE PASSIONS!

Let's Draw Olive!

GRAB A PIECE OF PAPER, A PENCIL, AND A MARKER—OR OPEN UP YOUR FAVORITE DRAWING PROGRAM IF YOU LIKE TO DRAW DIGITALLY.

KEEP IN MIND, THE FIRST FEW STEPS SHOULD BE IN PENCIL OR ON A "SKETCH LAYER" SO THEY CAN BE ERASED LATER.

START WITH SIMPLE SHAPES. SKETCH A CIRCLE FOR THE TOP OF THE HEAD AND ADD THE SHAPE OF THE CHEEKS AND CHIN UNDER THAT.

THESE LINES ARE JUST GUIDES AND DON'T HAVE TO BE PERFECT!

DRAW A LINE FROM THE TOP OF THE HEAD TO THE CHIN, CURVING IN THE DIRECTION THE CHARACTER IS FACING AND ANOTHER LINE ACROSS THE CENTER OF THE FACE.

OLIVE'S EYES KIND OF LOOK LIKE ROTATED COMMAS OR APOSTROPHES.

PUT THE EYES ON THE LINE GOING HORIZONTALLY ACROSS THE FACE AND PLACE THE NOSE AND MOUTH BELOW THEM ON THE VERTICAL LINE.

SKETCH IN THE HAIR AND ANY OTHER DETAILS.

OLIVE USUALLY HAS THREE POINTS ON HER BANGS AND THREE TIERS IN HER BRAIDS.

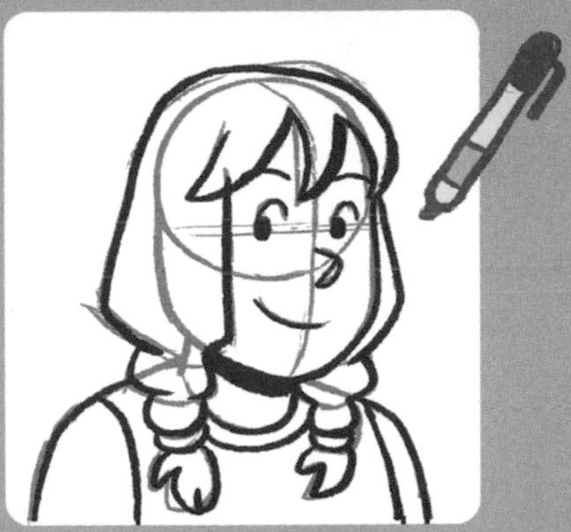

TRACE OVER THE SKETCH WITH A MARKER (OR ON A NEW LAYER IF YOU'RE DRAWING DIGITALLY).

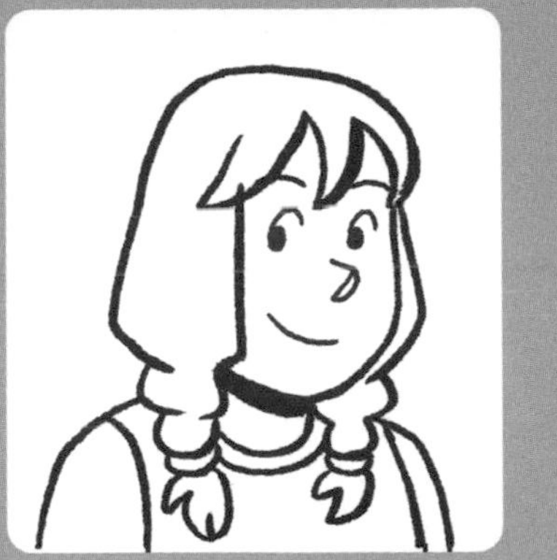

CAREFULLY ERASE YOUR SKETCH (OR TURN OFF THE SKETCH LAYER).

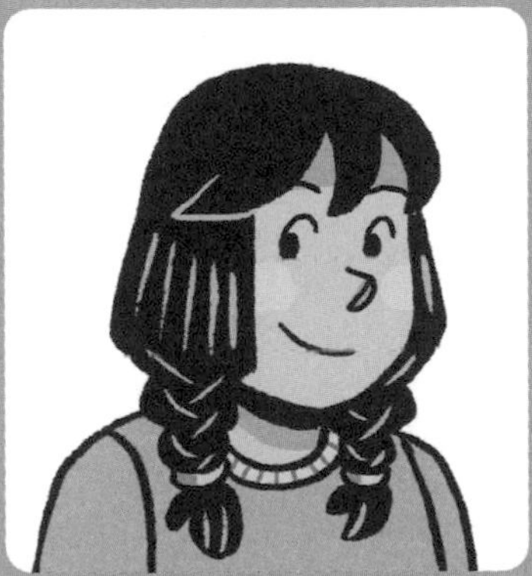

ADD DETAILS AND COLOR IF YOU FEEL LIKE IT!

OLIVE'S HAIR IS A SOLID SHAPE WITH THE DETAILS DRAWN ON TOP WITH A LIGHTER COLOR.

GEL PENS WORK WELL FOR ADDING DETAILS OVER BLACK IF YOU'RE DRAWING WITH MARKERS.

MAKE SURE YOUR MARKER IS PERMANENT IF YOU WANT TO DRAW OVER IT.

TRY DRAWING SOME OF THE OTHER CHARACTERS FROM THE SERIES, A SELF-PORTRAIT, OR A COMPLETELY NEW CHARACTER BY CHANGING THE FEATURES.

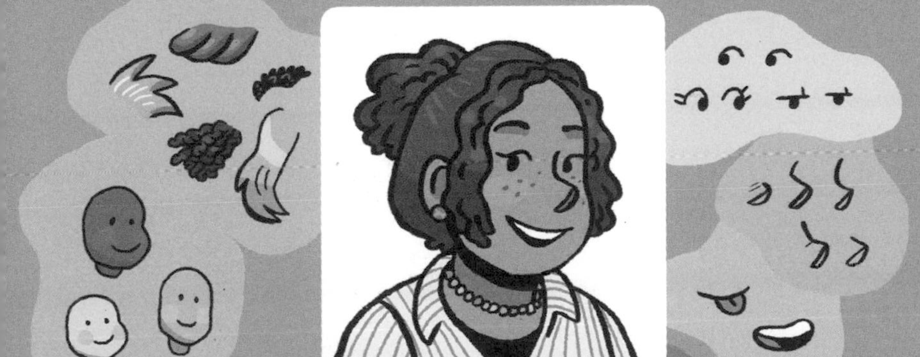

WHO IS THIS?
A NEW FRIEND?

Q: It's exciting to be so many books into Olive's story, as well as to see her overall world expand with the spin-off series, Besties. What has been your favorite part of expanding the Click universe?

KAYLA: Olive has a lot of friends, so the cast has been large since the first book—and of course she's always making new friends as she goes—so being able to expand on those friends' personalities and explore their lives more as the books progress has been amazing.

Q: How has your process evolved through the years of working on Click and Besties?

KAYLA: The main way it's evolved is that things have become more collaborative. When I first started working on Click, I was trying to do everything on my own with as little help as possible, and I was kind of afraid of letting other people in on the process because I'd never really collaborated with others on such a big project before. Now with both Besties and the Click series, I'm seeing that teamwork really does make the dream work. Working with collaborators is what makes the books possible—and it's also a whole lot of fun!

Q: As Olive is maturing and facing different challenges, how do you decide what her next adventure is going to be?

KAYLA: I think about things that were important to me as a kid, but also listen to the young people around me to better understand what they're concerned about. It's obviously been a little while since I was in middle school, and unfortunately it seems like there are always brand-new things for kids to worry about. I try to be aware of that while also having Olive and her friends tackle some of the more timeless challenges that every generation faces when it comes to school, friendship, and growing up.

Q: *This is the first time we've gone in-depth on Olive's relationship with her father. What do you think is different about Olive's journey in this story compared to previous books?*

KAYLA: This was a rough one for Olive! In the other books, even though there are some issues that were ultimately out of Olive's control like inequality or bullying, there were ways that she could take action and feel like she's helping. But when it comes to their own families, kids don't always have a lot of sway over situations. Honestly, it was difficult to explore this relationship where Olive feels this big disconnect with one of her parents for a good portion of the book. While Olive is a fictional character, the whole time I was writing I was thinking of the real people I love who have gone through similar situations in their childhoods, and all the young people out there who are experiencing similar feelings right now. But that's also why I wanted to tell this story.

Q: *What made Nat the right person to help Olive through this situation?*

KAYLA: Olive and Nat have a complicated relationship, but in a way I think that allows them to be honest with each other. Where another friend might be more comforting or just let Olive vent, Nat isn't going to do that, for better or worse. They're both having these difficult spring breaks and trying to figure out how to connect with their parents, so they can relate to each other on that level. But they also both have strong personalities and their own perspectives.

Olive and Nat still have a long way to go before they'd consider themselves friends, and they might never get there, but they're learning to understand and respect each other. I wanted Olive's journey with her father to have a similar ambiguity. Things aren't perfect with Dad and the conversation isn't over just because he offered an explanation and apologized. It felt important to write the dialogue in a way that Olive doesn't verbally accept his apology, because I don't think she should feel obligated to. They love each other and understand each other better, but things aren't resolved.

Q: Was it interesting to incorporate social media so heavily into the story? Is it a topic you'd like to explore more?

KAYLA: Social media is this amazing tool that brings people together, but it can also be pretty stressful. It's hard to get to a place where you're taking advantage of the benefits and not taking on any of the damage. It bums me out that it can feel like the trade-off for keeping up with current events and sharing funny videos with your friends is feeling left out of things, being bombarded with random drama, and constantly seeing advertisements. I think there are a lot of big emotions there and interesting stories to tell.

Q: Where do you draw inspiration from for your art/stories?

KAYLA: I try to draw a little inspiration from everywhere! The stories I tell aren't true events, but I do get inspired by the world around me. And in a more general sense, I get motivated to keep making art and telling stories by seeing the amazing creative things people around the world make every day. Back on the topic of social media for a second, I love being able to see, read, and listen to all the things my friends are creating—no matter how far apart we are—and to share what I'm working on with them.

Acknowledgments

Thank you to everyone whose passion and hard work brought this book into the world. Elizabeth, thank you for always offering your support, wisdom, and a listening ear. My editor, Mary, thank you for your guidance in creating the strongest stories possible. Many thanks to colorist Jess, letterer Lor, designer Steph, art director Elaine, and everyone at HarperCollins who I might not know personally but still work hard to get these books printed and into the hands of readers. As I tell kids when I'm visiting schools and libraries, making graphic novels is a group effort and I absolutely would not be able to do it on my own.

And as always, thank you to my friends and family. You keep me motivated and inspired on a daily basis. Making graphic novels is a lot of work...and so is everything else in this life, and I wouldn't be able to do any of that without all of you. I don't see any of you nearly enough, but the meals and talks and walks I have with you all mean the world to me and keep my heart strong/soft enough to write more books. Thank you to my online friends (shout-out to the YELMS chat) for keeping me laughing and letting me share every silly little thought that crosses my mind. Mom and Dad, thank you for being my parents for three decades strong and counting—love you. Jeffrey, I'm always grateful to have your eyeballs on basically everything I write from grocery lists, to comic scripts, to this very page probably—but I'd like to thank you for helping with this book especially.

Last but not least, thank you for reading! Making comics is always more fun when there's someone out there who wants to read them.

—KAYLA

JAN 2024

Read the *New York Times* bestselling series from
Kayla Miller

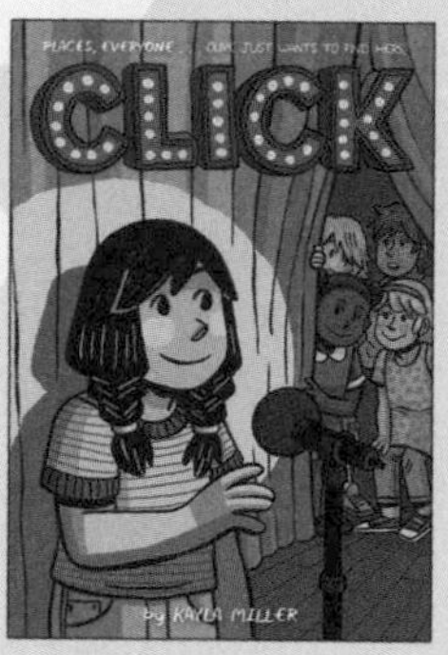
CLICK
by KAYLA MILLER

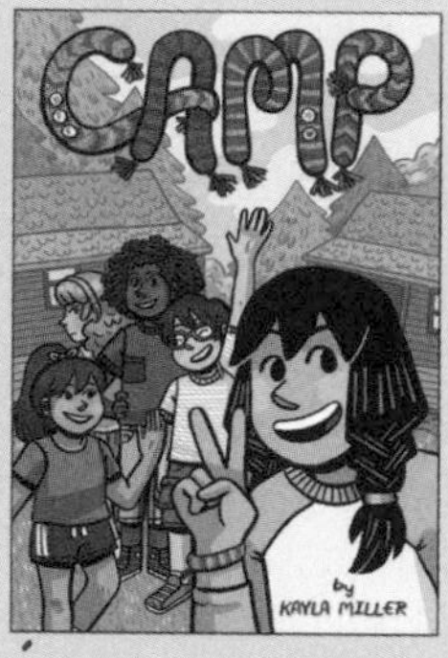
CAMP
by
KAYLA MILLER

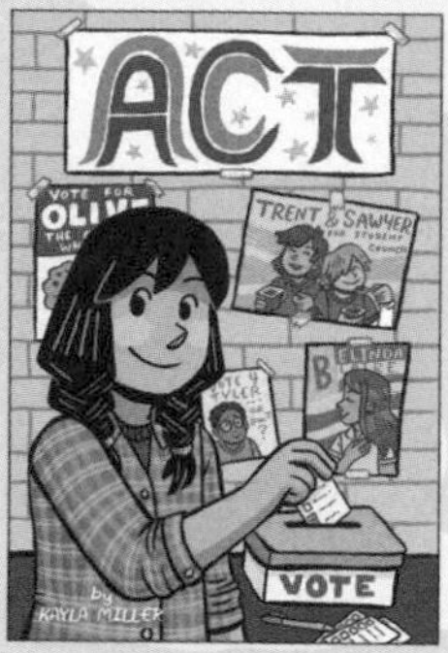
ACT
TRENT & SAWYER
VOTE
by
KAYLA MILLER

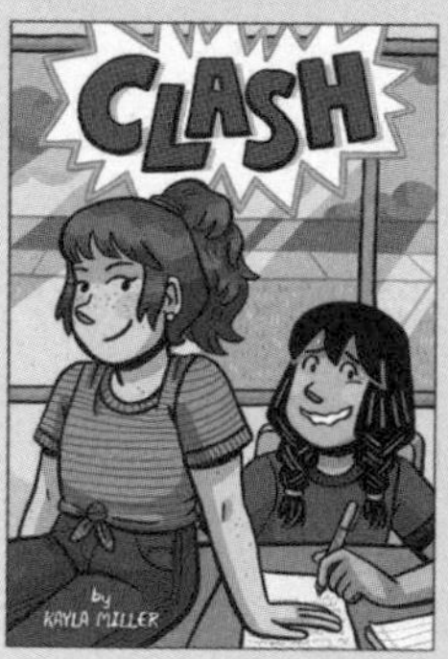
CLASH
by
KAYLA MILLER

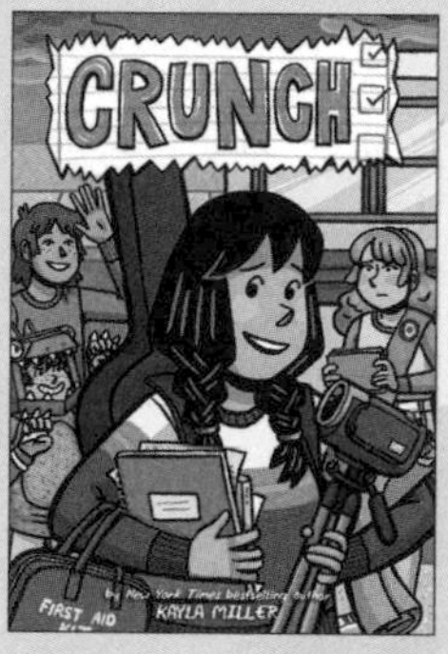
CRUNCH
KAYLA MILLER

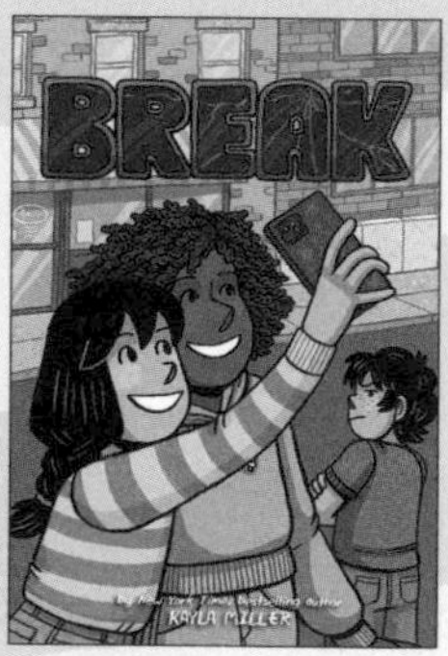
BREAK
KAYLA MILLER

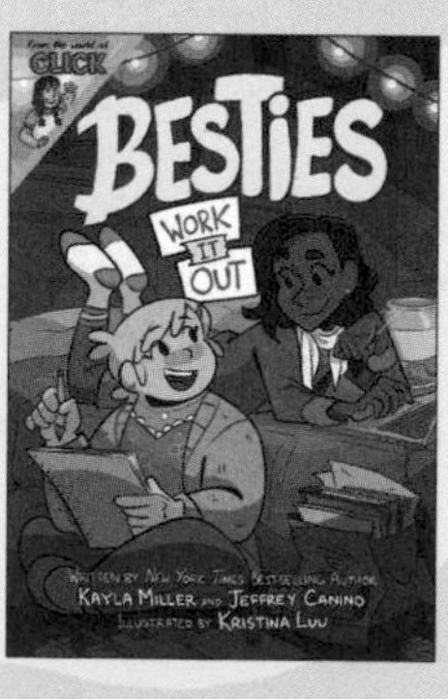
CLICK
BESTIES
WORK IT OUT
KAYLA MILLER AND JEFFREY CANINO
ILLUSTRATED BY KRISTINA LUU

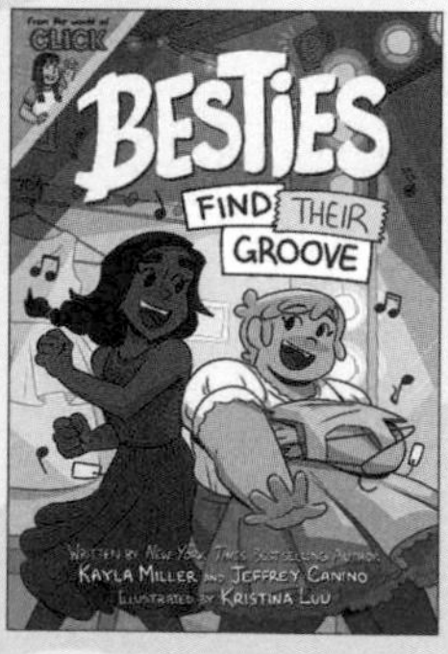
CLICK
BESTIES
FIND THEIR GROOVE
KAYLA MILLER AND JEFFREY CANINO
ILLUSTRATED BY KRISTINA LUU